DIANA TREGARDE
INVESTIGATES

Valdemar

Heralds of Valdemar
Arrows of the Queen
Arrow's Flight
Arrow's Fall
Vows and Honor
The Oathbound
Oathbreakers
Oathblood
The Last Herald-Mage
Magic's Pawn
Magic's Promise
Magic's Price
Mage Winds
Winds of Fate
Winds of Change
Winds of Fury
Mage Storms
Storm Warning
Storm Rising
Storm Breaking
Mage Wars
The Black Gryphon
The White Gryphon
The Silver Gryphon
Owl Mage
Owlflight
Owlsight
Owlknight
Alberich
Exile's Honor
Exile's Valor
By the Sword
Take a Thief
Brightly Burning
Sword of Ice

The Valdemar Companion (edited by
John Helfers and Denise Little)

The Dragon Jousters

Joust
Alta
Sanctuary
Aerie

Other Novels

Reap the Whirlwind (with C.J. Cherryh)
The Ship Who Searched
(with Anne McCaffrey)
If I Pay Thee Not In Gold
(with Piers Anthony)
Rediscovery (with Marion Zimmer Bradley)
Sacred Ground
Firebird
The Black Swan
The Fairy Godmother
One Good Knight

Elemental Masters

The Fire Rose
The Serpent's Shadow
The Gates of Sleep
Phoenix and Ashes
The Wizard of London

Bardic Voices

The Lark and the Wren
The Robin and the Kestrel
The Eagle and the Nightingales
Four and Twenty Blackbirds

The Halfblood Chronicles

(with Andre Norton)
The Elvenbane
Elvenblood
Elvenborn

The Obsidian Trilogy

(with James Mallory)
The Outstretched Shadow
To Light a Candle
When Darkness Falls

Bedlam's Bard

(with Ellen Guon)
Knight of Ghosts and Shadows
Summoned to Tourney
(with Rosemary Edghill)
Spirits White as Lightning
Beyond World's End
Mad Maudlin
Music To My Sorrow

DIANA TREGARDE INVESTIGATES

CHILDREN OF THE NIGHT

BURNING WATER

JINX HIGH

Mercedes Lackey

CHILDREN OF THE NIGHT   Copyright © 1990 by Mercedes Lackey
BURNING WATER   Copyright © 1989 by Mercedes Lackey
JINX HIGH   Copyright © 1991 by Mercedes Lackey

First SFBC Science Fiction Printing: November 2006

Published by arrangement with:
Tom Doherty Associates, Inc.
175 Fifth Avenue
New York, NY 10010

Visit The SFBC online at http://www.sfbc.com

ISBN 978-0-7394-7703-8

Printed in the United States of America.

CONTENTS

CHILDREN
OF THE NIGHT

Dedicated to
Melissa Ann Singer
for more reasons than I can count

ONE

Diana Tregarde sighed, propped her chin on her right hand, and leaned on the countertop. *Of all the jobs I could have taken, working in an occult supply store is not one I'd have chosen on my own. I like my profile low, thank you very much. Too many people know I'm into the Craft as it is. This just boosts my visibility.* She stared out the window and tried not to feel like some poor GI in a bunker, waiting for the next scream of "Incoming!"

I hate being exposed like this. But I owe Annie . . . She flexed her shoulders, forced herself to relax. *Your paranoia is showing, Tregarde. There's no reason to be this gun-shy. It's not that bad. This isn't like the Bible Belt, where I'd get crosses burned on my lawn for being a witch. And most people I run into here are either gonna take me for a flake, or a phony. Besides, I've learned my lessons about staying invisible but doing my job. Nobody's going to have to show me again, especially not the hard way.* She finally laughed at herself for being so nervous. *After all, what could possibly happen to me two blocks off Forty-second Street?*

Then again . . .

She sighed again. The noon rush was over at Bell, Book, and Candle; now—afternoon doldrums.

This is ridiculous; I'm letting this gloomy weather get to me. All is well. We made the rent at noon. Come three, it'll be profit. The turn her thoughts had taken reminded her of the morning rush, and she snorted, thinking what the reaction of most of the otherworldly types that frequented this occult emporium would be to the word "profit." *A profit is not without honor, save when it's not in your pocket.*

She yawned; stretched, looked at her watch. *Still got a little time.*

At least the lull gives me a chance to think about that stupid almost-seduction scene in chapter four.

She mentally reshuffled palm trees, sand, moonlight, hero and heroine one more time, made some internal notes—then looked out the shop window and stifled another yawn.

I should never have let Morrie set up this category-romance deal. I'm just not the type to turn out marshmallow white-bread story sandwiches. I know I need the money, but—this heroine is such a ninny. The stuff they want me to do with her is bor-ing. *And I don't need to be reminded about how awful the Apple is in the winter.*

"*Just follow the outline,*" *says Morrie.* "*It'll be easy, no thinking, just writing,*" *says Morrie.* "*Bubie, you can't* lose,*" says Morrie.* "*You need the dough,* they *want the book. You got 'em by the, you should excuse me, short hairs—they* need *this book and you're the* only *writer I got or anybody else has got that isn't contracted up right now.*" *Morrie, you shark, I'll get you for this. You owe me. I wanted to do another Regency. I wanted to have something with a little humor in it, and something like a bit of historical accuracy. Not Hollywood's idea of Caribbean pirates. You didn't tell me the editor with his ass on the line was your brother-in-law. You creep, you* knew *I was a pagan, you* knew *I wasn't gonna be doing Christmas stuff like everybody else you've got—or even Hanukkah stuff, you snake. You* knew *I'd have "free time." Gods, I'm gonna get you for this.* "*Limpid, heavenly-blue waters of the Bahamas, sparkling beneath the full moon, as she gazes adoringly [and mindlessly] into his ebon-dark eyes,*" *phooey.*

It all only made the filthy October weather and the drab New York street outside the shop seem bleaker and the possibility of making getting even with Morrie even more appealing.

I'll fix you, Morrie. I'm gonna write that honest-to-gods historical Blood and Roses *and I'm gonna make you sell it. And read it, too. Gods forbid you should* learn *something from it. Give you something to read on your Las Vegas vacation next year.*

"*I need a vacation,*" she muttered, while the wind flung dirty bits of paper past the grimy window. Grimy despite the fact that she'd cleaned it once this week. "Gods above and below, I need a vacation."

After a moment of self-pity, she chuckled and shrugged to herself. "But I also need to pay *my* rent. Morrie was right about that, anyway. I can't *quite* make it on writing yet, and the reserve is getting lower than I like."

I should be thankful I've got an agent as good as Morrie. I should be grateful I've got an agent at all. If it hadn't been for Itzaak tangling with that dybbuk and me bailing him out with fairly light damage, he *wouldn't have talked his good old uncle Morrie into taking me.* She grinned a little. *I'll never forget Morrie's face when he saw the bite mark on 'Zaak's thigh—and 'Zaak told him where it came from—and then told him where the dybbuk had been aiming in the first place . . .*

. . . like, forget about "be fruitful and multiply."

The glass rattled in a gust, and a listless spatter of rain drooled across the black and gold lettering. Even the storm predicted for this afternoon couldn't get up the enthusiasm to do more than threaten.

She rubbed her eyes, and shifted her weight—and sent a little more energy into the shield around the shop. *Umpty bizillion people in this city, and half of 'em unhappy at any one time. With weather like this, probably* most *of 'em unhappy. Yuck. Hell being an empath in the Big Apple. Hell being a big shiny target the way I am. Every time I do something arcane I feel like I've sent up a big neon sign—"GOOD EATS"—with an arrow pointing right down at me. "Hi, I'm the blue plate special." Too damn many things I can't handle. Too damn many things I can take, but only if I get 'em from behind.* She shook her head. *I've got to snap out of this mood. I'm getting paranoid again. This is ridiculous. It's probably just because I'm tired.*

After six hours behind the counter, her feet *did* hurt. She wasn't used to spending this much time on them.

And the thought of spending some time in someplace remote, isolated—and *warm*—

"Now if somebody would just give me enough money to *pay* for a vacation. And the rent. Now what's the odds I could find a sugar daddy . . . ?"

She laughed at herself. "Right, Tregarde. A sugar daddy and you. Sure. Being *real* bad at taking orders is the reason you don't have a mundane job. Oh well. I guess I'll have to settle for turning the heat up and putting the ocean record on when I get home."

Today had not been a good day to boost the mysterious and otherworldly atmosphere that Annie preferred to cultivate. "Mysterious and otherworldly" tended to be gloomy and chilly.

Not today. Di had turned on every lamp in the place, turned up the heat a little, and chosen cinnamon incense and spice candles and set them burning as soon as she opened. She closed her eyes and took a deep breath; it was as cozy in here as in a kitchen full of baking pies. *Could be worse, could be worse. I sure can use the cash Annie's paying me. Gods, I hope the baby comes soon, though. I want to get this damned freebooter romance out of my hair.* She tasted the cinnamon in the air, and thought about a hot cup of tea—

And looked up.

Looks like the afternoon rush just started.

Across the street she saw three people she knew so well she'd recognize them a mile away—and they were heading straight for the shop.

And in front of the shop was a young man with a notebook sticking out of his pocket and a peculiar look on his face. Curiosity and distaste.

Oh double hell. A re-port-er. Just in time for the afternoon rush.

The young man pushed the door open, and the string of bells over it jingled in the rush of cold, damp air. They chimed with a cheer Di could not force herself to emulate; the sour expression this lad wore did not bode well.

"May I help you?" she asked, making face and voice as neutral as possible.

He started; *she* could see the whole shop from where she was, but the arrangement and sheer volume of merchandise crowded into the tiny storefront tended to confuse the unwary—

She ran a practiced eye over him, as the bells on the door jingled again and Melani, Jorge, and Nita slipped in, heading straight for the "reserved" shelf and the books Annie ordered for her "regulars" in the back.

It isn't in yet, kids, but I'm glad you showed.

She watched the reporter carefully, keeping all her "feelers" tucked in, reading only body language. No use in advertising—and if he was marginally sensitive she might freak him.

Hmm. Caucasian, brown and brown. Um—twenty-five, tops. Gods. A "cub reporter." Betcha they sent him out to get him out of everyone's hair, after a silly-season fill story; he has visions of coming up with something weird enough that the wire services will pick it up. She gritted her teeth. *Gods, give me patience, and give it to me now. Why can't I get more like that nice chick from the six o'clock news last week?*

The classical station on the radio behind her finished baroque, and began modern, grating and interminable. *Not my day,* she concluded, and turned it down. The reporter looked for a path through the bookcases and standing racks of incense, notecards, and transparent "stained glass" window decals. He clutched his notebook to his chest possessively, and made his way toward the counter, emerging eventually from between two coatracks festooned with rainbow-colored "ritual robes," specifically made for the tourist trade.

Di smothered a grin at his grimace of distaste. The robes weren't real, and Annie was no dummy. Not with B, B, and C being just off Forty-second Street. The tourists and teenyboppers came looking for weird and outré, and she was perfectly happy to separate them from their money. These "magic robes" sold especially briskly just before Halloween and New Year's, and at twenty-five bucks a pop, the polyester horrors would buy a lot of diapers for Baby. And no one who patronized the shop for serious purposes minded—because Annie kept a stock of *real* robes, made by hand (and about as ornate as a monk's habit) in the back.

Di noticed empty hangers as he pushed past the rack, and made another mental note. *Going to have to remind Annie to get Jillian to do another batch of red, black, and purple, we're low.*

She knew before he even opened his mouth that *this* reporter was going to be one of the obnoxious ones.

"Are you Miz Sandstrom?" The very tone of his voice, strident and demanding, set her teeth on edge.

"She's on vacation," Di replied, polishing the counter with a piece of chamois and quietly signaling the trio at the back of the shop to stay out of the way for a minute. "I can probably help you."

She watched him out of the corner of her eye. His face fell, and he actually pouted. "I *expected* to talk to Miz Sandstrom. Give me her home address."

Without even a "please" attached. "I'm sorry," she said insincerely, wondering if he'd go away. "I can't give out that kind of information."

Because if I did, you'd print it, you little creep, and then Annie would have nuts trying to break her door down, to save her soul from the Devil.

He sulked, and glowered at her as if he blamed her personally for keeping him where he was, at the bottom of the journalistic pecking order. "My editor said she'd be here. My editor said to get an interview with a real witch."

As if Annie ran her life by the dictates of his editor. She smiled, a conciliatory, saccharin-dripping simper, and debated doing something to drive him off. *But if I don't give him something to write about, he'll make up a story. Then may the gods help us. He'll be certain we're hiding something, and he'll have us sacrificing chickens and drinking acid-doctored blood cocktails at Friday night sit-down orgies.* So she groveled a little, and batted her eyes, and said, in a confidential tone of voice—"But *I'm* a real witch."

The corner of his mouth twitched. "You are?" he asked, making no secret of his doubt.

"Uh-huh." She nodded vigorously.

"Well." He sulked a moment more, then said ungraciously, "I guess you'll do, then."

She caught Melani's eye and gave her the nod; the three of them swarmed the counter.

"Excuse me a minute—" she said. "Customers—"

Thank the gods for friends.

"What's up?" Jorge asked, making a big show of asking for some of the herb powders behind the counter.

"Reporter," she said sotto voce, and Melani grimaced. Di measured powdered dragon's blood into a plastic bag. *These* three were some of Annie's steadier customers—and if it weren't that they all *had* jobs, Annie would have asked one of them to mind the store for her instead of Di.

"Hey." Nita spoke up—a rarity. She usually let the other two do all the talking. "Tell you what—you bore him, and we'll carry him off, okay?"

"I love you," she said gratefully. "I go, I go—"

Di returned to the visitor and went fully into a character she'd created for moments like this one, the persona of "Gladys Eisendorf" (which was the name she gave him); the *dullest* human being on the face of the planet.

She gushed, she wheedled, she fluttered. She talked through her nose, so her voice was as whiny and grating as possible. She pitched it just on the bearable side of shrill. She giggled like a fool.

And she gave him *nothing* he wanted.

When he asked about Halloween ceremonies, she corrected him primly, like a schoolteacher. "It's Samhain," she said, deliberately mispronouncing it, then spelling it out for him. With a sanctimonious air she described a ceremony that made a Tupperware party seem licentious revelry by comparison. Before he could draw breath to ask another question, she proceeded to a tedious homily on Harmony, Peace and Love, and the Role of the Spirit in the Universe. It was a piece of tripe riddled with the clichés of every "The Universe is a *friendly* place, my child" type she'd ever had to put up with. And it was so boring that even had the young man possessed the temper and patience of Saint Francis he'd have thought longingly on satanic sacrifices before she was finished. With *her* as the starring attraction.

Both of these dissertations were punctuated by flirtatious asides and hungry looks—"I'm *single,* you know"—"If you'd like to come to the ritual, I'd be *happy* to vouch for you"—"We're allowed a guest, and I'm *single,* you know—"

It would have taken a stronger man than he was to shrug *that* blatant attack off.

He took notes—then *pretended* to take notes—and finally

stopped even pretending, waiting with growing and visible desperation until she paused for a breath. He flipped the notebook closed, shoved it into his pocket, and spoke before she could get started again.

"Thank you, Miss—" He'd obviously forgotten her name, and hurried on so that she wouldn't notice the lapse. "Thank you very much, you've given me *plenty* of information. I'm sure I can do a *terrific* article from what you've given me. Of course, I can't promise that my editor will *print* it—"

She hid a grin. *Weaseling out of it already, hm?*

"—but you should know, middle-class values, bourgeois materialism, chauvinistic prejudices—"

You rattle that stuff off quite well, laddybuck. Covered the peace movement lately?

"—but of course I'll try, sympathetic exposure, put a word in the right places—"

He was babbling now, and backing away, carefully, as if he were afraid that if he turned his back on her she'd throw a net over him. She encouraged that belief.

"You don't have to go—" she cried faintly, flapping her hands frantically. "I have *plenty* of time. No one *ever* comes in here this time of day!"

"No! I mean—"

The trio, who had been awaiting this moment of retreat, swooped down on him.

And suddenly, with Nita, exotic, dark-eyed Nita, Nita the professional belly dancer, cooing at him, "witchcraft" became a *lot* more interesting. And the shop a lot *less* interesting. And the absent "Miz Sandstrom" a creature of no importance. She watched the transition with veiled amusement. Before thirty seconds had passed, the "terrible trio" had him neatly bedazzled and were luring him out the door; notebook, the shop, Annie, and "Gladys" forgotten.

When they passed out of sight, she leaned against the counter and wheezed, laughing too hard to get a full breath, tears coming to her eyes.

She'd managed to get herself under control when the bells jingled again, and a middle-aged couple who had *tourist* writ across their expressions in letters of flame crept in. By now the classical station, as if in apology for the first two pieces, was playing Dvorak's *New World* Symphony.

That was usually a soothing piece, but—

I don't think they're soothed, Di thought, watching them inch their way into the shop. *I don't think they know what it is they've got-ten into. They're actually scared. Poor things. I'd better be gentle, or they may have heart attacks right on the threshold.*

"Hi!" she said brightly, when she was certain they'd spotted her. "What can I do for you?"

Mister Tourist peered at her while Missus Tourist clutched at his arm. "What is this place?" he asked, blinking. "This some kind of hip-pie store?"

She came out from behind the counter, so that they could see her. Mister was at least six feet tall, so he towered over her by a good foot. The disparity in height seemed to reassure him, as she'd intended. "Well, not really," she admitted. "We're kind of a religious supply house."

"You mean—" Missus Tourist whispered, looking over her shoul-der for demons, "—*Satanists?*"

Di laughed, projecting reassurance as hard as she could. "Oh, heavens no! We get a lot of people into Eastern religions in here," she told them, with perfect truth. "Some odd kinds of Buddhists, for in-stance. And we carry a lot of books on spiritualism and the occult. Fiction, too. In fact, the name of the shop comes from a play—" She beamed, and stuck her hands in the pockets of her jeans. "I bet you saw the movie version by the same name, I think it had Kim Novak in it—"

Both of them perked up and relaxed at the hint that she did any-thing so mundane as go to movies. And about then, Missus Tourist subconsciously noticed the cinnamon scent in the air, the familiar odor relaxing her still further. In about five minutes they were chat-tering away like old neighbors—

There was method to her madness. The *next* time someone back in Davenport, Iowa, said something about horrible hippies practic-ing witchcraft, it would be Di that Fred and Edna remembered. They'd think about the friendly, cheerful girl who looked more like a refugee from American Ballet Theater than anyone's notion of a "witch"—the girl who'd encouraged them to stay and chat until they'd warmed up, in a store that smelled like apple pies baking. And maybe, just maybe, they'd tell their neighbor a thing or two—

It turned out that they'd wanted something out of the ordinary in the way of a souvenir, and the hotel clerk, perhaps in a fit of mali-ciousness, had suggested Annie's shop.

That annoyed her enough that she went out of her way to be even nicer to them. Before they left, she'd *found* them their "unusual souvenirs"—a book on the ghosts of New York City, and another on the purported Viking ruins found up and down the New England coast—and she had Fred Blaine joking with her, while his wife, Edna, smiled at her and said she wished now that she'd had at least *one* daughter instead of all those boys.

"I always used to carry one of these," Fred remarked at last, while Di rang up his purchases on the store's ancient preelectric cash register. He had spotted, then insisted on buying, an overpriced rabbit's-foot key ring. "Dog got my last one, and I haven't felt lucky since. Of course it wasn't so lucky for the rabbit, now was it?"

Di laughed at the joke—no mean feat, since she'd heard it at least once a day since she started tending the store. But they were, at bottom, *good* people, and she felt a bit more cheerful as she wrapped their purchases and waved them out.

Her good humor lingered, which was just as well, because the rush was on.

The trio returned from reporter seduction just as the classical station moved on to Praetorius's suite from "Terpsichore." She was weighing out their purchases when the shop began to fill. There were a couple of book browsers, who would probably come back for another couple of days before they made up their minds, a couple of teenage girls, and three young men of about college age who scanned the store and came straight for her.

That was so out of the ordinary that for a moment she was taken completely aback.

"Hi," said the bespectacled blond who seemed to be the leader of the trio. "We need some help—"

She stiffened.

"Just a second—"

The loaded words hit her like a slap in the face with a cold washcloth. Her adrenaline kicked in, and her heart started racing—because those words held special meaning for her. *They need some help? Oh my god—what now?*

She rang up the trio's purchases, hoping they wouldn't notice how her hands were shaking. An innocent phrase like that shouldn't throw a scare into anyone—

Unless you were a Guardian.

"We'd like some books on Druidism and the Norse," said the second, a thin and dreadfully earnest type, while she handed Jorge the brown paper sack. "We war-game, I mean the hobby, and we're just getting into something called 'fantasy role-playing games.' Napoleonics we know, but we need *rules* so we know how to run magic and religions—"

Her knees went weak with relief. *Only a game? Lord and Lady, for a minute I was afraid they were Calling on me—*

"See you later, guys—and thanks." She waved her friends through the door, and turned back to the newcomers (trying to keep a weather eye on the two teenagers). "Is this something like—uh—re-creating battles with toy—I mean miniature—soldiers, only doing it, like, with Tolkien?" she asked, vaguely remembering a couple of her war-gaming friends talking about something like this just before they all graduated from college. *Gods, that was Itzaak and his lot, and the bunch of them were like kids with a new pony. What did he say? "A very new twist on traditional war-gaming. Using maps and miniatures—only you fight dragons instead of dragoons—"*

"Exactly!" The blond beamed at her as if she'd just come up with the unified field theory. "And we need some help, the guys playing clerics are getting away with practically murder—"

"We don't mean anything sacrilegious," the third, tall and beefy, and altogether looking like a jock, interrupted meekly. "I mean, we're not making fun of anybody or anything—honest!"

That set off the other two, who were nowhere near as shy as the muscle boy.

"Whoa!" She brought the torrent of explanation to a halt. *Lord, the intensity here, and for a game! Was I ever that earnest about anything?* "I know Tolkien and most of the other major fantasy works pretty well; why don't you just tell me what your game is closest to, and I'll tell you what books I think will suit your purposes best."

That pair of giggling girls that *couldn't* be older than fifteen watched her pull books down off the shelves, surrounded by the three boys. She ignored them for the moment; she was doing mental calculations and trying to keep in mind the fact that these young men probably didn't have much spare cash.

Lord knows Itzaak never did. Were we really ever this young? Has it only been two years—less—since I graduated? It feels like I'm a hundred years older than these kids. Itzaak, if I ever catch up with you, I don't know if I'm going to kill you or kiss you for getting me on Uncle Morrie's client list. Though right now "kill" has an edge.

Their finances, when pooled, got them the first four books on her list. "Believe me, that should hold you for some time," she told them, while the two girls whispered and eyed the young men from the shelter of the astrology section with predatory interest. "We're not talking a couple of hours of light reading, here. *The Golden Bough* has been used as a comparative religions text in more than one university." The talkative two looked a little daunted; the jock perked up.

"Gimme that one, okay?" he said, reaching for it. "And the Wallis Budge. You two can take the others."

Di raised an eyebrow at him. "You're tougher than I thought."

He actually blushed. "Hell, ol' Budge didn't put me to sleep with the *Book of the Dead* in Egyptology, I don't figure he's gonna do it now."

Di's other eyebrow rose.

Egyptology? Have we got a budding psi here?

But before she could say anything, they'd gathered up their books and headed off into the cold.

The two girls sidled up to the counter, killing her chance to call the boys back, and a tall and saturnine older man slipped in behind the exiting boys. She heaved a mental sigh and turned her attention to the girls.

It didn't take ESP to figure these two out. They were just like the bunch that had come in at noon, all cast from the same mold, so fierce in their nonconformity that they set an entirely original standard of sameness.

Bet if one started a sentence, the other could finish it.

"Hi," she said, when they just stared. "Need something?"

"Um," said the short-haired, aggressively made-up blonde. "Like, we're having a Halloween party, you know? Like, we kinda wanted something different, you know?"

"Like, spells and stuff, you know?" finished her partner in crime, a baby-faced redhead. "Like, it's just girls, and like, we wanta do love spells, you know?" She giggled, trying to hide obvious embarrassment.

Lady bless. Just what I needed. Well, at least they came here. They could have picked up something from that bastard Ulrich, and if there's anybody in that little clique that's got even marginal Talent—gods have mercy.

"Well," she said slowly, "you know the problem with doing stuff like that is that the ingredients are *awfully* expensive."

"They are?" the blonde said, beginning to look doubtful.

"Sure," Di replied cheerfully. "Take your average love spell—to *start* with you'll need a whole mandrake root—" She began naming off ingredients at random, taking care that they were some of the most expensive herbs in the shop. ". . . and you finish up by binding it all together with attar of roses."

At one hundred dollars an ounce. Sheesh. Good thing we seal the bottle with wax every time we have to open it.

Since the prices were all posted openly, she watched with amusement as the girls made some hasty mental totals.

"And *then,* of course, you have to take what you've made and consecrate it. The ritual's in here—" She reached out and snagged a copy of *Sword of Wisdom* off the shelf behind her. She picked it for its size and small print. The redhead turned a couple of pages and put it down, unread.

"How long would it take?" she asked, subdued.

Di shrugged. "Depends on the ritual you choose, and the stars, and the moon phase. Could take all night."

"Oh." This, obviously, was *not* their idea of a good time.

"On the other hand, there's always the folk charms—they're quick, and real easy, and a lot of fun."

"The what?" they chorused, brightening.

"Folk charms. Like the teenaged girls in Salem probably used to do—at least when their Puritan daddies weren't looking." She winked, and the two of them giggled again. "They're mostly geared toward finding out who your lover is going to be, and you'll find most of what you need in your kitchen. Here—" She snagged another book, this one on American folk magic, a book she *knew* was harmless. *No demon-summoning in here, thank the gods. I do* not *need a repetition of what Mark Valdez did to me.*

She opened the book on the counter, and the two girls put their heads together over it, whispering. She grinned to herself, wondering how many boys were going to get "love apples" the day after Halloween. "The book's three-fifty," she said helpfully. "And what you can't find in your kitchens you can get at the Arboretum if you ask the guys nice, or even in Central Park or the Zoo."

"Like, heavy! Okay," said the blonde. "And we want this, too—"

She put a Ouija board on the counter. Di stifled a groan. *I should have known. I should have known.* While she rang up their purchases—blessing, instead of cursing, the recalcitrant cash register, since it was buying her time—

She needed time. Time to cast a "quick" shield on the board. All it took was one Sensitive kid—one open, the way Mark had been—and one Ouija board—and you had a combination that spelled (in all senses of the word) Trouble in River City.

But with her shield blocking it, the only messages they'd get would be from their own dear little subconscious minds.

She promised her twisting stomach a nice cup of tea, and fought the blurring in her vision caused by the draining of her own power. *I shouldn't be doing this, even inside the shop shield. If one of the browsers is a psychic—if somebody's* looking *for a Guardian—damn, damn, damn. If I didn't have to work four times as hard to set this stuff so I didn't leave psychic fingerprints all over everything—*

All Di's internal alarms started shrieking at top volume—telling her that Real, *Living* Trouble was already *in* the shop, poised on the threshold.

Christ on a crutch—

Now she got a good look at the guy who'd slipped in when the three boys had left. Six three, if an inch, and dressed with expensive flash in a velvet Edwardian jacket and lace shirt, he was saturnine, brooding, and aquiline—and oozed charisma.

A baited trap if ever I saw one—

And he was a hungry hunter on the prowl. A "chicken hawk," which wasn't unusual, not this close to Forty-second Street—but this particular gentleman might well be hunting with other senses than the normal five. And in any case, in a moment he'd zero in on the girls and do his level best to reel them in—

He'd use them, however they let him, then use them up.

Over my prone corpse. Gods, I hate advertising my presence. He could be stronger, meaner than he looks. But if I don't deal with this— it'll come back on me. And when I'm not ready. Just like that—thing. She suppressed the nausea *that* memory caused, gritted her teeth, and prepared to challenge. *Let's see for certain if he's after more than the physical—*

Di slapped a barrier up right in his face; he started to take a step forward and encountered it, and his expression changed in a split second from bored to enraged, then to cautiously wary.

She flared her shield just enough to catch his attention, knowing that if he could be stopped by her barrier, he was more than good enough to catch a belligerent aural flare.

And if he could be stopped by her barrier, he probably was someone she could handle.

He responded, as she'd expected him to, and she trapped his gaze with her own.

He smiled, very slightly, and nodded.

She did not return the salutation. His eyes narrowed, and she saw his thoughts in his expression and body language as clearly as if she'd read them directly. He'd taken her at first for a fellow Hunter. Now he knew her for a Guardian. He was not amused.

Out, she thought at him, with just a touch of psi bolt backing the word, and saw him wince. She distracted the girls with a comment about the section in the book on love charms using apples, which sent them hunting it. While their attention was on the book, she drew a glyph in the air between him and the girls. It wasn't visible to outer sight, but to Inner it flamed as fiery as the candles behind her.

Out, she repeated. *Out, or I'll call Challenge. This is my Place, and you aren't welcome in it. Find another hunting ground.*

He tried to contest her will, locking eye to eye—

But in the end it was his eyes that dropped, not hers, and he turned and left without a word, though she could see a tenseness in his jaw that probably meant he was grinding his teeth in frustration.

Maybe if he had been on his own turf he would have fought her. But he wasn't—

Oh gods. She went weak-kneed and held on to the counter to keep herself standing; she was just as glad he hadn't tried to force the issue.

Maybe I'm stronger than him—but a Challenge is not the way to find out for certain.

And it wasn't *that* long ago that she'd forced the poltergeist out of Keith's workshop.

Thank the gods I didn't have to push things before I got a chance to recharge.

That incident was more than she wanted to handle this afternoon, and when the girls took their goodies and left, and the browsers—happily oblivious to the whole incident—followed, she headed for the front of the store and the "Open" sign in the window. It was more than time for a nice cup of strong tea—

Actually a nice shot of strong Scotch would be a lot more welcome. Oh well.

She had her hand on the sign and was actually starting to flip the plastic rectangle over when she heard a sound coming from the curtained-off entrance to the storeroom.

She jumped a foot, and came down in "ready" stance, facing the threshold and the intruder, halfway expecting it to be Mr. Trouble back for a rematch, and that he'd somehow gotten in the service entrance.

Facing the front of the shop—and panting a little—was a dusky, exotically handsome young man—

Or boy; after a moment she was no longer certain of his age. Gold glinted in his ears—and for one moment she thought, *Gay?*

Then he moved hesitantly into the light, and there was no doubting his antecedents; if he wasn't Romany she'd eat the scarf around his neck. The universal uniform of jeans, rock T-shirt, and CPO jacket did nothing to disguise his origins, nor his halfhearted attempt to look like "everyone else." He couldn't; even his curly hair didn't match, as it was a little shorter than the current standard.

His chest heaved, and he stared at her blankly, his forehead beaded with sweat in spite of the cold.

Oh my; oh yum. For that, I could be tempted into cradle-robbing. Hey, little boy, want a chocolate-chip cookie, hm?

Then she saw his expression, and her paranoia kicked into high gear. Her self-amused and slightly lascivious thoughts wafted away like fog in a high wind.

Because beneath his self-imposed calm, he was *terrified.*

"*Drabarni*—" he said, holding out a hand in entreaty, with an air of expecting to be slapped down. "Where—please, where is Annie Sandstrom?"

"*Drabarni*"—*I think that means "sorceress," or something like it. Which means he knows what I am*—

She weighed all the consequences, then dropped into the Sight, and felt her eyes widen as she sucked her breath in with surprise.

Ee-ha, he knows what I am, all right. He's got it, too. Lady bless, he reads Potential Power like a small nuclear reactor. He may be damped down now, but that's because he wills it that way. Talk about different—I thought it was only the women of the Rom that were into the Power. This one must be something really special.

"She's going to be gone for at least another couple of weeks," she said. "But I'm a friend. I'll help you if I can."

Relief made him go limp, those huge black eyes of his turning luminous with gratitude.

"Lady—" he panted, "there is someone—"

"After you? The law?"

He shook his head, and his curls bounced. "After me, yes. No one's law but his own."

Within the safety of the shop shields, she dared expense of power and augmented observation with a delicate probe. There was something of a "feel" of amorality about him—but then there was always that "feel" about gypsies.

Not surprising, given that by their lights God created the rest of us to support them.

She made a snap judgment in his favor. "Do you need sanctuary, help, or just an escape route?"

More gratitude, this time tinged with wry surprise.

"I told you, I'm Annie's friend. Those of us with Powers get hassled, too," she pointed out, letting one corner of her mouth quirk up for a moment. "Probably as often as the Rom get it. And we aren't as good at hiding as the Rom are."

He spread his hands and shrugged, acknowledging the truth of her statement, and admitting her as a kind of kindred, all with the same expressive gesture. She wished briefly that *she* could manage body language that eloquent. "I looked for a hiding place, for now," he replied nervously. "The shop will break my trail. The Hunter is good, not *that* good. I don't think that one will find my trail again, once broken."

Mr. Trouble? Naw, couldn't be. Too much of a coincidence. She pondered him a moment more.

Damn. He's into something deeper than he can manage—and he was hoping Annie could help him with it. Double damn. Granny always told me—"With powers like yours you got no choice. You either use 'em to help the ones that come to you, or the things after them'*ll come after you."* She shivered. *I wish she hadn't been so right.*

She dug into her back pocket and came out with one of her personal cards—the one with her name and home address on it. "Look, it sounds like you've been hunted by this guy before—am I right?"

He tilted his head sideways. "Yes—" he said, a bit warily. "So?"

She inched past the incense rack—for once it didn't snag her—and got close enough to him to hand him the little rectangle of pewter-colored paper. "So if you're in trouble in this neighborhood—" She shrugged, trying to look casual. "Allies are always useful."

He only then looked at the card, and smiled his gratitude at her, a brief flash of white in his dark face. "I—thank you."

"Better get while the getting's good," she said, pointing. He nodded, and moved—

He didn't *run,* not exactly, but he certainly wasn't walking. She saw little more than a flash of sneakers, then heard the alley door scream open and slam shut before the curtain had finished fluttering.

She waited for a moment to see if his pursuer would put in an appearance, but the street seemed oddly deserted. Perhaps it was the sky: dead gunmetal, going to red-lit charcoal; the threatening storm and the grim dusk were not likely to induce anyone out at this late an hour. Besides, with this much overcast it was going to be full dark in a very short time. No one ventured *here* after dark, not without an appointment.

Time for that tea—then, warmed and fortified for the subway ride, she'd be able to shut the shop down and go home.

She put the kettle on the hot plate in the dark, redolent storeroom, and hunted through the clutter of teabags for cinnamon. The incense had put her in the mood for it. She realized as the water started to boil that she hadn't turned the sign to "Closed" after all, or locked the front door.

Oh well. Nobody likely to show now—
The classical station on the radio behind her began something tinkly, precious, and baroque; with a grimace she turned it down a hair. As her hand left the knob, the phone rang; she reached out across the hot plate, and opened the miniature coffin where it lived. "Bell, Book, and Candle," she said, as brightly as she could.

"Hi, sweets," Annie Sandstrom replied, her voice thin and tinny. "How's tricks?"

"We've done a bit better than normal, and dammit, if your back hurts, lie down." Di could tell by the strain in Annie's voice that it had been a far-too-long day. "Drink some chamomile tea. Put Brahms's 'Lullaby' on the stereo and stick the headphones on your tummy."

"You really think that would make Baby settle down?" Annie sounded pathetically hopeful.

"Well, the chamomile should cross the placental barrier," Di replied absently, as she peered out the curtain to the front window and wondered if there was *anybody* out on the street. "It won't hurt her any, and it might calm her down. And What's-her-name swears by stereo headphones in the last month. You know who I mean, the one with the guy with the head shop?"

"Oh yeah, the one that changed her name to Azure Asphodel. Had any flakes today?"

Di snorted, and twined a strand of her hair around her fingers. *Damn mop's getting out of the knot again.* "Makes me glad I'm finally legal to buy hard liquor. I got a *mob* of teenyboppers in here at noon. One of them wanted to know how to throw a curse on somebody, and his girlfriend wanted a copy of the *Satanic Bible.* Just what we all need."

"I trust you threw a good scare into them?"

"Need you ask? You'd better spawn soon, lady. That fifth of Scotch I bought isn't going to last much longer. Why did I *ever* let you talk me into running this joint for you?"

"Because you have a soft heart." Annie chuckled. "You couldn't *bear* the notion of me fighting my way through the subway with a monster under my belt."

Di grinned, in spite of her sore feet, and leaned up against the wall. Three weeks ago Annie had resembled the Goodyear blimp. She hated to think what her old college friend looked like now.

"Besides," Annie continued, as the street beyond the glass grew perceptibly darker, "you're the only one I've ever Worked with that I'd trust to handle the nutcases that show up around Halloween. I mean, can *you* picture Siobhan with a reporter? Or Alicia with a teenybopper who wants to play at the Craft? Or Stazi with those two would-be black-magickers you had this afternoon?"

Di shuddered. "The spirit quails. Stazi would probably have sent them over to You-Know's place. And gods forbid they had any *ability*, guess who'd end up pulling their fat out of the fire."

"You or me, or one of the others. The Terrible Trio, maybe, they're good at—" The words were followed by a stifled gasp.

"Baby rambunctious?"

"She's taking after Auntie Di," Annie said, a little sourly. "She's doing karate katas. Listen, if it seems dead, shut down early, okay? No use in you sticking around for nothing, not with the weather like it is right now."

"Okay," Di agreed readily. "Bye-bye, darlin'. Give Bob a big kiss for me."

"Ciao, Bambi."

Click.

If she calls me Bambi one more time . . . Six days to Halloween. Feels like six weeks. Oh hell, I forgot to ask her about that gypsy boy. And the chicken hawk. Maybe I'd better call her back—

But the back of her neck prickled, and she had the strongest feeling that she really *ought* to check on the front of the store, just in case—

And when your psychic Gifts were as reliable as Diana Tregarde's were, you didn't ignore prickling on the back of your neck.

She sighed, turned the heat down, and stepped to the front of the store—

And saw *him* standing uncertainly in the light of the lamp in the window, peering through the glass, as if trying to make out if the shop was tenanted or not.

He was, without a doubt, the foxiest, *sexiest,* man she had seen in a year.

For a moment, with his eyes dazzled, no doubt, by the contrast between the dark of the street and the lighted shop, he couldn't see her—but she could certainly see him.

He was short—he probably wouldn't top her by more than a couple of inches—and lean; but it was the slightness and leanness of a panther that *he* put her in mind of. His face was that of a medieval angel; fine-boned, with high, prominent cheekbones and the most beautiful dark eyes she'd ever seen in her life. Those eyes—

Oh yes. Eyes that grab you by the throat and won't let go. Centuries. Like he's seen centuries pass, and he's learned from them, but he hasn't let them make him disenchanted or bitter—

His hair, like the gypsy boy's, wasn't long by modern standards, but it was dark as the boy's, and long enough and silky-looking enough to make her itch to run her hands through it.

For a tiny moment she indulged herself in a fantasy of doing just that—she *was* a romance writer, after all.

Then sighed. *Business, my dear.* She squared her shoulders, controlled her expression, and moved forward.

He was quick; she gave him points. She'd scarcely taken a step when he spotted her by her movement, and locked his eyes on her. She nodded; he tightened his lips a bit, and opened the door.

My gods, he should be freezing. No coat, nothing but a pair of jeans and a sweater—

He hesitated on the threshold; she had the oddest feeling that he was *waiting* for something.

She wanted to extend and "read" him, both intrigued and a little suspicious, but decided against it. *Odd. Very odd. I don't ever remember seeing him around here, and Annie would have mentioned a fox like him.*

He was still hesitating, one hand on the doorframe. It was his right hand, and the gleam of metal on his wrist above the cuff of his dark sweater caught her gaze for a moment.

He was wearing a very wide, heavy silver bracelet—and *that* was odd too, since he was wearing no other jewelry at all, and the bracelet itself seemed snugged to his wrist, but had no visible opening or catch. It might almost have been soldered onto his wrist.

And as he continued to hesitate, she remembered the gypsy boy, and became suspicious. What if *this* was what had been hunting the boy? It certainly seemed an odd coincidence that he should show up on *this* foul night right after she'd broken the boy's trail with the shop.

But even if he was after the boy, *she* could take care of herself, *he* couldn't know she'd aided the kid, and she *might* be able to buy the boy a little more time by occupying his attention for a bit. She smiled, and nodded.

"Come on in," she said cheerfully. "I don't bite."

He seemed to find the remark amusing; he chuckled as if to himself, anyway, then smiled back at her, slid his hand down off the doorframe, and glided gracefully across the threshold, closing the door behind him. She found herself envying him: he *moved* like a panther, too; both elegant and powerful.

"I beg to disturb you so late," he said, his words faintly accented. It took her a moment to identify the accent as French. "I am certain that you wish to close and return to your home—but could you tell me if there was a particular man here an hour or so ago? He is tall, taller than six feet, I believe; he is very dark, with narrow eyes and a prominent nose—he tends to favor somewhat flamboyant clothing."

She raised her eyebrow at him. *Mr. Trouble? Now what on earth could this one want with* him? *Unless this is just an excuse—or unless they're working together—*

One way to find out. "He was," she said shortly, admiring the graceful way his hand lay along the counter in the back of her mind—and taking notes on it for possible use in her book. "He left."

The young man sighed; and unless she was *grossly* mistaken, it looked like he was relieved. "Then he must not have bought—or found—what it was that he was looking for," he said, so softly that he might well have been speaking to himself. With his next words he raised his voice. "I do not suppose that you would be able to tell me his direction—would you?" He sounded wistful, as if he really wasn't expecting her to cooperate.

He didn't mention the kid. Maybe he's okay. Maybe he isn't. Still, it can't hurt to tell him. He aroused very ambivalent feelings in her; she was *certainly* attracted to him, yet he made her very uneasy. *I'd just as soon be rid of him,* she decided. *Better safe than up to my neck in kimchee.*

"He headed down toward Forty-second," she told him. "The less savory side."

"Ah." He nodded understanding. "My thanks. I shall not detain you any longer—"

As he turned away, she caught sight of his face, and the expression had changed completely. There was something so implacable about him now that she found herself backing up a step. She could readily believe that he would calmly commit murder if he felt the circumstances demanded it.

"If you're having trouble with him, isn't that a job for the cops?" she said, carefully, frightened by the change from urbane and quiet man to cold killer.

His eyes bored into hers, and she had the unsettling feeling that he not only knew *what* she was, but that he was weighing and calculating her every arcane ability down to the last erg of energy. "Do not," he said levelly, "play the fool with me, mademoiselle."

One moment he was *there,* the next, *gone.* And so quickly the bells above the door scarcely moved.

She stared into the dark for a moment, then moved carefully to the door and peered out at the street. There was no one, no one at all, in either direction.

"That is *enough* for one night," she said out loud. "Come to Mama—"

She held out her arms and gathered the shields *she'd* put on the shop back around her. They settled into place automatically, and she dismissed their presence from her conscious mind.

"Time to blow this popstand." She flipped the sign to "Closed"; in five minutes she had shut everything down, grabbed her coat, and was out the door—before something *else* could happen.

TWO

The wind muttered sullenly around the street lamps, and not even a mugger wanted to be out on a night like this one. Di shoved her hands down into the pockets of her jacket, hunched her shoulders against the bite of the wind, and wished she'd had the sense to hunt out gloves this morning. *It's colder now than it was when I left, it has to be. Gods, I'm freezing my tush off.* The echo of her boot heels on the pavement only made the street seem emptier. There should have been plenty of traffic, but not tonight. Only an occasional car blundered by, windows staring at her blankly. This was one of those night when she would have appreciated owning a car. *Thank heavens the subway station isn't too far from home, or I'd have to thaw my hands before I could type.*

She bit her lip as she got one of those unpredictable surges of homesickness. A night like this in Connecticut could be so shivery and delightful, with the wind twining around the trees, the clouds streaking across the moon, and a fire in the fireplace—

Home isn't there, anymore, kid. Home is here, *where people need what you can do. A real, honest-to-gods Home is where people who love you are, anyway, and by that measure you haven't really had a "home" since Granny died.*

When she reached her block, she could see the squat bulk of her building just ahead. The apartment building was ablaze with lights—it was *always* ablaze with lights, night or day. Considerably older than the buildings to either side of it, and several stories lower, Di's apartment house huddled in their shadow most of the day—so the tenants never turned their lights off except to sleep. No use putting plants in the window, not even ferns—there wasn't enough direct light available to keep *anything* alive.

Not that the occupants gave a damn about sunlight, direct, or otherwise. They were in hot pursuit of another sort of light. Footlights, limelights—and the dreamed-for, prayed-for spotlights.

With the single exception of Di, the building was tenanted, attic to basement, by dancers. All manner of dancers; jazz, ballet, modern, Broadway. They were crammed four and six to an apartment, and endured the cranky plumbing, the scarcity of electrical outlets, for two reasons. The lesser of the two was the heating—*unlike* the plumbing, it was utterly reliable. No small blessing in a New York winter. *That* was the reason everyone who lived here quoted when asked.

But the second and most important reason they stayed (and the one you never told anyone you couldn't trust) were the Living Rooms (capital L, capital R) in each and every apartment—

Di scampered up the grimy cement staircase, and dove into the entrance; unlocked the outer, then the foyer doors, and walked into a wall of warmth and dim yellow light. Before her was the only way up—no elevator in *this* building; she took the worn wooden stairs beyond the foyer two at a time. The fat, gleaming radiators lining the landing bathed her with heat, and already she felt better.

Cooking smells wafted past her. *Jimmy's on his liver diet again. Good thing he has tolerant roomies.* Somebody *baked brownies; naughty naughty.* Her apartment was only on the second floor and just off the staircase; a blessing on a night like this, when all she really wanted to do was get back and unwind. She unlocked her door and pushed it open carefully, just in case there was something in the way.

Sure enough, one of the others had picked up her mail for her and shoved it under the door. *A third reason; we're a family here. Mail gets picked up, packages get accepted, brownies get shared. And one noise out of character, much less a scream, and everybody in the building comes running with knives and baseball bats in hand. One "SOS" tapped out on the radiator, and our modern-dance fan, the super, checks every apartment in the building to see if somebody's sick or hurt—wonder how Kay's ankle is doing? Have to make some pea soup over the weekend and take her some.* She bent and scooped the mail up off the floor without breaking stride, and flipped on the living room lights with her free hand.

Before her, lined with mirrors on two of the walls, empty and equipped with a practice barre, was *her* Living Room—

Every one of the apartments in this building boasted a room

identical to this one; so big it echoed. She knew people who didn't have *apartments* this size. It had a solid wooden floor, gently worn, smooth, but not polished—and substantial enough that you could teach an elephant to tap-dance in here.

And as if that weren't wonderful enough, it was more than big enough and high-ceilinged enough that you could do full lifts if you were a ballet dancer. It was, point of fact, a small practice studio.

Rare was the dancer in New York who could have a studio at home to practice in. Rarer still was a home studio with a ceiling high enough to do full lifts. The Living Rooms in this building had both size and height; these apartments dated back to a time when people Entertained. The building itself had once stood in isolate splendor amid a carefully tended garden—true *garden* apartments. *That* had been very long ago.

The people that owned this building were unaware of the peculiar amenities of their property—if they ever found it out, they'd undoubtedly raise the rent to an unholy rate. So some time ago—how long ago, she'd never found out for certain—someone had set a certain small spell going here—

A spell of deception.

Maybe I'll collect karma on it, she thought, just a bit guilty. *I didn't set it—but—I don't know. Still, I couldn't survive long anyplace else. . . .*

Her predecessor had explained the workings of the spell to her; a sarcastic, gnarled old man they told her had danced with Ted Shawn. "You pay in personal energy," he'd said. "You maintain the spell out of your own strength, and you live here, and you have a safe harbor. And the landlords never learn what it is they're renting."

Because *this* apartment had always belonged to a Guardian. Guardians needed peace and space; occasionally enough space to conduct minor warfare.

There was no harm in allowing others to share that peace and space; on the contrary, it made excellent camouflage.

That a Guardian had retired just when *she* needed a base of operations—*that* was why she was *here,* and not elsewhere in some other city. Or so she suspected. Things like that happened to those with Guardian-level magic and psi powers. Maybe it was to make up for being such a large and inviting target.

Most people, even those as involved in the occult as Annie was, never even guessed the existence of the Guardians.

There's a good reason for that, if I can just think of it, she mused, pulling off her scarf. *Ah. Self-sufficiency, of course, and responsibility.*

If they knew about us, they might not be quite *so alert about covering their own asses. They might start* expecting *us to pull their fat out of the fire.*

Di suspected there had been Guardians as long as there had been cities; cities seemed to breed predators like Mr. Trouble. The Guardians could recognize each other—and Teachers, like Di's Granny, could recognize those born to be Guardians, and see that they got the kind of education they needed, the reassurance that they *weren't* going crazy because they saw and sensed things no one else did.

And Guardians become Guardians because they have no choice. Because you either use *what you have, or—or the things the Guardians Guard against come hunting you. Even if you want to be left alone, they'll come hunting you, and come for you when they are most ready. So you deal with them before that can happen.* She sighed. *Maybe I won't get karma from the spell. Maybe this pad is like hazardous-duty bennies. I pay for it in blood.*

She did a quick scan of the apartment, then the building; nothing whatsoever amiss. She hadn't expected there to be—but why take chances? She closed the door behind her and flipped the locks.

I just wish to hell one of the bennies was a salary, she thought wistfully. *Or at least job choice if I have to have a job. Or, for the gods' sake, choice of* projects. Then she gave herself a little mental slap. *Now dammit, I've only got myself to blame for that. But I swear I will* never *let Morrie talk me into category work again.*

Guardians and Teachers ran in her family tree—though the rest of the relatives rarely suspected anything. She was only one of a long line of practitioners of magic who protected the innocent from some of the things that could—and did—prey upon them. *Poor Mom; here she was trying to raise me a good Episcopalian, and there's Granny sneaking around behind her back, raising me a good pagan.*

Guess which stuck.

Then that drunk took Mom and Daddy both out, and the potential conflict was moot . . . things like that happen to Guardians, too.

More guilt, guilt that she had not been able to see what was going to happen, somehow—that she had not been able to stop it. As always, she stomped on the guilt with the only answer that made sense. *You do what you can, when you can, with what you're given. No one can be everywhere at once, not even a Guardian. And you weren't even half-trained back then.*

Di's Living Room was a studio, too; but she used it to practice karate katas—and, on certain nights, to hold Circle.

And on other nights, to save lives, and sometimes souls.

But not tonight. She stretched a little, and crossed the empty room to pass into the dining room (which had been set up as office, lounge, and *real* living room). *Not tonight. I've done my share for today.*

As she passed the door, she flipped on the living room lights without even being aware of the motion, and sailed on through into the hallway that led to the bedroom, flinging her coat into a chair on the way past.

Last set of lights, and she was staring at her unmade bed with a wince. *Granny would have a cat.* The bedroom held only her bed, a low bookcase that served as a nightstand, and a single bureau. She had an enormous walk-in closet that took up the entire wall opposite the door, but it was mostly empty. Clothing was of a lower priority than just about anything else. After all, hardly anyone ever saw her.

In a couple of minutes she'd stripped off her "good" pants and sweater, thrown them on the bed, and changed into a karate *gi*, tights, and a leotard.

Sensei would have a fit to see the ballet gear, but sensei isn't here. I like *leotards.* She stretched; thought about dinner; decided against it for the moment. *Katas first; I'm like a bundle of bridge cables.*

She trotted back out into the living room, centered herself, and listened to the life sounds around her. She didn't so much hear them as *experience* them. Others might find it maddening; she found it soothing: the sound of dozens of feet tapping, sliding, and leaping all around her. It reminded her of what life was all about—

She waited for the moment to be right and her *ki* to be perfectly balanced—

—and began.

It was a good workout; she was warm, and calmed, and all the knots were loose again when she finished and sank down to the floor in full lotus. She closed her eyes and let herself *feel* everything, then dismissed the sensations one by one from her conscious mind. The lingering hint of incense from the last Circle, the smooth, warm wood under her, the sweat cooling on her forehead, the heavy weight of her hair knotted at the nape of her neck; all dissolved and floated away, as she centered her *self* and let her mind still, let whatever was most important float to the surface to be looked at.

In other words, let's rewind the tape and look it over. What happened today that could come back and bite me later?

Not any of the kids—though she had a feeling she'd see that jock sometime in the future. *Good potential there. Good material. Open mind, cautious, but doesn't freak easy. If he's psi, or he's Talented, and he needs someone to teach him, he knows where to look now. Hmm. Might even be me.*

Mr. Trouble though, and the gypsy boy—*Bad juju. That certainly has all the marks of something that may return to haunt me. Oh well, couldn't have done anything else. I'd rather take him on my terms than his. Still.* She shivered, as a cold finger of premonition slid up her spine. *One nasty piece of work, that man, and the more I think about him, the nastier he seems. I wonder why he* didn't *Challenge me?*

That led her thoughts inexorably to the Frenchman, and she felt a pleasurable tingle about him—at least at first. *I don't know what he is, and under other circumstances, I wouldn't much care—that's one I sure wouldn't toss out of bed for eating crackers.*

Then she thought about the other face he'd shown her. *He* does *bother me. He's dangerous. Lord and Lady, if it was just me, I don't think I'd mind a little more danger in my life . . . but it isn't just me. Analysis. He didn't threaten me. He was going after Trouble, or at least that's what he said. He did show me that darker side of him. That alone is interesting. I'd better keep a weather eye out for him. Other than that, I can't see what else I can do. Except that I'd better warn Annie about both of them, and ask her about that kid. The last thing she needs is to find the shop turned into a battle zone.*

She let her thoughts roam for a bit, but nothing else popped to the surface, which meant there was nothing else likely to get in the way of work, at least not tonight. So she refocused on her *outer* self; felt the world come back with a tingle of returning awareness along every nerve—opened her eyes, and stretched, letting the stretch pull her to her feet.

Just in time; there was a knock on the door at that exact moment.

But since nobody'd buzzed to be let in the front—it had to be someone from the building. And since the knock had come at *precisely* the moment she was ready for it, there was only one person *really* likely to be calling on her—

This was home base, and safe to let some things "show." She extended a mental finger just a little and encountered familiar shields. Very familiar, since *she'd* put them on *him* less than six months ago, when he'd moved in upstairs, then homed in on her door with the surety of someone who knew *exactly* what he was looking for.

She strolled over to the massive wooden door, and threw all the locks. "What's kicking, pony?" she teased, pulling the door open. A lithe and light-boned young man who was the very image of Kipling's version of Puck, right down to ears that gave an impression of being pointed, and artistically tousled dark hair, waited indolently on the threshold. "I thought you'd have headed home to ole Virginny at the first drop of sleet this afternoon. Aren't you tired of cattle calls yet?"

"Bite your tongue," Lenny Preston retorted. He lounged decoratively against the doorjamb, posing for her appreciation, a bouquet of chrysanthemums in one hand, a thick bundle of candles in the other. "I *never* get tired of cattle calls. I just get tired of not being called back. I told you, I'm staying in this lousy town until I get somewhere. There's not much call for a dancer in Amaranthus, Virginia—not unless you want to spend the rest of your life teaching little girls to stagger around on pointe shoes."

"And watching the fathers of little boys *waiting* for you to make a move on their kids so they kin whup th' faggot upside th' hayde. A point." She took in the elegant sweater he was wearing, and gave him a raised eyebrow. It *looked* like alpaca. "Where *do* you get your clothes, you fiend? I *know* you don't have any more money than I do—"

Lenny chuckled. "If you're good, maybe someday I'll tell you. Here—" He flicked a lock of long hair out of his eyes with an elegant toss of his head, and handed her the flowers and candles. "These are from Keith."

She took them, rather surprised. She certainly hadn't expected anything from Lenny's friend. *These candles are beautiful—and I bet it's not accident that they're in the cardinal colors—but who told him what I needed? I doubt it was Lenny. Len is far too cautious about letting people know we're Wiccans. Unless—Keith did attract that poltergeist, and he's very psi, even if he doesn't know it—*

"*They're pure beeswax,*" Lenny said archly. "*Virgin* beeswax. Linen wicks. Hand-dipped."

Uh-huh. Nothing artificial, nothing man-made. "Working" materials. Something is going on here—

"Did you tell him?" she demanded.

Lenny chuckled, wrinkling his nose at her. "Not me, deary. *He* jumped on *me* the minute you were out the door, but I kept our little secrets to myself. Then yesterday he called me up and told me to come by the studio, he had something for you. The exact message is, quote, Thank you for getting rid of my houseguest, and I'm certain someone like you will get use out of these, endquote."

She laughed, as much in surprise as anything else. "Well. Are you suspecting what I'm suspecting?"

Lenny shrugged. "Could be he's Reading you subconsciously. Could *also* be he knows something about Wicca. I know he reads SF and fantasy, and there's a lot of that sort of thing showing up in the literature these days. I don't see any reason to worry about it."

She bowed to his judgment. "If you say so, I'll trust you on him. How's he doing? No recurrences, I hope? Any clients?"

Lenny made a face. "Business as usual. The candles are selling, the sculpture isn't. But no, he doesn't have things flinging themselves into the vats of melted wax anymore."

"Well, a poltergeist around flames, hot plates, and liquid wax is a Bad Idea; I figured I was just doing my bit to help enforce the fire codes."

Lenny grinned at that. "All *I* have to say is that if I didn't *know* what was going on, I'd be jealous. He's never given *me* candles and flowers!"

She spread her arms and gazed up at the ceiling for a moment. "Give me strength—" she muttered, then looked back down at him. "Play your cards right, and you won't have any reason to be jealous, nit."

Lenny straightened from his slouch, all his feigned laziness gone. "You think so?"

She snorted. "I'm a bloody *empath,* remember? *Some* of that poltergeist was him—and my suspicion is that he did it to get you to come around more often. He didn't get into trouble until he pulled in the real thing and he couldn't control what was going on anymore. *That* was when it stopped being a good excuse to have you come by and started getting dangerous. But I tell you, scared or not, every time he happened to look at *you* it got hot enough in that studio to broil meat. Speaking of food—I've got enough salmon for two—"

He started to shake his head. "Not—well. I have to be out of here *some*time tonight. I've got an extra rehearsal tomorrow. Choreography being made on me, for me."

She raised an eyebrow. "What, a *solo?* Coming up in the world, are we?"

He grinned again. "Not only that, but this show may actually open. Bob Fosse it isn't, but it's got its moments."

"But Off-off-off Broadway, no doubt."

His grin got larger. "Nope. Only Off. All the chasing's beginning to pay off. Not to mention hard work and dedication and kissing the right—"

"Feet," she interrupted him. "Keep it clean, m'lad."

He gave her a mock bow. "Anyway, I've gotta get some *sleep*. And *alone*."

"As if I were your type—get *in* here. I *won't* let you drink too much, and *I* have work to do tonight."

He followed her into the kitchen and draped himself over a chair and watched with acute interest while she broiled fish and steamed vegetables. "You look like a dancer, you *eat* like a dancer—I really don't know why you aren't a dancer."

"Because I don't get into pain," she replied wryly.

He winced. "Set, point, and match. We are masochists, aren't we?"

"You spend sixteen of the first eighteen years of your lives turning your bodies into machines, and your heads into a space where you can dance with injuries that would send a quarterback to the sidelines and do it with a smile on your face." She turned the fish, deftly. "Then you all come to New York and compete for a handful of jobs and starve so you can spend three evenings a week on a stage. And because of what you do to yourselves, you have a likely active dancing life of *maybe* twenty years. Hell yes, you're masochists. Go set the table; we'll eat like civilized human beings tonight."

He meekly obeyed; more than obeyed. When she brought out the food, the wine, and the coffee, she discovered he'd arranged the flowers and twisted the napkins into little—lilies, she thought.

"Nice."

He bowed, then held the chair out for her. "My pleasure."

"You know what made me decide *not* to go into dancing?" she asked, as she served. "Aside from the fact that there were other things I wanted more."

He paused in mid-bite. "What?" he asked, around a mouthful of salmon.

"Agnes de Mille's autobiography. The place where she talks about one of her teachers in London—I think it was Marie Lambert— showing the girls how to tape their toes, so that when their blisters broke and bled *it wouldn't leak through and stain the pointe shoes.* Not *if,* Lenny. *When.* That's when I decided the dance was *not* for me. Pain is *not* my friend. Besides, I like writing better."

"Different kind of masochism, but still masochism," he retorted, pointing his fork at her.

She sighed, thinking about the current project. "I wouldn't argue that point. Eat, eat, eat, you're too thin. How you gonna get a husband, you're so thin?"

He laughed, and speared a carrot strip. "I want to get serious."

"What?" She batted her eyes at him. "Are you proposing?"

"You said yourself you're not my type. *Serious,* Di. I have a question."

She sighed. "Fire away."

"How come I never See you unshielded?"

The non sequitur took her off balance. "What brought that on?" she asked, stalling for time to think of a good answer.

"You told me a year ago that if I was still here you'd tell me what you were doing here," he replied, contemplating a piece of broccoli, then nibbling it. "I've been waiting for a good time to bring the subject up, because you've got me puzzled as hell. You're the only odd one in this building, Di. Everyone else is a dancer. Everyone else has three roommates, or more. *Almost* everyone else is of a traditional religious background. *Nobody* but me is psychic. What's wrong with this picture?"

She waffled for a moment, debating whether or not to tell him— at least something. Like she told the gypsy boy, it's always a good idea to have allies.

"You may not like it."

"There's a lot of things I don't like. I can't imagine you being anything I wouldn't like." He put his fork down, and folded his hands. "I mean that. You and Keith are about the only real friends I have."

"It'll make you a target, if you know," she warned, concentrating on her plate, giving him a last chance to beg off.

"So?"

She checked and double-checked the shields on the room, the apartment, the building. They all seemed secure.

She dropped her personal shields for a moment; less than a minute, but Lenny gasped anyway. When she brought them back up, she deliberately finished the last of her salmon, and *then* looked back up at him.

"That's why," she said quietly. "I *have* to shield; otherwise I might as well strip naked and run through the woods in deer season with antlers tied on my head." She poked him with one finger. "Wake up. It looks more impressive than it is. There's plenty of things out there tougher than I am."

"What do you *do* with all of that?" Lenny whispered, eyes glazed and bedazzled.

"I fix things," she replied, shrugging. "I have to. If I don't use it, the power starts to leak through my shields and radiate. When that happens, I can be seen. And *things* would come after me."

"What kind of things?" Lenny asked, blinking.

"Things. Nasty things. Like that guy that came sniffing around you in high school. Like Keith's poltergeist." She pushed her plate aside and took a long sip of her wine. "Anything, everything. Stuff like Dion Fortune hinted about. Works like this, or so my grandmother told me—*anything* or anyone who 'makes a living' exploiting others psychically—or hurting or killing them—is going to be acutely sensitive to Power. They are *going* to see me. When they see me, they're going to know I'm well trained. When they know that, they're going to assume that I'm just like they are. A higher predator. A jaguar doesn't even allow its own mate in its territory except for mating—same principle holds. So—I have no choice; I either take care of *them,* when I see them and I'm ready, and they're *not,* or I stand around and let 'em come for me on *their* terms."

Lenny nodded and refilled her glass. "I never did believe in Superman," he said with a wink. "I kept wondering why he didn't just compress a ton of coal into diamonds and retire to Buenos Aires. Next question—why are you worried? Because you are, or you wouldn't be so secretive."

She sighed. "Well, I *was* kind of making a virtue of necessity, because I really do want to help people. Having abilities and not using them to help makes me—guilty, I guess. Maybe that's the same thing that makes a *good* cop. Then I broke up with my boyfriend over being involved with the occult and I wanted to quit. I tried."

"Why didn't you?"

"Because I found out that my granny was right the hard way. Right after she died; without her nagging at me to go play hero, I thought I could just lay back in some remote place and not be bothered. Maybe get to be like normal people. Wrong-oh. I got munched."

Something must have penetrated her light tone. "Was it bad?" he asked, just touching her wrist.

"Well—yeah. It was." She shook her head. "I managed to get away; it wasn't easy, and it only happened because I was lucky. It took a long time to—get over it." She shivered away the memory. "And now—I get panic attacks. I *can't* be alone, I *have* to have people around me. And I protect my rump like nobody's business, which means striking first and preventing that ever happening again. But I still want to help people, so there's still that business of making a virtue out of necessity."

But when my gut figures I'm in over my head—I'm helpless because of the attacks. I haven't had one for a while . . . but I'd sure like to have somebody around who knows I'm likely to freak.

"Last question." He raised an eyebrow. "Why are you pecking out ninety-five-cent romance novels? Seems to me with Power like that, you ought to be doing better."

The laugh she replied with was real. "Because, my good friend, playing hero is not lucrative. I *have* to make a living. Things happen if I use my Power—and Things will see the fireworks and come looking for what's smelling so tasty. So—I write romance books. I *like* writing; I'm all right at it, and I think I'm getting better. I like writing romance novels; they're fun, and I think maybe I can do a little something about the prevailing theme in them that 'anything He does to you is all right if He loves you.' Other than that, I *don't* take what I'm writing seriously, and it's a good escape from the feeling of something breathing down my neck."

"Good enough." He drained the last of his wine, and shoved away from the table. "Now I know to keep one eye on you and one on me. And I'm *not* so bad at Seeing danger and yelling 'Look out!' as you well know."

She was touched. She'd *hoped* for this reaction, but—she hadn't expected it.

"Now, I really *have* to get upstairs, get some practice in, and get to sleep."

"I'd like you to stay a while—but I have work to do, too." She let him out. "Break a leg," she said. "And don't forget to bring your robe to Samhain. I keep telling you, I don't do skyclad."

He pouted. "You're no fun."

She shrugged. "Let's just say it's a lot colder in Connecticut than Virginia, and I'm easily distracted. You know, you *might* see if you can talk Keith into coming. If you two do start to get serious, he should *know* about your strange tastes in religion, and not just guess. Besides, it might be a chance to do something to—um—cement the relationship."

Lenny went as big-eyed and innocent as a Woolworth painting. "What, *me*? Cast love spells? What on earth could you be thinking?"

She shoved him out the door, and he skipped off, laughing, doing a two-step up the stairs.

She turned on the classical station; retyped an offending scene and started up again where she'd left off, cursing at the typewriter when she mistyped "the" as "teh" for the third time. And mentally berating her heroine for being such a damned wimp. Such a damned *thoughtless* wimp, sashaying along the beach at midnight, never mind there were supposed to be pirates in the neighborhood. Sashaying along a *deserted* beach. With no dwellings around for a mile. She *deserved* to get ravished. *Oh to be able to afford a computer. Or a typing service. Helluva note; here I am with enough psi to stop Hunters on the threshold, and magical ethics forbid my using it to make my publishers give me bigger advances and more contracts!* She took a swig of Coke, and chuckled at herself. *My strength is as the strength of ten, because my heart is pure. Pure* what, *I don't think I want to know.*

The Halloween party swirled through every room of the luxe Village apartment. In the glitter and glitz and the occasional actual costume, the band members' beaded jeans and appliquéd shirts with "Wanderlust" embroidered across the back didn't look out of place. Dave Kendall leaned back into the corner of the couch he was sharing with his lead singer and Jason's acquisitions, and watched Jason Trevor make his moves—and suppressed a twinge of envy. The sensuous, classically handsome rocker had a girl snuggling up to him on either side, a brunette with a *nice* tush on his left, and a redhead with great kabambas on his right. And chances were the lucky bastard would not only lay *both* of them before the night was over, he'd get a third and go home with a fourth.

Dave felt a drop of sweat run down his back, and tried to ignore the faint headache that the babble of shrill conversation all around him was giving him.

"—so then *she* said—"

"—pure quill, my man, and big as my head—"

"—right there in *Billboard*—"

"—and I told him, 'Look, Morrie, you're a *good* agent, a fine agent, but—'"

They'd come straight over to the party from their gig; invites to parties like this one didn't come along too often. The party was hot, in more ways than one, and at uncertain intervals his grass-blown senses made the room seem too big, too crowded, and much too bright. Still—this was a good party to be seen at. Probably the best Halloween party in the Village; looked like everybody who meant anything was here. And they seemed to recognize the band members, which was a good sign.

So he'd stay. It was worth putting up with. Even if everybody else in the band seemed to be having a much better time than he was.

He looked over at Jason, taking up three quarters of the couch— and *shit*, he'd just collected a *third* chick, curled up at his feet with her back to Dave; a raven-haired chippie in a pair of tight leather pants that made it perfectly clear that nothing got between her and the leather. He took a quick check of the others.

The drummer, Jack Prescott, was off in the corner by the hot buffet, scarfing down egg rolls and schmoozing with the guy from *Rolling Stone* he knew from back when. That was real good; Jack had mentioned the guy before, but Dave had never been able to figure how good the acquaintance was. Looked like it was enough.

That ain't bad. That ain't bad at all. I'll remind Jason tomorrow.

Maybe Jack can get somebody to come by and give us a listen, or something.

He looked for Doug in vain for a while; then the bassist strolled in with a disheveled just-past-teenybopper hanging on his arm, and he had that funny grin on his face that he always got after *he'd* been laid. . . .

Dave sighed, and grabbed a hit off someone's doobie as it made the rounds. *What the hell, the food's great, the dope's good, and the wine sure as hell ain't Ripple.* He wedged himself back in the corner a little more as the brunette next to Jason shoved her tight little ass into his thigh.

It was getting awfully crowded on this couch. It fit four—if they were polite. This chick wasn't real polite.

She had her hands all *over* Jason, and Jason didn't look like he planned on stopping her anytime soon. The black-haired chick on the floor seemed oblivious; the redhead looked annoyed.

Dave wondered if the brunette was stoned enough to start something with the lead singer there and then.

Well, maybe she's bored. It's Halloween, and it don't look like any-body's gonna bring in apples for her to bob for.

He watched her for a moment longer—Jay was still dressed, but the clothing didn't seem to be slowing her down any—then his neck started to get hot, and his own pants started feeling way too tight, and he decided it might be a good idea to get up and get a drink or something.

The minute he got up, she curled her legs up on the couch where he'd been, and—

He decided enough was enough, and went looking for the potato chips.

He didn't find chips, but in the first room and near the door he found a marble coffee table holding the remains of some other munchies. In the rubble was an unclaimed bottle of wine and a bowl of cashews, and beside the table, a leather beanbag chair that seemed unoccupied. He took all three.

Just as he got settled, a latecomer arrived, with a fair amount of fanfare. The voice wasn't anybody Dave recognized, but about half the people in this room seemed thrilled to see him, effusing all over him, and calling him "Master" Jeffries. So many people swarmed over to greet the man that until he actually drew opposite Dave, the guitarist couldn't see him. When he did, he wasn't impressed.

The man would have been darkly handsome in a brooding sort of way, if it hadn't been for the two black eyes he sported, and the cast on his left arm. *"Master" Jeffries, huh?* Dave thought to himself, trying to get the man's measure. *Master of what, I wonder. He sure doesn't look like a martial artist.*

"Master Jeffries," asked a guy with an earnest and pained expression and a nose like a ship's bow. "Whatever happened to your arm—"

Jeffries gave the younger man a *look* that could have peeled paint. The offending party withered under it, and slunk away.

Dave became impressed. *Now that I wish I could learn.*

He was beginning to get the measure of this gig, but this Jeffries just didn't fit in any category Dave could come up with. The party was just about equally divided between the young and up'n'coming (like the band, a scattering of dancers, and a slew of writers and artists), some teenyboppers with daddy's bucks to blow, and the middle-aged and terminally hip, also with money to blow. One of the latter, a trendy ash-blond woman whose skin had the tight look of one-too-many face lifts, accosted Jeffries in the moment of silence left by the questioner's departure.

Dave couldn't hear exactly what she was saying, just something about a "reading." Whatever it was, Jeffries was all smiles again, and he took her beringed hand and led her over to the couch next to Dave's chair.

Dave was impressed for a second time: he didn't even look at them, much less say anything to them, but the current occupants of the couch abandoned it without so much as a murmur.

For a moment, Dave was afraid that the guy was some kind of writer, or worse, a poet, and that he was about to be involuntarily subjected to a reading of Literature.

But no.

The man held to the socialite's hand as they sat on the leather couch, spread her palm out in the light from the track-spot behind them, and began spinning her some kind of tale about what he was "reading" from her hand.

Dave was both relieved and amused. *Uh-huh. "Master" Jeffries, now I know what you're supposed to be. A guru. Just another phony mystic.* He listened a little, and poured himself another glass of wine. *He sure is good at body language, though. He's reading her like he could read minds.*

Jeffries segued from the woman's recent past to a description of her "past life" as a Roman slave girl. Interested now, Dave eavesdropped without shame—and had to stuff a handful of cashews into his mouth to keep from laughing out loud when he recognized *where*

Jeffries was getting the material he was using for the woman's "past life."

Shit, if that isn't The Last Days of Pompeii *I'll eat this chair. I thought every kid had to read that tripe. Guess not. She sure doesn't look like she recognizes it.*

The woman's eyes were moist and glowing, and her attention uncritical and total. She looked like a Moonie having a major religious experience.

After a few more minutes, Dave had to admit to himself that the man was *good*. He didn't miss a trick, and if Dave hadn't had some coaching on how to spot the phonies from that flaky ex-girlfriend of his in college—

Di might have been off in the ozone about half the time, but you couldn't pull one over on her—God, Di, why couldn't you have been fixated on something else, something I could have gotten a handle on?

But the memory hurt too much; their breakup hadn't been easy *or* pretty, and it had left enough scars that he hadn't written anything since. He shoved the recollection back into the corner where it came from, grabbed another jay making the rounds and took a big hit off it to numb the pain.

He looked around for the rest of the band, figuring that it was no bad thing for *somebody* to keep tabs on the others, and it might as well be him. Jason was nowhere in sight. Doug had another groupie, a blonde, and this one couldn't *possibly* be anything but underage. She was leeched onto his arm, rubbing up against his side, and running her hand through his shoulder-length hair, and he wasn't doing anything to discourage her. Jack had lost his friend from *Rolling Stone,* and drifted in just as Dave started looking for him. In a few minutes he was sharing a monster joint with some gay artist and his lover-of-the-week. *Keep that going, Jack-ol'-buddy. I've heard Burton has friends in the music biz.*

The murmur of the woman's voice brought Dave's attention back to Jeffries. She was thanking him, with tears in her voice, for "enlightening" her. There was something odd about her, and for a moment Dave couldn't quite place it. Then he realized, as she drifted off in search of other prey, what it was. When she'd accosted this Jeffries, she'd been lively to the point of manic, and quite vivacious. But *now* she seemed drained and exhausted. She looked depressed, and complained to one of her friends on the way out of the room that she had a terrible headache.

He took a quick look back at Jeffries, to see if the man had been affected in the same way.

He hadn't. In fact, he looked better. His black eyes seemed to have faded visibly—Dave would have been willing to swear that they were real shiners when he came in; now they were just a faded purple, and hardly swollen at all.

Dave shook his head. *I'm stoned, that's all. Too stoned to know what I'm seeing. Maybe it's time to go home*—

But a commotion over at the side of the room drew him and everyone else in the direction of their host, some kind of avant-garde writer, who was enjoying a wave of popularity for his current, terribly relevant novel of life on the streets.

He had something in his hands; from where Dave stood it looked like a bowl. A plastic bowl, with a cover on it.

What is this, a Tupperware party?

"All right, kiddies, it's trick or treat time!" he called over the party noise. That got him silence, and he smiled archly. "It's the witching hour, boys and girls, and you all know how witches used to fly away on Halloween. I've got you something that'll send you to the same place."

He pulled the lid off the bowl, and Dave could see that it was full to the brim with capsules; small ones, a maroon color that was just a shade under black. They bothered Dave for a moment; then he figured out why. They were the color of dried blood.

"Thought we'd all like a little *adult* trick or treat; the trick is that these little darlings are *new*—so new they not only aren't illegal yet, they don't even have a name yet. The treat is what they *do* to you." Their host smirked, and Dave saw that his eyes were so dilated that there was no iris showing. "I promise you, I previewed them yesterday, and they are *dynamite*. So share the wealth, kids—"

The bowl began to make the rounds, and Dave found he was reaching for it with all the others.

"—party left eight dead of unknown causes," the news announcer said. "Meanwhile, more news of Watergate—"

Di tuned him out. She'd only put the news on in the first place to see if there were any after-Halloween incidents that might involve her. But a druggie party in the Village had no consequences to anyone but the ones stupid enough to dope themselves into the next life, and Watergate was out of *her* league.

The news left her feeling very sour. Nixon would get off; you didn't have to be a fortune-teller—a real one—to know that. He knew where too many skeletons were hidden, and he had too many connections who'd be only too happy to make sure certain witnesses never got to testify. About the only *good* thing would be that he would never hold office again.

As for the fools who popped whatever came to hand—*I don't do Presidents, I don't do druggies, and I don't do windows. Eight dead. Damned fools. Some people never get beyond the stage of sticking everything they find into their mouths.*

She had more pressing difficulties; something she could and would have to do something about. How to get the ravished maiden on board the privateer *without* having the rest of the crew find out and demand a piece of the—ahem—action.

Hard to do when the smallest dory takes two men to row, and Sarah ain't bloody likely to help. She's too busy fainting. What a wimp!

She chewed on the end of her pencil and scowled at the typewriter. Inspiration was not forthcoming.

Why didn't they cover this in the outline? Maybe if Nicholas buys off the first mate—

Sound of the feet overhead. Hard little taps, running, and thuds. Ballet. Paul and Jill were rehearsing "Le Jeune Homme et la Mort" again.

Maybe I ought to go up and watch. They shook me loose last time I had a problem. Besides, they're so good on that piece—

She stood up and shoved her chair back—

—and suddenly found her knees giving; grabbed the desk and hung on.

Shield, shield, dummy—this is coming from right outside—

A wave of pure fear battered at her and drove any vestige of real thought from her mind. It took her a breath to fight back; another to get control of herself.

A third to realize that the wave of violent emotion was carrying with it an unmistakable call for help, magician to magician, psi to psi.

By the fourth breath, her keys were in her pocket, her ritual knife and flashlight were in her hands, and her door was gaping wide behind her as she took the stairs at a dead, flat-out run.

A second wave of fear broke over her just as she hit the landing—she stumbled, then recovered—

But when she reached the foyer, there was—nothing. Nothing at all, just a mental emptiness.

And that was more ominous than the fear.

She hit the outer door; there was nothing in either direction on the street. That left the alley. Which she did *not* want to go into—but there was no choice.

She scrambled around the corner and shone the flashlight ahead of her; it was a powerful light, heavy enough to use as a club if she had to. The light wobbled around the alleyway as her hand shook; then there was a flash of something pale off to the side.

She steadied the beam.

A person. The intruder was bending over something in a kind of half-kneeling position. As the light struck him, he turned, and snarled—

And vanished.

"Oh dear gods!"

Di nearly dropped the flashlight; she put her back to the cold brick of the alley wall and tried to make sense of what she'd just seen.

Because the "intruder" was the strange Frenchman from the week before. And when he had snarled at the light, she had seen—fangs.

And *then* he had disappeared.

She waited, heart pounding, for him, for *something*, to come after her, but as the moments crawled by, and she got colder and colder, nothing did. Finally she managed to scrape up enough courage to approach whoever was lying in the alley. *Whoever*, because she was dreadfully afraid that she knew who had called her tonight.

The powerful beam of light was pitiless, and cared nothing for her remorse. It showed her what she didn't want to see; that the thing in the alley was a body, that the body was that of the gypsy boy she had given her card to, and that the boy was dead.

She knelt beside him, sick with grief. *I failed him. He came running to me for help, and I was too late to save him. He thought I could protect him; I'd promised protection, and I failed that promise. Oh gods.*

That was enough to hold her kneeling motionless on the wet, filthy pavement for a long time. It was really only the *other* thing she'd seen that broke her trance of self-accusation and made her take a closer look at the boy to try to discover what had killed him.

And that was the Frenchman; the Frenchman with *fangs*.

Because she had just seen something that didn't, couldn't exist.

A vampire. A real, classical, blood-sucking vampire.

THREE

Patrolman Ron St. Claire stared into the murky brown of his third cup of coffee and hoped that he'd be able to *finish* this one. It hadn't been a good night for finishing much of anything; coffee, conversations, dinner.

"Hey, Ron."

He looked up from the coffee and grinned at the elfin waitress wrinkling her nose at him. "Hey, yourself. What's cookin', honey?"

April Santee, the third-shift waitress of Dunkin' Donuts number five-three-seven mock-glowered at him. "How many times do I have to tell you not to call me honey?"

"Till I stop."

"One of these days," the little brunette told him, pointing a threatening finger at him, "I'm gonna bring my girlfriend the karate champ in here, and you *will* stop." She saw then how tired he was, and dropped the banter. "Babe, you look like somebody's been giving you the short end of the stick all night."

"Something like that," he replied, rubbing his right eye with one knuckle. "It's a big night for indoor crime and craziness, and it isn't even half over. Three breaking-and-enterings, five assaults, two assault-with-deadlies, and seven domestic violence. And before you ask, here's the stats of the ones I think your gang should talk to." He pushed a half-sheet of lined notebook paper across the counter to her.

April frowned down at the list, and shook her head. "There's only three names here," she said, accusation shading her voice with suspicion.

"Two of the seven you already have. One walked out on her old man after clobbering him back with a cast-iron frying pan; I think that was the first time he took a hand to her, and I *know* it's gonna be the last. One was a woman beating up on her old man. That leaves you three. Better talk to number two quick; she had that look in her eyes. She's in a trap she can't break out of, and if she doesn't get some help there's gonna be a homicide."

"Gotcha." April folded the piece of paper and tucked it into her apron pocket. "I'll phone 'em to the hot-line desk on my break. Thanks, big fella." She refreshed his coffee without being asked. "You know, I never asked you: what do *you* get out of this? You could get fired if anybody ever found out you were passing names and addresses out to us. Never mind we're saving women from wife beaters, that's invasion of privacy."

"What do *I* get? Let me tell you what I *don't* get. Corpses. Bodies on my beat I don't need." He'd gotten two just before he met April; some poor, worn-out thing beaten to death by her husband—and a husband hacked to pieces with a cleaver by a wife who couldn't take it anymore. He looked up into April's muddy-brown eyes, the exact color of his coffee, wondering if she had any idea of what he was talking about. He needn't have wondered; the grim set to her mouth told him she'd seen a couple of corpses, too.

"Helluva job, isn't it?" she said rhetorically.

"Could be worse. I could be an MCP and be laughing at you gals, instead of trying to help." He drank half the coffee and smiled, wearily; April made *good* coffee.

About then the box at his belt squawked. "Oh hell," he groaned, pushing off the stool.

"Yo, Ron!" He looked up just in time to catch the plaid thermos April tossed at him. "Full, fresh, black, and sugar. Compliments of the Women's Shelter. Move out, soldier."

He grinned, transferred the thermos to his left, and saluted. "Yes, *ma'am.*" He turned smartly on his heel and trotted to the squad.

"Got a weird one," the dispatcher told him, when he reported in. The interior of the squad car was still warm; he hadn't even been inside long enough for the heat to dissipate. He started the engine, and grunted with relief when it caught.

"Weird how?" he asked, waiting for traffic to clear.

"Runaway bus—well, runaway driver, anyway. We took five calls on it before the captain decided it wasn't a prank, and we just took call number nine a minute ago; he says this looks like something we'd better step in on, especially after the last call."

"What's the deal?" Ron asked, backing out of the parking space and onto the street.

"Bus on route twenty-nine isn't stopping to pick people up. Sticking to the route, but not stopping. It's damn near empty, so that's not why."

"So?" Ron said scornfully. "Let them take care of it. Bus company's got radios and cars. So they got a stoned driver, let them handle it. Maybe he's pissed off at his bosses. Why should we mix into it?"

"'Cause the last call was a guy the bus *did* stop for. He was all alone, he started to get on—and when he happened to look over at the other passengers—he swears on his life they were wounded or dead."

A finger of cold ran up the back of Ron's neck. "You're sure this isn't a hoax?" He swung the squad onto a route that would bring it to intersect with the bus's in about ten minutes.

"Not hardly," Dispatch said wryly. "Caller number nine was Father Jim O'Donnel from Saint Anthony's."

"Hell." He turned a corner and saw the bus up ahead of him, lights shining harshly through the windows. "Roger. I've got 'em in sight."

He hit the lights, then the siren—

But to no effect; the bus didn't even slow down.

He swore, pulled alongside—

He fought a battle of "chicken" with the thing for ten minutes, sweat popping out all over him, his armpits getting soggy. He asked Dispatch for some help—but there were gangfights all over tonight, and a rash of armed-and-dangerous, and there was nobody to spare. Finally he managed to force the vehicle into a cul-de-sac.

The bus rolled to a gentle halt, stopped. As Ron flung his car in behind it, slewing it sideways with a squeal of tires so that the cul-de-sac was blocked, someone turned the bus engine off, the lights flickered, then went to battery—

And nothing happened.

No one got out; no one moved. Not even the driver.

Sweating, Ron called in what he was about to do, asking for backup. Just in case. Dispatch said they'd try. He waited a few moments; decided he didn't dare wait any longer. Then, before he had a chance to think about it, he pulled his gun, kicked open the squad door, and dove out, like a baseball player diving for home plate, into the meager shelter of a battered old Rabbit.

Silence, except for the ticking sounds of cooling metal.

He waited, while the sweat on him froze, and his chest went numb from contact with the cold pavement, and still nothing happened. He gathered himself, a human spring coiled tighter and tighter—then he lurched to his feet, and dashed to the side of the bus. He didn't slow in the least as he neared it, just ran straight for the side of it, plastering himself there with a thud as he hit the metal.

Still nothing. No sign of movement, and no sound.

This was getting spookier by the second. With sweat pouring down his back, and his piece cocked and ready, he inched along the freezing side of the bus until he came to the rear exit. He tested it, pushing on it. It gave a little, so it wasn't locked up. He took a deep breath, trying not to cough on the diesel fumes, and shoved it open, then flung himself inside, sprawled in the stairwell, elbows braced against the top step.

"*Freeze,*" he shouted, targeting the driver's head, thinking *Now it comes*—

But nothing happened.

Except that he smelled the burned-iron tang of blood, and his knee was getting wet where it was jammed against one of the stairs.

He looked down at the floor of the bus. He'd heard the phrase "awash with blood" before, and had laughed at it. He wasn't laughing now, not when blood was running down the aisles, and trickling over the stairs in a thin but steady stream, soaking the knee of his uniform.

He stumbled through the open door to the smog outside, clung to the side of the door and threw up.

They'd given him one of the soundproofed rooms used for questioning suspects so that he could concentrate. There was a pot of coffee on the table next to the stack of forms he had to fill out, also (presumably) to help him concentrate.

What if I don't want to concentrate? What if I just want to forget the whole thing?

The door opened and shut behind him. "St. Claire—"

Ron looked up from the pile of papers in front of him, his eyes dry and aching and foggy with weariness, his stomach sore from heaving. He'd never had a multiple homicide before; he'd had no idea there were so many papers to fill out for each victim. He had just completed Schetzke, Leona (Female, 45, Cauc, brown, brown) and was about to start on Paloma, Marie Annette (Female, 43, Hisp, brown, black).

And it's a good thing I didn't have to fire my piece, or I'd have had about fifty ballistics reports to fill in, too.

"Captain." He nodded as the precinct captain eased himself past the edge of the table and sat down in one of the old wooden chairs on the other side. A stranger in a suit so crisp it looked as if he'd just taken it out of the box gave him a long, measuring look, then took the other chair. Ron suppressed the urge to look at his shoes. Shiny black shoes would have meant he was FBI. If the Feds were mixed in this somehow, Ron didn't want to know about it.

"Ron, can you give it to us one more time? After you got back on the bus." The boss looked unhappy; Ron's hackles went up. There was something severely wrong—

"I got back on the bus," he replied, clenching his hands into fists, and feeling his gut clench, too. "I started taking a body count. First was a pair of females, that's right opposite the rear entrance. Second was an old man in a tailored business suit—"

The stranger took notes. So the FBI *was* involved. As he detailed the body count, working his way up to the front of the bus, he wondered what on earth could have happened to bring Feds into this. Was this a terrorist action of some kind? Something involving the Mob?

"—the last one was the driver, I guess," he finished.

"At least, he was wearing a bus uniform. He was the only one not cut up any, but he was as cold as the rest of them—and they were *cold.*" There was a snap and he looked down at his right fist, startled. He'd broken his pencil in half. He put the halves down, carefully, and reached for a new one with the same deliberate care.

"You're sure," the captain persisted. "You're *certain* that the last one was wearing a bus uniform."

"Yeah," he replied, too upset to be angry. "I mean, that's not something I'd make a mistake about."

"Was this him?" The stranger pushed a Polaroid across the table at him, the kind they took when they checked bodies into the morgue. Ron took a cursory look. It was definitely a picture of his corpse.

"Yeah, that's him."

"Thanks, St. Claire." Without any explanation, they pushed their chairs away from the table, legs grating on the linoleum, and started to get up.

"Wait a minute," he said belligerently. "Don't I get to know what's going on? You come in here, make me go over that—slaughterhouse all over again, and then you don't even tell me *why?*"

The captain paused for a moment; the stranger stopped halfway to the door.

"Go ahead," the stranger said, with what might have been a shrug, except that it was too slight a movement to even wrinkle the shoulders of his suit.

"We had some bus dispatchers in here to identify the man," the captain said slowly. "They got here about half an hour ago."

"So?" Ron prompted. "What happened?"

"He wasn't there."

Ron shook his head, thinking he must have misheard. "He wasn't theirs?"

"No—*he wasn't there.* He was gone. Vanished. Poof. Right out of a morgue drawer."

"Gone?" Ron said faintly, feeling very, very cold.

"Gone."

Suddenly the paperwork seemed very attractive indeed, as an alternative to thinking.

Di poured herself a double Scotch and picked up the phone, dialing the emergency number. In a voice that shook, she reported screams and gunshots in the alley beneath her window. No, she hadn't gone out to look. No, she didn't think it was cars backfiring, there hadn't been any cars down there at the time. No, she didn't know if anyone else had heard. The sexless, passionless entity on the other end of the line took down her name and address, and said someone would be around to check the alley shortly. They hung up; so did she.

Thank the gods Lenny isn't home tonight; he'd have been out there with me. She sagged against the desk chair. *He might have beat me there. He couldn't have missed the vibes. And he could have gotten* himself *killed.*

Then she drank half of that double Scotch in one gulp.

Her hand shook so hard that the ice cubes rattled against the side of the glass. She put it down, and stood beside the desk, bracing herself against it. She simply held that position for a long time, staring at the dark reflection of herself in the windowpane.

After a while there were sirens below, and red lights flashing against the bricks of the building opposite her. She took her drink to the kitchen, refilled it, and returned to her living room to curl up on her shabby old brown sofa.

She half expected the cops to come and pound on her door, but no one arrived, and eventually the red flashes went away from the window.

No. No panic attack, she told herself sternly. *Not now. I can't afford one.*

Fight or flight, fight or flight, adrenaline flooded her system, trying to override her ability to think. She *knew* the mechanism, *knew* it right down to the chemicals involved, and it didn't help.

No. Not. Now. It ran from me. I can handle this.

She had won. This time, she had won.

When her hands stopped shaking, she began sipping the Scotch, trying to get everything straight in her head.

There wasn't a mark on him, not one. But he was *drained; drained of psychic and emotional energy until his heart literally stopped. That is not "traditional" vampiric attack.*

Vampiric attack? What in hell am I thinking of?

But I saw the fangs, I know I did. I did not *imagine them.*

But it wasn't blood he was drained of, it was emotional energy. Like a "psychic vampire." Like the kind of person who walks into a party and leeches onto the liveliest person there, and when he leaves, he's feeling wonderful *and his "victim" feels like the bottom of the biorhythm chart. I've known psychic vampires that could drain you so low that you'd catch every germ that walked by, just because the immune system is so tied into the emotional system. And ones that left you ready to commit suicide but too tired to pick up the knife to do it.*

But that's psychic vampires. "Psivamps." Granny told me that "vampires" were a myth, that the psivamps were the only kind of vampires there were.

What if she didn't know?

That's crazy. That's not what killed the boy—

And psivamps can't kill. Or—can they?

What if there's very rare *psivamps that can? What if those long teeth are an outward sign of a really strong psivamp? What if I really didn't see fangs, what if what I saw was something my subconscious produced, so I'd make the connection between the boy's death and vampirism?*

I can't have seen a vampire.

But I did.

Oh gods.

She sipped, and got only ice, and she looked at her empty glass in some surprise.

What if I'm wrong? What if there are *real vampires?*

But if there are—who killed that boy? Why did they kill him? What made it so important that they kill him before he reached me? Did they know he was coming to me? Am I a target now? What did he know— and did he plan to tell me about it—or was this all coincidence, and was he simply running to the nearest safe harbor he knew of?

And if this man is a real vampire, a classical bloodsucker—why did the boy die of emotional drainage?

She wanted badly to have another drink—but if she was a target, she knew she didn't dare. She *had* to stay alert and on guard, and she could not give in to fear. Instead she spent the better part of the next two hours reinforcing every shield on the place, then showered and went to bed—

But not to sleep. She left all the lights on, and stared up at the ceiling, waiting.

Dave woke up—sort of—around five the next night. But his eyes wouldn't focus right, and he felt as if he hadn't gotten any sleep at all. He tried everything to jar himself awake, from a cold shower to downing a whole pot of espresso, black—but when he blanked for "a minute" and came to at midnight, slumped over the kitchen table (with a roach doing the backstroke in the half-empty cup in his hand), he decided to hang it up and go back to bed.

He was in that kind of half-daze for almost forty-eight hours; half waking, trying to get up, going back to bed again. And God, the dreams—

The dreams he had were real bummers; like no dreams he'd ever had before. Nothing visual, either. Just a blackness and the feeling that millions of people were shouting their most intimate thoughts at him. They were really repeats of the stuff those damned red pills had done to him. He felt like he was stuck inside of peoples' heads, feeling what they felt, eavesdropping on whatever they were doing.

Made him feel like some kind of damned pervert. Some kind of *Twilight Zone* Peeping Tom.

Finally, *finally*, he really woke up, around four on the second day after the party. And looked at the calendar on the wall above his bed, and realized they had a gig at a club they'd contracted to play in be- fore Halloween—in four hours.

Oh hell. Oh goddamn hell. I feel like shit warmed over.

He struggled out of his tangle of sheets and blankets and into clothes—gig clothes; he'd have to hustle his buns like crazy to get to the club as it was. He was a little surprised to see the clothing from the party-night tossed over a chair; he didn't remember doing that. Come to think of it, he didn't even remember getting home.

I must've taken a cab. Thank God I took the axe home before I went over there. Thank God Jack's got the amps in the back of his car—

He didn't have a stomach so much as a hollow, echoing cavern just under his ribs. His throat and mouth were dry as a critic's soul, but the hunger was worse. *God, I'm* starved—*I should be sicker'n a dog, but I'm starved—*

But there was no time—he grabbed what was in the fridge, threw baloney on bread, snatched up his axe, stuffed it in his gigbag, and headed out the door—

And at the door of the building, he hit sunlight, and it felt like hitting a wall.

He backed into the entryway for a second, and fumbled in the pocket of his jacket for his shades. *Is it just me, or did somebody clean out all the pollution while I was out? God, it's like stagelights.*

He got the shades on, walked out of the building again, and looked around—

And nobody else was even squinting, while to *his* eyes the sun was only just bearable with his shades.

Must've been that stuff. Damn if I ever take anything red again—

He wolfed the sandwich down as he loped to the bus stop, but it did nothing to ease the gnawing hunger in his belly. When he made his transfer, he stopped long enough at a newsstand to pick up half a dozen candy bars, but a sugar megadose that would have left him feeling bloated a couple of days ago didn't ease his sore throat or even *dent* the raging that was gnawing at his backbone.

Now *that* was even stranger than his sudden sensitivity to light.

Hell, I didn't eat for two days. Probably some kind of deficiency. Potassium, maybe. I'll deal with it when I get home.

Besides, he had a head that felt like a pumpkin—and he sure didn't need to add to his problems by stuffing himself and then turning sick. *That'd be a great way to end the act, barf all over the stage. Real impressive, Dave.*

Once he stopped moving, depression set in. He cradled his axe in his lap and stared out the grimy bus window, wondering if Wanderlust was *ever* going to get anywhere. The night of the party, it had looked like things were coming up, but now? God.

The sun crawled behind the skyscrapers, and he was finally able to stuff his dark glasses back into his pocket.

Three years we've been at this, and we're still basically a bar band. I wish I knew what the hell we're doing wrong. Maybe we should try moving to LA or 'Frisco—naw, that wouldn't do any good. Man, I can't take La-La-Land, even if we could afford the move, and nobody's picked up any new bands out of 'Frisco since I can't think when. Since Graham closed down the Ballroom. He slumped down in the slick plastic seat, and tucked his chin down on his chest, hoping vaguely that his head would stop throbbing. It didn't hurt—but the sensation was uncomfortable and disorienting. Maybe we oughta pack it in. Maybe I oughta go back to school. Finish out, get my degree. Go be an accountant or something. Shit, I haven't written anything in years, even. All the stuff of mine we're doing is three years old at best. Maybe I just can't cut it as a musician. Maybe I'm a has-been; shit, maybe I'm a never-was.

He was so sunk in depression that he almost missed his stop; shaken into alertness only by the flash of neon as somebody turned the club's gaudy orange and red sign on just as the bus rolled past. He yanked the cord just in time, crawled over a sea of knees, and escaped into the cold of the street.

The club wouldn't open till eight, so he had to take the alley entrance, and for some reason tonight his nose—that he'd thought was used to New York—wasn't handling the mix of rotting garbage and urine at all. He gagged, and held his breath until he got inside. The other guys were already there, setting up, though from the looks of things they hadn't been there long. Of all of them, only Jack looked in any shape to do anything.

"You look like hell," Doug said, as he hauled himself up onto the tiny carpet-covered stage.

"No shit, Sherlock," he replied sourly. "I feel like hell."

"Join the club," Jason muttered, setting up mikes with a clatter of metal. He was still wearing his shades; Dave didn't think he wanted to know what his head felt like.

"Next time Frazier brings out one of his treats, hit me if I take him up on it, okay?" he said to Doug.

"You too, huh?" The bassist pulled his baby out of her bag, and frowned at her—and Doug never frowned at his baby.

"Yeah."

"I dunno why that shit got to you guys so bad," Jack commented from somewhere behind his kit. "All it did was give me rainbows around everything for a while, and giggle fits."

"You checked in with the news?" Jason asked suddenly, turning to face them, and raising his shades to reveal eyes like two holes burned into the flesh of his face.

Dave mutely shook his head. Doug did the same.

"Nope," Jack seconded. "Didn't have time. Why?"

"'Cause we're the lucky ones. They took 'bout eight of Frazier's friends home in body bags."

Jack whistled; the sharp sound passed *through* Dave's head, and he winced.

Doug grimaced, though it was hard to tell if it was in reaction to the news or the noise. "Shee-it. Who?"

Jason paused in his mike placement, and pondered them both for a moment from behind the shelter of his glasses. "Only ones you might know would be that dancer, Tamara, and the two dudes she's been playing threesies with."

Dave started, and covered it by fiddling with the pickup on his amp. Because one of the few clear memories he had of when the drug kicked in was a strange hallucination of *being* Tamara and her two partners in turn, as they screwed each other's brains out. If it hadn't been so weird and embarrassing, it would have been an incredible turn-on—he hadn't considered that Tam's lovers might be bi; and he hadn't *dreamed* that there could be—that anybody could—God, the kind of things three creative and athletic people could do with each other!

That's crazy. It's just a coincidence. Just a real strange coincidence, and my own gutter-imagination.

"Christ on a crutch," Jack said, subdued. "Hey, next time we do one of Frazier's parties, we stick to what we know, okay?"

Dave swallowed, then nodded, considering what *could* have happened. No telling why or how they'd croaked, but that was *too* close. "Dig it. Man, we are just stone lucky we weren't on last night—we'd never have made it."

Jason pushed his glasses back down over his eyes. "Damn straight. And *that* would have spelled 'finito' to *this* band right then and there. So let's get this show on the road, huh? Or we may not make it out of *this* gig alive."

Privately, Dave had this figured for a Bad One. There was *no* electricity, *no* drive when they warmed up; they were just walking through the songs, making the motions, but not much else was going on. It didn't get any better, and when the hired hands showed and started setting the place up, *they* did not look impressed. The owner walked in halfway through, listened, and grimaced a little; the bouncer looked flat bored. Dave's heart sank.

The owner put the floor lights on, and vanished down the corridor behind the stage; a couple of seconds later the canned music started, and a couple of customers filed in.

The four of them wordlessly racked their instruments and jumped down off the stage; give the place half an hour to fill, then they'd be on.

Half an hour—too much time, and not enough.

They edged single file down the icy, cement-block hallway to the break room, each in his own little world. This one was like a little prison cell, painted cement walls, a couple of foggy mirrors, metal folding chairs and a table, a fridge full of soft drinks. Dave grabbed a Coke; his mouth was so dry now that it rivaled his hunger for discomfort level. He chugged it in seconds, then grabbed another—the ache in his gut eased up a little, and his throat didn't seem quite so dry. He chugged a third, beginning to feel better.

Damn if it was something missing—what's in Coke? Vitamin C maybe? Di always used to swear by vitamins, but I can't remember which ones.

Doug caught on, then Jason. Together they must have finished about half a case inside fifteen minutes. Jack looked at them with a funny expression for a minute, then went off into his trance, staring at the floor about five feet in front of him, air-drumming.

Dave actually started to feel like a human being again, and went into *his* preset ritual of pacing in little circles while going over every song, every riff, in his mind. He wasn't sure what Jason thought about, but *his* thing involved dance stretches. Doug just sat, eyes closed, so quiet you couldn't even see him breathing.

The overhead light flickered twice; moment-of-truth time.

If we can pull this gig off, lousy as we feel, then we've got it enough together as a band for us to keep trying, Dave decided suddenly. *Yeah. That's how I'll play it.*

He jumped up onto the stage feeling like a gladiator must have felt in the arena. Make it or break it—

They usually opened with the Stones' "Satisfaction," but Jason had decided they weren't going to do anybody else's work on this gig but their own. So they opened with one of Dave's pieces, the last one he'd written, "Crawlin' the Walls."

It began with a falling scream from the lead guitar, a monotone snarl from the bass, and a screech that rose to meet the lead from Dave's—then Jack's drums came in like thunder from the gods—

Out of the corner of his eye, across the thin haze of smoke, Dave could see every head in the place snap around to face the stage, eyes going wide with surprise.

Well, that sure as hell got their attention, anyway.

Then the lights came up on them, angry and red; Jack began

driving the beat like a manic pile driver, Doug pounded the bass line, and the rumble was on—

For the first half of the song it *was* a rumble; his line fighting Jason's for supremacy, the bass muttering threats underneath, and the lights pulsing on them in alternating reds and hot yellows. But the crowd seemed to like it that way; there were heads nodding out there, and feet starting to tap, and a couple of dancers, braver than the rest, out on the floor.

The drumbeats started to get inside Dave's head; to throb in his blood.

Then Jason started his vocal line.

Dave had been dreading this; Jason had a voice as smooth as chamois suede most of the time, but tonight he'd been awful. He'd wandered all over the landscape, pitchwise, and he'd been hoarse and rough—Dave had been real tempted to ask him to sit this one night out and let him and Doug handle the vocals.

But when the first note left Jason's throat, he knew everything was going to be all right.

I'm gonna buy stock in Coke, he thought, with wonder verging on reverent awe. *I don't* care *if they're capitalist pigs, I'm gonna buy stock in Coke. My God, our ass is saved*—

The song poured from Jason in a flow of molten, red-hot gold, every note round and perfect, every nuance shaped exactly as Dave had heard it in his head.

And Dave could *feel* the crowd responding; feel the energy rising up from the floor and beginning to build. There was a wave building up out there, in the dark, past the reef of light and sound—a throbbing power and a tightwire tension waiting to be released, *begging* to be released, and lacking only the trigger—

Oh God—

It was coming round to *him* now, he was supposed to come in with the harmony, and oh God, *how* was he going to match what Jason was doing? He was going to screw it up, he was, he didn't dare sing, he didn't dare *not* sing, he grabbed his mike like a lifeline and—

"Set me free!"

Oh dear God *in heaven*—

It was beautiful, it was cosmic—their voices rose together, so perfectly matched they even had their vibrato in unison. It was the Holy Grail, it was orgasm, it was everything he'd ever *dreamed* that song could be—everything he'd despaired of it ever becoming—

And the wave of energy from the crowd crested and broke over them.

Suddenly they were *alive*, like they'd never known what it was to *be* alive; and hot, and jamming like they'd never jammed before. He hadn't seen anybody move from the tables, but suddenly there was a sea of faceless bodies out there on the floor; they were packed so tightly in front of the stage there was no room to move, they just jigged in place, a sea of arms waving wildly over their heads, making eddies in the sweet grass smoke that billowed around them like incense around the altar. *They* were on the altar, the band was celebrant and sacrifice in one. *Life;* that's what was pouring from the audience into him. He soaked it up, his hunger ebbed away like it had never been there, and still the energy flowed into him, sweet as sin, more intoxicating than any drug.

He couldn't stop, not now. He threw back his head to toss his hair out of his eyes and segued right into the next piece, "No Time Out." Jason followed him like they'd planned it that way from the start. Doug moved in on his mike and they made the same kind of sweet harmonies *he* and Jason had achieved, and Dave just closed his eyes and let his fingers do the walking.

The flow was incredible—

They jammed on that song for a full ten minutes; it felt like no time at all, and when they brought it round, it *hurt* to have to end it.

Then it didn't end, because *Jason* licked right on into "FreeFall," and when Dave came in on the vocal line, all of a sudden *Doug* was in there too, and it worked, oh dear God in heaven, it *worked,* and Dave's throat ached with the purity of it.

Then from that straight on into "Meltdown," then "Breaking Glass," then "You, Baby, Too." They switched mood, they swapped leads—nothing broke the energy, the flow, it just kept coming and coming—

The next song was Jason's and the last of the set; all Dave had to do on this was lay down his guitar line and go with the flow. He was sweating like a racehorse, and feeling like a god—and when he *finally* really looked at the others to see if *they* were feeling the same way, Jack gave him a thumb's up and the wickedest grin he'd ever seen in his life. He volleyed the grin right back, and turned to Jason and Doug—

—and felt a cold chill walk down his spine.

Jason had lost the glasses somewhere; Doug was in shadow. Their eyes were closed—Jason's *and* Doug's. Doug was backed off right behind the lead, like his bodyguard; head down, and cranking that bass to her limits—Jason, face streaming sweat, hair plastered down to his skull, crooned into the microphone, bathed in a single golden spot.

They both wore exactly the same expression, right down to the quirk at the corners of their mouths—and it was that expression that made Dave's blood chill.

They were feeling that energy, no doubt of it. They wore the same expressions they wore after they'd just been laid. Sated, and no little smug.

But—they still looked hungry. Like they wanted *more.*

A *lot* more.

But there was no time to think of it; they were in the break room barely long enough to get drinks and dry off a little, then the crowd *pulled* them back out onto the stage just by sheer force of their collective will.

It can't be that good again, Dave thought, as Jack began to pound the solo intro to the next set. *It was a fluke. We've never done anything like that before—*

Then Doug and Jason hammered down, and the impossible happened.

It *wasn't* that good again. It was better.

The four of them were like pieces of a single machine; they'd toss changes at each other and no one ever missed his catch. They took a little longer rest this time; Jack had to have one, he'd played like he had eight arms up there, and one more song might have sent him into cardiac arrest. And Jason lay right flat down on the concrete floor, trying to dump some of the heat from his body. But within twenty minutes they were back out on the stage again, and it was like they'd never left it.

The manager finally had to get the bouncer to drive people out at closing. Nobody wanted to leave.

Dave tried the same trick with the floor that Jason had, hoping to leech the warmth out of his overheated body before he broiled; God, it was wonderful, feeling that cold concrete suck the heat right out of him. The club manager showed up at the door of the break room and started babbling; Dave groaned, and opened his eyes, and gave him the look that said *Not now*—but the guy wasn't taking that answer, and he started to lever himself up onto his elbow—

"I'll take care of this—"

The tone was commanding, even arrogant, and Jason rose up out of his chair like Apollo rising from the Sun-throne—

And suddenly there was a perceptible shift in balances.

Everybody froze for a moment, even the club manager. Only Jason moved, and only his eyes, which went to Dave's and locked with them.

Dave had seen that look before; from one gang member challenging for supremacy, from the beta wolf going for the alpha, from a stallion claiming another's herd.

Are you going to fight me for this?

Up until now, Dave had been the de facto leader of the band, mostly because nobody else wanted to be the one to make the bookings and give the orders. But suddenly there was a new set of priorities, and the world skewed about 90 degrees.

Do I want to fight him on this? Dave asked himself, and met those hard gray eyes—

Then looked away.

No. No, it's not worth it. Jason wants the hat, Jason can have it.

He lay back down on the concrete, but not before he had seen Jason's eyes narrow and then glint in satisfaction.

Dave closed his eyes and heard two pairs of feet walking away toward the manager's office. About ten minutes later, one pair came back. He opened his eyes, and saw Jason standing over him, with a dark bottle in one hand, offering the hand that wasn't holding a bottle.

"Lay there too long and you'll stiffen up," the blond said.

He took the hand and Jason hauled him to his feet without any effort at all, which surprised the hell out of Dave. He'd never suspected that much strength in that lanky body.

"So what's up?" Doug asked, as Jason grabbed a Coke, drank half of it, and poured dark amber liquid back into the bottle. Dave sniffed, caught the heavy scent of rum.

Not a bad idea. He swigged down half his Coke, snagged the bottle of rum, and followed Jason's example. He cast a glance sideways at both Doug and Jack as he did so; they seemed to have adjusted smoothly to "Jason as leader" instead of "Dave as leader." He wasn't sure whether to be annoyed or relieved.

"Needless to say," Jason said with heavy irony, "Clemson is pleased. I made money noises; he caved in. I made extension noises; he'd have given us till 2092 if I'd asked for it. I didn't, but I *did* let him talk me into staying on until after New Year's—"

Dave frowned. "Is that a good idea?" he said. "If we jam even *half* as good as we did tonight—"

"We will," Jason cut in, with a smile of complete satisfaction on his lips. "This is just the beginning."

"All right, then—we could fill a place *twice* the size of this, once word gets around"

"That," Jason replied, reaching across the space between them and tapping the table with his forefinger for emphasis, "is *just* the point, bro. We *could*—yeah, and we'd be competing with uptown names. But if we *stay* here—those people out there are gonna talk, and they'll bring their friends, and their friends will do the same— before long, there's gonna be a *line* to get into this joint, and that line is gonna get longer—and *that* is gonna bring in the media, and the high rollers—and who else?"

"Producers—" Dave breathed.

"Dig it. Scouts, execs, managers—all wanting to see what in hell is making people stand in line in *November* for God's sake. So they get in here—and we're on *our* turf, right? Not some pricey uptown gig, but this dive where our flash don't look like trash. You readin' me?"

"Loud and clear." *Jason, baby, you want it, you got it. No way am I gonna fight you when your brain just got up and kicked into warp drive.*

Jason leaned back in his flimsy chair and swigged rum and Coke with a grin, then threw his head back and shook all his hair out of his eyes.

"Gentlemen," he announced to the ceiling, "this band is on the move."

FOUR

Morning finally crawled across the city; a gray, grim morning that was just about gloomy enough to match Di's depression. She didn't want to get up—but she didn't have much choice.

And lying here isn't going to accomplish anything, either.

Fighting off a panic attack always left her emotionally, mentally drained. She'd had to fight off attacks three times last night. Now she didn't have much left to run on except nervous energy.

The alarm had jarred her out of enervated paralysis; her heart raced, pounding in her ears. It finally calmed enough that she could breathe freely after a few minutes. Showering was a matter of fatigue-fog and constantly looking over her "shoulder." She brushed out her waist-length hair; tied it into a tail, then bundled herself into a gray sweater and bleached-out gray pants that had once been black. Breakfast was a disaster. She didn't pay much attention to what she was doing, and set the toaster too high. As a result she burned the toast, but it didn't matter, she didn't taste it anyway.

I'd like to be invisible. She tasted fear again when her gut realized she was going to go *out there.* Where whatever had killed the boy waited still.

After several minutes of screwing up her courage, she left the dubious haven of her apartment for the uncertainty of the streets.

She paused at the stop of the steps for a quick scan of the neighborhood, but there was nothing out of the ordinary. Cold drizzle—a scant degree from being snow—wept greasily on her, penetrating her coat and chilling her until the bones of her wrists and ankles ached.

Physical aches came as a welcome distraction.

Guess I'd better get a move on.

She trotted most of the way to the subway station; she was sweating when she got there, but it wasn't enough to warm her, not *inside*, not where it counted.

The subway ride was a test of endurance, spent in a wash of sullen misery from the passengers around her. Shields that were normally adequate to keep her well insulated from empathic miasma had been thinned by the stresses of last night; they were barely good enough to keep the psychic muttering down to background noise. She hung to the overhead bar and made herself as small as possible. Tried to be inconspicuous. Tried to feel less afraid.

And tried not to breathe too much.

Her stomach churned with unease, and almost anything could set nausea off. Inside the swaying subway car, the odor of wet wool battled with perspiration, stale urine, and beer for ascendancy. Twice somebody stepped on her foot; once somebody tried to pick her pocket. Since she'd long ago learned to carry her purse inside her coat, all he got was a Salvation Army wallet full of pieces of newspaper and cardboard. This morning it certainly didn't seem worth the effort to try and stop him.

The street was quiet, with only other shopkeepers fighting the miserable weather. She opened the shop with her mind only half on the tricky lock; the rest of her stayed alert for possible danger until she was safely within the shelter of the shop's shielding. But nothing happened, not then—and not for the rest of the day.

She spent the hours that dragged by in self-recrimination and entirely alone. Not one customer, not even a teenybopper, and not one telephone call.

It happened that way, sometimes. With a store that sold things so esoteric, customers came at uncertain intervals. You couldn't close it, because you never knew when the stranger, the out-of-towner, would come in and buy something that would make the rent for the rest of the week.

Not a good situation when what she needed was company. And that idleness gave her plenty of leisure to examine last night in rerun, and find a hundred new things she had done wrong. Finally, mental and physical exhaustion drove her into a dull lethargy in which nothing seemed to matter. She was too depressed to be hungry, so the lunch hour came and went without her noticing. Even the weird radio story about a dead bus driver ferrying around a load of even deader passengers couldn't claim more than a few moments of her attention.

Until the phone interrupted the thin voice of the afternoon radio concert with its shrilling.

She started, her heart sent into overdrive. It shrilled again, and she caught it before the second ring was over. "Bell, Book, and—"

"Di? Di, is that you?"

She blinked. *Is it—it's Lenny—I think—*

"Di, it's Len—" He confirmed her guess, and he sounded panicked, hysterical. "It *is* you, isn't it? Di?"

"Len?" she replied, her brain still responding in slow motion. "Yeah, it's me. What—"

"Di, Di, you've gotta help me, please, I don't care what you do, you've gotta get over here and—"

Oh gods; the magic words, "you've gotta help me." I have one disaster on my hands already. I have one enemy—maybe after me—now. Unless this is related—

But the goad of Lenny's fear, of those words, was clearing her brain of fatigue-poison and fear-clouds. "Whoa, slow down a minute, Len—" She broke into his babbling. "What's happened? Where are you?"

"The morgue. Downtown."

"The *what?*" She nearly lost the handset in surprise. "You're *where?* Why? What's happened?"

"That bus, you know, the one last night, Keith's ex was on it, and he still had a card with Keith's name on it as emergency number—"

She concentrated as hard as she could; when Lenny got either drunk or freaked he tended to slur his words together and his accent got a lot thicker. When that happened, she couldn't always make out what he was saying through that Southern twang.

"The police called Keith and Keith called me, he said he couldn't face it alone, and I said okay and I understood and we went over here together and they pulled out the—and gods, Di, you've *gotta* get over here—the—I Saw something, I mean I used Sight and I *didn't* See and—"

His voice was rising with every word, and started to crack on the high notes; it was pretty obvious that *he* was teetering on the ragged edge. And that very loss of control on his part, oddly enough, gave her control back, and energy.

"Lenny—" she said, trying to get his attention; then, when he kept babbling, added the force of command-voice and will. "*Lenny.* Ground, boy. Slow down. One word at a time. What did you See?"

There was an audible gulp on the other end of the line. "*Didn't* See," he corrected, speaking slowly. "The soul—it wasn't there—oh gods—"

"Of course it wasn't there—" she began, reasonably.

"Gods, no, that's *not what I mean!*" He was getting increasingly shrill again, and she judged that she wasn't going to get any sense out of him over a phone line.

"Look, *stay* where you are," she told him. "I'll be there as fast as I can. Okay? Don't freak out on me. Okay?"

He took a long, shuddering breath. "Okay," he replied, voice trembling. "Okay."

"Don't leave."

"Okay."

She hung up; glanced at her watch and shrugged. Three-thirty.

No customers all day, not likely to be any now.

Besides, it gave her an excuse to think about someone else's problem.

And maybe—maybe the two were linked.

She grabbed her damp coat, shut everything down, flipped the sign over to "Closed," and headed out.

They weren't actually in the morgue itself, but in the waiting room; a place of worn linoleum, plastic chairs, and too-bright fluorescent lights. A room that tried to be impersonal but smelled of formaldehyde and grief.

The two young men sat side by side in cheap, hard, vacuum-formed plastic chairs. They weren't in physical contact with each other, although Di could see in the way he held himself Lenny's longing to touch Keith, to hold him and comfort him. And some of it leaked past her shielding; a longing so intense it carried over even the mingled swirls of fear and shock that she felt coming from him.

She had to reinforce her shield against him immediately. He was too close to her, his emotion was too strong; he was just too raw to handle. Keith was easier to deal with; purely and simply mourning. He slumped in his scarred gray chair with his elbows on his knees, hands dangling, head hanging, staring at the scratched and gouged floor.

Lenny looked up the moment she entered, and revived a little, his eyes taking on the pathetic brightness of a lost child sighting his parent.

And she could tell that was *all* he was thinking about.

Uh-oh. He's not going to watch his mouth.

She took a quick look around for possible eavesdroppers. The swarthy attendant was talking quietly to a cop; he glanced up at her curiously as she passed his desk.

"I'm with them," she said, pausing a moment, and indicating the pair at the end of the waiting room with a wave of her hand. "Lenny called me; he sounded a little unhinged so I said I'd get them home."

The attendant nodded in a preoccupied manner and returned his attention to the cop, dismissing her into the category of "not part of my job."

Lenny jumped to his feet and started stuttering something as soon as she got within speaking distance; she hushed him and took a seat between him and Keith. The artist's long, dark hair and black sweater would have made him look pale under the best of conditions, and the fluorescent lights washed color out of everything—but he was *white,* and when Di touched his hand, she got a distinct impression of "nobody home."

"Keith—"

He didn't respond, so she risked an exercise of Power and sent a little tingle, like an empathic spark, through the point where she touched his hand. He jumped, jarred back into reality, and looked at her sharply in surprise.

"Keith, are you going to be all right?" She pitched her voice in such a way that the question balanced equally between sounding concerned and sounding a little impatient. He blinked, and chewed on his lip—but then he looked over her shoulder and must have seen the strange expression Lenny was still wearing, and his eyes widened.

"Yeah, I—yeah. It's just—hard—"

She softened her tone and squeezed his hand. "That's okay, kiddo—I just don't need both of you falling apart in public on me. Wait until I get you home—"

She didn't wait for his reply, but turned back to Lenny; he was perched on the edge of his chair, hands clasped, face even whiter than Keith's. "Now, tell me slowly. One word at a time. What's wrong? What happened?"

He took a long, long breath, a breath that trembled and ended in a choked-off whimper. "You know I've got Sight," he whispered.

She nodded; the fluorescent fixture above her head flickered and buzzed annoyingly.

"Something didn't seem right so I, so I invoked Sight. I thought maybe Tom was hanging around, trying to tell me something. Like when Jo-Bob keeled over at rehearsal with a coronary. You remember—"

She frowned at him, thinking only that invoking Sight in a morgue full of bodies, mostly dead by violence, was probably one of the most outstandingly stupid things Lenny had ever done. He winced when he saw the frown, and said defensively, "I shielded! I'm not an idiot!"

She kept the reply she wanted to make—about not being so sure of *that*—purely mental. "Go on."

He closed his eyes and began to shake. "I, I Saw something. A hole. A hole where there shouldn't have been one. A—I don't *know*, but it wasn't like Jo-Bob, or my gramps, or the guy in the drugstore when I was a kid—not like somebody who properly died and the soul left—it was like the soul was torn out when the body died! And, and there's no *trace* of Tom anywhere—"

"Whoa—" She cut him off so that he couldn't spiral off into hysteria again. "Let me go have a Look for a minute. There's probably a good explanation."

Five minutes with the attendant convinced him to let her into the morgue. She managed to spin a realistic enough story that he didn't bother to check on her claim of being Tom's sister. Thirty seconds with the body, and she was as white as Lenny and just as close to hysteria.

Because he had been right. Something had killed Tom, but torn his soul out of him before he had properly "died"—and there were none of the traces that would have shown where the soul had gone.

Which meant it had been destroyed.

She managed to maintain an outward, completely false shell of calm all the way out to the waiting room; managed to call a cab and get both young men into it. Managed even to get them all into her apartment.

Then *she* had hysterics, but only when she had locked herself into the bathroom. And only after she had turned on the water in the sink to cover the sound of her own moaning.

This *was* a panic attack, and one she couldn't hold off; she knew the symptoms only too well.

She couldn't control herself, no more than she could have when that *thing* came hunting her and caught her alone, and offguard.

Nightflyer; that's what she'd found out it was called later. Much later. After it had almost killed her. After she'd found out the hard way that there were things too tough for her.

It had been a long time before she'd learned to sleep with the lights off again.

Once again her subconscious had decided she'd met another creature as bad as the Nightflyer.

Once again her body wanted to grovel and give up, held her prisoner in a sea of fear.

She hadn't had an attack for a long time, not since before she'd come to New York—

She'd managed to keep from having one yesterday.

That wasn't stopping her from having one now.

I can't do it. I can't do it. I can't handle this and it's going to come after me—

She huddled on the bathroom rug, hugging herself, rocking back and forth, and whimpering, tears streaming down her face. She was shivering so hard she couldn't stand, her heart was racing. Her mouth was dry, but her hands were sweating.

All the—the classic signs. Oh gods. Oh gods. I can't face this thing.

The bathroom was *the* most heavily warded room in the apartment; it was tiled floor to ceiling in sea-green porcelain, and all clay products held a charge as readily as anything man-made could. But the heavy wardings could not guard her against her own mind—

Only she could do that. And she *had* to. She was a Guardian. There was something out there that only a Guardian could handle. It would come for her if it got the chance—and she had been asked for help against it.

Time to pay the rent.

If she could just keep from falling apart.

She knelt on the tiny braided rag rug, bent over her knees, with her head hidden in her arms.

Breathe. Slow. Center. Oh gods.

Gradually the trembling stopped, and the tears; slowly her control began to return.

Think. You're not helpless. Whatever did that, it has to have enemies, vulnerability. You'll find its weak spot. Whatever it is, it's mortal. There was no trace of the Otherworld there. If it's mortal and vulnerable, it can be dealt with, destroyed if necessary. And you're not the only Guardian in the city. If you have to have help, you can get it. There's that guy in Queens, and Rhona in Jersey and Karl in Harlem—

Just the bare thought that there were other Guardians was comforting. No matter that Karl was in the hospital with a broken ankle, Rhona was seventy-odd, and the guy in Queens wouldn't leave his house if he could help it. For something that could destroy a soul, if it proved out that Di alone couldn't handle it, he'd find the courage to leave his house, Karl would grab crutches, ignore his pain and rise up out of his bed, and Rhona would have the strength of a teenager. Because if they had to, like Di, they would deal with it.

They won't have to. I'll handle it.

She had no choice, really, because Di *was* the youngest and the least handicapped of them all—and the best at troubleshooting. That meant she had *damned* well better do what she could on her own, first—

But that's all *it means. If I really* need them, they'll come—

Even if they kill themselves doing so. No. I can control myself. I can, and I will. I can handle this thing. It's been handed to me, *and I can handle it.*

She took three deep, slow breaths, and straightened from her crouch, tossing her hair back over her shoulder. *I won't have them on my conscience.*

She grabbed the cold, slick edge of the sink and hauled herself to her feet, biting her lip—her feet had been asleep and now they tingled and burned as life came back into them. She averted her eyes from the mirror.

No sleep last night, no makeup this morning, and now a crying jag. I probably look like I was buried two days ago.

She reached for the faucet and turned the water off; dipped a washcloth in the icy water still in the basin, and swabbed the tearstreaks off her face. She looked carefully into the mirror. Bags under the eyes, and white as a sheet, but not looking likely to break again.

I've looked worse, she decided. *Besides, they're so shook they won't notice.*

When her feet stopped tingling, she unlocked the bathroom door, pulled it open, and went from there straight into the kitchen.

The minute she opened the door to the bathroom, she could feel the two young men in the living room; Lenny like a sea urchin with sharp spikes of distress all over him, Keith a dull, gray blob of sorrow. She walled them out as best she could—

But there was something oddly comforting about them being there, despite their own troubles.

I'm not sure I could have faced an empty apartment . . .

I haven't had any food but that toast, and I'll bet neither have they. And there's something I need to be able to think this out—something I need a lot more than just food.

After a couple of false starts, moments that had her clinging to the counter and shaking, she managed to find three reasonably sized tumblers—and the bottle of vodka. And the frozen orange juice.

Damned if I'm going to think about this sober.

While the blender whirred, she cut up some cheese and half a loaf of French bread that was supposed to have gone up to the spaghetti party and hadn't. The orange juice went into a plastic pitcher that had seen much better days; the tumblers each acquired a few ice cubes. She brought it all out on a tray and plumped it down on the table in front of the couch. The two faces turned toward her wore such identical expressions of puzzlement that she would have laughed if she'd had the energy after her own bout with hysteria.

"Di—what—" Lenny stammered, looking from her to the glasses and back again.

"Gentlemen," she replied solemnly. "I have a proposition."

"W-what is it?"

She poured herself a *very* stiff screwdriver, took the armchair, and seated herself in it with care. "I propose," she said, after pausing for a long swallow, grimacing at the bitter undertaste, "that we get very, very drunk. Because at the moment there is nothing we can do. And because if we get very, very drunk, we might be able to come up with some kind of an answer—or at least a place to start asking questions."

Yuki pulled her coat collar up a little higher, shivering as the frigid wind curled around the back of her neck. She'd only had the Sassoon cut for a week and already she was sorry—her hip-length hair might have been a stone bitch to take care of, but at least it had kept the back of her neck warm!

And it was a *long* walk to the bus stop. Especially in the winter. *Most* especially in this micromini. There was nothing between her legs and the cold wind but her tights and boots. There were times—

But you couldn't work the kickiest boutique in the Apple wearing a *pantsuit* for God's sake. Not looking like some old lady from the Bronx. And jeans wouldn't do either. Not when Greg was such a leg man.

There *was* a stop right in front of the boutique, but taking that route meant a long ride in the wrong direction and a transfer, and a total of almost an hour and a half on buses. Whereas a fifteen-minute walk—if she hustled her buns—took her to the bus she *wanted*.

Just—it was dark, and cold, and at this hour, mostly deserted. You could probably shoot an M-16 down this street and not kill anybody right now.

She winced away from *that* unbidden thought. The war was over. Tricky Dicky had made one bold, bad move too many. There wouldn't be any more M-16's. No more Nams.

The wind moaned through the man-made cavern between the buildings and wrapped around her legs, and the streetlight just ahead of her flickered and went out. She shivered again, and this time not from cold.

They hadn't had but a handful of customers all day, and Greg evidently hadn't had enough Halloween. He'd started in on some real spooky stories that he swore had happened to people he knew—and when *he* ran out, he started teasing the others into telling ghostly tales. When Yuki's turn came, she'd tried to get out of it—but Greg had been insistent, and he was *so* foxy—it was impossible to resist him for long.

"You know Japanese ghost stories, don't you?" he'd asked coaxingly. "Things your grandma used to scare you with so you'd be a good little girl?" He'd winked at her over the shirts he was putting up.

"Well—"

She hadn't fought much, truth to tell. The stories had seemed so impossible in the well-lit boutique, with black-light Peter Max posters everywhere and rock music going as a background. And it had been a way to keep Greg's attention on her, and a way to keep from dying of boredom with nothing to do but put out new stock. But now—now she was beginning to be sorry she'd given in to him.

"I always did have too much imagination," she muttered, trying to bury her chin in her collar.

There was *no one* on the street, and still she could have sworn somebody was following her. Twice she whipped around to look behind her; in both cases the street behind her was just as empty as the street in front of her, which made her feel *really* stupid. Nothing in sight but blowing papers and the occasional headlights of cars at the intersections.

"Halloween jitters," she told herself aloud.

But the emptiness of the half-lit street, full of shadows and hundreds of places to hide, only contributed to her nervousness. It *should* have been reassuring and utterly normal; she knew every crack in the sidewalk, after all, she walked this way every night. But it wasn't; the echoes that were coming off the alleys were distorted tonight, and the way the streetlights kept flickering made those shadows look as if they were going to solidify and take on life. It didn't seem like the street she knew, but like something out of *Night Gallery*.

She kept glancing up, she couldn't help herself; she didn't really *expect* to see Flying Heads lurking on the windowsills above her—but she wouldn't have been surprised to find them up there.

"Bad drugs. God, I've *got* to stop letting Sasha talk me into going to parties with him."

She was speaking aloud just to hear something besides the

warped echoes of her own footsteps on the pavement. Her spine was crawling, for once again she could *feel* something behind her—and she was afraid, even as she scoffed at her fear, that if she turned around this time, she'd see a black cloud rolling down the street toward her, against the wind.

It wouldn't *be* a cloud, though; it would be the hunting form of a *gaki.*

She swallowed, and picked up her pace, the chunky heels of her boots making her feel a little unbalanced. *Gakis* were myths, no more real than Dracula. By day she could laugh at them. But in the deserted street—she couldn't laugh at them now. She had taken Greg a little too literally. *Those* were the stories that had kept her huddled in her bed at night, afraid even to go to the bathroom. The stories about *gakis,* the demons who could take the form of anyone they had slain—

"Dammit, those are just bogeyman stories!" she said, trying to talk some sense into herself. "There's *nothing* in them!"

—and when feeding took the form of a cloud of dense black smoke with eyes—a cloud that violated the rules of nature blithely, which was the only way you could tell what it was. The hunter who saw the smoke from his campfire acting oddly, the monk who noticed that the incense was not drifting away on the wind, the traveler encountering an unexpected patch of fog that refused to disperse—all those had been the heroes—or victims—of her grandmother's stories.

And a city the size of this one, with all the hiding places it contained, would make such a perfect hunting ground for a demon—especially one that could look like a cloud of smog.

She started at the sound of footsteps behind her; but she didn't turn around this time. That wasn't an echo of her own tread back there, keeping pace with her. There *was* someone following her, now.

And there wasn't a cop in sight.

Fear suddenly leapt out of her gut and into her throat. It had a life of its own, and she couldn't control it. It took over her body, and made her legs slow, and she found she *could not* get them to move any faster.

She glanced behind her; yes, there *was* a man back there, muffled in a dark overcoat with his face in shadow. Just seeing him back there gave the fear a little more control over her, made her knees go to water, slowed her pace further, until she felt as if she were forcing her way through glue. Even more frightening, she got the distinct impression that the man was matching his speed to hers, that he was toying with her.

The third time she looked back, she wanted to scream—but it only came out a strangled sob. She had been wrong. There wasn't *one* man tailing her—there were *two*.

And they *weren't* together.

She faltered—and broke; the fear took over her thinking, and she lurched into a wobbling run. With the high heels of her boots catching on the cracks in the sidewalk, she stumbled and caught herself before she fell into the wall. She paid no attention to where she was going; she couldn't really see, in any case. Fear skewed everything, made it all as surreal as a nightmare and she couldn't recognize her own surroundings anymore. She made a quick right turn, thinking she was finally on a street that had a regular cop on the beat—

And wound up staring stupidly at a blank brick wall. This wasn't a street at all, it was a cul-de-sac, and she was trapped.

She whirled and put her back against the brick, as footsteps told her that her first pursuer was rounding the corner.

Now she could see him; tall, swarthy, his complexion sallow in the yellowish light of the street lamp above her. A gust of wind blew paper past his legs. He smiled, but it was not a friendly smile, it was the smile of a hunter who had finally cornered his prey after an invigorating run. His eyes were dark, and so deeply sunk into their sockets that they looked like the eyeless holes in a skull; his mouth was cruel, with full, sensuous lips.

She was so terrified that she could hardly breathe. Her heart raced, and she fought against a faint—he smiled again, and licked his lips with the tip of his tongue, a gesture that was somehow repellent and voluptuous.

Then the sound of a second set of feet on the pavement behind him turned the smile into a feral snarl, and he pivoted to face the newcomer in a crouch.

She could still see the face of her hunter in profile—and that of the man who had interrupted whatever it was the first had intended to do to her. And as the second man stepped fully into the light, she began to hope.

Though he wore the studded black leather of a street-gang member, he was Japanese.

She started to speak; to stammer out something about being glad to see him, to try to pull an "us against the WASPs" number on him—but the words stuck in her throat.

Because he was watching her with a faint smile of amusement; a superior sort of smile that told her he had *no* interest in helping her. The smile broadened as he saw her read him correctly, and turned into one identical to the smile the man had worn—the look of the hunter, with the prey trapped in a corner and in easy striking distance.

He ignored the other man, whose snarl had turned to a frown of perplexity.

Then the first man straightened, and stood aside with a mocking bow—and she saw with dumb surprise that his perplexity had given way to a look of extreme amusement. The young man gave him a wary, sidelong glance—

And slowly began dissolving, becoming a dense cloud of dark smoke.

She choked, her hands scrabbling at the bricks behind her as she tried to press herself into them. This was, literally, her worst nightmare come true. She was face-to-face with a *gaki,* and one who, by his actions, could only be one of the three kinds of *gakis* that killed—those who devoured the blood, those who devoured only living flesh—or, worst of all—those who devoured the soul.

She had paid no attention to the other man, who had moved toward her as the *gaki* had begun to change. Now, as her knees finally gave out on her and she began to slip to the pavement, his hand shot out and grabbed her shoulder, crushing down on it with a cruel, hard grip that kept her from moving.

The cloud drifted closer; it still had eyes, and a kind of sketched-in caricature of a human face. The lips stretched in a suggestion of a grin. Only the eyes were clear, the sulfur-yellow eyes. The demon-eyes. The *gaki's* yellow eyes switched from her to the man and back again, and she wondered if the thing was going to take *both* of them.

If it went for the first man, would she have a chance to escape?

The man spoke, practically in her ear. "A moment—"

She yelped, started, and the man's hand held her in her place, shoving her against the rough brick of the wall, with the bricks prickling the backs of her thighs. His voice was deep and harsh, and it had the tone of someone who was accustomed to being obeyed.

"I think," he said, as the cloud paused, and the face in the cloud seemed to take on an expression of surprise, "that we seek something similar, but not identical, you and I. I think that if it were to come to a conflict, we would both lose."

The face vanished for a moment in a billow of the smoke, then returned. The face seemed less a sketch and more solid, and it was definitely frowning thoughtfully.

"I think," the man continued, as her shoulder grated beneath his hand, "that perhaps we might come to an accommodation. Could we not be—allies?"

The face vanished again, and the clouds billowed and churned. Silent tears poured down Yuki's face, blurring her vision; tears of complete hopelessness. She was doomed, and knew it. There was no trace of humanity in either of these—creatures. Unlike the heroes of the stories, there would be no Shinto priest or ronin versed in magic to rescue her.

Finally the cloud condensed—

And once again the young man stood a few yards away, just within the cone of light cast by the street lamp. He pondered them both, his face as impassive as a stone Buddha, with his head held slightly to one side.

"Perhaps," he said, after a silence that stretched on for years.

Yuki moaned—which brought his attention back to her.

And he *smiled* at her.

This was an entirely different kind of smile than the first; it was *horrible,* it was like being eaten alive and hearing your devourer make little noises of appreciation while he ate you, and it made her fear leap up and take control over everything—

And it froze her in place so completely that she couldn't have moved to run even if the way had been clear and a cop car in sight.

The *gaki* looked back at her captor, and blinked twice, his eyes glowing a sullen sulfur. "Perhaps," he repeated, and nodded. "Would you care to discuss the possibility . . . over dinner?"

It's A Beautiful Day sang something that was probably deeply meaningful if you were stoned instead of drunk. Overhead someone was practicing piqué turns, and falling off pointe every so often. Just out of reach, Lenny and Keith were still in full possession of Di's couch. The couch tended to sag in the middle, and the more they drank, the more they leaned toward each other. They probably didn't even realize they were doing it.

Di cleared her throat. "I've got an idea—"

Both sets of bleary male eyes turned toward her.

"Let's have another drink. I can still tell which foot is mine."

"Oh, Di—" Lenny groaned. "We're *supposed* to be—"

"Drinking." She held up her glass and studied it for a moment. The ice was holding up all right. "I told you I *wasn't* going to think about this sober."

"Why not?" he retorted. "*You* always told me that you have to have a clear head to do occult work."

She'd had just enough to be honest, and too much to keep her mouth shut. "Because I'm too scared to think about this sober. I'm on the edge, Len. On the ragged edge. I've already had one panic attack, and I'm trying to hold off another one. Okay?"

Lenny's eyes widened, and he moved a little closer to Keith. Keith gave her a look that showed no understanding of what she'd said. She ignored both reactions and poured herself another stiff one. She'd stopped tasting the vodka two drinks ago, which meant she was *almost* drunk enough to analyze the situation without triggering another panic attack.

Someday maybe I won't have to do this. But right now—She tossed it down.

Keith had demolished two to every one of Lenny's, matching Di drink for drink, and with as much reason, given the level of his grief and self-accusation. *He* was now numb enough that Di no longer had to wall him out so completely.

When this is over I have to talk him through all the guilt he's feeling about Tom—

Gods. I hope I'm around and in one piece.

He leaned forward a little, and fixed Di with an unfocused stare. "Diana?" he said, hesitation making his voice soft, vodka blurring it. "Diana, I don't understand—"

"You don't understand what?" She ate an ice cube, taking out some of her frustration by crunching angrily down on it.

"Why you're so upset. *You* didn't know Tom, so that's not it. And Len didn't know him well enough to get so—so hissy-fit—" He licked his lips, and looked at her with anxiety overcoming the alcohol. "So it has to be something else. That *other* stuff. Like the thing in my studio?"

"Yeah, sort of." She slumped a bit farther down in her chair.

"Is that why you're afraid?"

She pointed an armed finger at him, and fired it. "Bingo. I don't know what it was, or how to deal with it—and I *have* to."

Fortunately he didn't ask why. He studied *his* glass. "There was something wrong. It didn't feel right. I knew it when they brought me in there. Then Len"—his right hand reached for Lenny's left, and found and held it, without his seeming to be aware of the fact— "acted like somebody'd just dropped a box of spiders on him. Then *you* freaked out." He looked up at her with a hint of defiance. "Are you going to tell *me* what pulled your chain?"

"You won't believe it," she replied, without thinking.

"I believed in the thing in my studio. I *know* that you got rid of it. Why shouldn't I believe you now?"

"Because—because I'm not sure I believe it."

"Try me," he said. Lenny shivered.

She decided she was drunk enough now. "Something—something destroyed his soul."

He looked at her with his eyes getting bigger and bigger, his face getting paler and paler—and abruptly he reached for the bottle and poured himself a double-strength drink, gulping it down as fast as he had poured it.

Beautiful Day gave way to Buffalo Springfield. Di sighed, and tilted her head to look straight at Lenny. "What do *you* think?" she asked.

He shook his head. "I don't *want* to think. I don't want to know anything about something that could destroy a soul."

"Neither do I," she confessed gloomily, staring at the empty glass in her hand. Not even a panic attack was going to get through that much vodka. "Not really."

"I mean, think of the *power* it had to have."

"Yeah. And *how?* How did it *do* that?"

Lenny squeezed his eyes closed, solemnly clicked the heels of his sneakers together, and just as solemnly intoned, "There's no place like home. There's no place like home. There's—" .

"How could something eat a soul?" Keith interrupted, utterly bewildered, in his blurred state not making a distinction between being "destroyed" and being "eaten." "Why would anything want to?"

Lenny began to giggle, still too near hysteria. "Fillet of soul, anyone?"

Di squelched the threatening hysterics with a glance. "I didn't say 'eaten,' I—" She sat straight up in her chair; not an easy feat, since she had been sitting in it sideways with her legs draped over the arms. In faithful counterpoint, Lenny had echoed her movement a fraction of a second behind her.

"Soul-eaters!" he exclaimed, before she could say anything. "Ye gods. *Those* I know about!"

"The library—" She scrambled out of her chair, and wobbled to the workroom; he stopped only long enough to pull a very bewildered Keith to his feet, and followed on her heels.

"Egyptian—" she heard him call out as she snapped on the light. "Dibs on Egyptian."

"Grab the easy one. All right; I'll check the Celts."

She began pulling books down, scanning the indices, and putting aside those that mentioned soul-eaters. Lenny, who had secretly yearned to be an archaeologist, got the *Egyptian Book of the Dead* down and launched into a detailed explication of the Eater of Souls to Keith. Lenny tended to pontificate when drunk.

Di put up with it for ten minutes, then interrupted. "Lenny," she called sharply. "Can it."

"But—"

"I said, can it. I've got a lot of books, and I've checked ten while you've been blathering."

"I wasn't—" he replied.

"You were. Ten minutes' worth."

He shut up and got back to work.

Five A.M. and they had a list—a very *short* list, but Di's library was nowhere near as extensive as the one in the shop—and they had come to the end of the books. Di put the last of them back on the shelf.

She turned back to the other two.

Keith was sitting on a stool they'd brought in from the kitchen; he knew shorthand, so he'd been made secretary once he was sober enough to take notes. Lenny was looking over his shoulder and making a face at the scrawls on his notepad.

Di felt her nervous energy beginning to fade. After all that frenzied activity—

"Now what?" she asked aloud. Lenny looked up; Keith frowned at his notes.

"What do you mean?" Lenny replied, after sneezing, and rubbing his nose with a dusty finger.

"Okay, we've got a list—but a list of *what*? Of all the mythical and semimythical things on it, which one is *real*? And—what are we going to do with what we've got?"

Lenny bristled. "Are you thinking of giving this up? Leaving something like *that* loose in the city? How many of our friends is it gonna eat before you're willing to do something? Or are you afraid to try?"

She shook her head. "No. No, of course not. But if we don't go at this logically, we're going to get nowhere."

"This list isn't that long," Lenny pointed out. "And since our killer isn't likely to be a god or a demigod, like the Egyptian Eater of Souls, well—I think we ought to go hunting. We ought to look for other kills like this one; we ought to look for psychic traces—"

She was about to interrupt him, to object that "looking for psychic traces" wasn't that easy, when Keith cleared his throat.

She looked at him in surprise; she'd forgotten he was still there.

"Even if Tommy and I broke up," he said, carefully, "we broke up still being friends." He glared at Di, as if he defied her to contradict him. "I want you to count me in on this."

Di raised one eyebrow. Her head was starting to ache, and she was glad that today was her day off. "You're drunk," she replied mildly.

Keith shrugged. "Sure. So are you. So's Len. Drunk or sober, count me in."

Di rubbed her head and sighed. "All right. You're in. We can use all the help we can get. I just hope you don't live to regret this."

The bedside clock said five, and it sure as hell wasn't A.M. Dave opened his eyes a little farther, and winced away from the last red rays of the sun, light that was somehow leaking past the slats of his dusty venetian blinds, and groped on the nightstand for his sunglasses. The blankets were all in a knot; he must have been fighting them in his sleep again. He threw them off, sat up, and squinted at sunlight filtering past the blinds. Even with his shades on, it still seemed too bright; funny, only sunlight affected him that way. After the initial discomfort of the first gig after the party, stagelights gave him no trouble at all.

There was a hollow in the mattress beside where he'd been lying, but the little groupie he'd brought home was long gone; he'd made sure of that before he went to sleep. She hadn't liked it much, being hustled out the door like that; she'd wanted to snuggle and maybe go for another round—

But he kept seeing Tam in his mind's eye—

It has to have been a coincidence, he told himself again; it was getting to be a kind of litany, but he still hadn't quite managed to convince himself of its truth.

So out she went, and no amount of pouting made him change his mind.

He was still afraid—of what, he couldn't quite say, only that he was afraid he might *do something* to anyone who might be near him when he was asleep. Something awful.

Heebie jeebies. He ran his dry tongue over his dry teeth, shook his head a little, and caught his breath. As always, his head began pounding as soon as he moved, and his stomach was an aching void. He planted his feet on the cold floor, and sagged over his knees, willing both aches to stop.

His body wasn't cooperating.

His stomach growled; hunger so sharp it made him a little sick and light-headed—not a good combination on top of the pounding in his temples. He'd learned over the past week that nothing he ate would have any effect on his raging hunger. The only things that could keep him going were liquids; Coke, coffee as strong as he could brew it, coffee milkshakes. Sugar and milk and caffeine. Anything else just sat there, making him nauseous on top of hungry, like having a lump of frozen rock in his stomach.

So he reached out without looking up for the second thing he *always* grabbed when he came to; the can of Coke he'd left on the nightstand beside his sunglasses.

It was warm and acidic; that didn't matter. He poured the whole can down his dry throat in three long gulps, saving one last sip to wash down the bennies he kept beside the Coke.

In about twenty minutes, the sun was down and the bennies were doing their thing, making his blood dance and sparkle. His headache was fading, and he felt like he was going to live.

He tossed the glasses back onto the nightstand, then picked up his jeans off the floor beside the bed where he'd dropped them, and pulled them on, frowning at how they'd stretched. He belted them to keep them on, and began rummaging through his closet for a clean stage shirt. *Got to drop my laundry off,* he thought, wrinkling his nose at the stale smell of sweat rising from the hamper. Funny, how smells seemed so much stronger lately—bennies normally dulled your sense of smell, but—

Come to think of it, everything seemed sharper, more in focus this last week. The bells on his clothes seemed louder; the colors of the embroidery brighter.

There were vests, a lot of empty hangers, a couple sweats, but nothing he wanted to use on stage. Then in the back, *way* in the back, he found a fringed shirt he used to wear before he'd started putting on that weight. He pulled it out and frowned at it—it had been one of his favorites, with beads and Indian symbols all over it, and it had been made to fit skintight. Chicks had really gone for him when he wore it—and he didn't like to be reminded how much he'd let himself go.

Then again—he shrugged. *What the hell. Since I haven't been stuffing my face with junk food, maybe it fits me again. Even if it doesn't, maybe I can figure out something—*

He pulled it on, started to button it—and froze, with his hands on the third button.

It was loose.

Christ on a crutch—

He closed the closet door, slowly, and for the first time since Halloween, he had a good long look at himself in the mirror.

Christ on a crutch—

A near stranger stared back at him.

It wasn't just the shirt—and the jeans hadn't stretched. He must have lost twenty pounds the past week. He didn't look *bad*—not yet, anyway. But he sure looked different. Not quite strungout—he wasn't sure what to call the way he looked now. Wasted? No. Gaunt.

He turned away from the mirror and headed blindly into the kitchen; coffee was the first order of business. He made himself a pot, plopped himself into the metal folding chair next to the card table, and nursed his first cup—black as sin, with five spoons of sugar in it.

What in hell is happening to me?

He stared at the fluorescent light from the fixture overhead rippling across the surface of the coffee, and realized something else. *It isn't just me. It's all of us except Jack. I hadn't really thought about it, but Doug's lost as much weight as I have; Jason's lost more. None of us are showing at the club before the sun sets—except Jack. We're all wearing shades when we do show. From the way I've been seeing Jason and Doug chug drinks—*

He clenched his hands around the cup, then forced himself to relax; finally downed the last of the cup, and poured himself another. *God, I'm hungry enough to eat a—*

But the idea of solid food was revolting.

I might as well eat mud. Bennies help, a little; booze and drinks; and Coke—but the only time it ever really lets up is when the music's rolling and I'm grooving on the vibes.

Just thinking about the vibes—and the way the gigs had been going—warmed the coldness inside him a bit, and coaxed a little smile onto his face, and he began feeling a little more cheerful. *God. We're doing it. It's working. I thought there was no way we'd be able to repeat what we did the first night—but every night it gets better, tighter. Just gettin' higher every time we play.*

He thought about that for a moment. *It started right after Halloween, about the time I started feeling weirded out. Huh. Okay. Maybe it's not a coincidence. Maybe it's all tied together.* He nodded a little. *Okay. If this is what it took, this business of being strung out, to get the band to work—okay. That's okay. I can pay that. Oh yeah.*

He reached for the coffee, and found to his surprise that he'd drunk the last of the pot.

Oh well. I need to get on the road, anyway.

He bundled himself into his torn leather jacket, grabbed his gig-bag, and headed out. His footsteps echoed up and down the empty staircase—and there was no doubt of it; his hearing *was* more sensitive than before. Down on the street, the streetlight rocked in the wind above him as he hailed a cab; no more buses for him, not now—

Besides, he thought wryly, as he slung himself into the patched seat and gave the cabby the direction to the club, *I'm savin' enough cash on what I'm not eating to pay for all the cabs I feel like taking!*

He sat back in the darkness, surrounded by the odor of old leather and cigarette and reefer smoke, and watched the back of the cabby's head. Sweet-sour smoke drifted around and through the driver's thatch of long hair. It crept into the back of the cab with Dave and when the cabby turned his head, Dave could see the red coal of his jay. *We've never been so hot. It's like a dream. Weeknights we're filling the place the minute they open the doors—weekends there's the line outside Jason was swearing we'd get. I never could pick up chicks before, not the way Jason and Doug could—now, if I go home alone, it's 'cause I'm the one that wants it that way.* He closed his eyes and sank a little deeper into the seat cushion, cradling his axe against his chest. *And when everything comes together up there and the vibes come up, and I'm grooving—damn. It's better than anything; sex, drugs, booze—it's like being a god.*

"Hey, man—you wanta wake up back there?"

He started up out of his reverie. The neon of the club sign flashed just outside the cab window. He popped the door, overtipped the cabby, and scrambled out into the freezing wind.

And no going around the back anymore, he thought, smiling to himself as the bouncer held the front door open for him, and two chicks giggled and wiggled their hips at him just inside. No time for that right now, though. There was barely enough time to get into the back and get warmed up.

Because they didn't warm up out front anymore, and they weren't suffering the cold concrete break room. *Now* they took their breaks and warmed up in the manager's paneled, carpeted office, and the manager had moved his desk into the break room.

Jack raised an eyebrow as he cruised in the door. "Took your time," he said sardonically, not missing a beat in his silent practice.

The drummer was alone in the sound-baffled room. "Looks like I'm the only one," Dave replied, unzipping the black nylon bag, tak-

ing his axe out, and uncoiling the electric cord lying neatly inside.
"Unless—"

Jack shrugged; he didn't look worried, but then he never worried
about anything much. "They ain't here, man. Dunno where they are.
They'll show when they show."

Dave grimaced. "Probably stuck in traffic somewhere—Doug's
got the van, right?" One of the first things they'd done with their newfound prosperity was to buy a used van for the heavier equipment.

"Yeah, that's—"

The door swung open, then knocked into the wall, interrupting
him. Jason edged in, looking like nothing so much as a pile of flimsy
white cardboard boxes with legs. He was followed by Doug, similarly
laden. Doug kicked the door shut behind them.

Dave stared at the incongruous sight, and started to laugh. "What
the hell is this?" he demanded. "You guys raid Bloomies, or something?"

Jason put his load down carefully on one of the cocktail chairs
they'd "borrowed" from out front, and straightened up. His eyes had
the gleam of excitement that Dave usually associated with a good set
or a foxy chick.

"Better than that, man," Jason replied, his expression smug,
gloating.

He picked up the first couple of boxes, checked something on the
end, and tossed one to Dave.

"We're changing our image," the lead said, shaking his hair back
over his shoulder, and nodding at the boxes. "This is the new gear."

"What image?"

Jason laughed. "That's it, man, we ain't *got* an image. Last night
we looked like every other bar band in town. After tonight, they'll
not only remember how we sound, they'll remember how we look.
Go on, man, open it."

He did; broke the tape holding it together, pulled the lid off, and
nearly dropped the box, contents and all.

"Shit."

Jason grinned.

He put the box down carefully and took out a pair of pants. He'd
known from the aroma that hit him when the lid came off what they
were, but the supple and unmistakable feel of the material in his
hands still came as a shock. Leather. Black leather. *Expensive* black
leather, soft as a kiss, and from the look of it, tailored to be just short
of pornographically tight. He put them down *very* carefully. Those
pants cost more than his entire wardrobe—

And how in hell had Jason managed to figure out what was going to fit him—especially given that he'd just lost twenty pounds?

Jason smirked at his expression. "This week's lady is a theatrical costumer," he gloated. "She designed this shit, and she doesn't *need* a tape measure."

Dave couldn't think of any way to respond to that, and waited for Jason's next trick.

Jason tossed him a second box; this one had soft shirts in it, also black, and the label said something about them being one hundred percent silk, dry-clean only.

Doug got up out of his chair with a smirk, and dropped a heavier box on top of the shirts. This one held black leather boots—and the label on the box was from an uptown shop that *only* did custom work. No mystery there—he and Doug wore the same size, and these babies were straight-leg. The mystery was how they paid for all this.

He put the boots on the floor and picked up one of the shirts; it had huge sleeves, some very subtle designs in black beads and sequins on the shoulders and back, and it was open to the waist. Sex on the hoof.

He put it all carefully back in its boxes. The van was one thing—

"Jason—" he began hesitantly.

"What the hell does this mean?" Jack interrupted, looking at the pants and boots with a frown of puzzlement on his face. "Are we moving to a biker bar or something?"

He doesn't get it—Dave realized. *He doesn't have a clue how much this stuff costs.*

Jason shook his head. "Nope, we're staying here. Just like I said, we need an image. This is a helluva lot better image than jeans and fringe—I promise you, chicks are gonna go wild for this gear."

There was something about his expression that made Dave very uncomfortable when he said that. This wasn't Jason's usual casual, cheerful carnality—there was something cruel, and yet overwhelmingly sensual, in his half-closed eyes—

"We're changing our name, too," the lead continued. "I had somebody come over from the store and got the drums redone this afternoon. Picked it all up on the way here."

Dave shrugged; he hadn't been in love with Wanderlust, anyway. From the quirk of Jack's mouth, neither had the drummer. "What to?" Dave asked.

Jason turned slightly to face him, and his stance took a faint hint of challenge. "Children of the Night."

A whisper of cold touched the back of Dave's neck, and he bit his lip to keep from giving away his unease.

This is getting real spooky. That name—the gear—hell. Man, it's like that mind-trip stuff Di was in; that occult crap. I hate that stuff; dammit, that's why I broke up with her in the first place. All that freaky weird-out stuff, mind reading and that other shit—she ended up spending more time chasing ghosts than she did with me, out half the night sometimes, then too tired to do anything when she did show. That's why I told her it was Ouija boards or me—

He shied away from the memory; it *still* wrenched his gut to think about that last scene he'd had with her. It hadn't been a fight, exactly. In a way, it was too bad; a fight would have been easier to take than the stricken look in those dark eyes, the silence in which she walked out.

He waffled for a minute, trying to come up with a good reason *why* he felt uneasy about the rigs, the name—and couldn't think of one. So instead he launched the only objection to the "new image" that seemed sane. "Look, Jason—I know we're startin' t' do all right, but man, this stuff, this's *money*, man, *I* can't afford this kind of rig."

Instead of replying immediately, Jason looked over at Jack, who just shrugged. "I don't much care what's on the front of the kit," the drummer opined, "and I don't much care what you put me in—just as long as it ain't comin' outa *my* wallet."

Jason grinned in triumph; Doug's smile an echo of the lead's. "Stay cool, man," he advised Dave. "There's not penny one of *ours* tied up in this."

He didn't follow; it didn't make sense. "Huh?" he said. "What do you mean, we've got no cash in this?"

Jason's grin widened. "We have a patron," he gloated. "We got ourselves a patron. And this is just the beginning of what he's gonna do for us. Just wait and see."

Di stared resolutely at her coffee, or her hands, or the faces of whichever of the two guys she was talking to, and *not* at her surroundings. Keith was into superrealism, and his studio looked like Doctor Frankenstein's workshop. Body parts in fiberglass were everywhere—and they were frighteningly lifelike.

Panic was behind her—for now. Whatever it was, it hadn't come for her yet. Those realistic body parts were only realistic *looking*.

Too bad Keith couldn't be a little more realistic in what he expected of her.

"Dammit, Keith, it's a *big* city," she protested, trying to get past his barricades of ignorance and emotion. "This *isn't* a TV show! I can't just wiggle my nose and make things happen! Magic doesn't *work* that way. Magic isn't *easy* in the first place; it takes more energy to do something magically than it does to just *do* it, always assuming you *can* do it mundanely. And this—it's worse than trying to find a grain of rice in a warehouse of wheat—"

Not like Five Corners, Connecticut, population 2,500 and ten cats. And two psychics. And no empathic interference. Hell, even New Haven was better than this—a much smaller area to scan, and it still took me months to pinpoint Emily.

"—the thing could be anywhere," she continued, worrying at a hangnail on her thumb with her fingernail, "and if it knows how to hide itself, I'd never find it unless it slipped up at the same time I was scanning right where it was."

And where does that gypsy boy fit into this? I can't believe it's coincidence. Maybe that—that vampire—if that's what he was—maybe if he can eat emotional energy, he can eat souls, too. I wish I'd paid more attention to him when I saw him the first time—

If he isn't involved somehow, I've got no clues. Everything on our list is either a god—and I can't believe there's a god running around out there, sucking the souls out of scuzzy bus passengers—or something vampiric. Like the Greek vampires—people they latched onto never showed up in the afterworld, so the implication is they got eaten. That Egyptian demon, the "Eater of Souls." Those African whatsis-things—

There's vampiric swords too, but—no, I can't buy that one. Besides, I haven't seen a single instance of one in the occult literature that predates Michael Moorcock, which leads me to think the notion got "borrowed," lock, stock, and copyright.

Does it know it's being hunted? Does it know me? Is it only lying low until it can choose the time and place to meet me?

Keith frowned, and fiddled with a snag on the sleeve of his sweater. "It's been five days—and we still haven't gotten anywhere. You didn't have any trouble with that thing that was in here," he protested. "Maybe I'm being dense—but it looked to me like you just sort of zeroed right in on it, trapped it, and threw it out. Why can't you find the thing that way?"

Lord and lady, she groaned to herself. *The man wants me to turn myself into a soul-eater detector. Just flick a switch, set a dial—*

"I can't, because I don't know what I'm looking for," she tried to tell him. "I knew *exactly* what I was going after in here; I knew what it 'felt' like, what it 'looked' like. I'm—I don't know how to describe

this, exactly—I guess the closest thing would be like a bloodhound.
I need a scent. I need to know what this thing 'feels' like, or I can't
track it."

"That's what's called a signature, babe," Lenny said, trying to be
helpful. "It'd be like you setting up to do a portrait bust on a verbal
description; without the signature, Di's moving blind."

She sipped her coffee; Keith was into herbal teas with cosmic
names, and the coffee he kept around for guests was awful. And Keith
still didn't look convinced. Water was dripping somewhere back behind her; it was beginning to get on her nerves.

"Can't you just look for something that doesn't look like a regular person?" Keith persisted.

She sighed. "I could do that, yes. It'd be just like going out into the
street and *looking,* physically, for someone who didn't quite look human. How many people are in the Apple? New York is just *too
damned big* for me to go sifting through it, looking at people's auras.
I'd die of old age before I found anything. And that assumes that
whatever we're looking for *doesn't* know how to shield itself from detection, which is probably a real bad assumption."

"But—" Keith began again.

Lenny touched his shoulder, interrupting him, and gave her a
look of understanding and patience. "Di," he said, "why don't you go
on home. You look tired to death. I'll explain it to him."

I hope you can, she thought pessimistically, *but I'm not going to
bet on it—*

But Keith finally seemed to *see* her—and she knew damned well
she looked like hell. She was just as glad Annie wasn't around to
mother-hen her. Too little sleep, too much going—it was taking its
toll. She wasn't sure how long she was going to be able to keep burning her candle at both ends *and* the middle.

*Just please, no more panic attacks. Not now. Not when I'm so low
already.*

"Take a rest, Di," Lenny said quietly; Keith nodded, and he
looked just a shade guilty. "You aren't going to get anywhere if you
burn out on us."

She nodded. "I know, I know. I should know better, and somehow I never learn." She wanted to smile, or something, and just
couldn't manage it."

"Out—" Lenny ordered sternly. "This is an order. Go home. Get
some rest." He pointed across the glaringly lit studio to the black
mouth of the door.

"I'm going, I'm going—" She grabbed her beat-up wool CPO jacket and obeyed, but only to the extent of leaving the building.

She was too restless to go home; too much nervous energy, and she couldn't face the thought of the empty apartment. Being alone could trigger another attack.

Besides, she thought, hunching her shoulders and burying her chin in her coat collar, *if it is looking for me, a moving target is a lot harder to hit.*

The wind was cold, though; there'd probably be snow soon. Not tonight, but soon. Would snow drive this thing into a lair for the winter? Somehow she didn't think so.

Keith's studio was just outside the Village proper; after a prowl of two blocks, she turned a corner and reached streets that were populated. There were clubs here, and restaurants that were popular enough to have customers despite the cold wind and the late hour, and the fact that it was a weeknight.

And it's harder to see a moving target around other targets . . .

She had no particular destination in mind; she just wanted to walk, and maybe shake something coherent out of her thought processes. And despite being among people, despite having just left about the best friend she had in the city next to Annie, she was feeling very alone right now.

And sorry for yourself. Snap out of it. Depression isn't going to get you anywhere but into a rut. Meep, meep, meep, you sound like Sweet Sarah, Soppy Sobber of the Spanish Main. Or a Guinea Pig.

She crossed a street against the light—not enough traffic to worry about—and suddenly her shields went up and her internal "bad" detectors went red.

Whoa! That wasn't unusual. The last time it had happened—had been just before the Nightflyer—

But that had been when she was alone, not with people all around her.

It occurred to her that she was feeling more alert by the moment; as if fear was spurring her now, instead of enervating her.

Oh please, let that be true.

She stopped cold, saw she was just outside a rock club. It had a flashy neon sign that buzzed annoyingly; in the few moments she stood there, she watched several people going in, opening the door just enough to slip inside, but not enough to let her see or hear what was going on in there.

Just another club. What in hell could have—

The door opened again, this time as wide as it could get, and a blast of hot air heavy with pot smoke and music hit her. And it was the music that sent the "wrong" feeling a little more into the red. There was something she couldn't put her finger on—it was like the smile of someone who's secretly into sadism and bondage. A nasty sort of knowledge lay behind the lyrics and the heavy backbeat—

Maybe it didn't have anything to do with the soul-eater; but that bus's route *had* gone through the Village. And there was something predatory about this music. It was something that needed looking into.

She pulled the door open slightly, and slipped into the club, moving as quietly as she could—

Which is "very," thank the gods.

A massive bouncer in the entryway nodded at her driver's license without ever taking his eyes off something at the back of the club.

You could get a stark-naked fourteen-year-old hermaphrodite past him and he'd never notice—Ye gods. *This is beyond weird. The cops have been coming down on the clubs in the Village lately;* he should be really *watching IDs. What in hell is going on here?*

The club was jammed to the walls; she had to inch her way through the elbow-to-elbow mob inside, it was literally standing room only. The very faint spots over the bar and the stage lights were all the illumination provided, but that didn't matter to the audience; their focus, like the bouncer's, was *all* on the tiny stage at the rear of the club.

Di regretted—for once—being as tiny as she was. She couldn't *see* the stage over all the heads. She wormed her way between people, putting out a "don't notice me" aura with all her concentration. There was something in here—and she didn't want it to have any notion that she had walked into *its* territory.

As she got to the bar, she was *very* glad she was shielding and hiding.

Speak of the devil and he shall appear—

Enthroned on a stool at the far end of the bar was Mr. Trouble himself; he looked very elegant—and Di would far rather have been swimming in a tank with a tiger shark than be in this room with him. He was in full "hunter" mode; other than that, she couldn't tell anything without probing him, which she did *not* intend to do. This was no place for a confrontation. And it was all too likely, from the relaxed way he was sitting, that this was *his* territory.

Not tonight, thank you.

He was trolling for something a bit older than chicken tonight—but his intent was undoubtedly the same, and his plans. There were more than enough "the universe is a friendly place" types to serve as fodder for someone like him, and a club was a good place to find them. There was a hint of movement just beyond his shoulder; she waited a moment for her eyes to adjust to the light over the bar before trying to pierce the shadows beyond him.

Well, he's hunting in tandem tonight. I can't say as I like that—

Beside him was a young Oriental woman with a short, stylish haircut that shrieked "in"; she was dressed sleekly in a black leather jumpsuit and a heavy gold metallic belt.

Japanese, I think. And about the trendiest chick in this bar.

The woman's eyes were hard, but opaque, giving nothing away. She swept the crowd with her gaze for a moment, and Di ducked behind a tall blonde student-type. When she looked again, the woman had gone back to watching the band.

Definitely not chicken. Definitely shark. Sharks don't usually run in pairs; I wonder why this one's teamed herself with Lover Boy? I wish I dared scan them—

But there was something about the music that seemed to be damping her ability to think and to read even the surface of those around her, as if it were setting up some kind of jamming or interference patterns that were scrambling anything psi outside her shields.

Another good reason not to pry just now. The trouble is, it's also making it damned hard to think.

She withdrew from the area around the bar and let the crowd pull her deeper into itself. Too late she realized that she'd gotten caught up in an eddy that was heading for the dance floor, and there was no way to get free of it without drawing attention to herself.

Crap.

She gave up, and danced with the rest of them, letting the dance take her nearer to the stage.

I ought to get a look at these guys anyway. I don't like the music or the feelings they're putting out. They're hot—and they're damned good—but there's something wrong with them. It's all "take" and no "give." And—damn, but I could swear I've heard the guitar work on this song before somewhere—

She was concentrating so hard on the song's arrangement, that she didn't realize how close she'd gotten to the stage—not until a wild guitar lick screamed out of the second in answer to a growl from the base—a solo riff that was *paralyzingly* familiar.

I know that style!

Her head snapped up, her mouth open in shock, her body frozen in place.

At first she couldn't see him; the tangle-haired lead was in the way; she noticed then that the entire band was done up in black leather and silk in costumes that were meant to evoke absolute raw sexual attraction.

There were patterns in black beads or sequins on their shirts—patterns that stirred vague memories that wouldn't quite come to the surface, but which made her shiver. They *were* occult; no doubt of that. Some of the animal magnetism the group was putting out was being generated by those patterns. But there was something else there that went deeper—

The name on the drum kit—Children of the Night—that bordered on the occult, too.

The lead stared off into the crowd over her head, his eyes focused somewhere other than the interior of the club. He seemed to absorb the stage lights, and the strange, *hungry* smile he wore actually frightened her. Then he lunged for his mike as the second guitar screamed again in that hauntingly familiar way—and she saw who was behind him.

Oh my god—

Dave Kendall.

Her heart stopped as he smiled, and closed his eyes—a smile she knew better than her own—a smile that took her back to—before. If he'd smiled like that, instead of getting angry and *demanding* that she choose him or magic—

Oh god. I'd have given it up. I'd have given it all up to keep him. Oh god—

But he hadn't; he'd forced her to make the choice before she was ready—more than that, he'd *forced* her to make the choice. Then before she could begin to explain, he'd gotten mad, called her crazy—then walked out on her.

It hurt then. It *still* hurt. *Davey, Davey, if you'd just* waited, *waited till I was finished—I was almost at a nexus point. I had a replacement online. I think—I think I could have taken a break, given it a little rest and been patient until you understood—but you wouldn't wait—*

She could hardly breathe, her chest was so tight; the club was stiflingly hot, but she hugged her arms to her chest and shivered, and couldn't move—

Then he looked down, and saw her.

He froze for a heartbeat, staring down into her eyes—and from the dumbfounded look in *his* eyes, she had no doubt that he'd recognized her.

Oh god—

She broke the contact; forgot all about trying to be unobtrusive, forgot why she'd come in the first place, forgot even the hunters at the bar. All she wanted was to get away, away from him, away from the pain.

She bolted for the exit, shoving her way across the dance floor and into the crowd, elbowing aside anyone who stood in the way too long. The door loomed in front of her; she didn't wait for the bouncer to open it; just hit it with her breath sobbing and her chest on fire, and burst out into the cold and the wind and the dark—

But even that wasn't far enough for her. She *kept* running; ran all the way back to her apartment—slammed and locked the door behind her—

And dropped to the floor right beside the door. She was so exhausted she could go no further, could not even get as far as a chair or the couch. And she cried like a child until her eyes were sore.

And *then* she went to the kitchen, found the Scotch, and got drunk for the second time in a week.

Dave's world stopped.

Di? My god—

All he could see were those eyes, those huge eyes, deep brown and haunting—

When the world stopped, so did he; it wasn't long, no more than the first half of a heartbeat before she wrenched her eyes away from his, and tore off into the crowd. No more than a single downbeat.

But that was enough; he *felt* Jason's glare as the lead looked over his shoulder. It was the kind of look he'd expect to get for infanticide and it jarred him back into reality like a slap in the face. He picked up where he'd dropped his line, still smarting under the hot lash of that snarl—

Shee-it, it's just a damned song—

Yeah, but it was *Jason's* song, one of the very few he'd written. As Dave tried to make up for his screw-up by *really* getting down, the sting faded.

It's Jason's baby. I know how I feel when somebody drops the line on one of my babies. And I almost "killed" his baby there. I guess it was infanticide.

His fingers were flying, and Jason seemed happy again—at least his shoulders weren't angry-tight, and he looked in profile about the way he always looked, lately. Waiting and hungry.

Wonder if his sex drive's gone up the way mine has? Given what he was like before—hell if I wouldn't look hungry too, I guess. And sex does seem to take the edge off, like getting stoned does. Just—ah, the hell with it.

His concentration was gone, and he knew from experience that nothing was going to bring it back for a bit.

The last person I ever expected to see in the Apple was Di. Christ on a crutch.

Shit, she looked so good—

And I look like hell. Bet she took one look and figured me for wasted.

Anger flared, and he let it run out his fingertips into the guitar. Jason turned around again, but this time the look he threw back over his shoulder was one of approval.

Hell with her. Hell with what she thinks. We're doin it, we're hot an' gettin' hotter. I'll be doin' champagne an' up t' my neck in groupies while she's still playin' those stupid mind games—

The anger didn't last. It couldn't last, not when she hadn't really been at fault. Maybe he should have been a little more tolerant. She'd never really gotten on his case about his drugs—

He hadn't had a steady girl after her. Lots of chicks, but no girl.

He settled the second part back in behind the lead, and just followed what Jason was laying down. His thoughts were definitely not on the music.

Seemed like nobody else could touch him inside, down deep, since he'd broken up with her. Not the way she could—had—anyway.

His best stuff had all been written while they were together. It was like she'd been able to do things to the way he was thinking that just turned on the creative juice and let it flow like there was no tomorrow.

Except there had been a tomorrow, and when she was gone, the stuff he wrote just sounded like The Elevator Version of the Greatest Hits of the Dentist's Office. No juice, no excitement.

Like part of him went into deep freeze when he'd walked out on her.

Jason gave him another *look;* and he realized he'd been doing noodles instead of riffs.

Shit; this is getting me nowhere. She's gone, and that's all there is to it. And from the way she tore out of here, she ain't likely to want me back. Screw her. I don't need her back.

Jason had his eye on him, for sure, and Dave felt his anger coming back; fire in his gut and coals in his soul.

Who the hell does she think she is, anyway? What the hell did she think she was doing? Worthless bitch, off in the ozone and wanting me

out there too, because she couldn't handle the real world! Christ on a
crutch, I didn't need that! I never knew where she was going to be, never
knew when she was going to be home—never knew when I was going to
find the living room barricaded by some jerk that wouldn't even let me
talk to her 'cause she was off communing with the spirits or something.
I don't need *that kind of shit!*

The anger rose, and his face set in a frown; he attacked the guitar
line, attacked it like it had offended him, and Jason stopped watching
him.

After that, it was a clean run to the end of the set.

L ookin' good, man."

Pausing on his way into the back to count up the night's receipts, the club owner gloated at Jason, while the four of them broke things down and packed up their instruments and the precious—and expensive—new mikes.

More largesse from this "patron," whoever he is.

"I *like* the new look. So did the crowd. Many more nights like this one and I'm gonna have t' start chargin' a cover on weeknights, too. You guys on some kind of diet or something? I wouldn't mind losing a couple of pounds."

Jack raised a sardonic eyebrow. "Been wondering myself," he commented.

Jason chuckled. "No diets, just fast living. You go right ahead and charge that weekday cover, so long as we get the percentage, just like we agreed."

Dave stowed the last of the mike stands away at the back of the stage, and chanced at that moment to look up, and caught Jason's veiled smirk. No doubt about it, Jason was very pleased with himself.

"You make us happy, we'll make you happy," the lead continued, his voice shadowed with irony. "Otherwise we can go someplace else—"

"Yeah, sure, no problem," the man said hastily. "Just like we agreed. No reason I should rip you off."

"Exactly." Jason stood up and stretched, his posture deceptively lazy. Dave blinked his eyes; for a moment there it had seemed like the lead was glowing darkly in the smoky backlit tunnel of the club; sleek as a full-fed panther, and no less dangerous. Dave could feel the danger, a hot radiation of thinly veiled threat, and the back of his neck prickled.

But the club owner was gone, and the air of controlled threat faded.

Then a pair of shadows detached themselves from the end of the bar, and approached the stage, moving silently, sinuously.

Dave blinked at them in amazement, because he *knew* the bouncer had run everybody out. He couldn't imagine how he'd missed these two.

Then again—he caught the gleam of gold at hand, waist, neck. The bouncer wouldn't have missed them—unless they were too important to be booted out with the rest of the rabble—

The dark and shadowed strangers entered a cone of light thrown by one of the dance-floor spots, and shadows resolved themselves into a man and a young woman, both in black. The man wore an elegant variation on their own costume, sans beads and sequins, the young Oriental woman at his side a black leather jumpsuit that *was* pornographically tight. The man looked naggingly familiar. In another moment, Dave knew why. He'd been the guru at that ill-fated Halloween party, the guy who'd been sporting a cast on his arm.

The one all those people had fawned over, calling him "Master."

And Jason dropped what he was doing to greet them like a pair of old friends.

"Master Jeffries!" The lead jumped down from the stage and approached the strangers—but oddly, did not touch either of them. "I was hoping you'd be here tonight!"

Dave caught movement out of the corner of his eye, and turned enough to see that Doug was standing quietly—nodding a silent but respectful greeting to the two.

Doug—respectful?

The idea was unbelievable, but Jason drove that wisp of a thought out of his head with his next statement. "Dave, Jack—this is the patron I told you about. Right, Master Jeffries?"

The man smiled urbanely enough, though Dave thought he detected just a hint of irony behind the smile. "Nothing so important as a *patron,* Jason. You know I can't do anything about getting you contracts. All I can do is get you contacts with the right people, and help you showcase yourselves."

"Which is more than we were able to do for ourselves," Jason replies, his smile as broad and bright—and ironic—as their "patron's." "Let's face it, you can't get anywhere these days by just bein' good, you gotta look good too, and you gotta know the right people an' the right things."

"A sad commentary on our times," Jeffries said, while the girl beside him remained as quiet and still as an icon of ebony and ivory.

Except for her eyes, which never stopped moving. Flick, flick, flick—she covered the whole room within a minute, then began over—as if she were watching for something.

"I think we ought to celebrate the successful debut of the new image, don't you, Jason, Doug?"

Dave was so fascinated by the girl's ever-moving eyes that he didn't realize he'd agreed to go with Doug and Jason to the man's apartment until the words were out of his mouth. Then he was suddenly, inexplicably, afraid. He racked his brain savagely for an excuse to beg off, but couldn't think of anything that didn't sound lame. He turned toward Jack and hoped for a refusal from the drummer—but he only shrugged. "Sounds good to me," he said. "I never turned down somebody else's booze or grass in my life, an' I don't plan on starting now."

The man smiled sardonically, as if he found Jack naïve and amusing. "It's all settled, then," he said, turning away with the aplomb of a king who has just completed an audience. "I'll see you there."

Not in this lifetime—Dave thought.

How do I get myself into things like this? Ten minutes later, Dave found himself sandwiched on the front bench of the van between Jason and Doug, and very grateful the van didn't have a stickshift, or he might have lost a kneecap somewhere along the trip. Doug was driving, which was enough of a thrill for twenty lifetimes. Not even cabbies would challenge Doug's kamikaze attacks on the traffic patterns.

And he had a foot like lead. They were always either accelerating, or being thrown against the dashboard as he slammed on the brakes. Good thing Jack was in the back, keeping the guitars from getting smashed. Dave didn't envy him back there.

Jason was paying no attention to the suicidal maneuvers Doug was pulling. He kept up a calm but steady colloquy on the subject of "Master Jeffries," all praise. Doug chimed in from time to time with grunts of agreement.

"—lucky," Jason was saying, as Dave pulled his terrified gaze off the cab Doug was running up onto the sidewalk.

"Huh?" he said, when Jason paused, expecting a response.

"I said we're lucky. To have gotten his attention."

"Uh, right. Lucky."

Jason heaved an exaggerated sigh. "Just wait. Wait till you see his place. *Then* you'll understand."

I'd just as soon pass—Dave thought—then Doug wrenched the van around, brakes screaming in an abrupt right-angle turn. He flung the van down a ramp that opened up in front of them, leading into the bowels of a dark parking garage. The ramp bottomed out— and so did the van—and Doug hurled it at the back wall, where Dave could see written in huge red letters the words "Visitor Parking Only."

Sweet Jesus Christ—he's not gonna make it—

He squeezed his eyes shut as Doug applied the brakes and the brakes howled in protest—and the wall came at him at fifty per.

The van shuddered to a stop—without Dave eating the wind-shield. He cracked his right eye open, slowly, and saw the beam of the headlights bouncing off concrete *one inch* away from the front bumper.

He sagged with relief. *Christ.*

"Come on," Jason said, bailing out of the passenger's side of the van, and grabbing Dave's arm to haul him along. "Master Jeffries doesn't like to be kept waiting."

"I'm coming, I'm coming."

If I can walk.

His knees were not exactly what he'd call "steady." In point of fact, he wasn't sure they were going to hold him for a minute when he climbed down out of the front seat. Jack clambered out of the back, and Doug could see he wasn't in much better shape—which made Dave feel a little less like a wimp.

On the other side of the van, Doug was holding an elevator open for them; white fluorescent light glared out into the half-empty garage, and the door kept trying to cut him in half. Jason hustled them inside, and Doug let the door do its thing.

If this is supposed to give me an idea of how well heeled our patron is, I'm not impressed.

The elevator was an industrial, bare-bones model; gray linoleum floor, gray enamel walls, two cheap, buzzing fluorescent tubes behind a plastic panel in the ceiling.

This isn't exactly your Fifth Avenue address, either. I dunno exactly where we are, but we're someplace west of the Village.

Jason punched 2, and the elevator cage rose, a bit jerkily.

Jack shoved his hands into his jeans pockets and looked around with a slight frown. "I thought you said this dude lived in pretty good digs." The frown deepened. "I hate to tell you, guys, but I'm pretty underwhelmed."

Dave definitely saw Doug and Jason exchange a strange look. Secretive? There was something of that in it. Also a hint of something more, both shadowed and knowing.

It was very peculiar—and it vanished from their faces before Dave had a chance to be certain he'd really seen it, and not misinterpreted a frown of puzzlement or the crease of a headache.

The door slid open; they escaped the metal box before it could snap its jaws shut again and trap them. The hallway was as utilitarian as the elevator had been, gray plaster and dark gray carpet, and Dave began to wonder if his idea and Jason's of opulent surroundings were *that* far apart.

Jason paused outside a plain brown doorway and knocked; it swung open soundlessly to admit them before he'd knocked more than twice.

As the door swung shut behind them, Dave immediately revised his earlier impression. If this wasn't opulence, it was a damned fine substitute.

The place *was* heavy-duty weird, no doubt about it; it was done up like some kind of ashram. There was very little furniture in the living room; mostly low tables and piles of pillows everywhere; one long table against the far wall with an incense burner and a couple of dishes on it. Four low-wattage lamps, one on each wall, supplied a dim and amber-tinged light.

But the lamps were heavy bronze and hand-leaded glass; custom-built, and no doubt of it. Dave had never quite believed in the "carpet so thick your feet sank into it"—until now, now that his feet were sinking into one that was so thick he literally couldn't feel the floor. The walls shone, papered in an expensive mottled metallic, and the pillows gleamed a rich ebony, like the same kind of heavy silk their stage shirts had been made of.

Incense hung in the air, making the dim light a bit dimmer—and it had an odd smell to it. It wasn't like anything he was familiar with, it was sweet with an undertone of sour; and—was it making him high? He seemed to be getting light-headed—

"What's that stuff?" he whispered to Doug, who had moved in close behind him. He waved at the dish on the table, which was sending up a thin streamer of bluish smoke.

"Belladonna," Doug said shortly. "Don't worry about it."

The name tickled a memory at the back of his mind, but it eluded him before he could bring it up to the surface. Something-something about some friend who'd—smoked it? OD'd on it? It worried him for a moment—but the worry slipped away, and in a few moments he couldn't remember why he'd been concerned.

Jack was looking around, his uneasiness now plain for anyone to read. "Listen," he said to Jason, ignoring Master Jeffries. "All of a sudden I'm hungry. Why don't we go grab a burger or something?"

There was a whisper of sound behind them—no more warning than that.

The Japanese girl materialized from the shadows behind Jack—except that she had inexplicably turned into a Japanese *boy*—and before Dave could move or even say anything to warn him, he (she?) had pinioned Jack's arms behind his back.

Christ—what in hell?

Dave *tried* to move, his *mind* wanted to spring to Jack's aid, but his body would *not* obey him. He struggled against a dark something holding his mind and his body, like a fly trapped in glue. His body wasn't *his* anymore, it was obeying someone else, and that someone wanted him frozen where he was.

No one spoke—not even Jack. Dave could see Jack's eyes, though, and they were terrified.

Like maybe he can't even wriggle, either?

Suddenly Jeffries, Doug, and Jason were moving in on Jack like sharks circling in on a tasty baby seal.

Dave started shaking—at least inside—because he could *feel* Jack's fear, exactly the way he could *feel* the vibes in the club when they played.

His hunger was fading.

The way it did when he made love to a chick, or even more, in the club when they played—

His stomach heaved as he realized what that meant. He'd been feeding on the vibes, oh Christ, he'd been *living* off the vibes at the club—no wonder he'd been losing weight. No wonder he hadn't needed to eat.

And now his hunger was being appeased by a different, darker sort of vibe.

I think I'm gonna throw up—

Jason turned to him, and smiled. It was the same kind of smile that he had exchanged with Doug in the elevator; sly, knowing. "You can feel it, can't you?" he said softly, with just a hint of seduction in his voice. "It's better than the vibes in the club, isn't it? Like the difference between stale bread and steak—"

He walked over to one of the low tables, and when he returned, there was a knife in his hand, black of hilt, silver of blade. The blade reflected amber from the wall lights all along its length, the light flickering and moving as Jason turned it in his hand. Dave stared at it in horror and fascination.

Doug smiled and nodded, and Master Jeffries wore an expression of proprietary approval.

Jason ran his finger down the back of the blade in a measured caress. "I can make it even better, can't I, Master? Better than steak. Better than anything you can imagine." He reached for the front of Jack's shirt, and tore it open in a savage parody of some TV melodrama. "Oh, I can make it *much* better."

He extended the knife blade like an artist's paintbrush, and used it to draw a thin line down Jack's chest, leaving behind a thin thread of blood. "I can make it ambrosia."

Jack's pain and terror surged.

Dave felt a vile wave of satisfaction.

Oh God—he's right—I'm gonna be sick—

Dave's hunger was almost gone now—it was being rapidly replaced by a warm glow of pleasure and a satiation that was better than the afterglow of sex.

Jason extended the knife again, and drew a second line parallel to the first. Jack whimpered.

"Poor Jack," Jason said conversationally, his head cocked idly to one side, his tone as ordinary as if they were all sitting around the break room. "The rest of us woke up supermen—but *he* just woke up hung over. And we *can't* have a Child of Day jamming with the Children of the Night, now can we?"

Then Jason laughed, and touched Jack's throat with his free hand.

Jack threw back his head and screamed, a lost howl of pure, animal terror.

The sound gave Dave his body back.

He found he could move—and he did. He turned his back on the awful tableau, and ran.

He didn't remember hitting the door; he didn't remember taking the elevator—all he could hear was Jason's laugh, and the rest joining in; all he could feel was wanting to vomit and being unable to. This couldn't be happening—his friends had turned into something out of a horror movie. He didn't know them—

He didn't know himself.

He ran down dark streets until he couldn't breathe and his side was in agony. How long he ran, he didn't know, there was no time, only terror, shadow, and cold; a cold in his gut that nothing would ever warm again. He finally stumbled into the better-lit streets of the Village, aware only of blurs of light and dark and nothing else—until he caught the yellow haze of a cab light out of the corner of his eye and stumbled into the street, frantically waving it down. Miraculously, it stopped. Somehow he got into it, fell into the back seat, gave the cabby directions to his apartment—and tried, without success, to forget that horrible laughter that had followed him out into the street.

They slipped me something. Windowpane, yellow sunshine. It's all a trip. Tomorrow I'll go back to the club, and we'll all have a good laugh.

He huddled on the back seat of the cab, disoriented and sick, wincing away from the moving shadows outside the cab windows, but watching longingly for the signs that he was back on his own turf. He saw them, but they gave him no comfort. His heart pounded so hard he could scarcely hear the cabby; he didn't understand what the man was saying until he realized that the cab had stopped in front of his own building. He paid the man, crawled out of the cab and up the stairs to his apartment.

Only when he reached his own door did he begin to feel safe. Only when he had opened it did he feel as if this had *really* all been some kind of mad nightmare; he turned and closed the door behind him with a shudder of relief.

And then stepped into the living room—

And saw Jason and the Japanese standing there, waiting for him.

He started to scream—only started, for Jason reached out and seized him by the throat, choking off his cry.

Dave went limp with fear, and whimpered. Jason's hand on his throat was *terribly* strong. He could scarcely breathe, and he couldn't even imagine trying to fight.

"Now," Jason said, softly, fiercely. "You just keep quiet, and you listen to what I'm gonna tell you, bro. You're gonna keep your mouth shut about what happened tonight, and you're gonna go with the flow. You're *one of us* now. You've had a taste of the good stuff—and *believe* me, friend, that taste made you *ours*. The vibes from the club won't keep you going anymore. Once you've fed on fear, *you have no choice.*" He shook Dave the way a man would shake a rag doll. "You hear me, man?"

Dave swallowed; the crushing grip on his throat relaxed just enough so that he could nod. *I'm not like him. I can't be like him. I won't—I can't believe that—but I'm sure as hell not going to tell him that.*

Jason let him go, and he stood as passively as he could, rubbing his bruised throat. "Too bad about Jack," Jason said with a faint smile. "But—well, we haven't *really* lost him, have we, Hidoro?"

The Japanese boy nodded—then *blurred*, as if he were melting, or Dave was watching him through a mist. Dave's gut did a kind of backflip in revulsion as the boy briefly dissolved into a cloud of smoke, then faded back in again.

Only it wasn't the boy standing there now.

It was Jack.

Dave staggered back as the familiar face grinned, and familiar hands flexed long, bony fingers. "Beats the hell out of getting somebody new to learn the sets," Jack's voice said pleasantly.

Darkness came down over Dave as the ground came up to meet his face. The darkness beat the ground by a fraction of a second.

He came to in his bed—with the rays of the late afternoon sun streaking through the cracks in the blinds.

He blinked—and chuckled.

"Shit, nightmares at my age," he said out loud, grabbing his shades off the nightstand, and reaching for the Coke he left there the night before—

Only his hand met nothing. No Coke.

Fear clenched his gut, and he scrambled out of bed.

"I forgot it, that's all," he told himself. "I was stoned, and I forgot it—"

And he almost had himself convinced—until he turned on the bathroom light.

Scrawled across the bathroom mirror, written in what looked like dried blood, was a single word.

"Remember."

The hunger rose, clawing at him, like a weasel trying to tear its way out of his stomach. He clutched the bathroom sink to hold himself up—and cried.

Di paced the space behind the counter, too restless to stand, too unhappy to really want to think.

But the "activity" of pacing was doing nothing to stop her brain from working.

She'd just hung up on Annie's husband, Bob; he'd been babbling, truth to tell. *But then, you kind of expect the new daddy to babble. Little Heather Rhiannon is going to be spoiled rotten if he gets his way. I'm kind of glad he was so wrapped up in being New Daddy; if he had been his usual sharp self, he'd have picked up on bad vibes from my tone of voice before I'd gotten three words out. Then he'd have wanted to know what was wrong. I don't want any of them in the line of fire. It's bad enough having Lenny there.* She turned, and stared out the window for a moment. *Thank the gods Annie's going to be able to take over again soon. I can't take much more of this, maintaining protection on two places, dividing my attention like this.* Her lips twitched. *Two weeks at most. Bob at least remembered to tell me that.*

She registered a twinge, and her lips shaped an ironic grimace. *I think I'm jealous.*

Because Bob was *so* supportive of Annie, and *so* happy about everything—and he'd been just as terminally mundane as Dave when he and Annie met.

Her spirits sank another inch. *That whole conversation just made me more depressed than I had been, if that's possible. If it were Annie in this mess—Bob would be right in there slugging away beside her.* He adjusted—then he accepted—and now he joins in.

Oh hell. The situation isn't *the same.*

She leaned against the counter and buried her face in her hands. It was one thing to know intellectually that her peculiarly strong psychic talents put her into a class by herself, that she was *always* going to be forced into the front lines by the very strength of those gifts. *Along with the rest of the fortunate souls who have the dubious pleasure of being Guardians.* But to know it viscerally—that had to come very hard. *Oh, very few fortunate souls, we are. I couldn't tell you if we're cursed, or blessed. All I know is that we're different. Annie's not in my league; why should she have had to make the same choices? I'm an F-15, a Sherman tank; Annie's a Piper Cub, a VW bug.*

But seeing Dave again—

I thought I'd gotten over him. The wounds weren't healed, they were only scabbed over. Now they're bleeding again.

All the little demons of loneliness she'd thought she'd been ignoring successfully were coming back for their revenge. And it sure didn't help that Dave had looked *incredibly* sexy. Leaner, his eyes dream-haunted and soulful, like the poet *she* had always known he was, even if he didn't believe it.

It's probably drugs, she told herself savagely. *I'm probably seeing only what I want to see. He's probably burned-out, not soulful. That's not the spirit of a poet looking out of those eyes, it's the fact that there's nobody home in his skull.*

She squared her shoulders and raised her head, staring at the tumble of books on the shelf opposite her, but not really seeing them.

I've got to snap out of this. I've got more important things to do than moon about my lack of a love life. I still don't know who—or what— killed that gypsy boy. I still don't know what killed Keith's ex, or where it is. I don't know if the two deaths are related. I don't even know if it knows about me.

She went back to pacing again, her mind going in circles, fruitlessly, until it was time for closing.

As she began locking up, her eye fell on the display case of jewelry, and because of the way the light fell on some of the silver pieces, she suddenly *noticed* them, gleaming softly in the shadows. Bell, Book, and Candle catered to folk of a multiplicity of esoteric religions—and some of them were nominally Christian.

There were at least three heavy silver crucifixes in that case. And legend swore to the efficacy of a crucifix against vampires.

The gods knew she hadn't anything else to go on but legend.

Before she could change her mind, she opened the display case and took the largest and heaviest of them, shoving it into her coat pocket.

Gods, I feel like a fool—

But that didn't stop her from walking out the door with it tucked into her pocket.

Di slunk her way along the route between the subway station and her apartment building. Every nerve was alive to changes, movement. She felt like a sentient burglar alarm.

If something doesn't break soon, I'm going to look like a Brillo pad made of nerve endings.

It had been another overcast day; the sun had set about the time she closed the shop, and this was one of those nights when the air seemed to devour all available light, leaving the eyes confused by shadows that wouldn't resolve into substance.

Shadows that could hide anything. Hunter, or hunted . . .

For the first time in weeks, that line of thought did not bring a crippling surge of panic.

She had been expecting one; braced for it. When it didn't come— the confusion made her stop dead about ten feet from the steps of the apartment building.

The street lamp on the other side of the steps cast long, murky shadows, shadows that hid the side of the building and part of the sidewalk. Before she could shake herself out of her stupefaction, a man-shaped shadow solidified out of the murk and blocked her path to the steps.

She didn't think—just acted. Street-smart instincts and a karate sensei far more interested in keeping his pupils alive than in perfect form had gotten her to the point that under a given set of conditions, her body took over, no matter what state her mind was in.

In fact, she could *hear* her sensei even as she struck.

"You don't ever warn, you don't re-*act. You act.*

She knew that—but more importantly, her *body* knew it.

She was analyzing his stance without having to tell herself to do so; doing it as fast as her eyes could react to him being there; her *ki* was balanced and she was ready to strike as soon as he took that critical step that brought him within range.

He did.

She struck for the throat, not the (expected, and consequently, often guarded against) groin shot; she already knew as she was moving that she would follow that up with a kick to the knee, and once he was down she'd get past him and into the building—

Except that it didn't happen that way.

He didn't move out of the way; didn't pull a weapon. He just reached out and caught her wrist before she connected. And held it.

She'd never seen anyone but her sensei move that fast. And even her sensei couldn't have caught her wrist and absorbed all the energy of the strike without showing *something*.

But that wasn't the last of the shocks she was going to get; the man turned slightly so that his face was no longer backlit by the street lamp, and she saw *who* it was that had her prisoner.

The Frenchman.

He smiled grimly; a smile that showed, without a doubt, the ends of very elongated and *very* sharp canine teeth.

"You are Miss—Tregarde, I presume?" The voice was soft, faintly accented. Neither it, nor the man's expression, gave her any clue to what he wanted, or what she could expect. But the moment he spoke, she had no doubt that this was the same man who had stopped briefly at the shop; the same one she'd seen bending over the gypsy boy's body in the alley.

Cold wind making her knuckles ache penetrated the fog of fear. One hand was still free—

It might be stupid—but it might be her only chance. She thrust her free hand into her jacket pocket, yanked the silver crucifix out so fast that she heard the sound of ripping cloth, and shoved it into his face.

He stared at it for a moment, still holding her wrist captive; stared at it with his smile fading and puzzlement creeping into his expression. He looked from it, to her, and back again—and she actually saw his eyes widen with sudden understanding.

With a real smile, one tinged with sadness, he took the crucifix from her shaking hand. He took it gently, unwinding her fingers from the base; kissed it in the old manner, and just as gently replaced it in her untorn pocket.

"I have nothing to fear from the Son of God, mademoiselle," he said, patting the pocket. "Only from the sun that rises at dawn. I did not intend to frighten you, but I see that you are very frightened indeed. If I release you now, will you consent to remain and speak with me?"

I don't exactly have a choice, she thought. *If he can move like that—he can get me before I run two steps.*

"Mademoiselle," he said softly, "I have no means to reassure you, I can swear by nothing you would trust. But I mean you no harm. I only wish to ask you questions. No more."

I'm toast if he wants it that way. What have I got to lose? Besides, I'm getting tired of having my arm hanging in the air. She nodded assent, and he released his manaclegrip on her wrist.

She let her arm drop and rubbed it surreptitiously, as he fished in his jeans pocket and came up with a business card.

What is this, he's handing out cards? Have hemoglobin, will travel? She was close to hysteria; so close that she felt wired, and inconsequentials kept getting in the way. *Cripes, he's still not wearing anything more than a sweater—don't vampires get cold?*

"This is yours?" he asked, showing her the card.

She successfully throttled the hysteria down and squinted at the card. She didn't have to give it more than a cursory glance; it was creased and smudged, but hers. She nodded, and shift her weight to her left foot.

"You gave it to Janfri—the young man who—perished here?"

She nodded again, and tried not to shiver as a cold gust of wind went down her collar.

He turned the card over; written on the back was some kind of sign or glyph in red felt-tip. "Have you any idea what this means?"

She shook her head. "I don't know much about the Rom," she replied, her voice little better than a whisper. "That's A—"

She bit off what she was going to say. *If I tell him about Annie, she could be a target—*

"I know of Lady Annie," he told her, as if he had read her thoughts. "She is in no danger from me or mine. This sign—it is a Romany sign for—oh, I think the concept of 'sanctuary' or 'safehouse' is the closest. Did you say or do something that might have implied an offer of such sanctuary to Janfri?"

Another cold breeze cut right through her jacket, and she shivered, nape to knees. She nodded again; swallowed, and dared a bit more. "Look," she said, trying to keep the shaking out of her voice. "Is this all you wanted to know? If it is, I'm freezing; if it isn't, I'm *still* freezing."

He gave her another one of those measuring looks, the kind he'd given her the night she'd first seen him, as the icy breeze ruffled his silky hair. "Is there somewhere nearby where we may go to talk?" he asked finally. "I—it is only fair to tell you that there is truth in some of the legends. Truth in the one concerning thresholds, for example. Until you *invite* me to cross yours, I cannot. Once you do, I can enter at my will. Public places, however, are no problem. If you would prefer it, choose some place neutral to both of us. A bar, perhaps."

She narrowed her eyes, thinking. *He's giving me information. He hasn't done anything to me except stop me from hitting him. And he could; strong as he is, he could have had me around that corner and into the alley in seconds, and have been breaking my arms until I told him what he wanted to know.*

"Is that legend about wooden stakes true, too?" she asked finally.

He nodded, and flicked his hair out of his eyes with a long, graceful hand. "It is. I shall give you this freely—any weapon of wood can harm my kind, and it will take long to heal of the damage. Days; sometimes weeks. Metal will harm us not at all. The sun—as I said—can kill."

A snowflake fluttered down and landed on her nose. She shivered again in the wind, and a second flake landed on her arm. She sneezed. That decided her.

"Come on," she said, taking her keys out of her purse, and heading for the steps.

"You—wish me to follow you? Into your home?" He sounded more than surprised, he sounded flabbergasted.

"Yeah, you might as well." To her own amazement, she could feel herself smiling as she turned back toward him. "I've had everything else in my apartment, I might as well have a vampire, too."

Out of the corner of her eye she could see him watching everything with suspicion. *I think he's more paranoid than I am,* she thought in surprise, and for some reason the thought was comforting. Nevertheless, before they entered the (small 1) living room, she took a wooden knife from Africa down from the display of weaponry on the wall of the hall, and when she sat down in her favorite chair, she put the knife on the table beside her.

He gave it a cursory glance; made an ironic little bow in her direction, and seated himself on the couch, pointedly ignoring it.

He didn't just *sit*—he *took* his seat; made it his own, for the moment. *Gods, if I live to be a hundred I'll never be that graceful—what am I thinking? He probably* is *a hundred.*

"So—" she said, pretending to a bravado she didn't feel. "I have a vampire in my living room. It would be nice to know the vampire's name, and if he'd like anything to drink besides the usual. *I* wanted some hot tea."

"The vampire's name," he replied, with a ghost of a smile, "is André LeBrel. And the vampire would very much enjoy tea. It is a most civilizing custom, tea. I regret, however, that I cannot enjoy any hospitality other than liquid."

"Let's just stick to tea, shall we?" she replied hastily.

Unless she was dreadfully mistaken, the smile grew—just a hair—and there wasn't so much as a *hint* of anything other than playful amusement in it.

This is weirder than snake shoes.

He maintained his silence through the first half-cup, as she slowly thawed and slowly grew used to his presence across from her. He was just as foxy as she'd remembered him; maybe a little more, now that he had a reason to be charming to her. Completely composed; completely confident.

He should be. This oversized splinter isn't going to do me any real good against him unless I happen to hit a vital spot. She watched him out of half-closed eyes; his very calm was calming her. *I don't want to hit a vital spot. I've never seen a more attractive man in my life. If I didn't have to worry about unauthorized nibbles on the neck . . .*

But he's not pushing; he's doing his best to put me at ease. He's succeeding. He's trying to convince me I can trust him.

And it didn't ring false.

It was he who first broke the silence, speaking in a voice of brown velvet that she'd have paid to hear on the stage. "Can you tell me, Miss Tregarde, what you know about Janfri, and why it is that you gave him your card? I can tell you that he already was great friends with Lady Annie—" He smiled again, this time ironically. His wide brown eyes held a hint of amusement. "Well, as great as any Rom can be with *gadjo.*"

She put the cup down, carefully. "I don't know much of anything; Annie's never said anything about him, and I haven't had the chance to ask her. He came in that afternoon by the service entrance. I think he was expecting Annie; I think he was startled and maybe frightened to see me instead. But he probably figured if Annie'd left me in charge I was okay, so he stayed back there until the customers had all gone, and then came out."

"Yes?" André prompted patiently. "What did he tell you?"

"That he was hunted. He didn't tell me who by; I didn't ask. But he looked to *me* like somebody who'd gotten himself into unexpectedly deep kimchee, and I didn't want to leave it at that."

"So you gave him your card?"

She nodded, and sipped at the cooling tea. "I told him if he was ever in trouble in my area he could come to me for help."

André raised his eyebrows. "Are you often so impulsive, mademoiselle?"

She flashed a look of anger at him, and he grimaced. "Pardon. I tell you not to toy with me—now I play the word games with you. You are one of those who guards, yes?"

She didn't reply. *Does he know about the Guardians? Who told him?* She looked at him with a new wariness. He waited for her answer; coiled strength, dark grace. She truly wanted to tell him—

She couldn't. Couldn't expose herself and the others.

He shrugged. "Janfri was hunted, as he claimed. I was attempting to find him so that I could deal with the hunter. He did not, or could not, return to his people, so that I was following the rumor of him only. I was—too late in finding him."

She realized suddenly that she had let down her personal shields in his presence so that his emotions—if a vampire *had* emotions— could get through. And that only happened when her subconscious had analyzed a situation and deemed it safe.

And there are times when my subconscious is smarter than I am. It's usually more paranoid than I am. So why has it taken my shields down? She analyzed what was coming from him, and found herself assessing him in an entirely new light. There was guilt there; and mourning, and a deeply felt depression that seemed a great deal like her own. His eyes held shadows within shadows; shadows of pain, and a loneliness that had endured longer than anything *she'd* ever known.

He had emotions all right; as real and as unfeigned as her own. This was an amazingly patient and gentle man, under most circumstances, but there was a steel-hard core to him. Like the dancers she knew, he would smile and do what he had to, and you'd never know he was bleeding.

"So *you* didn't kill him—" she blurted.

"*Le Bon Dieu* forbid!" He looked angry now—and she sensed he was profoundly unhappy. She felt the claws under the velvet, but felt also that they would in no way be turned against her. "*Mais non.* It was as I told you. I was hoping to protect him, as I have pledged to protect all of his clan."

"Protect him from what?"

"In this case—one who wished to use him. That one found him, I think. But how he was killed—"

"Who did it? Who was chasing him?" The words tumbled out, and she leaned forward in her eagerness to hear the answer to one of the mysteries plaguing her.

"The man I asked you of, the one I described to you." His jaw clenched, and his anger smoldered just under the surface of his words. She winced a little at the heat of it. "I feel sure of this. The man is called Jeffries. 'Master' Jeffries by some. Master. *Merde.*" He brooded for a moment, eyes fixed on his mug. "He wanted something of Janfri, of which revenge for a plan I thwarted was a small part. Janfri's death was that revenge. But I do not know *how* he murdered the boy. You say that he never actually reached you?"

"No—do you know what an empath is?" He nodded, and she continued. "That's—one of the things I do. I 'felt' him calling for help before he died. I think you saw me; I reached the alley after you did, so I don't know who murdered him, or why—but I *do* know how he died."

"How?" Her words galvanized him; he raised his head and stared directly into her eyes as if he could pull the knowledge directly from her mind into his. She couldn't look away; didn't want to.

She described psychic vampirism in detail, as André sat tensely on the couch and clenched his mug tightly in both hands, as if he wished he could lock those hands around one particular neck.

". . . so it looked to *me* as though this time the psivamp drained his victim so completely that he killed him," she concluded. "The boy was a burned-out husk, psychically speaking."

Now André shook his head, doubt beginning to creep into his troubled eyes. "Not possible—" he objected. "This thing—it cannot be possible."

"Huh." She snorted. "This afternoon I would have said *you* were impossible. Not possible? Tell that to Janfri. It happened, guy."

She was interrupted by a scratching at the door—and cool, collected André LeBrel jumped a foot, and pivoted as though expecting an enemy to burst through the door at any second.

Di was secretly pleased to see him shaken up a little. "I'll take care of that," she said, before he could object, and rose to let in the building cat—because 'Tilly was her final test of character. If this super-natural creature sitting nervously on the end of her couch could pass 'Tilly's judgment, then he could be believed, and trusted.

"Attila the Nun" was the cat's full name; a registered Maine Coon, she weighed in at nineteen pounds, all muscle (hence "Attila") and was a neutered female (hence, "the Nun"). They hadn't had a bit of trouble with rats since Jerry the super had brought her home, and she was allowed the run of the entire building.

Theoretically she "belonged" to Jerry, but she was fed by every-body and spent at least half her sleeping hours in Di's apartment. She was also the surest judge of character, occult or otherwise, that Di knew.

Tilly greeted Di with a single rub of the head, and strolled imme-diately into the living room as if she knew exactly what she was wanted for.

And for all I know, Di thought wryly, *she does.*

She headed straight for André. He extended his hand, palm up, toward her. She leaned forward a little to sniff his fingertips.

Now she's either going to take off two of his fingers, or—She rubbed her head on his hand, and leapt into his lap, where she promptly made herself at home.

He relaxed as the cat began to purr, then looked up at Di with a shrug, one hand busy scratching the cat's chin. "Well, mademoiselle—if I do not mistake you, this was something of a test. Do I pass?"

Di nodded, and smiled and realized that it was the first time she'd really smiled in days. "You pass."

He put the other hand to work on the cat's ears. 'Tilly increased her volume. "Then tell me again of this 'psychic vampirism.' If it happened—it must be true."

She went back over the phenomena in more detail—and as she did so, she found herself silently agreeing with her guest that "Mr. Trouble" (aka Jeffries) *was* the most likely candidate. He *had been* a psychic vampire when she first saw him. And if something had hap-pened to make him even more powerful than he was already . . .

She said as much.

"But what?" he asked. "What could do such a thing?"

She sighed, and contemplated the clean line of his jaw. "I don't know," she said, finally. "But I know it's possible. A couple of oc-cultists have hinted about things like that in their works. And—" *I want to trust him. I want to trust him. I want this man for a friend.* She mentally shook herself. *Gods, what am I thinking? He's a vampire*—

"—let's just say I've heard of things that could amplify a psivamp."
Like certain magics only the Guardians are supposed to have access to.

Finally André nodded in reluctant agreement. He removed the
cat (who protested sleepily), set her down on the couch, and rose. "I
must go," he said, his expression a sober one. "It seems that I have a
great deal to do before dawn."

Di stood too, and moved toward the door. As he followed, she half
turned so that she could say something to him. "I could help—" she
offered hesitantly, then paused, her thoughts a welter of confusion.

He's a vampire—*I'm not sure I really want to help him, I'm not
sure I should—but there's already been one death. It was a death I
could have prevented if I'd been a little quicker. I've got an obligation—*

"No, thank you," he replied curtly. "This will be difficult enough
for one who knows what to do."

She drew back, a bit nettled by his assumption that she was some
kind of clumsy amateur. And that bothered her, too.

Now I am really *confused. I like him; I want his respect. And he's a*
vampire, *for gods' sake! But he did pass the 'Tilly test—*As she opened
the door, she admired the lithe way he moved, the graceful curve of
his back. *And he sure is sexy. A lot more attractive than anybody I've
ever met—except maybe Dave—*

Hell, I'll never see him again.

That thought actually caused a twinge. She wanted to see him
again—

*Yeah, and I want other things that aren't good for me. But at least
one of my mysteries is solved . . .*

"Thank you, mademoiselle," he said at the door. "For your
time—for your help. *Au revoir.*"

And he turned and slipped down the stairs, obviously eager to get
on with it.

She closed the door behind him; locked it, and leaned on it for a
moment.

*One mystery solved. But not the big one. I have my real vampire; I
have my psivamp—but neither of those is the soul-eater.*

She shuddered.

And I still have no notion where it's going to strike next.

SEVEN

While the other three headed for the break room, Dave slipped behind the bar and passed the barkeep another ten. The gaunt, sad-eyed scarecrow of a man gave him a dubious look, but poured him a six-ounce tumbler of straight vodka; no ice, no mixer. Dave tossed it off in a couple of swallows, and waited, eyes closed, elbows planted on the bar, for the shaking, the hurting to stop.

It didn't stop, but it became bearable. He waited a moment longer, while the canned music rolled over him and pounded his brain cells, but there was no further improvement. So he pushed away from the spotlighted bar and wove his way back through the crowd to the break room.

He could *feel* every body in the place; their excitement when he brushed past them, the life in them. The white-heat of them; vibes that had fed him up until last night.

No more. No more.

Jason was right; it wasn't enough anymore. The vibes only whetted his appetite, and he had felt something inside him reaching out for those warm, glowing sources of food.

He'd pulled back every time, before he did anything. But. *But.*

It was harder every time to pull back.

And the gnawing, devouring hunger kept rasping away at his self-control. He'd sought, with limited success, for something to hold it off. Booze helped; so did drugs. Snow worked the best, but he only had one hit in his stash and he'd used it this afternoon to get to the club without—consequences. Booze and drugs *numbed* the edge of the clawing hunger in his gut. *Nothing* made it go away.

This was his third drink tonight, and the gig was only half over.

Three shots of straight vodka, six ounces each, and he was just *barely* able to keep from grabbing one of the little teenys trying to cling to him, and take her out into the back, and—

He shoved open the door to the break room, and three pairs of cynical eyes met his. He flushed, and ducked his head, wondering if they'd guessed how he was trying to fight this—thing—he'd become.

"Poor Davey," Jason said silkily. "Poor Davey. I don't think he's happy, Hidoro."

"He has a conscience," the thing that wore Jack's face said, complacently cleaning his fingernails with a knife. "Inconvenient things, consciences. Expensive to maintain."

"Maybe he needs another lesson," Jason lounged further back in his chair, and half closed his eyes. "I think maybe he ought to be assigned to get you your dinner, Hidoro."

"Aw, come on, Jason," Dave said weakly. "I'd really—give me a break—"

The blond lunged up out of his chair and had Dave by the throat before the other could blink. "There *are* no breaks, Davey," Jason whispered, pulling Dave's face to within an inch of his own. "It's us, and the sheep. Sheep were made to be slaughtered. Get used to it."

Dave cringed, hardly believing the power in Jason's grip, the speed with which he'd struck. *Oh God, oh* God—*he's so strong*—

"I'm stronger than you are, Davey," Jason continued, as if reading Dave's thoughts. "Mind and body, I've got the jump on you now, and I'll always have the edge on you. That's because I'm *not* pretending to be a sheep. Now you'd better start acting like a wolf, Davey-boy—or one of these days we might mistake you for one of *them*." Jason grinned. "And that'd be too damn bad, wouldn't it?"

He let go of Dave and shoved him at the same time; Dave staggered back into the door, his heart pounding, his mouth dry with fear. He tried to say something; found that he couldn't. Jason resumed his chair, and surveyed him with a little smile, crossing his arms over his chest and narrowing his eyes.

"Go out there and help Hidoro," the lead ordered, after a long, excruciatingly uncomfortable moment. "Go cut him out a nice little lamb. Hidoro will wait for you at the van; just find some chippy and get her to follow you out there." He waved one hand carelessly. "Pick up a runaway. You're good at that."

Dave's face flamed at the reminder that the last two girls he'd picked up here had been underaged teenyboppers with forged IDs. *I seem to attract the kids in women's bodies. Oh God. Kids. I can't*—

He's not going to take any excuses—

"Please, Jason—I—I don't think that's too good an idea," he stammered. "We shouldn't be doing this where we hang out. What if somebody notices? What if somebody comes looking for—"

He couldn't finish. But Jason just shrugged. "A hundred runaways vanish a day in this town. Nobody's gonna notice one or two more dropping out of sight. Who's gonna remember 'em, or tell anybody they were here? 'Sides, Hidoro doesn't leave anything to find. Ain't that so, Hidoro?"

The thing just gave Dave a cynical look, and half smiled.

"Go on," Jason ordered, ice suddenly coating his words. "Get out there and do what you were told."

He found himself outside the door and in the hallway—pushed out by the uncompromising command in the lead's voice.

He leaned against the wall, and shook; shook with the effort of holding back sobs, shook with the terrible hunger that was beginning to take over his very thoughts.

I should just walk. Get the hell out of here. Get out of their reach—

And do what? Oh God in heaven—and do what? *I'm trapped. This thing inside me, this* appetite—*it's a monkey on my back, and I'll never be free of it, no matter how far I run—*

Jason was right. He pounded his fist white on the concrete blocks of the wall. *Oh God, he was right. I'm one of them.*

Pain finally made him look at his hand, at the damage he'd done to himself, in dazed bewilderment. He watched in fascination as blood seeped to the surface and collected in tiny beads on the scraped skin of his knuckles.

Then the hunger cut through his daze, and he stumbled back into the club, onto the mobbed dance floor, into the blacklight and the flashing spots.

He saw her at once, knew *this* was going to be the one, this hard-faced old-young chick with frightened eyes, sensuous mouth, and a calculatedly bored, jaded expression. He moved in on her as she writhed in her own little space on the dance floor; watched her watching him, hoping he was heading for her, not believing he was.

Out of the corner of his eye he could see Jason, leaning against the doorway, keeping him under his eye.

He synched his moves with hers, and the old sex drive went into high gear; now he had two hungers goading him on, and his brain wasn't in the driver's seat anymore. He felt himself smile, saw her eyes widen; slipped his arms around her waist and ground his hips into her leather mini, and watched her melt.

And hated himself.

"Hi," he said, just loud enough to be heard over the pounding drums and screaming guitar of Iron Butterfly. "Tired of dancing yet?"

"Sure." Her mouth shaped the word, though he couldn't hear it.

"How 'bout we go outside—" He jerked his head in the direction of the back exit, and let her go; began parting the squirming dancers and moving out, *knowing* she'd follow him.

Jason was gone by the time he reached the door into the hall; *she* was right behind him. He reached back and took her hand, and it trembled a little in his.

"What's your name, sweet thing?" he said, giving her an arch look and a slow, sexy, ultramacho half-smile.

"Sherrie. You're Dave, aren't you? With"—a worshipful pause— "the band?"

"Uh-huh." He squeezed her hand. "Glad I saw you out there; I thought the evening was gonna be a total loss." She glowed, and he squeezed her hand again. "You want a toke? I got some good stuff in the van."

"Sure—"

He interrupted her, saying what he *knew* she wanted to hear. "You doing anything tonight? After the gig?" His thumb caressed her palm knowingly, and she shivered, her eyes got soft, and her lips parted a little.

"N-no," she stammered, moistening her lips with the tip of her little pink tongue.

"You're pretty new to the Apple, aren't you?"

She looked dismayed. "Does it show that much?"

He stopped just inside the entrance, under the glaring "Exit" sign. "Yeah, just a little. You on your own, honey? You got friends, a guy, anyplace to stay?"

She shook her head, avoiding his eyes.

"Hey." He caught her chin in his right hand, tilted her face up to his. "It's no big deal—just—I got this place, and nobody but me in it—"

He bent and kissed her; she parted her lips readily enough when he tongued them, and he probed her mouth, slipped his hands behind her buttocks and crushed her hips against his—

—and could see everything in her head—

She was fifteen and a runaway from Pennsylvania. She thought in New York she'd make it big, maybe as a model. But looks that had been outstanding at home were nothing here. Then she thought she could make it as a dancer, but the only offers she got were from strip joints.

She wasn't shacking up with guys for money, yet, but in a way she was even more desperate, she was doing it for food and a place to crash.

Dave's conscience cringed. *Either she's found out that most of the crash pads are just recruiting stations for pimps, or else she hasn't made a crash-pad connection yet.*

That *he* should be going for her was more than she dared dream now—though when she'd come running out here it had been in the hopes of finding someone like him—somebody to match her daydreams and the lyrics of all those songs.

His body kept putting the screws to hers; his mind writhed and grew more nauseated by the moment.

He broke the clinch when she was hot and gasping, and more than ready. "Hey," he said, smiling falsely into her eyes. "You're okay, Sherrie."

Her lips were wet, her eyes dazed and soft, her cheeks flushed. "So're you—" she breathed.

"Let's go out to the van, huh?"

"Okay—"

She shivered in the blast of cold air that met them when he opened the door; but she didn't complain, and she snuggled against him when he put his arm around her.

His conscience was giving him no mercy. *You traitor, you goddamn Judas—*

He was still inside her head. *The alley was dark; just the one, dim light over the back entrance.*

Yeah. To Sherrie's eyes it was dark—not to his. To his, the alley was in clear twilight, and he could see Hidoro waiting for them beside the van.

The van loomed up on their right, a dark blot against the painted brick of the alley. It cast a long, deep shadow—and Sherrie gasped when Hidoro materialized out of the shadow.

He was still in the band costume, but wearing what Dave presumed was his own face, that of the young Japanese boy he'd seen in his apartment. He smiled, cruelly, and Sherrie shivered.

"Dave?" she said, bewilderment plain in her voice. "Dave? What—"

He let go of her shoulders and stepped away from her. She turned to look at him with her face set in a mask of confusion.

"Sorry, Sherrie," he said, choking on the words. "You shoulda stayed home in Pennsylvania."

Her confusion turned to fear as Hidoro approached her; she was trapped between the Oriental and Dave, with nowhere to run that wasn't straight at one or the other of them.

Dave could taste her fear—and so could the need inside him. Before he could stop himself he was drinking that fear in, holding her paralyzed and weakening as he fed, and the hunger finally stopped gnawing at his spine—

No!

He cut himself off from it, from her; doubled over as a cramp hit his gut.

Freed from what he was doing to her, the girl screamed.

None of them, not Hidoro, nor Dave, nor (from the despair in her mind) Sherrie expected a response to that scream. But one came.

"Hey!"

The voice from the street startled all three of them. Sherrie reacted first, screaming again, louder this time.

"Hey! Y'all leave that gal alone!"

Heavy running footsteps echoed in the alley, preceding Sherrie's would-be rescuer. He was a big man, dressed like a construction worker; with Amerind features and long, straight black hair in a ponytail that waved behind him like a battle banner. He was carrying something—a length of pipe, it looked like, and he was holding it like someone who knew how to use it. With a snarl, Hidoro launched himself at the girl, shoving her into Dave's arms, then he whirled toward the attacker, and dissolved into a cloud of evil, black smoke.

The man ran right into the cloud, seeing only Dave under the light, and probably taking him to be the only threat.

He didn't come out on the other side.

A choked-off cry of agony came from inside the cloud, oddly muffled and distant—then the thud of something heavy hitting the pavement.

Sherrie was shaking in Dave's grip; she whimpered, and the fear flooded from her, and it was so *good*—

Half of him wanted to throw up; but the operable, unparalyzed other half of him was sucking it in as fast as she put it out.

The cloud condensed, slowly, revealing the man sprawled face-down on the pavement as it coiled in on itself. The cloud took on man-shape, then color—then became recognizably Hidoro. The Oriental was frowning.

He shoved the body aside with a booted foot; it rolled, arms flapping limply. "*Most* unsatisfactory," Hidoro said, glaring at Dave as if he were somehow to blame. "I only got the kill. I had no time to feed before he escaped me."

He transferred his frown to the girl, who wilted with fear, shrank in on herself, and cried silently.

The frown turned to a smile, and he reached toward her with one long, pale hand. She whimpered, and his smile deepened. The whimper choked off as Hidoro touched her face, and the fear coming from her was so strong Dave couldn't even feel the hunger gnawing at him anymore.

"Still—" Hidoro said caressingly, "there is this one. Young, and vital. I think she will do."

He made a peremptory gesture, and Dave shoved the girl at him, turning quickly away before he could see the creature transform again.

He stumbled blindly toward the rear door of the club as Hidoro chuckled behind him.

Bile rose in his throat, and he flung himself into the shelter of the shadowed hallway.

And straight into Jason. The iron of the lead's hands catching his shoulders shocked him into cold silence.

"Greedy, greedy," Jason chided, as his stomach roiled. "Jumping the gun on us, huh?" He laughed out loud as Dave tried unsuccessfully to control the revulsion on his face and the turmoil in his gut.

"You should be in *good* shape now, huh? Ready for action?"

Only Jason's hands gripping his shoulders kept him on his feet.

"Good. But action is gonna have to wait." Between one moment and the next, he was shoved down the hall toward the dance floor. Jason stayed on his heels, and gave him no chance to falter.

"It's show time, baby."

"Davey-boy got a little greedy and had some appetizers," Jason told Doug as they herded Dave back into the break room at the end of the last set.

"Well, good," the dark bassist snickered. "Then he won't mind helping you and me get ours, will you, Davey?"

Dave shook their hands off him and headed for "his" corner of the room, refusing to answer their baiting. He mopped his sweating face and neck with a towel, then put his gear away with slow, precise care, hoping that they wouldn't see how much his hands were shaking, or guess how close he was to tears.

God, god, kid, I'm sorry, I really am, I couldn't help it, I didn't have a choice—

He caught Jason raising his head and staring toward the closed door, for all the world like a hunting animal sniffing the air.

"Nothing tasty out there," he said to Doug, who grimaced and nodded. "What do *you* think?"

The bassist frowned, and shook his sweat-damp hair out of his face. "Wall Street?" he ventured. "Some pretty high rollers work out of those brokerage houses. They run just as strung and uptight as coke and uppers can get 'em. On the wire, for sure. A lot of 'em work late. We did Mad Ave last night."

Jason nodded, a tight little smile on his lips. Dave turned away— but felt a hand grab his elbow and turn him around. Doug was holding out his jacket.

Jason pushed him at the bassist, then released him. "Move it, man," he said coolly. "You're driver tonight."

He shrugged into the jacket, the familiar weight of the leather across his shoulders giving him no sense of comfort. "Where's Hidoro?" he asked, stalling.

"Out." Jason pulled on his own jacket.

"But what about the stuff—"

"That's what Master Jeffries hired us roadies for," Doug interrupted, not *quite* sneering.

Right on cue, a silent and painful anonymous figure in a Led Zeppelin T-shirt came in carrying Dave's axe. He was followed by a second, as like to him as a twin, carrying the mike boxes.

"They'll be picking up the mikes and the instruments and stashing 'em for us every night from now on," Doug elaborated. "If you'd been listening instead of wallowing in self-pity, you'd have heard him tell us that before the first show. Come on, get a move on. I'm hungry."

He laughed at the look on Dave's face, and shoved open the door to the hallway.

It seemed strange to be in the driver's seat for a change; he headed in the direction of Wall Street while Jason and Dave watched the streets and buildings intently, eyes narrowed in concentration, as if they were listening for something. He entertained a brief fantasy of flooring the gas, whipping the wheel around, and smashing the van with all three of them in it against the wall of some apartment or factory—

I can't. I can't. I haven't—

"You haven't got the guts," Jason said coolly in his ear. "So don't even play with the idea."

He jumped a foot, fear cramping his gut, along with the hunger that was growing again.

"You shouldn't've cut yourself off from the flow, shithead." Jason laughed as the lights from cars in the other lane made a moving, changing mask of brightness and shadow out of his face. "Well—maybe we'll leave you a little something."

"Stop here," Doug said suddenly, as they moved into the business district and cars all but disappeared.

"Pull over," Jason ordered.

He longed to disobey, prayed for a reason to be able to keep the car moving, but a parking place loomed up like an unpaid debt, and he was forced to pull into it.

He waited in cowed silence for the other two to leave the confines of the van, but instead of opening the door, Doug looked over at Jason with a nasty grin on his face. "Want to try what we were talking about?" he asked. "I think we got two candidates coming down the elevator now."

Jason nodded; echoed the other's grin, then closed his eyes, a line of concentration appearing between his eyebrows.

Dave—*almost* heard something.

Something in the back of his skull, like a radio with the volume turned too low to make out anything but a vague murmur of voices. Except the voices were in his head.

Oh God, now what?

He gripped the steering wheel and tried to concentrate on the streetlights reflecting off the bumper of the car parked in front of him, but the voices were still there, and they were making the hunger worse.

Footsteps on concrete made him look up; he saw two people, a man and a woman, emerge from the building, talking. They were both dressed conservatively, but expensively; both carried briefcases. The man had an umbrella, one of the expensive oversized English imports with a sturdy steel shaft, meant to last a lifetime. That was all he got to see before the fireworks started.

They paused on the curb right in front of the van; they didn't seem to notice that there was anyone *in* the van. Jason's frown of concentration deepened and the hand that had been resting on his knee tightened into a fist.

And what had been a quiet conversation burst into a violent argument. Within seconds the man and woman were shouting at each other, screaming at the tops of their lungs, oblivious to their surroundings.

Dave could feel the flow of anger pouring out of them—anger that flowed at him and around him, anger that the hunger inside him leapt up joyfully to devour.

And there was something else—

Only *that* "something" was flowing from *Jason and Doug* to *them*, not the other way around. Something wild, bestial. Something that was throwing what should have been a mild disagreement out of any contact with reality, and turning it into something deadly.

Jason and Doug opened their eyes and exchanged a smug little smile; then, as Dave stared stupidly, they got out of the van and bracketed the couple.

Who never even noticed they were there.

Unthinking anger flowered into pure, killing rage—and as Dave watched without understanding, the man dropped his briefcase and took his umbrella in both hands.

Fury roared in Dave's ears and sang in his blood, and unnatural, irrational wrath gave the man unnatural strength. He took a step backward, then shoved the umbrella like a sword—

—right through the woman's body.

She made a little mew of pain—her hands scrabbled at the man's face, then her mouth gaped in a silent scream.

Pain, pain, pain. Rage and lust and hate—

Dave just sat there, too shocked to move, as the man pulled his umbrella loose, and the woman doubled over and fell to the pavement. She lay curled around her wound, on her side, a dark, spreading stain pooling around her, black against the white of the concrete. He stabbed down at her, again and again, until the umbrella collapsed and he trampled the body in a dance of insanity and triumph.

And beside him stood Jason and Doug, pulling it all in, their faces as transfigured as saints in rapture, shining with unholy joy and perverse beauty.

With a little cry, Dave cut himself off, and buried his head in his arms, sheltering behind the steering wheel—

Then, suddenly, there was nothing. He looked up in surprise, and Jason and Doug came back to the van and climbed up beside him. For one wildly hopeful moment he thought maybe this *thing* inside him was gone—

No. He could still *feel* the other two, radiating satiation. It was only that the man had gone psychically, emotionally dead. Burned out. Nothing but a husk.

His hands lost their grip on what was left of his umbrella, and he dropped it beside the body. He stared dully at his own feet, plainly feeling *nothing*.

"There's nothing left for him to feel with," Jason said smugly. "*We* got it all. Pull out and go around the corner. I want to see what happens."

Shock set in, and Dave obeyed, too numb to think about doing otherwise. The man continued to stare at the ground, and didn't even look up when the van engine started beside him.

He pulled up to the corner, and hung a U-turn. With no traffic on the street they could wait as long as Jason wanted.

"Worth putting a little out," Doug said, with a sleepy, satisfied smile on his face. "Just like the Master said." The headlights of an approaching car appeared up the street, and Doug's smile grew sly. "Give the zombie a shove, bro. Wouldn't want to leave too many loose ends."

Jason nodded; Dave *felt* something again, and the man shambled out into the middle of the street—

Right into the path of the oncoming cab.

Dave cried out, flung his arms up, and hid his eyes in the crook of his arm as tires shrieked and there was a distant thump from the direction of the headlights.

Doug laughed, and Jason grabbed his elbow and pulled his arm away from his face. He shuddered, and didn't bother trying to hide it.

Jason slapped him, sharply.

"Get used to it," he said roughly. "Sheep and wolves. If you won't be a wolf—"

He let the sentence hand unfinished. Dave clutched at the steering wheel and got his shudders under control.

"Better." Jason leaned back, ignoring the commotion in the street ahead of them, and put his hands behind his head.

"Now what?" Dave managed to croak.

"Home, James," Jason replied. "Home." Then he grinned. "And we'll see if the Master has anything for you to do."

"Home" meant Jeffries's place now, at least for everyone but Dave. As Dave pulled the van into Jeffries's parking place, he wondered how long it would be before he was coerced into giving up his apartment and moving in, too.

He climbed out of the van and tossed the keys to Doug; turned, and started to head for the outside again. But Jason blocked his exit.

His gut went cold.

"Not this time," the blond said, reaching for his shoulder. "You and Master Jeffries need to have a little talk."

Dave backed up a step, avoiding Jason's hand. "What about?"

The lead shrugged. "What do *you* think? Your attitude Davey-boy. You're just not coming along the way the rest of us are. You better start shaping up fast."

Dave took another step backward.

"Indeed," said a cynical baritone voice behind him. "I would say you lack—ah—enthusiasm."

Dave stumbled, trying to pivot too fast for his sense of balance to cope with. Jeffries stood less than a foot away, and he'd come up behind Dave too quietly to be heard.

Dave was trapped now, between Jason and Jeffries. Nowhere to run. His head spun, he caught himself with one hand on the garage wall and licked dry lips.

Jeffries held out his hand without taking his eyes off Dave, and Doug dropped the keys into it. He was as pale and unfeeling as a granite statue in the cold, flickering fluorescent light of the parking garage. "I would say you are less than committed to us," he continued, his voice echoing slightly, his eyes slitted, his mouth a hard line slashed in his face. "I think perhaps you need to truly learn where your loyalties and self-interest lie."

Then Dave went blank for a minute—

No longer than that—he thought.

But one moment he was standing there, facing off Jeffries. The next, he was driving the van out of the garage, with Jeffries lounging tigerlike on the passenger's side of the bench. And he had no memory of anything in between.

He waited for Jeffries to give him instructions. The man remained silent—yet Dave found himself making turns as if the man had directed him explicitly—until he found himself parking the van outside a quiet, obviously private, club.

A mote of surprise penetrated his misery. *Gentility, antique leather, and old school ties. What in hell are we doing here?*

"Hobbyists," Jeffries said, answering his unspoken question. "These men are all numismatists and philatelists." He sneered silently at Dave's look of incomprehension. "Coin and stamp collectors," he explained, as though to a particularly stupid child. "Wealthy ones."

Stamp collectors? After the atrocities of this evening—

Stamp collectors? What's he gonna do? Stroll in, introduce himself, and—and—show 'em a naked penny?

Dave giggled hysterically, and Jeffries glared at him. "You—you're kidding!" he gasped. "A bunch of dried-up old men like *that?* What in hell good are *they* going to do you?"

Jeffries pointed a finger at him—and his throat closed. He couldn't breathe. And ice ran down his spine when he saw the man's eyes.

"They have passion," Jeffries said coldly. "These 'dried-up old men' are *full* of tortured passion, passion they never gave to a living creature. If you get your mind out of your crotch sometime, you might learn something."

He made a gesture of dismissal, and Dave fell against the steering wheel, gasping for breath. Jeffries slid smoothly out of the van, and stalked into the bar.

Dave huddled in the van, shivering with cold and emotion and not daring to move.

I hope to hell Jeffries takes his own sweet time. I hope he falls flat on his face in there. I hope—

Realization began to sink in of how entirely helpless and without real hope he was. *Oh God. There's no way out of this. No way at all.*

He pillowed his forehead on his arms and shook. He never even saw Jeffries emerging from the bar with a second man. Didn't realize he was standing beside the van until another surge of fear/lust/greed washed over him from 'outside,' and he looked up, startled, to see Jeffries holding out his empty hand, and a stranger staring into it as though it held the Hope Diamond.

And the thing inside him reached out to feed—

The wave of emotion built, fully as high as the rage and bloodlust shared by the couple Jason and Doug had devoured. Dave clutched at the steering wheel, unable to pull himself away this time, as it built higher still, like a scream that went on and on, and showed no signs of stopping.

But it did. Something *snapped*—

Jeffries shoved the man aside and climbed into the cab of the van. There was *nothing* inside the victim now; he was a dead and blackened hulk, emotionally. There was not even so much as a single spark left. It turned empty, unseeing eyes on the occupants of the van, then shambled slowly, aimlessly away.

"Start the van, David."

Feeling benumbed, overwhelmed, he did so; then pulled out into the street.

"The boys are so crude," Jeffries said smoothly. "It isn't necessary for us to kill to get what we need. That fool will go wander off somewhere, get himself killed or join the winos in some alley. It doesn't matter; he can't betray us, and he's as good as dead. Killing is—a waste of energy. Except for Hidoro, of course—but he cleans up after himself."

Dave began shaking again. The bodies—the girl, Sherrie, and the guy—they *had* disappeared. He wasn't sure he wanted to know *how*.
At least they aren't in the van . . .

"I think you should stay with us from now on, David," Jeffries said, as Dave pulled the van into his parking space. "It's too dangerous for you to be staying on your own."

The tone behind the words left no doubt in Dave's mind that this was no request—it was an order.

He wanted to weep; wanted to tell Jeffries where he could put the whole idea—

He found himself nodding meekly and handing over the keys to the van.

He'd thought his spirits couldn't sink any lower. He now discovered there were further hells below the one where he'd been.

—trapped—

He followed in Jeffries's wake, obedient as a child, his mind cursing and railing at a body that would no longer obey him. The hall was miles long, a throat that swallowed his soul by inches.

At the end of the seemingly endless journey, Jeffries turned to his door and put his key in the lock—but the door opened before he could turn it.

"Master—we had a visitor."

It was Jason. Light glinted off Jason's hair. Jeffries pushed Dave in ahead of him, but Dave froze at the sight of the lead guitarist's condition.

Jason—disheveled, clothing torn, and with a bruise purpling under his left eye—unceremoniously grabbed Dave's arm and hauled him in, allowing Jeffries clear passage of the door. Jeffries stared at the blond with the first hint of surprise Dave had ever seen him show.

"Jason—what on earth—"

Doug emerged from the living room. "Like he said, we had a visitor, Master," the bassist said carefully, touching his own cut and swollen lip. "He just about took us apart. He'd have gotten away if Hidoro hadn't shown up when he did."

Jeffries got a strange look on his face, and strode into the living room; Jason moved around behind Dave, and double-locked the door. "Don't even think it, Davey-boy," he said quietly, though without his earlier sneer. "You just go on inside."

Dave hunched his shoulders and obeyed.

Jeffries was already there, standing beside the prone, unconscious body of a young, dark-haired man. His face was again registering surprise, but that was fading into something like intense satisfaction.

Dave took a closer look at the intruder; he was slim, his apparent age about twenty-five. He didn't *look* all that formidable—which made it *very* odd that he was tied hand and foot with airplane cable, cable that had once been used to secure a bicycle from theft.

"Well," Jeffries said, his voice rich with pleasure, nudging the prone man with one toe. "Well, well. The young man who— threatened me in the matter of that gypsy trash. But—Jason, why the wire cable?"

"That's all that'll hold him," Jason replied sullenly, emerging from the entry hall behind Dave. "He got away from us twice. We tried everything, and he went through us like the Front Four of the Green Bay Packers."

The lead was rubbing his arm, and Dave guessed at other injuries besides the black eye.

"Hidoro had to put him out," the blond continued. "We couldn't. He threw *me* clear across the room."

"He did?" Jeffries looked startled. "I knew he was strong but— where *is* Hidoro? Why didn't he *kill* this man?"

There was something under Jeffries's startlement; after a moment, Dave recognized what it was, and nearly lost his teeth. Because it was *fear* that stood in the Master's eyes, and colored his words.

"He went out hunting again," Jason supplied. "He told me to tell you that he used up a lot of strength subduing this guy. I swear to you, Master, if Hidoro hadn't been here, this—whatever he is—*would* have gotten away. Hidoro said he *can't* kill him. Said you can't kill the dead—whatever *that* means."

Jeffries puzzled over that statement for a long moment—then suddenly grinned. "Well. Well, well, well. If that means what I *think* it does, I know what will take care of him for us."

He cast a look around the living room, then shook his head regretfully.

"No wood," he said, and sighed. "Not a stick of wood in the place. I never thought I'd come to regret my Eastern tastes in furnishings. Ah well. I think there are other ways, things that won't leave any bodies to explain."

What in hell is he on about? Dave thought; he saw Doug and Jason exchange puzzled looks and shrugs.

Jeffries pondered the young man at his feet a moment more.

"Never mind," he said finally. "I don't need a stake; the sun will serve my purposes quite handily."

"The sun?" Doug asked hesitantly.

"Exactly. Jason, Doug, take our importunate young vampire up to the sun porch and chain him there." Jeffries raised his head and stared at the closely curtained windows—and smiled. "It can't be more than a few hours till dawn, and that porch faces due east. I *hope* he's aware by then." He smiled; a shark's smile. "I want him to savor his experience."

"Vampire?" Doug squeaked—and Dave began to giggle hysterically again at the look on his face.

"Of course." Jeffries raised one eyebrow. "What did you *think* he was? For that matter, what did you think *you* were?"

Dave's giggles died, and his heart chilled. He stared down at the young man's slack face with horror as Jason and Doug began to drag him out to the French doors leading to the porch. Jeffries took in the stricken expression on his face, and smiled.

"Indeed, David," he repeated. "What *did* you think you were?"

EIGHT

D i opened the useless little corner cabinet above the sink and
contemplated her brand new bottle of Scotch for a moment
with her fingers resting on the handle. Bought just this afternoon, it stood in splendid isolation on the otherwise empty middle
shelf, replacing the one she'd finished in two bouts of—

*Self-pitying indulgence. There's no other term for it. And both in-
side of a week.*

She quietly closed the cabinet, leaving the bottle where it was.

*I don't need it, and I've been hitting on it far too often. It doesn't
solve the problems, it doesn't make them go away—all it does is make
me forget about them. Temporarily. And when I'm drunk on my butt,
I'm not doing anything productive about problems or mundania. It
isn't helping, and it might be hurting.*

She filled the kettle, put on hot water for tea, and gave thought to
what she should do with the rest of the evening. When the water was
boiling, she picked out some bags of Red Zinger, put them to steep in
the hand-thrown pot Lenny had given her, and carried the pot out to
her desk. She looked at the pitifully small pile of manuscript pages,
then sat herself down at her desk, and resolutely turned back to the
tribulations of the lovely, languishing, and thrice-ravished Sarah.

*Tomorrow is Sunday, which means I can sleep late. Dave—the
wound is raw. I know that. I'm going to have to figure out why and what
to do about it. I can't do anything about the soul-eater tonight. I don't
know anything more about it now than I did before, I only know what it
isn't. I'm not going to go play bait out on the street for it. The only thing
I can think of doing is something involving group magic—and I'm not
sure about trying that. I want to think hard about running a group-*

magic Circle on it and weigh all the factors, pro and con, before I even broach the idea to Len. So—let's do something about paying the rent.

Besides, work is supposed to be the best cure for the jitters. That's what Granny always told me, anyway.

All right, Sarah. Let's see if we can get you out of the Captain's cabin and into a little more trouble ...

Di bent over the typewriter, cup of hot tea at hand, pot of tea on the warming plate beside her. Sarah was disposed to cooperate. Within an hour, Di was humming while she typed. Within two, she knew she was on a roll. By midnight the tea was gone, and Sarah was showing sign of a backbone. By three A.M. the Captain had a sense of humor. Not *precisely* within the outline, but if Di tweaked it gently, she doubted anyone would notice. And it sure made working with those two characters a lot easier.

By five she could hardly keep her eyes open, but the first mate had just begun his mutiny plans and she wanted to get *that* set up properly before she called it a night.

Six A.M. and she was at a point where things would be easy to pick up and run with when she started again.

She stretched, and her shoulders popped; she was a little amazed at all she'd done. *Tomorrow—no, today—I'll have plenty to deal with.* She regarded the pile of typed paper with a bit of weary satisfaction. *The hardest part is going to be keeping this monster inside their specs. I'd just as soon that Sarah challenged the whole lot of them to duels, ran the first mate through herself, took over the ship, and left Tall Dark and Macho to stew on that island.* She yawned hugely, and rubbed her gritty eyes. *Time to pack it in.*

She was too tired to worry about anything past finding the bed without falling over her own feet and breaking her neck, much less that she had been hostess to a creature of myth the night before. There could have been twenty vampires hanging upside down from her window ledge, and as long as the apartment wardings held, she wouldn't have cared.

She peeled off her clothes, pulled on the oversized T-shirt that served her for a nightgown, and fell into bed without even tying up her hair.

I'm gonna regret this when I have to comb it out—

That was her last thought.

A feeble rattling at the kitchen door, the door that let onto the fire escape, woke her up. She listened to it a moment, confused, before she was able to identify *what* was making the noise and *where* it was coming from.

The wind? No—if it was blowing that hard, my windows would be rattling, too. The cat? Not bloody likely! Attila hates the fire escape.

In defiance of reason, the rattling continued. She rubbed her eyes and peered at the clock beside the bed.

Noon. Not likely to be a burglar either, not in broad daylight. What in hell is out there? Some stray? When Attila finds it, it'll be cole slaw.

Without probing beyond the wardings she couldn't tell for certain—but if "it" was alive, it was at too low an ebb to "feel" from inside the apartment.

So that lets out just about everything, including a stray on Attila's turf. It must be the wind. Maybe something just coming in from an odd angle.

The bed was *so* soft and warm; she was just about ready to ignore the noise and drift back into sleep, when the rattling stopped—and she heard the door swing open, creaking, followed by a soft thud, as something large and heavy hit the kitchen floor.

There was a baseball bat under her bed, and a knife in the bookshelf in her headboard; both were in her hands a millisecond after the creaking stopped.

She slipped into the hall without a sound, avoiding the floorboards that creaked without having to think about it—having run this drill at least once a week since she'd moved into the place.

Sometimes paranoia pays off.

She kept herself plastered to the kitchen-side wall of the hallway, eased up on the open door noiselessly, her feet growing cold and numb in the chill air that was blowing in the open door. She peeked carefully around the edge of the doorframe, exposing as little of herself as she could.

There was a dark-haired, slender man sprawled facedown on the worn yellow linoleum of her kitchen floor.

He was half-naked; at least it looked that way to *her.* So far as she could see, he was clothed in nothing more than a pair of mangled blue jeans, more rips than whole cloth; barefoot, and battered, but he wasn't a street bum. Those jeans had been clean and not too worn before whatever it was that got him had hit him.

And he looked like hell. Where cloth didn't protect, he was *covered* with livid burns; she hadn't seen anything that bad since the accident in chem lab back in college with the overcharged gas line. Already parts of his back were blistering.

She stared in horrified astonishment, and the sun came out from behind the clouds, framing the stranger in a square of yellow-gold light. The man moaned then, then scrabbled feebly at the cracks in the floor, as if the light *hurt* him. He succeeded only in getting himself turned onto his back—

But now she could see his face, twisted with pain. Her uninvited visitor was the vampire, André LeBrel.

She dropped the bat, and jammed the knife into the crack between the wall and the doorframe beside the kitchen door. She ran into the kitchen; when her feet hit the icy air from the open door they ached with cold. She just barely registered the pain; she vaulted André's body to get the kitchen door shut, locked, and the curtains over the window closed.

The moment the light was no longer falling on him, the young man stopped moving. He moaned as she knelt beside him, but she could see that he was no longer truly conscious.

She hated to do anything to him; winced at the thought of how her lightest touch would send waves of agony through his body. His chest and arms were worse than his back; terrible burns that had blistered and broken open.

And beneath the burns—a set of ugly slash marks and brutal bruises, clear signs of some kind of fight. His face was battered, one eye blackened, his lower lip cut and swollen, his throat mottled with bruising.

"Gods—" She spoke aloud without thinking.

He stirred, movement making his hair fall limply across his forehead; opened his eyes, and there was sense in them.

His lips moved a little, as if he were trying to speak; his right hand curled in a painful attempt to gesture, but he couldn't raise it more than an inch.

"Don't talk," she said urgently. "Don't even try. You'll only hurt yourself more. I'll get you to a doctor—"

His eyes widened, and he gurgled in a frantic attempt to convey something to her—it was a futile attempt, but the fear in him penetrated even past her shielding.

"Wrong idea, huh? Okay, okay, I understand. I won't take you anywhere." She chewed at her thumbnail in frustration as he relaxed, closed his eyes again, and lapsed back into unconsciousness.

She was frustrated and frightened. Helplessness churned down in her stomach. She didn't know what to do for him, and she didn't know what had *done* that to him. The sun of course—but how had he been caught out by day? Those burns—they were second-, maybe third-degree burns, *not* within the scope of her rough first-aid training. And the other injuries were just as daunting; the slashes looked as though they needed stitches, and she couldn't tell if the bruises were indicative of internal damage. Someone, something, had attacked and beaten him, mauled him, then left him out in the sun to die. Who? Mr. Trouble? But André had been strong enough to take the man down before. *She* had been strong enough to daunt him. If it *was* Mr. Trouble, and he had gotten backing—who could it have been? The Oriental she'd seen him with in the club?

She sat back on her heels, chilled, and shivering with more than cold, twisting a strand of hair in both hands. *What do they do for burns in hospitals? Gods,* think, *Tregarde. Burns—the skin is so damaged already you have to prevent more injury. You've got to cushion them. Aren't they using water beds now? What do I have that I could use? Maybe that air mattress. I've* got *to get him out of the kitchen, anyway. If nothing else, I can use the air mattress to move him. I sure's hell can't carry him.*

She dove into her bedroom and dug the thing out of the back of the closet and sat down on the floor beside him with it spread out in a scarlet splash on the yellow linoleum. She blew into the valve to inflate it until she was dizzy. It *always* seemed to take forever to fill, but this time was worse than all the others combined.

It was plastic, not canvas. *At least he isn't going to stick to it,* she thought, surveying it and him dubiously. *Provided he survives the next few moments.*

She steeled her nerves, and rolled him onto the mattress, her own flesh wincing at what she was doing to him. He whimpered a little, but did not wake again, even when she dragged the whole mess into the living room.

She was tired and sweating by the time she got him into the warmth and darkness of the living room. She sagged down next to him, and stared at his pain-ravaged face. *Now what?*

He was still unconscious, and it seemed to her that he was weakening. His breathing was shallower; the whimpers and moans of pain he made were fainter, though his face was set in a grimace that told her he *wasn't* lapsing into relaxation, but into further agony.

Dammit!

She pounded her fist against the wooden floor in frustration, striking again and again at the unyeilding surface until she managed to scrape her knuckle.

"Crap!"

She stuffed the injured finger into her mouth reflexively; sucked at it and tasted blood—

And froze.

Blood. What if they drained him of resources to where he can't *heal himself?*

If I stop long enough to think about this—I'll panic.

She got to her feet, and ran out into the enormous empty room beside her living room, headed straight for the tiny altar on the eastern wall of the Living Room.

Living alone as she did, she no longer had to hide her ritual implements as she had when she was in college. Arranged carefully on the plain wooden table were a cup, a dish of salt, an incense burner, a small oil lamp, and her atheme. Made by her own hands—and used more than once in mundane *and* arcane self-defense, it was a black-hilted, perfectly balanced throwing knife.

Good thing I always keep my atheme sharp. The ritual knife was honed to a razor edge and she maintained it in surgical cleanliness. It should be safe enough—no need to worry about blood poisoning the way she would if she used the knife she'd left stuck in the wall.

Think about blood poisoning, and not about what you're going to do—

She shivered anyway as she fought back the early symptoms of another panic attack. *I've got this situation under control. I think. Mostly.* She picked up the blade and returned to the living room.

He was still there, and there was no doubt in her mind as to the gravity of his condition. He was fading by the second.

She knelt at the young man's side and made a careful nick in her wrist.

Now, before I chicken out.

She leaned over, her hair falling across her arm and his chest, and held the bleeding cut to his lips.

There was no warning; one minute she was fine—

The next, she was graying out; her eyes unfocused, and she was overwhelmed by a wave of pleasurable weakness that washed over her and made her sag limply over him—

Then the weakness became *all* pleasure. She closed her eyes and shuddered uncontrollably, caught in overwhelmingly sexual bliss that was like *nothing* she had ever experienced before, and which had no room in it for rational thought.

It ended as suddenly as it had begun. One moment she was all animalistic pleasure, the next, herself.

She opened her eyes, and blinked.

André was conscious, holding her wrist in both hands, keeping pressure on the wound she had made there. It had stopped bleeding, and the edges were sealing together.

He already looked better. His burns were red and painful to look at, but they weren't blistered, broken open, or seeping fluid. The wounds were closed; and his bruises were fading even as she watched.

There was intelligence in his warm, brown eyes—and shame or guilt, or both.

He released her wrist and looked away, past her shoulder, unable to meet her eyes. "I beg your pardon," he whispered softly. "I never intended—that."

She snatched her hand back, and her cheeks burned; she felt embarrassed and confused. *Like I'd been caught writing a porn novel,* she thought. *I don't understand*—She was acutely conscious that she was wearing nothing more than the thin cotton T-shirt; she, who hadn't been body-conscious since before college.

"What—happened?" she asked, getting the words out with some difficulty. She didn't want to know—and yet she did.

"It—what you felt—that is our protection, and the coin with which we pay for that which we must have to live." He whispered still, and there was an equal amount of embarrassment in his voice. That made it easier for her to look back at him.

"If I had known," he continued. "If I had known what you would venture—I would have forbid you—"

That killed any shame.

Oh you would, would you? she thought, anger sparking and burning away the last of her reticence. "You and who else, laddy-buck?" she snapped. "You weren't in any damned shape to do anything to stop me! And I've got a hot news flash for you; *no one* tells me what I will or won't do!"

She tossed her tangled hair back over her shoulder, picked up her atheme, and lurched to her feet, doing her best *not* to show the dizziness that was making the room do a little waltz around her.

"I'm going to put a bandage on this," she said, holding the cut, which her abrupt surge of movement had reopened. "I'll be right back. *Don't you move.*"

The room was still showing an alarming tendency to rotate, and her vision kept fogging, but she managed to flounce indignantly off to the bathroom despite these handicaps. She ignored some strange sounds behind her that might have been anything from gasps of pain to muffled chuckles.

She took advantage of the opportunity to change into something a little more dignified than an oversized T-shirt.

When she returned, wrist neatly bandaged, she felt a bit more in control; sweater and jeans and hair neatly knotted at the nape of her neck made her feel at less of a disadvantage.

Less exposed.

Already André's burns had faded to no worse than a bad sunburn—but he did *not* look good. He was lying flat on his back with one arm over his eyes; his mouth had a pinched look about it, and under the red of burn, he seemed terribly bleached.

She studied him for a moment with her head tilted to one side, trying to assess what she saw with the little she knew—or thought she knew—about vampires. "Are you *supposed* to look that white?" she asked, finally. "I think you look pretty wretched right now, and I don't remember you being *this* pale, but the only vampires I've ever seen were in the movies."

"I—attempted to disobey you, mademoiselle, Diana," he replied, his voice thin with strain. "I met with great lack of success. And to answer your question: no, since I confess to you that I feel quite horrible, I suspect that I do not look as I should. Or if you will, I suspect I look as miserable as I feel. It would be difficult for me to make a comparison, however—the mirror legend is also true."

"Oh," she said, remembering Christopher Lee movies and not much else. "Um—so you, uh, need to get back to your coffin or something?"

He began shaking silently, and she was alarmed. She started to ask what was wrong, when her alarm turned to annoyance.

He's laughing *at me, the little creep!*

He took his arm away from his eyes and caught her expression, and his laughter died in chagrin. "I beg your pardon," he said contritely. "I seem to have offended you yet again. I—am a fool. There is no way you could know what is truth and what is silliness. We do not require the props of bad theater, Diana. Only a bit of one's native soil, and that is safely *here.*"

He tapped the wide metal bracelet he was still wearing.

"This is hollow, and contains what I require. My enemies would need to remove my hand to remove this. *If* they had known it for what it is. Now *that,* I suspect, would have killed me. As it was, the sun only hurt me, as did the injuries they dealt me when I was bound and at their mercy. I was stronger than they were, even then; I managed to release myself from the bonds when the sun became too much for *them* to bear."

"You came here," she said, sinking down onto the floor beside him, cross-legged. "Why?"

"I dared not go to my usual shelters," he replied unhappily, his mouth tightening. "I remembered you; and that you had invited me to cross your threshold. I had nowhere else to turn; I hoped that you would help me, or at least not cast me out."

That much talking seemed to have exhausted him. He was still plainly in pain, and every word seemed to take a little more energy out of him. She was alive with curiosity—but it could all wait.

"So," she surmised, "you won't have any problem staying here as long as I keep you out of the sun?"

He nodded, and closed his eyes wearily.

"What do you need besides rest?" she continued. "More—uh, nourishment—"

Now she blushed again.

"Animal will suffice," he said faintly.

"Huh. But not as well, right?"

He cleared his throat uncomfortably. "I cannot lie to you—no. Not as well. But—"

"But nothing. Just leave a little for me—and tone down that 'protection' bit next time, okay? It's a little hard on your donor." She found that she was smiling.

He's too gorgeous for words. And—if he didn't do anything to me when I nearly passed out, I can't see where I'm in any danger from him at all. That—experience—wasn't exactly bad. Just so I don't make a fool out of myself. Lawsy, it would be easy to make a fool out of myself.

He opened his eyes and saw her smile, and returned it, shyly.

"Okay," he ventured. "I *can,* if I am aware."

"Which you weren't—not even conscious. Or whatever it is you call 'awake.'" He blinked at a strand of hair in his eyes; she reached out absently and flicked it to one side for him. "Probably last-ditch defense mechanism," she hazarded. "Make sure your energy supply doesn't get away from you before you get what you need. Hm?"

"Probably," he agreed, softly, looking away. A faint flush crept across the tips of his ears.

She chuckled to herself. *Made you blush, did I? Serves you right.* "Look, stay awake for a bit longer, and stay *put.* I'm not going to leave you all night—I mean, day—on a cold plastic air mattress."

She got the spare blankets from the hall closet and made up the couch into a fairly comfortable bed, while he watched with fuzzy interest. She could tell from the glaze over his eyes that he was hanging on to his wakefulness with teeth and toenails. When she had finished, she helped him onto it—and was acutely aware, with his warm body so closely in contact with her own, that he was wearing next to nothing. The shredded jeans hardly counted.

But if *he* was as aware, he was too worn and hurting to show it, or for it to affect him much. His eyes were closing and his breathing growing shallow even as she tucked him in.

She straightened, sighed, and looked down at him. He was already out for the count. His breathing was *very* slow, *very* shallow. Imperceptible; only knowing what she was looking for enabled her to see it at all.

I can see why the legends say they're "dead" by day.

She touched his forehead lightly; his skin was cool to the touch, and she remembered how he had been wearing nothing more than sweater and jeans both times she'd seen him before. *Maybe he didn't need the blankets—well, he didn't object. Do vampires get cold?* She wondered about that for a moment, then drifted over to her desk, and Sarah—who now seemed utterly unreal. From another world altogether.

There's a vampire in my living room. There's a vampire *in my* living room. *I feel like I'm living in Stephen King's head.*

His left eye was still a bit purple, but now that most of the bruises and burns had faded, she could see the dark rings of fatigue beneath both eyes. That only made him look more vulnerable.

Gods, is he ever a fox. Captain Sommers, eat your heart out.

There is no way I can concentrate on Sarah while I've got the vampiric hunk of the century lying on my couch.

She busied herself with domestic chores; her stomach finally woke up from shock and complained to her, demandingly. The cravings that arose were—not surprisingly—for red meat, spinach—

Iron, of course. I wonder how much he got? I feel worse after I've donated blood to the Red Cross, so it probably was less than half a pint. Still.

Physical activity allowed her to get used to his presence; by early afternoon—particularly since she had her back to the couch—she was able to get back to Sarah.

The mutiny was engrossing enough—*action at last!*—to get her involved. Once again, she was on a roll, totally held by what was in her head and going onto the paper, until her stomach growled.

She looked up in surprise, saw that she'd turned on her light without even realizing she'd done so. It was after sundown. *Well* after sundown.

Huh. Best I've done since I started this monster.

Her stomach complained again; she wrinkled her nose and headed for the kitchen, with a brief glance at the couch. No movement, no signs of life.

Or is it signs of undeath? Who knows.

She turned the classical station up enough so that she could hear it in the kitchen as she worked. It was obviously getting on toward Christmas, because they were doing selections from the *Messiah*. She sang happily along with "Unto Us a Child Is Born" until the couch creaked—

Well, the undead hunk is back among the land of the conscious.

"Welcome back," she called, waiting for her soup to heat. "I'll be out in a minute."

"Do you realize how fortunate you are?" a soft, melodious voice replied from the depths of the couch.

He must sing like an angel. "Non sequitur?" she answered.

"The music. I have been listening while you worked. You turn a knob, flip a switch, and *voilà*. Beethoven, Berlioz, Verdi. Accessible to any with the price of a radio, and at all hours."

Bet it's the "at all hours" part that he likes. "Not to mention Pink Floyd, Led Zeppelin, and Crosby, Stills, Nash, and whoever they dragged in this week," she countered. "And I hate to think what the price of *their* concert tickets are. Classical at least you can get the cheap seats."

"*Mais oui,*" he replied agreeably. "Also those. And records, by which a memorable performance may be held for all time. Who would believe Woodstock without recordings, *n'est-ce pas?*"

She left her soup to poke her head around the kitchen door and stare at him. "You mean to tell me that a thousand-year-old vampire is a closet rock fan?"

The top of his head and his eyes appeared over the back of the couch. "Not a thousand years," he said, a chuckle in his voice, and a smile in his eyes. "And not a 'closet' fan."

"Oh, really?" She smelled the soup beginning to scorch, and yelped, pulling back into the kitchen to rescue it.

She emerged a few moments later with a mug of soup in one hand, and two mugs of tea in the other. "Here," she said, handing him one of the tea mugs. "You said yesterday you could drink things. Besides the usual."

He accepted it with what looked like gratitude, cupping his hands around the mug as if drawing warmth from it. "Yes, I did. You remember things well, mademoiselle."

"Comes with the territory. Do you get anything out of this besides the taste?"

"Sadly, no." He half smiled. "It seems that to be nourishing, my drink must be from the living."

"Too bad." She settled herself in the chair beside the couch and sipped her soup. "Now, about your taste in music—"

He brightened, and launched into the subject with cheerful abandon. This young man was very different from the aloof, otherwordly creature she'd sat across from just the previous evening. There was no doubt that love of music was one of his ruling passions.

And no doubt that his tastes were as catholic as hers. And remarkably similar.

Both loved rock; both abhorred country and western ("Unless they keep their mouths shut—" Di amended, and André bobbed his head emphatically. "Indeed. So long as they do not—attempt to sing—" He shuddered.) and both loved orchestral and ethnic music.

The only place their tastes did not coincide was within the classics. *He* loved opera—which *she* could well do without.

"You mean you loved the little opera-ballet girls," she said accusingly, remembering that at the turn of the century the Paris Opera Ballet had been little better than a recruitment center for expensive mistresses.

He flushed, slowly, beginning with the tips of his ears. "Well," he admitted, under her unflinching gaze. "Uh—yes. But—"

She chuckled heartlessly, and his flush deepened.

She, on the other hand, adored medieval and renaissance music, which he dismissed with a flip of his hand as "mere caterwauling." They argued about that for a good half hour before she decided to change the subject.

"You look better," she observed, finishing off the last of her soup, and relaxing into the arms of the chair.

He held out his hand. It shook, despite his obvious effort to control it. "I do not think I should be much of a challenge to M'sieur Jeffries," he replied wryly. "Not that I was before."

She toyed with a wisp of hair that had escaped from the knot. "Are you going to tell me what happened?" she asked, after a moment of silence.

He looked at her dubiously.

"That's *my* couch you're lying on," she pointed out remorselessly. "You're under *my* roof, sheltering under *my* sanctuary, with *my* blood running around in your system. If you get tracked here . . ."

She pointedly did *not* finish the sentence. He sighed, and inclined his head.

"Very well," he acquiesced. "But—first, a bath? Perhaps clothing?"

She raised her eyebrows, but smiled faintly. "Well, I don't think that's too much to ask. The bath I can manage, at least. I don't know about the clothing—though I think we aren't *too* dissimilar in size. If you don't fit mine, you're out of luck. *I* don't keep men's clothing in my closet for chance visitors."

"The bath would be enough." He pointedly ignored that last sally, held out his hand—which still shook—and she climbed out of her chair and pulled him to his feet with it.

"I thought vampires didn't like running water—" she said, draping one of his arms over her shoulders so that he could lean on her to steady his uncertain steps. No doubt of it, he was weak as a boiled noodle.

"A foul calumny," he replied. "Having only to do with the fact that we are territorial, and tend to mark our ranges by landmarks. They might as well have said we do not cross mountains, or lakes, or major highways."

"Oh, okay." Once again she was acutely conscious of him, and concentrated on getting him into the bathroom with the door safely closed between them.

Not at the moment. If Dave and I couldn't make a thing work how in hell *could I have a good relationship with a vampire?* A dozen answers to that question occurred to her, but she pushed them all aside, hastily, and returned to her bedroom. *He's awfully lean, and not that much taller than I am. Those jeans Annie gave me that turned out to be too big might fit him fine. I've got a couple of baggy sweaters that ought to fit about anybody. He's going to have to do without underwear, though.*

Boy, I can think of a lot of things I'd like to do to him without underwear . . . Jeez, what am I thinking? She blushed, and dug into the back of her closet where she kept clothing that didn't fit but was too good to throw out.

"Are you still alive in there?" she called through the closed bathroom door.

"A reasonable facsimile, mademoiselle," came the muffled reply.

"I'm leaving some clothes outside the door," she told him. "If they don't fit, you're on your own. And it's chilly in the living room."

She didn't wait to hear his answer, but went back to the typewriter and Sarah, before she lost her momentum.

I'm a lot better at this than I used to be, she thought, rereading the last few pages, and chewing the end of her pencil. *I didn't used to be able to immerse myself like this, no matter what. Sure never thought I'd be writing category romances; I used to think it would be historical mainstream, occult thriller, or nothing. On the other hand, if I wrote what I* know—*people could get hurt. Either that, or it'd get rejected as being too unreal. I seem to have a knack for this, anyway, enough so that Morrie thinks it'll pay all the bills by next year. Thank the gods for Granny's nest egg, though. Paid for college and my last year and a half in the Apple.*

She flung herself back into Sarah's tribulations, and didn't come out again until André touched the back of her neck with a leaf-brush of a caress.

She shrieked and jumped, and whirled in her chair to meet the imagined threat.

He stared back, equally surprised, and tripped and landed on his rump when his shaky knees wouldn't hold him.

"Don't *do* that," they cried in chorus. Then they stared at each other for several minutes—

—and dissolved into helpless laughter.

She got herself out of her chair, still shaking with laughter, and offered him a hand up. He accepted it without any evidence of shame, and she helped him back to the couch.

"Now," she said, settling into her chair again. "About what happened to you last night—"

He made an expressive and completely Gallic shrug. "I followed this M'sieur Jeffries to where he lives. He left, but knowing now where he laired, I decided to confront him while I still had the advantage of surprise, to ambush him as it were, before he could arrive again. He was, however, no longer living alone. In fact, there were *three* young men in the apartment, one of them Oriental. I saw them first, and attempted to conceal myself, but they somehow detected me. That should *not* have been possible. The two attempted to detain me. They were amazingly strong. *Too* strong, Diana. It is not natural, their strength, it is uncannily like my own. Nevertheless, I nearly managed to evade them. Then the Oriental appeared."

He tilted his head, and his eyes darkened. "What happened then is not clear to me. Something disturbed my mind for a moment. The Oriental—did *something* to me. I think I recall a cloud, or smoke, but my memory is not clear. My head was turned all about, and I was within the smoke, and *it* was within *me*, and it seemed alive."

"A drug?" she hazarded.

He shook his head negatively. "No. No, it was not a drug; drugs do not affect us. Certainly they would not affect me like this. It was terribly cold, terribly painful—it was like a blow to the soul, like— like the closest thing I can remember . . ."

His voice trailed off, and his expression became strange, a little fearful, and very distant.

"*Like?*" she prompted, sharply.

"It was very—like—dying. Only not dying. *Mon Dieu. Very* like dying."

His voice faded again, but she did not prompt him. His eyes looked lost, haunted, and she let him sort out his thoughts himself.

Finally he recollected himself and his surroundings. "Whatever it was," he continued, "it injured me, deeply, who—very little can harm. The touch of the sun, hurts inflicted by wood—and not much else. I was not altogether unconscious, but I was not aware of a great deal when Jeffries returned. He recognized me for what I am, and determined to have his vengeance. Fortunately, he could find no wood to—"

He shivered, looked off beyond her shoulder, and rubbed his long, slender hands over his forearms.

I don't think stake jokes would go over very well right now, she thought.

He looked back at her. "Luck was with me in that. His minions chained me upon an east-facing porch and took revenge upon my body for what I had done to them in the struggle. When the sun rose, I could see that they began suffering nearly as much as I was. When I feigned unconsciousness, they departed, and I freed myself."

He shrugged again. "The rest, you know already."

"You called them 'minions,'" she said thoughtfully. "How sensitive are you to—uh—nonnatural phenomena?"

"The psychic?" he supplied.

She raised her eyebrow, and he smiled faintly.

"I am rather well read, mademoiselle. There are two places in these modern times that are safe for my kind to spend the daylight hours—those of us who have not the means to purchase a secure sanctuary, that is. Can you guess them? Two places safe from sunlight, and from the curiosity of men."

Funny, it never occurred to me that a vampire might not be independently wealthy. She shook her head.

He chuckled, and held up a slender, strong finger. "Public libraries," he told her, and held up the second finger. "Movie houses. I can recite the plays of Shakespeare, Euripides, and Voltaire in two languages. I can also recite the dialogue of every B movie ever made. *And* I am an excellent picker of locks."

He grinned, a kind of lopsided, quirky grin, and she giggled.

"On the other hand, I believe I have read every book on psychic phenomena ever to enter the New York Public Library system. So: to answer your question of 'am I sensitive to these things,' I can answer you, very. I read these books because I needed to understand what I was, and I did not always have teachers when I needed them."

She licked her lips thoughtfully and nodded a little. He continued. "To answer your *next* question, the one you have upon the tip of your tongue, the other young men, or at least the two who first attacked me, they 'felt' as Jeffries now 'feels'—and I can pledge to you that he did *not* 'feel' that way before All Hallows' Eve. Halloween."

He sobered again. "I was able to deliver a clear warning to Jeffries on the hazard of threatening those I protect before that night, with no difficulty. I do not know that I could take him now."

"Not a pleasant thought," she ventured.

"No. And now I believe in your 'psychic vampires.' I did not wish to, before. Jeffries has become one, as, somehow, have those young men."

"What do you mean, 'those you protect'?"

"Ah. There is a particular tribe of the Lowara Romany with whom I have had a—partnership. An arrangement that is beneficial to us all. This has gone on for many years." He quirked one corner of his mouth at her little snort. "Truly, it is of benefit. They are noted for producing *drabarni* of great power. *I* protect them from those outside the Rom who may be attracted to this power, and seek to exploit them. I also protect them in these latter days from others who would—ah—I believe the term is 'hustle' them."

"And what do you get out of all this?"

"They protect me during the daylight. Not always, it is not altogether wise for one of my sort to spend every day in the same place, but—three days out of the seven, yes. Janfri was one of their tribe, and would have been one of the most powerful if he had chosen to flout custom and exercise the power. Usually it is only the women who so choose. But Jeffries—"

She grimaced. "Jeffries saw a nice little thermonuclear power plant and couldn't resist trying to take over the control room. All right, I can understand what happened to Janfri now. And I can see why Jeffries might band together with the two others. I think I could even suggest how to handle them. But what about the third one?"

"The Oriental?" He shuddered, and closed his dark eyes briefly in a grimace of pain. "I do not know what he is. But he *can* harm me. Harm me so that I ache even now."

He *was* in pain; that much was certain, from the faint sheen of sweat on his brow and the pinched look about his mouth. Equally certain was the fact that he was trying to conceal from her how *much* pain he was in.

I could—no. Let him keep his dignity. I bet he isn't used to feeling vulnerable.

He opened his eyes at that moment, and caught and held her gaze. "Mademoiselle Tregarde," he said soberly, "I have never asked help from another creature, living or otherwise, since I became what I am. But I am not a fool, or not so much of a fool as I was before last night. I am asking now, what you offered before. Will you help me?"

She trembled in that dark gaze; something about him was touching her profoundly, in ways she didn't understand, and wasn't certain she wanted to think about.

But he said the magic words. And I am a Guardian. I don't think he'd have asked unless he knew he was at the end of his own resources.

"Yes," she replied simply. "But not now."

"No." He sighed, and sagged back against the couch cushions. "I am scarce able to walk across this room. And I asked you to *help,* not to do it all yourself."

The exhaustion he had been trying to conceal was all too plain when he relaxed. "Do you need—"

"I—should not ask it," he interrupted, a pinched look about the way he held his mouth. "I should not. Not so soon—"

"So much for my scribbling. You need to feed again, right?"

Something flickered in the back of his eyes—first a raging hunger—then determination. "I—will not—demand. I will not take. I will have only what you offer freely. I have, at least, self-control enough for that—"

"Self-control be damned. You *need* it, and you asked for my help. I *give* that help with no strings attached. Except for one condition." She stood up, and he opened his eyes and looked up at her.

"And that is?" he asked.

"That you call me Di. Partner."

He smiled; a smile sweet enough to bring her heart right up into her throat, and leave it pounding there. "*That* will be my pleasure— Di. But—"

"But?" She stopped on her way to the couch.

"The Oriental—bothers me. Me, he can hurt, but he could not destroy me. I fear his power over the living. My memory returns, bit by bit—Di, I believe he was trying to devour my soul when he—"

—I believe he was trying to devour my soul—

The icy hand of a panic attack seized her throat, and the room blackened.

NINE

P anic had her heart in its bony fist; it squeezed her and toyed with her, and would not let her go.

She huddled, kneeling, on the floor beside the couch. She was clutching her knees so hard her fingernails were leaving little bloody half-moons in her skin even through the thick fabric of her jeans, and she was bent over and squeezing herself into a tight little ball, with no memory of the past few moments. There was room only for the fear and the memory of the Nightflyer that had triggered it. She sobbed and shivered, reduced to near mindlessness by the uncontrollable emotion that crushed her. She barely recognized her own living room. There was *nothing* in the world but fear.

Nothing to hold on to, nothing to protect her, nothing she could do to save herself.

This was the worst panic attack she'd had in years. She buried her face in her hands, sobbed and moaned. Completely paralyzed, mind and body.

The memory dominated the dark of her mind. *Like a grotesque mockery of a humanoid bat made of tattered black plastic. It had stood tall against the moon for a moment, then it had her wrapped in its folds as it sucked away at all that* was *her, trying to absorb her into itself—*

The Nightflyer; it wasn't wounded anymore, and there was no way to trick it this time. It was coming back. It was coming for her. This time there would be no escape.

A frightened voice. "Diana—Diana—"

She cringed away from a touch on her arm—

But those weren't the Nightflyer's talons on her shoulders, they were hands. Human hands.

"*Chérie, petite,* come to yourself. These are shadows that you fear. You are safe, in your own home."

Someone was holding her against his shoulder; someone was stroking her hair, gently. The panic ebbed a little, gave her a moment of respite.

Then returned, shaking her like a dog with a rag. She whimpered, and tried to pull away, huddled back into herself, but the hands would not let her go.

It took an age, an eon, before the panic finally faded, leaving her sobbing, limp, and wrung out.

And cradled in André's arms.

She was too exhausted to feel any embarrassment; too drained to do anything except to continue to allow him to hold her. She was shaking too much even to speak, her mind so fogged she couldn't have mustered words even if she *had* been able to speak.

—gods. If he hadn't been here—don't want to move.

Even her thoughts were coming slowly, fighting their way up to the surface of her mind through the sludge of exhaustion.

Finally her trembling eased; her hysterical tears dried. She opened her burning eyes, made as if to sit up, and the arms about her shoulders loosed.

But he took her shoulders in his hands as she pulled away from him, and looked searchingly into her face.

"Are you yourself?" he asked softly.

Her hair had come undone, and it fell into her eyes when she nodded. "I think so," she replied, her voice hoarse and thick with weeping.

He brushed the hair away from her face with a touch so light she hardly felt it, and tucked it behind her ear. "Will you tell me?"

"Panic attack," she said shortly. "It—happens, sometimes."

"Sometimes? When? What is the cause? Was it something that I said?" His eyes were bright and his brow furrowed with concern.

"I—" She began trembling again. "I—can't talk about it. I can't! If I do—"

"Diana, *chérie*—forgive me, I think you must. Does a soldier go into battle with a weapon that may fail him at any moment?" He shook her a little. "You cannot continue like this. *Tell* me."

"I can't—" she wailed, pushing feebly away from him, unable to face the possibility of triggering a second attack so soon after this one.

"You *must.*" His voice took on urgency. "Listen to me. I depend on your strength, your mind, your abilities. Many others must also. If you permit this fear to rule you, you will *fail* them, and at the worst possible moment."

He was right. She *knew* he was right. It didn't help. She squeezed her eyes shut, and tears leaked out from beneath her tightly closed lids.

"Diana—" She felt a gentle hand lift her chin. "Open your eyes. Look at me."

She did, though her vision blurred with tears. He cupped his hand against her cheek, and spoke slowly and carefully, in a voice tremulous with compassion. "Listen; you *can* overcome this. I can help you. I *wish* to help you, as you have helped me. I know how to help you defeat this fear."

"You do?" She blinked at him doubtfully.

"*Oui.*" His voice admitted no possibility of failure; he seemed utterly sure of himself, and of her. "It will be very hard for you, but it is not impossible. And we shall do nothing for the next several moments. I wish you to hear what I have to say and decide for yourself if you are willing to carry this through."

He rose carefully to his feet, pulling himself up with the help of the couch; she looked at him standing beside her, trembling with weakness, and yet willing to lend her the little he had left—

Oh gods. He's braver than I am—

I have no choice. He's right.

She pushed away from the floor and staggered to her own feet. He backed up to the couch and let himself collapse on it. She joined him. The tendency of the couch to sag in the middle had a predictable effect on their positions—she found herself leaning against his shoulder again.

She made a halfhearted attempt to move away from him, then gave it up. He waited for a moment, then slowly, hesitantly, put his arm around her shoulder.

"Now," he said, after giving her a chance—which she did not take—to object to the presence of his arm about her. "You have these attacks of panic. I hazard it is because of something that happened to you in the past, *non?* Something—something that nearly killed you."

She nodded, unable to trust her own voice, and stared at a spot on the lampshade across the room.

"So now, when something else occurs that brings this into your mind, the fear overcomes you again."

Put that away, the attacks seemed reasonable, inevitable. "Yes," she whispered, fixing her gaze on that spot.

"We—my kind—our passing into this state is often traumatic. It is not uncommon for my kind to have such spells of fear."

Surprised, she twisted so that she could look at him. He smiled a little and nodded at her expression. "Indeed, I speak the truth. Nor can we, who must keep all our wits about us to survive, allow ourselves to be so debilitated. So—we learned how to cure this."

She sniffed, and rubbed at her eyes, frowning in disbelief. "You're—you're kidding, right? I mean—" She thought about it for a moment. "I guess you'd have to, wouldn't you."

He nodded. "And as it happens, these doctors of the mind that have sprung up of late have chanced upon the same remedy we use. Truly. But it is not a pleasant one."

"So—what is it?" she asked, pretty certain she was not going to like the answer.

"We—you and I—will invoke the fear. Deliberately. We will do so until it no longer controls you. We will wear it down, as treading upon a rough place in a path wears the roughness away. But that is not entirely all, Diana—" He held up his free hand to forestall her objections. "Your fear has been creating considerable energy. That will still *be* there. We must find a way to use it, to channel it into something useful, else it will continue to paralyze you."

"Oh gods—" she moaned. "I—André, it—"

He waited, patient, silent—understanding, but as implacable as her granny had been.

"There are no excuses, child."

She could hear the voice in her mind even now.

"There are reasons, but no excuses. And when there are reasons, there are usually causes that cancel out those reasons."

"What happens on the day you meet an enemy, and then are paralyzed, Diana?" he asked softly.

I have no choice. One of these days I will get caught outside a safe shelter by one of these attacks—and then what? I can't be like Josey, hardly able to leave his house.

She shivered, she started crying again—but she nodded.

Taking that as her assent, he prodded her with a question.

"This thing that you encountered—where and what was it?"

She held her arms tightly to her chest. "It—it was after my grandmother died, right after I graduated from college. Just before I moved here. Things had happened in college—I—I'd broken up with this guy over my doing magic. I wanted to quit it. I couldn't see why I couldn't. Shouldn't. I was tired of pulling other people's fat out of the fire. So I decided I was going to say to hell with it; that I was going to take care of me and nobody else."

"So—" he said, satisfaction in his voice. "You *are* one of those they call Guardians. I thought perhaps you were. I thought perhaps that might have been why you offered Janfri shelter."

She swallowed, and hung her head a little. "I am. I was," she said, feeling an echo of the old bitterness even now. "I was *sick* of it, André; it had cost me the only guy I'd ever been happy with. I wanted out. I didn't believe my grandmother, who'd told me that if I wouldn't act to protect others, I'd find *myself* a target. I thought I could go into hiding, you know? And when I found out about this guy who was planning to conjure up some nasty stuff—I didn't stop him. I didn't even try. I just ignored him, and figured he'd ignore me."

She closed her eyes and spoke around clenched teeth. "It wasn't my business. That's what I told myself. So when what he called up aced him and came after me, I not only wasn't expecting it, I wasn't ready, and most of my defenses were down."

The panic was starting to rise, trying to choke off her words.

"They—they called it—a—Nightflyer—"

That was all she managed to get out, before the panic hit her again, and she broke.

Dimly she heard André talking to her; she tried to answer, tried to fight it. She heard something about channeling—

Useless. She rode the attack through, and came out again on the other side spent and drained.

But—*but*—this attack had not been *quite* as bad as the last. He was right. So she gave herself no respite, and no chance for second thoughts.

"Let's—do this again," she said, when she could speak again.

He nodded. "This Nightflyer—describe how you came to encounter it—"

She had been reading. She'd heard something outside, and had thought it nothing more than a stray cat. The Nightflyer had been very apt at cloaking its presence.

The sound repeated, and she decided to investigate, because it hadn't felt quite right. If she'd stayed inside, the house wards would have kept it out, especially in its weakened condition. Perhaps the Nightflyer had sensed this. Surely it had been driven nearly wild by the proximity of a relatively unprotected Guardian with all the energy potential a Guardian always possessed. She would never know, exactly.

She only had a glimpse of it, the black that absorbed everything and gave nothing up, moonlight showing through the places where its gliding members had been torn. Then it was on her, wrapping her in its substance.

It began to devour her, just as a Venus'-flytrap devours a living insect.

But it was weak; the struggle with the fool that had summoned it had damaged it. It was desperate, and therefore a little careless in its hunger. It gave her a tiny opening, and in desperation, she took it, accepting again her Guardianship and opening herself to the energies and knowledge only a Guardian could tap.

There had been an instant of light and terrible agony—and when she woke again, she was lying on the ground; exhausted, wracked with pain, but alone. And still alive.

Had she banished it, or destroyed it? She didn't know. All that she did know was that she could never feel safe again.

This time, as she cried and shuddered, she was able to *remember* where she was. She was able to bring up the full memory, though she still couldn't *tell* André about it.

"Again—" she said, while she still shook, and her eyes dripped tears.

The strange "therapy" was working. Through it all André held her, soothed her, spoke coaxingly to her when she needed it—and shook her, scolded her, when *that* was what she needed.

There finally came a point where she could see what André meant—about the amount of hysterical energy she was producing, and how it was holding her in chains of her own forging.

That time through she couldn't do anything about it—but the next—

The safest way seemed to be to direct the hysteric energy into her shielding. And as André talked her through attack after attack, and she found she *could* stay in control, she started trying to do just that.

She had been keeping her eyes tightly shut so as to be able to concentrate, and she didn't truly notice anything out of the ordinary until André gasped and she realized that she no longer felt the light pressure of his arm on her shoulders.

She opened her eyes, and found herself alone on the couch—surrounded by a brightly glowing aura about an inch above her skin.

Glowing brightly enough that she was making the furnishings around her cast shadows.

"*Chérie*—" came a strangled voice from the other room. "If you would be so kind—that is painfully similar to sunlight."

She bit off a curse and dismissed the shield, and André poked his head cautiously around the doorframe. "I think," he said, carefully, "that we can count you as cured."

She licked lips that were salty with tears and sweat. "The patient," she replied hoarsely, "survived the treatment, at least."

He made his unsteady way back into the living room and sagged down onto the couch beside her. "Do you think that you will be able to handle your fear from this moment on?"

She made a careful internal assessment. "I—think so," she said, a little surprised.

"*Bien*. Because I think so also."

She managed a weak and trembling smile. "Now about your overdue—uh—meal . . ."

He shrugged, and put his arm around her shoulders again. "Let it wait for a little."

"He *what?*"

With Jeffries's anger filling the room, the apartment living room seemed far too small to hold them all, even with Dave sitting on one of the cushions over in the corner. Jason stood in front of Jeffries, with Doug slightly behind him. Master Jeffries wasn't shouting, but there was something deadly in the tone of his voice that made Dave shrink back into the shadows of his corner of the living room, glad that he wasn't delivering the bad news, even gladder that *he* hadn't been entrusted with handling the intruder.

That had been Jason's job. And Dave watched as Jason paled at the menace in Jeffries's voice.

"He's not there," the blond said faintly. "He's gone. Just the airplane cable and the locks. No body, no bones, no nothing."

"So. He escaped, despite your assurances that he was going nowhere." Jeffries radiated controlled violence, and Hidoro at his side could have been a statue.

Jason didn't actually move, but he seemed to shrink, somehow.

Dave was amazed: he'd never seen Jason back down from *anyone*, not even the time they'd played a biker bar and one of the locals had taken exception to the way Jason was singing at the biker's old lady. And now that Jason was—whatever they all were—he was twice as cocky-tough.

Jason had been deferential enough with Jeffries, but Dave had wondered how long *that* was going to last. Jason didn't much care to play second to anybody, and he'd let Dave handle the business end of the group only because *he* didn't want to be bothered. For as long as Dave had known him, if Jason saw a lead position he wanted, he'd challenge for it. Dave had expected that to happen here, too. But Jason was backing down from Jeffries.

It looked like the leader of the pack had just found somebody bigger, meaner, and tougher.

That surely was sticking in Jason's craw—but he wasn't showing any signs of it.

"Yeah," Jason ventured, looking away from Jeffries's angry eyes. "It kind of looks like he escaped. I dunno how. I *can't* see how—we worked him over some, so he'd be out of it when the sun came up, but we couldn't stay out there in the sun long enough to see him finished off—"

Jeffries remained silent, and the lead's words trailed off into uneasy silence. Suddenly the man rounded on Doug. "How big is your apartment?" he demanded.

"Not very," Doug stammered, backing up a pace. "It's an efficiency. Jason's got a loft."

Jeffries smiled at them both, and although it hadn't been directed at him, Dave shrank back even farther from the malice in that smile.

"Appropriate," Jeffries said softly, "since *he* allowed the creature to escape. Get your things and mine into the van; we're moving. If my enemy survives, he'll be back here. That young man is not so young, nor is he a fool. When he returns, he won't be alone."

Hidoro, who had been silent throughout this conversation, nodded gravely. It was plain that he agreed entirely with Jeffries on both Jason's culpability and Jeffries's assessment of the situation.

"That is what I would do," the creature said, his voice betraying only a hint of accent, and no emotion whatsoever. "But is there anything we can do *besides* flee? Could we also not move to neutralize him?"

"You mean, take the offensive?" Jeffries raised an eyebrow in skeptical surprise. "Against a true vampire powerful enough to escape in full daylight? How could we, and what could we do?"

Hidoro shrugged. "If we cannot deal with him directly, perhaps we can control him through others. Is there nothing that *he* cherishes, that *he* would protect?"

Jeffries thought a moment—then smiled again.

"Oh yes." He chuckled. "Oh yes, I think so. Jason?"

"Sir?" the lead said promptly, while Dave lost his jaw. He'd never heard Jason call *anyone* "sir" in all the years he'd known him. *We have definitely just become beta wolf, haven't we, Jas?*

"Leave the packing to the others. You're coming with me, and we're taking the van."

Jeffries was unmistakably grinning now, and Dave did *not* want to know what the man was thinking of.

"We're going to see about taking a bit of a counteroffensive," he heard the Master say to Jason, as they headed out the apartment door.

———

Di rested her head back against André's shoulder, and he tightened his arm about her.

"What time is it?" she asked quietly.

"Nearly four, I think."

"I am *too* damned tired to open the shop—"

"Then do not," he interrupted. "Will your friend grudge you one day? If she does, I cannot think she is much of a friend."

"Good point." She sighed, thought about moving, decided not to. "I could sure use an afternoon on the book."

"So. I should get you to your bed, I think." So he said, but he made no move to rise, and neither did she.

She closed her eyes, and felt his free hand smoothing her sweat- and tear-soaked hair.

"Thank you, André," she said, putting as much sincerity into her voice as she could produce around her exhaustion.

"For what?"

"For being something I don't have many of. A friend."

"A friend." His tone was wistful. "I have few enough of those, my own self. The Rom respect me, but they do not offer their friendship. I am still *gadjo*. And my kind are few. None in this city that I am aware of, though it does not necessarily follow that there actually are none. Have you friends beside your lady Annie?"

"Lenny. He's a dancer that lives upstairs. A couple of people in Annie's Circle. No one else."

"Circle?" He sounded surprised. "Are you then a practicing witch?"

"Of course I'm practicing, how could I get to Carnegie Hall if I didn't practice?" She was tired enough that the feeble joke made her burst into giggles. She doubled over her knees, and wheezed. Every time she looked back up at him, his nonplussed expression only made her start laughing again.

He was tired enough that after a few moments of staring at her he joined her in laughter. They leaned against each other, keeping each other propped up, chortling like a pair of fools.

"What—what I meant was—" He gasped for breath. "What I meant was that—how can you be a witch and a Guardian, too?"

"When they handed me my enrollment form I checked 'other' under 'religion,' and they passed me on through," she replied, then burst into laughter again.

He snatched up a throw pillow and hit her lightly with it, unable now to *stop* laughing.

She retaliated by scooting over to the corner of the couch, leaving him to topple over, helpless with mirth.

"*Mon Dieu,*" he said, finally catching his breath. "I have not laughed so in—I cannot think how long."

"Me, either." She let gravity take her back to his side, and laid her head and arm along the back of the sofa. "I should let vampires across my threshold more often. Even if they go and trigger a—"

The sudden recollection of *why* the first panic attack had occurred made her sit up. "Ohmigod. That Oriental. The one that *wasn't* a psivamp. You said what he did to you felt like *what?*"

"As though he were trying to pull my soul away," André replied, his face gone still and sober.

She was putting two and two together, and coming up with a figure that she did not in the least like. "Listen—I haven't *just* been trying to track down the creep that murdered Janfri. I've been after bigger game—"

She detailed the story of Keith's ex-lover and the bus full of dead bodies.

"And you think that this soul-eater may be the one they called Hidoro?" André finished, his eyes focusing somewhere within him.

"What do *you* think?" she countered.

"I think—I think that we need more information. I think also that neither of us is capable of going beyond these walls until tomorrow at the best."

She eyed him speculatively, then held out her hand. It shook and she couldn't get it to stop. He gave her a wry look and held out his own. It did the same.

"We *are* in sad shape, are we not?" he said.

She sighed. "Very sad. I don't like this, but I'm afraid you're right. And I should get to bed."

His hand rested over hers on the couch between them. He seemed to be thinking very hard. "Diana—if this is no business of mine, say so. Have you a—a young man?"

"Me?" She coughed. "Not hardly. Not after the last one. Our breakup was pretty painful, and I swore after the Nightflyer that I was never going to get involved with someone who didn't believe again. Now the only men I *might* be able to tell what I'm into are mostly already paired up, and the rest are yo-yos."

"But what of this Lenny?"

She choked on a laugh. "Len? Good gods, André, he's *gay*. He and Keith are on the verge of becoming a very tight item. I am *not* his type!"

"So. Am I a—'yo-yo' would you say?"

"No. You're not exactly normal, but I've known vegetarians with weirder diets." She began giggling again, until the look on his face sobered her. "Why are you asking me these things?"

"Because—because I follow a kind of code, myself," he said softly. "I do not accept—what I need—from the same person more than twice, unless it is given with—affection." He coughed a little, and looked down at their joined hands. "There is a reason for this. It is the reason I did not wish to believe in your psychic vampires. My kind are something of psychic vampires also. It is not only the blood we need, it is the emotions."

"You mean you people are psivamps, too?" she whispered.

"Of a sort. We who follow the code do not *take*. We only accept what is given. That protection—that is what triggers what we need. It is so for all of us who follow the code. Those who do not—are the origin of the legends, I suspect."

"So not all of you are good guys; yeah, I'd figured that. But the stories claim going vamp *makes* you evil."

He shrugged. "A person who was good before the change generally remains a good person. One who was evil—him, we hunt down and destroy ourselves, for his excesses will put us all in danger."

She nodded. "So what are you asking of me?"

"More than I should," he said quietly. "More than blood. Liking. And if you feel you cannot offer that—I shall regain strength more slowly, then seek what I need elsewhere. From those among the Rom who are willing, probably." He took her hand in his. "I will not demand what I have no right to, Diana. You have already given me more than I can repay. I will understand if you tell me no."

When she didn't reply immediately, his face fell a little. With a resigned sigh, he lifted her hand to his lips.

"Go to your rest, mademoi—"

She turned her hand in his so that his kiss fell upon her palm and not on the back, and she cupped her hand around his cheek to raise his face to meet her eyes just as he had done with her, earlier this evening.

"As easily as that?" she asked, wonderingly. "You go back to loneliness as easily as that?"

"I have," he said, fixing his dark eyes on hers, and covering the hand on his cheek with his, "had a great deal of practice."

"You make me ashamed of myself."

"Why?" he asked simply. "What is there to be ashamed of?"

"I've been doing a great deal of feeling sorry for myself," she pointed out. She freed her hand from his, and took it into both of hers, marveling at the long, graceful fingers, the strength that was in it.

"You have had reason."

"Maybe." She bent her head a bit, and her hair fell into her eyes again. "Gods. I must look like a three-day-old corpse."

"You look—"

The tremulous tone of his voice made her glance sharply up at him, and she held her breath. She hadn't seen a man look at her like that since—since Dave. No, not even Dave. There had always been desire in Dave's eyes—but never the warmth of humor, and never, never, the respect and admiration she saw in André's.

"You are—very attractive to me. Will you consider me as a friend, Diana?"

She felt herself smiling. "I thought you already were a friend, André."

He reached out and traced the line of her cheekbone with one gentle fingertip. "Do you have any fears of me?"

She shook her head, and let the couch take her into his arms. "No. Not anymore. Just two questions."

"Ask."

"The first—I was under the impression that getting bitten too many times makes you a vampire."

He nodded. "A good question. The answer is, not. M'sieur Stoker was correct in that, at least. I *could* kill you, but I could not make you one of us by feeding. For that, there must be the blood bond—the exchange of blood. Which we have not, and could not, without your consent and cooperation."

She sighed. "Okay, I'll accept that. Now the second. Can a friend offer you a—drink? Maybe a little more than a drink?"

He laughed, and kissed her eyes.

It was six when she went to her own bed. Since she knew Bob would be awake already, she called him and told him that she had spent a hell of a night—the truth, after all—and that she wouldn't be opening the shop.

"That's okay, Di," he said. "I got some vacation days coming—I'll tell you what, make tomorrow your last day, take your pay out of the safe, and go back to book writing. If Annie isn't ready for work, I'll take it for a week. Annie said she thought you were sounding stretched a bit thin."

She sighed. "Annie was right." Some of her mental, physical, and emotional exhaustion must have leaked over in her voice; he queried her sharply, recommended a dozen vitamins, and told her in no uncertain terms to get herself into her bed.

She did; and woke about two. She had expected to feel depleted; instead, she felt relatively alert, and a great deal easier in her mind and heart than she had in years.

Certainly easy enough to get back to the perils of her heroine, and let the problem of the man called Hidoro stew in the back of her mind.

She noted with a half-smile that André had repaired the mess that the two of them had made of the couch last night. That little nip of his had quickly led to other things.

A neat fellow, not a slob like Dave was. If I have to have a vampire in my living room, it's nice to have one willing to pick up after both of us.

I wish I could figure out what to do about The Problem. Gods; killer psivamps and a soul-eater—it's like the worst nightmare I ever had.

Jeans and a leotard were the order of the day, seeing as she had no intentions of going anywhere but her living room. While she showered, she mulled things over.

If what André says is true, the psivamps are at least as vulnerable to sunlight as he is. Did he say anything about them getting burned, *though? I don't think so—that means it must be visual sensitivity. Okay, that gives us a weapon. If my shield-glow gets him, it'll keep them blinded, too. They can't jump me if they can't look at me. Hmm.*

She thought about that for a moment. *I would bet that my shields will keep them off my head, too. So all I have to worry about is that enhanced physical strength. I'm martial-arts trained. They aren't. That may work against them, if they're counting on simple strength. I won't make the mistake of attacking first the way I did with André.*

She was ravenous—not surprisingly. That was twice in twenty-four hours she'd "donated," and though André hadn't taken much, it was enough for her to feel *some* aftereffect. After an enormous sandwich, she felt much more inclined to deal with work.

She took her place behind her typewriter, turned on the radio, and resolutely turned off the rest of the world for a few hours.

It was time for Captain Sommers to rescue himself from his exile on a desert island. When the telephone shrilled at her, just past four, it broke a concentration that was so intense that she jumped and squeaked, her heart pounding.

Who on earth—

She picked up the receiver.

The voice on the other end was very familiar.

"Hi, Morrie," she said wearily.

She listened with half her concentration while Morrie danced around the question he wanted to ask.

"No, Morrie. I really *can't* give you a firm turn-in date right now."

She stared out the window at the darkening sky until he slowed down again.

"Well, my life just got a lot more complicated. Like with your nephew and the dybbuk. Only more so."

Silence. Then, as she had *known* was inevitable, Morrie got excited. When Morrie became excited, half of his words were Yiddish and the other half mostly unintelligible. Only working with him as long as she had enabled her to understand him. He produced a choked-off phrase that only experience enabled her to interpret.

She bit back a smile. *I can't resist this.* "Well, for one thing, there's a vampire on my living-room couch."

A squawk.

Poor Morrie. He wasn't ready for that one. "Calm down, Morrie, this one is on the side of—you should excuse the phrase—the angels. A good guy."

Another squawk.

Well, what do you expect? You knew *about me when you took me as a client.* "How did I get tied up with Itzaak? These things just *happen* to me, Morrie."

A whisper, in which she caught one word.

She softened. *Morrie, I never knew you cared.* "Morrie, you're a sweet man, but I don't think your rabbi could help. This one's a Catholic. I think. As Catholic as a vampire can get, anyway."

A gurgle.

Now we come to it. She sighed. "Look, Morrie, I *promise* I will do my very best not to die and leave you with a half-finished novel on your hands."

Morrie did not sound mollified.

Di made a few more soothing noises, and finally got him to hang up, She went back to work, only to be interrupted a half hour later by someone buzzing her apartment from the foyer.

Now what?

She went down to the foyer herself, not trusting *anything* at the moment. If Jeffries had tracked André here—

But it was only a messenger from Morrie's office. She half expected some kind of written remonstrance from Morrie—but the boy had brought only a large white paper sack from the deli on the first floor of Morrie's office building.

Now what on earth? she thought, thoroughly puzzled now.

The mystery was not to be solved until she got the sack and opened it.

There was a note inside. *You sounded like shit, kid. To hell with the damned book; take care of yourself. If I can do anything, tell me. Itzaak is in Seattle, or I'd send him over with his special stuff, which I don't want to know anything about. You should only eat. And keep that guy on your couch away from your neck.*

And inside the sack, under the note—garlic-laced chicken soup, garlic bagels, garlic-and-chives cream cheese, and a half loaf of garlic bread.

She had to put the sack down, she was laughing so hard. If she hadn't, she'd have dropped it.

"It doesn't work, you know," said a soft voice from the living room.

"What doesn't work?" she called back, conveying the sack into the kitchen with care. The chicken soup was making her stomach remind her that she'd been skipping far too many meals lately.

"The garlic. It does not work the way the legend says. Before you inquire, I can smell it from here."

"I should think they can smell it all over the building. Bernie's Deli makes one *powerful* chicken soup." She couldn't stand it. Her mouth was watering so much she was about ready to take a hunk out of the sack and scarf it down. "Are you *sure* it doesn't bother you?"

"Not at all." André sounded positively cheerful. "Only—I would like some company. If you would be able to spare the time."

"I can't eat and type. Hang in there a mo."

Food in hands she returned to the living room. André looked *much* better, and he accepted the mug of tea she brought with her with a sweet smile that she found herself returning.

"Diana, I hope that you will excuse the impoliteness, but I also made use of your telephone. I needed to tell my Lowara where I was, where I could be reached—"

"No problem. I'm in the phone book," she said, settling herself in her favorite chair. "Better the Rom than a carpet salesman."

"Thank you," he replied simply.

"You know, you're very quiet," she said. "I know you were listening to the radio before dawn, and you picked up the living room, for which I thank you, and you just told me you used the phone—and I didn't hear you out here at all."

"I have had practice," he pointed out. "Many years of it."

That was an opening if ever she'd seen one. "How many years? I'm nosy."

He chuckled, and a lock of hair fell charmingly over one eye. "You have the right, Diana. A bit under two hundred. I was *almost* a victim of Madame Guillotine."

She sipped her soup, then cocked her head to one side. "Almost?"

He sighed. "I came under suspicion as a Royalist sympathizer, and with no one to speak for me, and no gold with which to bribe the proper officials, I was destined to be an example to the New Republic. Except that a certain young lady with unusual appetites had a habit of bribing her way into the prisons—"

She laughed. "Aha! The woman in the case! It's those big brown eyes of yours."

He blushed. "Perhaps. It may just have been that I was young and cleanly, and to tell the truth, very frightened. She was in the habit of offering only a painless death—to me, she offered the blood bond."

"And that's the exchange of blood that makes—"

"The change, yes." He nodded. "So, to shorten the tale, the jailers found one more poor fool dead of fear in the morning, and buried me with the rest in a shallow common grave. Except that I did not remain there long."

She finished her soup. "When did you end up over here?"

"I came over with my tribe of Lowara—they adopted me after I engineered their release from a provincial gaol. That was—let me think—shortly after Napoleon crowned himself Emperor. I have been here since."

He smiled at her; his eyes had softened, and there was nothing of the ice-knife killer about him at the moment. His long hands were laced around one knee, and he seemed completely relaxed and at ease.

Which pose lasted about thirty seconds more.

There as a knock at the door—and his expression underwent a change to alert, wary, and cold as sharpened steel.

"There is someone out there—" he breathed, "—and it is someone I cannot read. There is a wall I cannot pass—"

TEN

A chill of fear crept down her back. *Could it be one of them? But how—and how did they get in the building? How—*
     She saw out of the corner of her eye that she was beginning to glow a little, as fear translated into shields—

Then she realized what an idiot she was being, and the glow vanished as she laughed at herself. André gave her a curious and bewildered look.

"Diana? What is it that is so amusing?"

"Andre, why would an enemy *knock?* Why would he come in the front door? I think I know who this must be. Hang on a minute." She extended and *touched,* and chuckled again.

"It's more than not an enemy, it's a friend," she said, and put her mug down as she headed for the door to let Lenny in. "You couldn't read him because *I* put shields on—"

She flipped the locks, and the door swung open. Lenny stood framed in the doorway, white with fear; every muscle tensed, a baseball bat in one hand, a sharpened piece of wood in the other.

*Good God—I'd better defuse this, fast—*She raised an eyebrow at him. "That's a strange way to come visiting. I know you promised me a steak dinner for Christmas, but that wasn't what I thought you had in mind."

He hadn't been expecting *that* kind of reception, that was certain. He looked at her with his mouth dropping open for a moment, then deflated, and shuffled his feet sheepishly. "I thought—Morrie called me. He seemed to think you might be in trouble."

She cast her eyes upward. "Good old Morrie. I should *never* have given him your number. Come on in. I'm in trouble, but not with my visitor. André is likely to be part of the solutio—"

She caught a hint of movement out of the corner of her eye and realized that André was *there,* beside her, pressed up against the wall where he would be hidden from anyone in the doorway.

Enough already! Her nerves were worn down enough that this was beginning to make her angry. "Will you two *stop* trying to save me from each other?" she snapped—and both Lenny and the vampire jumped, startled.

She grabbed Lenny's wrist and dragged him inside; shut the door and turned him so that he faced André. "Lenny, this is André. André, Lenny. Shake hands and be nice."

Lenny swallowed, and reluctantly extended the hand holding the stake; then realized what he'd just done, blushed, and fumbled awkwardly with it. André recovered first, and saved the moment by taking the piece of sharpened wood from him, clasping his hand with a chagrined smile. "I think we are both fools, *non*? I am pleased to meet you."

Di waited, hoping Lenny would see the man, and not the mythic monster.

"Funny," said Lenny, after a long pause, plainly responding to that smile. "You don't look Transylvanian."

". . . So that's what we know so far," Di concluded. "And I would bet any amount of money that by the time we get back to this Jeffries's place, he'll be long gone. I would be if I was him."

"I agree," André seconded. He was curled up next to Di on the couch, but on the end. There was a space of a couple of feet between them, and he was all business. Not even Lenny, who was highly sensitive to body language, would be likely to read anything into his behavior.

All of his other masks were off, though.

He's allowing Lenny to see that he's not all-powerful, that he's vulnerable, and I bet it's because he's figured Lenny will be receptive to vulnerability.

Lenny digested all this, his eyes fixed on the coffee table. "So you figure this 'Hidoro' creep is the soul-eater."

"He certainly fits the profile." Di edged back into her own corner of the couch, and tucked her feet under her.

"Okay. You gonna let me and Keith in on this one?" He looked up at her, belligerently.

She started to say no, then caught André's eye. The vampire was nodding ever so slightly, and she did a quick rethinking of her answer.

"It's bound to be dangerous—" she began.

Lenny interrupted her. "We've already *been* in danger," he told her. "We've been busy. We thought about what you told us, about how you weren't likely to be able to pick the thing out of all the people in New York, and we decided to see if we couldn't stack the deck some. We've been out every night, cruising some part of the bus route; one of us in Keith's car, one on the street playing bait. Trolling for soul-eaters."

It took a minute for the meaning of his words to hit her; then she bit back a curse. "You *idiots!* You're crazy! You could have been killed—no, *worse* than killed!"

He shrugged. "We talked; Keith figured if just thinking about the thing sent you into a panic attack, you weren't in any shape to do anything about it."

Her anger ran out like water from a broken pot. "I deserved that, I guess," she replied, biting her lip. "I guess I wasn't being very effective. But I *was* trying—"

"Di, if you'd found the thing, could you have done anything about it?" Lenny countered. "At least we weren't likely to freeze like scared rabbits."

"That isn't going to happen again," she told him firmly. "I've worked things out. You've got my word on it."

He gave her a doubtful look, but didn't say anything.

André shrugged. "I cannot see where that makes any great difference at this moment. We may know *who* they are, but we do not know *where* they are, nor do we at this moment know *what* Hidoro is."

"I've got a start on that," Di said, grateful to finally be able to bring something useful into the nebulous plans. "Annie has the most extensive occult library in this city, and she keeps it in the back of the shop. I'm going in for my last day tomorrow, and I'll have plenty of opportunity to research the subject. She's got a lot of Oriental stuff, and I'd bet if the soul-eater isn't in some book in there, he's something so rare we'll *never* find anything on him."

"In the meantime—"

"In the meantime—believe me, friend Lenny, you do *not* wish to encounter this man—or whatever he is." André leaned forward, his hands clasped, his mouth a thin, tight line. "You would stand no chance with him. I am stronger than even the finest athlete by virtue of what I am, and *he* was stronger than I am. In his other form, I do not know if anything could harm him. I would not send a squad of armed soldiers against him at the moment—not without knowing his strengths and his weaknesses."

Lenny sat back a little. "Oh," he said, reluctantly.

"I don't believe in coincidences anymore," Di said into the unhappy silence. "Especially the kind of 'coincidences' we've been getting here and now. There has to be a reason why the four of us have met on this. *I* sure couldn't have dealt with it alone. I *still* can't. I think all the signs point to the fact that we need to work on this together, as a team. Len, can you get Keith over here as soon as I come back from work tomorrow?"

"No problem." He lost some of his obvious unhappiness with the situation.

Her head ached, and she was suddenly very tired. "Then let's see what we can do about this tomorrow. I hate to let it go another day, but I don't think we have a choice, frankly. We need information we don't have, André isn't fit to travel, Len, you don't know where the shop *is*, and I'm not prepared to hit the subway at night. It isn't going to do us any good for me to get myself killed by a mugger."

Lenny sighed, but nodded. André gave her a wry smile.

"All right, it's agreed. We meet here tomorrow night." She got to her feet, and tossed her hair over her shoulder, gazing at Lenny. "Out, you. I have a lot of sleep to catch up on. I haven't gotten much the past couple of days."

When the doors were all safely locked behind him, she headed back into the living room. André was still curled up on the couch, staring at the reflections in the darkened window, a frown of concentration on his face.

"I'm ready to crash," she said, quietly. "I can't keep my eyes open anymore."

He looked up, his face haunted for a moment, as if he saw someone other than herself standing beside the couch. "That is a common—complaint," he said softly. "It will pass, if you get a full night of sleep."

She was reluctant to leave him. "Will you be all right out here alone?"

He nodded, slowly, and touched her hand. "*I* will be fine. I think your protections will be enough, even should anything come at us—and I think that is most unlikely at the moment. Tomorrow? I cannot say." He interlaced his long fingers around his knee and favored her with a little grimace. "We have many problems, and I would like to think about them."

"Then I'll crash—if you don't need anything?"

For a moment his expression clouded, and Di sensed that he was struggling with himself. His eyes went cold, and unreadable, and she forced herself to remain where she was, despite the little chill of fear that masklike expression gave her.

Finally he shook his head, and that one unruly lock fell over his eye. "No, Diana. And so soon—that would not be wise for you."

She sighed mentally with relief, then shrugged. "All right then, I'll see you in the morning. You should still be conscious when my alarm goes off."

This time he did smile. "Oh-dark-hundred, is the phrase, I believe. Yes, I shall still be aware. *Bonsoir, chére amie.*"

Good friend. She sighed again as she headed for her bed. *If only—*
But she did not allow herself to finish that thought.

I'm in hell, Dave thought bleakly, staring out the windshield of the van. The dark streets were no longer dark—for him, or for any of the others. The glare of light on ice patches bothered him a little, that was all. He was truly a child of the night now.

I'm in hell, and I'm not even dead yet.

They were keeping a tight eye on him, all of them, from Hidoro on down to Doug. He wasn't allowed out of their sight for more than a few hours—and no matter where he took himself, they always seemed to be able to find him when they wanted him.

Like tonight; he'd been sitting on a bus-stop bench when the van pulled up beside him, and Jason stuck his head out of the window.

"Time's up, Davey-boy," he'd said with gleeful cruelty. "You've had your little wallow in guilt. That's all you're allowed for tonight. Get your tail in the driver's seat. It's time to go hunting, and we don't feel like driving."

This time they were cruising a lower-middle-class, ethnic neighborhood. Rows of little brownstones, dim streetlights, lace curtains in the windows; Archie Bunker territory. Dave went where they told him, and stopped when they told him, and tried not to think about what he was doing.

The hunger was getting past all the grass and booze he'd been doing, and he hadn't been able to make any connections to get anything stronger. It was gnawing away at the base of his spine; beyond an ache, it was so pervasive and invasive it was hard to think of anything else. And all the audience vibes did anymore were to increase his appetite; the scent of cooking food to a starving man.

"Pull over," Jason ordered. Dave obeyed numbly, sliding the van into a spot beside a fireplug.

The only possible target in view was a couple walking down the street; he had noticed them out of the corner of his eye as he'd passed them. He watched them in the rearview mirror as they approached the back of the van. The woman, who kept a careful two paces behind the man, was so self-effacing as to be invisible. The man, a great, stocky bull of Middle-European peasant stock, radiated hostility that Dave picked up with no effort at all.

"What d'you think?" Jason asked in an undertone to Doug, ignoring Dave. "Let 'em pass, or take 'em?"

"Huh. The woman's hopeless. But the man's got enough for both of them." Doug scratched his chin thoughtfully, and peered into the rearview mirror on his side. "We could work him, but not her."

Jason frowned. "But if we don't work the stockbroker scenario on them—"

Doug laughed maliciously. "I know what will work. My old man was just like that old fart. You see the wife? Take a close look at her; she's a good twenty years younger than he is. He wants her barefoot, pregnant, and one hundred percent *his*. You want him keyed up, we just stroll on up and make him think one of us has been poaching. That'll get his blood boiling in no time. Once we get him started, it'll be a breeze to crank him up."

Jason grinned. "The Don Juan'd be me, right? I think I'm gonna *like* this."

Doug closed his eyes for a moment, and a sly smile crept across his face. "This's foolproof, Jason. You won't have to lay a finger on him. He's got a shaky heart. We'll get what we need out of him, and cut out. Heart attack will take care of the rest."

"Good deal. What's the woman's name?"

Doug frowned, his eyes still closed. "Hmm. Hannah, I think."

"Close enough." Doug climbed out first, then Jason slid out of the van just in time to block the sidewalk in front of the man. He was radiating sensuality, and he greeted the woman effusively by name, ignoring the man entirely.

In a maneuver Dave had seen too many times of late, Doug slipped around behind the van to intercept the woman in case she ran. Jason moved toward her, brushing the man aside and touching her arm. She shrank away, bewildered and frightened, and the man's temper exploded in violence, with a roar like a wounded bear's.

Dave closed his eyes and huddled behind the steering wheel.

He could shut out the sight and sound of what was happening, but not the rest. He knew the moment the man tried to grab his wife's arm, and Doug stepped between them. He knew when the man rounded on Jason, and Jason eluded his blows, laughing at him, taunting him with innuendo.

And he knew the moment that the two of them began exerting their wills on the man, building his anger into a red rage that blocked out all attempts at rationality, that sent his blood pressure soaring—

Pain, constricting his chest. Terrible pain, getting past the anger that had been blackening his vision.

The hunger inside Dave sucked at the pain, chortling to itself.

Anger was gone. There was only pain, disbelief, and more pain. Pain that choked off his breath, that made him clutch his chest in a futile attempt to ease it.

Dave shuddered, and wept silently, but made no attempt to keep the hunger from feeding. It controlled him, now. He could no more stop it than stop a hurricane.

Falling. Impact on cold concrete. Clawing at the icy concrete, trying to rise, unable to move for the pain.

Fear. Fear that enveloped him as the anger had. Fear that choked his breath in his throat, that constricted a chest already tight with agony.

The hunger eased a little, reaching for this richer, stronger mix.

Jason and Doug stood, one on either side of the writhing man, laughing at his struggles to breathe, to live.

Laughter of devils, mocking at him.

Then the abyss. Then—

Nothing.

The hunger, now satiated, curled up in the pit of his stomach, humming contentedly to itself. Jason and Doug climbed back into the van as the woman stared at the body of her husband, mind so numb Dave couldn't even feel surprise in her.

"Get us out of here before she thinks of getting our license number," Doug ordered. And when Dave pulled out too slowly, growled, "*Move* it, dammit!"

Dave started, cold sweat suddenly springing out on his brow, and in his armpits, and floored the gas pedal. The screech of tires on the pavement echoed the woman's scream as they roared away.

Ten minutes later, Jason directed him to pull over again. Since there was no one within sight or sensing in this rundown business district, Dave was momentarily puzzled and no little relieved—until Hidoro materialized out of the shadows between two buildings, wearing his girl form.

"Trolling for rapists?" Jason asked genially, rolling down the window of the van. Hidoro nodded, a Mona Lisa expression of smug satisfaction on his face.

"Have *you* fed full, brothers?" the Oriental asked, in a breathless soprano.

Say yes, Dave prayed silently, staring at the crumbling facade of a building farther down the street. *Oh God, say yes!*

Jason looked back over his shoulder at Dave as if he could hear what the other was thinking. The movement made Dave glance at him out of the corner of his eye. Jason smirked, and winked at him.

"Not yet," he replied, as Dave writhed inside. "There's three of us, after all. We need more than one kill."

"Then I shall be pleased to assist you." Hidoro chuckled. "Shall we try the Village?"

"Good idea." Jason opened the side door, and Hidoro climbed in, draping himself over the back of the bench seat. He retained his girl form, which somehow made him all the more uncanny.

"You heard the man," Jason said to Dave, addressing him directly for the first time since they'd pulled away from the first kill. "Head for the Village."

"Ours is a good alliance," Hidoro said conversationally, while Dave tried to concentrate on his driving and keep his thoughts blank. He feared the Oriental more than all the others combined.

"I'm inclined to agree," Jason replied. "Makes it easier to work if you know you've got somebody watching your tail."

"True—but that is not all that I meant." Hidoro leaned closely over the back of the seat, his black eyes glittering in the streetlight, shiny, cruel chips of onyx. "In time past those with powers such as yours and mine could become something more than mere hunters."

"Oh? And what did you have in mind?"

The Oriental laughed, a laugh like the bark of a fox. "Say that there is a powerful man, a politician, or a powerful criminal. Say that he has an enemy. What would it be worth to such to have a means of eliminating such an enemy without suspicion?"

"Plenty," Doug supplied thoughtfully.

"And again, with your gift at enhancing violent emotion—say that the man does not wish his enemy eliminated, only disgraced. So—he debates his opponent in public, and the opponent becomes incoherent with anger. Who would elect such a man? Say that the opponent is a churchman—who one day is incited to rape. Who would put further trust in such a man? The possibilities are many."

"Fascinating," Jason said dryly. "Have you told the Master about these notions of yours?"

"I have indeed, and he is cautiously in favor. However, he felt that in this case, since the stakes are so much higher, you should hear and think of these things yourselves. He would have no one involved who is not willing."

Jason laughed, throwing his head back, showing his teeth in a bloodthirsty grin. "Oh, even Davey-boy would be in favor if we put it to him the right way. Wouldn't you, Davey? You used to be a real wheel in the peace movement—think about it. Wouldn't it have been a rip to take Tricky Dicky down? How about that jerk that's mayor of Philly? Just think of all the *good* you could do, Davey."

Dave stared unhappily at the traffic and the street ahead, trying *not* to think about it. *How many innocents would we take down in the meantime, just to—feed? How could anything justify that?*

Jason laughed again. "Poor Davey. He's thinking about the sheep again. Think of us as wolves playing sheepdog, Davey. Isn't it worth a few sheep to keep the whole herd safe?"

His head swam with confusion. *I—God, I don't know. I just don't know.*

"Never mind." Jason's voice sharpened. "We'll worry about that later. I've got a target dead ahead. Pull over. *Now*, Davey."

As he pulled in, he saw what must be the "target" Jason mentioned. Two women on the otherwise deserted side street, one fair, one dark. Bundled up against the cold, but their voices sounded cheerful and lively.

Dave could see what made them a choice quarry in Jason's mind. There was so much energy in them that they glowed, and a powerful bond of affection flowed between them—

Christ. Torture one and make the other hurt worse for not being able to help her. Two for the price of one. Jason, you're a bastard—

Last of all, from the scraps of thought Dave was picking up, they were tourists who probably wouldn't be missed for a while. Canadians, which would muddy the trail back to them even further.

Oh God—not again. Dear God, not again!

"Oh, yes," Jason said caressingly. "I think they'll do *very* nicely. Hidoro?"

I can't let them do this.

"Suitable," the Oriental agreed. "I cannot feed, however. I can only kill while I am full-fed."

"Could you—*hurt* them a little?" Doug asked.

Maybe if I throw the door open—yell at them to run.

Hidoro laughed, and it echoed ghoulishly in the empty van. "My good colleague, I can hurt them a great deal."

The hunger that Dave had thought quiescent rose up and

growled in anticipation, and he realized in despair that it had him in thrall again. He couldn't move.

All three of the others slid out of the van, Hidoro coming around the rear to cut them off as the other two closed in from behind.

The one closest to the van, the fair one, threw herself at Hidoro in a doomed attempt to clear the way for her companion to escape, shouting something at her. Something about running for it. And a name, or a nickname. "Fi—"

But Hidoro changed into his cloud shape just as she reached him—and she vanished into the dark smoke.

She shrieked, her cry coming muffled and dim from inside the cloud, as the other two caught and held the other woman trapped between them, helpless even to move.

Dave closed his eyes, and cried, as the pain rolled over him and his hunger fed.

The shop had been blessedly quiet; customers few, and not inclined to gossip. When Di got back from the shop, André was still asleep— or something. She stood beside the couch, looking down at him, little tag ends of thoughts going around in her head.

He looked so young—not much more than twenty-five, if that. And so—vulnerable. It was strange, thinking of him as vulnerable. It wasn't a word she would have thought to apply to a man like him, and yet she'd used it twice in thinking about him in the last two days.

On the other hand, I've seen him at his most helpless, so maybe that isn't surprising.

A knock at the door interrupted her reverie, and by the time she had answered it and brought Lenny and Keith into the living room, André was awake and in the armchair that stood opposite the one she usually took.

Huh. Tactful of him.

She got everyone settled and brought in tea; then got down to business.

"All right," she said, waiting for her tea to cool enough to sip. "We've been dealing with two kinds of victims and multiple killers. We'd just about decided that for ourselves—and what André told us seems to indicate not only that there are psivamps *and* something else, but that they've all linked up. Not that improbable a coincidence, actually. Predators can be pack animals as well as solitary, and pack animals hunt more efficiently. Provided there was no quarrel of leadership rights, it actually make a certain amount of sense for them to have met and for them to decide to band together."

Keith nodded. "I wondered about that. It just seemed like too big a coincidence."

She took a sip of tea, carefully. It still was hot enough it nearly burned her, but she was chilled to the bone. The long walk from the subway station seemed longer in the dark of winter.

"It may not *be* a coincidence, as such," André said quietly. "If you think of the areas both must hunt—relatively deserted, yet with *some* people upon the street—it was inevitable that their paths must cross, soon or late. There are not that many places which qualify as hunting grounds."

He turned his attention to Di. "I take it you did find something that fits the soul-eater, then?"

She nodded. "When I looked up Oriental vampirism in Annie's library, I didn't have a lot of luck, until I acted on a hunch and cross-checked in Japanese folktales. That's when I ran across something called a *gaki*."

Andre considered the word for a moment, then shook his head and shrugged. "I do not recognize the referent."

She rubbed the handle of her mug with her thumb, thoughtfully. "They're—well, we don't *have* an equivalent," she said. "It was hard to make out exactly what they are, and since I don't know Japanese, I couldn't cross-check in the original texts. The word is translated as 'spirit,' 'vampire,' *and* 'demon'; take your pick. They are *not physical*—that is, they didn't start out as human beings, like the *real* Japanese vampires do. Most of them seem to be harmless, and they feed on other things that are not considered 'physical'—like perfume, music, incense, the smoke from cooking, even the emanations of a monk's meditations."

"So far, nothing like our killer," André observed, tracing a little design on the arm of his chair with a long finger.

"I said *most* of them. There are three kinds that aren't harmless— the 'flesh,' 'blood,' and 'soul' *gakis*. The flesh *gakis*—those make Jack the Ripper sound tame." She shivered. "They have to devour the flesh of the victim while the victim is still living."

She swallowed to moisten a throat gone dry with fear. Knowing what she had known—reading those folk tales had been very unpleasant. Annie's books had not been written or translated for kids. She wondered what conventional scholars made of them.

And what would they do if they knew the stories were something more than stories? That the bogeymen were real, a real as the scholars themselves? She felt a little finger of cold touch her back, as she had when first reading the stories, but ignored it as best she could.

"The blood *gakis* are just like the Western notion of Count Dracula; absolutely evil, seeing humans as no more than his rightful prey. Then there are the soul *gakis*. The tales were very clear on two points. First, they *do* devour the spirit after killing the chosen victim, and they seem to delight in making the death as frightening, violent, and painful as possible."

"Which would account for the mangled victims in the bus," Lenny said, after a moment. "I couldn't figure out why this thing would want to do that if it just wanted to—" He gestured helplessly, unable to complete the sentence. Keith just went a little pale, and clutched his mug.

She nodded. "The second thing is, they're able to take on the physical appearance and attributes of anyone they've killed by absorbing the body when the soul has been devoured. Remember the missing bus driver?"

Keith nodded, holding tightly to Lenny's hand. Lenny patted his arm absently, all his attention fixed on Di.

"Let's assume that the bus driver was the first one killed, and that the *gaki* took his form by absorbing him."

"He'd have a rolling deli if he did," Lenny said bluntly, as Keith winced. "The temptation must have been too much to resist."

"Exactly. The *gaki*'s so-called normal or feeding form is like a cloud of fog or smoke, and it supposedly takes time and concentration to switch from that to human and back. When the cop forced him to pull the bus over, he might have figured it was safer to 'play dead'—and once they put him in the morgue, he just went into his other form and got out the ventilation system."

"The cloud!" André exclaimed. "The cloud of smoke that struck me!"

"That's it. That's the only thing that makes sense, and fits in with what you told me. That's why the Oriental boy vanished before the cloud showed up. The only reason you're here now is because you can't 'die' twice—I actually have some theories, but now isn't the time. Now, our problem in going after them is that since the *gaki* has hooked up with the psivamps that killed André's gypsy friend, we're at a bad disadvantage—because they're covering each other's weaknesses. The *gaki* can only be hurt or killed when it's in its human form. The psivamps can drain you down to heart-failure level, probably without even touching you."

"Concentrate on the psivamps, and the *gaki* will go into cloud

form and get you. Go for the *gaki,* trying to get him before he becomes a cloud, and the psivamps could drain you." Lenny nodded,
frowning. "I don't much like this."

"Do you suppose they are sharing victims?" André asked.

"I would be surprised if they weren't. The psivamps don't give a
fat damn about the soul. It's like two kinds of lions, one that only
wants the hindquarters, and one that only wants the fore. They complement each other; it makes sense for them to work together."

"How have we got *anything* going for us?" Keith asked unhappily.
"This looks hopeless!"

She reached over and patted his hand encouragingly. "Not yet, it
isn't—for one thing, there's four of us now. For another, they only
know for certain that André is on their tail."

Lenny was thinking; Di could tell by the way he was chewing his
lip. "Could we get them to split up or something?" he asked. "Like
maybe we could do something to exhaust one of them, so it has to
go hunting before the rest of them are ready. Then we could get
him."

"Might work. I had some other ideas," Di replied, rubbing the
back of her neck. "Most of them *did* involve catching at least the *gaki*
away from the psivamps."

"First we must learn where they are," André pointed out. "Did
you—"

"Yeah, I checked the address you gave me. Not so much as a
mouse; even the cockroaches bailed out."

"So. They have moved, as we both expected. And they will be on
their guard. Jeffries will no doubt be waiting for me to return."

She nodded, and put the cold mug of tea down beside her; she
hadn't taken more than a few sips and neither had anyone else, so far
as she had noticed. She sighed, then a memory she had been *trying* to
bring up all day drifted into the front of her mind.

"Well, *hell!*"

"What?" the three others chorused.

"I don't know where they are now, but I bet I know a good place
to pick up their trail. I saw Jeffries there just the other night, and he
was acting like he owned the place. Not only that, but there was a girl
with him, a Japanese girl, and I'd be very surprised if she wasn't your
gaki, André."

"Where was this?" André asked, looking a bit more lively.

"A club, a rock club down near the Village. It's called HeartBeat."

The phone shrilled.

Jeffries was hiding something. Dave had no doubt of it.

When he and the others returned—they had, thank God, been satisfied at last, and Dave had managed to get himself under control before they returned to the van—Jeffries took Doug aside to tell him something that none of them wanted Dave to hear. Well, that wasn't that unusual, but—

The back half of Jason's loft was one big room; it had been an artist's studio, Jason said. They'd used it for rehearsals for a while—until they got the steady gig at HeartBeat; now they used the club itself. It had always been open, though empty of everything but odd bits of gear.

But now the door was closed and locked.

He discovered the locked door when he got up the next afternoon, and stared at it without doing more than touching it to confirm it had been locked.

There was unhappiness and fear on the other side of the door. And something that filtered that unhappiness and fear so that very little of it could be detected on the other side of the door.

Like they're trying to keep it hidden. And I'm the only one they'd want to hide it from.

He backed away, then returned to the dubious shelter of the room Jason had assigned him, a little cubby barely big enough to hold a cot.

He was recalling the talk of a "counteroffensive" against the intruder—and it frightened him.

He paced the narrow confines of his room, thinking furiously. *They've got people back there. More than one. Oh God, this is wrong, it's wrong—and I don't know what to do about it. Everything I've done is wrong. The booze isn't helping enough, neither is the grass. I—I haven't done anything but drive the van—*

His lips twitched. *Right. And feed off their leavings.* He flung himself down on his cot, and covered his eyes with his arm. *I haven't hurt anyone—but I haven't stopped them. Get real, Dave. Standing by and watching while they kill is just as bad as doing the killing yourself. Oh God.*

He groaned, turned on his side, and curled into a fetal position. *I can't get away—they always know where I am, and they'll come after me. If they think I've blown the whistle on them, they'll kill me. If I go to the cops, anyway, they'll lock me in the loony bin—they'll track me, and then* they'll *send Hidoro after me.*

"Hey, Davey-boy." Jason interrupted his misery with a sharp rap on his door. "Up and at 'em. Gig time."

He dragged himself to his feet, pulled his door open, and joined the others in the living room, his throat swollen with misery. *And through it all I have to make music—or they'll kill me.*

His guilt gnawed at him all through the gig. Even the wild vibes from the floor couldn't penetrate his misery. As Jason turned on the heat and they screamed through "Why Oh Why," he sang the chorus with real feeling.

If only there was someone he could turn to for help—

That thought—and the coincidence of *that* song, and a girl dancing on the edge of the floor, a dancer with hair down to her ass—all combined to trigger the first hopeful thought he'd had in weeks.

Di.

My God—she *knows all about this stuff, and she was* here, *I saw her—which means she's living in the Apple.*

He finished the set in a rush of impatience, and headed straight out the back door afterward, mumbling something to Doug about going for cigarettes. The bassist didn't care; all through the last set he'd had his eye on an aggressively made-up dolly with the look of someone who'd trip a guy and beat him to the ground. Now he was headed for the dance floor. As Dave passed him, Doug made a dismissing motion, and moved out, intent on his own game.

And Jason was nowhere to be seen.

Hidoro and Jeffries, Dave knew, would be holding up one end of the bar. The coast was clear.

He ran the three blocks to the nearest phone booth, closed the door behind him. The cold wind cut off, he fumbled out a dime with numb fingers, praying that she hadn't gotten an unlisted number.

Well, there's a D. A. Tregarde listed. The only one. If it isn't her—

He didn't want to even consider that notion.

He dialed, his fingers feeling fat and clumsy, and waited while the phone trilled. Once. Twice.

On the third ring, someone picked it up.

"Tregarde residence," said the voice he'd been hoping to hear.

"Di?" he said, suddenly uncertain. "It's Dave. Dave Kendall." *Yeah, kid. The guy you used to be in love with. The one who dropped you like a hot rock 'cause he didn't understand what you were into. That it was important—maybe more important than him. The guy who needs you right now, like he's never needed anybody before.*

"Oh. Dave. Nice to hear from you." Her voice sounded cold, preoccupied, and a little strained. "Look, I'm afraid you caught me at a bad time right now."

"Di—wait, please, don't hang up on me. I—I need to talk to you."

He stared at the stainless steel of the tray under the phone, and willed her not to hang up."

"We're talking now," she said.

Not going well. "Please, Di, it's important, and I don't want to talk about it over the phone. I need to talk to you in person."

There was a long pause, during which he could hear, faintly, something on a crossed line—some other conversation between two women with strident voices. "It's late," she said, finally.

He forced himself to stay calm; told himself that screaming wouldn't do any good. "I know—please. Di—it's not about us, it's about—about something I've gotten into. The kind of thing you—you know. I'm in over my head. I *need help,* Di. I wouldn't lie to you, not about this." More silence. "We could meet someplace if you don't want me around your pad, okay? Someplace neutral?" He swallowed. "I—I was a lousy macho bastard. If you don't want me to come around, I wouldn't blame you. But I don't know where else to go."

"Someplace neutral?" She sounded a little less cold. "Well, I don't know. I—suppose so. As long as I can bring friends."

He leaned against the cold glass of the booth, weak-kneed with relief. "Sure, sure thing, anybody you want. Tonight?" Desperation sharpened his voice. "Please, can we make it tonight?"

There was another long pause, during which he could hear her talking to someone with her hand over the mouthpiece of the phone. "All right," she said at last. "I guess it can't hurt." There was another pause, and he clutched the receiver to his ear to catch every word. "There's a bar over in the club district where a lot of folk musicians hang out. It's called Logres. You know it?"

"Yeah, yeah, I know it."

Oh there is a God. It's only ten blocks from here.

"When do I meet you there?"

"In—" He checked his watch. There was one more set left, then they packed it in for the night. Doug he *knew* had a target in mind, Hidoro would be good for a couple of days yet, and Jason took somebody out in the alley after the first set. If he went off on his own, quickly, they might think he was running off to feed—or to brood. In either case, they'd give him at least two hours before coming for him, and they wouldn't go into a crowded bar after him, they'd wait until he came out. "In two hours. Is that okay?"

She made a little sound of speculation. "This had better be good, Dave. Two hours from now is damned late to be dragging somebody out in this weather. If this is some kind of a gag, my friends aren't gonna be real happy."

"Yeah, I—"

"You played enough head games with me, Dave. I'm not as forgiving as I used to be. If you're pulling some cute trick, I *might* let my friends have you when I get done with you." Another pause. "I'm a brown in karate now, Dave. I can wipe the floor with you if I want to, and I'm not kidding."

"Oh God, I swear it, Di, I need your help and it's not some kind of stupid frat joke." He looked at his watch again. Ten minutes left in the break. "I gotta go. I'll see you in two hours."

He hung up the phone without waiting to hear her say goodbye, and ran all the way back to the club.

ELEVEN

Di hung up the phone, all too aware that her palms were sweating.

"What was *that* all about?" Lenny asked, very bewildered. "I've never heard you threaten to beat somebody up before."

"That's because my ex-lover never called me up before," she said, flushing, and wiped her hands on her jeans before she sat down again.

"Oh." Lenny looked embarrassed. "Uh—I—"

"The one," she continued, allowing herself no wallow in self-pity, "that dumped me in college. I told you about him when we both got drunk that one time you really screwed up an audition."

"Yeah, you did." Lenny grimaced. "I know this's supposed to be the era of peace and harmony and all that, but—let's just say I don't blame you."

She managed a wan smile. "Thanks. Well, it sounds like he got his, anyway. I was just bringing it home to him that I'm not the same girl he dumped. He *says* he's in trouble, *my* kind of trouble. He was practically crying, and I don't think he was faking it."

"What goes around, comes around," Keith put in. "Thing is, can you afford to mess around with his problems when we've got this other stuff on our hands?"

She frowned, thinking. "That's the odd thing. The last time I saw him was just about a week ago, maybe two—his band was *playing* at HeartBeat. That was the same night I saw Jeffries and what I *think* is the *gaki*. I told you that I was beginning to think that there isn't *anything* connected with this business that's a coincidence. Seems to me that if Dave's in occult trouble it would be damned odd if it's *not* connected to those two." She rubbed her hands together, trying to massage cramps out of her fingers. "Anyway I said I'd meet him—with some friends—at Logres." She tilted her head sideways a little, and looked pointedly at Lenny and Keith. "You don't have to go if you don't want to."

"I said I was in," Lenny replied firmly. Keith nodded. "I go along with your take on this," the dancer continued. "I can't see how your ex's problem could be occult and not be tied in with something as nasty as those two, not when you've *seen* them lurking in the same club. You know, maybe they own it."

"*That* is an interesting thought, friend Lenny," André said, drumming his fingers on the arm of the sofa. "An excellently baited trap for the catching of unwary mice, *non?* One could pick and choose, and not need to prowl the streets at all—"

"Only part of the time," Di interrupted, sure of her ground here. She'd hunted too many predators not to have learned how they thought. "You don't want to draw too much attention to a particular area by taking all your victims from there. But it *would* be a good place to mark people out for later."

"A lot of runaways hang out down there," Keith put in, face very quiet and thoughtful. "Anytime one of the clubs gets lax about checking IDs, it's all over the street. If you're looking for nameless, faceless victims—"

"Yeah. With a vested interest in *not* going to the cops." Di grimaced. "I think we've got a lead. Now all we have to do is keep from spooking him."

Di saw to it that the four of them arrived early for the meeting at Logres; early enough to set Lenny and Keith up in a booth at the front, and to have a few words of warning with Jim, the bartender and part owner.

She felt sick to her stomach. *I don't want to do this. I don't want to see him, or talk to him, or any damn thing. And I don't have a choice.*

"You have storm warnings up," the swarthy bartender observed sotto voce, when she leaned over the bar and gave him their orders.

Yeah, no kidding. But I didn't think it showed that badly. So much for the Great Unflappable Tregarde. Another illusion shattered. "You're very perceptive, as usual."

I wish I wasn't involving Logres, but there's no place else that's this well protected. And I don't *want Dave in my home. Sorry about this, Jimbo.* She stuffed her change back in her purse but did not touch the four glasses of Harp on the counter in front of her. "I'm meeting somebody," she told him, in a voice that would not carry beyond the two of them. "There could be trouble."

"Physical, or 'other'?" Jim flexed his enormous biceps unconsciously as he gave a quick glance toward the door. She smiled a little. *Oh Jim, you never stop hoping for the day you can ride to the rescue on your white steed, do you? No medieval brawls tonight, Sir Severale. Sorry about that, too.* He was a Medieval Society knight, a well-trained fighter with rattan blade and shield, and big and brawny enough to take care of most troublemakers without resorting to anything worse than intimidation—which occasionally disappointed him.

"Other. Who's in that might catch fallout?" *I've got to get the innocents out or shielded, just in case—a Guardian does not leave innocents undefended.*

Logres wasn't *just* a place where a lot of folk musicians hung out—or Medieval Society members, though there were plenty of both that spent their time here. It was the watering hole of a fair number of occultists and sensitives—psis like Di, who had mundane jobs and mundane lives, and extramundane interests. They *had* to have mundane jobs—the bill of drink at Logres was mostly imported, and not cheap.

"Nobody, at least not tonight. Anybody like *that* cleared out an hour ago. You'd think they were psychic." His broad grin invited her to answer it, and she did. "We have the Baron and the Count playing chess in the last booth, and four folkies drinking Guinness like they know what they're drinking right behind you. That's all."

*The Baron and the Count are so headblind I could let off a psionic nuke in here and they'd never look up from the game. The folkies—*She put a quick shield on them, and sighed. *One more erg of energy I'm out in case I need it—one more time, no other option.* "Bad news for your cash register, but good for me—"

He shook his shaggy, dark head. "Nope; guess again. We had a big crowd in here until about an hour ago. For some reason they all cleared out just before you got here. Not to worry, m'lady. Just try and keep the fireworks contained, hmm?"

"Good enough." Now she took the four glasses, sides slick and cool against her palms, two in each hand. "Jimbo, I'm sorry about visiting possible havoc on your place—"

"Forget it. Logres can take care of itself."

She thought about that; thought about how *she'd* been drawn in here, her very first day in New York, drawn by the warm and friendly atomosphere (psychic *and* mundane); how the place seemed to hold people in protective arms—and how anyone that was *really* trouble had always been dealt with. Summarily. By Jim—or by fellow customers—and a time or two, *she* had helped with the "dealing." And she wondered if the other owner—the one she never saw— might not also be a Guardian . . .

"Listen—" she said, shaking herself out of ruminations. "This guy, when he comes in, get a good look at him. He *might* be bad news, and not just because he's my ex. He told me on the phone that he's in deep kimchee, and I *think* it might be real heavy. You might want to find reasons to bounce him on out of here if he ever comes in on his own."

Jim raised his eyebrow—he only *had* one, a solid bar that stretched across his forehead—and wet his lips. "I've never known you to say that about anybody, m'lady, even people I know you don't much care for. I'll *take* that advice."

His trust of her word warmed her. "It could be mistaken advice—" she felt moved to warn. "I'm sure's hell not infallible."

"And I could be Elizabeth Taylor. Right." He snorted. "I'll have my eye on him, so figure your back's covered. Oh—don't forget; another hour and all I can serve you is juice. Okay?"

"Yeah. And thanks." She bestowed a grateful smile on him, and took the drinks to her friends, Lenny and Keith at the front booth, André parked at a table two booths away from the folk musicians, who were waving their hands in the air and talking taxes.

Gods, my throat is dry. Nerves, nerves, nerves. Maybe I should have taken something. No. I can't be less than sharp.

André turned the glass in his hand and held it up to the light. "Ale?" he asked, sniffing it interestedly. Di was in the middle of a drink and couldn't immediately answer him. He sipped. "Harp!" he exclaimed with delight.

"You have an educated tongue," she said, amused in spite of her worry.

"Practice."

He was sitting with his back to the door; an odd position, but he had assured Di that nothing would be able to take him by surprise—

Of course, the fact that the back wall was one long mirror made that statement something less of a boast.

The door opened and closed silently, and someone was standing uncertainly in the dim light.

He moved, and the light fell on his head and face.

Dave.

Her heart began pounding, and it hurt to breathe. *Gods. I am not ready for this. Oh gods—he looks like hell. He wasn't kidding. He needs me. And I just want to go away.* Her stomach knotted, and her palms began sweating again.

André caught the change in her expression immediately, and his smile faded.

There was a pull from Dave that had nothing to do with sex or her old feelings for him. *I knew it the minute he opened the door,* she thought, angry at herself for allowing her emotions to blind her to what had been in front of her. *And I should have known it when I saw him on stage. Psivamp. He's trying to drain right now, only there's nothing here that isn't protected.*

Dave gave Lenny and Keith a cursory glance, then headed toward the next occupied booth—theirs.

*He doesn't have an aura—he's a whirlpool, a vacuum, feeding on whatever he can grab. Gods, he's strong! He always was a little in that way—why didn't I see it before? He couldn't always have been this strong, could he? And if wasn't—*She felt fear chill her and knot her stomach further. *If he wasn't, what in the name of all that's holy did he do to get like this?*

"Hi," Dave said weakly, stopping beside their table. "I—uh—"

"You!" André exclaimed coldly. "I *know* you—"

Dave started, then turned a little to look at André, as if he hadn't really known he was there until the Frenchman spoke. He started again when he saw André clearly—then stared, his face displaying an odd expression compounded equally of guilt and relief.

"You got away—" he said, in a whisper. "They said—I wasn't sure you had—they lie a lot." He flushed. "I—I'm sorry. God, I'm sorry. I wish I could undo that whole night."

André's expression lost a little of its chill. "Why?" he asked, rubbing his wrist absently. "You did nothing. At least, not to me."

That's it, she thought, clenching her hands. *He's with them. Oh gods, Dave, how could you be so* stupid *about this?*

Dave flushed again, and stood looking at the surface of the table, hands shoved into his pockets. "That's just it. I didn't do anything. I should have stopped them. I should have at least tried to stop them."

André made a sound of contempt. "Oh, *bon*. With *what* would you have stopped them? You are not a match for the weakest of them."

"I take it," Di interrupted ironically, hoping her voice wasn't shaking too much, "that you've met." Dave looked briefly at her, but could not meet her eyes. He mumbled something she couldn't hear.

"Well." She clasped her hands on the table in front of her, and looked him up and down. *He looks like he's been through more than anybody should have to take. What am I going to do about him? Dave, Dave, why couldn't you have just gone off to L.A. or 'Frisco like you wanted to?* "Just what is it you want *me* to do for you?"

He managed to meet her eyes once, then looked quickly away. "Can I sit down?" he asked unhappily. "It's a long story."

André slid out of his side of the booth, and indicated Dave should take his place with an ironic half-bow. When Dave was seated, he slid in beside Diana, carefully positioning himself so that there was neither too much nor too little space between them.

And enough room for me to go for him over the table, if it comes to that, she realized. *Bless you, André. Now somehow help me stay together for this little interview.*

"All right," she said to Dave, pleased to hear that her voice sounded calm. "Let's hear it."

Jim brought a third glass of Harp, unasked. Dave looked at him in surprise, then paid for it. He turned the glass around and around in his hands, while they waited patiently for him to make up his mind to say something.

She tried not to look at him; tried to think of him as a stranger. It didn't work. *Why did I say yes on the phone? Why didn't I just have one of the boys talk to him? Stupid. Because it has to be you, Tregarde, There's no coincidences here. You ended up nearly screwing up your life over him. Now it's come back around, hasn't it? You have to prove your life is back on track.*

"I guess it happened Halloween," he said softly. "I was at this party—the guy holding it had some stuff, new stuff, you know? So we all did it."

You never could keep from taking anything somebody offered you, could you, Davey? I told you that was going to get you into trouble someday. Her heart seemed to have lodged somewhere south of her larynx. *I never thought the trouble would come like this. Gods, if I'd stayed with you—would this have happened?*

"It did some real strange shit to my head," he continued. "Like I thought I was seeing what people were thinking, and when I went home, I didn't wake up for a couple of days. When I finally did— nothing I ate did me any good. Just sat in my stomach like a rock. I couldn't figure it, thought maybe I had the flu or something. We had a gig that night, and I thought it was gonna be a disaster for sure—"

He continued with frequent pauses that stretched over several minutes.

Those pauses twisted her up inside until she thought she

couldn't take any more without screaming for the exit. It was all just too raw—

Then André put one hand unobtrusively over hers, and she began to feel calmer. She wasn't alone; she had friends she could trust—one she could trust with her real secrets. And Dave wasn't the same person who'd dumped her. *He'd* gotten more feckless, judging by the story he was telling.

She hadn't gotten over him—not by a long shot, judging by the gyrations her insides were doing—but she'd gotten at least a little more responsibility. She gave André's fingers a little squeeze, and began to pay attention to what Dave was saying.

He began to stammer under Di's scrutiny, and spent more and more time staring at the glass in his hands.

But he told them enough.

Enough to know that the drugs combined with the fact that he was already marginally psychic had somehow made him into a psychic vampire—and that André had been right. That there were three more of them, plus the *gaki*.

Enough for her to know that the psychic vampires weren't killing too many—at least not yet, and not directly.

But what they're doing is worse than killing, she thought unhappily, watching him turn his glass around and around, like the mindless pacing of a caged animal. *He doesn't realize that the people they drain that way are burned out for life, not just temporarily exhausted. He hasn't figured out that once they shuffle out of his life, they probably end up street bums, unable even to care about living anymore. If they ever told him, he doesn't want to believe it. Gods, this has got to stop. I have to stop it.*

Dave, how could you have gotten yourself tangled up in this? Why didn't you come to me earlier? And—if I'd run after you, really tried to make the effort to make you see what I was into—would you be here now?

Am I to blame for you?

"Di?" he said in a small voice, after one of those long pauses.

"I haven't run off," she replied thickly. It was hard to get words out. *Dammit, he's responsible for him, and I'm responsible for me. He's sitting there because of things he did, not things I did.*

He grimaced. "Please, you've gotta get me free of this. You've gotta help me. Please. I can't live like this. Jason an' Doug *like* it—I—I just wanta be sick every time I—you know." He put the glass to his lips and gulped, the first time he'd drunk anything since he came in. When he put the glass down, it was half empty. "I'd rather be dead," he finished flatly, concentrating on his own hands. "I can't keep doing things like this."

Oh gods, Dave—"I thought you were used to using people," she said, as coldly as she could. *I have to know if there's anything left of you to save. If I can save it.*

He winced. "I had that coming, didn't I?" he replied, his deep-set eyes shadowed with emotions she couldn't read through the chaos that surrounded him. "I dumped you when you wouldn't be my little cheerleader, when you told me that there was something out there besides music. And here all along you were right." He laughed hollowly. "Talk about your instant karma. Dump you, get dumped on. And the only place I can go for help is you. Di, this stuff is *wrong.* I'm doing things that are horrible. If I don't stop now, I'm gonna do things that are worse. I can't take this anymore."

There are times I wish I'd never taken up Guardianship, she thought, aching inside so much that she wanted to cry. *And most of them seem to be tied up with Dave.*

"If I had any choice—" she began.

"You should not aid him," André interrupted coldly. She looked at him in surprise, and read true hate in his eyes. "He caused you pain, and doubt, and indirectly threatened your very self. He has participated in the deaths of many. He does not deserve your concern."

"André, he hasn't gone over completely; he's salvageable, and he asked me for help." *That's true. All of it's true. I just wish it wasn't me that has to give the help.* She touched André's hand, then looked back at Dave, trying not to show how much she hurt.

"Your boyfriend's right," Dave said, head down, voice muffled. "You should throw me out. Out of your life, out of here."

She stiffened. *It's my job; it's my life. And I won't let a thing like what you did to me mess that up a second time. That's not the way a Guardian does things, dammit.* "I don't have a choice, Dave. There are pledges I made a long time ago that I have to fulfill. You *asked* for my help, I *have* to give it. And André isn't my boyfriend."

André frowned, but made a little gesture, as if to say, "It's your decision."

I might as well get this over now. Either I can do something for him, or I can't. I'd rather know. I'd rather not have to go through this again.

Forgive me, Lord and Lady. I don't know which I want. I still can't forgive him, even now. I know I wanted him to get hurt enough someday to see how right I was—but I truly don't think I wanted anything like this. Did I?

She swallowed hard as he stared at his glass. "So—let's see what I can do," she said, flexing her hands, then digging into her purse for some of her "equipment."

"Here?" Dave looked up, eyes startled. "Now?"

"Here's as good a place as any," she replied. "We won't be disturbed—" —*and I* don't *want you in my home. There's nothing to remind me of you there now, and I don't want anything of you there, ever.*

She glanced over at the bar, and hand-signed "Do not disturb" when she caught the bartender's eye. Jim, who among other things, was a fluent "signer," nodded. "Okay," he signed back. "Keep it quiet."

She half smiled. "Will try," she signed.

She turned her attention back to Dave, and throttled down tears at the haunted look in his eyes. "Now—let's see what you're made of these days—"

It was a good thing Logres never seemed to close.

Di tried every trick in the book—and plenty that had never *been* in any book. Jim ignored the aural flares, the shield probes, the spectacular attempt—which failed—to reverse the complete unconscious drainage. He could most assuredly See all of it; Di had ascertained a long time ago that he had Sight. But he ignored it all, trusting her to keep it within the confines of the booth.

Which she did, though not without cost.

I'm not getting anywhere. Oh gods, I can't do anything with him—

She even considered trying to invoke Guardianship—but *that* came when it wanted to, and tonight it didn't feel like it wanted to. *I guess Dave doesn't rate. He got himself into this—maybe he's supposed to deal with it by himself.*

Finally, when her hands were shaking and her vision blurred, André put his hands over hers, and said, in a quiet voice, "No more."

She sighed, and closed her eyes for a moment.

It's no good. I can't block him without starving him. And I can't reverse what's been done. Oh God, Dave—no matter what you ever did, you don't *deserve this!*

It hurt; not her pride, there was little enough left of that after defeating her panic attacks. It hurt *inside,* it hurt to know that there was nothing she could do for him.

I'm a Guardian and Guardians are supposed to be able to help people. And I can't help him.

Maybe when I started this it was because I didn't have a choice, but now—there's a hunger. I need to be able to help. And this time I can't. Oh gods, it hurts!

"I'm sorry," she said, propping her elbows up on the table and bowing her head into her hands to hide her tears of frustration. "Dave, I'm sorry. I've tried everything."

Silence. "You can't help me," he said, voice dull.

She couldn't look at him. "I can't help you. At least, not now. Maybe before—I don't know. That stuff, that drug you did, it changed your metabolism, so that you were living on bioenergy. You were all right as long as you were feeding off the high frequencies, the positive emotions—but the minute you started taking in the lower frequencies—you changed *again*. Your receiver's been retuned, if you will. I can't change you back. It's like—like weaning a young animal. Once you get them off milk, they can't digest it anymore; their body's changed. Yours has changed, and I can't reverse it. I'm sorry."

"I'm sorry" sounds so damned pathetic.

He laughed, bitterly, and her throat tightened with tears. " 'Once they get the taste for blood,' " he quoted, and laughed again. "God."

She looked up, over her entwined fingers, and his face was bleak and utterly without hope. Her eyes stung and blurred, and she blinked the tears away, silently.

He didn't seem to notice she was crying. "So you can't fix me. Can anybody?"

She shook her head, sniffed, and rubbed the back of her hand across her eyes and cheeks. "I don't know."

He slumped a little farther, huddled in on himself. "So—what do I do now?"

"I don't know that, either," she confessed.

"You were supposed to *help* me," he said bitterly.

Then, suddenly, she was angry. Angry at him, angry at the attitudes that had gotten him into this mess in the first place. If he'd *once* been willing to take charge of his life instead of letting other people make his decisions for him—

"You always wait for somebody else to do your thinking for you, and to bail you out when you get in too deep," she snarled. "And that's why you're *in* this mess in the first place! Why don't you try thinking for yourself for a change?"

Oh gods—now what have I done? She bit her knuckle, wishing she could unsay those last words. *I didn't mean—oh shit. Tregarde, you and your big fat mouth—*

Silence engulfed the booth, silence in which he stared at her as if she were some creature from another world entirely. As if he and she were the only people at the table, in the room, in the world.

"Maybe—" he said, slowly, something stirring in the back of his eyes. "Maybe that's exactly what I ought to do."

She sat frozen in her seat, as he rose slowly from his. As he rose, his face changed; from bleak and hopeless, to thoughtful and determined.

He leaned over the table and kissed her, lightly brushed her lips with his. It felt like a promise.

"I never could hide anything from you, could I?" he said, smiling, in a falsely frivolous tone that broke her heart. "I couldn't even hide where I was. Used to make me so damned mad at you—remember?"

He eased out of the booth, as Di stayed rooted to her seat. "Ciao, baby," he said, saluting her with two fingers. He looked over at André, and his smile faded. "Take care of her," he said.

Then he turned, and before anyone could make a move to stop him, he was gone.

Lenny was the first to recover—he squirmed out of his booth and dashed out the door at a dead run.

He returned in a few minutes, face like a thundercloud, and slouched over to their booth.

"Gone?" André asked, his voice sympathetic.

"Shit yes." Lenny looked so disgusted at himself she didn't have the heart to say anything. "I don't suppose he told you where he's holing up, did he?"

André shook his head. "Regrettably, no."

Di's mind was slowly coming unfrozen.

"*I never could hide anything from you. I couldn't even hide where I was. Used to make me so damned mad at you—remember?*"

She *did* remember. Now that he'd reminded her. Deliberately reminded her—

"He didn't have to tell me," she said slowly, her heart aching so much for him that she held back tears only because she knew tears would do him no good. "He didn't have to tell me. No matter where he is, I can find him. Even if I didn't already know where the band is playing, now that I know he's in the city, I can find him wherever he goes. I could from the minute we'd been lovers. *And he knows that.* He went out of his way to remind me. Maybe it was so I could find him if I figure out a way to help him—but it doesn't much matter, does it? I can find where they're *all* hiding. All I have to do is stay within range of him. And—"

André nodded, sudden understanding lighting his eyes. Lenny's eyes widened, and his mouth formed a soundless O.

André touched her arm and slid out of the booth. She followed. He looked in the direction of the street door. "It is perhaps three in the morning," he said conversationally. "Perhaps four. Is that time in which to accomplish anything?"

She took a deep breath and steadied herself. "No," she said slowly. "No, I don't think so."

Lenny took a good look at her face, and wordlessly put his arm around her shoulders. She leaned against him, so grateful for his support that she couldn't possibly have put her feelings into words.

Evidently she didn't have to. He gave her shoulders a squeeze, dropped a gentle kiss on the top of her head, then let her go.

Keith spoke up for the first time since they'd arrived. "Should we head on back, maybe get some rest, and see what we can do tomorrow?"

"I—" Suddenly she was tired; tired enough to drop. Certainly tired enough to break down on the spot and cry. "Yeah," she said wearily. "I'm not even up to magicking my way out of a wet paper bag."

"The car's just around the corner," he offered.

She shook her head. "No—no, I'd rather walk. I've got a lot of things to think about."

"Tomorrow night, then." Keith slipped out the door, Lenny beside him. André hesitated.

Before he could say anything, Jim spoke up from the darkness behind the bar, where he'd been standing without her noticing him.

"I'd feel better, m'lady, if you didn't take that walk alone. Lots of nasty things out this late; some of 'em don't take to being exorcised." He grinned, and his teeth shone whitely. "Hard to exorcise a switchblade."

She made a halfhearted attempt to laugh. "Too true, Sir Knight. Well, André—feel up to a walk with a—"

"Yes," he said, before she could call herself any of the uncomplimentary terms she was considering. "I do not think you really want to be alone, *non?*"

"True," she said, sighing.

It was snowing, little flurries that sifted down and melted when they hit the salted sidewalk. He waited until they had gone at least a block, and the cold wind that cut through her coat had at least restored a little clarity to her mind, if not her heart.

"You knew him very well, once," he ventured, hesitation in his voice. "One assumes, that is. Lovers do not always know one another."

She sighed, and studied the deserted street ahead of them. There didn't seem to be any traffic at all out tonight. The sky was still heavily overcast, given the falling snow; in New York it was sometimes hard to tell, since you almost never saw the stars even on a clear night. There was a hint of damp in the air. "Well, I thought I did," she replied after a while. "I sure thought I was in love with him."

He reached for her hand and took it; he held it tentatively, at first, then, when she didn't pull away, he interlaced his fingers with hers. His hand felt warm and comforting, even through her glove. "Something happened to change that?"

She sternly told the ache in her throat to go away, and concentrated on putting one foot in front of the other until she thought she could respond without choking on her words. "Until tonight I thought I was still in love with him. Now—I don't know." She sighed, and her breath made a cloud that wisped away on the light breeze. "I feel sorry for him—*gods*, I feel sorry for him—but there's nothing *there* anymore but pity."

They passed beneath a streetlight, and she squinted against the brightness for a moment. "Perhaps you grew up," André suggested quietly, after they had walked a few more paces, footsteps echoing together on the concrete. "Perhaps he did not."

A car passed; a cop car. The cop inside gave them a brief glance, saw only what looked like a couple out for a little walk, and didn't even slow down. "I—I don't know, André," she answered absently. "I'm not sure of much of anything right now. You know about the way we broke up."

"Hmm." His fingers tightened a bit on hers. "As they say, messy, *non?*"

"Yeah. Messy. Very messy. He wanted me to give up what I was. Am. Magic, being a Guardian, all that. He didn't understand any of it, and didn't want to, because it took me away from him. And he didn't want to share that with me. I guess, anyway."

They reached another streetlight, passed beneath it, and turned the corner. She stared at the sidewalk a few feet ahead of them, at the way their shadows lengthened as they moved away from the streetlight. The flurries were turning into a real snowfall.

"Allow a stranger to correct?" he said tentatively.

A siren howled somewhere in the distance, moving away from them. She hunched her chin down into her coat collar, feeling a chill of the spirit as well as the body. "I'm supposed to 'know myself.' I mean, that's one of the rules of being a Guardian, so I don't get stuck in head games. Sure, go ahead."

The wind picked up strands of her hair and played with them. She thought about freeing her hand from his long enough to tuck them into her collar, and decided she didn't want to.

"He wished, I think, not for a partner nor an equal." He paused for a moment, as if searching for the right words. "I think that what he wished for—at that time—was for you to give up your identity, and become a mirror that reflected him. I think, however, that tonight—perhaps tonight he saw *Diana* for the first time, and not the thing that he wished you to be. I think perhaps that you forced him to truly *see* you for the first time. It was something of a shock to him. It was—an experience for him."

She turned that thought over in her mind, examining it from every angle she could think of. *It feels right. It feels like he's got it pegged.*

They crossed the street, and she stumbled a bit on the curb when they reached the other side. He caught her elbow, steadied her, then let her go when she had her balance.

"How did you know?" she asked. "You don't know him at all, you hardly know me—how did you manage to get all that figured out?"

She looked at him out of the corner of her eye, and saw him shrug. "I have been about for no few years," he said wryly. He looked at *her* sideways; their eyes met, and he raised his eyebrow ironically. "I have seen his kind, the young and popular male musician, many, many times. It seems that they are either supremely sensitive, or supremely *insensitive*. Sometimes both. There seems to be little or no middle ground with them." He chuckled. "One could do worse than be or choose a shopkeeper, *n'est-ce pas?*"

"Right now I wish I *was* a shopkeeper," she replied sadly. "I wish I was ordinary. Ordinary people don't seem to come in for as much pain."

They walked on in silence, as a steady fall of snow drifted down from the sky, becoming visible only as they entered the cones of light from the street lamps. Her nose was getting numb in the cold, and she sniffed. The snow was beginning to "stick," and as the ground whitened, light reflected both from the ground and the low-hanging clouds. It began to grow noticeably brighter.

"Does it hurt you so much, the past?" he asked softly.

"Not as much as it did, I guess." She took internal inventory, and came up a bit surprised. "Not as much as I thought it should. The present hurts more. Being helpless. Being unable to *do* anything for him."

He raised his free hand, and rubbed the back of his head with it. "As with an injury," he mused, "you have feared to look at it, to test it, until it has mostly healed—and *voilà*, it does not pain so much as you had feared."

"I suppose so."

The apartment building loomed at the end of the block, as always, brightly lit. "You intend to follow through with this—to eliminate the killers."

She swallowed hard, and tightened her fingers on his. "I don't have a choice, André."

"If it means eliminating him, as well?"

"I—yes. I hope it won't. But if I have to—"

The thought of that—*oh gods. Oh dear gods. Please don't make it come to that*—A sob forced its way out of her throat, and she bowed her head. *But—it may. It may, and I have to face that.*

"*Chérie*—" He stopped, and tugged on her hand to make her pause beside him. "Diana, look at me."

She did; she hadn't expected to read what she saw in his face. Pity, sadness, understanding—compassion.

"He knows this, Diana. I do not think he is deluding himself. And I do not think he meant the words in jest when he said that he would rather die than continue as he is." His lips curved in a faint, and infinitely sad, smile. "I did not care for him, not at all, nor did I pity him—until the very last. Until he said goodbye, and told you what you had forgotten. Then something extraordinary—he began changing at that moment, I will swear to it. He is becoming something worthy of admiration, *chérie*. I do not know *what* he will become, but it will not be either petty or evil, whatever end he goes to."

She stared at him a moment longer, and then the tears began in earnest. He took her in his arms, and she sagged against his shoulder and cried while her tears froze on her cheeks.

"I have lost those I cared for, *chérie*," he murmured into her hair. "It is not an easy thing, and becomes no easier with time. Do not be ashamed to care, or to weep."

So she wept. And he held her, carefully, patiently, until she had cried herself out.

They entered the front door in silence. She shrugged out of her coat and threw it at a chair; it missed, and slid down to the floor, and she was too exhausted, mentally and physically, to care.

She didn't bother to turn on the lights; the steady snowfall outside had built up to at least an inch on the ground, and all the reflected city light made it nearly bright enough to read inside the apartment. When they had climbed the building steps, she had looked back over her shoulder at the street, peaceful beneath the frosting of white. It was beautiful, serene, and somehow pure.

And filled with soft light.

She hoped it was an omen.

They both stopped in the hallway, halfway between her room and the living room, and the silence became awkward.

"André—" she began, and flushed. *I don't know how to say this. I'm not used to asking for things. I—I'm not used to a lot of things.*

He waited, saying nothing, merely waiting.

"André, I—I'd rather not sleep alone tonight," she whispered, looking at her feet.

"I think," he said, quietly, but with a hint of humor, "that I am about to make a great fool of myself."

She looked up at him, startled. "What?"

"Ah, come—"

He took her hand, and led her to the couch. When she had taken her seat, he sat beside her, still holding her hand. "I told you, did I not, that my kind—are something of 'psychic vampires' ourselves?"

She nodded, and chewed at her lip, wondering what was coming next.

"I told you that we take only what is given freely and no more? And that I, I have made it a pledge that I take nothing without some feeling between myself and the other, after the first few times?"

She nodded again.

He sighed, and shook his head. "Diana, Diana, I have done so *very* well for so very long with casual encounters—until now."

She blushed. "Until now?"

He reached out, and just barely touched the back of the hand that was resting on her knee. "You have made casual encounters somewhat—distasteful. Am I a very great fool, or have you been something other than indifferent?"

His lips smiled, but his eyes begged for her to tell him that she had *not* been "indifferent."

She shivered. "I'm not sure what to say. I—you're very special to me, André. More than I ever thought anyone could ever be. But—"

His eyes had brightened with her first words—now they looked wary. "But?"

"André—I can't stop being a Guardian. I might not make it through this next one—or the one after that—or the one after that. I don't want to ask you to get involved with me when you could end up hurt. And I don't just mean physically."

He smiled, then his smile broadened until it turned into that lovely silent laugh of his.

Gods, he could stop my heart when he laughs like that—she thought longingly.

"How very odd." He chuckled, reaching out and cupping his free hand around her cheek, without letting go of the hand that he held. "How very odd. That was *precisely* what I was going to say to you!"

She threw caution, bitter memories, and a fear-darkened future to the wind. "Would you consider sticking around—if we make it through this one?"

His laughter faltered and died. "Oh, *chérie*—" He searched her face, looking for something—she wasn't sure what it was, but he must have found it, because he smiled again, and moved his hand around to the back of her neck, burying it in her hair and tugging her closer. "Diana, dear, sweet lady—*chérie, mon amour,* I will stay for as long as you wish me to stay—"

Whatever else he might have said was lost as their lips met.

There was too much tangled up in that kiss for her to sort it out; so she didn't even try, she just gave herself to it, and to him. And when he let her go, whispered, "I still don't want to sleep alone."

He looked deeply into her eyes, and smiled—and before she realized what he was up to, he'd scooped her up in his arms as effortlessly as if she were no heavier than one of the throw pillows.

She gasped, and clutched his shoulders. He chuckled. "This is another legend that is true," he said to her widened eyes. "The strength. *Chérie,* if you do not wish to sleep alone—"

He glanced at the clock on her desk. "It lacks an hour to dawn," he told her, impishly, and began making his way toward the door leading to the hallway and her room. "You shall not *sleep* at all, for a bit—hmm?"

TWELVE

C iao, baby," Dave said, trying to keep his tone light, trying to keep his despair from showing on his face.

If I look into her eyes again, I'll fall apart. I don't want to do that, not in front of her. It'll only make her feel worse than she does now.

So he focused on the dark guy, the one with the French accent, instead. *The vampire. Christ.* The man's eyes bored into his; sable, solemn eyes, measuring eyes. Thoughtful eyes.

I've lost her for good—but then, I threw her away, didn't I? I had my chance, and I blew it. You—feel like a good guy, even if you are a bloodsucker. I think you'll back her. I know you understand her better than I ever did. I'm glad she's got you. Before this is over, she's gonna need you.

"Take care of her," he said to the vampire, knowing the man would read more than just that in his tone. Then, before any of them could stop him, he turned on his heel and headed out of the door.

I've got to get out of sight, he thought, shivering in the cold wind, and shoving the door closed behind him, *or one of them is likely to chase after me.* He gave a quick look around; the street in front of Logres was deserted. *I can't let them follow me. If any of the others got hold of them, they'd be cole slaw. Maybe if I duck around the cor—*

He blinked in surprise.

My God, it's a miracle.

At precisely that moment, a cab pulled up to the curb, right at the front door of Logres. A single man got out, muffled to the ears in an overcoat. He paused for a moment, handing money to the driver; then turned and looked directly into Dave's eyes.

He smiled. For one moment, Dave felt all of his problems fall away before the warmth and understanding implicit in that smile—

Then the man was hurrying past, not into the bar, but opening an unobtrusive door at the side of the main entrance.

Dave shook his head—and dived for the cab, ducking inside before the cabby could pull away.

He slammed the door shut, and the cabby pulled out just as the door to the bar began to open.

"Where to, mack?" A cloud of pungent cigar smoke filled the front of the cab. The cabby didn't seem the least interested in anything except the nonexistent traffic on the street.

"Central Park—" He blurted out the first destination that came to mind.

He could feel the cabby's eyes on him; looked up at the rearview mirror and saw that he was, indeed, being stared at. Not surprising— Central Park at four A.M. was hardly a common destination. He slumped down into the back seat, ignoring the stare.

The cabby's massive shoulders shrugged when he didn't respond to the stare. "Okay. You're payin' th' fare."

Dave closed his eyes, tried to steady his mind down, and slouched a little lower. Getting under control—oddly enough—seemed a bit easier now than it had been when he'd first walked out of the bar.

Okay, he thought, deciding to take his problems apart and analyze them. *Di can't help you.* Now. *That's not to say she might not be able to find someone else who can. Wasn't that why you reminded her that she knows how to find you, no matter where you are? So maybe—*

He suddenly flashed on Di, walking, say, into the club. *This* time knowing what Jason and the rest really *were.*

Oh shit. Oh holy shit.

She knows about the others. What they've been doing. She's not likely to sit around and let them keep eating people alive. She's gonna use that line to you *to get at* them, *shithead. She's gonna come after them.*

And then they're gonna kill her.

He bit back a moan of anguish. *God, there is no* way *she can take any of them out! They're gonna have her for* lunch—

—if she's lucky. If she's not—

—Hidoro's gonna get her.

Oh God, what have I done?

His gut knotted with anguish. Bad enough watching them take on strangers, but *Di?* He couldn't even bear thinking about it. *She's gonna die—or worse—and it's gonna be my fault.*

Oh God, what can I do? What—

He suddenly froze, as he realized what he was thinking. *What can I do—*

I've got to think for myself. There has to be something I can do.

He opened his eyes and stared out the window of the cab at the street passing by, not really focusing on what lay behind the glass. Light—dark—light—streetlights and shadows made an abstract patterns that he scarcely noted. Except that there was so much darkness. So little light. So much cold, so little warmth.

So little hope.

He was hardly more than Jason's shadow. If Di couldn't do anything about *him,* how could he expect her to stand up to the others? Even Doug was stronger than he was—

Because Doug hasn't been trying to hold back, he thought bitterly at the dark city. *Doug hasn't been trying to stay a good guy. They all think I'm a fool for fighting this. Shit, I could be as strong as any of them if I would just give in to this thing. Dammit, it's not* fair! *I shouldn't be penalized for trying* not *to hurt people!*

He gritted his teeth. *Maybe I should give in and go their way. It sure looks like good guys do finish last.*

The spluttering neon of a sign made him think of what he'd *seen* when Di had been trying to help him. Flashes of white light, flickering shadows, the strain on her face, and through it all he felt nothing. *Good guys finish last—and Di isn't gonna finish at all—*

The cab paused at a stoplight, an angry red eye glaring above the corner. Below it, waiting for the light to change, Dave saw a young girl, clad far too lightly for the cold, in bell-bottoms and a fringed denim jacket. Flurries of snow fell on her granny glasses, and on her long, straight hair, hair bound up hippie-style with a headband; she slouched against the lamppost with her hands shoved deeply into her pockets. Her face was absolutely blank; either from dope or despair, he couldn't tell which, and he *didn't* want to "reach" for her to find out. She was probably just another anonymous runaway—*like all the others I've—taken—*

She was certainly too young to be out this late legitimately. Another innocent, or once-innocent; another morsel for some shark in the city to gobble up. *A shark. Like me. Like my "friends."*

Dave turned away from the window, biting his lip to keep the gnawing in his gut at bay.

I've got to do something. I can't just sit there and watch them destroy Di, like all those poor kids I helped destroy.

The light changed, and the cab pulled out with a cough and an explosive backfire. The girl jumped, and stared at the cab with the eyes of a frightened rabbit—started at *him?* Maybe, maybe not. She didn't look much like she was seeing any kind of reality. Her wide, startled eyes were like holes burned into her face.

Then the cab moved across the intersection, and she ran across the street and was swallowed up in the darkness.

Poor kid. If not tonight, then tomorrow, or the next night. Mugged, raped, eaten alive, she's a target, and she'll get hit. The stock situation, the setup, reminded him of a comic book. *But if this was a comic book, she'd be playing target on purpose. And when the bad guys moved in—wham. Too bad she isn't Hidoro,* he thought, sour taste of bile in the back of his throat. *Too bad. What was it Jason said? Trolling for rapists? It almost made me like Hido—*

My God. Trolling for rapists.

I've been holding back, but what if I didn't have *to? What if I made like a comic-book hero? What if I went out looking for other predators?*

Like in—Central Park.

It all fell together.

It might work.

He chewed his lip, thinking hard and furiously. *I'm stronger than any mugger, even if I couldn't take on Doug or Jason.* Now.

I could—go hunting. Now, tonight. Then when I came back, they'd believe *me if I let them think I'd given in, gone over to the wolves. And meanwhile, I'll be getting stronger. Maybe strong enough to be a match for them. One of them, anyway.*

Then when Di shows up—which she will—she's got somebody behind the lines.

He nodded to himself. *It's stupid. It's suicide. And damn if it isn't better than doing nothing.*

The cabby looked at him very oddly when he actually got out on the edge of Central Park, near one of the bridle paths—but a fifty convinced him that he wasn't curious. A second fifty convinced the driver to return in another two hours.

He probably thinks I'm a dealer, Dave thought wryly, turning his back on the cab to face the park. He took a deep breath of icy, exhaust-laden air. Behind him the cab coughed and backfired again as it pulled way; he ignored it and turned his attention to the new senses inside him—and let that strange hunger within him loose for the first time, to go hunting out among the trees.

The trees made a lacework of black, darker than the buildings around them or the sky above them, and seemed to go on forever. The snow, dirty gray by day, was white and pristine in the dim lights of the park, the reflected light from the city itself. It all looked so peaceful, so untouched. And it was all just another kind of trap.

Snow began falling in earnest; fluffy, fat flakes instead of flurries. He raised his head and walked slowly into the park, ignoring the paths, his feet crunching on the granulated snow. He sent that *thing* within him out again, and felt something after a moment. He paused to identify it.

He got feelings first. *Hunger. A clawing in the gut that matched his own. Pain. A man with a monkey on his back, a habit to feed, a habit that was killing him.* He could feel the death waiting inside the man— waiting, biding its time. It wasn't ready yet. It had a while to grow.

Dave's lips curled in something that wasn't exactly a smile, and he moved deeper into the park, slipping between the trees. The cold penetrated his thin boot soles; he hardly noticed it except as a minor annoyance. He was in his element at last. Tonight a predator was about to become prey.

Now he was getting images along with the feelings. *Body shaking, need screaming along his nerves, making him wired to the max. But not so wired that the hands holding his knife weren't rock-steady.*

The feelings, the images strengthened. Dave sensed he was nearing his goal. He peered ahead through the dim light, looking for a particular place . . .

There—that clump of bushes beside the concrete path. Now, how to flush the quarry—

The pain the other was suffering was giving *him* strength and energy. He opened himself to it, and shivered in poisoned pleasure as it poured into him, flooding him, filling his emptiness.

But it wasn't *quite* enough. The hunger within him snarled, and wanted more.

Well, it was going to *get* more.

He slipped silently from shadow to shadow, stalking his prey's hiding place, nearly invisible among the underbrush in his own black clothing.

The other was waiting in ambush—though it was an ambush based more on hope than on planning. Now Dave could *see* the thoughts in his head, just as he'd been able to see the thoughts of the chicks he'd picked up at HeartBeat. *There was a pimp that used this path; so did his girls. So did their tricks. Any of them would do. He was hoping for a john—a john would have more cash than one of the girls, and a john wouldn't be expecting trouble or paying protection—*

Dave smiled hugely, and licked his lips, and the hunger within him purred in anticipation. Of course. The best way to flush *his* quarry—

—would be to look like prey.

He slipped over to the path; paused a moment, then began walking confidently toward the bushes, his boot heels clicking against the concrete. He sauntered along as if he suspected nothing, expected no trouble, hands shoved carelessly down into his pockets.

And all the while he was using his line into the guy to hold him back, just as Jason used *his* line into prey to pull them out into reach. He could *feel* the junkie's eyes on him, burning into him; felt the elation when the guy first saw him, and the junkie realized he was alone, he was dressed expensively, he was unarmed.

It was hard not to look at where the junkie was hiding. Dave knew exactly where he was, how he was crouching in the center of that clump of privet just off to the right; how his legs burned, and his feet were going numb.

Not yet, he whispered into the junkie's mind. *Not yet. Let him get past. Come at him from behind—*

He closed the distance between himself and the bushes. He could feel the junkie's eagerness, straining against his control, a crazed greyhound on a lead of gossamer, with the rabbit in sight.

Five yards.

Not yet—

Two.

Past.

Now—

The bush rattled. It might not have alerted a *real* victim.

But Dave wasn't a real victim. He whirled to meet the attack before the attacker had a chance to realize that something had gone wrong.

The junkie slashed at him, his reactions thrown all to hell by the games Dave was playing with his mind and his balance. Dave danced aside from the clumsy knife stroke, and *reached*—

Touched fear.

Set it aflame.

The junkie froze—

His mouth opened in an utterly silent scream, and he dropped the knife, collapsed to his knees on the concrete. Dave walked toward him, slowly, feeling every step he took echoing in the man's mind, echoing back as the footsteps of everyone he'd ever feared in his life.

The junkie moaned and fell over sideways, quivering mindlessly at Dave's feet. Dave reached down and grabbed his greasy collar; hauled him upright as if he weighed nothing. Transferred his grip to the front of the man's jacket, hauled him up further, and forced the junkie to look right into his eyes.

The junkie wept, unable to look away, and a dark stain spread over the front of his jeans.

Dave smiled.

"Hello, sucker," he said.

And *reached* again.

It was like being reborn.

So much for appetizers. Now what's on the main course?

He left the junkie where the cops would find him the next time they came through. In a pile of greasy rags and limp limbs in the middle of the walkway.

Clearly, most sincerely dead.

And I feel—incredible. No wonder Jason gets into this. It's like—

Like sex. Only better.

His mind was clearer than it had been in weeks. The hunger was no longer a factor that drove him—although he was far from being sated. He felt like a god. And the whole world existed for him alone— for his pleasure, to take as he chose, when he chose, *how* he chose.

He froze between one step and the next, and slammed down on that thought.

This's like the first time you did acid. Remember? You thought you were playing so hot—that the lyrics you were coming up with were the best thing since Lennon. So you turned on the tape player.

And the next day he played that crap back. He couldn't understand a word he'd been singing—and he'd written better tunes when he was in kindergarten.

This isn't real; no more real than the acid dreams. It's just a different kind of high. Don't let it fool you the way it's gotten to Jason and Doug.

But the pleasure as the sweet essence of fear had poured into him—*that* had been real. And the new strength, the vitality—that was real enough, too.

Okay, so keep your mind on what's real, why you're doing this, and on business. And business is getting yourself ready. Which you aren't, not yet. You need to hunt again—

He sensed movement, rather than saw it. A car on one of the roads that threaded the park. Running without lights.

Lawful prey.

He sent out his questing senses again; now that he was no longer half-starved, the hunger answered his demands tamely, obediently. He gave himself over to it, confident that it was under his control, and let himself *feel.*

Three. One rigid with fear, two pulsing with lust. One helplessly weak, two cruelly strong.

He almost laughed. Trolling for rapists—

Pain-fear-pain.

He drank it in. It was wine—but he needed something stronger. And he needed a clearer target.

Frustration-lust-impatience.

He moved in on the impatient one; got a fleeting impression of a steering wheel. He began running surefootedly, through and around the trees, on a course that would bring him out of the trees somewhere ahead of the car. He couldn't even feel the cold anymore, even though his breath was forming clouds in the snow-laden air.

Pull over, he whispered into the burning mind he touched. *This's a good place to stop.*

He could hear the car engine somewhere off to his left; heard it coming nearer, and got a better impression of *where.*

There, he whispered insidiously. *There. The picnic tables. Time for a nice little party.*

He broke through a thin line of bushes and vaulted a snow fence. The snow had melted when it encountered salt-covered pavement and the roadway lay black before him. They weren't too far away—he could *feel* them so clearly—

One—fear so strong she can't move. Two—sense of power and joy in the fear and pain that surges as strongly as the lust. Three—thoughts swirling, blind chaos, nothing clear but the erection that throbs hunger, throbs need, through his body, his brain, in time with his heartbeat.

Dave skirted the edge of the roadway; if he moved out onto the cleared blacktop, they'd see him. He was a match now for both of them in strength—but he wasn't a match for two thousands pounds of moving metal.

Ahead, the engine sounds stopped. Car doors slammed twice. He thought he could hear muttered words.

Here—he whispered. *Now.*

Laughter. Tearing cloth. Pain-sounds, shrieks of pure agony filtered through cloth until they were hardly more than whimpers.

He could see the cluster of picnic tables through a thin screen of young trees. See the dark moving shapes clustered at one end of the nearest.

Grunts and whimpers in time with each other, with the rhythmic movements of one—

Here—he called the other, the one who watched and waited and joyed in the pain. *Here—there is something waiting for you. Just for you. Better than that—*

It turned, dark amorphous shape, and took the two steps needed to come into his reach—

Dave took that one quickly—turning lust into pain, pain into fear, and fear into silent paralysis. Dave held him down with the strength of his mind alone, drinking in the bliss of pure terror. But when the fear was everything, when it screamed through the first one's mind and soul, something snapped deep within the brain, and brought paroxysm and death.

The last agony of death was ambrosia—but it came too quickly, it wasn't *entirely* satisfying, and although new strength swelled his muscles, his hunger sulked and complained—

Not enough. Not enough.

But there was still the other, who, oblivious to the fate of his companion, was grunting his way to orgasm.

Until Dave interrupted his pleasure with a well-placed punch to the kidney.

And a knee in his chin as he collapsed.

Followed by a carefully calculated kick to his larynx. And a lovingly placed boot grinding into his privates.

He opened himself to the agony, standing over the writhing blot on the ground, letting it flow. *Oh yes*—

The pain was exquisite. The man took a gratifyingly long time to die, strangling on his own crushed windpipe. His fear and pain built *much* higher than his partner's had, and Dave was only too happy to enhance it for him. He played with the fear, the anguish, carefully, teasingly, making absolutely certain that the rapist sustained *everything* he was capable of feeling until the very end.

Dave lost all track of time, lost track of anything except the *feeding,* until the last sensation faded away—

A whimper behind him caught his attention—a new source of pain and terror—

And he *almost* reached for it—

Only the girl's eyes, seen clearly, stopped him. The eyes, wide and blank with disorientation and misery, beneath long, lank hair—

Eyes he'd seen just this evening, less than two hours ago—

The child on the corner.

Recognition stopped him cold, and he pulled back before he had *touched* her.

She had been gagged with her own headband; while he'd fed off her rapist she'd stealthily freed herself, huddled her torn clothing back on. Now she stared at him, expecting—more of the same treatment from him. He felt her thoughts pounding their way into his skull.

He's going to kill me. He's going to rape me again and—and—and—

He backed up a step, as his hunger complained mildly at him that he was cheating it of dessert. She stared at him, waiting for him to move on her, stared at the way he was just standing there—motionless, not coming *at* her—

At first she didn't believe. Then—she made the wild jump from seeing him as another attacker, to seeing him as *savior*.

Relief flooded her—she sobbed, and started to throw herself at him—

OhGodohGodohGod—

He couldn't tell if the thought was hers or his.

He backpedaled away from her so fast that she sprawled face-down in the snow at his feet.

"Get out of here—" he snarled at her, holding himself in check by only the thinnest of margins. *If she touches me, I'll kill her too—oh God, somebody, help me—I can't hold it back if she touches me—*

She made some kind of a sound. The hunger coiled to leap.

"*Out!*" he screamed at her, backing up until he ran into a tree trunk. "Go! *Run*, you stupid bitch!"

She stared, she scrambled to her feet—and she ran.

He slid down the tree trunk and huddled on the cold, bare dirt at its roots. Snow fell on him, melting and dampening his hair—fell on the body beyond him, dusting it, then slowly coating it with a shroud of white. He fought with himself with his head on his knees and his arms wrapped around his legs until the hunger subsided, and he stopped shaking.

The cabby arrived as promised. He was a little surprised to actually find Dave waiting there, but the lure of another fifty at this time of night—

Had been more than even Harv could resist.

Oh God, now I'm picking up everything—even passing thoughts. Got to shut down . . . got to.

He smiled stiffly, passed the cabby the promised fifty, and settled into the back seat of the cab. The cabdriver's greed nearly triggered the hunger again.

He shut his eyes and savagely throttled down on it. If he hadn't fed so fully already—

But he had, and it subsided within him with scarcely a struggle.

"Find what you wanted, mack?" the cabby asked conversationally.

"Yes," he replied. "Yes, thanks. I did. Sometimes the only place you can find what you're looking for is in a park at night, I guess."

Let him try and figure that one out.

A fierce cloud of cigar smoke rose to fill the front of the cab as the driver pondered.

Dave sat back and stared out the cab window beside him. The hunger coiled at the base of his spine, a sleeping serpent, no longer pushing him, and no longer opening him to the thoughts of others. He hadn't felt this—good—in years.

I feel fantastic, he thought wonderingly. *Like I could run a mile and never be winded. Like I could do an all-night gig and never need a break.*

And what did it cost? Two rapists and a junkie.

People nobody will ever miss. Scum that the world will be better off without.

The cops would probably thank him. Certainly that girl did.

I could go on like this very easily. How many muggers are there in New York? How many junkies? How many perverts?

What was so bad about exterminating vermin?

I'd be doing the world a favor.

He could do what the law couldn't. Serve the world and save himself.

Like one of my old heroes in the comic books.

It would be easy.

I may not need Di's help after all—

It would make the world a better place.

And what was it Hidoro was talking about? Using my power to get into people's minds, to tilt them one way or another? To—

His conscience supplied the word. The ugly word. *To manipulate them. To use them.*

His conscience supplied something else. The frightened eyes of the rape victim. Her fear. And how *her* fear had tasted just as sweet as that of her abusers.

How close he'd come to taking her, the innocent, after he'd disposed of the guilty.

Bile rose in his throat.

No. Oh God, no. If she hadn't run, I'd have killed her. I'd probably have raped her first myself, just to get the most out of her.

It rang true. It rang with more truth than what he'd *been* telling himself.

Snow continued to fall; it was coating the street and the sidewalks, lying along the branches of the trees. It made the city look pure and pristine. Dave bit his lip, and really *looked* at what he'd done tonight.

I hurt those people; I made them hurt as much as I possibly could. I enjoyed it.

He swallowed nausea.

I'm no better than they are. It was just that I picked my victims a little more carefully.

And what about the day when there's no mugger, no rapist around, and the hunger demands to be fed? That day *would* come, sooner or later.

If I can't get this thing that's happened to me reversed—one day I'm not going to be able to stop myself in time. I'm going to take the innocent victim along with the scum. And from there—

I'll probably move straight on to taking the innocent. There are so many more of them. And they're so much easier to hurt, to frighten.

He clenched his jaw tightly against the sickness rising inside him. *No. No. I won't let myself do that. This can't last much longer. Di will make her move one way or another soon. And after that—*

After that, I'll see this ended—no matter what.

And no matter what it takes.

"Well," Jason drawled lazily from the couch beside the door. "The prodigal returns. Out helping old ladies across the street, Davey-boy?"

Dave smiled, and moved into the light from the overhead fixture. "Hardly," he said dryly. He let his eyes meet Jason's, slowly—and gave a little mental *shove*. Not much. Not enough to challenge. But enough so that the blond lead *knew*.

Jason sat straight up, as if he'd been shocked awake. "*What* in—" he began.

Dave's smile widened. Jason's eyes narrowed for a moment, and he looked Dave over appraisingly.

"Well," he said, and began to chuckle. "Well, well. Been busy tonight, have we?"

Dave folded his arms across his chest and sauntered over to the couch. "Could be," he replied enigmatically, examining the finger-nails of his right hand with studious care.

"It would appear," said a lightly accented voice behind him, "that the little lamb has developed teeth."

Dave controlled his expression, told the chill walking down his backbone to go away, and turned to face Hidoro. "Shall we say in-stead that the little lamb has discovered he never was a lamb at all?" He tilted his head to one side, and narrowed his eyes down to slits.

Which makes them harder to read, monster.

"There's a story somebody told me when I was a kid," he contin-ued. "It was about a lion that got raised by sheep. The little guy grew up thinking he *was* a sheep. Then one day the sheep were attacked, and he found out what he really was."

Hidoro nodded, seemingly pleased. "And so you have discovered that you are not, after all, a sheep?"

He yawned; *that,* he didn't have to fake. Dawn was very close, and he was beginning to feel it, to feel how much the night had taken out of him in terms of mental exhaustion, despite all his newfound en-ergy.

"I guess that about sums it up," he replied. *And you obviously never heard that story—or you'd know what the ending really is. How what attacked the flock was a wolf pack. And how the little lion de-fended his flock and killed the entire pack. I hope my remembering that story is an omen, you bastard.*

He yawned again. "Now, if you've got no objection—"

"How many did you take, David?" That was Jeffries, coming up from behind like the silent snake he was. Dave avoided starting, and turned to face him.

"Three," he said, and shrugged. "I'm afraid I killed them. I don't have as much practice as the rest of you."

Jeffries nodded slowly, and Dave felt *something* brushing at the edges of his mind. He hardened his barriers, and pushed back. Jef-fries's eyes widened for a moment before his expression resumed its usual bland cast.

"Finesse will come with practice," he said, his lips twitching a lit-tle, something that *might* have been a smile on anyone else flickering briefly across his handsome face. "All male, however. I congratulate you. Your friends cannot seem to realize that the male gives a much stronger and more satisfying reaction than the female. They persist in taking only those men who are already with women." He shook his head. "Homophobic. And foolish. Absolutely foolish. Although the male is harder to frighten, when he *does* become frightened—the male has *such* a store of rage buried within him." He smiled again, this time at Jason, and the smile mocked the blond and dared him to respond.

Jason's face twisted in distaste. "I'm not a damn queer."

Jeffries's face hardened, and his voice acquired a coating of ice and steel. "Are you implying that I am?"

This time Jason didn't back down. "How should I know? Are you? You and Doro sure spend a lot of time together. Were you, before you—"

Jeffries strode deliberately across the room, reached down and took Jason by the throat and hauled him to his feet. "Would you like to find out, Jason?" he hissed in the blond's face. "Would you like to find out the hard way? Let me warn you, the *sweetest* prey is another predator—"

Jason wrenched himself out of Jeffries's hands, stumbled backward a few steps, and took a defensive stance.

"You want to try?" he snarled. "I'm ready for you—you just make your—"

"*Enough!*"

Hidoro moved between them, with a leap that told Dave that, no matter what else he was, the creature was no stranger to the martial arts. He drew himself up to his full height and glared at both Jeffries and Jason, and the cold calculation in his face made both of them pause.

"I find our current arrangement much to my satisfaction," he said softly, but with an unmistakable undertone of threat. "But you should be aware that I need *very* little other than a safe haven. I have continued in this alliance because I approve of your plans, Jeffries—"

He stared coldly and dispassionately at Jason. "You, on the other hand, seem to have hardly a thought in your head beyond your next woman and your next feeding."

Jason glowered, but clenched his jaw tightly on whatever it was he might have wanted to retort.

"Until you prove otherwise, Jason-san"—he delivered the honorific with an ironic little bow, his tone so sarcastic that Jason snarled—"I accept and follow Jeffries as the leader of this group—*and I will back him.* I assume you know what that means."

Jason dropped his eyes, and muttered.

"Better." Hidoro stepped from between the two. "Now, if you wish, you may continue your discussion *as* a discussion. I will retire to my resting place. I expect not to hear any further disturbance."

Interesting, Dave thought, watching the *gaki* walk down the hall to disappear into his room. *Very interesting. He's closer to being invulnerable than any of the rest of us, and he's certainly stronger in a lot of ways. He stays with us for convenience—but he could take us over if he wanted. But instead, he lets Jeffries play master. I wonder why?*

He dropped into a chair as Jason muttered an unmeant apology to Jeffries, and the "Master" glared and uttered insincere words of acceptance. Jeffries took over the couch before Jason could resume his seat. Since he obviously didn't want to sit next to Jeffries, and there was nowhere else to sit except the floor, Jason retreated from the living room with the air of someone who had been defeated, but not vanquished.

I figured it was going to come to this sooner or later. Dave pretended to read a magazine, but he was watching every move in this little dance of ascendancy with keen interest. *And we're in Jason's loft, on his turf. Not surprising that he'd challenge. But Doug's no match for Hidoro—assuming Doro stays on Jeffries's side. How smart is Jeffries, I wonder?*

Jeffries might have been reading his mind, for as soon as Jason shut the door of his room behind him, the man asked quietly, "And whose side are *you* on, David?"

Dave tossed the magazine aside; it landed on the coffee table, slid across it, and spilled onto the floor. He looked at Jeffries measuringly for several moments before answering.

"My own," he said, truthfully. *We won't mention that it's also Di's.* "None of you have done anything likely to make a bosom buddy out of me."

"True." Jeffries steepled his fingers together. "I regret the things I said and did to you, but you surely must admit that you were not cooperating. But now—"

"Now is different."

"Obviously. Tell me—just how intelligent is Jason?"

"Smart," Dave replied, seeing no reason to hold back information. *Especially if it's going to help make a schism here.* "Smart, but lazy. I was the group's leader for the last year and a half. Until we all—changed. It wasn't until Jason linked up with you that he took over. He doesn't make a move unless he thinks he's got something to gain by exerting himself. And then—he's damned hard to stop."

"Interesting. That parallels my own observations." Jeffries stared off into space for a moment. "You do realize that I have larger plans for you all that go far beyond where you are now—"

Dave nodded, keeping his silence.

"I do not think we have even begun to explore the kinds of things we can do. If we can enhance pain—can we not also enhance pleasure? And what would *that* do to your audiences, David? Think about how self-induced hysteria in their young fans carried the Beatles into prominence. And that—could be the opening to a much wider field of endeavor for all of us. The world of entertainment can lead to so many other things . . ." He smiled. "Who would *ever* have dreamed that politicians would listen to actors? Who would *ever* have believed that a half-rate B-movie actor could ride his 'fame' like one of his horses to a governor's mansion?"

Dave snorted. "What makes you think—oh. Yeah. We can play with their heads, can't we?"

Jeffries nodded. "Exactly. I believe Hidoro is cautiously in favor of the plan, so long as we stay discreetly in the background and never actually assume the position of power ourselves."

"Hard to go hunting," Dave pointed out, "when you have a bodyguard or a Secret Service guy in tow."

Jeffries smiled. "Precisely. And I am not entirely certain that Jason has a subtle enough mind to comprehend that."

He does. He's already thought of all this. But I'm not going to tell you that.

"So what do you want out of me?" Dave asked.

"For now—nothing. If Jason should make a move again—" He shrugged. "Well, not *quite* nothing," he amended. "We have some hostages to the vampire's good behavior. I am holding them in the studio. Gypsy children. He seems to set a certain store by them."

Dave carefully schooled his face to betray none of his thoughts.

"I had been leaving them in Jason's charge—but I'm not certain I wish to continue to trust him. He might turn them loose—after all, the man's quarrel is with *me,* not Jason. You see my quandary?"

"Yeah," Dave replied. "Yeah, I can. So you want *me* to keep an eye on them?" *Maybe I can turn them loose when Jeffries goes out. I can at least let Di know they're in here.*

"If you would." Jeffries's tone made it clear that this was an order, not a request.

"How long are you planning on keeping them?" he asked.

"Not more than another week at most. By then the new safehouse will be ready, and we can get rid of them." He lifted an eyebrow. "Already they're more trouble than they're worth. But once we do not need them, for one night, at any rate, we won't have to hunt."

Somehow Dave managed to smile. "Sounds good to me," he replied. "I take it I move into the room next to the studio, then?"

"Indeed." Jeffries tossed him a set of keys. "Hidoro feeds them. All you need to do is make sure no one bothers them."

"Like Jason."

"A hostage is valueless if it's dead," the 'Master' pointed out. "Or gone. I rather think Jason would turn one or two loose to lead the vampire back here, then feed on the rest. I want you to prevent that."

"Oh, I think I can do that." Dave nodded.

And as soon as I'm in the clear, I call Di. Looks like this thing is going to come to a head faster than I thought.

God help us all.

THIRTEEN

D i yawned, and drifted up toward consciousness gradually—
rather than being shocked awake by the alarm. There was a
warm and silent presence at her back. It was strange, after all
these years, to wake up with someone else beside her in bed. Besides
Atilla, of course.

It was comforting, and comfortable. And what had gone on between them before they'd drifted off to sleep had been considerably
better than that. Considerably. André was certainly living up to the
legend of the French as great lovers. Of course, there was the effect of
his feeding—and the fact that he'd had plenty of time to practice . . .

I could easily get used to this, Di thought drowsily, and smiled to
herself. *And vampires don't snore.*

By turning her head just a little she had a wonderful view of him.
Legends aside, he did *not* look like a corpse. He didn't look as wan
and ill-used as he had when he was recovering, either. Though he
didn't move at all, once he'd actually fallen asleep—

—*"Is this comfortable?" he'd asked, words a little blurred with exhaustion, holding her with her head resting on his shoulder.*

*"Nice," she'd replied. It had been more than nice, actually, but
"nice" seemed like a reasonable thing to say at the time.*

"Good . . ." His voice had trailed off sleepily.

*"I'll probably wiggle away," she'd warned, watching the gray out-
side the window begin to lighten. "I toss a lot. I kick too, sometimes."
She'd chuckled. "You may wish yourself back on the couch."*

*"I won't feel it," he'd replied, with that silent laugh of his. "I assure
you, I won't feel it. You could push me onto the floor and I would not
awaken."*

"I may try that sometime."

"If you do, chérie," *he'd warned, then yawned, which spoiled the effect, "I shall conjure cold frogs onto your pillow."*

"Can you do that?" she asked, believing him.

"Well, no—" Yawn. *"But it makes . . . a good . . . threat . . ."*

He was quite a hormonal experience, just to *look* at. He lay slightly turned on his side, his hair tumbled in his eyes, the arm that had been holding her curved as if he still cradled her. He looked absurdly young, too young, really; she wondered what his real age had been before he changed. Not that it mattered.

A faint smile still hung about his mouth.

I could get very used to this.

But with that thought came full waking. Reality intruded, the reality she'd kept at arm's length with lovemaking *Assuming I have any time to get used to anything.*

Assuming there's anything left of either of us when this is over.

She turned on her back and stared up at the ceiling, at the pattern of acoustical tiles the Guardian before her had installed.

All right, let's look at the opposition. They have three full psivamps. Enhanced strength, and if they touch you, or get through your shields— they've got you. Vulnerabilities are just to sunlight, and maybe— probably—to physical damage. A gun could probably take them out. If I still had a gun. After mine got melted—no, I didn't have the cash to replace it. Stupid move, Tregarde. You should have eaten brown rice and macaroni for a couple of months, saved your pennies, and gotten another. Now it's too late.

She tried *not* to let fear cloud her ability to think, but it was hard. It had been bad enough *not* knowing what they were going up against. It was worse, now.

Then the gaki. *As far as I can tell, vulnerable only when he's in human form. I've got Len and Keith, Gifted, but not even in Annie's league. One real vampire. Me. Four against four, the numbers say it's even but the abilities sure aren't. So what do I do with what I've got? There has to be a way to use all of us to our best advantage* and *still utilize their weaknesses against them.*

Cold chilled the pit of her stomach as another scenario occurred to her. *What if they put the screws to Dave when he got back to them? What if they know that I know? I'm in the bloody phone book—*

She refused to panic. Not when there was no reason to. *No, wait, think about this. We're safer here than we are anywhere else. The* building *is shielded* and *warded, and my apartment is under shield and* ward on top of that. *Maybe Guardian's magic wouldn't help me cure Dave, but with all these innocents in this building in the line of fire—*

Staying here is probably better than moving into a hotel. At least I know this place, and it's got generations worth of protections on it.

But what am I going to do about confronting these bastards? I don't know. All the scenarios I can come up with end up with me on toast.

She shivered, pulled the blankets up a little higher, and glanced over at André. *Is that why I went to bed with him? Sort of on the order of the condemned prisoner's last request? Is that why he went to bed with me?*

Does it matter?

She reached out hesitantly, and traced the curve of his cheekbone with one finger. *Yeah, it matters. This may not be True Love, but I care for him, I respect him, and he turns me on like nobody's ever done before. I can trust him at my back. I want him around. We complement each other. He's a great partner.*

Even if he does need a little nibble every now and then.

She touched a silky lock of his hair, and bit her lip.

This isn't accomplishing anything. I'm just delaying things.

She eased herself out of bed, moving carefully so as not to disturb him, but he showed no sign of being disturbed. The garment she took from the closet was not her usual jeans; it was a simple, black sleeveless robe, calf-length, on the order of a Greek chiton. Her ritual robe. Her fingers tingled a bit when she touched it.

Still plenty of zap left from Samhain. Good; I need it.

She showered and changed—and, with a glance of regret at her typewriter—

I said I'd try, Morrie. I didn't say I'd succeed. Figures, just when it was getting fun. Wonder who else he'll sucker into this? Wonder if they'll use my notes?

—she headed for the Living Room.

For full ritual, every tiny bit of ceremony. No skimping today.

She laid out the altar; included the Sword, something she hadn't done for two years. Pulled out every talisman she had. Robed and armed, she cast a full Major Circle and invoked every protective Power she could think of—and *then* got into the serious Magick.

It was late afternoon when she finished. She'd been a little surprised at the amount of energy she'd managed to raise. A lot of it had gone into reinforcing the building protections; a good piece of the rest had gone into passive shields for Lenny and Keith.

The little that was left, she simply formed into a plea and released. Nothing specific—asking for specifics was a lot like wishing on the Monkey's Paw—"Please let me live to be two hundred," and waking up as a Galápagos tortoise.

No, nothing specific. Just—

*Just "Please, I don't want to die—and I don't want anyone I care for to die, either." But if it comes to a choice—screw it, I'll throw myself on the grenade. And hope—*Her thought faltered. *And hope it doesn't hurt too much.*

She changed back into jeans and cleaned up carefully afterward; cleaned the Living Room, then the office/living room, then the kitchen, the bathroom—methodically, thoroughly. Thinking about mundanities kept her from frightening herself into a limp imitation.

And if it comes to that, I don't want to leave my replacement with a mess—she thought bleakly, putting the last of the cleaning supplies away, *if I don't make it—I'd rather have a tidy sort of ending. Tie up as many loose ends as I can—*

A knock at the door interrupted her before she could go any further down *that* mental path to the Slough of Despond.

She put her palm against the door and closed her eyes; ran a quick check, recognized *precisely* who she'd expected, and opened it.

Puck, looking not very Puckish. Puck, after the last of his kind had gone over the water. Puck, ready to put on Oberon's armor and defend the elvenlands alone.

"Hi," said Lenny in a fairly subdued voice; he looked at her sharply when she didn't immediately respond, his eyes narrowed.

He motioned to Keith (who was right behind him) to go in, and when his lover had passed, took her face in both hands, and kissed her, very carefully, very gently; forehead, eyes, lips. Then he held her. That was all—but it helped.

"Are you going to be all right?" he asked quietly, no trace of mischief at all in his expression or his voice.

"I think so," she said, looking into his eyes. "I'm just scared to death, that's all."

He let her go. "I'd be worried if you weren't," he told her. "I think we're facing a bad set of odds. But if we're smart—maybe we can beat those odds. I've been thinking about this—Keith and I spent this afternoon talking about it."

He took her by the elbow and steered her in the direction of the living room. "Do you want out?" she asked him as they passed the doorway, not able to guess what his answer would be.

Though I wouldn't blame him if he did—

"Get serious," he said roughly, letting go of her when they

reached her chair, taking his preferred seat on the couch next to Keith. "And leave you to handle it with nobody to help except Count Dracula? Two of you against four of them? No way. Besides, we *still* want a piece of the soul-sucker's hide, or had you forgotten that?"

"Oh," she replied weakly. "I—thanks—Lenny, I didn't expect you to buy in with me on this."

She sat down quickly; no telling when nerves might turn her knees to jelly.

He shrugged. "You didn't get a choice. There are times when the sensible route isn't the right one. Think I'll take right over sensible. Now, the sixty-four-dollar question is—just *what*, exactly, are we going to do?" He took Keith's hand in his, and studied it for a moment. "I'm sort of short on ideas. And all Keith could come up with was to trap them all in a barn and set the barn on fire."

"Barns are a little hard to come by in New York," she pointed out.

"I thought of that," Lenny admitted. "There's the notion of setting their *apartment* on fire, but setting buildings on fire would get us arrested for arson."

"Not to mention all the innocents we could take out that way," she reminded him sternly.

"And besides," said a soft voice behind her, "the *gaki*'s other form is a cloud of smoke. I do not think a fire would cause him more than a moment or two of discomfort."

As she turned toward the doorway, André moved out of the shadowed hallway and into the living room. "At the risk of being sacrilegious," he said, flicking on the lamp nearest the end of the couch, "let there be light."

She blinked at the sudden flood of warm, yellow light; glanced out the window, and realized that the sky was a deep gray, slowly turning to black.

"So," André continued, "let us make more reasonable plans, *non?*" He moved around the end of the couch to perch on the overstuffed arm of Di's chair. It felt unbelievably *good* to have him there. "Such as—oh—weaponry. What physical weaponry have we at our disposal?"

"How much money have you guys got?" she asked, recalling her earlier thoughts about guns.

Pockets, purse, and checkbooks were all turned out and the total made. Unfortunately, all *three* of them had just paid bills and the rent. André, of course, had no rent, but neither did he have any money. Among the three of them, they could scrape up a grand total of one hundred and fifty-three dollars and twenty-seven cents.

"Not enough." She sighed, and waved at the two young men to take back their portions.

"Enough for what?" Lenny asked, pocketing his billfold, then putting his arm around Keith.

"For a gun," she replied with vexation, mostly at herself for not thinking of this sooner. "We couldn't have gotten a handgun on this short a notice, but I *could* have picked up a shotgun. With all the equipment in that studio, Keith could have found a way to saw the barrel off—"

"But we don't know how to shoot!" Lenny protested—then saw her expression of irony. "Do we?"

"What do you mean *we*, masked man?" she replied with the tag line of an old joke. "I *had* a very nice thirty-eight that used to belong to my granny up until a few months ago."

"What happened to it?" Keith asked quietly.

"The barrel got melted," she answered. "Don't ask. It's not something I'm ready to talk about."

"Oh." He took her at her word, but gave her a very peculiar look. "Why a gun? Aren't we dealing with things that a gun won't hurt?"

"Are we?" she retorted, and sat back in her chair. André put one hand on her shoulder, unobtrusively. "I wouldn't bet on that. The psi-vamps are just changed humans. I would tend to think that an ounce of lead would make it a major bad day for any of them. And André was handling the *gaki* well enough until it changed—the books say it's vulnerable only in human form. I'd bet a chunk of bullet could at least make it stop and think about what had just happened to it." She shrugged. "It doesn't matter. We don't have the cash."

But if I live through this, I swear, I'm never going to be without mundane arms again.

"So. What are the arms we *do* have?" André asked.

She licked her lips and stared at the ceiling. "Start with me, since I'm probably the best armed of all of you. One two-handed broadsword, sans sheath, which we can't carry out of here without getting arrested, and can't be concealed on anybody's person."

"But—" Lenny interrupted. "We could put it in the car, couldn't we?"

"No 'buts,' sweets. The cops are being real nasty lately. If *anything* happens and they see it, we'll get hauled in. If it's in a sheath, it's 'carrying concealed,' if it's not, it's a blade longer than six inches, which is major bad news. Sir Severale told me a couple of his friends just got their favorite dress blades confiscated last week, and *I* don't even have a Recreation Society card to save me getting my ass locked up."

Lenny sighed. Di did, too. "To continue. Assorted knives, some of which, ditto, but which I'm going to pass out to you guys anyway because they're a bit easier to hide than a broadsword. All of them are blessed in one tradition or another. I don't know if that will make any difference."

"It could not hurt," André said.

"True. I did my level best to transfer most of the whammy from my sorceror's sword into my witch's atheme, but I can't swear it'll take. Assorted clubs, including one cane with a silver-plated handle. Good against werewolves, one would assume, but not against psivamps or *gakis*. We'll all take our choice of those. Except for me, I don't need a club. I have my own hands and feet, being a brown belt in karate." She paused for breath. "That's the physical weaponry. Nonphysical, I have assorted talismans, none of which are going to do us any good because while our enemies may be evil, they aren't creatures of *spiritual* evil. I have psi bolts and levin bolts which *will* probably do us some good. I mentioned the blessings on the knives, the power in my atheme. I have some of the best shields in the business and in a few minutes, Lenny and Keith will, too."

She paused for thought. "I also have a glow-in-the-dark shield aura which apparently radiates at the same frequency as sunlight and gives André fits—so it *might* work on the psivamps. All I have to do is get scared enough."

Keith gave her another strange look. "That's the *oddest* form of transference I ever heard of."

"Is that what it is called?" André said, looking interested. "I knew that these psychologists were—"

"Guys," Di interrupted, "can we talk about Freud *after* we survive this little Kaffeeklatsch? Hmm?"

André actually blushed. "Pardon," he said. "Is it me, then?"

She nodded.

"Very well. First, I am very strong. Stronger than any of them alone. Second, I have some knowledge of *savate*. Third, it appears that the *gaki* cannot digest me. Fourth, I see almost as well by night as by day. Fifth, I can be so very silent that I cannot be detected if I choose. Arcanely—I suspect my shielding is as powerful as yours, *chérie,* and I am sensitive to emotions, to thought under some circumstances, and to magic in use. That is all."

"No turning into bats, or fog, or wolves?" Lenny said in disappointment.

He shook his head, his lips twitching. "No, I fear not. Not that anyone I know has ever taught me."

"Rats."

"Nor those," André obviously could not resist saying. Di wondered *how* he was keeping up his spirits, given the odds against them.

"Guys?" Di prompted.

Lenny cleared his throat self-consciously. "No mundane weapons, except one switchblade and the fact that I know how to break just about anybody's knee. Helps, being a dancer. Not much arcane, either."

"Ditto," said Keith. "All I've got is assorted lengths of pipe. I was figuring we'd probably work best as bait and a distraction."

"That is no bad thought," André opined.

"You'll do that better if you're shielded," Di told both of them firmly. "Come, my child." She crooked her finger at Lenny. "Sit at my feet."

"Yes, Great Lady——" He ducked as she cuffed him.

"Hold still, or I'll get distracted, and if I lose this thing, it's gone," she warned, as he settled himself at her feet, back up against the chair.

Something small and light clicked against the windowpane; they all jumped. André was the first to rise and look outside.

"One of my Rom," he said, his voice troubled, although Di could not see his face. "I must go——I will use the back door."

He was into the kitchen before she could protest that that back door only gave out onto the fire escape.

Then she realized that he'd already used that door as an entrance once.

He knows what he's doing. Better concentrate on what I can do.

She held her hands just above Lenny's head, and carefully invoked the passive shield she'd built expressly for him, earlier today.

It came into being just under her hands, Looking like a misty veil. She settled it over him, then released it, and it drifted down and melded with the shields he already had in place. He knew when she was finished, he was more than sensitive enough for that. He opened his eyes, and tilted his head back.

"Want to give it a test?" he asked. She nodded, and probed at the shield; gently at first, then harder, and finally with all her strength, trying to get *through* it to affect him with projective empathy.

"Anything?" she asked after the last probe.

He shook his head. "Not a thing."

"Good. I was trying the same thing on you I think they'll be using, given what Dave Looked like. Keith, your turn."

She repeated the procedure on the young artist, but got something of a surprise. When she probed at him, he went psychically blank. To her Sight, he simply wasn't there.

She opened her eyes, and saw that his eyes were tightly closed and he was frowning in concentration. "Hey," she said, tapping his shoulder. "Leonardo. You, with the mean look. What in hell are you doing?"

"I'm trying to pretend I'm not here," he responded, opening one eye to look at her.

"Well, it's working. You and Lenny had better start having a long, serious talk someday soon. You're Gifted, m'lad. Very. When this is over, I want you to do something about getting your Gifts controlled."

He got to his feet and resumed his seat on the couch. "Okay," he replied, as if not sure what he was agreeing to. "Now what?"

"Now—"

The phone rang, and they all jumped a foot.

Lenny answered it, and handed it wordlessly over to Di. *Dave,* he mouthed, as she took it.

She noticed that her hand was shaking as she took the handset from him. "It's Di," she said.

"Yeah, listen, I haven't got much time." His voice was low, and the noise in the background suggested a kitchen or a nightclub in the process of being set up for opening.

"Go."

"Jeffries and the Jap took hostages to make sure your boyfriend stays quiet. Gypsy kids; around a dozen, I think. So far, they're okay, but they're scared. I thought about trying to get them out; I figured out that I can't. Jeffries figures on using 'em for dinner when he doesn't need 'em anymore, and that'll be in about three days by the plan, but could be sooner if the new place he's putting together gets finished before then. There's also the fact that Jason may make a try for the kids. He's low enough. Got that?"

"Yeah," she said, her stomach sinking. *Gods. He's upped the ante, hasn't he. Now we've got no choice. It'll have to be tonight.*

"They've got me scoped for playing guard tonight, after the gig, so the Master and the Jap can go hunting first. Hot item—Jeffries and Jason are at each other's throats—"

"Dave—I hate to ask you—"

"Ask. But make it quick."

"Can you see to it that the Japanese goes out hunting alone?"

Brief silence, and the sounds of moving furniture. "I think so. Won't take much. Egg Jason on, so the boss figures he'd rather have him under his eye. Maybe hint I've seen Jason scoping out the door to where the kids are stashed. Tell him I'll go out last, with Doug. You're coming in?"

"You know I can't tell you that," she replied.

Dave paused for a long moment. "Listen, baby," he said softly, "I'm on your side. And I—did a little hunting myself; tried to get ones that had it coming. Last night, after I left you. I'm up to strength, like maybe as good as Doug. They figure I've bought into their scene, so they trust me now. I'll see if I can't keep people from hunting until after the gig, like hint to Doug that Doro is keeping an eye on 'em, hint to Doro that Jason may try something; that should get 'em all good and irritated with each other. You've got an ally behind the lines; one who'll do whatever it takes. Okay?"

"Dave—" Her voice broke.

"Do what it takes, baby. I will, too. Dig? There's a point where you gotta commit." A long pause. "I think I found mine. I know you had yours a long time ago."

There was a muffled voice in the distance. "Yeah?" she heard Dave call back. "Okay, I'm on the way." Then, "Do it, baby. You got more people to think about than just us. Ciao."

Click.

She hung the phone up, slowly, feeling as if somebody had just hit her in the back of the head with a board.

"Who?" she heard André say. She hadn't even heard him come back. When she didn't immediately reply, he shook her shoulders impatiently. *"What did he say?"*

She blinked, and focused on his anxious face. "That was Dave. The leader has taken hostages, André—against you. Gypsy children—"

"Sacré merde—"

His face had hardened, chilled—became the face of a practiced killer who knows better than to get angry.

"That is what the *Rom baro*—the leader—told me. What else did he say?"

He could kill with just the look in his eyes, right now.

She swallowed. "Dave said he expects Jeffries to hold them for another three days or so; evidently he's keeping them until their new safe house is ready."

"The *Rom baro* did not know where the children were taken, although he said that those who took them made an effort to ensure he knew *why*," André muttered. "Bastard, preying upon *children*. His quarrel is with me, not them. My poor Rom. They rightly fear for the children."

"Dave also said that he doesn't trust Jason not to go after the kids if he thinks he can get away with it."

André swore, then bent his head and rested his chin on his fist, face brooding, obviously thinking. "Definitely tonight, then, do you think? *I* would prefer it so."

"Tonight or not at all, love. I don't think we'll have a better chance," she told him, choosing her words with care. *I don't know that we have any chance, but the odds get longer with every hour. They haven't figured out Dave's gone over yet—but they could.* "There seems to be dissension in the ranks, and Dave's going to play on it. He's going to use it to keep them all from hunting until after they're through at the club. Then he thinks he can get the *gaki* to go out alone. He says—" She swallowed hard again. "He says that he'll back us. *He* thinks that we should move tonight. I think that since Jeffries must know that you know about the hostages by now, he won't expect you to make a move."

Oh, Dave—

André raised his head, his eyes hard and unreadable. "Is there any chance, do you think, that this could be a trap?"

"There's always the chance; I don't think it likely."

He brooded again. "The four of us when freshest will face the strongest and most dangerous of them."

"Exactly," she agreed. "If we have any chance at all against them, it will be if we can take out the *gaki* first."

"And we have the ally in the rear," he reminded her, his momentary glance at her sharpening, then remaining, while his expression softened. "*Chérie,*" he said quietly. "I now like the young man very much."

She wiped her burning eyes with the back of her hand. "So do I, love," she replied, thinking of the last words on the phone. "So do I."

They waited in Keith's car, parked by the mouth of the alley behind HeartBeat. André and Di had made brief forays, each in the places they were strongest. The band van was parked in that alley; André had made certain of that. Jeffries was *not* at the club, for Di had gone just inside the door to quick-scan the whole building, and had come up with only three psivamps. Presumably he was guarding the hostages.

The alley dead-ended at the other end. None of the band members were going to get past the car. True to Dave's promise, none of the band members left the club itself. They *might* have taken victims inside the club or the alley, but Di didn't think they would. Not if they were as divided as Dave seemed to think. They wouldn't want to turn their backs on each other.

None of the four in the car entered the club after Di had scouted and reported that the "Master" had not joined his protégés. It seemed safest that way.

Di and André huddled together under a quilt in the back seat, Keith and Lenny in the front. It was cold; well below freezing outside the car, and not that much warmer inside. They were trying to keep their heads down, trying to make the car look empty, so they didn't dare run the engine for the heat.

Di held her watch up to catch the light from the street lamp on the corner, sighed when she saw the time, and tucked her numb hands under her arms. In the front seat, Keith and Lenny were talking, murmurs far too soft to be really heard, but the tone sounded suspiciously like pillow talk.

She closed her eyes for a moment, and put another glaze of protection on them. André's arm tightened around her. "They will have those two only through me," he said softly in her ear.

She twisted a little so that she could whisper to him without the lovebirds in the front seat overhearing. "How did you know what I was thinking?"

He stroked her shoulder. "I told you, I am sensitive to thought under some circumstances. *You* are falling under those circumstances, *chérie.*"

"So you know—"

"How very long our odds are? *Certainement.* I knew it all along. Nevertheless, we shall strive to beat those odds. I am, and always have been, a gambler."

She had to know. Even if it hurt. "Last night—"

"Was *not* because of the long odds." His lips brushed the top of her head. "It—was—is—because I have come, foolishly perhaps, to care very much for you. It is because I wish very much to have the pleasure of repeating last night with you many times in the future. Provided you have no objection."

She let out the breath she had been holding in. "No objections here."

"*Bien.*"

"But those two—" She nodded at the front seat.

"Come first. I have been a man of war, Diana. Civilians, however well intentioned, are to be protected at all costs. As I said, they fall only when I am no longer capable of interposing myself. Or you are. Yes?"

"Yes." She stared at the glare of streetlight on the dirty window, and wriggled her numb toes in her boots. "We think very much alike. I just hope if that happens they have the sense to run instead of playing hero."

"So do I. The time, *chérie?*"

She pulled her arm out from under the quilt and squinted at the watch dial. Her heart began racing, whether from fear or anticipation, she couldn't tell.

Probably a bit of both.

She cleared her throat and raised her voice a bit. "The club just closed. Figure fifteen minutes, max. You hear that, guys?"

Keith answered. "We hear." The seat creaked as they disentangled themselves from blankets and each other. Di and André sat up and did the same. At that moment she felt more alone than she ever had in her life.

"I think my nose is gonna fall off," Lenny mourned. Keith laughed, and said something too low for Di to make out, but Lenny hit him mockingly.

She caught the sound of an engine starting from the alley, and extended a tentative probe—

—void. Hunger. Anger, held barely in check.

"Heads up, people," she warned. "Or down, rather. Here they come—"

Lights flooded the alley; van lights on bright, plus fog lights. The van pulled out of the alley mouth with a blast of horn, and screeched around the corner on two wheels. If there had been anything on the street, it would have been forced over.

"—and they're not happy," she concluded.

"Good for Dave," Keith said quietly. "All right, go for it, Di. I'm on their tail." He pulled quietly out into the street, making no attempt to keep up with the van. That wasn't the plan; they weren't going to have to follow the van itself.

She closed her eyes, and reached for the sense of *Dave*. She found it; she hardly recognized it. Tonight, unlike last night, he had himself under control, no longer torn by the terrible hunger—

For one joyful moment she thought that perhaps she *had* done him some good. Then she remembered what he'd said, that he'd hunted last night. And she Looked more closely, and Saw that the only reason he was in control was that the voracious hunger was still sated.

She felt a tear trickled down her cheek; felt someone wipe it tenderly away.

"Di, I just lost the van," Keith said softly.

She oriented, eyes still closed. "North," she said distantly. "They've turned north. One block, I think."

"Right." The car swayed and André braced her as they made a turn. "Still no luck. They're not in sight."

She located herself; located Dave in relation to that. "A little more west. About two blocks. Then north again."

"Right."

Dave wasn't driving; one of the others, the one not in so much of a rage, was. That wasn't anger driving, it was just recklessness; the one driving had a fine disregard for the safety of anyone or anything else. His carelessness was so much him that she suspected he'd always been that way. The third seethed with anger, and with hunger; given the feeling of temper, that one must be Jason. Dave must have been baiting him tonight. The fourth—Di couldn't read. It wasn't even remotely human. She caught a touch of smug superiority, and a sense of detachment and a great deal of alienness. She pulled away before it could sense her and scanned it from a comfortable distance.

It. Definitely it. This thing had no more sexuality than a snail.

A snail.

That thought sent her back, probing delicately, so caught in concentration that she wasn't even aware of her own body.

It was a hermaphrodite, the gaki, *both male* and *female. Capable of reproducing all on its own.*

And, in this new home, protected on the hunt by its allies, with a secure base to operate from, and an abundance of prey, it was contemplating doing just that.

"Di—"

The shaking of her shoulders brought her back, with-drawing as carefully as she had probed.

"What?"

"I've lost them again."

She shivered with reaction, now that she was no longer in contact with the thing. "Two more blocks west," she said absently. *Do I tell them? Would it do any good?*

André spoke into her ear. "*Chérie,* what is amiss? You tremble."

She opened her eyes again, sure of her line to Dave, and leaned toward him. "The *gaki,*" she said, her teeth chattering, her heart in her throat. "It likes the setup it's got. As soon as things get settled, it's going to spawn. It's a hermaphrodite."

"*Merde.*" His lips were compressed into a tight line. "I had a thought that if the thing was not human, it might not have human motivations. And I wondered if it might be looking to nest. But I had hoped the damned thing needed male and female."

"No such luck."

She heard him take a deep breath. "We had little choice before, Di, but now we have none. We must destroy that thing."

He finally called me Di. "You took the words right out of my mouth."

"Whatever it costs."

She closed her eyes. *Even my soul. Lady have mercy on me.* "Whatever it costs," she repeated sadly.

"Except that." He touched her cheek, and her eyes flew open. "No, *chérie.* Not that. I shall see to it."

A little of the tension inside her eased, though not the fear. *At least I've got somebody who cares enough and is levelheaded enough to give me the shiv if it all goes sour. And probably make sure it's painless. That's something. That's a lot.*

"*Chérie—*" he breathed in her ear. "I am as frightened as you. I truly am. I am frightened *for* you. You may rely upon me—I shall not let that thing have you."

She groped for his hand, found it, and squeezed it.

"Di?" That was Keith, from the front seat.

"What?" she asked, clamping her jaw down to keep her teeth from chattering.

"They're pulling over."

She sat up straighter and craned her neck to see over the back of the seat. They seemed to be in an area of former small industries; lofts, mostly—some of the places still had business signs in their windows, but there were too many cars parked on the street for this time of night, and more than one of the lofts had hanging plants in the windows, and psychedelic posters visible from the street.

A few blocks ahead of them, the band van was pulling over to the side of the street. Just as Di caught sight of it, the lights went out.

"Okay, we know where they're stopping. Don't slow down or speed up, cruise right on by. I'll catch where they're going."

As they passed the van, the last of the musicians was getting out of the back; the rest were nowhere to be seen. Light shone momentarily at a door that opened and closed, giving a brief glimpse of a staircase leading up. Di narrowed her eyes, and briefly brushed Dave's mind.

Third floor. Empty up, empty down. Okay.

   She didn't dare stay any longer than that—she had no notion of Jeffries's capabilities, nor the *gaki*'s, and no idea if they were or were not sensitive to psi or magic.

   "Down three blocks, then over two," she told Keith. "Then find a place to park."

   She felt André take her hand and hold it. She squeezed back, and tried to feel brave.

   But she couldn't help but notice that she was beginning to glow, very, very faintly.

FOURTEEN

For once there weren't *enough* shadows.

In fact, there wasn't much cover at all around here.

This was not a good area to be trying anything covert. But if truth were to be known—it was a safer place for a confrontation than a real residential neighborhood would have been.

Safer on the noncombatants, that's for sure.

Di was about half a block behind the boys, plastered into the three inches worth of concealment offered by one of the doorways. *Plenty of time to work into position, too.*

Keith had pulled over into a parking space about six city blocks from their target. André had moved out first—

And once he was five feet from the car, I couldn't spot him. No wonder the legend is that vampires turn into bats or mist. I have no idea where he went.

She could hear the boys' footsteps up ahead of her, echoing through the clear, cold air. She centered, and paused to assess the situation ahead.

And I can't tell where André is now. I can't Feel him at all. Nothing up there but the boys. He was right; his shielding is at least as good as mine, if not better.

Which reminds me; better start thinking like a brick wall.

Behind André were Keith and Lenny, playing bait to the *gaki.* Sooner, rather than later, Hidoro would leave the apartment. He'd be hungry; she had Felt his hunger as they trailed the van. She hoped that he would be looking for something right on his block, if he could get it; the alliance had no stake in keeping things quiet in *this* neighborhood, not when they intended to leave it in a few days.

Seeing Lenny and Keith strolling toward him—that would be like a kid hearing the bell of the ice-cream truck.

That's what Di and André were counting on, anyway.

Di followed behind the boys, since she figured she was a lot more likely to be detected by the *gaki* than André was. That bracketed the boys with protection. When the *gaki* spotted them and moved in on them, she and André were going to get the boys out of the way and trap the *gaki* between them. Short of flying, it wasn't going to get away from them.

And maybe, just maybe, it had gotten so used to hunting with a partner on watch it would forget about being careful. Maybe it was so used to being invulnerable it would forget that it had a couple of weaknesses.

Di peered cautiously out of her doorway; to her left, silhouetted in the streetlight, the boys, just sauntering along as if they were out for a little midnight stroll. To her right, empty street. Nothing in sight but piles of dirty, granulated snow hiding the curbs. She peered left again, sizing up the territory. One streetlight on the corner; the alley that the boys were just now reaching. A couple of parked cars, and more hummocks of dirty snow. Not much in the way of conceal-ment until she reached that alley.

Now—do I scoot for cover like a commando, or act like somebody who belongs around here?

Act like I belong, I guess . . .

She stepped out of the doorway; paused, as if she had just gotten into her coat, and tugged her jacket sleeves down, then headed in the boys' wake. Her next hiding place was halfway up the block—that al-ley mouth, a black slash across the middle of the block of industrial brick.

But before she got there, something stepped out of its shadows.

Hell—don't tell me there's a civilian insomniac strolling right out into the middle of—

She reached for it—touched *alien.*

Hidoro.

Oh, shit! Now *where do I—there.* She threw herself to one side and managed to squeeze herself behind the bulk of a parked car be-fore he glanced her way. She peered out from beneath the rear bumper, keeping her head at street level. The *gaki* stared up her side of the street for a long, uneasy moment, before turning to look after the boys.

But once he'd spotted them, he headed purposefully in their di-rection.

She gave him a few minutes to get past that alley, then scrambled from behind the car, sneakers getting soaked and slipping in the snow. She launched herself at a dead run after him.

And her heart spasmed when she saw the tableau beneath the white glare of the streetlight.

Lord! Too late—no!

The boys clung together; Hidoro faced them. The *gaki* had them pinned somehow; he wasn't more than five feet from them, and they weren't moving, weren't even trying to escape. Their faces were white and blank with fear.

The thing was already turning into its other form—

Gods!

She *reached* and readied a levin bolt, not sure it would do any good, but it would get there before *she* would—

Someone else beat her to it.

Between one blink of an eye and the next, André was *there.*

She didn't see him *anywhere,* but he was there, shouldering the boys aside so hard that they fell to their knees, placing himself between the *gaki* and them, so that they were sheltered behind him.

Relief—

It made her stumble, but she caught herself, and she didn't slow; she still had to bracket the thing herself, still had to take her place on the line. André was counting on her.

"Come, m'sieur," André said clearly; his eyes glittered, and his mouth was a tight, thin line of anger. He was in a half-crouch, balanced on the balls of his feet, like a street fighter. He made a little beckoning motion with his right hand, and smiled, a hard, furious smile. "Come, you want them, you take them through *me.*"

Lenny scrambled farther out of the way, grabbing Keith's sleeve and taking his lover with him. Keith shook his head dazedly; then managed to get to his feet and hauled Lenny up by the back of his coat. They began backing away, step by slow step, eyes still on the *gaki.*

Come on, *you guys—you're supposed to get out of the way and watch for the others while we deal with the soul-sucker!*

They were arguing about that, it seemed—Lenny shaking his head vehemently, and continuing to back away, Keith stalling, pulling at his sleeve, their breath puffing about them in white clouds—

But she had no time to worry about them, because the *gaki* was reaching for something, something under his jacket, stuck in the waistband of his pants—

—pulling out a set of *nunchaku.*

A weapon of wood—

Which, as André had told her, was the *only* thing besides sunlight that could hurt or kill him.

"*No!*"

She launched herself desperately at them, not hoping for anything more than to knock André away from the deadly weapon. She did better than that; she knocked him to the pavement *and* managed to intercept the chuk heading for his temple with her shoulder.

They tumbled together in a heap; she rolled, cursing as she hit her bruised shoulder, and came up on her feet, and at the ready.

Her shoulder throbbed, which did nothing to improve her temper. "*My* turn, you bastard," she snarled, and put her shields up to full. Predictably enough, she started to glow. Not enough to put André off, but enough to notice.

The *gaki* held the chuks in both hands and smiled—she Felt something battering at the outside of her shields. Behind her, she heard André climbing to *his* feet.

"Nunchaku," she said shortly, never for a microsecond letting her attention slip from the *gaki*. "Wood, André."

She heard a muttered "*merde,*" and his footsteps retreating slowly.

The creature before her seemed puzzled that whatever it was he'd tried to do to her had no effect. "What are you going to do, *gaki?*" she asked in a growl. "If you stay in *that* form, you have to deal with me. If you go to the other, André can take you. You're trapped."

It stared at her, face utterly *blank;* it might as well have been a department-store mannequin. It was wearing black, head to toe; in this light she couldn't tell if it was the band's stage gear or not. "I have to give you a choice," she said to that expressionless face. "I don't like it, but I have to. If you give up, I'll see what I can do about you without killing you. If you choose to fight me—"

It didn't give her a chance to finish, not that she cared, or really *thought* it would give itself up. But the gesture *had* to be made, regardless.

It charged her, chuks blurring in its hands. She danced out of the way, sneakers making a scuffing sound on the salty sidewalk. *Barely* out of the way, and barely in time.

Oh gods—

He whirled around his own center and lashed out at her as he recovered.

Oh gods—he's better than I am.

She ducked out of the way, then had to make a dive and a roll to get out from under a side kick.

I'm in very deep trouble.

She flung out her hand, and hit him with the levin bolt she'd held in readiness. As she'd half expected, it had no effect.

His magic doesn't get through my shields, mine doesn't get through his. I could try a psi bolt instead—

But first she had to get out of the way of the chuks.

She scrambled back and blasted it at him. He shook his head and faltered a little, but a bolt that would have left Lenny blinded and on his knees with a headache only gave the *gaki* a moment's pause.

André could get him, if he didn't have the chuks—

The *gaki* grinned toothily at her, and moved in again. She dodged the chuks, only to run right into a hand-foot combination that knocked her to the pavement. She rolled with it, and came back up—but got to her feet with a muffled cry as pain shot up her left leg from her ankle.

Oh shit. *He's better than me, and now I'm handicapped.*

I'm not gonna survive this one.

Fear flooded her. Her aura flared; he squinted a little, but it didn't seem to affect him the way it had affected André.

All I can do is buy time and wear him down.

The hilt of her atheme, the little knife she had at the nape of her neck, reminded her of one more option. *And maybe take him with me when I go. Betcha there's enough power in there to make him notice if I do a kamikaze with it in my hands.*

That last thought steadied her, oddly enough. *When you've got nothing left to lose*—The light around her dimmed, and finally died, as she concentrated on surviving the next encounter—taking them one at a time.

She evaded two more attacks with increasingly less success, acquiring two more bone bruises on her forearms. She concentrated with all her might on the *gaki's* eyes, waiting for them to tell her what his next move would be—

:The greatest swordsman in the world fears not the second greatest, but the worst. Why?:

She shook her head and danced back in surprise at hearing a voice in her mind, and flung a psi bolt at the thing to distract it a little while she recovered. That thought had *not* come from her, not even her own subconscious!

Who then?

André—? Telepathy was *not* one of her strong suits—she got feelings, not thoughts—usually. But André had said something about *that* this evening, too . . .

:Think, woman! Why?:

But she knew; it was exactly like one of sensei's riddles. The greatest fighter fears the worst, because an amateur can't be predicted; he'll make the "mistake" that creates an opening—

So make a mistake—he knows exactly how good you are. He won't be expecting a dumb move—

She feinted, working him around into range, luring him closer. This wasn't a trick she'd be able to repeat—so it was going to have to *work*—

He drove the chuks straight down at her. Only this time, instead of diving *away* from the blow, she lunged *into* it—and caught the descending stave in her left hand.

The *crunch* of her own bones breaking was the second-worst sound she'd heard in her life. Before her hand had a chance to start hurting, she closed it as best she could, curled her whole body around it, and pivoted, carrying the chuks out of his hand. They clattered to the ground, and she finished her pivot inside his guard, thrusting upward with all of her momentum behind the heel of her right hand. It impacted with his nose—

A second *crunch,* and a scream like nothing she'd ever heard before. But now her hand was screaming in its own strident voice, and she collapsed to her knees, folding up around it.

No matter. André took the place she'd surrendered—proving that he did, indeed, have "a knowledge of savate."

One kick took out the *gaki's* left knee. A second to his chin snapped his head back as he was falling.

A third pulped his temple, and when he hit the pavement, he did not rise.

André stood over the prone body, his face a mask of cold rage, panting slightly. Di struggled to her feet, her hand protesting every movement. She staggered to André's side; he caught her and held her as she stumbled into him, her hand clutched to her chest.

"Anything?" he asked quietly.

Recklessly she abandoned shielding, opened herself up completely.

Nothing.

Then—

One moment there was a body there.

The next, an evil cloud of black smoke.

"Jesus H. Christ!" she shrieked, scrambling back away from it, expecting it to follow her. Her aura flared, making patterns of light and shadow dance.

André grabbed her elbow and shoved her behind him—

—and the cloud billowed up, rising, coming at them—

—but it was losing color, losing cohesiveness.

Even as they took that in, it faded, thinned, and finally drifted away on an errant little breeze.

She stared at the place it had been, still sensing nothing. André walked forward, slowly, until he was standing where the body had been, where there was now nothing but a pile of black satin. He poked it with his toe, frowning.

"Nothing?" he said, finally.

"It—it's gone," she replied through the throbbing of her hand, around teeth gritted against the pain. She got her jacket open and pulled her left arm out of the sleeve, then zipped the jacket back up with her arm held against her chest by the tight fabric in a kind of improvised sling.

"*This* one—" Suddenly he looked up, and looked around. "Lenny and Keith—where are they?"

"They were supposed to—"

But there was no sign of them on the street.

Their eyes met in a flash of realization.

"They didn't—" André began.

She scanned, quickly—and found them precisely where she had not wanted them to be.

"They did—oh gods—it's them against *three* psivamps—"

André cursed, and grabbed her good hand; he set off at a run down the street, pulling her after him.

Her heart sank when she didn't see the boys waiting for them at the foot of the staircase. There was no one guarding the door either, not from their side nor the enemy's; they pounded up the splintery wooden stairs without hindrance. Over the racket of their own feet they heard the sounds of a fight above. André kicked at the door on the third landing and it slammed open. The two of them flung themselves without hesitation into the chaos beyond.

Light from overturned lamps spotlighted two knots of struggle, and the shadows of the fighters sprawled huge and inelegantly on the wall. Di identified the combatants in a glance—first and foremost, there was no sign of Jeffries. To the right, between two chairs, one on its side, was Dave, grappling with a slim, dark-haired man. It looked to Di as though they were evenly matched, both of them locked into a stalemate. To the right, on the floor next to the wall, Keith was down, and not moving. At the same moment as they burst through the door, Lenny crashed into the wall beside him, thrown there by a tall blond. Lenny started to struggle to his feet; the blond, his face contorted with fury, vaulted an overturned chair and strode across the wreck of the living room toward him, oblivious to the two newcomers.

"André—the children—" That was all she had time to say before she launched herself at the blond. There was a flicker of motion at her right—and André was gone.

Pain shot up her leg from her maltreated ankle; she ignored it. She knew she had no second chance, and didn't dare miss. So no fancy stuff, no flying sidekicks. Just a rush as primitive as a football tackle, meant to knock him off his feet; one she could control enough to turn into a roll to bring her back *up* on *hers.*

He saw her coming at the last moment, but not in time to get completely out of the way. She hit him sideways, which sent him spinning into an overturned couch. She didn't land quite the way she wanted, and her hand howled at her when she hit the ground with more of a jolt than she'd intended.

It shook her; she was a shade late in getting to her feet, and a shade shaky when she faced him again. She edged sideways, knees bent, in a posture equally suited to attack or defense, until she stood as a defiant wand of protection between him and the boys.

He had already gotten to his feet. He hesitated for a moment, only now *seeing* her—she used his hesitation to study him, look for weaknesses. He was a good foot and a half taller than she was, with an insolently handsome face, and long, wild blond hair. His eyes were narrowed in anger, his jaw clenched. Plainly, he did *not* like being downed. He doubly did not like being downed by a woman the size of the average ballet dancer.

This is Jason, she decided. *And I hurt him in his macho. That's going to make him even madder than he was—which will probably enhance his psi abilities, even if it takes away from his control. He could be more than I can occultly handle now . . . . This may have been the wrong thing to do—*

Sure enough, a delicate probe in the long moment they stood staring at one another had to be retracted quickly inside her shields before it got swallowed up.

He's not stronger than my active defenses, but he is stronger than the passive shields I put on the boys. He'll be able to unravel those shields and feed on them before he actually takes the boys. Oh gods, I can't, I don't dare let him get near them or he'll have them—

Somewhere beyond Jason's shoulder, in the darkness that marked an open doorway, there was a muffled pounding. André, presumably, had found the children, and was trying to break down the door to their prison.

Jason didn't seem to hear the noise, didn't seem to notice Dave and the other band member thrashing in a tangle of arms and legs on the other side of the room. He was targeted in on Di, with a single-mindedness that was uncanny and completely inhuman.

She shifted her stance a little, watching his eyes follow everything she did, seeing his very posture shift to match hers. *It's more than that he's mad at me. It's—a lot more than that.* She shifted again, winced at pain from her ankle, and caught a surge of hunger from him.

Oh gods—he's gone into feeding mode. And I'm the chef's special—I've got to break that, if I can. At least for a minute, long enough to distract him.

"Jason," she said aloud, as forcefully as she could.

And reached behind her head, pulling out the atheme.

I'm not about to throw it, and lose my only weapon. But a knife is a knife. But Power is Power.

The blond started, his head jerking a little, his eyes dilating briefly. Then those chill eyes focused again on her. There *seemed* to be a little more sense in them, although he didn't reply.

"Jason, we took out Hidoro, so don't expect the cavalry to come charging over the hill."

—But where the hell is Jeffries? I don't like it that he's not in sight.

He smiled; actually smiled. "Don't expect *me* to shed tears over that," he replied. "Doro was no buddy of mine."

There was a cry of pain from the struggling knot at the side of the room, but the struggle continued. Jason's eyes flickered briefly in that direction, but returned to her before she could take advantage of the distraction.

She gestured with the blade; if he could sense Power—

He could; his eyes widened.

"I'm no flyweight. I've been at this game longer than you have. I'll offer you what I offered him," she said, with a calm that she did not feel. "Give it up now, and I'll see what I can do for you without taking you out. You *have* to see at least some of what I am. If there's a way to help you—"

He interrupted her with a peal of laughter, his expression harsh and sarcastic. "*Help* me? Why in hell would I want *help?* Christ, chickie, you're a bigger fool than Davey is—"

"Or you are," she retorted angrily. "What goes around, comes around, Jason. If you make yourself into a big bad shark, sooner or later a killer whale's gonna come by that figures *you* look tasty."

"I'll take my chances on that, honey." He grinned. "That little toy is cute enough, but you haven't convinced me that *you're* any big threat."

He'd relaxed just the tiniest bit. *Probably figures that if I'm talking instead of attacking it's because I'm not in any great shape.*

Which I'm not—but I'm probably not as badly off as he thinks. Besides, all I have to do is buy time for André to get those kids out—

The pounding ended in a crash. Jason jumped, and his head swung around. It was enough of an opening.

She crossed the space between them in a limping sprint, ending it with a kick with her good foot aimed to take out one knee, and a slash at his face. It would have worked, except that he was faster than she'd thought; he ducked the slash, and the kick went into the couch frame instead.

She bounced back, staggering a little, blinded for a moment with pain and unbalanced with one hand immobilized. When she could see again, Jason's eyes were pits of rage, and she could Feel him battering away at her shields, seeking a weak spot to exploit. "Bitch!" he snarled. "I'm gonna—"

She drew on the stored Power in the blade and gave him no time to elaborate on what he was going to do to her.

Because she heard the sound of many faint footsteps from the dark—and over on the side, Dave was on the *bottom* of the struggle.

She feinted with the knife, then lashed out with an elbow strike and caught Jason in the breastbone with it, gritting her teeth against the screaming of hand and ankle. He grunted and staggered backward. She came on, tiring, and in pain, but this was the only advantage she was likely to get and—

Crack.

In the confined space of the room, the explosion sounded like the impact of a lightning bolt. She jumped back as a bullet struck the floor between herself and Jason, and pivoted on her bad ankle to face the new threat.

Jeffries.

With a gun, and a sadistic smile on his face.

She froze. The fight in the corner had stopped; now the guy she didn't know separated himself carefully from Dave, and backed away. Dave didn't move from where he was sprawled on the floor, in the lee of an overturned armchair.

"I believe it is game and match, hmm?" Jeffries said smoothly. "David, David, I had hoped you had come to your senses—well, apparently not. I do suggest that you, and *you*, young lady, place the witchblade on the floor and surrender. Not that you and your friends won't meet ultimately the same end, but your choice is between painful and excruciatingly painful." He raised his voice. *"And you can take those children back where you found them, young man—"*

Her mind, which had gone into stasis, unstuck. It took a moment to register. First came shock. Then immobility.

Then fear. Overwhelming fear. The kind that used to paralyze her. And didn't. Not anymore.

Light.

Her shield aura flared, high in the UV and illuminating the room like a floodlight, brighter than a photo flash, and *much* more potent in that moment than the weak winter sunlight.

Jeffries screamed.

There was a clatter as his gun fell to the floor. The man was moaning in pain, and by squinting through her own glare, she could see that he was clawing at his face. He collapsed slowly on his knees, babbling and weeping now, as if the light were cutting right into his brain.

She fed the light with all her strength and the last of the stored Power in the atheme, knowing the brightness to be her only defense. *Maybe it is eating into his brain. I hope so. I hope it burns your neurons to a crisp, you sonuvabitch!*

But she was weakening; running out of energy fast, and maintaining the light was taking a lot more out of her than she had guessed it would. She heard a scuffle of feet behind her, and kicked backward without looking. The impact of her foot in someone's solar plexus told her that her instincts were still working, although the move cost her in red agony from her abused foot. The flare of pain through the black hole of hunger told her she'd gotten Jason.

I can't keep this up much longer—

"André, *the kids—*" She gulped; it was even getting hard to breathe. "Get them out of here."

Running feet; half a dozen shadow shapes flitting across her own glare, one of them leading a taller one by the hand—

Right, he can't take this either, he probably can't see a thing. But the kids are getting him out. Thank the gods.

She sheathed the atheme behind her neck and backed up, feeling her way across the floor, kicking aside lamps and unidentifiable debris. She moved step by slow and uncertain step, until she reached the area where she *thought* Lenny and Keith were, and felt around with her bad foot until she hit something soft. It groaned.

She knelt, carefully, and reached out with her right hand, and shook the leg she encountered. It was too well muscled to be Keith. "Lenny. *Lenny.* Come on, wake up—"

Her light was fading discernibly, and with it, her strength.

"Uhn—" Finally a moan that was a response. "Di?"

"Get up, get Keith, and get out. I can't hold these jokers much longer."

"But—"

"*Move!*" she snarled, nerves ready to snap, and not inclined to take any back talk.

She could make them out now, and that was a bad sign. Lenny pulled himself slowly to his feet, then reached down and helped Keith up. The artist was not in good shape; he leaned heavily on Lenny, and didn't seem more than half conscious. She kept herself interposed between them and the others—

But the light was fading faster, and they were *not* going to make it to the door before it was gone.

Then, like the voice of an angel, Dave spoke out of the shadows cast by his overturned chair.

"Di, baby, I've got the gun. I can't see *now*, but I wasn't looking at you when you flamed on. Get your two buddies out of here, and I'll take care of my *good friends.*"

The last two words were spoken in a snarl of hate.

She hesitated. Lenny and Keith did not. They were almost at the door—

"Davey—" she began. "Davey, I—"

"Don't *worry* about me, just *go!*" She took one step toward him, and saw him shrink away.

"Davey—"

"Go." Then, very softly, "It's okay, babe. It's okay. I know exactly what I'm doing. Listen—be happy, Di. Just—be happy."

One of the others nearest Dave started to move; now she could see perfectly well, her light was no worse than sunlight. She pointed. "Dave!"

He whirled. "*Forget it,* Doug—Di, get the hell *out* of here!"

Seeing that he was looking away from her, toward Doug, she put the last of her failing strength into a final flare, and fell out the door, slamming it behind her and overbalancing, and tumbling down the first flight of stairs—

Dave was waiting for one of them to make a move when Di slammed that door—and sure enough, Doug rushed him, his face an inhuman mask.

Calmly, dispassionately, Dave sighted and pulled the trigger.

The bassist made a choking sound, his eyes wide with surprise as the bullet hit him in the chest. He jerked once and collapsed, his momentum carrying him to Dave's feet.

Silence, and the smell of cordite. Dave kept his eyes on both of the other two. Jason hadn't gotten up yet. Jeffries stared at him out of red, watering eyes, his mouth hanging open in dumbfounded surprise, bloody scratch marks on his cheekbones where he'd clawed at his own face.

"Didn't think I knew how to use one of these, did you?" Dave asked softly. "Funny thing, you know? *She* taught me. Big wheel in the peace movement, and she taught me how to shoot a handgun. I thought she was crazy."

"David—" Jeffries began, his mouth working for a moment before the words came out. "David, there's really no need to be hasty—"

Dave took a deep breath, steadying the fury inside himself. "You asshole. No, I suppose you'd figure that, wouldn't you?"

"David, there is no reason why we can't use our power the way I described to you—"

"Yes there is," he interrupted coldly. "There damn well is. Because I'm going to kill you."

He pulled the trigger a second time; shooting for the head, not willing to take anything from Jeffries, not even the energy his slow death would give—

He heard the noise of unsteady footsteps beyond the door. Someone was limping painfully back up the stairs.

Dammit Di, I told you to get the fuck out of here—

He rounded on Jason, who was just rising from the floor where Di's kick had put him. He kept the gun trained on the blond, making his way slowly over to the door, where he locked it one-handed and shot home the bolt.

Just in time.

Di began pounding on it, crying out his name.

Crying.

No, babe. No.

"Hey look, man," Jason wheezed, spreading his hands wide. "Dave, we been friends a long time, right? Just—get on out of here. I'll—"

The vision of Jack's terrified face rose up between them, and the sound of his screams and Jason's laughter. Abruptly he couldn't take another word. *"Shut up!"* he screamed. "You goddamn dirty son of a bitch! You got us *into* this! Friends? What the hell was Jack, *friend?* You guys *ate* him!"

More than one shoulder was hitting the door now, and he could hear the wood splintering behind him. The doorframe was industrial grade, but it wasn't going to hold much longer.

"I'd like to make you hurt the way *he* hurt, the way those kids you ate hurt, you piece of shit," he said clearly and carefully. "But I don't have the time."

Jason's eyes widened, then narrowed for a moment, as if he were gauging the distance between them for a rush.

Dave didn't give him the chance.

"See you in Hell, you bastard," he said—and pulled the trigger a third time.

Silence filled the room now, a silence that had nothing to do with the clamor outside the door. A silence that said—

You can do it. You have the strength. You can be careful to take only the guilty, only the ones who prey on others. Or maybe Di'll be able to help you. Maybe she'll love you again, maybe not, but—you know she's always been able to pull you out of things before. Why shouldn't she be able to work a miracle this time?

It was such a seductive promise—so sweet—and so easy—

Then the hunger, that thing that coiled at the base of his spine, grumbled and roused from sleep. It raised its head, and looked about—

And felt Di outside the door. Unshielded, unprotected. Who would never know what hit her if he just *reached*—

Just reached. Like it was reaching now.

He pulled it back, even as it was reaching—and knew that he would never have the strength to do so a second time.

"No—" he said aloud. "No. Anything is better than that. Even Hell."

He put the warm barrel to his temple; took a last deep breath, and looked toward the door.

Oh, lady. Still trying to pull my fat out of the fire.

"Not this time, babe," he said. And squeezed.

She heard the first shot when she was still on the landing, and began to crawl back up toward the door. The second came while she was still on the stairs. By the time she reached the door and began pounding on it hysterically, it was locked.

When the third shot came, she redoubled her efforts, not sure why, only having a premonition—she never knew exactly when André arrived to lend his shoulder to hers, but suddenly there he was, and the door was yielding—

When the fourth shot rang out.

She cried out—Dave's name, or André, she didn't know. All she knew was blackness descending to end the pain.

Blackness, shot through with red lightning bolts of pain. Sometimes the sound of her own voice, strangely calm. Then—there was the car, for a moment, and Lenny's voice saying "Saint Francis. I know it sounds strange, but we've got a neopagan on the ER night shift. Ask for Doctor Grame."

Yeah, that's right—she thought, the realization fighting through pain into her conscious, then there was blackness again.

Another interval of darkness.

Then another interval of lucidity—the white lights of a hospital, and a vaguely familiar face. "Does it hurt when I do this?" the face was saying.

Someone did something unpleasant to her hand.

She knew him—from somewhere; the name "Doctor Grame" swam up to stare at her, and another, "Gwalchmai," one and the same person, confusingly enough—so she refrained nobly from kicking his teeth down his throat, or from screaming. "Yes," she whimpered, and felt nebulous shame at the tears pouring down her face.

Why am I crying? she thought. *It doesn't hurt that much—*

Then the doctor did something else, and it *did* hurt that much. She blacked out again, and only came to when someone did something equally rude to her ankle. *That* time she struck out, blindly, not remembering where she was, and only aware of pain and blindingly white light in her eyes. A hand caught her wrist and held it in a way that *should* have evoked a memory, but the memory couldn't get through the pain.

"I advise you," said an accented baritone, "to recall that she is a brown belt, and a bit delirious."

Baritone? I don't know any—Errant memory returned. *Oh. André.* She stopped fighting, and the doctor said something she couldn't hear. There was a pinprick in her arm—and the pain went away.

She floated for a while in a sea of haze, keeping her eyes closed, because to open them was too disorienting. They—whoever "they" were—were doing things to her hand and ankle, they were arguing

with André about admitting her to the hospital, but she no longer
cared. She was trying to recapture the past few hours. Bit by bit,
memory came back.

The gaki. *We got it alone, and fought it. I got hurt, we took it out.
The apartment. I went into full shield flare. I'm in power-drain shock.
Okay, that's why my brain isn't working. We won. Sort of.*

Davey—

She began crying again, this time without shame. It was cold by
now, and there was a sensation of movement. She opened her burning eyes briefly on darkness, and saw after a bit that she was in the
back seat of a car. Being held. By two somebodies.

Her mind, working in slow motion, finally identified them. André. And Lenny. Both holding her, both trying to comfort her. But
there was no comfort; Davey was dead, and all his beautiful music
dead with him, and she had failed him . . .

Weeping passed into exhaustion and exhaustion into more aimless drifting; after a while, she swam back up to consciousness again,
and noticed that someone was carrying her. She opened drug-hazed
eyes and saw the steps of her apartment building to her right; Keith,
supporting Lenny, just ahead of them. "I can walk—" she protested
to whoever was holding her so firmly. "You don't have to carry me."

"I believe the expression is, 'the hell you can,'" André replied dispassionately. "The doctor was most adamant about not putting
weight upon that ankle, and even more so about not allowing you to
walk where you might slip."

She closed her eyes, because the moving steps were making her
dizzy, and when she opened them again, André was putting her carefully down on her own couch.

Her brain was working slowly, but now it *was* finally working.
And a hundred consequences of this night's work were flashing
across it. She grabbed his arm as he started to move away, and peered
up at his sober, worried face, into his expressive eyes.

"I'm beginning to wake up," she said. "André, what happened . . .
after? What excuse did you give the hospital?"

"You do not remember?"

She shook her head. "Not a thing."

"When—we heard the last shot, you pushed me down the stairs
ahead of you; told me to get Keith while you and Lenny brought up
the rear. We ran, but when we were a block away, you told us to stop."
He gave her a very strange look. "You truly do not remember?"

"No. Honestly." *Bizarre. My gods. Sounds like somebody took me
over for a while. I sure wasn't that copacetic.*

"So, you told us to stop, and—'act casual, man,' is exactly what you said. You began singing, loudly, as if you were very drunk. Something about a 'whiskey bar'; young Lenny joined you. And at *precisely* that moment the police arrived. They passed us by without a second look. We reached Keith's car, and you proceeded to faint dead away." He grimaced. "Unsurprising, since the doctor informs me that you have torn the ligaments upon that ankle."

"I thought it hurt a little bit more than a sprain," she replied vaguely, still trying to figure out what had happened. *She* didn't know any songs about a "whiskey bar."

"We took you to the hospital; we asked for Doctor Grame, but before he could arrive, a most officious young man attempted to deal with you. You nearly"—his mouth twitched—"relocated his private parts to somewhere near his larynx."

"I don't remember that, either." *Her* mouth twitched. "Too bad."

"When Doctor Grame arrived, he wanted to put you into the hospital. I convinced him that this would not be wise; that your friends could care for you adequately. You were kinder to the doctor, although there was a point where I had to restrain you."

"I think I remember that—André, the fight—"

"Is already upon the news; there was a radio in the emergency room." He took her hands, and his eyes grew infinitely sad. "It was a good thing, your David did, that he locked the door against us. The police have no notion that there was anyone in the place except the four they found. They are reporting it as a quarrel over drugs."

"André—" Her throat closed. "All of them?" she whispered. He nodded, and looked down at their linked hands.

"He was very brave, and very wise, at the end. And at the end, he chose rightly. I shall treasure that memory of him. I think I shall always admire what he became." He sighed deeply. "He did what few have the strength of character to do; to overcome the consequences of his mistakes, and to take responsibility for them."

"There was so much he never had a chance to do—" She mourned for that as well as for him. Tears came, slower tears this time, like a quiet rain. André hesitated for a moment, and then took her into his arms, holding her close when she didn't resist him.

"*Chérie,*" he said quietly, "I did not guess he meant so much—"

"No." She sobbed into his shoulder. "No, it isn't that—it's that I failed him. I couldn't help him, André—I couldn't save him—"

"Ah," he replied, and held her until she had no more tears left.

———

She was resting in his arms, completely spent, when it occurred to her that the sky was growing lighter. "André—it's almost dawn," she said into his sweater.

"I know, *chérie,*" he replied. "I thought that I might avail myself of your couch once more before I return to my Lowara."

Once more? Then he's going—I never pictured him not being here.
She pulled away, slowly, and sat up.

"I thought you said something about last night not being the equivalent of the condemned man's last meal—"

"I did. But—" He looked away. "I did not intend to make an infernal nuisance of myself. I—I wish to give you time to consider things."

"Things?"

"Consequences, *chérie.*" He smoothed her hair behind her ears, and smiled faintly. "There are always consequences. For instance, you know, my Lowara feel that they owe you a great debt. They will not be happy until it is repaid."

She sighed, momentarily distracted. *Just what I need. Another karmic burden.* "I'm sure it'll all even out one of these days. Maybe I can hit them up for a lot of tarot readings."

He quirked an eyebrow at her, and settled back against the arm of the sofa. "You know that they call you the Starchild? For the brightness. They are almost as afraid of you as they were of the captors of their children."

She grimaced. "Lovely. So now I'm a Rom bogeyman."

He touched her cheek, gently, with one of his long, graceful hands. "Oh, not that. Something lower than a saint, but not so low as a 'bogeyman.'" He stood up, and faced the window, looking out at the false dawn. "Well, it is over. We worked well together, I think—"

He began to walk away from her.

"André—"

"I shall take my leave after sunset. Young Lenny said that he and Keith shall look in on you—"

"André—"

He stopped in mid-sentence, and looked back over his shoulder at her, expression unreadable.

"Top drawer of the desk. The brass box."

He turned around and walked slowly to the desk and put his hand hesitantly on the drawer pull, opening it as if he expected something to leap out at him. He took out the little brass box and opened it just as gingerly.

And held up the set of keys with an enigmatic frown on his face.

"I don't like the idea of somebody as vulnerable as you spending his daylight hours in public libraries and cheap movie houses," she said, trying to put her thoughts in order. She spoke slowly and carefully to keep the pain that was returning from creeping into her intonation. *I don't want his decisions based on the fact that I'm not exactly in top shape.* "Especially not—somebody I care for. Someday someone who knows what you are is going to feed you a nice thick stake."

Despite her best efforts, some of her pain must have shown in her face, if not her voice. He took a tiny white paper envelope out of his pants pocket and silently handed her a pair of pills, and she swallowed them dry.

"I thought we had agreed that it might be dangerous to become—entangled," he said, standing between her and the light, so that his face was in shadow. Just as it had been the night they met.

Children of the night. All of us. Him, me, Davey ... the night brought us together. Be damned if I'm going to let it take him away without a fight.

"We did," she admitted. "But we didn't discuss how dangerous it might be *not* to be entangled. You mentioned consequences. There are consequences there, too."

"True." He returned to her side, dangling the keys from his long, sensitive hand. "And would that be dangerous?"

"It might." She waited until he seated himself. "For you, because living the way you do, you're vulnerable. For me—" She faltered. *I hadn't thought about this, not really. But it's happened all the same. What I swore wouldn't. Ever.* "You're tied into me on a lot of levels, André. I like you, and I don't have to hide anything from you."

She took a very deep breath, and made the last confession. "I've been alone too much, and too lonely. You changed that, and I—I don't want to be alone anymore. I'd like you to stay. I'd like you to be with me. Please?"

He looked down at his hands, at the keys held loosely between them. Her heart sank when he didn't immediately reply.

"Well," he said finally, not looking up. "I prefer thinking that I am not a parasite. There is an ugly word for that, *chérie.*"

"I—could use some help—" she said ruefully, raising the plaster-encased bulk of her left hand.

"So I see." He looked a little happier.

She gave him a wry grin. "So tell me what you can do, besides the obvious."

"Well, so this is an interview?" His smile appeared, tentative, but there. "Very well, mademoiselle, I *can* type. And take dictation. I play

the violin passably well, so I might entertain you. I fear, however, that
I cannot cook."

"You said yourself we work well together. Would you be willing
to give me a hand with things like tonight?"

Please say yes—

"Hmm. Indeed, I could help you with other things. I do have certain talents." He tilted his head sideways, and his smile faded as he
considered her. "It will not be easy, Diana. I am what I am."

"So am I. No one's ever claimed *I* was easy to live with. Please,
let's just try."

He cupped his hand under her chin, and finally gave her that
slow, sweet smile she'd been hoping for. "Very well, *petite*," he said
softly. "We will try."

The drugs hit her then, and she swayed toward him. He caught
her in his arms—and then he caught her up, lifting her easily.

"Wh-what are you doing?" she gasped.

"Putting you to bed, *chérie*. Where you belong. If you will insist
on my being here, you must put up with my insistence upon certain
conditions." He looked at her sternly out of the corner of his eye as he
carried her toward the bedroom. "And one of those is that you must
spare your maltreated ankle."

She sighed as they passed the bedroom door and he flicked on the
light with his elbow. "I suppose I don't have any choice."

He put her carefully down on the side of the bed, pushing aside
the tumbled blankets. "No, you do not."

"But neither do you—"

She still had her arms around his neck, and she pulled him down
beside her, cast and bandaged ankle and all.

"Wh-what do you mean?" he asked, eyes going wide.

"I mean," she whispered into his ear, "once I get to feeling a bit
better, you're going to *have* to help me finish this blasted romance
novel—"

"I am?"

"Uh-huh." She nibbled on *his* neck. "Especially the research—"

BURNING WATER

Dedicated to
Mary Jean and J. R. Holmes,
who gave Diana a place to grow up

ONE

Lupe sobbed harshly, her voice muffled, as if smothered by the darkness all about her. She clawed at the rubble that hemmed her in; her finger-ends were surely raw and bloody, but *she* couldn't see them, and she was too hysterical to feel much pain. All she felt was panic, the panic of a trapped animal—for she was trapped helplessly beneath tons of rubble, rubble that, less than an hour ago, had been the twenty-story hotel in downtown Mexico City where Lupe worked as a maid.

Today was September 19, 1985. Mexico City had just experienced one of the worst earthquakes in its history.

Ironically enough, it was also Lupe's birthday.

Less than an hour ago she'd been happy. It had not much mattered that she'd had to work on her birthday; she had known that she was lucky to have this job at all. Less than an hour ago, she had descended the stairs to the cellar storeroom singing. It would only have been a few more hours, and then she'd have been off, free for the evening. There was going to be a party, cake—and handsome Joachim, who worked as a bellman, had promised to come. She had a new dress, red and soft, like rose petals, and Joachim liked red. One of the tourists had already given her a tip for bringing extra towels. And there had been a full, unopened bottle of wine left behind after the party in room 1242. She'd hidden it in her locker, for *her* party. It was going to be a good day, with a better evening to come.

The ashtrays she'd come seeking were kept in boxes next to the stairs; cheap little metal things that the tourists were always taking. Somebody had overfilled the particular box she reached for and several of them had fallen out and rolled under the staircase. She'd had to wedge herself under the staircase to reach them. She hadn't minded; the cellar was well lit, and she was small enough to fit beneath the staircase easily.

That was what had saved her.

For with no warning, the floor began to buck and tremble like a wild horse; the lights sparked and went out. She screamed, or thought she did—she couldn't hear her own voice in the shrieking of tortured metal and concrete. She'd been flung backward and against the wall, and hit her head, seen multicolored flashes of light, then nothing.

When next she could think, she was hemmed in on all sides by concrete and debris; trapped in the dark—a darkness so absolute that there was nothing she could compare it to.

The reinforced staircase had protected her; kept her from dying beneath the crumbling hotel.

She knew at once what had happened; Mexico City had suffered earthquakes before. But she had never been caught inside a building by one; never known anyone who had been buried alive like this.

Lupe had survived the quake. Now as she stared into the darkness, she realized slowly that she faced death in another, more painful form: suffocation, starvation, thirst—

Madre de Dios, she prayed wildly, *I'm only seventeen! I have always been good—I can't die—*

The air in her tiny, sheltered pocket was already growing stale. She panted in fear, and the air seemed to grow thicker and fouler with each breath. The sound of her breathing was a rasping in her own ears, for the silence was as absolute as the darkness. She rested her forehead on the wall in front of her, feeling her chest constrict and ache. How long before the air became unbreathable?

That fear was enough to make her tremble in every limb. But worse than the rock that hemmed her in, worse than the thickening air, worse than any of it was the terrible, menacing darkness all around her.

Lupe was afraid of the dark; she had been afraid of the dark for as long as she could remember. It was a vague fear she couldn't even define, just a feeling that there was *something*—waiting for her. Watching. A something that lived in the dark—no, it *was* the dark.

And it wanted Lupe.

But it was rarely "dark" in Mexico City, even in the early hours of the morning. Certainly it was never dark in the two-room apartment she shared with her sisters; the neon signs of the nightclubs across the street saw to that. Her night-fears had been easy to laugh at until this moment.

Now she was caught in the very heart of darkness; thick, hot darkness that seemed to flow sluggishly around her, seemed to be oozing into her very pores and trying to force itself down her throat until she choked on it.

She could feel it now—

She gasped, coughed, and frantically scrabbled again at the wreckage hemming her in; whimpering and hardly realizing she was doing so. She had barely enough room to crouch; impenetrable rubble formed a tiny pocket around her—like the pocket holding the larvae of a tourist's "jumping bean." But the larvae would grow wings and escape—

She never would. She would die here, and the dark would eat her bones.

She wailed, and pounded at the wall before her with aching hands. Trapped—trapped—

Lupe's mother had had no patience with her child's phobias. The census said they were Mestizo—but Paloma had told all her children that they were truly Azteca, and descended from priests. "Look for yourself, if you don't believe—" she had told them all, and more than once. "Go to the museum and see for yourself." And so, dutifully, they had gone—to see their own high-cheekboned, beaky profiles (so unlike most of their schoolfriends' round faces and snubbed noses) echoed at them from pots, from paintings, from bas-relief. "You are of noble blood, the blood of warriors," she had scolded Lupe when the girl confessed her nightmares. "How can you be so afraid?"

Mamacita, she cried out in her mind, *what good is noble blood when the earth shakes? What good is descent from priests when the dark comes to steal my breath?*

She sobbed, the thick air tasting of her own fear. The smell of her own sweat was rank, thickening the dark further. Her eyes were burning with tears as she continued to beat at the unyielding wall before her. She knew it was useless—but what else was there to do? It was either that, or curl into a ball of misery and die or go mad.

Maybe the Virgin would grant a miracle, and someone would hear.

She forced herself to pound on the wall, while her arms grew weary, and fists numb. Pound—pound—pound—

Then the wall moved.

She started back, hugging her bruised fists to her chest with an involuntary intake of breath, afraid now that she might have trig-

gered a fate worse than the one she sought to escape—a second
falling of rubble that would crush her.

When nothing else happened, she reached out with one hand,
heart in her throat, and pushed tentatively at the spot that had
yielded.

Again it moved—moved outward just the slightest bit. She tried
to think, when the movement brought no corresponding descent of
stone on her head—what direction had she been kneeling? What lay
before her?

Carefully now, she felt along the wall; it was flat, or nearly.
Cracked, cracks she could stick a finger in up to the first knuckle, but
mostly flat. It must be the basement wall, then, rather than a tumble
of concrete. She must be facing the back of the staircase.

Maybe the quake had opened up a hole next to the foundation!
Maybe—maybe it was even a way out—

Lupe didn't hesitate any further; the thought of a way out gave
her arms a new and frenzied strength. She shoved at the yielding
place with all her might, bracing herself against the wreckage that
held her trapped; shoved until she thought she was going to tear herself in two. And when the wall suddenly gave way, she was unpre-
pared, and went somersaulting headfirst down a pile of dirt and
rocks, hitting her head on a stone and nearly knocking herself out a
second time.

She sat up, after a long moment of dazed blinking at the false
lights thrown before her eyes by the blow on the head. Then she
moaned and groveled in the dirt, for she realized she had merely exchanged one prison for another.

It was just as dark *here* as it had been *there*; the only difference
between "here" and "there" was that now she could no longer touch
the walls that held her prisoner.

That, in its way, made "here" even worse. The darkness was growing colder with every passing moment; she was somehow certain of
that. Colder; and flavored with the taint of evil, like a nest of snakes.
She could almost hear something breathing out there beyond the
reach of her groping hands. The thing that had always waited in the
dark for her was *here*, she *knew* it!

She scrambled backward, inching a little higher on the mound of
dirt, trying to reach the pocket in the rubble of the hotel basement
that now seemed a haven of safety and sanity. But the dirt was loose,
and slipped and slid under her, and she could get nowhere near her
invisible goal.

She became aware of a strange smell; sweet at first, then repellent.

Rather like the smell of the old catacombs where her mother had taken them all on the Day of the Dead.

But with the smell came something so welcome she ignored the faint charnel odor.

Light!

There was light out there—

Or was it only that she thought there was light?

She scrambled to her feet, peering hopefully into the no-longer-threatening darkness, clawing sweat-sticky hair out of her blinking, burning eyes. Yes, there *was* light, a dim, reddish glow—and it was coming from somewhere ahead of her.

So was the odor—but she ignored the smell in the rush of elation she felt at the promise of light.

With her hands out before her, she stumbled blindly forward, tripping on rocks she had no chance of seeing, until at last there were no more rocks and the dirt under her feet was level and smooth. Then it was no longer dirt beneath her feet, but stone, smooth stone, that the heels of her shoes clattered against like castanets.

Abruptly her hands encountered stone at eye level.

She squinted, and made out the dim bulk of a regular outline against the dim glowing. She had found the top of a low doorframe. Perhaps—perhaps another part of the cellar; perhaps the cellar of another building. There was no way of knowing what kind of a jumble the quake had made of the buildings. She ducked, and passed the threshold—

And the glow flared up, angry and hot before her eyes. It was like molten iron, red and glaring, so that she cried out involuntarily and hid her face in the crook of her arm.

At nearly the same moment, she felt something slam down behind her, closing off the doorway practically at her heels.

She whirled, going to her knees, and beat on the slab of stone that had fallen down to seal off her exit, seeing only now in the raw red light that her hands were bloody, the nails split to the quick, the skin gashed and the flesh torn and lacerated.

Something laughed soundlessly behind her.

Again she pivoted, plastering her back against the cold stone slab that blocked the door, mouth dry with fear.

She saw she was in a low-ceilinged, stone-walled chamber. Although there was no apparent *source* of light, the chamber was bright enough that she could easily see the colorful paintings on three of its four walls. She couldn't look at them for very long, though; the garish colors and the light that pulsated with every beat of her heart made it seem that they moved. They made her dizzy. The floor was black and crusted—and it was plain that *this* was the origin of the sickly sweet stench. And on the fourth wall—

On the fourth wall, the wall opposite the door, was a block of stone like an altar, and behind it, a statue. The statue, the paintings—they were like the ones she'd seen in the museum, only untouched, undamaged by years of profaning hands.

Things of the Ancient Ones, the Azteca. She seemed to remember, vaguely, that all of Mexico City had been built on ancient ruins, the ruins of the Aztec capital, Tenochtitlan. And hadn't some of the museum artifacts been unearthed when they had dug the foundations of this very hotel?

The statue was of a dead-black stone that reflected none of the light in the chamber, and pulled at her eyes until she could no more look away from it than escape from this place. She knew, in a way beyond knowing, that the statue was of the rarest unflawed black jade. Priceless, and peerless.

With that knowledge, a voice insinuated itself into her head; it hummed behind her eyes, seductive, hypnotic.

She listened; she couldn't have escaped it even if she'd wanted to. And she didn't want to. It promised, that voice, even if she couldn't yet understand *what* it promised. It soothed; it began to drive out her fear. It was so good to listen to that voice, full of more promises than Joachim's, even. Almost, she could almost understand it. It was telling her—that she was brave, and good, and beautiful. That she was awaited here, long awaited. So good not to think, just to listen—thought ebbed away, and pain, and finally, the last chill of fear.

In the moment her fear left her, she saw that the *statue* was the source of the chamber's illumination; in that moment, the stench of the room vanished, replaced by a subtle perfume. The hurting of her hands and arms ebbed away as well, and she looked down dumbly at her hands to see them not only healed, but flawlessly groomed and soft, as only the hands of the lady tourists were. She looked up again at the glowing statue—and now it seemed to represent the very pinnacle of desire. Fearful no longer, she approached it; the sweet, hypnotic voice still humming behind her eyes, cajoling, promising.

"Sherry—"

Sherry Bryce Fernandez knew that exasperated tone of voice only too well. She braced herself for another inevitable sample of her husband's sarcastic wit, and winced in anticipation.

"Are you quite finished?"

"Not quite—" she ventured, and Robert sighed dramatically.

"So what," he asked, with carefully measured venom, "makes this tourist trap any different from all the other tourist traps we've gone past today?"

Sherry shook back her straight blond hair, held out the brightly brocaded *huiple* in nerveless hands, and attempted to explain. "This is Tenejapa work, Bob—I had no idea there'd be any this far north— it's the Chiapas women that do this kind of weaving—"

"Never mind," he interrupted, boredom and irritation showing only too plainly on his handsome face, somehow getting past the concealing sunglasses he affected. "Don't get started. I suppose now you're going to spend the next two hours dickering for that rag?"

"You know we don't have much to spend," she retorted, flushing. "And this could be very useful to me."

"All right, all right—don't go throwing *that* argument in my face. I'll see if I can find something worth shooting—" Robert backed out of the tiny cranny of the shop as Sherry turned her attention to the keeper.

It wasn't as if he hadn't been getting plenty of pictures, she thought resentfully, as she concentrated on bargaining the price of the *huiple* down to something she could afford. That was just about *all* they'd been doing on this trip—shooting roll after roll of film, spending hours in the broiling sun until the light was "just right"—it might be April, but April in Mexico was as hot as June in Dallas. This was the first time Sherry had been able to track down anything in *her* area of interest—

She felt an immediate surge of guilt, and tucked a wayward strand of ash-blond hair behind one ear with nervous habit. That wasn't fair—this was supposed to be a working vacation. And it was *Robert's* assignment that was paying for it, not hers. She was just lucky that the magazine had been willing to pay for two plane tickets, otherwise she wouldn't be here at all. And Robert would be the only one enjoying the sights of Mexico City—

And the temptations.

Now it was her turn to fight down exasperation. Robert couldn't help himself; he just wasn't made for monogamy. If he just wasn't so damned good-looking—one of his models had likened him to a "young Fernando Lamas."

And that little slut was right—too damned right. He attracted women the way a rock star attracted groupies.

He had all the smooth moves, too; women practically threw

themselves into his arms. *Especially* his models, once they figured out (and it didn't take long) that he wasn't gay.

She stole a glance into the street, and saw that he was totally engrossed in setting up a shot of another vendor's wares; pacing restlessly up and down, trying out camera angles, totally immune to the curious glances of passersby. Her heart lurched as it always did when she caught a glimpse of that craggy profile, especially now that his sarcastic expression had been erased by the concentration he was maintaining. And God, that body—even after six years and a child, the sight of his muscles rippling as he moved was *still* a turn-on!

She dragged her own attention hastily back to her bargaining, grateful for her fluency in Spanish. To have a blond *Americano* begin a sharp bargaining session in their own tongue usually threw shopkeepers off balance enough to give her a real advantage.

To this day, she still didn't quite know why Robert had married her. God knows he'd gotten everything he wanted out of her without *that*.

Maybe he had been telling the truth when he proposed; maybe it *was* love. Half the time she was sure it was—half the time she wasn't sure of anything.

This trip had seemed like a godsend, a chance to prove to Robert that she was still just as attractive as she had ever been. Bobby stayed with his grandparents; she'd made a conscientious effort to leave behind every T-shirt and pair of blue jeans she owned; to slough, if only for two weeks, her holdover hippie image. It was supposed to be the honeymoon they'd never been able to afford.

And this was Robert's big chance, too—the chance to get his work seen by everyone who meant anything in the Dallas fashion scene. Granted, he was just out here on spec for *TravelWorld*—cheap airfares and cheaper off-season hotel rates had made their benefactors seem more generous than they really were. But *TravelWorld*'s execs had an experiment they wanted to make—their hopefully innovative notion was to take destinations thought to be "overexploited"—like Mexico City—and make them look interesting again. Mexico City was chosen as the test case because it was near *TravelWorld Magazine*'s Dallas headquarters, it was inexpensive, and it was probably the *last* destination any experienced traveler would choose. If this test issue generated interest—and income for the advertisers—the project would go into full production.

And Robert—*if* his work passed muster—had a chance of becoming a staff photographer—a chance for a secure position. That was the carrot, the big prize he was really hoping for.

Security—Sherry had never thought there'd come a day when that was something she longed for.

God, it all depended on Robert, and whether he could work enough magic with his camera to make tired old sights seem new and entrancing.

Or so he thought. Sherry had experienced enough disappointment in her marriage to Robert to convince her that this trip was the time to further an idea of her own.

Once upon a time Sherry really *had* been a holdover hippie; her handcrafted clothing outlet had a small, but devoted clientele, though Sherry had been more interested in the craftwork itself than the money it brought in. But that phase had ended three years ago. . . .

The whole world and what was important had changed for her the first time Bobby (poor asthmatic little baby) had gotten seriously ill. The hospital had wanted money in advance, and Robert hadn't worked in weeks. They'd ended up borrowing from Robert's parents (who weren't all that well off themselves), after a frantic midnight phone call.

It was then that Sherry realized that it had been *her* money, not Robert's, that had been paying most of the bills. It was then that she decided to take her work seriously, and began researching craft techniques and expanding her circle of customers. She had gotten the feeling lately that she was on the verge of a breakthrough—what she needed now was something new and different in the folkloric look to make *her* own name. Research had convinced her she just might find what she needed right here.

The ancient Aztec garb of brocaded *huiple* and wrap-skirt was timeless, practical—and might be just different enough to provide the answer she hoped for, once updated for the eighties. The Aztec wrap-skirt with the double ties and pleats was looser, easier to move in than contemporary skirts—and far less apt to "get away" from the wearer. And the *huiple*, a loose, sleeveless blouse held close to the body in front, but loose in back to catch the breezes, was—so far as Sherry was concerned—the ultimate in summer comfort.

She finished her bargaining in a rush, and hurried out into the street with her purchase clutched under her arm. Robert was glancing around with a crease between his thick brows; she knew that look. There was something not quite right about the shot he wanted to take. He spotted her coming toward him as she slipped between two plump, gossiping women, and smiled.

Her knees went weak again. God, that smile—it was like Apollo parting the clouds and bestowing his blessing. No matter how feck-less, how unfaithful, how neglectful he was, all he had to do was smile and she knew she'd never have the guts to leave him.

"Sunshine! You're *exactly* what I need! Go stand over there and look touristy—" he pointed toward a display of Aztec-replica pot-tery. This lot was rather better than the usual; it looked real. She draped the *huiple* gracefully over one arm and posed artlessly, seem-ing totally unconscious of the camera. She was an old hand at this—she'd started out as Robert's very first model, after all.

And as usual, Robert was right. Her pink sundress (her own design—*that* might do her some good, too) and long blond hair con-trasted nicely with the dark pottery and white adobe, making the scene seem more exotic than it really was. Robert snapped off a dozen shots from as many angles in a few minutes, passed the grin-ning potter a couple of pesos, and took her elbow with an expression of satisfaction.

"Now where?" she asked. She was perfectly content to be dragged anywhere he wanted, now that he was in a good mood again, and now that she had a prime example of exactly what she was looking for in her possession.

"The ruins, I think." He eased the strap of his camera case a little further up on his shoulder.

"Haven't they been done to death already?"

"Maybe—that's what I want to check out. Maybe some different angles, dramatic lighting—I don't know, maybe I can stage some-thing. . . ."

He went introspective and brooding on her, with one of his typi-cally instant mood-changes, and she knew better than to interrupt his train of thought.

The earthquake had been eight months ago, and parts of the city *still* looked like a war zone. The plunging prices of oil had brought as much economic disaster to Mexico's economy as to Texas—more so, in some ways. The earthquake had just been the mud-frosting on a rock-cake. Recovery was going to be painfully slow—

"Robert—" she tugged at his arm, bringing him out of his reverie. "Over there—quick—"

"Over there," in a courtyard complete with the week's washing hanging out to dry in the hot sun, was a group of eight or ten kids dancing. For the moment, if you couldn't hear the rock beat coming from the ghetto blaster (fortuitously just on the edge of the group), you'd swear they were performing some quaint native dance. For a wonder the girls were in skirts instead of jeans. Granted, they were cheap Cyndi Lauper imitations, but they were also colorful, border-line folky, and rather cute. Robert got half a dozen shots before one of the boys started moonwalking.

"Good eye, Sunshine," he applauded as he waved down a cab. "I'll have to crop the radio out, but that was nice composition."

She couldn't help herself, no matter that he'd probably be snarling at her before another hour was over. For now, she had his approval, and she glowed.

Robert stared at the ruined pyramid as if it had personally offended him, and Sherry sighed. There was *no* shade out here; the sun was bearing down on both of them mercilessly, but Robert showed no signs of wanting to move on. She squinted into the glare; sunglasses weren't helping much. She wanted a margarita and a cool place to sit, badly.

She knew what his reaction would be to her suggestion that they come back later—a sullen snarl. He had taken these old ruins as a personal challenge. He was obviously bound and determined to make something interesting out of them, or die in the attempt.

She shifted uncomfortably on the crumbling stone step, and scanned the few other people she could see, hoping for something interesting. Unfortunately they seemed equally divided between earnest and impoverished college students and pudgy middle-aged American tourists, all of them squinting against the sunlight reflecting off the white stone pavement.

The Ugly American lives, she thought wryly, wondering for the thousandth time why it was that the skinny students wore the jeans, and the pasty, middle-aged monuments to cellulite exposed their thighs for all the universe to gawk at.

She fanned herself with her hat, wishing she could somehow capture the incredible blue of the sky in a dye-lot that didn't look garish. White stone, green vegetation, blue sky—sun so bright it had no color at all, and not a cloud to be seen. It was gorgeous, and looked as if it would make a perfect photo. But that brilliant sun was the problem; any pictures taken now would look washed-out by the bright light.

Besides, they'd look like a thousand other pictures of these ruins. What Robert needed was a setup that would convey the age and awe-inspiring quality these ruins had, without looking contrived or like every other picture of an Aztec ruin. Or worse, come off a poor second to the latest round of adventure-movie stills.

Too bad I can't convince some Aztec ghosts to show up and pose for him, she thought idly, brushing damp hair off of her forehead. *It would be just what he—*

She started as a girl came around the corner of the pyramid she sat on.

My God—

For a moment, she thought the girl *was* a ghost. The features, the profile—she could have posed for any of a hundred paintings and carvings back in the museum. Hair so black that it held turquoise-blue highlights, smoldering eyes that took up most of the upper half of her face, a complexion like gourmet coffee lightened with the smoothest and finest of cream. And her costume—

My God, it looks like she copied it from that painting of Smoking Mirror and his priestesses—

The colorful, elaborately brocaded *huiple* and wrap-skirt were perfect replicas of those in the painting, so far as Sherry could remember. And the workmanship of both made the blouse she carried in her bag seem like the fumblings of an amateur weaver.

The girl moved as gracefully as a hunting cat, carrying herself with a dignity that was totally unconscious. Sherry knew a handful of dancers who moved that way, but not many. She was about to say something to get Robert's attention, when he turned and spotted the girl himself.

He froze; just stopped moving completely. Sherry had been steeling herself for his inevitable reaction to an attractive girl—but this was an entirely new response, or at least one *she'd* never seen from him before.

He might not even have been breathing; he didn't even twitch when an enormous fly landed on his arm. It was like the old cliché of being turned to stone.

His reaction was so abnormal she found herself thrown entirely off-balance by it, so that *she* froze in place.

While they stared like a pair of idiots, the girl approached both of them, head held high, the image of some ancient goddess deigning to take notice of a pair of mortals.

"Señor?"

The liquid sound of her voice snapped the strange trance that held both of them. The girl held out an arm draped with silver necklaces that gleamed in the sunlight—not with the highly reflective glitter of most of the jewelry that had been offered to them, but with a soft, subtly textured shimmer, like antique satin.

Or—like scales.

Sherry was suddenly struck by two strong and mutually antagonistic reactions. Half of her wanted to reach out and touch those bright garlands of metal—and the other half shuddered with revulsion at the thought.

That jewelry—it's like dozens of skinny little snakes wrapped around her arm—

"Silver, señor?" The girl struck a pose within touching distance of Robert, and smiled up into his eyes. "Very fine, very cheap."

"My God . . ." he mumbled; the girl did not seem to notice that he had said anything at all. She simply continued to pose, patiently.

He continued to stare; the girl, strangely, did not seem in the least disturbed by his scrutiny. "My God . . ." he said at last, "you could have come down off one of these walls—"

"Pardon?"

Robert pulled himself together with an effort clearly visible—at least to Sherry. "Señorita," he said, in Spanish far better than Sherry's, "I will buy your necklaces, on one condition—that you pose for me here—"

The girl regarded him measuringly.

"Señor," she asked, "are you wishing for a model?"

"Well—yes, I suppose so." For the first time in Sherry's experience a woman had succeeded in making him uneasy.

"You photograph for the American magazines?"

"Sometimes—"

"Then," she said coolly, "I make *you* an offer. I will pose for you, and my sisters—all tomorrow if you wish. You need buy no silver. But you must see that important people see the pictures, and know who we are. You must see that we are given more jobs, so that we may have green cards. My sisters and I look much alike—it is our resemblance to the Ancient Ones you wish, no?"

Both Robert and Sherry stared at her, more than a little surprised at the strange turn the bargaining had taken. The girl smiled again, a serene, slightly superior smile.

"You see," she said, "I am no ignorant Mestizo. I have some learning. I know what a camera like *this*—" she gestured gracefully at Robert's hands, the necklaces chiming softly with the movement "—means. We wish to come to America, and as legals; we wish to be models, and rich. You will take such pictures that will make us famous—"

"There—there's no guarantee of that—" Robert stammered.

The girl shook her head, dismissing all doubt. "You will make us famous. *And* yourself."

Now she turned to Sherry, who had been totally ignored until this moment. Her eyes were just as enormous as Sherry's first impression had painted them, and so dark that they looked black. Sherry could not look away from them—and found her suspicions ebbing away. Why—of *course* all this made sense! What a clever girl, to have thought of a practical way to make it into the States, instead of sneaking across the border!

The girl smiled a little more broadly, and Sherry smiled back. There was no reason to distrust such cooperation. There was no doubt that the girl would do everything in her power to help Robert.

"Señora," the girl spoke softly, still staring deeply into Sherry's eyes, "you are a lady who has admiration for the old ways, yes, I can see it. I see that you long to examine the work of my people's hands—" She smoothed the front of her *huiple* with her free hand, a movement totally free of any hint of coquettishness. "I should be gladdened to bring with me more such pieces tomorrow, if it would please you—and I see that it would."

Somehow the girl had taken total control of the situation; in a way that left Sherry bewildered and breathless. There was no doubting her, somehow. She had succeeded in hypnotizing both of them.

"So. I shall come to your hotel."

"The Sheraton—" Robert breathed.

"The Sheraton." She nodded, turned with a grace that would have called up raw envy in a prima ballerina, and began to return along the same way she had come.

"Wait—" Robert called, as Sherry sat, still bemused and unable to think. "Your name—"

She cast a glance over her shoulder, arch and full of amusement.

"Lupe, señor. Lupe."

Robert spent the remainder of the afternoon among the ruins, a man obsessed, talking to himself and scribbling notes at every possible setting. Sherry knew better than to interrupt him. He'd been like this only a handful of times before—but those times had produced some of his best work. If the girl had inspired him to a new height, then *she* was not going to argue about the result. For the first time she began to really believe that he might pull off the hoped-for coup of attaining the pinnacle of a permanent position with *TravelWorld*.

They ate in the hotel restaurant, Robert still scribbling away in his plan-book. He could have been eating cardboard, or a plate of fried bugs, for all the notice he took of the food. And *she* just wasn't there for him. Back in their room he checked over every piece of his equipment, then rechecked, then paced the balcony, muttering to himself.

Sherry hardly felt like herself; found herself able to think of little more than the promise of having *her* goal delivered on a platter. So while he paced, she charted patterns—then, unable to concentrate on anything else, dialed room service and turned on the television.

He was still wrapped in thought and never noticed the arrival of the waiter with the drinks she'd ordered. She offered him his share, but he didn't even look at her.

She was too used to him in this mood to be piqued—and she'd done without for too long to let the pitcher of margaritas go to waste. So she ignored him, and curled up to enjoy the margaritas and a Mexican vampire movie. It was one of the worst flicks she'd ever seen, boasting a professional wrestler as its star. Maybe—probably— she was drinking too much. But to see Robert so *enthused* was such a relief that she wasn't paying as much attention to her intake as she usually did. By the time one of the hero's opponents in the ring turned into a werewolf, she'd drunk so much it seemed the height of hilarity.

When she crawled into bed, more than a few sheets to the wind, Robert was still pacing.

In the morning it seemed like a dream, especially with a tequila-head to conquer. She was more than half afraid Lupe was a fraud; that she wouldn't show up at all, and Robert would crash down from his creative height to spend the remainder of their stay in sullen apathy in the hotel.

But the strange, queenlike girl and her three sisters arrived with the dawn.

And they were incredible, all four of them, two shorter and one taller than Lupe herself, but otherwise nearly identical. As they stood in the lobby, they looked like a quartet of ancient Aztec princesses— and it was their surroundings that seemed disjointed from time, not them. They made the gleaming modernity of the hotel lobby seem tawdry and contrived—poorly conceived and cheaply executed.

The youngest and smallest carried a neatly wrapped bundle, which she pressed into Sherry's arms wordlessly, with just a slow, coy wink of her eye. From the moment her hands touched the fabric, she found herself unable to think of anything else—and her hangover inexplicably vanished.

Sherry's obsessions returned full force and then some, and when she saw the patterns woven into the fabric that held the promised clothing, she could not restrain her impatience to get back to the room. She answered Robert's absent farewell with equal distraction, and did not even wait to see the odd procession leave.

The contents exceeded her wildest hopes; not just *huiples* and skirts of the finest and most intricate brocaded patterns, but an unsewn garment in the first stages of construction. Not only would she have patterns for the brocades and embroideries, but she would have a working pattern to adapt for a modern set of garments. It was more than she had dared dream for.

She had brought her own camera and film; she spent the entire day closeted in the hotel room, photographing every inch of the intricate brocades, the construction techniques, and how the garments were meant to drape. She didn't even miss eating lunch; her notebooks were full of sketches and instructions and she'd used every last frame of her film by the time Robert staggered in the door, sweaty, dusty, and totally exhausted.

"My *God*, Robert—" His appearance alone served to shake her out of the trance she'd been in all day. She took his equipment from him and he stumbled over to the bed, throwing himself down with an utter indifference to anything that might have been in his way.

She glanced out of the hotel window to see with a feeling of shock that it was already growing dark.

"Where on earth *were* you?"

"God." He groaned, and turned himself over. "I think I've been over every square inch of ruin from here to Cancun. I haven't one frame of film left. God, Sunshine, those chicks were in-bloody-credible!"

"Good?"

"Good isn't in it. That Lupe was right on. If what's in those cans doesn't set both *TravelWorld* and my agency on their collective asses, I'll eat my equipment and go push Big Macs for a living." He sat up, wiping a film of dust from his forehead. "You mark my words, Sunshine—half the agencies in the Southwest are going to be fighting for the right to offer those girls their green cards. And you and I are about to hit the fuckin' bigtime, because Lupe told me they aren't gonna work with anybody *but* me."

"Robert—" The strangely intense, inward-looking expression he wore frightened her a little. "Robert—you've never talked like this before—"

"That's because nobody ever handed me the way to the top on a platter before." He looked absently down at his filthy hands, and seemed to see the dirt for the first time. "God, I look like a pit. Get room service to send up a sandwich while I shower, will you, lover? Oh—Lupe said to leave the stuff at the desk; she'll get it in the morning."

He kissed her with a kind of preoccupied gentleness, peeled off his shirt, and dropped it on the carpet, drifting into the bathroom in a half-trance.

She picked up his shirt, feeling her own bemusement return to make all the questions she wanted to ask him seem irrelevant. After all, she had *her* treasures now—

But later that night, Robert woke her from a sound and dreamless sleep, tossing restlessly in a dream from which no amount of shaking could wake him, and crying out—

Only one word was clear, and that only because he repeated it so often.

"Tezcatlipoca," he cried out as if he were calling for someone, "Tezcatlipoca!"

TWO

Detective Mark Valdez ignored the horde of harried travelers crowding up against him and searched the TV monitor for the Amerine Airways flight from Hartford. Thanks to being shoved he managed to overlook it twice before finally spotting the entry.

Every time you turn around, they're changing schedules, changing flight numbers on you—oh great. It's coming in at the other terminal, of course. Halfway across the county. I hate DFW. It was bad enough before, but when they started letting everybody back inside the terminal five years ago, it turned into a zoo. Sometimes I wish they'd go back to the old security system: nobody gets inside without a ticket.

He elbowed his way out of the crowd and trudged along the concourse thinking longingly of a cold beer.

Huh-uh, Valdez. No beer. You're still on duty.

He spotted a concession stand that hadn't a line of customers twenty deep and settled for a large Coke instead. His head hurt, and he hoped the caffeine would do him some good. His feet hurt, too; well, that was par for the course for a cop. Normally people gave cops a wide berth, so he'd have been spared the pushing and shoving—but he wasn't in the uniform. He was plainclothes division, and good God, he especially wouldn't wear the monkey suit on *this* pickup. So—he'd gotten jostled just like everybody else.

There was a sickly *beem-boom* right behind him, and a mechanical, pseudo-female voice bellowed—

"Amerine Airways shuttle cart in motion. Puh-leez stand clear of the cart."

He jumped, scuttled out of the way with the rest of the shell-shocked walkers, and the cart sailed by. He felt like cussing the driver out, but he was just too tired. His ribs were sore where somebody had elbowed him, and his shoulder was aching because he'd pulled a muscle restraining the reaction that would have sent the elbower crashing into the wall. That would have been a little hard to explain to the Chief, seeing as said elbower had been an eightyish old lady with blue hair. And *very* sharp elbows.

I hope to hell Di is traveling light. This hasn't been a good day.

He'd been up since four ack emma, so he was tired enough that when he got to the moving sidewalks linking the two terminals, he let them carry him along, squashed over on the right side so that stews and athletic types could pass him. He savored the cool bite of his drink, ignoring the annoyed glares of those who squeezed past him. The echoing and re-echoing of voices along the concourse was enough to drive anybody with sensitive hearing right into catalepsy. And all the crossechos distorted the boarding and arrival announcements into unintelligible gibberish.

Sounds like a bunch of religious yo-yos speaking in tongues. You'd think they'd do something about the acoustics of these places while they're on the drawing board. I think this terminal was designed by a reincarnation of Torquemada. God, I hate DFW!

By the time the third walkway terminated, he had finished the Coke down to the ice—of which there had been considerably more than cola. He dumped the cup in an overflowing trash receptacle, and headed for gate eighteen.

He was way early, and found himself a seat in the no-smoking section away from everyone else, loosening his tie and collar as he sagged into the uncomfortable plastic chair. Dallas was experiencing an abnormally hot spell—eighty degrees in January. It seemed rather like they'd gone directly from fall into summer, with no spring, and only a nod to winter. And as usual, the air-conditioning system of DFW Airport was not coping well. In fact, knowing the current state of things, it might not be working at all. Certainly it was hot, damp, and smelly in the terminal—not much different than the atmosphere outside.

He slumped and tried to relax, then sat bolt upright as a horrible thought hit him. He hadn't talked with Di since he'd asked her to come. She'd sent him her flight number—which had changed, of course—but other than that he hadn't heard a word from her. While Diana wasn't exactly chatty at the best of times, he should have heard something more than this—

There wasn't anybody at his gate yet (DFW was so hectic that agents frequently didn't materialize until ten minutes before boarding), but there was an agent manning one of the others nearby. Mark jumped to his feet and sprinted over before she could move away. He pulled out his shield and ID and shoved them under her startled eyes.

"Can you tell me if a Diana Tregarde is on flight 185 from Hartford?" he asked before she could muster a question. Unless you were a cop, dispensing that kind of information to questioners was strictly against airline regs. There'd been a couple of cases of irate wives and husbands showing up at airports with mayhem in mind when they'd found out about certain trips. . . .

But the agent frowned worriedly, almost anxiously—more so than the question warranted—as she punched the query into her terminal.

"Yes sir, she is—" the woman replied after a moment. "At least she got a boarding pass about five minutes before departure." She bit her lip, and wouldn't quite look at him. "Is—is there something wrong?"

"No, no, not at all," Mark sighed, then smiled. "She's a special consultant, and I wanted to be sure she made the flight, that's all. We kind of got our wires crossed, and then you guys changed all your flight numbers on me, so I wasn't sure if I was making the right one or not."

The woman's answering smile was bright with relief, and she bent her dark, curly head over her keyboard as he turned away and walked back to his chair.

Oh shit, he thought, suddenly having his memory kick in. *I shouldn't have startled her like that.*

Because everybody in DFW was bound to be a little jumpy lately; only last month there'd been a hostage situation. Some crazed Iranian trying a ground hijacking. It had tied things up for half the day, and the whole incident was fresh and raw in the minds of anybody who worked here. Probably they expected bomb scares whenever they saw a shield at this point.

He slouched back into the ill-fitting seat, trying, without much success, to find a comfortable position.

Man, this is the last thing I ever expected to be doing—bringing Di in as occult *consultant, of all damned things. To think that she told me I'd be doing just this years ago—and I didn't believe her.*

He could still hear her final words when they'd last seen each other, as if it had been days ago instead of years.

"You'll see me again," she'd said, giving him that Mona Lisa smile. *"You'll need my expertise some time in the future. You'll call me. Trust me, I'm sure enough to put money on it."*

Which parting had been a damn sight more peaceful than their meeting. . . .

Mark was looped; Tim, Phil, and Quasi were a good bit farther along than that.

Quasi—short for Quasimodo—was carrying the booze-box, for the reason that he was the only one of them capable of toting that much, drunk or sober. Quasi was built like a gorilla, and just about as hairy.

He was also on a full academic scholarship to the anthro department. Phil claimed it was because he was the only living specimen of Neanderthal and they wanted to study him; Mark knew better—he'd seen Quasi's midterm marks. Im*pres*sive.

It was three flights up to Quasi's apartment, and this old wreck of a building didn't have an elevator. Normally, this was no big deal, but half blitzed, it was an adventure. The staircase was lit only infrequently, and poorly; the stairs were worn and slippery. Mark was clinging to the banister with both hands, but frankly wondered if it would stay attached to the wall if it had to take his full weight.

"This," Tim announced to no one in particular, "is 1970. The Age of Enlightenment. The Age of Illumination. This is the dawn—"

"Of the Age of Aquarius, Age of Aquar-i-uuuuus—" Phil warbled. He was, as usual, off-key.

"Shut up, dork," Tim said, glaring at him from under an untamed thatch of thick black hair.

"Sir, yessir!" Phil saluted—which struck Mark as hilarious, since Phil, flatfooted, four-eyed, and a genuine asthmatic, had about as much chance of being drafted as a nun.

"You were saying—" Quasi prompted, shifting the box a little, and pointedly ignoring Mark's snorts of laughter.

"My point is, what the hell are we doing having a seance?" Tim demanded, squinting almond eyes at their host.

"One," Quasi replied amiably, "This *is* Halloween. It is traditional, as it were, and I am *all* in favor of tradition. Two, I'm curious about that 'spell' I dug up. My anthro prof claims he's seen magic work—you know, stuff that had no rational explanation. The way I see it, if a magic spell ever works at all, I'm betting it will work on Halloween. Three, I'm paying for the booze."

"And very good booze it is," Phil agreed, nodding so hard his glasses slid down his nose. "Well worth a bit of cavorting and chanting."

"Okay," Tim replied, mollified. "That's a good reason."

"Hey, we're here—" Mark interrupted, hauling himself up the last few stairs and getting to the door on the landing ahead of them all. "I want to get this over with."

He held the door open for the other three. Phil had been entrusted with the key to the apartment, and skipped to the front of the group. The hallway was even dimmer than the staircase; Mark suspected that the bulbs in the light fixtures were at best fifteen-watt refrigerator bulbs. It was probably just as well; by the musty smell, nobody had cleaned the hall carpet for years. Mark was just as glad he didn't have to look at it. It might be growing something.

Phil fumbled with the lock while the other three made rude comments, and finally got the scarred and gouged door open. Quasi shouldered him aside impatiently; Mark trailed in behind his three friends.

Quasi had obviously been hard at work earlier today; his usual clutter of Salvation Army furniture and books had been pushed up against the wall. The couch was shoved against the wall next to the door they'd entered. It was absolutely covered with junk. The chairs and orange-crate tables were piled up against each other on the back wall. The curtains were tightly closed and then pinned shut with enormous safety pins.

It was, without a doubt, the cleanest this place had been in weeks.

Drawn on the anonymously brown rug in colored chalk was an intricate diagram. Placed at the four corners of the design were rickety candlesticks apparently salvaged from a church; they stood as tall as Mark's shoulder and held black candles as thick as his wrist. In the center of the diagram was a hibachi stoked with instant-starting charcoal. Beside the hibachi was a sheet of newspaper with a neat arrangement of little piles of unidentifiable flotsam on it.

The three invitees stared at the bizarre setup. Quasi set the box down on his cracked vinyl sofa and took control of the situation.

"Okay, since you want to get this over with, let's move it. Phil, you go stand in the south—"

"Right." He made a face. "*Which* way is south, Leatherstocking?"

"Behind the candlestick in front of the record player." Quasi cast his eyes up toward the ceiling. "Give me strength."

"If you're gonna raise a demon, you should be looking in the other direction," Tim pointed out.

"How many times do I have to tell you cretins? We're *not* raising a demon, we're trying to contact a dead person. That's what this book says—" Quasi waved a thick paperback at them; the cover said *Voudoun Today*. Mark squinted at the letters, which wavered in front of his eyes.

"Voo-doon? What's that?" Mark wanted to know.

"It's not 'voo-doon,' dummy, it's *voodoo*. Sheesh. You go stand to Phil's right."

"Over here—" Phil flapped his right hand helpfully. Tim took the other open position without being directed.

"Shouldn't we be wearing robes or something?" Mark asked, looking down at his jeans and Grateful Dead T-shirt doubtfully. It didn't seem like the right outfit to be talking to a ghost in—even if he didn't believe it would work. Well—the skull on the front was okay, but the outfit itself seemed kind of—disrespectful.

"Nah—you'll be okay." Quasi dismissed his objection with an airy wave of his hand, and took a healthy slug of whiskey directly from the bottle. "Now, don't move, or you'll ruin the pentacle."

Quasi moved unsteadily around the diagram, closing up lines they'd erased by walking on them, lighting the candles, and giving each of the participants a carefully printed slip of paper.

"Okay, when I point at you, say what's on that. I wrote it down pho-net-ic-al-ly—" he had a little trouble getting the word out "—so just say what's there. If this works—"

"If? Why shouldn't it?" Phil wanted to know. "My sister gets answers on her Ouija board all the time!"

"Well, I didn't have everything, so I had to make some substitutions in the formulas," Quasi admitted. "But I did it logically, okay? So it should work. Anyway, if it does, the ghost will show up in the middle, in the center of that five-pointed star. I'm trying for Julius Caesar—" He lit the hibachi; there was a sharp chemical smell and a sparking line traveled across the surface of the charcoal.

"You wanted me 'cause I know Latin, right?" Phil blinked owlishly.

"I wanted you 'cause you're a Scorpio, okay? Now shut up, I'm gonna start." Quasi palmed the light switch, and suddenly the only illumination in the room was coming from the four candles and the hibachi.

Mark went very cold; with the lights out this was beginning to seem like something other than funny. The Scotch he'd downed had worn off all too quickly, and with it his bravado. He wanted very badly to walk out that door, but didn't dare. He *knew* what the other three would say if he did. He'd never live it down. He was supposed to be studying criminology; it wouldn't look real cool if he couldn't handle a spooky situation.

Quasi, looking warped and sinister in the flickering candlelight, began chanting and throwing various substances on the coals in the brazier. Some of them smelled vaguely pleasant; some stank to high heaven. All of them produced a good deal of smoke, further obscuring vision. Mark could scarcely see when he pointed dramatically in his direction.

He stammered out what was written on the notebook paper, not feeling at all ashamed that his voice shook. This *wasn't* funny anymore. He waited, feeling a cold chill ooze down his backbone, as Phil and Tim said their pieces. Then Quasi intoned a final sentence—

Everything—just stopped. No sound, no nothing. Then Mark's stomach lurched, and every hair on his arms stood straight up. The temperature in the room dropped at least twenty degrees. But that was only for openers.

Without warning a soundless explosion in the center of the diagram knocked Mark right off his feet.

By some miracle, he *didn't* turn over the candle behind him; as he staggered upright again he saw that Phil and Tim hadn't been so lucky. His candle and Quasi's were the only sources of light—

Then something at the heart of the diagram flared greenly; the remaining two candles were snuffed out by the hurricane wind that followed that flare of sickly light. For with the light came a tempest.

Mark dropped back down to his knees and sheltered his head in his arms. There was a whirlwind raking the room; it was centered by a vortex in the heart of the diagram. The wind was sucking anything loose into that vortex—papers, bits of herb, posters torn loose from the walls. Quasi was staring at his handiwork with a face that was panic-stricken and utterly dumbfounded.

There at the heart of the vortex was the source of the evil light—it was—

Mark didn't know what it was, only that it was a dark, amorphous blot that smelled utterly foul and made him sick to his stomach. It had eyes that glowed a vile, poisonous green; eyes that he *could not* look away from.

He found himself rising again to his feet, and realized with cold and helpless horror that he was being pulled toward it.

Phil screamed; an incongruously girlish sound. Mark heard him clearly above the howl of the wind.

And then Mark heard the sound of his footsteps fleeing toward the back door. A splintery crash marked the slamming of the porch door against the wall—then Tim followed Phil, backing out slowly, unable to take his eyes off the apparition. Tim was not screaming, he was giggling hysterically. Quasi held out a few moments longer, but when the thing turned its horrible eyes on *him*, Quasi howled like a mad dog and followed the other two.

Mark fought the fascination as best he could, but found himself taking a slow, deliberate step toward the thing—then another—and another—

He was too frightened to cry out, too terrified even to pray. He could only fight against the pull, and know his fight would be, in the end, useless.

The creature in the vortex chuckled wetly, and Mark felt his whole self become one inarticulate and soundless cry for help.

And—like a miracle—help arrived.

The front door literally exploded inward, with a force that dwarfed the initial explosion that had brought the thing, and the compulsion and the whirlwind weakened as the thing turned its attention to the newcomer.

Light—light against the awful darkness.

Brilliant, clean white light poured in the open portal. Standing in the light—or had she brought the light *with* her?—was a young woman. A very *angry* young woman.

Some unencumbered part of his mind recognized her as one of Quasi's upstairs neighbors.

Her waist-length hair stood out from her head as if she had taken hold of a static generator. She was wearing ballet slippers, a leotard, and an ancient Japanese kimono that whipped wildly about her in the screaming wind.

She was holding what could only be a broadsword.

The sword *was* glowing. Blue-green flames flickered all up and down the blade. The thing in the vortex saw that, and snarled at her.

The girl sidestepped into the room, slowly; she looked like she knew exactly what she was doing. She was holding the sword in both hands, and Mark had the relieved feeling that this was *not* the first time she had fought this particular battle. She eased along the edge of the diagram until she stood a few feet from Mark—

Then she suddenly dashed the remaining few feet toward him and slashed the fiery blade down into the space between him and the thing, as if she was cutting a line that was binding him and the thing together.

The compulsion to join the thing snapped so abruptly that he stumbled backward into the wall.

The girl was shouting words that he couldn't quite make out—

and didn't really want to—above the howling of the wind and the higher wailing of the apparition in the vortex. He crouched and covered his ears with both hands, unable to look away. She gestured with the sword, drawing fiery lines in the air between herself and the creature, lines that glowed and continued to hang suspended before her long after any afterimage should have faded. The thing's wailing grew in intensity—and so did the sucking wind. Mark huddled against the wall, his heart pounding with absolute panic.

Then the girl changed her stance, balancing the pommel of her sword in her hand as if the whole massive piece of metal was nothing more than an oversized throwing-knife.

Mark stared at that; the back of his head was insisting that you couldn't *do* that, but his eyes were telling him that she was, and logic be damned.

She held it that way for only an instant—then cast it, throwing it as if it had no weight at all, aiming it at the darkness between the thing's eyes.

There was a third explosion and a flash of light that left Mark half-blinded and half-deafened, and not a little stunned.

When he finally came to himself again, the electric lights were back on. There was an awful stench filling the apartment, like burned and rotting meat.

There was nothing in the middle of the room except a blackened spot in the center of the rug, a spot that had a sword sticking out of the middle of it. Mark stared at the blade with a slackened jaw; it had buried itself into the floor for a depth of at least two inches. He couldn't imagine how the *hell* she had tossed it that hard.

The girl was again standing between him and the spot where the thing had been, surveying the wreckage with her feet slightly apart, and her hands on her hips. As he stared stupidly at her back, she turned to face him.

She was *not* happy.

"Well," she said at last. An angry frown marred her otherwise pretty face as she grabbed the hilt without looking at it and wrenched the sword from the floor with an audible *crack*. "You sure blew *my* study plans all to hell. I'm not too thrilled about having to drop everything to rescue an almost-damned fool. What have you got to say for yourself?"

"Uh—" He swallowed hard. "Thanks?"

She stared at him for another long moment, then began laughing.

So it was that Mark Valdez, criminology student, and Diana Tregarde, expert in the occult, first met.

She never did let me off the hook for interrupting her midterm studying, either, Mark reflected wryly. *Recruited me for her ghost-hunting squad before you could say "poltergeist." Lord—ghosts, phony mediums, the Celtic Nightmare—half the time I thought I was making a mistake in letting her boss me around like that, in letting her railroad me into her Spook Squad. I should be, I am, just as glad—now. She told me once that she always helps if anybody asks—that she has to—and unless my instincts are all wrong, we need her, and badly.*

"Amerine Airways flight 185, service from Hartford, Connecticut, with continuing service to Phoenix, now arriving gate 18. . . ." The announcement broke into his recollections and brought him to his feet, pushing forward with the rest of the modest crowd awaiting passengers from the plane.

He had to watch for her carefully—even after all these years he was *still* vaguely amazed at how tiny she was. She'd certainly been impressive enough when she'd rescued him; she'd seemed ten feet tall, no matter what her true physical size was. But for all that she loomed large in his memory, she scarcely topped five feet, about the height of the average ballet dancer. She looked like a dancer, too—or at least she used to—

He saw her finally; nearly the last one down the jetway. She had a pair of turquoise nylon carry-on bags and a hefty purse slung over her shoulders, and was wearing an outfit that he remembered was almost a uniform for her, a black leotard and jeans. She waved at him and eased her way gracefully toward him through the throng of embracing relatives and friends.

She hadn't changed a bit; still wore her long, silken brown hair waist-length and unbound, still had the same piquant, heart-shaped face with her high, prominent cheekbones and brown eyes so huge she looked like one of those stupid velvet paintings of big-eyed kids—and she still had her dancer's grace and dancer's figure.

"Hello, love!" She dropped her carry-on bags, threw her arms around him, and gave him a very thorough and shamelessly hearty kiss.

"You had me worried for about five minutes," he said, when he'd recovered from the inevitable effect. "I realized I hadn't heard from you since you told me your flight number, and for one long moment I wasn't entirely sure you were going to be *on* that plane."

"Oh ye of little faith," she chuckled, picking up her bags and indicating with a nod of her head that he should lead the way. "I'm sorry; I was smack in the middle of a particularly tangled love triangle, and

I had to get it sorted out and in my publisher's hands before I left. I literally finished the damn thing at the last minute. I *did* drop the FedEx package with the final in it at the pickup box at the airport. Good thing I have an account with them, or I *wouldn't* have made it."

It was Mark's turn to chuckle. Diana took no compensation for her occult work—and being unable to live on air, had a perfectly non-arcane way of paying the rent and grocery bills.

She was a writer—but not of horror or even books *about* the occult, as might be thought.

She wrote romance novels. Sentimental, wildly entangled, and blatantly melodramatic romance novels, with never an unhappy ending in sight.

"So what was it this time?" he asked, taking one of her two bags and leading the way to the baggage-claim carousel.

"Regency." She laughed as he made a face. "Oh, you might have liked this one. The heroine was a tomboy, the hero was a smuggler, and the complication was a duke."

"A dastardly cad, no doubt."

"But of course, aren't they all? You're looking for turquoise-blue rip-stop nylon, like the rest of my gear."

She shrugged at his raised eyebrow. "Hey, it was a bargain, and it's certainly easy to see in a crowd."

He spotted and retrieved the appropriate bag—and he almost suspected her of a little spell-casting, it came off the plane so quickly.

He gave her a long sidelong glance, and she laughed.

"Don't give me that look—you *know* I don't work that way," she admonished.

He continued to give her a teasingly skeptical stare.

"Honestly, some people—work it out for yourself, Sherlock."

"Huh?"

"Lord, I thought you were supposed to be *good* at figuring mysteries out. I told you myself that I was in a hurry, so much so that I posted the FedEx package at the airport. Ran on the plane at the last minute. Simple airline procedure, silly. Last baggage on is first off. No hocus-pocus needed. Except maybe a little nudge at the handlers to make sure my stuff got on at all."

"Okay, okay, I believe you." By way of apology he relieved her of one of her carryons. "After you—" he gestured grandly.

They headed out the door, to be met by a blast of heat, light, and noise.

"Good *Lord*! This is like walking into the ninth circle of Hell!"

"Welcome to January in Dallas," he shouted over the screeching of tires and the roar of motors. "So you were up to your eyebrows in love triangles right up until you left, huh?"

"Uh-huh. The best is yet to come—I wangled an advance on a five-book contract, all five to be set down here. That's who *paid* for these plane tickets, m'lad. I am ostensibly doing research even as we speak."

He shook his head with admiration as they approached his battered little red Karmann Ghia. Diana handed him her burdens silently, then said, very softly, and with just a faint hint of mockery—

"I wondered how long it was going to take for you to call me. I've been keeping track of your weirdo killer in the news items. That's the reason I went after that contract in particular—I was about ready to call you up and volunteer."

Mark sighed. "If it had been up to me, I'd have called you in sooner."

She waited until he unlocked the passenger door before replying. "Why don't you pretend I don't know anything about this and start from the beginning. What I've gotten so far has been what's hit the national news, and it's probably pretty distorted."

She waited quietly for him to organize his thoughts, while he negotiated the Ghia out of the parking garage and onto the superhighway. A quick glance to the side told him that if she was feeling any impatience she certainly wasn't showing it. But then, she rarely displayed signs of emotion; she kept her feelings, like her private life, to herself.

"Like I said," he told her, finally, "if it had been up to me, I'd have called you earlier. The feeling of the whole area has been *real* weird for the past month or so."

"How so, weird?"

"Off—just—off. Unsettled, and not in a good way. You know I'm not real sensitive, that's the best I can tell you. But we've been getting all those signs of 'bad ju-ju' you always told me to watch out for—"

"Increased violence at mental institutions, an upswing in the number of nasty cultists coming out of the woodwork, an increase in psychiatric admissions?"

"All of the above. And the fourth—an increase in certain kinds of people finding excuses to bug out of the area."

"Like?"

"Most of the Rom are gone. Flat *gone* is what Bunco tells me. So far as we can tell, the great majority of our regular gypsy population pulled out and headed north last September. And we're down to half the usual population of 'psychic advisors,' and it ain't 'cause Bunco is busting 'em. It's getting so that Bunco can't even find them. I figure the real ones left early, the marginally sensitive bailed out this month, and all we're left with now is the flimflam artists, or the ones too desperate poor to leave."

She pursed her lips, looking thoughtful. He hit the brakes as a pink-beige Cadillac with a vanity license plate saying TOMMY H and an "I love Tulsa" sticker cut right across his front bumper.

"Asshole," he muttered under his breath. "I heart Tulsa. Jerk."

"Accident looking for a place to happen," she supplied, absently.

Then, a fraction of a second later, the look of abstraction vanished—and she seized the steering wheel and yanked it violently right, sending the Ghia careening across three lanes of traffic with a shriek of tortured rubber. Behind them came the sound of frantic horns and the scream of brakes—

And at exactly the same moment, the driver of the Cadillac that had cut them off made a fatal misjudgment.

He tried the same maneuver that he'd inflicted on them a moment earlier, only this time it was with the semi-rig in the far left lane. Unfortunately, the driver of the semi chose the same instant to accelerate.

The semi clipped the rear of the Cadillac, sending it spinning right across the slot they'd occupied until Diana had wrenched the wheel over.

Before Mark even had time to blink, the Caddy spun across their lane behind them, rolled, rammed into an overpass, and burst into flame.

"My God—" He started to pull over; the automatic reaction of any cop. Diana, face as white as skim milk, forestalled him.

"Go—just go," she choked. "He—you won't help him."

After one look at her deathly pale face, he obeyed.

He had forgotten that—among other things—Di was an empath—sensitive not to thoughts, but to feelings and emotions.

My God—she must have felt *the whole thing—*

Silence reigned for so long that he finally reached over and turned on the radio, unable to stand it any longer.

"Ah—" After a song-and-a-half she shook her hair back and massaged her temples; her color was returning. "That was *not* good. That's what I get for unshielding on the highway."

"Yeah, well." He negotiated a tricky bit of driving to get around an elderly Buick doing forty. "I'm glad some of your other talents are still working."

She grimaced. "Not as well as I'd like, nor as predictably."

"You—" He took another glance at her. She looked okay, now. Pretty well back to normal. "You ready for the debriefing again?"

"No—but go on, anyway. Instinct says I'm late getting on this one as it is."

"Okay. So far as the Chief is concerned, this whole mess started about three or four months ago—"

"I take it you think differently."

"Uh-huh. I think it began about eight or nine months ago. We started to get the cattle mutilations about then, and I'm convinced that they're related."

Now she looked at him, quizzically. "There's something you're not telling me. About *why* you're convinced. Confession time."

He blushed. "One of the ranchers getting hit was an old rodeo cowboy; you know, the oil economy isn't the only thing that's in trouble down here, the ranchers are having problems with keeping their spreads. This guy—damn it, I felt sorry for him; he spent half his life risking his neck just so he could save up for a place of his own—then these sickos start wrecking his herd. Well, I couldn't get anyone to stake out the place, and I had the feeling this was more than just the work of a garden-variety sicky, so I snuck out there on the full moon—"

"And?" she prompted.

"I—I warded it." He could feel his face burning. Good Catholic boys didn't go around casting pagan magic. Good cops didn't either.

"Well?"

"They never hit *his* place again."

"Hmm. If it looks like a duck—"

"Yeah. It *wasn't* just some sicko; a sicko wouldn't have cared squat about a warding, right?"

"A sicko wouldn't have noticed it, right. He might even have been caught by it; that's the thing about the warding I taught you bunch of refugees from the loonybin, it's a little like a watchdog. If somebody sensitive comes, it warns them off; if they come in anyway, it bites them; if they're wearing armor or just don't notice it, it raises hell with the master. If it had just been a nonsensitive sicko, the minute he crossed the boundary with ill-intent, your cowboy would have felt a pressing need to go visit that pasture—armed."

"Well, we've had animal mutilations before, just not so close to

Dallas or so many; the Chief was inclined to let the county mounties handle it. But then it escalated, and we started getting dead people."

"Ah. So our weirdie upped the ante."

"They," he corrected, pulling off on his exit ramp. "What we've been seeing is too much work for one person alone. And—I know you told me that my main psi-talent is mediumism and not sensitivity, but—well, I've been *feeling* something around the murder sites. Something—I don't know—"

"Evil?"

"I guess. Something *I* don't want to touch, anyway. Makes my skin crawl, and frankly scares the shit out of me."

"How's the shielding I put on you holding up? Any chance you could be getting leakages? That might account for it. Violent death tends to make for violent spirits. And you *could be* a very sensitive medium if you ever unshielded. Spirits could just slide into you like they were coming home. That was why that critter was targeting *you* the night we met, not one of the others."

He shook his head. "No way; that's the first thing I checked for. Shields are as good as when you put them on me right after that Halloween party. Anyway, that's when I talked to the Chief and managed to get him to agree to your coming in on this."

"Not under my true colors, I take it?"

"Are you kidding? I don't want you burned on my lawn! This's Bible-thumper country; one hint of the stuff you're *really* into, and we'll both end up covered in tar and feathers if we're lucky. No, you're an 'expert on modern cults.' That double major of yours in anthro and psych helped convince them you had the credentials. They still think this is just another Manson thing."

"Gah. I wish. Not by all *my* preliminary investigation. Yeah, it's cult-related, I'm sure of it—but I'm also sure there's a purpose and they know exactly what they're doing. But I was hoping it would just be one person. Group-minds are a lot harder to pin down, and a lot better at covering their tracks."

He shook his head. "Sorry. All our evidence points to at least three."

"So your department is feeling out of their depth, huh? They must be pretty antsy; a little bird in the Hartford PD told me they'd been making inquiries." She grinned. "I suspect they liked what they heard."

"Liked it enough that they're going to put you on a retainer. Your rep for never getting involved with the press or blowing your own horn helped."

"God—" she shuddered. "No thanks. I have enough problems without getting followed around by Astral Annies. Good; at least they're going to be predisposed to listen to me. Now, how big is this retainer? *You* know I'm not exactly rich."

"Hey—what about all those books?"

Her face was shadowed for a moment, and her eyes darkened with unmistakable sorrow. "I—I've got some very expensive things to take care of."

Then she brightened again, though he had the impression that it was a forced brightness. "Expensive—honey, I got expenses you wouldn't believe—have you seen the price of crystal balls recently? Things *I* need you *don't* find at Kmart. *And* they don't come cheap. And I *still* have to eat and pay the rent. So what's my retainer, hm?"

"Well—we're under a budget crunch. Not real big. It'll cover a hotel bill or food. Not both."

He pulled into an old residential neighborhood; houses that dated back to the mid to late 1800s—which for Dallas, was old. The street was tree-lined, quiet; a considerable relief after the highway.

"I have a couple ideas, though."

"Hm?"

"I've got an old maiden aunt that takes in student boarders, and one of her 'girls' just headed out for overseas study last semester. She's got a room free. And she's a darn good cook. I already asked her—she said she'd be happy to have you. My apartment isn't too far from here—it's in the Rose Point complex. She'll give you bed *and* board for the amount of the retainer."

"Okay. Or?"

"You could stay with me. But I've only got a studio. One bed."

"Uh-huh. And I don't think you picture either of us sleeping on the floor." She shook her head. "No, I don't think so, love. I'm not the one you want, so I'm not going to settle for being the one you're with."

His mouth dropped open. "I—uh—" he felt himself blushing again, this time all the way down to his toes. Despite the earlier reminder, he'd completely forgotten that picking up odd information about people's emotional states—apparently out of thin air—was one of her most unsettling habits. Her *primary* psychic talent, the one she relied on most, was empathy—as she had so amply demonstrated back on the highway. It was a very useful gift, but did tend to cause some consternation among her friends.

Especially when she blantantly *said* things like that.

"Uh—okay, well I kind of figured—Aunt Nita is pretty much waiting for us."

He pulled into the driveway of an enormous Victorian home, painted light gray with darker gray trim, and genteelly shabby. The lawn was the usual withered brown of Dallas grass in midwinter, but was showing some signs of reviving in the unseasonably warm weather.

The driveway was obviously a relic of earlier times; it was cobble-stoned, and barely wide enough for the Ghia. Mark would never have wanted to pull a standard-sized vehicle in here.

His aunt—as he could have predicted—had been watching for them. As he and Di got out of the car, a white-haired old woman in a gray, lace-trimmed dress opened her front door and descended the steps of the porch with the same dignity and poise Queen Elizabeth exhibited when treading the steps of Parliament—and with a good deal more grace than most monarchs ever displayed.

Mark waited respectfully; Aunt Nita was not a woman that any-one treated lightly. She was a ramrod-straight, iron wand of a woman of aristocratic *hidalgo* blood. Her parents and grandparents had held *rancheros* the size of counties. Her great-grandparents had been vir-tual monarchs.

All that had vanished, either at the hands of greedy Texas politi-cians, or in the Depression. All that was left her was her dignity, her pride, and this enormous house.

"Aunt Nita," Mark said, "this is the young lady I told you about, Diana Tregarde. Di, this is my Aunt, Juanita Valdez."

Di offered her hand with a smile whose warmth surprised Mark. He was even more surprised to see that his aunt was wearing a smile of identical warmth.

"I believe I have read one of your books, Miss Tregarde—*Blood and Roses*—"

"Good heavens, Miss Valdez! I didn't think *anyone* had bothered to buy that one!" She smiled ruefully at Mark. "That was one of my rare attempts at a serious historical—and it was a total failure. *I* thought it was a natural, it was set during the Spanish Campaign of the Napoleonic Wars, and done from the Spanish viewpoint. I guess I didn't get enough fainting and ravishing in it."

"It may have been an economic failure, Miss Tregarde," the white-haired lady admonished, "but it was an artistic success."

Di laughed. Mark wished she'd do so more often; it was such a musical laugh, like a clarinet arpeggio. "If you're going to praise me so extravagantly, Miss Valdez, you've earned a friend for life, and you're going to have to call me Di."

"In that case, you must give me the pleasure of hearing you call me 'Aunt Nita,' as Mark and my young ladies do. Would you care to come in and see your room? You *are* staying—"

Mark sighed. "Yes, Aunt; Di's staying. Her virtue is safe."

Di gave him a warning look, but his aunt merely smiled.

"Has Mark told you why I'm here?" she asked, as they climbed the stairs of the ornately carved wooden porch.

"You are some sort of expert in the occult, and he thinks you can help with these dreadful murders," she answered, obviously surprising Di.

Di looked back over her shoulder at Mark, who was following with the luggage. By the look on her face, she was no little taken aback.

"Aunt Nita's a believer," he said. "She actually tried to warn me about being too open before I went off to college, but I had no idea what she meant."

"A believer, but not a practitioner," his aunt agreed. "Poor young Mark was so puzzled—he thought I just meant that he was too trusting!"

"Anyway, she knows a good bit about you—"

Di sketched a pentagram in the air and looked back at him with an inquiring expression. He shook his head negatively.

"In that case," Di said, turning back to his aunt as they climbed the staircase to the rooms rented out to the boarders, "my work will be a little easier. I might do some odd things from time to time—I might ask you some odd questions. I promise that whatever I do or ask, I won't compromise any of your beliefs. If you feel any doubt or any discomfort at all, just say so."

"That statement alone confirms my welcome to you," the old woman replied, as Mark heaved a mental sigh of relief. They were hitting it off just fine. That had been his only worry.

After all, both Di and his aunt were very strong-minded individuals. "Alpha bitches," was what Di would have said. There could have been only two endings to this meeting—mutual respect or mutual antagonism. It was, thank God, mutual respect.

"Whatever else you are, dear, you are certainly on the side of the angels. I'm certain my parish priest would be shocked, but my people spent a great deal of time among the *indios*. There is good, and there is evil, and whatever other differences there may be are window dressing."

Mark smiled. This was going as well as he could possibly have hoped.

The old woman led the way down a white-painted hallway; the

wood floor was highly polished, and bare of rugs. She paused before the door at the end.

"This will be your room, my dear, for as long as you care to stay," she said, unlocking it and handing Di the key.

Di just stared. "Oh—my—"

"It is rather nice, isn't it?" his aunt said, pleased at her reaction.

Mark dropped Di's bags just inside the door. He had seen all the rooms at one point or another; he'd known this was one of the better ones. The furniture was all antique; sturdy stuff that had been hand-made by local craftspeople. It was of the dark wood and simple style found in most of the early *rancheros*, but having seen originals like these, no one would ever be content with the copies. The walls were painted white, with Indian rugs carefully mounted on them. The tall, narrow windows were curtained with loosely woven beige material. The bureaus and desk held fine examples of Indian and Mexican pottery.

"Aunt Nita is fairly careful about who she takes in," Mark said wryly.

"I trust my instincts," his aunt replied, just as dryly. "With one exception, most of my young ladies are graduate students in classical music and anthropology. They appreciate a good environment."

"What's the exception?" Di asked, plainly amused.

"I rent the basement to a young lady who is a dancer with the Fort Worth Ballet. She has a studio set up down here—which, she tells me, you are welcome to use."

Di grew immediately thoughtful. "That's very welcome; I'd rather not do my karate exercises around all these antiques. I suppose—" now it was her turn to look wry "—Mark told you about that, too."

"Good guess," Mark grinned. "You'll find you don't have a lot of secrets Aunt Nita doesn't already know."

"I won't even try to keep any, then. Why waste energy?"

"I save the best for last," Aunt Nita said with a smile all of mischief. "And I had intended to use this as an inducement to tempt you to stay here instead of risking your 'virtue' as Mark would say, with him. That door here is the closet, but the one next to it is your own bathroom."

"Oh, Aunt Nita—you know your sex only too well!" Di laughed. "Given the choice between having my own bathroom and sharing one with *anyone*—much less a man, who is likely to leave the cap off his toothpaste—what would *any* sensible female do?"

THREE

Mark was still a little flustered by Di's too-accurate reading of his emotional state. As he watched her unpack, he thought about the mess with Sherry, and wondered if she'd mind giving him a sympathetic ear on that one, too.

He decided, given that *she'd* brought it up, even if obliquely, that she probably wouldn't mind. And he wanted badly to talk to her about it. Di had a way of asking the right questions that let you at least get a new handle on things.

So he waited for her to finish getting her things put away, and watched patiently for the right opportunity.

It didn't take her long at all to get settled in; Mark noted that she still tended to travel light. Jeans, underthings, the ubiquitous leotards—one good suit, the fancy shirts and gear that went with it.

There really wasn't much that was out-of-the-ordinary in her wardrobe; none of the trappings of occultism so beloved of movies and bad novels. No dark, hooded robes or strange costumes, although one of the things she'd brought with her—the lab coat— raised his curiosity. She had everything neatly stowed away in less than an hour. The only bag she did not unpack was the smaller of her two carryons. He remembered that she had never allowed him to take it. What *that* signified he had no idea, although it did suggest that she had come prepared for trouble of a nonphysical nature. Certain of her "tools" were very sensitive; things of that ilk she generally kept at home, where she could be certain they would remain uncontaminated. To have brought them with her proved that she was taking this whole problem with deadly seriousness.

That unopened bag went into the closet, still packed.

"Well," she said, folding her arms and pivoting to face him as he lounged on the room's short couch, "I don't know about you, but I'm hungry. I'm not sure what it was they were serving on that plane, but I doubt it was ever alive. I have the feeling that my so-called Reuben sandwich had been on enough planes to earn a frequent-flyer trip to Hawaii before I ever saw it. What are my options?"

"Aunt Nita will feed you breakfast and supper—lunch will be on the department, and probably either hot dogs or our godawful cafeteria slop. But tonight—how about Italian? My treat."

"You're on—" Her purse was lying on the bureau by the door; she grabbed the strap and slung it over her shoulder in one smooth motion. On the way out she turned to check the door as she shut it behind them to make certain it had locked.

Then she dug briefly in the purse and came up with a vial of colorless liquid. Dipping her finger in it, she traced a wet line around the doorframe, then drew an invisible but intricate diagram on the door itself.

She accomplished the entire bit of rigamarole in something under thirty seconds; if he hadn't been standing right there and watching, he probably wouldn't have guessed she'd stopped long enough to do anything.

She glanced over at him as she stoppered the vial, and grimaced. "As they say—'just because you're paranoid, that doesn't mean there isn't anyone out to get you.' When I get back I'll do a more thorough job and include the windows—but the patterns on those ceremonial rugs will be enough to keep 'things' out for the short time we'll be gone."

"The—*what*? The rugs?"

She grinned. "That's what you get for being a medium instead of a sensitive. Or else you're so used to the vibes you don't notice them anymore. More of your aunt's instincts, I suspect—those aren't just any rugs on the walls, those are medicine blankets. Good ones, too. I'd give a pretty to know how she got them."

"They were mostly given to her grandparents by the local Indians," he said, slowly. "They were pretty enlightened for their times, and unusual in the way they treated the natives—like equals."

"I bloody well guess! There must be an interesting story there— damn! I *wish* I had more time—"

"You could always write her and ask when this is all over," Mark pointed out. "Aunt Nita is one of the old-fashioned type of letter-writers; for her, six pages is short. She'd love to correspond with you."

"Good thought." Di brightened. "Well, I think I hear a lasagna calling me—don't you?"

Mama Antonia's was a little family-operated place; Mama cooked, Papa was the waiter, three of the daughters were waitresses. It was a longtime favorite of Mark's. Papa welcomed him with a sly grin when he saw that Mark wasn't alone, and showed them to a table in the back corner, hedged in with ferns and lit mostly by candles.

"The lasagna is a good bet, provided you aren't worried about gaining weight."

She shrugged, and tossed her hair over her shoulders. "You'll be running it off me, I have the sinking feeling. Lasagna it is."

"Two—" Mark told hovering Daughter Number Three, a pretty, plump little child of barely seventeen, named Angelina, "and the house red."

One dinner and half a bottle of wine later, Mark felt the last of his reticence vanishing. Di sipped her own wine and looked at him with amused expectation.

"You have, I suspect, a personal problem?"

"I've got a question for you, first."

"Shoot."

"You're holding out on me." He'd known that from the way she'd clouded up when she'd talked about having heavy expenses. "Something's into you for a chunk of your income; I'd like to know what it is."

She looked uneasy and uncertain. "I—"

"C'mon, Di, I'm a friend. I'm *also* a cop. Maybe I can help. You being blackmailed or something?"

"No." She looked at him, long and hard, then seemed to make up her mind. "No—I've got—a sick friend. Too sick to work anymore. He's got major-medical, but I'm covering his nonmedical bills for him. Lenny's done me some pretty hefty favors in the past; I figured it was my duty to do the same. So I am. Besides, like I said, he's a friend, and right now, he hasn't got a lot of those."

Mark put two and two together, and made the jump to twenty-two. "AIDS, huh?" he said, making it a statement.

Her eyes widened. "How did you guess?"

He shrugged. "Put 'male,' 'friend,' and the fact you were pussy-footing around the subject together. I've got no argument with that—not like I'd have if somebody was putting heat on you. You do for friends, but you damn well don't pay danegeld."

"Well it'll sure help if I can get as many of my expenses paid for as possible."

"No sweat; I'll figure a way to squeeze as much out of the department as I can. Like—we're good for long-distance calls so long as they're partially business, okay? And if you need to FedEx something, we can probably put that on the account."

It seemed he had relieved her of a certain stress with his matter-of-fact acceptance of her situation. "Very okay. Now—what about that problem of yours?"

He sighed. "It seems pretty trivial stacked up against six corpses."

"But you'd like to talk about it anyway." She looked at him sharply, and bit her lip, as if to hide a smile. "Mark Valdez, I do believe you are in love!"

"Yeah—I guess so—" he said gloomily, and stared at his half-empty wineglass. "Problem is, the lady is married. *And* has a kid."

"Oh, boy—" She raised an inquisitive eyebrow.

"I do *not* go around seducing other people's wives." He glared at her, daring her to challenge him.

"I never suggested that you should."

He traced around the squares of the checked tablecloth with his finger. "The other problem is who she's married to. An old friend of mine—going back to when I could barely toddle. He's a professional photographer, Robert Fernandez."

"The *wunderkind*? I'm impressed. You can't open a magazine without seeing his models these days." She gave him a second, sharper glance. "Mark, you are *miserable*, aren't you?" She shook her head sympathetically.

"I guess so."

"How long has this been going on?"

"Oh—almost a year. Since he hit the bigtime. Back before then, I'd never met Sherry—I knew about her, but I'd never met her. Robert—well, he wasn't doing real well. I used to get him freelance work for the department when I could—I fed him lunch about three times a week. Then he went off on that Mexico City trip, and came back with a portfolio full of gold."

"The travel spread. I heard about it—set the Dallas sportswear mavins *and* the tourist business on their respective ears. Even made *Time*, as I recall. I've got a friend who has a travel agency—those photographs more than doubled her Mexico bookings, and she told me it was the same across the country. Those four girls are just incredible—"

"And they won't work with anybody but him, so he's got it made. He's banking enough to keep him comfortable from now until the end of the universe, even if he never works again. So he decided to start paying me back."

He laughed, but his heart wasn't in it. "Took me to—you wouldn't know the name—a fancy restaurant. The only reason I didn't get thrown out was because I was with him. I've never been so uncomfortable in my life. Rob figured *that* wasn't going to work, so he started inviting me over to his new place in the Bear Creek complex for dinner and drinks, and for the parties he's been throwing. That's when I finally met Sherry."

He sighed, and chewed his thumbnail.

"How often are you seeing them?"

"A couple times a week; she's got a thing about being the gracious hostess. It's driving me nuts—and I can't seem to stay away."

"Hm. I've heard that excuse before." When he looked up, the velvety brown eyes that met his over the candle flame were cynical.

"Yeah, I know." He sighed again. "It's just—when I'm there the girls aren't. Rob's a real Don Juan; I know he's sleeping with all four of them, because he told me himself. Sherry knows too; it's making her wretched. She still loves him."

"One wonders why," Di remarked dryly, playing with a bit of candle wax. "It doesn't sound to me like he's worth keeping, money or no. I still don't understand why *you* keep inflicting mental pain on yourself by hanging out around her. Last time I looked, you weren't a masochist."

"Because the girls never show when I'm invited. Whenever I'm over there, Sherry can forget about the girls for one evening, pretend they don't exist. It may be driving me insane, but it gives *her* a break, so I keep coming. Gives Bobby a break, too—poor little guy. They keep wearing perfume and stuff that he's allergic to, and he's asthmatic. I think he's picking up on the tension between his parents; Sherry says he's been having really bloody nightmares every night. I like the little house-ape, anyway, and he knows it; thinks I'm better than Magnum P.I. And Rob sure doesn't pay much attention to him. Shit, I'm not sure Rob's even sleeping in the same room with Sherry anymore. But I won't take advantage of the situation, dammit, I won't!"

Di echoed his sigh. "Lordy—it's as bad as one of my novels. What a mess! I wonder—"

She suddenly broke off the sentence to stare out the window, brow creased with puzzlement and something akin to pain.

"Di—"

"There's—something wrong." She frowned, her attention focusing inward, eyes plainly not seeing him.

"What?"

"I don't know—it's too nebulous—but—Mark, I think we'd better be leaving, and fast—"

Dwight Rhoades *should* have been a happy man. He'd been promoted to DP manager of Ransome International just this past year—the goal he'd been aiming at since he'd hired on. Data Processing had assumed an extraordinarily high level of visibility since the new director took over. The new man on top was convinced that the DP department was the one likely to make waves and save money in the future. So Dwight was in a position to make his mark.

He closed and locked his gray office door, and shuddered. The way things looked now, the only mark he was likely to make was a blot when he hit the sidewalk.

The gray carpet muffled his footsteps as he passed the row after row of identical cubicles that held his staff during the day. If only he could make them over the way the corporate planners had made over the DP complex—take away the spouses, the kids, the outside interests; make them into perfect servants of Ransome. Take everything away from them except a need to spend sixteen or twenty hours out of every twenty-four sitting in those little cubicles and producing the miracle that would save him.

Because it was going to *take* a miracle to save him.

He shouldered open the outside door, stepping out into the balmy evening. It slammed shut behind him of its own weight, the *thud* of its closing echoing across the parking lot.

It had a very ominous sound, like the lid slamming shut on a coffin.

He headed for his car, his own footsteps echoing in the silence.

Damn the new tax laws! That's what had gotten him into this mess in the first place. He'd agreed to a deadline set by guess and then undercut, a guarantee to get them into the system, a reckless deadline that had made the director's eyes light up—the programmers had tried to tell him it wasn't possible, but he knew better. He'd seen them, seen the way they worked. They were too used to taking it easy, too used to putting in their eight hours and heading home. They thought they could put one over on him because he'd been in data management, not programming. But regs said salaried personnel weren't entitled to overtime pay, and that compensatory time off was up to the discretion of the manager. And *this* manager had had every intention of showing them what it was like to hustle.

Besides, jobs were scarce in Dallas, what with the oil business bottoming out. He had wagered they wouldn't dare revolt if they wanted to keep getting their paychecks. So when things began to get tight on the schedule, he'd just handed them the appropriate ultimatum—put in the overtime, or look somewhere else for a job.

But now the project was weeks behind, every new body he'd hired had either quit ("You can take your six hours a day of uncompensated overtime and shove it up your wazoo," one had screamed at him, throwing his resignation on the desk) or gotten transferred. The director was beginning to wonder why he had such a high rate of resignations, and why the DP department had suddenly become such a hotbed of discontent. Antimanagement cartoons were showing up on bulletin boards—and little signs and stickers ("Poor planning on your part does not constitute an automatic emergency on mine," read one) were appearing in the director's interoffice mail. The old employees, the ones who had too much time in to quit, had come up with a new twist—they were getting "sick" as soon as five o'clock came around—migraines, allergies, nothing catching, nothing you could or couldn't prove. They went home "sick," and didn't "recover" until eight the next morning. And since they weren't getting "sick" during regular working hours, none of the regulations intended to keep salaried employees from pulling "sick-outs"—like forcing them to come up with doctor's notes proving they were *really* suffering from some infirmity or illness—could be enforced.

And as one told him insolently—"You want to force me to work when I'm sick? Go ahead and try—my lawyer says that would make me very rich."

Somehow, somewhere, he was going to *have* to find somebody to blame for this mess—before the director landed the blame squarely on *him*.

He was so involved in trying to think of a scapegoat who was high enough in the hierarchy to be credible (but low enough that when it came to claim versus claim, the higher rank would win out) that he never heard the footsteps behind him and never felt the blow that knocked him out.

When he woke up, the first thing that he noticed besides his aching head was that he was terribly cold . . .

He opened his eyes slowly, and moved his head just enough to look down at himself. He discovered that he had been stripped of all his clothing. He dropped his head back down; he'd been left lying on his back. He found himself staring up into a lacework of naked tree branches against the starry sky.

My God—I've been mugged—

He started to lever himself up into a sitting position; his head throbbed so painfully it was all he could do to roll over onto his side. For a moment he couldn't even see; his eyes fogged over and his stomach churned sour bile.

When his vision cleared, he realized that it *wasn't* an ordinary mugging.

He could see quite clearly in the moonlight. He was wearing—something. Not much. And *not* his underwear. A *loincloth*, the kind TV Indians wore; some strange jewelry. When he moved his head slightly, he realized there was something fastened on it, tied under his chin. He felt along his head, and encountered feathers. He grabbed the feathers and pulled the thing off—it was some kind of weird headdress that would have looked about right on a Las Vegas show-girl. He dropped it on the sandy ground beside himself. There were more feathered things on his upper arms and on his ankles, but he ignored them since they weren't bothering him.

He tried to get his feet under him, and felt a tugging at his right ankle. That was when he discovered that one of the feathered ankle things concealed something else. He was tethered by his ankle to an enormous boulder beside him.

He felt his stomach contract with fear, and ignored the throbbing of his head to sit up and seize the tether. He tugged at it, with no result; it wouldn't break or pull loose. He could feel the knots, but the thing was made of what felt like leather, and he couldn't even get the knots to loosen. He looked around the ground next to him for something to cut it with, but there was nothing there, not even a shard of glass or a sharp rock. The ground for as far as he could reach had been literally scoured. There were four sticks with feathers stuck along the edges lying next to him, but nothing useful.

He cast about frantically for help—or whoever had put him here. This place looked like a park—

And parks were patrolled. The cops went through every park in Dallas once an hour.

"*Help!*" he yelped, so scared his voice jumped an octave. He got halfway to his feet, clawing at his tether. "Somebody—help! I've been mugged—somebody help me! Police! Fire! Help!"

"No one will hear you," a deep voice said behind him, startling him into silence, "or heed you if they heard you."

He wrenched around on his knees, the sandy soil grating against his skin.

Out of the shadows beneath the trees behind him stepped a figure so strange Dwight was halfway certain he must be hallucinating it.

The man was wearing a loincloth a bit longer than Dwight's. His armbands and anklets were made of flowers instead of feathers. He must have been wearing forty pounds of elaborate metal jewelry, jewelry that gleamed silver in the moonlight. And his eyes peered out from the shadows cast by a bizarre helmet-like headpiece, like nothing Dwight had ever seen before. It seemed to be shaped like a snarling cat's head, with the man's face coming out of the open mouth.

He was carrying sticks like the ones lying in the dirt beside Dwight—except that instead of feathers, the edges were set with bits of something dark that glittered in the moonlight.

"What—what do you want?" Dwight stammered. "I'll give you whatever you want, anything you want. I've got money—I've—"

"I have what I want," the man interrupted, with heavy calm.

"But—"

"You are here for another purpose. You are a man in a position of power; you must have had courage to fight your way to that position. You are here to prove that courage."

"What—"

The man moved to the edge of Dwight's patch of bare earth, his sandals making a grating sound in the sand, and toed the feathered sticks.

"Take up your weapons," he said, "and defend yourself."

Dwight scrambled backward until his back encountered the cold, smooth boulder. He edged into its protection, mouth dry and heart pounding with fear.

My God, I've been caught by some kind of nut—

"I—I—" he stuttered.

The man came toward him and struck him lightly with the stick he carried. The blow looked almost playful—but Dwight felt sharp pain and looked down, startled, at his shoulder. There was a long gash there, and blood welling up and glittering blackly in the moonlight.

Suddenly it began to hurt—a *lot*. He nearly vomited. His stomach turned over, and he gasped as he swallowed down the bile of fear.

"I said to defend yourself." The man hit him again, opening up another gash to match the first. "Comport yourself with honor."

Dwight whimpered, and cowered into the shadow of the boulder.

The man's eyes glistened wetly in the moonlight, and he smiled. It was the most terrible smile Dwight had ever seen.

Terror overcame him. He flung himself, groveling, at the man's feet, blubbering like an hysterical child, begging for mercy.

"Please—" he wept shamelessly. "Please, I've never done anything—I don't know how to fight—I've never hurt anyone—"

He ignored the nagging memories of the careers he'd destroyed—or tried to—to get his current position. He pushed out of his mind the recollections of the hours he'd stolen from the private lives of the people beneath him—

That wasn't hurting anyone. That was just good business; good management. Any good manager would have done the same.

The warrior spat at him, impassively. The blob of spittle struck his cheek; he winced, but he was too frightened to wipe it off.

"Dog. Son of dogs," the man said, "you shame your family; you shame your gods. If you will not delight the Great One with your courage, then you must pleasure him with your pain."

He made an abrupt summoning gesture, and from out of the shadows behind him ran four wildly garbed young women, bedecked with flowers and feathers, wearing headdresses even more astonishing than the warrior's cat-helmet.

My God, it's a Manson-cult—

Before Dwight had a chance to react, they had seized his arms and legs, and were dragging him back to the boulder, sand grating in his cuts and getting into his eyes and mouth.

He tried to fight them, but they were far stronger than they looked. He accomplished nothing more than getting more dirt into his mouth.

They dragged him onto the boulder, and it scraped the skin from his back—

They stretched him out over the top of it, one on each limb, pulling his arms and legs so far apart he thought he was going to scream. They had him pinned, back bent over the rock; spread-eagled, unable to move enough to see anything except sky and tree branches and the heads of his captors.

The warrior loomed over him; in his right hand there was a knife-shaped object that glittered blackly in the moonlight.

"What—" that was all Dwight managed to get out.

The man studied him for a long moment, then reached out with the glittering thing, and drew it in a slow, deliberate line down the middle of Dwight's chest.

After that, all he could do was scream in agony.

Mark felt vaguely sick. *This is number seven—and it doesn't get any easier with repetition.*

Diana had gotten into his Ghia and—tranced out, was the closest Mark could come to figuring out what she'd done. It was a funny kind of trance, though; not like anything he'd ever seen her do before. She was sort-of "there" and sort-of "not there."

She'd told him, in a foggy, preoccupied voice, to start driving. After about ten minutes she'd told him "left"; then "right." He'd gotten the idea in fairly short order. Any time he'd ever been with her in the past, she'd always *known* where she was going. This time, she was evidently having trouble pinpointing her goal. So she had turned herself into some kind of detector; circling in on whatever she was sensing.

That had been a couple of hours ago; about the time that *he* figured out that Bachmann Lake Park was probably their destination, they'd gotten an "all points" on the radio in his car.

He and Diana had arrived on the scene at about the same time as the first squad car.

There wasn't much doubt in his mind that the victim had—quite literally—been sacrificed. What was left of him was lying spread-eagled and stark naked across a huge flat boulder—a boulder whose shape made it a kind of natural altar. In due course his belongings—all of them, including wallet and pocket-change—were discovered neatly folded and stacked, under a nearby bush. So robbery was out as a motive.

Mark figured he either died of shock or blood loss. Either would have done the trick. He had been mutilated with some incredibly sharp instrument, and with an almost artistic precision. Only "swimming" through a vat of broken glass could have produced lacerations so extensive.

The coroner agreed with Mark about the lacerations, but disagreed about the actual cause of death. *He* felt that the poor fellow had still been alive when his heart had been neatly removed from his body. Maybe even conscious.

The heart was lying in a little depression in the boulder, next to the victim's head.

The park patrol was a couple of rookies—more used to dope dealers and muggings than anything like this. One of them was still over in the bushes, throwing up. Mark had taken charge as soon as they arrived on the scene, much to the intense and obvious relief of the two patrolmen. He had made sure that the area around the body stayed unmolested until the arrival of the Homicide squad and the coroner. Once they arrived, Mark stayed out of the way. He was *not* a Forensics man; his forte was legwork. These days even detectives specialized.

The boulder and its burden were the center of a pool of glaring white light now, light so bright that the entire scene looked phony, like a movie setup. Mark found it easier to think of it that way; he wondered with macabre curiosity what the Parks Department was likely to do about the boulder. It was sandstone and the victim's blood had soaked into it so deeply that there would be no removing the stains. Would they leave it for the curious to gawk at, or would they break it up and remove it?

Mark had seen more than his share of ghastly corpses in his time; it was only the tortured expression branded on the man's face and the extent of the mutilations that disturbed him. He was somewhat queasy, but under control. The same could not be said for some of his colleagues—several of those who had arrived before the Homicide squad had joined the first officer in the bushes.

What rather surprised Mark was that Diana—except for a pronounced pallor—seemed about as unaffected by the grisly scene as he was. Once he had established the appropriate perimeter, she had gone straight to the edge of it and begun examining everything as minutely as she could from the distance permitted her. Mark watched her for a moment, trying to figure out just what she was up to.

She stood carefully and quietly at the border of string that marked the point-past-which. She made no attempt to get any closer, or to touch anything—but she spent long minutes studying the body, what portions of the boulder she could see, then finally getting down on her knees and examining the ground with the same care as the Forensics experts.

They had regarded her with some suspicion—but when she made no moves to interfere, and no comments—and when, in fact she had unobtrusively pointed out a bit of something they had overlooked— they began to regard her as—possibly—one of their own.

About that time Mark's boss arrived on the scene.

He was a balding, overweight man, incongruously dressed in a Hawaiian shirt and jeans. He looked far more like a particularly dull and dense redneck county sheriff than the owner of one of the sharpest minds Mark had ever worked under. It was an image he took pains to cultivate. Being consistently underestimated gave him a hell of an edge in interdepartmental politicking.

After making his own examination of the body and the proceedings, he wandered ponderously over to Mark's side.

"That your pet expert on wackos?" he asked, nodding in Diana's direction and taking out a cigar. He did not light it; he was trying to quit smoking, and claimed that just holding the thing in his teeth helped curb his craving for tobacco.

"Yes sir—"

"Huh." The cigar migrated to the other side of his mouth and he nodded, thoughtfully. "More brains than I'd'a thought, just to look at 'er. Got sense enough not t' touch anythin' , and not t' get in th' boys' way."

He watched as Di made a close examination of the mutilations on the victim's legs. "More guts, too. M' wife'd been halfway t' the Panhandle by now."

"She didn't get where she is by being squeamish," Mark felt compelled to point out.

"Yeah, Hartford PD sets pretty high store by 'er." The Chief clasped his hands behind his back, and continued to watch her. "I was kinda disinclined t' believe everythin' they told me, them bein' damnyankees an' all, an' her bein' a Yank too—but I think I'm changin' my mind."

Mark thought about what *he* knew about her. "Diana has that effect on people," he agreed.

At that point she got up from the ground beside the boulder, and walked slowly toward them, one eyebrow rising inquisitively when she saw that Mark had company.

"Diana Tregarde," Mark said as soon as she was within earshot, "Chief of Detectives Samuel Clemens Grimes."

She took the outstretched ham masquerading as a hand with no sign of hesitation, and Mark could tell by the slight widening of the Chief's eyes and the slow smile that she had returned his attempted squeeze with interest.

"Any relation to Mark Twain?" she asked as he released her hand.

"Somethin' distant on m' mother's side; she slapped it on me t' annoy some uppity aunty of hers back East," the Chief replied with perverse pride. "Well, missy—you bein' the imported expert, what y'all think?"

Diana gave Mark a look that held just a hint of amusement and that said quite clearly, *I'll tell you more, later.*

"I have absolutely no doubt that this was a ritual sacrifice, with all that implies," she said slowly—so slowly that Mark got the distinct impression that she was choosing each of her words with utmost care. "I think it was very carefully planned and executed, possibly with this specific individual in mind as the victim. I also would judge that it wasn't timed randomly—I think whoever did this had some specific goal in mind."

"Like what? What th' hell good's a stiff t' anybody? Unless y' think this ritual stuff's a cover-up fer a paid hit."

Diana looked at the Chief, measuringly. "Try to think like someone who'd do this sort of thing for a moment—there are any number of traditions that place a very high power value on a ritual sacrifice carried out with precision and according to a ceremony as involved and elaborate as a Catholic High Latin Mass."

"Huh. So—why?"

"If you think of magical power as a tangible force—and these people *do*—you want to accumulate as much of it as you can *without* having to give anything up yourself." She made a half shrug. "There are two traditional ways of raising power, both involving sacrifice. The first is *self*-sacrifice: abstinence, chastity, the accumulation of power by *not* using it for the pursuit of pleasure. That's the kind of thing that a Buddhist monk, a Shao-lin priest, or a *real* yogi would do. And that's the hard way; it isn't in these people to do anything the hard way. So the other way to get power is to take someone's power from them. The easiest way to do so is to murder—with as much pain inflicted as possible."

"So you don't think this was just some isolated nut?" Mark prompted. He knew that, like himself, the Chief was convinced that they were dealing with a group, but it was interesting to see how he was taking what Di told him and integrating it with his own suspicions. Mark could almost see the wheels going around in the Chief's head.

"No—nor do I think this is some cult that's sprung up on its own," Di replied soberly. "Everything points to a group with an established and elaborate ritual to complete."

"Like—what? What's tippin' you off?"

Di waved her hand at the boulder and its burden. "Just about everything over there. The mutilations, for instance; they're absolutely symmetrical to fractions of an inch; the order in which they were made argues for following an established pattern. The area around the boulder is completely clean of *any* sign of footprints; they obviously cleaned up after themselves. There were a couple of flower petals—I couldn't identify what kind—and bits of feather in the grass beyond the dirt, which leads me to think that the victim was decorated and the decorations removed to avoid their being traced.

The petals were fairly fresh, so they probably weren't from anything brought into this area during the day, and there's nothing in bloom around here, so it looks as if whoever did this brought them *and* remembered to remove them. That's the kind of thing amateur Satanists and the like don't think of doing. They tend to be very sloppy—and sometimes they even leave things behind on purpose, since one of their goals is to terrify the believers and nonbelievers alike. It's part of their power trip to frighten people."

The Chief chewed on the end of his cigar, thinking furiously. "All right, missy," he said after a long pause. "I'll buy what you're sayin'. You do seem to know—"

"I've made something of a study of it," Di said modestly. "I managed to point the Hartford cops in the right direction once or twice, anyway."

"Okay—then you tell *me*—*is* this Satanists an' witches? We got some kind of coven thang going here?"

Mark choked, and quickly turned it into a cough as both of them glared at him. Di had told him the very night they met that she was a practicing witch. "Famtrad," she'd said, "which means 'family tradition.' I was trained by my great-grandmother; the psi-senses skipped two generations in my family. It was kind of funny; Mom was raising me as a good little Episcopalian, and Grandy was giving me another sort of education altogether—and although it may seem to be a contradiction, in her way she was as devout as Mom. Grandy's generation kept everything as secret as in the Burning Times. Well, witchcraft is about the only way *I* know of to train psychics; at least they're the only folk around with a fully developed course of education."

Di did not seem in the least discomfited by the Chief's question, nor did she read him the same lecture she'd given Mark when he'd confused witchcraft—"Wicca" she called it—and Satanism. "It doesn't correspond with any ritual of dark witchcraft or Satanism that *I've* ever heard of," she said, shifting restlessly from foot to foot with an unobtrusive swaying motion, the only real sign that she was deeply disturbed. "For one thing, it's the wrong time of the month; both types of cult would have set this at moon-dark, and we're halfway between full and last quarter. For another, both place a great deal of emphasis on binding a blood-victim, and the only place I saw the mark of tethering was on his right ankle."

"What if they're mavericks?"

She shook her head, tucking a flyaway strand of hair back in place. "I told you, this kind of sacrifice *has* to follow strict formulas, or the practitioners consider it ineffective. Blood-sacrifice *has* to take place at the dark of the moon, otherwise the power just isn't released properly. Now there *is* a superficial resemblance to certain Druidic rites—but—"

"But—" prompted the Chief.

"Well, the sacrifice in *that* case either has to be a willing victim, in which case he would have been a member of the order, and he'd have been drugged to keep him from feeling pain—"

"Well, that sure don't match this."

"—or he's an oathbreaker, a violater of the laws—which again would mean that he would also be a member of the order. They just don't do this sort of thing to nonmembers."

The Chief looked speculatively in the direction of the corpse, now shrouded and soon to be taken away, and shook his head with a little regret. "No sign of that; Mr. Rhoades was a good Freewill Baptist boy, an' what time he didn't spend in church or with 'is fam'ly 'e spent at work."

"Well, there's also something like this in Norse ritual—a punishment for someone who has truly made an implacable enemy of a cult-member."

"Now that sounds promisin' ," the Chief said, nodding. "From what I make out, Mr. Rhoades wasn't too well liked by his people. Seems he's been pushin' 'em pretty close t' the breakin' point."

Di sighed and shook her head. "The problem there is that if he had angered some practicing Norse pagan cult, they'd have either hung him from an oak, or performed something on him called the 'blood eagle.' "

"Which is?"

"Are you sure you want to hear this? Don't say I didn't warn you—the victim is put on his stomach, not his back—slits are made between his ribs, and his lungs are pulled out through them. He is left that way until he dies—which is usually hours to days; basically, until he dies of shock or his lungs dry out."

The Chief was taken a bit aback by her matter-of-fact recitation. "Whoa—nice people. That *is* a little like this 'un, ain't it?"

Again she shook her head. "I told you, these people are absolutely serious and absolutely fanatical about what they do. This just doesn't match the 'M-O,' as you'd say. The closest I can come—and what I'm going to be following up on if you want me to—is this is something like the rites Aleister Crowley developed. Or maybe—just maybe—some outlawed Hindu cults. The thugee cult in particular."

"Who's this Crowley? Can we get aholt of 'im?"

"Well, his followers would say 'yes,' but I have severe doubts about their sanity." Di managed a wan smile. "I'm afraid he's been dead for a good long time."

"But he does still have followers?" The Chief pounced on that bit of information.

"As they say, 'there's one born every minute.' Yes, Crowley still does have followers. The main difference between what we have here and Crowley's rituals, is that Crowley left the sacrifice alive, rather than cutting out the heart as a grand finale—presuming the poor devil he'd been slashing didn't bleed to death. It was the spilling of blood that was important, not the death. The Hindu cult of Kali is almost a better bet; they *did* cut organs out of their victims, they *did* tend to torture before killing, and they *also* decorated their sacrifices. Trouble is, I haven't heard even a rumor of a single *thug*—that's what they're called—in the entire United States."

The Chief carefully removed his mangled cigar from between his teeth and smoothed it between his fingers while he looked Diana up and down.

"Well," he said, canting his head to one side, "you seem to know what you're talkin' about, anyway. Tell me somethin' missy—can you take orders? Take 'em when they're given, and not go asking questions until there's time fer questions?"

Di nodded emphatically. "Of course," she replied. "You don't joggle an electrician's arm—and you don't ask questions when you might be under fire."

The Chief grinned and stuck the cigar back in his mouth. "Missy, you got a good head on you fer a woman an' a nut-case expert. I'm thinkin' we're gonna get along. All right, boy—"

For the first time in this conversation he acknowledged Mark's presence.

"—your little lady here is on; no holds barred, she's ours, she gets what any critter on the squad gets. I want you two in my office 'bout ten ack emma. I'm thinkin' this case is gonna need some special handlin', and I'm thinkin' I'd better set somethin' up now t' do that, 'fore it's too late."

"Yes sir," Mark responded. "Ten A.M. it is."

The Chief wandered off to see to the removal of the body. Feeling that they had been dismissed for the evening, Mark gave Di a quizzical look.

"In the car," she said shortly. "This place is literally making me sick."

Since the Ghia was parked only a few yards away, it wasn't long before Mark's curiosity was satisfied.

They sat, side by side, in the silent car, until Di cleared her throat and began to speak, hesitantly.

"I've seen uglier corpses, love," she said, staring out into the darkness beyond the windshield and rubbing her hands along her arms as if she felt chilled. "This was more than just an ugly death. Everything I told your chief was true—this *was* a ritual of power. It was more than that. It was a ritual of invocation."

"Invocation? Of what?"

"I don't know; it doesn't correspond with anything I've ever run into before, either myself or by hearsay. I can get a general sort of picture just from the power currents that have been set in motion, but every time I try to get something more than a generality, I just pull a blank. This is just one of a series of rituals, I think; there have been some before, and there will be more unless we can put a stop to them. They will *all* be blood-rituals culminating in death, and intended to bring *something* into full manifestation. What—I don't know. But the manifestation—it's close; it's very close."

She regarded him with troubled eyes, light from the parking-lot lamp contrasting with shadows in the hollows under her cheekbones.

"There's something else bothering you—and I think I know what."

"Hm?"

"I've been with you on other hunts; you've never had problems pinpointing bad vibes before this. You're good; you may be the best I've ever seen, inside or outside the law. So why did you have so much trouble even *finding* this place—especially with the amount of emotional anguish that must have been here? Why was the trail so cold to you? *That's* what I think bothers you the most."

"Bingo," she said soberly. "Right on target. This thing has me badly worried because—even though this must have released a tremendous amount of *power* as well as the emotional turmoil—I didn't pick up a thing. Not a glimmer. I tracked this by a snatch of precognition and a 'dead' spot that shouldn't have been here."

Mark whistled. "Good Lord—whoever they are, they're shielding like crazy! Then that means they really do know what they're doing!"

She nodded unhappily. "Exactly what I told your chief. These people—whoever they are—are for real. And because they're for real, they are far more dangerous than your chief realizes."

After they had watched the Homicide and Forensics crews clean things up and shut the operation down, there didn't seem anything

more that either of them could do. Di wasn't being particularly talkative, and it was getting late. . . .

"I'll tell you what," Di said finally, "I think my best bet would be
to start at the beginning. Why don't you get me all the records on
'John Doe' homicides and animal mutilations for the past six
months—no, make that a year—"

"Sure," Mark agreed, stifling a yawn with the back of his hand,
and turning the ignition key. "Just—Di, I've been up since 5:00 A.M.,
can't it wait until tomorrow?"

"Where's your stamina?" she teased. "You used to be able to do
better than this!"

"Darlin' ," he drawled, "let me tell you a simple fact of life. After
thirty, the warrantee runs out. After thirty-five, parts start falling off.
And I need some sleep—before my radio runs my battery down."

"Okay, okay. Can you stay awake long enough to get me back to
your aunt's place?"

He backed out of the parking slot and sent the Ghia sedately on
her way. "I don't have to—the Lady in Red already knows the way.
You know, just like old times."

Di shuddered theatrically.

As he'd half expected, his aunt was waiting up for them. Mark suspected that she was not at all certain that Di's presumed virtue was
safe in the hands of her nephew. She opened the front door before Di
could get her key out of her purse.

"Heavens, you're awfully late," she said, with a world of unspoken
questions in her eyes. "I thought you'd just gone out to eat."

"We did—but Homicide found what looks like one for us at
Bachmann Lake Park," Mark answered. "You know I've got a radio
receiver in Lady. We've been out there most of the night."

Aunt Nita ushered them both into the entryway; Mark was about
ready to fall over, but he answered all of his aunt's questions with
fairly good humor. After all, now that she'd found they'd been out examining mutilated corpses, and not assuaging Mark's lust, she was
rather embarrassingly relieved.

"Not that I was worried, mind," she said, realizing that her concern had been a bit too obvious and attempting to cover herself.
"But—"

"It's all right, Aunt Nita," he said, too tired even to tease her. "I
should have warned you that we might be keeping some really oddball hours. I just didn't think that it was going to start this soon."

"Heavens, here I am keeping you standing around in the hall—Mark, would you like some coffee, tea—"

"Something with enough caffeine in it to get me home safe would be right welcome about now," he admitted, as she led them back into the kitchen. "Di?"

"Tea, I think," she replied. "If it's not an imposition. I've got some research to do before I hit the hay—I wish I could have brought more in the way of books with me than I did, but I can at least make a start."

"I wish you'd been able to finish your degree work, Mark," Aunt Nita said wistfully, as she started hot water for tea. "I know you do a lot of good where you are, but I wish there had been enough money for you to have become a lawyer like we planned."

"Is *that* what your original major was?" Di asked curiously.

Mark shrugged, and selected a teabag from the assortment his aunt offered. "I'm not certain now I would have gone through with it, especially not after getting involved with your little group. As it was, instead of detective work I *almost* went into Bunco—"

"You'd have been wasted there," Di admonished, spooning honey into her tea.

"Maybe—but I would have been able to separate the phonies from the few with real abilities, and see that we hustled the ones that deserve being hustled."

"Small potatoes," she replied, as Aunt Nita dropped into a third chair at the table, plainly fascinated. "Just because we rousted out a couple of phony mediums at college, and it seemed like it might be interesting—you can take it from me, it gets old real fast, Mark."

"One of those phony mediums was a *real* killer!"

"And who was the one that pegged her? 'Twasn't me. You're where you belong, love." She turned to Mark's aunt, tapping her spoon against her cup to emphasize her point. "Your nephew has a real gift for sensing things wrong, Aunt Nita. That was why he called in the Hartford cops on that wretched creature back in college. She was preying on sick little old ladies, first running the usual seance scam on them, then getting all their portable wealth away from them under the pretense that she needed it to keep the 'contacts' going. She'd take everything: cash, jewelry, even the family silver. Well, that's not unusual, as Mark could tell you, but when she'd taken them for all they had, this lovely lady gave them farewell cups of foxglove tea before anyone found out she'd milked them dry."

"Simulated heart failure," Mark nodded. "And Hartford PD hadn't seen the connection."

"That's because they weren't working our end of it," Di pointed out. "They hadn't known the old dears were even *seeing* a medium. We were the ones who saw them coming and going, and it was *you* who noticed how many of Madame Thelma's clients ended up on the obituary page."

He shrugged.

"And I have the feeling," Di continued doggedly, "that it's going to be connections where no one else has noticed connections that is going to hand us the answer to this one. It may be my knowledge and my gifts, but it will be your ability to put chestnut hulls together with feathers and see a stuffed and roasted goose."

"Maybe—" he yawned again. "But if I don't get some shuteye, I'm not going to be able to tell the chestnuts and the feathers apart."

FOUR

The phone rang.

Mark was nearly half awake; he tried to ignore it, to bury himself somewhere in the middle of his mattress, but it wouldn't *stop* ringing.

"Go away," he growled at it. "Shut up!"

It didn't shut up. *Somebody* was very persistent.

Cursing Alexander Graham Bell and all his descendants unto the ninth generation, he reached for the handset on his nightstand, missed, reached again, and got it finally on the third try.

"If this is a siding salesman," he mumbled, "I'll be sending a hit man around to take you out in one hour."

"It's Di, Brighteyes." The voice in his ear sounded far too alert and cheerful for his liking. "Having conquered the intricacies of the Kabala and the twisted philosophy of the mad Arab, Abdul Alhazred, I have crowned my career by mastering the Dallas bus system. I'm down at the stop at the entrance of your complex. I figured I'd better give you warning before I pounded on your door. You *might* have shot me."

"I *still* might," he grumbled.

Her only reply was a trill of laughter as she hung up.

He fumbled the phone back into place and peered at his clock. Seven A.M. The Chief wanted them in his office at ten. Gag. Better go stand under the shower for a while.

After five minutes of hot water followed by one of cold, he was feeling somewhere around the level of *Homo erectus*. With a transfusion of coffee he might reach *Homo neanderthalis*.

Clothing.

He'd managed to find everything but his shoes—and more important, drag the clothes on over his weary body—when Di tapped on his front door.

He knew it was Di before he even got within five feet of the door, and not by any paranormal method, either.

"Pardon me, sir," came a high-pitched, squeaky voice, only partially muffled by having to pass through an inch of wood, "but I'm working my way through Gramarye School, and I wondered if I could interest you in a complete set of the translations of the *Necronomicon*? Bound in genuine simulated humahide with fourteen-karat goldlike tooling? A priceless heirloom designed to be passed down to future generations, should you live so long?"

Less than ten hours ago the owner of that voice had been kneeling at the side of a very mangled corpse, doing a valiant job of not throwing up. Now she was making jokes . . .

Damn, she's got the same defense mechanisms cops do, Mark thought in surprise. *Which tells me she* has *been poking around some pretty grim situations the past few years. Well. She always was tougher than she looked—I think I can stop worrying about her taking care of herself—*

"Does this translation include the commentaries and footnotes by Robert Bloch?" he called back.

"I—don't think so, sir. August Derleth, but not Robert Bloch."

"Not interested." He opened the door.

Di was leaning up against the doorframe, an impish grin transforming her face to pure gamin. "Well, how about some Gargoyle Scout Cookies, then?"

"Only if they have caffeine. Get in here, before my neighbors start to talk."

She skipped inside and he closed the door behind her. "You mean they don't talk now?"

"Of course they do—but if wholesome types like you start showing up, making me get up *early*, they just might think I've gone respectable."

"Good God, we can't have that." She took a quick look around the living room; there wasn't much to see. Mark's one extravagance was his entertainment center; the rest was Salvation Army tables, foam flip-chairs, and futons. "Lord, Mark, you're slipping—this is cleaner than my place."

"Don't look in the bedroom; there's things growing in the corners." He staggered into the kitchen to start the coffeemaker; she followed noiselessly behind him.

"Well now," he asked, before she crossed the threshold, "how is the one love of my life?"

"I trust you don't mean me—"

"Bite your tongue," he replied, scooping up a small, furry handful of delicate charm from the middle of the kitchen floor and turning back to Di. "You forfeited your claim on that position when you called me at 7:00 A.M. Di, meet Treemonisha."

"What a love!" she exclaimed, holding out her hand for the cat to sniff. Treemonisha, a dainty sable Burmese that Mark had found in an alley one night, examined the proffered fingers with aristocratic care. She determined that Di was appropriate company for Mark, and bestowed her approval with a tiny lick and a rub of her head.

Mark put her down on the floor and filled her bowl with chopped chicken from a bag he extracted from the refrigerator. The acknowledged queen of the household resumed her stately progress toward breakfast, a progress she'd interrupted when the doorbell rang.

"Getting to be a real homebody, aren't you? Furniture, cats, microwaves—"

"Bite your tongue. Coffee?"

"I don't suppose you have it in IV? No? Black, sugar."

Ten minutes later he was feeling alert enough to deal with Dallas traffic, and they were on their way to headquarters.

"Had any inspirations since last night?" he asked, as they pulled onto the freeway, figuring he might as well get the ball rolling.

She shook her head. "There's nothing in any of my books that even bears a superficial resemblance to what we saw last night except the Kali cult, and I have a hard time believing I wouldn't have picked up on *thugee* moving in. What I want to do now is to winnow out the deaths and mutilations that really *are* the work of our cult—"

"Can you do that?" he interrupted.

"Oh sure, that's not the problem. That aura I picked up last night will *still* be lingering around the sites; I'm a good enough empathic clairvoyant to pick it up off a map or a photograph. You don't wipe away the stain of something like that in a few months, not even in a big city. No, the problem will be coming up with a good rationalization to give your chief about *why* I'm going to pick that particular set of cases as our string. I *hope* that between us we'll be able to find the common link to satisfy him. I want him thinking I'm doing this scientifically, not by esoteric means."

"Tall order." He sent the Ghia flying for the exit ramp.

"I never said it was going to be easy," she pointed out. "My work is a lot like yours—I've learned bunches from the Hartford PD about investigative procedure. All right, once I do pick out the cult-kills, I'm going to try to fit them into some kind of lunar/solar/stellar pattern. I *did* bring full ephemerides with me, and a sort program and astrological database I developed with the Hartford PD on diskette. If I can find a pattern, that might tell us something about what tradition the cult is working in."

He pulled into the HDQ parking garage. "Sounds good to me. I'll drop you off with the Records people; I've got paperwork to do on the murder last night. I'll come get you in time for the meeting."

"She's in the back," Sara told Mark in a nasal Bostonian accent, looking up at him over the rims of her bottle-bottom glasses. "I thought she'd be a real flake, but she's okay. Knows the retrieval system, so I just gave her the spare terminal and a laser printer and let her rip while I check out this program of hers and see if it's compatible with our system. It should be, both us and Hartford have nearly the same setup, but you never know. When are *you* gonna get computer-literate, goat-roper?"

"As long as I have you around, why should I?" he asked over his shoulder, as he headed to the back of the Records Room. "That's what damnyankees were created for."

"One of these days, Valdez—the *least* you could do is buy me lunch sometime!"

"Sure—the day you learn to appreciate real food. Chili, *chimichangas*, and *fajitas*—not sushi and tofu."

"Get *real*."

"I happen to like sushi," Di admonished, not looking up from her terminal. "Although tofu isn't on my all-time favorite list. Looks too much like Styrofoam."

Mark shuddered. "Woman, the day the Pope told us we didn't have to eat fish on Friday anymore was the happiest day of my life—and why anybody would eat the stuff *raw*—"

"It isn't raw, it's marinated; you only ruin the flavor by subjecting fish to heat. You've just burned out all your taste buds with jalapeño peppers, that's all." She shut the machine down, turned it off, and spun her chair around to face him. "All right Daniel, let's go beard the lion in his den."

"A li'l bird down in Records tells me you been puttin' in a good mornin's work, Miz Tregarde." The Chief regarded her thoughtfully over his loaded desk. " 'Specially since we ain't payin' ya'll jack."

She spread her hands deprecatingly. She had the good chair; the one with wheels that stayed on when you moved it. Mark stood, rather than chance the other. "You asked for help," she said. "When you ask *me* for help, you get it; I don't do a job halfway."

"Uh-huh. Mark, I gotta tell you, I gotta allow as how this young lady is comin' off mighty impressive. I didn't think much of the notion when y'all talked me inta it, but she didn't lose her cookies last night, an' she ain't gone flappin' her beak t' the newsboys—I didn't necessarily trust them damnyankee cops, but she's been livin' up t' what they told us."

Mark was a little uncomfortable with the Chief talking about Di as if she weren't there, but the amused wink she slipped him eased his embarrassment somewhat. "She has a tendency to surprise people, like I told you last night."

The Chief chuckled. "Damn well told! Okay, I done some thinkin' on this mess; you ain't the most senior, but you got a better feel fer this thang than anybody in the department. I got a gut feelin' this ain't gonna get solved real quick. So you an' Miz Tregarde are on special assignment as of right now. I'm puttin' you on detached duty; y'all report straight t' me fer the duration. Y'all are on free rein; take as long as it takes, an' I'm figgerin' on months. I'll have a reg'lar team on this too, somebody t' give th' newsboys somebody t' watch and nag at. Maybe we'll break this thang the reg'lar way, but I ain't bettin' on it. Y'all are my ace in the hole. An' I ain't gonna admit y'all even exist."

"Thank God," Di said fervently. "The *last* thing I need is to have some yazoo from *National Enquirer* climbing in my bedroom window. Trust me sir—"

"Y'all might as well call me 'Chief.'"

"If you'll call me Di. Chief—I don't want to be known for this any more than you want me attracting attention. If nothing else, I have a living to make—I assume you know I don't do this as a career. I can't write if every time I get into a juicy love scene the phone starts ringing and it's some jerk who wants me to find Judge Crater or something. I've had friends who ended up on the scandalrag sourcebooks as 'experts in the occult.' They had to change their names, finally. Those bozos *won't* take 'no' for an answer, not even when it's backed with a club."

The Chief chuckled again. "Okay, Miz Di. Now what I'd like from you right off'n the bat, is t' check out th' fruitcake angle. I don' wanta mess y'all up if you got a lead—"

"Not yet," she said, shaking her head. "I'm just getting organized.

I don't see a problem; mind you, I told you last night that this probably *isn't* the work of some known fruitcake, but it *will* help to be able to eliminate them right away."

"Fine—I'll get you the makesheets on 'em an' send 'em on down. The first one's th' head somethin' of the Church of Satan—he's been pretty mouthy 'bout the homicide last night, denyin' his flakes had anythin' t' do with it 'fore anybody could even ask 'im. The second, he's got a porn palace; goes in for the leather an' whips an' chains bunch. Vice tells me he's got some other stuff in th' back that ain't strictly porn, stuff that looked pretty spooky t' them. Mark, Ramirez sez he ain't goin' back there without seein' his parish priest first if that tells y'all anythin'. "

"Maybe, maybe not; Ramirez spooks pretty easy since Vice broke up that cathouse with the voodoo woman for a madame."

"Maybe he's got a good reason to be spooked," Di put in thoughtfully. "This might tie in with voudoun; I hadn't thought about that here, it isn't the territory for it. Louisiana, Florida, I'd expect—Texas, no."

The Chief raised his eyebrow. "You kin check for yourself, I reckon; see what th' ol' boy has on his shelves. I kin tell you this much—when y'all spouted names at me last night, I checked with Vice; their report sez this ol' boy has got a lotta stuff by that Crowley fella."

"Now *that* is interesting; it wouldn't hurt to see if the killings fall anywhere around where this guy lives. The archives and the computer could tell me that fast enough. By the way, you wouldn't mind my adding a little program of my own to your base, would you? Sara said to ask. It could end up being useful on other cases like this one."

"Depends. What is it?" the Chief asked suspiciously.

"Just another search program; this one is based on moon cycles, seasonal cycles, and star charts. I told you loonies like this try to do things to match patterns—this program will help you find out if there are any matches."

"Jes' make sure t' check it out with Sara; if she says it's okay, then it's okay by me. I gotta tell you, Miz Di, I was right pleased t' find out you was down there with your nose in th' archives. I figgered out a helluva lot more cases doin' snoopin' and pryin' than I did playin' Dirty Harry. People round here get touchy when you start leanin' on 'em wrong—an' you go wavin' a piece at 'em, they're likely t' wave a piece of their own right back at you." He warmed to his subject; Mark stifled a sigh. He'd heard this all before.

"You start actin' like some yoyo on th' tellyvision, you ain't gonna get nowhere. . . ."

Mark could practically recite the monologue in his sleep—not that he disagreed with the Chief on any of his points. It was just that you got a little tired of hearing it after a while.

And there were times when it was *so* tempting to forget the Miranda decision ever existed—

Then again, from what he'd read about the late Mr. Dwight Rhoades, it had probably been *real* tempting for his former employees to create Rambo fantasies. That was why *he* didn't think it was an employee, current *or* previous, and not just because there didn't seem to be a tie-in to some of the other cases. If *he'd* had Dwight Rhoades for a boss, and *he'd* gone around the bend, Mark knew what *he'd* have done. He'd have gotten himself a nice legal semiautomatic rifle and filled Dwight Rhoades with so many holes he'd have looked like a lace tablecloth . . .

He shook himself out of his reverie. Di was still looking attentive, but the Chief was winding down.

"Anyway," he finished, "y'all know what you need to do, so I ain't gonna get in your way. When you think you can go give those loony-tunes a look-see?"

"Tomorrow soon enough?" Di asked. "By then I'll have my data together, and I can put a preliminary report in your hands."

The Chief whistled. "Miz Di, I wasn't expectin' anythin' in writin' *that* fast—"

She smiled as she stood up and Mark got ready to leave. "Chief, I have one real advantage over your staff—I *write* for a living. I may not be a detective, but I'm hell on wheels over a keyboard!"

He laughed. "Lady, you better not let any of th' other boys know that! They'll kidnap you, an' never let you see th' light of day again! Hellfire, *I* might—what's a felony when I got somebody t' do all my paperwork?"

"All right Yankee, how do you like your hot dogs, and how many?" Mark asked as he and Di pushed open the door to Records.

"Two and everything. Large diet cola, easy on the ice. Sara, what do you want?" Di said before he could interrupt, smiling sweetly. "Mark's buying."

"Like hell; the Department is buying, and—what the hell, I'll pick up the tab this time. Four-eyes?"

"The same, wetback. Di, I've been looking over that correlation program of yours, and I don't see any problem; if it ran on the Hartford mainframe, it should . . ."

Mark made his escape while he could; technese was worse than Greek to him.

When he returned, Sara was involved in a search for somebody from Legal, and Di was back at her terminal in the rear. Mark dropped Sara's lunch on the desk—careful to leave it in a clear place; he'd never forgotten the day he'd left a coffee cup on one of her precious little disks—and headed for the rear.

Di was just sitting; the terminal was mostly blank, with a tiny *running* in the upper left-hand corner. He touched her shoulder and she jumped.

"Lordy—I shouldn't have let myself blank out like that—"

"Any results?" he asked, plopping down into a chair beside her and starting on his own lunch ravenously.

"Here." She tapped a pile of folders to one side of the terminal. "I got hard copy because I figured we might want to consult some of the data when we're away from here. Everything else I looked into was either copycat or garden-variety loonies. Either one you'll catch eventually; they'll slip. Our cult—they're too careful. We'll get them only by being smarter than they are."

He picked up the top folder and began leafing through it. By the time he reached the bottom of the pile, he had noticed one thing: there were no dates earlier than April of the previous year.

The cases had not been arranged in any particular order. On a hunch, he sorted them in order of the dates of occurrence.

He felt a line of cold run up his spine when he saw that there was a second pattern—

The incidents started with the mutilation and killing of a single animal; the next was like the first, and the next. Then came the slaughter of half a dozen animals. Following that one was a similar slaughter, but this time the carcasses had been carefully laid out in a pattern afterward, and the mutilations on their bodies had been very precise.

Then came a series of single "John Doe" murders: winos, addicts, bag ladies. The pattern with the animals was being repeated—first simple murder, killing that almost looked as if it had come as the result of a fight. Then something more elaborate. Then mutilations before death—

And now, tonight—

"Is it too much to hope that this is the end of it?" he asked Di, praying that the answer would be yes.

"No, I'm afraid this is likely to be just the beginning of a new phase for them," she replied thoughtfully. "And it looks to me like *I* am going to be in trouble. I'm running the correlation program to make sure, but take a look at the dates, and compare them with the chart I made from the ephemeris."

Mark put the dates of the incidents on a timeline, then compared it with Di's hastily scrawled chart. He stared at the result, chewing the end of his pencil as he tried to find a pattern.

"If there's a correlation there, *I* can't find one," he admitted finally.

"Me neither," she replied, surprising him. "Nor can the computer, I'll bet, though the job isn't finished yet. There isn't any pattern following any cycle that I've ever worked with—yet there *is* a pattern of self-consistency within the incidents; they are all about three weeks apart until the end of the animal series—then they're about every day. There *is* a ritual being followed; I have no doubt of that whatsoever. You'll notice the other pattern—"

"Increasing violence," Mark said grimly.

"Exactly. It goes from simple death to real atrocity with the animals—then starts the pattern all over again, but this time with human beings."

"The last couple of John Doe killings have been groups of two and three—until this one."

"Now we get the elaborate ritual murders." She sighed. "Everything I can see points to more to come."

"No," Mickey's mother whined. "You kids stay out here."

Mickey stuck his lower lip out and pouted. "I wanna book."

Robin and Lisa jumped on that. "We wanna book! We wanna book!" they chanted, jumping up and down and pulling on their mother's arms.

For once their mother didn't cave in. "There *aren't* any kids' books in this store. Besides, I thought you wanted some G.I. Joe stuff."

Mickey stuck to his guns. "I wanna book. I wanna book *too*."

"You just *stay* out here and play. I'll get you a G.I. Joe book at Kmart."

"But I wanna book—"

"Mickey—" His mother got that pinched, angry look around her eyes. The one that said she was about to forget her EST and nonviolent parenting and smack him one. "You wanna live to reach nine?"

Mickey hadn't made it to eight without learning the danger signs. Mommy would be real mad at herself for smacking him, but he'd *still* get smacked. He shut up, and dragged seven-year-old Robin and six-year-old Lisa with him. Their mother vanished into the bookstore, heading straight for the romances.

Mickey walked away from the bookstore, and looked for something new to try. Experimentally, he shoved at a big metal cylinder three stores down. It didn't take him long to figure out that while one kid couldn't knock over the big freestanding ashtrays, three kids working together could. The stainless steel tubes made a clang you could hear all over the mall when they hit the floor, and they flung sand and cigarette butts out in a spectacular shower of white that reached for yards.

Now *that* was exciting!

They got a total of three turned over before Mickey spotted the rent-a-cop hurrying down from the upper level. He led the other two on a fast end-run around to the play area.

There were about a half-dozen other kids in the play area, but no mothers. That was a good sign. Only two of the kids were playing together; that was good too. It meant that the three of them could take it over, easy.

They pushed the two kids on the teeter-totter right off; one of them ran away crying, the other looked ready to fight until Mickey sucker-punched his stomach. The ones on the swings took one look at this junior Mafia and left to find their mothers. The one on the slide wasn't so easily intimidated; they had to follow him around for nearly five minutes, glowering and muttering threats, before he gave up and left. They never did see where the sixth one went, or when she left. She just vanished when they weren't paying attention to her.

That left them the complete masters of the play area. With no strangers around to intimidate, their unity fell apart, and they began fighting with each other.

They finally decided that wasn't such a good idea when Mickey managed to tear the whole sleeve off Robin's jacket.

"Oh-oh—" Lisa said, as he stood looking at the sleeve in his hands and trying to figure out a way he could blame someone else for doing it without having Robin tattle on him. He looked up, and saw trouble.

There, sniffling kids in tow, were two mothers with determination in their step and fire in their eyes.

Time to make a quick exit.

They scrambled out of the play area before the adults could reach it, and headed for the escalator at a dead run.

Once on the second level, Mickey remembered he had two dollars in his coat; enough for some hot pretzels. The pretzel place just

322 · Diana Tregarde Investigates

happened to be right by the top of the escalator, and Mickey knew from experience that if you were buying something or had just bought something, adults left you alone. Especially if it was something to eat.

Six pretzels later—and in the wake of the pretzels, a trail of mustard on the coats of unsuspecting grown-ups—they were at the far side of the mall wondering what to do next.

"Mommy's gonna be in there a long time," Robin whined. "An' they won't let us in the toy store here anymore."

No kidding. The clerks in the toy store knew Mickey and his siblings by name, and had orders to chase them out if they came without an adult.

Lisa sat down in the middle of the concourse, forcing everyone to walk around her. "I wan' somethin' t' *do*," she sniveled. "I'm *borded*."

Mickey thought, knowing he had to figure out something or Lisa would start to howl. That would bring an adult, or worse, the cop. Then he heard a strange sound, like a whistle.

He glanced up, looking for the source. The sound resolved itself into a peculiar song, one that sounded a lot like it was being played on one of those weird whistles they had for music class—"ocarina" his teacher called them. The kids called them "sweet potatoes," 'cause that was what they looked like.

The teacher never let Mickey play one of those. She never let him play the drum or the cymbals, or even the triangle. All he ever got to play were the notched sticks and the blocks with sandpaper on them. And not even the blocks since he'd tried to sand Jimmy Kreske's face with them.

But the kids at school never got any music like that out of their whistles, not even nerdy Elen Atkins, who was taking clarinet lessons. It was weird—but real neat.

He finally spotted the player, and was amazed that he hadn't seen her before. She couldn't have gotten to the middle of the mall without passing them at least once. It should have been pretty hard to miss someone dressed like that, in a kind of coat or cape made out of bird feathers. It was wild, like something out of a Conan movie, and like the music she was playing. Mickey wanted a coat like that—he could just imagine what the other kids at school would say when he swept in with it over his shoulders.

The flute player had painted designs on her face and looked like a punk rocker. Mickey liked punk rock. Maybe this girl had a band! Maybe she'd want him in the band!

She sort of nodded her head at him when she saw he'd spotted her, and stopped playing.

"Wow—" said Lisa in awe, scrambling to her feet. "*I* wanna look like that—"

The girl tucked her whistle away somewhere out of sight, nodded at them again, and vanished through the door behind her leading to a service corridor.

Robin pulled Mickey's sleeve. "You think she wants us t' go with her?"

Mickey was certain of it. This was just how neat things happened in cartoons.

"What d'you think? Come on, or we're gonna lose her!"

The three of them scrambled after the girl; when they got to the alcove she'd been in, the door to the service area was closed—but it was also unlocked.

"See?" Mickey crowed with triumph. "What I tell you guys? Let's go!"

"Hey wetback?" Sara called from the front, her voice echoing hollowly in the nearly empty room.

"What?" Mark answered absently.

"I'm off—but you might get some bodies down here. We got a couple of missing kids—"

"Every time the weather gets warm we get missing kids, so what's new?" Mark stared at his map, and frowned.

"These have been gone a while. All from the same family. Dan Rather even picked it up. Big-time stuff."

Mark grunted something in reply. He was trying to see if there was a pattern to where the cult-killings showed up on the map.

"Anyway, third shift may be busy, but Chief reserved that terminal for you guys, so don't let them bully you off of it, okay?"

"Fat chance," Mark replied, replacing the pins that represented single kills with ones with blue heads, to see if anything stood out that way. "But thanks for the warning, Yank."

"Just buy me lunch again."

"On *my* salary?"

"It's bigger than mine." Sara sailed out the door, he heard it *thunk* shut behind her, and Mark promptly forgot her.

Di was keying more data into her astrological database after a quick trip to the public library. The "normal" cycles hadn't come up with any more of a match than could be accounted for by chance, so now she was trying some more esoteric ones.

"If this doesn't work," she muttered at Mark, who was switching pins around again, "I'm going to *have* to make a long-distance call. A couple of them, actually. One at least to my voudoun contact in New York to establish some credibility for me with whoever's local. Probably one to my house sitter if I can find a modem; I need more stuff from my database."

"I didn't know you knew so much about computers—" he looked sideways at her in surprise.

"I don't, actually," she said, keying like one possessed. "The real work was done by my house sitter. André is very good, and since he has a lot of time on his hands *and* knows what my 'other job' is, he set me up a number of programs and databases."

"Hm. Boyfriend?" That was news. Di had always been pretty much of a loner.

"Sort of. Off and on. More me being flaky than anything else; I don't really see where I can settle down right now."

He chuckled, and leaned back to see if he could see a pattern from a distance. "I have a hard time picturing you with a hacker."

"God forbid!" She actually took her eyes off the screen for a moment to glare at him. "I have better taste than that! André is just good with computers. He's 'just good' at a lot of things—he plays violin very well, he's a damn good dancer—"

"Ah, but can he *cook*?"

"He burns jello. Can you?"

"Burn jello? With the best—look, do *you* see any pattern here?"

"No," she said finally. "Have you tried a chromatic from blue with the oldest kills first?"

"No—" he bent over his map.

It was hours later, Sara's warning notwithstanding, when they were interrupted.

"Mark?" came a call from the front of the room. "You guys still at it back there?"

"Yo, Ramirez," Mark called back, his voice fogged with fatigue. He craned his neck to see over the low wall of the work station. "What's up?"

A short, thin, intense young man in faded jeans wormed his way back through the desks and terminals to their position. "You guys up with the news?"

Mark stretched, feeling his shoulders pop. "Couple kids missing?" he hazarded. "Sara said something before she left."

"Three," said Ramirez grimly, "and dead. Chief sent me after you. He thinks your nut case just became a baby-killer."

"Ah *shit*," Mark cursed; his tone, if not his words, conveying anguish—the anguish a cop was supposed to stop feeling after a while. The anguish he couldn't help feeling when a homicide victim was under twelve. "Man, I *hate* it when stuff like this happens."

Ramirez just nodded; he felt it too.

Mark couldn't force himself near the site; just couldn't. Couldn't handle itty-bitty shapes under those olive-drab sheets. It made his gut twist up inside; made him want to go pound on something. Made his eyes sting—

So Di had gotten her clearance and was with the Forensics team without him.

This time the location was a half-abandoned ranch just outside the Fort Worth city limits—well outside the range of any of the previous human deaths that they knew of—but within the range for the cattle mutilations. Mark made a mental note to ask the Narcotics boys if they'd been finding any John Does out here since April.

The kids had been found in an old cattle tank, a tank that the caretaker swore on his life had been left dry, with the drainhole unplugged.

It wasn't dry now. It was full to the rim, and the water was fresh. It wasn't rain water, either; there hadn't been enough rain in the past week or two to put more than a couple of inches on the bottom of the tank.

Somebody had come out here and deliberately filled the tank; and they'd have had to fill it by hand, bucket by bucket, from the tap fifty yards away. Somebody had gone to a lot of work—and done it undetected, unseen—so that somebody could drown three kids here this evening.

Again, undetected, unseen.

They'd taken the old caretaker away about an hour ago; Mark hoped they'd reached the hospital in time. The shock of finding the kids had thrown the former ranch hand into a heart attack.

"Hey Valdez—" one of the Forensics boys hailed Mark, who waved him over. "Look, this is none of my business, but what makes you guys sure that this is the same loony? The kids weren't slashed up or anything—"

"This—" Mark held up an envelope that Melanie Lee, one of the other Forensics folk, had given him. There was more than enough of the flower petals this time to go around. "We looked back over all the records; nine times out of ten you guys found plant stuff, and I suspect the tenth just meant the cult was either real good at cleaning up after themselves, or there was already native stuff in bloom on-site. None of the copycats or the lone loons left flowers behind."

"Weird." The Forensics man shook his head. "I like that chick you guys brought in; you never know she's there unless she finds something—then she just points it out and waits for us to deal with it."

"Yeah, she's okay," Mark admitted. "She find anything this time?"

"Naw. Look, if this is gonna help you—it'll be on the coroner's report, but I can tell you now. This is real bizarre. It doesn't look like anybody laid a finger in violence on these kids until they put 'em away. Doc thinks they were maybe drugged; he'll be looking for that in the autopsy. I figure they *had* to be—see, before they were croaked, somebody painted 'em with rubber cement."

"With *what*?" Mark hadn't seen the pathetic little corpses, so this took him by surprise. Ramirez, who had, just nodded.

"Honest to God, thick rubber cement, or something a lot like it; painted 'em about half an inch thick everywhere except their mouths, and I mean *everywhere*. Like that old story about the gal who got painted gold—kids would have died from that if they hadn't been drowned. Whoever it was sealed everything shut with the stuff, in fact, before it dried; eyes, nose, genitals, the works, all but the mouth. Thing is, it wasn't messed up much; they really don't seem to have struggled."

"Which bears out the drugging. Prints?"

He shook his head. "Just like all the rest; partials only, damn near worthless, and what little we get doesn't match any files. We've sent 'em to the FBI, but—"

"Yeah, I know, even if our birds have passports or were in the armed forces, *those* records aren't on-line. Means searching archives."

"Which could be months."

"No shit. And even then, working only with partials we're gonna match half of Texas." Mark shook his head. "Man, I wouldn't have your job—at least I can make some motions like I'm doing something."

"Yeah, well I wouldn't have yours. I'd just run in circles. In the lab I can maybe figure something out." The Forensics man nodded, barely visible in the gathering darkness. "Luck, Valdez."

"Thanks. Same to you."

Mark and his colleague watched the Forensics crew begin breaking things down in silence until Di separated herself from the rest and made her way across the dusty stockpen to them. In the near-dark after sunset she looked like a thin, wispy ghost.

"Mark, I need to—" She stopped, noticing the third person.

"Sorry, I didn't have time for formal introduction before. Ramirez, this is Di—Di, Alonso Frederico Ramirez, fellow slave in the department; was Vice, now with us—Homicide, I mean. Us guys with names that end in Z gotta stick together."

Ramirez smiled thinly. Until lately, that hadn't been too far wrong. Then the Chief had been made Chief—and things had gotten better. The old fart hadn't given a fat damn about affirmative action—but when he saw potential being wasted, he saw red, and did something about it.

"He's currently clawing his way up despite the efforts of the rest of us to keep him down."

Ramirez grinned a little more genuinely.

Di gave him a long appraising look. "So what's that got to do with creative esoterics?"

"He's cool, Di—he was on that voudoun cathouse bust, and the madame cursed him."

"Made *me* a believer, let me tell you," the young man said fervently. "Ended up taking a vacation across the border, looking for an old-time *brujo* to get it off me."

"Did you ever find one?" Di asked, curiosity evident in her voice. "In my experience you have to fight like with like."

"No—no, I got lucky. Dispatch hired in a little bitty gal from Baton Rouge. Ran into her in the hall one day—she took one look at me, freaked, and practically bludgeoned me into accepting a date with her."

"*You* sure freaked when you found out that the date included her *and* her granny. . . ." Mark could still remember the sour look on Ramirez's face when he'd confided the details to Mark.

"And a soon-to-be-deceased rooster and a mess of other shit. Damn good thing for me her granny was visiting."

Di chuckled. "Damn good thing for you that she and her granny have a soft spot for cops. A lot of voudoun practitioners won't even *talk* to cops."

"Yeah, well, maybe I did 'em a little favor or two, like passin' on down the grapevine that the old lady is okay and maybe Baton Rouge Bunco shouldn't hassle her."

"Well, I need a favor; I want to do a full unshielded probe and some other things, and do it without attracting attention. Can you two keep me standing up and pretend to talk to me for about five minutes?"

"You gonna go limp or rigid?" Mark asked.

"Rigid."

"No prob. Ramirez, grab her elbow—okay Di—"

One second she was "normal"—the next, stiff as a corpse; eyes staring, teeth clenched. Mark and his companion pretended to make small talk, watching covertly for anyone approaching them, but no one did. Four or five minutes later they could feel her muscles relax, and she was "back."

She leaned up against Mark, shaking. "Oh *hell*. Mark, I hit problems. Feels like I've been run over. I—nasty stuff. Worse than the last time."

"Get anything?"

"In general, yes—it *is* the same bunch, and this time I got enough to identify five signature auras. But in specific, no, I got hit in a major way. In very specific—they know about me, and they're blocking me."

"Huh?" Mark was startled out of speech.

"They know the Chief's brought in an expert," she replied grimly, "and they are actively working to prevent me or anyone else from pinpointing what tradition they are working in. I could *feel* it; I'd get a clue, start to get close to identifying them, then I'd hit a booby trap, and it would be gone. Knocked right out of my mind."

"You sure it wasn't, you know, the 'on the tip of my tongue' phenomena?"

She shook her head, and her long hair brushed his sleeve. "No—and it wasn't just that floaty forgetfulness you sometimes get in trance. This was deliberate—first redirection, then getting forced off the track, losing the entire train of thought. Then sabotage when I got *too* close. Multiple times. Mark—they're good. Frighteningly good."

"Good enough to beat you?"

She sighed. "I don't know. They were good enough to sucker me—and I'll tell you more about that later."

FIVE

There were no jokes the next day.

Di called from the bus stop again, but Mark was already awake. He hadn't slept much that night; he'd spent most of the night hours wondering what he could have done to prevent what happened. When the phone rang he was lying on his back, staring at the ceiling, feeling every muscle in his shoulders ache with tension.

This was the first time *his* work, *his* assignment, had involved dead kids. He'd been feeling wretched: and not only miserable and torn up inside, but unaccountably guilty as well, even after getting home last night. It had taken a double shot of bourbon to put him to sleep, and his dreams had been nightmare-haunted.

He headed for the shower after Di gave him his wake-up call, hoping, somehow, to wash some of the depression away. It didn't work. But at least he was showered, shaved, and dressed by the time Di rang his doorbell.

He let her in; she looked just as blue as he felt. She followed him to the kitchen without a word, moving as quietly as Treemonisha at her sneakiest. She took a seat and watched him feed the cat. They brooded at each other over coffee until she finally broke the silence.

"It isn't my fault," she said grimly, "and it isn't yours. It happened, it could happen again. If we can prevent it, fine. If not—well, dammit Mark, we're *trying*. If we've got to lay some guilt, let's put it on the bastards who drown little kids! We shouldn't *have* to be protecting every innocent creature in Dallas."

"But—" Mark tried to articulate his own guilty feelings. "Di, we're the only ones who really know what's going on. Doesn't that make us responsible for preventing things?"

"No, dammit," she replied, strain in her voice. "Okay, we're the best shot the law has at catching these lunatics—but there's only two of us, and the bad guys are at least as good as I am. That's gonna make it harder; we'll do it anyway. But we aren't going to do anyone any good if we wallow in guilt that we don't deserve."

He thought about that; thought about it hard. They *were* trying; doing the best that they possibly could. Finally he nodded, slowly. "Okay," he replied. "You're making sense; you're making sense to my gut as well as my head. I think I can deal with that."

She sighed as his tension eased, and the line of anxiety between her eyebrows faded. He gave her a questioning look.

She shrugged. "One of the problems with being an empath is you get caught in positive feedback—I felt wretched all last night, and once I got inside your influence it was worse. And we can't let this stop us—that's exactly what 'they' want."

He nodded. "Okay, changing the subject. Tell me something, you said you were being 'blocked' last night. Shielding I understand, but how can anybody block a thought?"

"You *would* ask about theory at seven in the morning, wouldn't you." She stirred a little more sugar into her coffee and contemplated the dark fluid for a minute. "You never used to be interested before—it was always 'Don't tell me, I don't want to know—just tell me what to do.'"

"People change; I've been getting curious."

"Okay, on your head be it. You want theory—you're going to get chapter and verse from now on. This is crazy stuff, so get ready to suspend your skepticism," she said. "I'm going to give it to you like it's fact—I don't know if it is or isn't fact, it's not provable, but it works this way for me, and in magic, that's what counts. The whole of the way I work is a half-baked combination of my Wiccan tradition and some of the parapsych experiments they're doing now, *and* a little tad of particle physics and of traditional psych."

He raised an eyebrow. "Strange bedfellows."

"In spades. It goes like this—Jung was almost right. There *is* something like a collective unconscious, sort of a human database. Only its 'memories' don't go all the way back to the cave, like Jung thought—they're only as old as the oldest human alive. Got that so far? There's another 'historical' memory that *does* go back that far, but that's not what I was after last night, and I have to go through a whole song-and-dance act to get at it. Still clear?"

Mark nodded again and sipped his coffee. "Think so."

"Okay; I can tap into the current memory bank, but I can do it

consciously, deliberately. It isn't telepathy; I'm not a telepathit's—
something else. I think of it as data retrieval, and that's how it works
for me. Most anybody can do this, you do it yourself when you
dream, I just do it on purpose. *But* if you know what you're doing—
and if you're dealing with a very small area of collective knowledge—
you can also lay roadblocks in the collective mind. Essentially that's
what I hit. When I'm dealing with something arcane that I don't recognize, I generally take a dive into the collective mind and trace back
what clues I do have to the source. Except that this time—"

"You hit the roadblocks," Mark supplied.

She sipped her coffee before answering. "Exactly. Now comes the
tricky part; behind the roadblocks were traps, traps I sprung on myself when I tried to get around the blocks. You know that 'tip-of-
your-tongue' phenomena you were talking about? Where you *know*
you know something, but the harder you try and work to get it, the
farther away it wiggles? Whoever is doing this knew that an occultist
was going to be called in, and laid a trap to do just that to any similar
knowledge the occultist in question possessed. They can't really wipe
it, the way I implied, but they made it damned near inaccessible to
me."

She looked angry and frustrated, and Mark didn't blame her
one bit.

"I am royally ticked off at myself for not anticipating traps. Now
the only way I'm going to figure out what magical system they're using is to come at it from the side, find it by process of elimination, or
get hit in the face with a clue so broad the trap doesn't work."

Mark polished off the last gulp in the cup. "Well, where do we
start?"

She managed a wry quirk of her lips. "The hard way. We spend
long enough at HDQ for me to work up that report I promised the
Chief and for you to collect the preliminary on last night from
Forensics. I called André last night; we aren't going to chance a modem because I might lose data to the phone lines—he doesn't much
like the quality of the lines down here, he told me. He's arranging for
a package of books and some dump-down diskettes to come to HDQ
via FedEx. I assume I can arrange for that to get billed to the department? You said I could, and I warned you I'm not exactly rolling in
money."

He nodded. "We've got a little account for stuff like that, I'll warn
the mail room that it's coming."

"Good, thanks." She bit at a hangnail, eyes dark with worry. "After that, we'll get the files the Chief promised on that Satanist and the

other jerk, and go check them out. By now André has called my New York voudoun expert—"

"And if I know how these things work, you should have a contact here by nightfall?"

"I think so; depends on how paranoid the locals are getting." She sighed. "If I were local, I'd be either gone or hiding so deep it would take a backhoe to dig me out."

"You want me along?" Mark asked, when they pulled up outside the former massage parlor that was now the First Dallas Church of Satan.

"How unobtrusive can you get?" she asked. "How good is your poker face these days?"

He considered that question for a moment, staring through the windshield. "I think I can probably still manage the 'Mr. Nobody' routine we used to use. The one where I'm your wallpaper boyfriend—"

"Then it wouldn't hurt to have you along, although I really don't expect much of anything. Put out your antenna for a minute, and you'll see what I mean."

Mark did his best to get the "feel" of the place, even though he wasn't nearly as sensitive as she was. "Nothing," he reported. "Not a damn thing."

Di smiled wryly. "That's because there's nothing there. High Priest Azarel, alias Thomas Harden, is about to conduct a Black Mass in there right now. He has a full weekday lunch-hour congregation— all seventeen of them—and if there was ever going to be any power being built even *you'd* feel it now. Fact is, there's not a thing there to be sensed. It isn't shielding, either. There isn't a person in that building that could magic their way out of a wet paper sack, or shield against *you* on your worst day."

Mark snorted. "But I'll bet they've convinced themselves that the world is trembling in fear of them."

"Bingo. Well, come on. If you can keep your stomach steady and keep from laughing your head off, we'll go play eager converts."

The Black Mass was about as exciting as a Knights of Columbus luncheon. The nude female serving as the altar looked as bored as Mark felt; by her garish blond hair and makeup, and a certain feeling that he'd seen her somewhere, Mark guessed she was one of the local stripper-cum-b-girls from one of the clubs in the neighborhood. The

congregation of middle-class, middle-aged businessmen and house-
wives did appear to be enjoying the "thrill" of doing something
wicked, though. Mark wondered how long it would take to wear off.

He and Di were the only people in the entire room under the age
of forty. Di's exotic good looks were drawing a lot of attention from
the male contingent and one of the ladies; for that matter, there were
a couple of the hausfrau types that were watching *him* out of the corners of their eyes.

Probably wishing this was the Saturday night orgy, and not the
weekday ceremony, he thought, finding himself rather grateful that it
wasn't. One of that lot looked like she'd enjoy devouring him whole if
she got the chance. He edged closer to Di, and caught disappointment in her expression before she turned away.

The founder of the cult had stolen from just about every ceremony he could lay hands on. The form was almost a parody of the
Catholic Mass; the main differences lay in the philosophy as well as
the ceremony. The nude woman as a living altar was the most obvious. Substitution of deity was another. But the main point of the ceremony was exaltation of the flesh instead of the spirit, and selfishness
instead of selflessness. The entire thrust was toward "do whatever you
want, whenever you want"—the old sixties "let it all hang out" credo
dressed up in semiliturgical costume and taken to its furthest extreme.

The congregation stood the entire time; Mark wasn't certain if
that was part of the ceremony or if it was because Azarel was too
cheap to buy chairs. Mark was fairly certain that beneath the various
robes, which were as motley as those who wore them, they were also
nude. Full nudity was reserved for Saturday night, Di had told him.

In the light of day the congregation looked like a bunch of
moulting crows.

The weekday "mass" was mercifully short. Afterward Di grabbed
his elbow and hauled him with her to accost the High Priest before
he could pull a vanishing act.

"Mr. Azarel?" she asked breathlessly, "I'm Sally Bradey, the one
who called earlier—"

The "altar" had already done her vanishing trick. The man's face
had brightened the moment he saw an attractive young lady hauling
Mark along toward him—and if he was disappointed that "Sally" had
a male companion, he didn't show it. He was altogether a rather pathetic little man, Mark decided after a moment's perusal. Thin, short,
and balding, with a bit of a potbelly; he was trying to grow a mustache and goatee in imitation of the founder of the cult and failing

miserably. His "robes of ceremony" were only too obviously salvaged
choir robes with moon-and-star appliqués sewn to them. His watery
blue eyes reflected a lifetime of not-quite-failing. Mark decided that
he was sorry for the little nerd.

*Just exactly the kind of jerk who'd get taken in by an operation that
was founded by a flimflam artist. Poor geek. Probably believes everything they told him.*

"—would you like to come around to my office, Sally?" the little
man was saying, in a kind of faded baritone. "I think we can probably
answer all your questions in an hour or so."

"Oh *wonderful*," Di gushed. "We were afraid you wouldn't have
any time—I'm sure you must be *terribly* busy."

The Dread Azarel smiled smugly. "We always have time for worthy converts. Back through there, Sally, the door on the right; I'll join
you in a minute."

The "office" was decorated in floor-to-ceiling bookshelves. The
shelves themselves (the inexpensive board-and-bracket type) held
not so many books as a plethora of other junk. It looked like a bank-
ruptcy sale at the demise of a horror-movie company. The shelves
were crammed with plaster skulls, "voodoo dolls," odd and badly executed statuary, black candles, incense burners, and the inevitable inverted crucifixes. The place reeked of cheap incense and low-grade
pot.

Mark felt his lip curling with contempt. It was all so tawdry—like a
tired old stripper in a carny geekshow, doing the "Ugha the Ape-
Girl" act because her stretch marks showed too much for her to work
the peep shows anymore.

"Priest Azarel" made a would-be dramatic entrance, flinging
back the worn velvet curtains at the rear of the office and striding
through. He was no longer in his High Priest costume; he wore black
pants and turtleneck, both polyester, and an inverted crucifix around
his neck. He didn't look sinister—or even worth a second glance on
the street. If anything, he looked like a burned-out old hippy who
wouldn't let the sixties go.

Within a few moments it was plain even to Mark that neither
Azarel nor his followers could have had anything to do with the
killings.

For one thing, he knew less about them than had been printed in
the papers. For another, despite his boasting about how much power
he and his followers had raised through "evil," his idea of "evil"
seemed to consist of holding weekly orgies spiced with a little grass
and coke, casting "curses" on the enemies of those within the congre-

gation, and pulling petty "acts of vengeance" on those so-called enemies that were somewhat on the level of teenaged pranks. Sugar in
the gas tank; slimy, fecal things in the garden.

Then Di pulled the last trick they'd planned on him.

"Do you mind if I smoke?" she asked, reaching into her purse
without appearing to look. Mark knew what she was up to, though,
and was not surprised when she cursed and pulled her hand back out
with a cut across the thumb.

"Dammit!" she exclaimed, holding the freely bleeding thumb out
before her. "My damned *mirror* broke! I don't suppose you have a
Band-Aid in your desk?"

Azarel stared at the blood, and paled; the kind of greenish pallor
that accompanies nausea.

"N-no," he stammered. "I—"

He gulped and gripped the edge of the desk.

"You're going to have to leave," he said unsteadily. "You're in
danger—I feel myself under psychic attack from my enemies, and
they would feel no remorse at striking at *you* as well—"

Di squealed, and stood up hastily. "Psychic attack! Oh how *horrible*! Thank you Mr. Azarel, we'll leave right now! Will you be all
right?"

He tried to look haughty as Di waved the blood-smeared thumb
practically under his nose. He succeeded only in looking sicker. "Of
course. I am far stronger than they—it is only that I have to extend
myself to protect you—"

"Then we'd better go—" They practically ran out of the office
door—their haste due mostly to the fact that they didn't want to
blow the game at this point by laughing in the man's face.

"What a wimp!" Mark exclaimed with contempt when they got
to the haven of the Ghia.

Di gave a little snort of disgust and agreement. "Why anyone
would bother with that turkey—" She fished in her purse for the razor blade she'd used to cut her finger, wrapped it and put it back into
a little plastic box so that it couldn't bite her again. "Well, at least
we've got a good solid reason to write him off."

He nodded. "I doubt even the Chief will want us to bother with
him after we tell him about the way Azarel nearly threw up when you
cut your thumb."

She grimaced, and sucked daintily at the cut. "The things I do in
the line of duty! Ah well—let's go check out Jorden MacKever and the
House of Dark Desires."

The House of Dark Desires was in Fort Worth, not Dallas; thirty minutes as the crow flies, but it took them slightly more than an hour to wind their way through all the back streets. It was in a neighborhood similar to that surrounding the Satanist Church; an area of porn purveyors, stripper bars and pawnshops.

"Ho boy—*this* I did not expect."

Di stared at the front of the shop with a look of startled surprise on her face. Since the storefront was nothing more than black glass with the name ornately lettered in gold, Mark didn't think her surprise was caused by the decor.

"What is it?" he asked, as the bucket seat creaked with his efforts to get a better look at the store.

"This *isn't* one of the five signature auras I picked up—but this guy knows at least something of what he's doing," she said, turning to him with an utterly sober expression. "No, don't unshield, take my word for it—I'd rather not chance you getting caught by what he's got going. He's got what we call a 'glamour' on the store; it will attract anyone with psychic gifts, unless they know enough to see through it. This is a hunter, Mark; and the store is his trap. And I think I know why and what he hunts."

"*Could* this be our pigeon? Could the others—the signature auras you talked about—be involved with him?"

She shook her head. "I don't think so; what he's done is a little crude by my standards, and it certainly lacks the finesse of the traps I ran into. If this were the number-one person behind the killings, he should have more subtlety. Besides, one of those five auras had an incredible feeling of power and the lust for power in it; and I can't see *that* person playing number two to anyone. But this guy is *not* a nice man, and if we can find something to hang him with, we should do it. *If* he's into Crowley, and it feels like he is, he's drawing in unawakened psychics, using their potential, and throwing them away when they're drained and ruined."

Now Mark was worried. "You want me in there with you? You think you can handle this by yourself?"

"Near at hand, but not *with* me, okay? If two of us with shields come in at once, he might spook. If just one comes in, he might figure they're unconscious shields, and he might bite." Her expression firmed into determination. "This isn't our prime target, but I *want* him, Mark. He's been using people—using them up. In some ways, that's worse than killing them."

Mark nodded. "All right then; I'll be right outside if you need me."

———

Diana edged her way into the porn shop, feeling her skin crawl with every step she took. The man who owned this place—and the people who frequented it—were genuine sadists. No masochists allowed. At least not here. In the back room—that was another story.

Power through pain—as long as it isn't mine. Maybe the ultimate in self-centeredness.

And at least some of those people—the owner included— understood the theory and practice of raising occult power by the in- fliction of pain far, far better than she did. They were doing as others before them had done; draining the power of unawakened innocents for their own uses, and throwing away the husks afterward without a backward glance. A psychic, even one who'd been abused physically and spiritually, *could* recover from that kind of ethereal rape—but it wasn't easy, and they had to find expert help right away. Too often the wounds just festered until the psychic ended up on a couch some- where, trying to explain things no classically trained psychiatrist would believe.

The aura of the place made her nauseous. Like a fish tank when the gravel has been stirred; the psychic atmosphere was muddy, murky, and tainted.

"Can I help you?"

Dressed all in black, he—appeared—from between two rows of high bookshelves. He had meant to surprise, even frighten her; she locked down her startled reflex before it could betray her. With eyes half-lidded and feigned boredom she said, "I suppose you might. I was told I could find a copy of Crowley's *Moonchild* here—"

He could have posed for a recruiting poster for the SS; though middle-aged, he was in superb physical condition, from his black- booted feet to his blond crewcut. Blue eyes, pale as watered milk, seemed to bore right through to her soul. She strengthened her shields a bit as she felt him probe at her. This was the kind of creature High Priest Azarel only dreamed of being.

His eyes narrowed as she resisted his probing. "Are we playing games, little lady?" he asked in a near-whisper. "I know what you are."

She dropped all pretense. Since he'd seen through the act, per- haps she could startle truth out of him with bluntness. "No games, not today. Not unless you had anything to do with three dead kids."

"Those children on the news last night?" He shook his head. "We don't do children. Only consenting adults here, white-knight lady. We don't kill, either; that isn't the Way."

She got a flash, then—from him, there was no doubt of it; it reeked of his aura—full of emotions. First of fear (another's), then of sexual arousal, then fear (his own). Then a picture, carried to her by the emotion, and a name. A woman—

And she heard herself saying, "Then what happened to Dana Grotern last week?"

Oh hell, she thought belatedly, as his cool surface vanished. *That's torn it! Some day I am going to* have *to put a governor on my mouth!*

"That was an accident, bitch—" the man was snarling, "but I doubt that much matters to you—"

She put up full shields just in time; he hit her with a psi-bolt that would have knocked Mark to the ground. She gave a little with it, judging his strength, then recovered. She had his measure now; if this was his best, then he was far below her level of expertise.

The first bolt was followed by two more, equally ineffective; she could see them hitting her outermost shields and dissipating in a shower of sparks.

He wasn't slow on the uptake, though, not this one; after three levinbolts it was obvious that she was stronger than he—so he rushed her, hands poised to strike, his multiple shadows cast by the many overhead lights rushing crazily with him.

Tae Kwon Do, she recognized with the back of her mind. The front was preparing to meet his attack.

She ducked under and around the strike; she made her own, felt her foot connect solidly, the side kick making her miss a breath.

Bad form—sensei *would have your hide, fool! Tighten up; balance, center your* ki, *dammit*—

But she did send him reeling into his own bookshelves with sore ribs. The shelves went over in a crash of splintering wood; he went with them. Using the momentum of the kick, she spun around to face him as he scrambled up out of the wreckage of books and wood. Unfortunately, since he'd been moving in the direction of the kick, she hadn't done him any real damage.

He circled her warily, his boot-soles making scuffing sounds on the linoleum as he moved, looking for an opening. Behind her she heard the street door slam open, and then close; she heard the sound of running feet—she went alert for an attack from behind, then recognized Mark's step, and dismissed the need for wariness in that direction.

But Mark stopped just outside the combat area.

There was no further sound from him; after a moment, she realized there wasn't going to be.

That creep! *He's going to stand around and* watch! *I'll* kill *him!*

She gave Jorden a sucker-opening. He took it. *This* time he wasn't moving in the direction of the force; but even as she delivered a neat chop (*Good! Solid!*) that must have numbed his arm to the shoulder, he got in an unexpected blow of his own. He missed her throat, but got her eye—with the side of the hand, thank the gods, not a thrust.

Agh!

She hissed in pain; her head rocked back. She danced away, her sneakers squeaking on the floor; seeing stars, and getting mad. She felt the blood rushing to her face, making her flush with outrage, and making her eye throb.

Lock it down; you know what the sensei *says. The one who brings anger into the circle is the one who will lose. . . .*

With an effort she shoved her anger back into its proper compartment, felt herself cool, and faced off her opponent again. He was grinning with satisfaction at having scored; she locked down another surge of anger called up by that insolent grin. She could feel her eye starting to swell, the tissues puffing and the vision out of that eye narrowing to a slit.

Dammit, that hurts.

That hurt and that loss of vision would put her at a little disadvantage.

Not as much as he thinks, though. . . . I wonder if I can sucker him twice? Well, nothing ventured—

She faltered a little, shaking her head, though it made her eye hurt and throb to do so, feigning that she was having trouble seeing. The second time she did so, he rushed her; *exactly* the way she wanted him to.

She ducked, came up in low-line—foot to the stomach—he folded around it, then started to unfold—then she executed a spin, and foot to the crotch.

Both hits were clean; felt absolutely solid, and looked textbook pure as she connected. She felt a little more redeemed for getting the black eye.

As he bent over, mouth open in a silent scream, she finished him off with a chop to the base of the neck.

Forgive your unworthy pupil, sensei. *I don't want to kill him,* sensei—*I just want to hurt him. I want to hurt him a lot. I want him to know what it feels like to be hurt instead of inflicting the hurt.*

He went down on his face and didn't get up again.

From behind her came the sound of applause.

———

"Thanks a bunch, Magnum," Di said sourly, as Mark applauded the end of the fight. "You're always there when I need you."

"You were doing okay," he replied with a grin, still leaning against the bookshelf. "It didn't look to *me* like you needed help."

"This ain't chopped liver," she retorted, gingerly touching the edges of her rapidly blackening eye. "Ah—this is going to be a bad one. Put the cuffs on that jerk and go call the office, huh?"

He pulled the cuffs out of his back pocket and walked over to be-straddle the body on the floor. "What're we charging him with?" he asked, bending over the unconscious porn peddler and snapping the cuffs on his wrists, locking them behind his back.

"Assault, for one; he came after me. I'll be perfectly happy to press charges. You might even get him on assault with a deadly—I don't know how they view martial arts in this state, and he's had more than a bit of Tae Kwon Do. I've got more than that to pin on him, though. You might want to talk to your friends in Vice; there'll be a gal named Dana Grotern in a coma in one of the hospitals—he put her there. She was playing M to his S last week, when they had a little accident. Seems he didn't bother to find out she had allergies be-fore he gagged her. She was choking, he thought she was acting."

"Huh," Mark said, shaking his head as he gave Jorden a quick pat-down. "Yeah, we look hard enough, we can probably find enough to get him on that. Any link to our cult?" He stood up.

Di's eye was becoming rather impressive. "No, worse luck. This lot follows standard Crowley, right out of the book. I got some em-pathic flashes from him, and I'd know the signs of that backward and blindfolded. It ain't our bunch."

"Okay, I'll get on the horn, then I'll take you back to Aunt Nita. You look like you could use some TLC."

"And I'll tell her," Di replied, both amused and annoyed, "that *you* are the one who did this to me!"

Crazy Jake followed Timbuktoo into the no-man's land of the old railyard with a mixture of hope and disbelief. Timbuktoo claimed he'd found this stash—

"Cases, man, cases! Just waitin'! Man, I'm tellin' you, cases!"

It was a bum's dream—Jake just hoped it wasn't a dream.

Timbuk said he'd found this stash of wine in the culvert under the abandoned S&P rail line. He'd spent last night trying to empty it by himself, but reason and guilt had got the better of him, and tonight he'd invited some friends to help him polish it off. Crazy Jake, Tonto, old Dusty, and Pete.

Certainly Timbuk had been *somewhere* last night; he hadn't shown up to panhandle the johns on porn row, and he hadn't shown up at the mission to crash. And he smelled like a distillery right now; his walk unsteady, his hands waving expansively as he talked.

Jake didn't have a thin dime to his name, and he was starting to get the shakes. Before too long he'd start seeing them snakes. He shuffled along last in line, and hoped that Timbuk wasn't seeing snakes of his own; he *needed* a good snort, needed it bad.

They trudged single file down the abandoned right-of-way, weeds higher than their heads in places. Jake could remember when nothing would grow on the right-of-way. He could remember bumming on the S&P freighters that had come roaring out of here under great clouds of steam. He could even remember back to where all the bumming had started, the Big One, the Great Depression. Kids these days didn't know what a real depression was. A real depression was not walking too close to tall buildings, 'cause somebody might be taking a notion to jump. A real depression was meeting bankers on the bum. A real depression was finding a kid dead of starvation 'bout once a day along the line. Nobody starved in the US of A these days, unless they were too damnfool stubborn to get help. A lot of folks starved back then. A lot of folks froze to death, up north, Chi-town way, where Jake came from. Nowadays, someone froze, it made national news.

The weeds rustled, and out of habit Jake started, looking over his shoulder. He scolded himself afterward. No railroad bulls, not here, not these days. Nobody here but five worn-out old bums, hoping for a boozy miracle.

"Down here—" hissed Timbuk through the gap in his teeth, and he led his buddies on a skidding slide down the top of the embankment and into the culvert. The weeds crackled and snapped as the others plowed through them as best they could.

It was dry down here this time of year. Dry and sheltered from the cold winds. Of course, the weather had been real weird this year; hot as summer, it was, hot as hell. But you never knew when the weather was going to turn, and when it did, it was no bad thing to have a tidy shelter lined up.

Especially nowadays. All these kids, all this fallout from the itty-bitty depression they were having now. These kids, they were taking the good spots away from the regulars; taking the bridges, the underpasses in town. And they were too healthy, too young to fight. It wasn't fair. It wasn't any damned fair. An old bum oughtn't to have to fight for the place he'd always been able to claim as his own. An old bum hadn't ought to turn up at the mission to find all the beds gone.

Jake was last; he slid down the slippery grass to land beside the feet of the other four. They were staring at the darkness beneath the culvert, jaws dropping. Jake's eyes followed theirs, and he felt his jaw drop in imitation of his fellows.

"Ho-lee shit—" he mumbled, gazing with benumbed satisfaction at what was under the plastic tarp that Timbuktoo was holding up. Timbuk was grinning from ear to ear, the gap in the front of his mouth wide enough to drive a truck through, his whole body saying "didn't I tell you?"

"What I tell you guys, huh?" he crowed. "What I tell you?"

"Timbuk, ol' buddy—you were *not* wrong," Dusty hacked.

Beneath the plastic tarp were cardboard boxes, each one holding twelve big beautiful bottles of vino. It was gonna be a cracklin' rosie night for sure. There were—Jake counted—six, seven, *eight* cases. And that didn't include the case already opened, that Timbuk had started on last night.

"Oh *man*," Jake said reverently. "Oh, *man!*"

"Help yourselves, boys," Timbuk said magnanimously. "Drinks is on me."

Before Timbuk could change his mind, Jake had a case open and had grabbed up four bottles. *Twist-off caps too—oh man, the livin' don't get any easier than this.* He found himself a nice, comfortable spot in the culvert, opened the first bottle, and poured it down his throat as fast as he could gulp. The shakes were hitting pretty good, and he had to steady his bottle with both hands—but he didn't spill a drop, nossir. He waited for the booze to hit; as soon as he stopped shaking, he relaxed into his chosen spot and began sipping at his second bottle.

The third brought a pleasant buzz to his thoughts. The fourth brought oblivion.

So he never saw the five barbarically clad figures step into the culvert to see what their baited trap had caught this time.

Pablo tossed back his beer and waited, sullenly, for the stranger to speak. He couldn't see the man's face in the shadows of the smoky bar; he had no idea who he was talking to. The note with the folded bill had just said that he wanted to talk, not what about.

But fifty bucks buys a lot of attention in the *barrio*.

The clothes were okay; loose white suit, like about any other dude. The color of the hand holding the beer bottle—which was all he could see of the man—was okay. Of course he wouldn't have gotten past the door of *this* bar if he hadn't looked like he fit. Pablo remembered last year, when some yuppie gringo reporter had tried to get in. Broken jaw don't do a dude much good on the six o'clock news.

Maybe the man was in dope, looking for runners, dealers, protection. He didn't smell like "cop" to Pablo. But if the man was new in dope, Pablo was going to think hard about turning him down. The big boys wouldn't deal nice with somebody pushing in on their turf.

Then again, maybe Pablo *would* deal with him. There was a power about this man—a power Pablo wished he had. This man could hold your attention just by sitting there drinking a beer. Somehow Pablo knew that when the man spoke, he would *listen*. He would have to. Like a puma, the man was; like a jaguar. Which was a good sign; Pablo's gang was the jaguars.

"I hear," the man spoke at last, "that you *hombres* think you're pretty good, you Jaguars. I hear other people think the same."

Pablo had been right about the voice. It was deep; you felt it as much as heard it. It was a voice that could issue a command and be obeyed without an argument. It was a voice that would put chicks on their knees. *Power*, said the voice to the back of Pablo's head. *I have Power. More Power than you dream.*

"We're okay," Pablo shrugged, not indulging in any of the usual bullshit. You didn't bullshit a man like this one. "We got a good turf, and we hold it."

"I hear you don't take anybody but *Mestizo*."

"You hear right." He toyed with the beer bottle, making little wet rings linking together into a chain on the tabletop.

"You got a reason?" the man asked—and Pablo knew he'd have to tell him.

"We're the first people; we were here before anybody," he said, becoming more passionate with each word. "Everything we had got stolen from us; first by the Spanish, then the whites. So—we're takin' some of that back, the Jaguars. Takin' back what's ours by right."

"So." The man leaned forward, and Pablo got a good look at him. He nearly died of envy. The man—looked like a movie star, a statue, a god! That manner, that voice—and now that face! What couldn't *he*, Pablo, do with a combination like that?

"I hear passion in you, *hombre*. I hear a heart, I hear guts. I hear a warrior. Tell me something, man—you interested in *doing* something about this, something real? Something *big*?"

Oh man—give me a chance—Pablo thought, and said, as level and cool as he could, "Try me. Try *us*."

The man smiled; predator's smile, jaguar's smile. "You ready to go back to the old gods—the warrior's gods? You ready to give them what they need? You gotta pay for power, *hombre*. You think you can come up with the coin? Warrior's coin?"

Pablo nodded, but before he could answer, the man rolled on, his own words hot beneath the ice-cool of his tone.

"You think you can handle yourself smart—be a warrior *and* deal with the new world? You think you can deal in the big time? You think you can handle more than a gang?"

"Like?"

"Like maybe an army?"

Tuf couldn't figure out where he was. One minute he'd been following this chick—oh man, *that* had been an armful, long black hair, round and soft in all the right places, a come-on look in her eyes, and a promising wiggle to her hips—the next minute, *bonk*.

No idea who hit him; never saw them. Now he was waking up cold and confused, and God knew where.

It looked like a warehouse, or something. He was just about bare-ass naked except for a single strip of cloth. He was lying on cold cement, and his head hurt like hell.

Whatever it was, wherever he was, the building was empty; there was real dim light coming from a couple of exit signs, but that was it. Enough to hint at a high ceiling, far-off walls. The echoes when he moved told him *empty*.

He started to get to his feet, and found that one of his ankles was tied to a support beam. He tried to get the knots undone, but they were too tight, and he didn't have anything to cut the rope with. He swore and struggled, but only succeeded in ripping one of his fingernails off.

Suddenly—light.

Blinding light from a fixture directly over his head struck him with an almost physical blow. The light was so bright that it threw everything outside the circle it delineated into absolute darkness. Tuf cringed, and shaded his eyes, but with no result; he couldn't see the rest of his surroundings anymore.

Footsteps; sound of bare feet scuffing against cement. Into the circle of light stepped an old enemy.

Pablo. Chief of the Jaguars. Tuf suddenly recalled that he'd been on Jaguar turf when he'd been coldcocked.

Better brazen it out.

"Say hey, Pablo." Tuf was trying to be cool, but it wasn't easy. Pablo looked rigged out for some kind of costume party; fancy loincloth, ropes of flowers on his wrists and ankles, for chrissake; some kind of helmet shaped like a big cat's head under one arm, about a ton of silvery jewelry. He should have looked stupid—he didn't. He looked *mean*.

"Say hey, Tuf." Pablo sounded cool; sounded amused, like he was laughing at Tuf. He moved a little, and Tuf could see his other hand come into the light. He was carrying what looked like two sticks.

"What th' hell's all this, man?" Tuf asked, trying to sound casual.

"Like, you're my enemy, man. I caught you on Jaguar turf, fair an' square. Like, I coulda killed you, but I'm gonna give you a chance."

Tuf snorted. "What chance, man?"

Pablo just grinned and threw one of the sticks at Tuf. "Like we fight, man. You an' me, *mano-a-mano*." He pulled on his helmet, and his eyes looked darkly out of the big cat's mouth, shadows within shadows. "Like you haven't got a choice, man. You fight me, or you die."

Tuf had caught the stick almost reflexively, and took a good look at it. It was flat, polished wood, and along both edges were set feathers. Feathers?

"I'm s'pposed to fight you with *this*? For what? Turf?"

"Honor, man. For the gods. For the old ways." Tuf did not much like the way Pablo's eyes were burning down in the deep shadows of the cat's mouth. "We fight for Burning Water, man—or you die for Burning Water. You take your pick."

"With a stick? What if I lose?"

Pablo laughed. "You die, you just die quick. You don't fight, you die slow. 'Member that dude they found down to Bachmann Lake? Like him."

Tuf swallowed fear. "And if I win?"

"I die; you kill me, you take my place." Pablo sounded as if it were a matter of supreme indifference to him.

"Who says?" Tuf asked belligerently.

"Burning Water." Pablo nodded at the area outside the circle of light to Tuf's right. *Something* stood there, or somebody. Dark and shadowy—and powerful. Even from here Tuf could feel the power—like the power of a black sun.

"So who's this Burning Water dude? Huh?"

Pablo's eyes shone with fanatic devotion, and his face was transformed by a vision only he could see. "He's gonna make us free, man. He's gonna make us *warriors*. He's a god; no lie, an old god. He's gonna wipe out the white man, he's gonna give it all to us. I'm tellin' you."

The smart-ass retorts on the tip of Tuf's tongue died before he could speak them. Somehow—that vague shadowy power seemed capable of all of that. That shadow was the shadow of Fear—of a hunger that could eat the world. Tuf could feel the force of that hunger, and it was squarely behind Pablo.

"You gonna fight, man?" Pablo was sneering, "Or you gonna die like a sheep?"

Tuf took a better grip on his stick, his hands slippery with the sweat of new fear, and went into a fighting crouch. This was no more than a fool's chance, but it *was* a chance. And whatever—*he* was not going to go down without a fight. "What you think, man?" He gestured with his fist, and Pablo laughed at the obscenity. "Come on, man—I ain't waitin' all day. You gonna rumble or not?"

And only when Pablo stepped fully into the circle of light did he notice that where the edges of *his* stick were inset with feathers, the edges of Pablo's glittered with something dark and sharp-edged.

And knew, with despair, exactly how much of a fool's chance he'd been given.

SIX

Flies, fat, lazy and engorged, and now disturbed in their feeding, rose in clouds from the end of the alleyway.

LaRoss took one look at what they'd been feeding on and nearly lost his lunch.

"My God—" Greeley whispered.

You don't patrol the barrio *without getting a tough hide,* LaRoss thought, holding off shock and sickness at a desperate arm's length. *But this—this isn't death, it's carnage. It's like a slaughterhouse.*

"I'll call in—" he gulped. Greeley just nodded wordlessly. LaRoss assumed the nod meant "okay," and got out while he could still control his stomach.

He left Greeley at the entrance to the cul-de-sac; his partner had gone pale, but it seemed like he was taking the sight better than LaRoss. But then Greeley had seen a fair share of mangled bods in 'Nam and maybe he could handle this a little more calmly than a guy who'd been too old in the sixties to draft.

LaRoss did not walk to the car—he ran. Without really thinking about it, he found himself reaching for the radio handset through the window of the squad car. He spoke a few words into it—not really conscious of what he was saying, but it must have been the right thing, since he got the promise of more help on the way. He couldn't really concentrate—kept seeing the pile of bodies—

—just like carcasses at a packing plant, just piled up on top of each other. Cut up like they'd been rumbling with razor blades and hopped on PCP at the time. But my God—those eyes; those punks, they saw Hell before they died. God help them.

There was a buzzing near his face; absently he brushed it away, then with a shudder of realization of why the insect was so lethargic, smashed the fat fly against the hot, shiny enamel of the squad.

Can't leave my partner alone back there, he thought, and shuddered again. *It's not the first time we've picked up after gang fights. Pull yourself together, man!*

He made himself return to the cul-de-sac, feet dragging. "Must have been hopped up for sure," Greeley said casually, as LaRoss forced himself to look at the pile of bodies until numbness settled in. "Get dusted bad enough, you don't feel nothin' , you know? Buddies must've been just as high."

"Buddies?" LaRoss replied dumbly. There were only six or seven bodies, but his mind kept multiplying them.

"Sure, how d'you think they got here? Had a rumble somewhere else—not enough blood around here— winners hauled the losers off and dumped 'em for us t' find. They gotta know we always check this alley."

Greeley's calm was infectious; LaRoss felt his stomach settling, his mind taking over. "Last night, you figure?"

Greeley shook his head. "Huh-uh; I'd figure some time around shift change."

Now LaRoss was focusing enough to take in the insignia on the back of the jackets, disfigured by blood and slashes though they were. "Hey pard—you notice something else, something weird?"

Greeley nodded. "They're from at least two, three different gangs."

"Must have been a *hell* of a rumble!" LaRoss brooded. "With that big a rumble, wonder how come we didn't get wind of it?"

"That," Greeley seconded, "is exactly what I've been thinkin'. "

Mark stood a little to one side and watched Di wading in like a trooper—and wondered how in hell she had managed to cover up that black eye of hers. The swelling had gone down, but it had been a real beauty last night when he'd dropped her off. He was able to keep his stomach under control as long as he was thinking about that and not too closely about the reason for the all-points.

The Forensics team had welcomed Di like one of their own when the two of them had responded to the call; now Mark knew why she had packed a lab coat. When she was sure of her reception she'd gone back to the car for it—and with the coat on she looked just like one of them; just melted into the crowd. Which was no bad thing for someone who was trying *not* to be noticed by the press.

"Look at this—" Di muttered to Mark, pulling up the cuff of one corpse's jeans with a pencil.

"Holy—rope burns—"

"And just on one ankle," she replied. "They're all like this."

"Like the stiff at Bachmann Lake. You were right about coming out here; these have got to be ours. You picking up anything?"

Somewhat to his disappointment she shook her head as she rose from her crouch. "Nothing strong; certainly no signs of any of my five signatures."

He stood, crossed his arms, and thought. "So I'll ask a dumb question. Can psychic traces be wiped out?"

She stared at him, and her eyes widened a little. "Not so dumb; I didn't think of that. The answer is yes—but only—only if you are very, very good. I can't do it."

He nodded; he was no telepath, but he knew what she must be thinking, because he was thinking the same thing, with a sinking spirit. *We could be getting out of our depth fast.*

Before he could say anything else, he heard one of the Forensics people swear under her breath.

It was a welcome distraction, and since she was practically at his elbow, he looked over in her direction. "Problems, Jean?"

"Just the arrival of a chronic pain in the ass," replied the curly-haired technician. "See that blond?" She nodded in the direction of the gathering of vultures behind the police barricade. "German reporter; thinks he's God's gift to journalism. Making a prime pain of himself, and we've been given orders to make nice with him."

A throaty chuckle from his other elbow sent his head swiveling in Di's direction. "But *I* haven't been given any such orders," she said. "Would you like a demo of my foolproof way of getting rid of snoops?"

Jean's mouth quirked a little, and she raised her eyebrows. "Is the Pope Polish?"

Di rose to her feet, and began walking toward the barricade, making notes on her clipboard. Predictably, the blond reporter intercepted her as soon as she got within grabbing distance, catching her by the sleeve and erupting with questions.

They were too far away to hear what she said at first—but then she pulled paper containers out of the copious pockets of her lab coat and began waving them under his nose—her voice rising with every word.

"—fecal samples!" she enthused. "I tell you, it's plain as day! It's all here, in the fecal samples!"

The German backpedaled so fast he nearly ran over another ghoul.

"I'll be *happy* to show you—" Di pursued him, still waving the containers.

"I—I do not think that will be required, Miss—" he gasped, eyes darting this way and that as he searched for an escape route to get away from this madwoman. "I haf enough information now, thank you—good day!"

For just at that moment he saw an opening—and all but ran out of the crowd. Di contrived to look disappointed, shoved the containers back into her pockets and returned to Mark's side.

If the situation had been less gruesome, it would have been hilarious. As it was, Di was greeted with a mixture of relieved, grateful, and approving looks.

"If we dared," Jean whispered, "we'd give you a standing ovation. Lady, you can work with us any day!"

"Any sign of flower petals or feathers this time?" Di asked, getting back down to business.

"Not around the bodies or in the clothing—but yes, flower petals stuck in the dried blood and actually *in* some of the wounds," one of the others replied. "And it looks, at least superficially, as if some of these boys were reclothed after they were killed. We won't know until we get the bodies back to the lab and map everything, but the lacerations in the clothing aren't always matching the lacerations on the bodies."

"Huh." Di folded her arms around her clipboard, and frowned with concentration. "Now *why* bother to put clothes back on them?"

"Red herring?" Mark suggested. "At least a temporary one? Make it look for a little while as if this *wasn't* one of the cult killings?"

"Buying them time for something—could be. Could be." The look in Di's eyes told Mark enough—that what the cult had been buying time for was to wipe out psychic fingerprints *and* psychic backtrails.

"I don't like you going out there alone," Mark protested, as they levered themselves into the Ghia.

"Mark, one look at you and my sources are going to smell 'cop' and spook on me," Di said, a bit of an edge of exasperation creeping into her tone. "And I won't be alone; you'll be within yelling distance. Besides, the first few are safe; my voudoun contact has been vouched for and knows I'm coming, and after that I'll be talking to people who can 'read' me. They'll know I'm on the level—and unless one of them is a renegade, I'm in no danger from them."

There had been an unexpected bonus; Di's voudoun practitioner lived within blocks of where the bodies had been found. And Mark could tell that she wanted *badly* to know if anyone sensitive to such things had sensed any otherworldly stirrings last night.

"I still don't like it," Mark grumbled, turning the ignition key. "Why voudoun, anyway? Why not some nice innocent Druids or something?"

"You don't know much about Druidism—if you think they're *innocent!*" She gave him a sidelong glance and shook her head. "Oh, I might as well level with you. Two reasons. One—those who work with blood magic tend to be sensitive to it. Two—I have *no* ties into the pagan network here. I work solo too much—and a lot of the pagan net frankly doesn't trust strangers much. You said it yourself; this is Bible-thumping country, they might end up out of a job or worse. *I* will have to be vouched for by a local, and the only local contact I have now is Noble Williams."

"Okay." He did not immediately pull out into traffic when the Ghia had rumbled to life; Di cocked her head at him quizzically.

"Something else wrong?"

"Are we biting off more than we can chew?" he asked somberly.

Her lips thinned, and she turned away from him, staring broodingly out through the glare of sun on the streaky windshield.

"Well?" he prompted.

"Possibly. Very possibly," she admitted after a moment of reluctant silence. "I've been trying to think of all the ways I know to eliminate psi-traces. Using running water to wash them away; that's out, obviously. Working insulated so that there never *were* any traces is *probably* out, it's too hard to maintain good insulation, and all it would take is one leak. That leaves one alternative that can be worked a half-dozen ways: using pure, raw power to blank any individual signatures. A kind of psychic bleaching. And that's something *I* can't do. If they can—I'm not sure I want to think about that too hard."

Mark gripped the steering wheel hard enough to turn his knuckles white, feeling real, honest fear. Fear like he hadn't felt since that long-ago night in Quasi's. This was exactly the reason he'd gotten Di involved in the first place; to have his *expert* out of her depth was enough to leave him gut-clenched. "Should we—think about pulling out of this?" he asked slowly.

"Let me counter that with a question of my own: Dare we?" she returned. "So far these people have killed ten victims *that we know of*, and three of those were little kids. Do *you* want more deaths on your conscience? I don't." She swallowed, and bit her lip. "I do this probably for the same reason that you became a cop, Mark—there are things out there that people need to be shielded from. Since I have the talent and the knowledge—it's almost a duty for me to stand in the line of fire. And unfortunately I *don't* know of anyone better equipped than I am who isn't already out fighting fires of his own."

"Unless I'm very much mistaken, this could get fatal."

She nodded, and twisted a strand of hair around one finger. "It could. We have one advantage going for us, though—"

"And that is?"

"That everyone who's been killed has been attacked *physically*, not by magic. And between the two of us, I truly do not think that there is anything *physical* that we can't handle."

He nodded, and forced his hands to unclench. "Okay, I'll grant you that. Can you shoot—" he bit off the rest with a blush of chagrin.

"How quickly we forget," she replied with a hint of irony. "The more appropriate questions would be, What can you get me in a hurry, and can you manage a permit for me to carry concealed?"

"You're asking a Dallas *cop*? When you're working for the force? What do you *want*? I recommend against a howitzer, they're awfully hard to hide." He put the car in gear and eased it into traffic.

"My current personal is a Colt forty-five; a revolver, I like to keep things simple. And button that lip on any smart comments about it being too big a piece for me to handle; I *happen* to have stronger wrists than you do, and I never fire it one-handed. I did *not* bring it with me—I never thought I was going to have to contemplate putting holes in people, and I've always figured that traveling with a firearm is a Very Bad Idea, since you never know who is going to be able to get at your luggage when you check it through. And you are not heading for my voudoun contact."

"No, I'm heading for HDQ. We are going to get you armed right now; you're *already* dangerous." He accelerated and squeezed the Ghia into a gap between two pickups. "What we have mostly are Browning nine-mil autos; that's close enough in weight to your forty-five for you to make the transition."

"I'll take your word for it. I should warn you, there are going to be some situations where I will refuse to carry the thing."

"It's your skin." He hit the freeway on-ramp and piloted the Ghia into the traffic flow with the ease of an Indy 500 driver. "I'll feel better knowing you've got it. Now answer me true, lady—what do we do if we get in a situation where we *are* out-magicked?"

"*You* run like hell. And don't argue; if our positions were reversed, I'd run while you covered me. In a case where I'm the expert, don't you try to be a hero."

"Agreed. But what am I supposed to do if you get put out of action permanently?"

"Now that," she replied, so softly he could barely hear her over the traffic noise, "is something you will not have to worry about. If I go—and I swear to you by all I hold sacred that I *can* do this—I take whoever's behind this *with* me."

It was late afternoon when they headed back out; Diana was now armed, checked out on the police range as being competent, and equipped with all the appropriate permits for the weapon now clipped to her waistband over her right hip. With her jacket on, even Mark had a hard time spotting it.

And that was weird—because a Browning nine mil is not an easy gun to hide.

"Now I feel a little better—" he admitted. "It isn't rational, but I do. Now tell me how in hell you're making it look like you're not carrying anything bulkier than a fat wallet!"

She smirked. "Trade secret."

"You *could* walk."

"Creep."

He growled threateningly; she winced and ducked. "Okay, okay, I'll tell you. I'm projecting harmless innocence; as an empath I'm very good at that—your mind doesn't expect Snow White to be packing, so it refuses to see the bulge."

"Huh." He shook his head, not sure whether to believe her or not. "Is that how you're hiding your black eye?"

"No. I'm using the same stuff they use to cover strawberry birthmarks. Would you like to know the color of my underwear too before you let me out?"

The sharpness of her answer told him how much on edge she was, so he kept the retort he'd wanted to make behind his teeth. "Where do you want me to wait for you?"

"Halfway down the block." They were approaching the address, which proved to be a tiny storefront on the corner. Late afternoon sunlight glared off the window, and Mark couldn't quite make out what was painted there.

"What is this place, anyway?"

"An herbalist—which around here is *admitting* you're an arcane practitioner."

Mark contemplated the denizens of the area, and felt a twinge of serious mundane misgiving as he parked the car. "I don't want to sound racist, but aren't you a bit pale to be wandering around this block?"

"I would be," she replied, slipping out before he could stop her, "except that they aren't going to see *me*. They're going to see only what they expect to see. Watch. . . ."

And sure enough; as he watched her saunter off, he could see that not only was she attracting no attention, but the glances of the loiterers and passersby actually seemed to slide right off her.

He sighed, and scrunched down in his seat, making himself comfortable. *If she could bottle that,* he thought, *we'd make a fortune.*

Di sighed, feeling some of the weight of the need to stay constantly under shields drop from her shoulders. She had known from the moment that she stepped in through the door of the tiny, fragrant, shadowy shop that she was in the presence of a friend, even though she had never met Noble Williams in her life. And the silver-haired, wizened, ebony man behind the counter had responded to her hesitant self-introduction as if she had been a long-absent relative, locking the shop-door, pulling down the shade that said Closed and ushering her into his own sitting room in the apartment behind the shop.

Before she had time to blink she was enthroned in a wicker chair and plied with a very impeccably British tea.

The shields he's got up on this place—she thought, a little in awe. *Granted, he's been at this game twice, maybe three times as long as I have, but still—you could hit this apartment with a psychic nuke and not penetrate.*

And the atmosphere within the shields was genuinely welcoming and friendly; as an empath she was doubly sensitive to things like that. It was the first time since she'd arrived in Dallas that she felt *safe*.

As she sipped her tea, she smiled at her host across his tiny hardwood table. "I must say," she told him, "that of all the things I was anticipating, that very *last* was a Mahatma Gandhi clone with the voice and accent of Geoffrey Holder! Noble, I could listen to you read the phone book and enjoy the experience to the hilt!"

"You are far too kind," Noble Williams laughed richly. "But my dear Miss Tregarde," he continued in mock protest, "our surprise was mutual! From my colleague's brief description, *I* was expecting a six-foot-tall Amazon warrior, wielding a mighty flaming sword—only to be accosted by—what? A music-box ballerina in blue jeans! Do have more tea, won't you?"

"Please—" She held out her cup, deciding that if *he* wasn't going to mention the Browning—which he had *most* certainly noticed—neither was she. "And—this room—something tells me you've really *read* all these books, and at least twice each!"

For the room was wall-to-ceiling bookcases, everything from books Di had in her own arcane library to Shakespeare to Tolkien to *War and Peace.*

He laughed again. "It is a hunger with me, books. I had rather read than eat, I do think."

"How on earth did you ever meet up with Marie? I didn't think the Haitian practitioners and the Louisianans even spoke, much less kept up a regular correspondence."

He let his eyelids droop, stirred another spoonful of honey into his tea, and smiled slyly. "My dear child, we aren't going to tell you *everything*, you know! We must keep *some* secrets!"

She returned the smile. "I have been rebuked. I'm just glad you were willing to talk to me. This is turning out to involve a lot more than I thought it would."

"Indeed." He set his cup carefully down on the saucer and steepled his fingers thoughtfully, his puckish expression turning serious. "But—you remind me, rightly, of business. This present situation calls for a great deal of cooperation among *all* the blessed. Ask—I shall answer with honesty, and with as much information as I possess."

She set her own cup down, and looked into his depthlessly dark eyes, allowing the last of *her* shields to drop completely. "By now you've heard what turned up a few blocks away—did you, or anyone you know, *sense* anything last night? Or any other night, for that matter?"

The voudoun priest shook his graying head regretfully, a genuine regret she could feel quite strongly. "No. Nothing at all. And it is a source of wonder and concern to me that we have not. Those of us who *are* in tune with feelings have only experienced the fear and sickness of those discovering the bodies of the victims. None of us have sensed the deaths themselves, which *surely* must have been horrible."

"You've felt *nothing*? Not even anything like a power-point where there wasn't one before?"

"No—we have felt threat, and strangeness. But what we have had is a feeling of growing—not *evil*; it is hard to quite describe what we have felt. It is a kind of hunger, a kind of violent, and very angry hunger. And—" he hesitated a moment before continuing. "The *loas* have been warning us of danger for some time now."

Di sat up a little straighter at that. "So *they* knew of something. Danger to your folk specifically?"

"Again, no." His eyes looked off somewhere into the far distance, to a place far removed in time and space from the pleasant little sitting room. "No, they have only warned us of places to beware of, and times when it would not be wise to be alone. I trust you have deduced that all the victims *were* alone?"

"Except for those three children—"

"Who were scarcely able to protect themselves; I think they could be counted as being 'alone.' And again, they were not—as the old phrase of my childhood went—'persons of color.' Have you not noted this also?"

"No," Diana replied, blushing with chagrin at missing something so obvious. "I hadn't. You're saying there's a connection—"

"One I do not yet understand," he said, looking vaguely puzzled. "It is subtler than I am stating; I feel sure of this. But this much I do know; there is a powerful anger, a hatred that this—being—has, and it is *not* directed at the black population. For once in our lives, *we* are not the target of rancor. If this thing were to take one of us, it would be because, like Mount Everest, we happen to be there. We are not immune—but *we* are not the preferred targets, either. Given a *choice* between a black and a white, this thing would slay the white and allow the black to move on unmolested. But this is not anything of ours, either; I can swear this to you. I *do* swear this to you, by all that I am."

Di let out the breath she had been holding in a soft whistle. "I believe you. But *that*—the hatred for whites—is not only interesting, it's something I didn't even consider. So *that's* why you haven't buttoned up, like the 'readers,' or run off, like the Rom."

"Not all the Rom have fled," Williams told her, shifting a little so that the wicker of his chair creaked. "And that may be significant as well. It is certainly significant that the Gitano, who normally do *not* wander, have left the city. Yes, the few Gitano we had are all gone, and the Kalderash with them, and *most* of the Lowara—"

"But not all?" If there were still some Lowara—the Lowara *owed* her. It might be time to collect.

"But not all," he agreed. His eyes now seemed to be looking inward, not outward. "Miss Tregarde—"

"Diana," she said firmly.

"Diana," his voice deepened, and took on a heavier coloration of accent—and a firmness of tone that almost *forced* her to believe every word she was hearing. "You are in most perilous danger. Believe this. There is present threat, and peril to your life."

She went still, almost frozen inside. Power moved here; had moved in so subtly that she had not noticed it until it was there. What was speaking now was *not* Noble Williams.

"This thing has the scent of you—and while it is *now* in the position of the quarry, it may well turn hunter, especially if you press too hard. It knows you, and it can find you if it chooses. Be wise. Do *not* walk anywhere unshielded, or unarmed. Keep all your weapons about you at all times. Guard your back."

A chill of fear threaded down the length of her spine, for she *knew* that it was the height of stupidity to ignore that advice. Especially from a *houngun* whose *loa* was Ogoun, god of war and warriors—and statesmanship and craft.

"Yes?" she breathed, making of the word a hesitant request for further help.

"Until now it has walked in the shadows, in hiding—but the sunlight does not weaken it, and it does not fear the day. It is as strong in sun as in moonlight, so do not presume to think that daylight will protect you."

"What *is* it?" she pled, not really hoping for an answer.

"We do not know," came the bleak reply. "We do *not* know. It is nothing we have ever known—but it is very old. Old in blood and old in death; old in strength and old in cunning. And it has never known, never wanted peace. You must keep it from making a home here for itself, Diana—or it will make of this city a Hell of blood and pain. For *every* living thing." And the far-off gaze faded from the old man's eyes. At her mute look of inquiry, he shook his head.

She sighed, and forced her shoulders to relax, telling herself that she would not give in to the fear and feeling of utter inadequacy until she was forced to. But she wanted to cry so badly that her throat hurt with the effort of holding the tears back; wanted to go running back to Hartford and André and forget she'd ever heard of Dallas. Wanted to pack it *all* in and let someone else take over.

But she knew that there *was* no one else to take over. She was all there was; she and Mark were all that were standing between a city full of innocents and something a major Power feared enough to warn her against.

I'm not good enough for this. I'm just a troubleshooter; a competent magical hacker. This—it's out of my league. I can't handle this—oh gods, and I have no choice, I have to.

But she was careful to let none of that show. She swallowed a sip of tea, exerted the iron control that had gotten her a black belt in three years, and forced herself to regain an outward calm.

"Well, that was more than I expected, anyway. Every scrap of information helps."

He picked up his teacup and stared thoughtfully into it for a moment. "I believe I can give you another contact," he said finally. He rose before she could say anything and flitted silently back into the shop. When he returned, he had an index card with a handwritten name and address on it.

"One of my occasional customers," he said, as she copied the address into the notebook she dug out of her purse. "I doubt that she has fled the city; I do not think her purse would permit it, nor her employer. If my own judgment is anything to go by, I would say she is practiced, though not as practiced as you."

"Which means she is pretty well entrenched in the local neopagan movement?" Di hazarded, since the name on the card was a simple "Athena."

"I believe so," he nodded. "If you will give me a day or two to contact her, I shall try to smooth the way for you."

Mark relaxed when he saw Di emerge from the herb shop and sprint for the Ghia. He was beginning to have uneasy feelings whenever she was out of sight. "Got anything?" he asked, as she pulled the door open and slid in beside him.

"A bit," she replied, as he drove off, noting that the neighborhood denizens *still* didn't seem to be giving him, Di, or the car a second glance. "Whatever, whoever it is seems to have it in for Caucasians. And I was told that it is 'very old'—which could mean a lot of things. But it *isn't* voudoun killings; Noble said not, and I believe him."

"You think he'd fink on his own people?"

"In this case—yes," she said firmly. "We *might* want to look into Middle Eastern or Asiatics though, after all. I'm sure as hell not infallible—there's a lot of room *there* for nasty surprises, and those are not areas that I know much about. I mean, despite that I thought not, we could have a new Kali cult going; the heart-cutting-out certainly fits *that* profile, and it fits the pile of bodies in the alley—"

"But not the drowned kids?"

"I don't know; I told you, I'm just not familiar with that brand of occultism. The flower petals *would* fit, though."

"Okay, what else did you get from this guy?"

"I've got a contact into the local neo-pagan network, but Noble wants to warn her I'm coming, first. And there's another 'but.'"

"Which is?"

"That I really do not think this thing has any ties into the neo-pagan movement. It just doesn't feel right; it feels independent."

Mark whistled tunelessly for a moment, squinting into the late-afternoon sunlight reflecting off the windshields around them. "Okay, I had a pair of thoughts myself while you were in there. One of them actually dovetails with your feeling. Thought one was that there is a fourth way to do things without leaving psychic finger-prints."

"So?"

"Use tools. In this case, human tools."

Di hit her forehead with her palm. "Oh *hell*! The oldest trick in the book, and I *forgot* it! My God, that's Crowley's old trick—*and* the Kali cult's, *and* a dozen others! How could I forget?"

"Did you?" he countered. "Or were you led to forget? Couldn't this have been an effect of one of those 'traps' you sprung on yourself?"

Silence from her side of the car as he shifted gears and dodged around a double-parked cab. "It could have been," she finally said, sagging a little. "Only the gods know what blank spots I've got in my memory now. It's enough to make me want to throw in the towel and hang it all up. What the hell good am I? What *use* am I?"

"Don't," he said forcefully. "Don't say things like that. And don't blame yourself. That's exactly what 'it' wants you to do—you told me yourself how easy it is for you to get caught in a downward spiral. We'll just realize you may have gaposis, and deal with it. Okay, thought two was—maybe we ought to check on a couple of the mav-erick tea-leaf readers. The ones that don't feel right, you know? There's still a couple with their shingles up; not many, and all on this side of the tracks, but a couple."

"And?" she prompted, looking very interested.

"And there *are* a couple that give me the willies—but Bunco's never caught 'em out on anything. Like—there's this medium not six blocks from here. . . . You game?"

"M'love," she said slowly, "that is *not* a bad notion."

Diana stared down the barrel of a gun, tasting fear—cold fear—in the pit of her stomach. The business-end of the thing looked as long as the Lincoln Tunnel and twice as black.

It was a .357, to be exact. It was pointed at her midsection, held in the hand of a *most* nervous gentleman who was not, and had never been, a medium.

She refocused from the weapon to the man behind it; thin, very dark—Cuban, she thought. Little scraggle of mustache; crewcut. Hyper to the max. She could feel a trickle of sweat down her back as she tried to think at lightspeed.

I can't pull my piece. He's too far away to jump.

She kept her eyes fastened on the man's face, knowing that his eyes would warn her before he pulled the trigger—

Sensei says I'm good enough to dodge bullets, but this isn't how I wanted to find out!

She froze her expression into a mask of total fear as her mind ran through the position of every stick and exit in the room. The sour reek of mildew and the dust in the air almost made her sneeze— which she didn't dare; that would *surely* trigger him to shoot.

"Please," she whispered in Spanish, pleadingly, "I don't understand. . . ."

The man spat something in *Cubano* dialect so thick she couldn't make out the words. Something about informers, she thought—

There was the door behind him; a window behind her.

If I could throw myself backward—no, it's barred on the inside.

To right and left, two cheap dinette chairs, aluminum and red vinyl. One had been hers, one his. Nothing else but the table—just bare board walls and rough wooden floor, sagging in the middle. The chairs?

Not heavy enough to stop a bullet.

Between Di and the gunman, there was only the table draped with a stained red velvet tablecloth. On the table lay something other than a crystal ball.

A sealed baggie of white powder, to be precise. *Not* what she had expected—and her face had given her away.

Smack. Gods help me, a heroin dealer. Where in hell is Mark? Never mind that; you're an empath—project, dammit!

She oozed innocence, helplessness, from every pore, projecting with every erg of energy she had to spare.

Hey man, I'm nothing but a stupid chick looking for a fix on the future, not a drug fix. I just walked in here by dumb accident. I look just like your airhead kid cousin—

She held out her hands, empty, imploringly. The gun wavered. The man's thin face turned puzzled, then predatory.

Good—oh good, I hit a nerve. C'mon, sweetie, remember how you used to want to get into your cousin's pants?

She turned down the innocence, turned up the sex. "Please," she stammered, "I'll do anything you want—"

It was working. She could read it in his eyes, in the flavoring of his emotions. He was *still* going to kill her—but now he was thinking that he was going to have some fun, first.

Mark, where the hell are you?

The man grinned; his teeth were stained and yellow, and too large for his thin face. He looked like a horse, truth be told. An *ugly* horse.

The muzzle of the gun moved a little aside; it was no longer pointing at her, but at the floor to her left. The man was relaxed now, his finger easing a bit on the trigger—

And there was a familiar *presence* at the window behind her.

Mark!

She waited; prayed he'd see the opening she had created. Held her breath and felt the tension behind her arc to a peak.

A welcome shout. *"Down!"*

She obeyed, throwing herself to her right, rolling on her shoulder, and coming up with her own gun in her hand as three shots crashed through the window to take the drug pusher in the head, neck, and chest.

The man was thrown back by the impacts, jerking with each hit—his face and torso blossomed into ruined meat. The last shot sent him sprawling on his back in the doorframe. The body twitched, then stilled.

She fought down nausea. *Oh gods—I can't—I—dammit, I've seen plenty of bodies before, I—oh gods.* She swallowed, tasted bile, swallowed again. *I've got—calm, calm, back to balance—*She managed to distance herself for an instant; it was enough—

She started to holster her own gun with hands that shook, then thought better of the notion.

That bastard might not be alone. Just because you don't feel anybody in the house—

So she stayed right where she was, crouched in the darkest corner, ears alert for any sound, however small.

It seemed an age before she heard a footstep she knew, and Mark's whistle.

Di sprawled on the passenger's side of the Ghia, half in, half out, holding her hands out in front of her with a look of exhausted concentration.

Both hands were trembling like cottonwood leaves in a high wind.

The block had been cordoned off and Narcotics was dealing with the mess inside. There must have been ten squads parked, and half as many unmarked cars; the place was swarming with cops, uniformed and plainclothes. So far as Mark was concerned, he was overjoyed to have them around.

"Well that's a new one," Mark mused, as Di slowly brought her shaking hands under control. "A pusher setting up as a medium—"

"I'm not too surprised he gave you the creeps," she replied, her voice dulled with fatigue. "My god, what a scam. You just trot up to the door, and say you need help—that got you in the door. Then you say that Angelita sent you. That got you to the table. *Then* I guess whatever your 'problem' was told him how much and what you wanted."

"And you just stumbled on the code words—here—" Mark reached behind the seat of the Ghia, took out a thermos, and poured her half a cup of lukewarm coffee. She took it from him, and managed not to spill any.

"Not quite—I was extended and feeling for trigger phrases. Sometimes I can do that if my subject is pretty hyper—"

"Considering he was dipping pretty heavily into his profit margin, I should *figure* he'd be hyper!" Mark replied, looking up to see the shrouded body bag being carried out to the ambulance. "He was heavy into coke. From what I found in the other room, he'd done two, maybe three lines before you came tapping on his door, and *his* stuff wasn't cut much."

She shuddered. "That—gods. That's the closest I've ever come to getting ventilated, honestly. Arcane danger I can deal with but—I swear, Mark, if I'd had any idea what was going on in there I never would have walked into that one. That was *not* a job for me—that was for the pros. Gods, it was worse than *anything* occult."

"Shit, *I* wouldn't have let you walk into that. But you did okay, spooky," he said softly, sincerely. "You did okay. You did everything exactly right, like we'd practiced it. Narcotics is real happy with both of us right now."

She glanced over at him, and he saw that the makeup covering her black eye was beginning to run. She managed a wan smile. "We pick up some points, partner?"

"More'n a few. You about ready to call it a day?"

She sighed and handed back the thermos top. She'd drained it so dry there wasn't even a hint of liquid left in it.

"It's a day," she said.

Sherry woke before Bobby's moans of fear grew loud enough to really *hear*. But she heard them—as she usually heard them.

Mother's instinct, she thought, feeling what was shamefully close to relief when she realized that the other half of the bed was as empty as when she'd gone to sleep. At least Robert wasn't back yet; he was more hindrance than help when Bobby was in one of these states, growling at him that he was being a baby and that it was time for him to grow up—

She slid out of bed without bothering to turn on the light, using only the dim illumination from the readouts of the various high-tech goodies in the bedroom to see by. As she hurried down the hall, the carpet warm and soft beneath her bare feet, Bobby began to cry.

She sat on the edge of the bed and began stroking his forehead, waking him gently. She'd found out the hard way that waking him at once left him dazed and petrified with fear for nearly an hour, and that turning on the light made things worse.

She murmured his name, softly, as she gentled him—and finally the dull, weary crying stopped. "M-m-mommy?" he faltered.

"I'm here, baby," she said, only now taking him into her arms. "It's okay, you just had another bad dream."

Thank God this dream hadn't been as bad as the ones of the past three nights—where he'd woken up drenched with sweat and screaming about blood. He was just a little warm, and clung to her with trust rather than the despair he'd shown then. She hugged him close, breathing the soapy-clean scent of his hair as he tucked his head under her chin.

"Better?" she asked.

He nodded a little. "Mommy?" he asked, finally. "When's Mark going to come over again?"

"I don't know, munchkin," she replied, wishing that she did know the answer to that question, and shifting a bit so that the bedsprings creaked. "What brought that on?"

He sniffed, and she felt him scrub at his eyes with the back of his hand. "The Mean Ladies," he said, finally.

"Is that who you were dreaming about?"

He nodded again, his hair tickling her chin. "They don' come over when Mark's here."

Perceptive little lad, aren't you? she thought, startled. Two of the three models *had* been over after dinner this evening; Lupe and the youngest, Conchita, the one with the come-hither eyes and the air of a girl who'd trip a man she wanted and beat him to the ground. . . .

Sherry stroked Bobby's hair and schooled herself not to tense up; he would read that, he was *very* good at body-language. No doubt, that was what had kicked off tonight's nightmare, his picking up the tension between herself and Robert.

The initial tension, anyway; once Lupe had decided to exert her charm, she'd succeeded in lulling all of Sherry's ugly suspicions away until she and her sister had left with Robert—ostensibly heading for the studio.

But once they had gone, the suspicions returned.

Bobby went limp, which told her he'd fallen asleep. She eased him back down into the bed and tucked the covers around him, carefully and slowly, so as not to wake him again. But when she returned to her own bed, it was to lie wakefully staring into the dark.

Robert had gotten so—strange—since last year. Yet the personality changes she thought she was seeing were hardly fitting any pattern. Some might have thought them positive. He'd become almost a workaholic—sure, he was playing around with the girls, but a good many of those photo sessions really *were* what they were supposed to be; Robert had the photos to prove it. He hardly slept more than three or four hours a night anymore; the rest of the time he was out—at the studio was what he said. . . .

But—the relationship he had with the girls went far beyond the flings he'd had before. The five of them seemed to be able to communicate without words, and to be wrapped up in some secret project or other that obsessed all of them. It was a relationship that left Sherry totally on the outside, and feeling like a stranger.

She longed for the times when Mark appeared for an evening; then Robert went back to his old self, laughing, joking—relaxed, with no signs of the cold intensity that frightened her so much.

Mark was such a *good* friend; so compassionate, trying so hard to be the buffer between Robert and herself. He was giving Bobby the male affection he needed, the affection Robert couldn't seem to show. But then Robert was an only, with an ultra-macho father, and Mark came from a huge family, all of them used to showing their feelings openly. It was too bad Mark's family had scattered all over the globe—parents in California, one brother in Minnesota, one in Vermont, two in the Navy, and the sisters in Seattle, Chicago and Florida. Only his aunt remained—

But Mark's loss was Sherry's gain. She didn't think she'd have been able to cope without his help, now that Robert had gotten so strange.

She turned restlessly, and stared at the glowing numbers of the digital clock without really seeing them. She wondered where Robert was tonight. He never bothered to tell her where he was going anymore.

But it wasn't as if he was being cruel—it was more that he was preoccupied with whatever was obsessing him.

She suddenly wondered if the girls could be getting him involved in some kind of cult—

It would certainly fit the symptoms: the preoccupation, the personality changes, the way he behaved when he was with the girls, like they were all part of some in-group.

If it was a peyote or mescaline cult, that would make even more sense. It would account for the reason he was sleeping so little, and for the incredible energy he seemed to have these days. Psychogenic drugs had caused positive personality changes before this—but if they were giving him delusions of grandeur, that would account for the way he'd been distancing himself from Sherry and Bobby—

In the next moment the notion seemed stupid. Robert had *never* been interested in any sort of religion, not even back in the sixties, and he'd been loudly and impatiently scornful of those of their friends who'd been into the drug scene. She couldn't see any reason why he'd change now.

Maybe it was her.

Maybe—maybe she had just gone dull since Bobby was born. She used to share in what he was doing, even to helping in the darkroom; she hadn't done that in at least a year. In fact, she'd closed *herself* off from *him*—letting her jealousy of the girls drive her out of the room when they appeared, dismissing shots of them with a feigned boredom. She'd been closing herself into the workroom more and more—and God knows Robert had always found her craftwork yawnacious.

Maybe it was her fault that they were drifting apart.

She wished she could talk with Mark; he always listened so patiently. And when he did give advice, it was generally good. And she could always count on him to be honest; if this was her fault, he'd tell

her. And maybe he could tell her how to get Robert to show a little affection to his son—

Dear, sweet Mark, she thought, as she finally became tired
enough to drift into sleep. *He's always there when I need him.*

SEVEN

The windowless room was darkened, shadow-shrouded, and echoingly empty. Oddly shaped metal structures, like robotic mantises, were pushed into one corner. Dim reddish light came from somewhere behind a massive chair, the only piece of furniture in the room. There was a man in that chair, a man hardly more than a deeper shadow within a shadow.

The door opened, then closed softly again, and a woman stepped into the barren room, her footsteps echoing from the pale, blank walls. Her name *had* been Lupe. Now it was Chimalman; fitting, for that had been the name of a great woman warrior—and she was now a warrior of a different sort.

She had come straight from the street without pausing to change into more suitable garb. Although it was not fitting, she was clothed as these northern invaders were. She hurried to the thronelike chair, and once there, prostrated herself at the feet of her lord and god.

He brooded, unspeaking, his shadows and silence taking on a palpable weight, that his priestess might feel the ponderous bulk of his power before he acknowledged her presence.

Her costume did not please him; she knew that—he had more than once rebuked her for appearing before him in such clothing. He was making her feel the weight of that disapproval before he would move on to the business that had sent her out into the street.

"Speak," he said at last, in the old tongue. The single word filled the room.

"The witch is still baffled," the girl replied, not daring to raise her head from the floor. "But she is not deterred. She is more stubborn than I had anticipated—and the man—"

"What of the man?" Some vague emotion sharpened his tone, and she trembled.

"He is clever—and he is working *with* her, warrior with warrior. He is as much of a danger as she—"

"No!" The god leaned out of shadow, and his servant, now gathering her courage enough to raise her face a trifle, could see conflicting emotions at war within him by the subtle clouding of his eyes.

"Lord?" she replied tentatively. When the god warred with himself, sometimes it boded ill for his handmaidens.

"No." He settled back into his seat, back into the shadow. "No, the man is not to be tampered with. Nor, for now, the witch. So long as she remains baffled—"

"And if she does not?" she ventured tentatively.

"Witches—" he pondered that for a moment. "They are chancy to deal with at best. I do not know the powers of this one—and this land is *her* home. I know not who or what she may call upon. The wise warrior does not waste his strength. She could cost us more than we can afford at this early stage. Yet she is only one—hear me; if she sniffs too closely upon our trail, warn her off in a way that she cannot mistake."

"And if she will not heed the warning?"

"Kill her."

The priestess sat back on her heels. "To your glory?"

"No," he replied. "That is too dangerous. Kill only."

"But the man, lord—"

"Enough, leave be." The impatience in his tone made her prostrate herself again. "Without the witch, he is of no importance. I say you shall leave him alone. Let us seek another, more easily obtained sacrifice."

It was sunset, and Ben Bronson whistled as he headed up the cement walkway to the ultramodern glass-and-steel RemTech building; he was feeling very pleased with himself, and looking forward to a few pleasant hours *away* from his wife and kids. He'd headed over here as soon as supper was over. RemTech was more home to him than his house was—especially with the youngest teething. Julie seemed to think *he* should help out with the kids when he was home. Fat chance; that was woman's work. He hadn't married her just so he could become a babysitter. There were lots more important ways to spend his time than in fooling around with a drooling little brat. Kids were for showing off when they were clean and acting intelligent, not for hassling over when they were being pains.

"Hello, Ben." The voice made him jump.

Lanky, nerdy Steve Barrigan materialized out of the door-alcove, letting the door close and lock behind him. Ben sniffed in annoyance, and reached for his keycard; after startling him like that, the *least* the jerk could have done was to hold the door for him!

"Steve," he responded shortly.

"About those enhancements to the Pancyber project—"

"I told you I'd get back with you on that." Barrigan *would* bring that up. Ben had hoped he'd forgotten. He pushed his way past the tech into the alcove.

"Yeah, you did," the tech replied, pushing his glasses up on his nose. "You said they were probably not going to want my enhancements. Funny thing, I found out tonight that you took all my programs and implemented them with your initials on them. Is that why you got a raise this week and I didn't?"

Ben jerked his head around so quickly his neck nearly snapped. "How—"

"You forget, *I'm* the one that coded the production protections, you lying bastard," Steve said pleasantly. "I can track anything I need to—and I figured it wouldn't hurt to check up on what *you'd* been doing lately. Glad I did." He held out his clenched hand, and opened it. Pieces of cut-up keycard fell to the cement with tiny clicking noises. "By tomorrow morning everyone else will be onto you, too. I added a little warning to everyone about you on the sign-on bulletin, one you can't get rid of. I don't think you'll be able to get away with that trick again. By the way, you'll find my resignation on your desk. *If* you can get in."

"What do you mean if—" Ben was too stunned by the tech's revolt to really take in more than the last sentence.

Steve had started to walk into the gathering twilight, but turned just long enough to answer. "You also seem to have forgotten that I used to work on the security systems. They never took away my access. So Ben, ol' buddy, the lock don't recognize you no more. Bye."

Then he was gone. And Ben jammed his keycard repeatedly and with growing anger into the reader—with no more result than if he'd used his MasterCard.

Finally he began circling the building, looking for someone to let him in, trying to think of ways to *get* that arrogant little sonuvabitch.

I'll see he never gets another job in DP again—he's gonna be washing dishes for the rest of his life!

He found lit windows—and beyond them, a cluster of two or three people from another department—he knew them, vaguely. He sighed with relief, and pounded on the window.

They looked up—and must have seen him, seen him clearly. But they acted as if they *hadn't* seen him, and went back to their discussion, ignoring further window-pounding. Ben's temper and blood pressure rose.

They were all in this together, the jerks! By God, he'd have them *all* on the carpet!

If he could just get in.

There were lights on in inner offices, but no one came to see who was making the noise. And by the time he'd circled back to the office where he'd seen those three Judases, the lights were off and they were gone from view.

After circling the building fruitlessly until it became full dark— after calling every number he could think of inside and getting no response, he finally gave up. He was so angry he could hardly think.

He was certainly too angry to hear the soft footsteps behind him as he headed for his car.

This "Athena" was not living in luxury accommodations. The bus had passed through a pretty dubious neighborhood to get to hers; Mark would not have been amused. As a matter of fact, Di rather doubted that Mark would have let her come here at all if he'd known where she was going.

But this was going to be tricky enough without having him along, bless his pointed little head. She'd left her gun behind, knowing that if the woman was good enough to spot it through Di's disguises, she'd freak at worst, and clam up at best.

It had taken an hour and a half by bus to get this far, and she still had six blocks to walk. She huddled in her denim jacket and concentrated on being invisible. But there was a palpable aura of *hunters* all around here, an aura she could taste, a hint of hunger in the back of her mind. She felt as if she was swimming in a pool filled with sharks.

The address was one more battered little stucco house, surrounded on all sides by similar buildings. The only real difference between this place and the ones to either side of it was that Athena's house didn't have three cars up on blocks in the scrap of front yard, or growling dogs chained in the back.

Di picked her way across the cracked sidewalk and up to the porch. There had been some effort at keeping the weeds and lawn under control here, as opposed to next door. There was no doubt in Di's mind just where the "threshold" of the house was; as soon as she climbed the pair of crumbling concrete steps and got onto the porch she could feel the barrier—

No bad idea; extend your threshold out a little beyond the house walls, and maybe people won't break in, she thought with surprise and approval. *I'll have to try that one myself.*

There was a tiny, faded, hand-lettered sign taped over the doorbell—"please knock, bell does not work." She tapped lightly on the metal frame of the storm door, and almost before she brought her knuckles down for the third time, the inner door cracked and a single blue eye peered out at her from around the doorframe, a security chain stretched tightly just above it.

"I'm Diana—" she said to the eye. "Noble said that he was going to call you about me."

"Yes—I've been expecting you. Just a minute, please—" The door closed for a moment and Di heard the scrape of the security chain being undone. Then the door reopened, and a slender, short-haired blond woman beckoned her to enter.

The living room was furnished mostly in floor pillows, brick-and-board bookcases, and books. Hundreds, thousands of books. There was New Age synthesizer music playing softly from a cassette deck, and the lighting was entirely by candlelight. Di took it all in with a single glance, and turned around to face her hostess.

The young woman was perhaps three or four years her junior; she was slender, but fairly strong-looking, with the kind of balanced grace that told Di she was no stranger to the martial arts herself. Her eyes were so intensely blue that there was no doubting their coloring even by candlelight, and her pale blond hair, styled almost in a crew-cut, was plainly that color without help from Lady Clairol. She was wearing a faded blue T-shirt and equally faded jeans. She was, to Di's eyes, teetering on an edge between fear and nervous curiosity.

"I don't bite," Di said with a chuckle. "At least not often, or hard."

The young woman echoed the laugh shakily. "Well, pick a spot," she said. "Noble did call—he said you were to be trusted, and he told me what you wanted."

"But you're still not terribly sure of me. Don't blame you," Di replied, seating herself cross-legged on one of the nearer pillows. "I could be anybody; I could get you fired for having a weird religion."

The woman's eyes turned bitter as she took a seat herself. "No, that you can't do. I've already been fired, because I wouldn't take the nightshift. Shit, it's bad enough on graveyard when everything's normal—but now—Lord and Lady, if I put myself out on the street when *that's* prowling—"

"You've precoged?" Di asked quietly, "That you're in danger after dark?"

Athena nodded, flushing. Di's immediate acceptance of the situation—and her easy familiarity with paranormal talents—seemed to reassure her.

"Some. But not clear enough to *do* anything. I mean, I know I'm on the menu if I go out after certain hours, but I can't tell when *it's* going to hit, or where. But to go out night after night, during the prime time for *that* to be hunting, I'm going to be narrowing my odds to the point of suicide! But they didn't give me a choice, and they wouldn't listen to my arguments. It was my turn on third, I had to take it or get fired. I'm—I *was* junior computer operator, low man on the totem pole."

Di frowned. "You've got grounds for a protest—"

Athena shook her head. "Unfortunately not. I'm fourth *dan* black belt; I could probably protect myself better than some of the men if this was just a slasher or a rapist. This neighborhood isn't that bad—it's only if you have to take the bus that you go through *its* hunting areas. And I would be, coming and going. There's one place where it's hunted over in the *barrio*, and another near the industrial park where I work. That's where some of the victims came from, those two places. Mass transportation isn't real good around here. You know where the bus stop is—I didn't hear a car so you must have taken the bus here. The other end for me is still a mile from the center. But when I protested, they just told me to get a car."

"Lovely," Di said sourly, as she lowered her shielding a bit. "Real caring folks, your ex-bosses. So terribly concerned about the welfare of their employees."

"I'm *trying* to save up some cash—and I don't make enough to buy anything but a junker, anyway nothing reliable, nothing that wouldn't eat me out of house and home with repair bills. So what do I do, say that I *know* if they put me on third, the local bogeyman'll get me?" Her eyes were defiant, but her mouth showed despair. "We aren't union; the only lawyer I could afford would lose, and I'd be out twice. Look, this isn't what you came for—"

"No, it isn't," Di agreed. But she was now beginning to have a stirring of certainty that meant she'd been brought here for a purpose.

Not what she'd thought to come for—"But maybe we can help each other."

Athena looked askance at her. "Well—I can tell you right now that nobody's getting anything, and we've done Work to try and pin this bastard down. I'm talking major circles here, several groups working together. All we get is warnings. Everybody that could afford to, left. The rest of us are trying to keep our butts down. What happened to your eye?"

"My what?" Di was startled by the abrupt change of subject.

"Your eye—" the woman began, then shrugged. "If it's none of my business say so—but my Prime isn't precog, it's healing."

The blackened eye sent a dull stab of pain through Di's skull. "When you turn over rocks," she replied wryly, "things tend to crawl out. One bit me. The one that owned House of Dark Desires."

"Old Creepy-Crowley-Clone?" Athena exclaimed. "I hope you gave as good as you got!"

"I think so—"

"Look," the woman said abruptly, "I'm being rude to keep interrupting you, but I can't help it, it's the way I am. I can't see things like that eye without reacting—can I fix it for you? It's driving me bats, staring at me and hurting."

Di raised a surprised eyebrow, and cautiously let down the rest of her shields.

She was startled again by the depth of what she sensed.

Ye gods, what is a major healing talent doing wasting away out here?

"If you really want to—" Before she could finish the sentence, Athena had stretched her hand out across the space between them, and was holding it less than half an inch from Di's injured eye. Almost immediately she felt the area begin to grow perceptibly warm—

—then hot—and it began to throb, but not painfully. Di had been on the receiving end of psychic healing before, but this was *strong.* And it argued for a substantial energy base.

"Don't tell me; you're an HP, right?" she asked.

"Well—sometimes," Athena replied absently. "My group tends to share high priestess duties around. I guess you could call me that."

Which means she's the best information source I could have found—and if she doesn't know who our quarry is, then it probably isn't anyone in the movement here. Oh well. Di closed both her eyes and relaxed, setting her mind on "blank."

Some timeless span later she felt a little internal signal that said that whatever had been done was over, and opened both eyes again.

Athena was shaking the hand she'd used vigorously, as if getting rid of something.

Di felt the eye that had been blackened, gingerly. It was just a scant bit more tender than the other. No swelling, no real soreness. She knew that if she looked in a mirror, she'd see only the faintest of bruises.

Well— She stretched out her empathy again. *Still waters run deep. I wonder—I wonder if I've been given something here for my other problem?* She allowed herself a trickle of hope.

"How likely are you to get another job soon?" she asked before she could change her mind.

"Not. The economy is depressed." Athena looked about ready to cry; from what Di felt from her, she'd been on the verge of it for a while.

What was she doing as a computer operator? She was damn well wasted on those jerks! Hm—I would lay odds she was confessor and counselor to half her co-workers. And peace-spreader. Bet they find with her gone that everybody is going to be at each other's throats. Serves them right.

"Considered moving?" she asked quietly.

"Sure. To where? With what?" Athena bit her lip, as if to bring herself under control. "Sure, I'd move if I could. I've got no real ties here, I'd go about anywhere, but—"

"One more question"; Di took a deep breath. This woman was something very special; all she trusted told her that Athena was worthy of anyone's faith—dependable, reliable—and something more. Compassionate far beyond the norm. She didn't get *feelings* this strong very often—and when she did, by the gods, they never proved out wrong. So Di asked The Question. "Would you be willing to take on something—not a job, but it would get you moved out of here without costing you anything—that meant being constantly exposed to someone with active AIDS?"

Athena looked at her with eyes gone round. "I wouldn't go making love to anybody with it—but—I *am* a healer. What I was saving for was med school, and the whole AIDS thing was what started me on it. I mean, here were all these MD jerks refusing to treat— *somebody* has to! Maybe I haven't taken the Hypocratic Oath, but what I am is oath enough. And when somebody's in pain, I *have* to help."

"Listen—I've got a friend, he's—" Di swallowed the lump in *her* throat. "He's got it. He's sick, he's alone; his family disowned him, his lover died a year ago. He needs somebody to take care of him."

It was hard, at first, to reveal her secret; the words had to fight to get around the lump in her throat. But as she told Athena about Len, and the woman's compassion reached over into *her* heart, the words came faster, easier, until they were almost spilling out of her.

"I hadn't been a real *good* friend until all this happened, but—when Keith got sick and Len was diagnosed positive, it seemed like everybody bailed out on them. I—couldn't do that, I just couldn't."

"You'd have been awfully petty-souled, if you had," Athena replied heatedly.

The wave of sympathy and care Di sensed flowing from her was so incredibly deep that she hardly dared credit it. "I was always closer to Len than Keith, so for a while I just sort of hung around, being there. Len wasn't showing any symptoms until last year, so he was taking care of Keith. They were basically coping until Keith died. Then Len fell apart—then he got too bad to work. That's more or less where I took over."

"This isn't meant to be crass—but how's the money situation?"

Di shook her head. "It's not—I know what you meant. It's something that you have to think about. Medical for both of them was covered by insurance, and I'm handling the other bills, I've got it to spare—and I'll tell you the truth, with what I get into I rather doubt I'm going to have to worry about old age, you know? So I can't see anything to save for, frankly."

It was to Athena's credit that she did not make empty noises meant to comfort. "Not if you go around chasing after things like—what's out there now. Someday something is going to be too good for you. . . . Okay, so where do I come into this? I hope to hell you don't think I can cure him—I could probably ease some of his pain, but anything else—"

"No." Di shook her head. "No, I'm not asking for miracles. It's that I can't always be there physically for him—like now. I've got other things I *have* to do—like you, I sometimes don't have a choice. He mostly needs not to be alone—to have somebody to care, to talk to. Somebody of the same religious persuasion, like us. And a stranger might be better at this point than a friend. He can be scared, be angry, break down with a stranger, where with me, he's trying to keep *me* from breaking down. Would you—consider—"

Athena touched Di's hand lightly, and the compassion she had felt earlier was nothing to what she felt now.

"How could I not?" she said simply. "Being what I am, how could I refuse, and still call myself a healer, a true child of the Lady, or even a *human*?"

Di bent her head to hide the tears. It was a few minutes before she could control her voice enough to ask, "Can I use your phone?"

Two hours later, and a substantial number of charges on her credit card, and the arrangements were all made. Athena would be flying out tonight; André would get her at the airport and take her to Lenny's. Di had known from Lenny's voice when she called him that it had been a bad day—he nearly made both women cry with his gratitude when Di told him she'd found him "a companion" and introduced Athena over the phone. He frankly sounded as if he would have welcomed the company of a drug-crazed mass-murderer, much less someone like Athena.

A moving company would pack Athena's gear and ship it off to her later this week, after picking up her key at a friend's house.

And Di's bank balance was going to be lighter by a couple thousand dollars.

She didn't care; it was money she was glad to spend. For once she could make a problem a little better by throwing money at it. That kind of solution was rare.

And the last thing on my conscience is taken care of. If I go down before Len does—he's got my insurance money, and *somebody to lean on.*

She knew Mark was puzzled; though he was sympathetic, he still couldn't understand *why* Len was so important to her. And how could she tell him? How could she explain all the times she'd felt that she'd failed other friends—how *this* time she was determined that she would not?

The last thing they did was painstakingly copy Athena's contact list into Di's notebook. Di wasn't figuring on getting a lot of information from the locals—but maybe somebody would have noticed more than Athena and her circle had.

"Just the psychics—" Di said—then amended even that. "Just the *real* Talents. Not the ones who play at it. I don't care if they're flakes, but they've got to be in practice, or they won't be able to distinguish a power-drain from a potassium imbalance."

Athena had cracked a smile at that. "Well that first narrows you down to about a tenth of the neo-pagans in Dallas, and the second to half of that," she replied. "Maybe less. Amazing how easy it is to let the mental muscles go as flabby as the physical ones, isn't it?"

It was nearly eight when she put Athena and baggage into a cab, and headed back to the bus stop.

No solutions, but—*Well, I didn't get what I came for—but I found what I needed.*

She was thinking so hard about Len that she forgot to stay alert. The streets were very quiet, almost like Hartford; it lured her into a false sense of security. She didn't notice that she was being followed until it was too late to do anything about it.

It was the sound of several pairs of sneakered feet in her wake that finally woke her to danger.

She risked a glance over one shoulder, and saw a handful of young men, all in ornately decorated jackets, following about half a block behind her. They *felt*—yes, they were after her. Predators. Hunters. And a quick probe ahead told her that there were more of the same lying in wait around the corner.

Oh, shit. No, don't run, that'll just set them off. Cross the street first, see what they do.

Half of them followed, the other half moved up to parallel her. She stumbled over broken concrete, cursed under her breath, and thought furiously.

Great, now I'm cut off in all directions. Okay, confrontation time; that's not what they're expecting, it'll buy me delay.

She stopped dead where she was, and whirled to put her back against the wall. Broken glass and trash scrunched under her feet; the brick was rough under her hands. They stopped, and milled uncertainly for a moment. She used the time to think.

Okay, no gun. I'm no karate champ; I can't take out all of them. Any help around?

She risked a glance up and down the street. It was deserted in both directions, not even a stray car in sight. And the streetlight nearest her was out.

Ain't nobody likely to even look out to see why the yelling's going on if I start raising cain. Oh hell. That leaves just one option. Now are they sensitive enough, or *hopped up enough to be sensitive?*

She dropped shields and touched at the surfaces of their minds. It was like touching rotting wood and cobwebs. No doubt about it, they'd been doing *something*. That was in her favor.

Gah. They're sensitive enough. Here goes nothing. Boy, I am going to regret this in a half an hour—

She gathered the power within as they regained their gang unity and began to move in on her from both sides, laughing and spitting obscenities at her. She waited, feet slightly apart, arms down at her sides, and hands clenched, until they were just about to rush her— the moment that they were most off-balance.

Then she struck, grateful that there *were* no witnesses.

It was a two-pronged attack; she flouresced her aura in the visible range, bright as a photo-flash, and followed that by psi-bolts to the minds nearest her.

Three of those she hit grabbed their heads and collapsed, moaning. Those of the rest that had been looking straight at her yelled in surprise, temporarily blinded.

She cleared the path for escape with a couple of handstrikes and a kick to those disabled, and ran—

Behind her she could hear commotion, but it didn't sound like anyone was going to follow immediately.

Oh gods, don't let me fade out now!

She ran as fast as she could manage, her breath rasping in her throat, her feet uncertain in the half-dark on the street; her side hurt already, drained as she was by the energy expenditure. It was three blocks to the haven of the bus stop.

She stumbled, recovered, stumbled again. Two blocks—she could see it up ahead, brightly lit, with three or four people waiting wearily for the last bus of the evening. And they looked like cleaning ladies, gas-station attendants, not crazies.

Thank you, Lord and Lady.

One block; was there pursuit yet? She touched back—not yet, but they were thinking about it. But she was almost out of breath, lungs and side on fire. She had to take a break—she let herself slow, her sneakers making slapping sounds on the pavement.

She staggered the last few steps, reaching for the side of the bus-stop shelter blindly, and sagged against the stanchion. She was well into the lighted area, but totally winded, panting like an exhausted hound.

The four—yes, four—other would-be passengers looked at her curiously, but said nothing.

Just don't let those punks get their courage up and follow, please—

A hand touched her arm; she yelped and jumped away, ready to defend herself.

And felt like a real fool, staring into Mark's disapproving eyes.

"Now that you're finished proving you can do without me, you want a lift home?" he asked quietly.

She blushed, knowing she'd been an idiot this time. But she couldn't say anything; just nodded, and followed him docilely to where his Ghia was parked down the block.

"You could have gotten yourself in big trouble, and *not* just from the you-know," he said angrily when they were out of earshot of the bus stop. "This is *not* a neighborhood to be wandering around in alone at night. You could have asked—you could have told me where you were going. I found out from Aunt Nita that you were gone, and I had to call up that voudoun guy and get the address out of him. And it *wasn't* easy. He made me go meet him in person so he could check out my vibes first."

"Mark, I admit it. Mea culpa; screwed up—" she said, exhaustion making her voice dull and lifeless. "Honest, I'm sorry. I won't do it again." The Ghia was within a few steps; she'd never been so happy to see a car in her life.

He snorted, then unlocked the car door and held it open for her. She literally fell into the front seat.

He climbed in on his side, and took a good look at her. "What in hell have you been doing, running the marathon?"

"Almost," she managed. The inevitable reaction to using that much power without preparation or proper channeling was setting in. She did not want to move, think, or talk much.

"I think I'll take you home, and leave the lecture for tomorrow," he said abruptly, turning the ignition key.

She felt the psi-bolt backlash headache beginning to start, just behind the middle of her forehead, and figured he *might* just have saved his own skin with that statement. . . .

Bridger was heading back to his camp under the bridge in a sour mood. Panhandling had been none too good today; he'd be sleeping with an empty belly if he hadn't found that half pizza in the trash. As it was, it wasn't gonna be easy to get to sleep; his teeth hurt and the pepper on the pizza was still burning down in his guts. The sunset was glorious; he couldn't appreciate it.

No money, no booze, he grumbled to himself. *No jobs, either.* He'd take a job if he could find one, not like some of the other bums out here. He only drank enough to keep his teeth from hurting so damn much. If he could get 'em fixed, he wouldn't drink at all.

No work for a roughneck, 'specially one that can't read but his name, he gloomed. *Maybe I oughta take them Bible-thumpers up on that offer. . . .*

He considered it, then shook his head. *Naw. Can't stomach listenin' to 'em preach at me every other minute. I'll go get mad, an' maybe sock one of 'em, an' be out on the street again.*

He sighed, longing for the smell of petroleum and dust and sweat that was the oilfields at full production. *Never thought I'd miss that in a zillion years.*

He trudged on, feeling the rocks through his thin bootsoles, so lost in melancholy recollection—interrupted from time to time by his aching teeth—that when he saw Jimbo and Billie waiting for him by the bridge in the blue half-light of dusk he half thought he was still daydreaming.

He only realized that he wasn't when they spotted him, gave a whoop, and rushed him.

Seeing his two old buddies was enough to make him forget his teeth hurt. They cussed, and pounded on each other, and carried on like lunatics for a good five minutes before he got calmed down enough to talk sensible to them.

"You jerks, you lookin' good—I never reckoned I'd'a missed you bums—" He suddenly remembered why they weren't supposed to be in town. "Hey, I thought you boys had a job—"

Billie shook his head, his hair flopping down into his eyes the way it always did. "Didn't pan out; some wildcatter, I guess. Went bankrupt about the time we hit the site. They gave us 'nough bus money t' get back here, an' that was it."

"Well, shit."

"Big ten-four," Jimbo agreed, scratching a two-day beard.

"Hey, I ain't got but a mattress but—"

"No man, that's what we came lookin' fer *you* for," Billie interrupted. "Hey, you et?"

"Could stand some more, iffen y'all got it."

"Lissen—you got anythin' back there in that hole you want?" Jimbo asked suddenly.

Bridger thought, and shook his head. "Naw. Anythin' any good got stole a long time ago."

Billie was wearing a backpack that Bridger didn't remember. He pulled it off and rummaged in it. "Here, when the chick gave us eatin' money, she tol' us t' get what we wanted, and I thought I'd pick up somethin' fer you—" He held out a cheap plastic thermos-cup, the kind they gave away in convenience stores, and a slightly squashed hoagie. "Triple cream in th' coffee, an' turkey an' mayo. You an yer touchy gut, gah. Do I forget my friends, or what?"

"Oh man—" Bridger did *not* snatch at the sandwich, but he did bolt it and the lukewarm coffee so fast the others had hardly time to grin. "—Billie, you are a helluva buddie, that's all I gotta say," he managed, wiping his mouth on his sleeve. Already the mild sandwich and the cream in the coffee were calming the storm in his gut. "Now—what chick? You find a soft touch, or a bleedin' heart or what? Hey, you lookin' to be Midnight Cowboys or somethin'?"

Jimbo grinned. "Shee-it, no. Ugly suckers like us? Gimme a break. Naw, we hit somethin' better'n that; we got us three real live jobs."

Bridger snorted. "Pull th' other one."

"No shit," Billie insisted. "We was sittin' at the bus stop, tryin' t' figger if we got 'nough to pick up a burger or if we gonna have t' hit the Bible-pushers. 'Long comes this car; fancy one, man, a Caddy. Chick drivin'; stops, pulls over, asks us if we're roughnecks."

"We said yeah," Jimbo took up the story. "She says, 'You wanta try drillin' fer water steada oil? Boss's lookin' fer men useta bein' on rigs.'"

"Well, we figgered, sure. But she give us a card, said t' meet her over by White Rock Lake Park t'night 'f we're innerested," Billie continued. "She give us some eatin' an' bus money, an' that's when we thought, hey, maybe this's okay, y'know? Like, she just *gave* us the bread. She weren't wearing no fancy suit, but she weren't wearin' no bluejeans, neither. Looked like some gal might work outa an office."

"She said no more'n three," Jimbo finished. "That's us an' you, we figgered. An' we looked th' card up in th' phone book. It's real, man. Real comp'ny, real rigs."

Bridger just stared. "I—"

"Yeah, no shit, feel th' same," Billie nodded. "Look, it ain't that far, last bus's due, what say we head out? Nothin' else, we c'n maybe sleep in th' park, and we et—"

Bridger laughed. A *job*! A real, live *job*! "Sure, why the hell not! Maybe our luck's finally changed!"

"I am *not* taking you back to Aunt Nita in the shape you're in now," Mark said, trying to keep one eye on Di and the other on his driving. "She'll have my hide!"

"I'll be all right in a bit," Di mumbled, sunk in the seat next to him, with both hands over her eyes. "I just need a few minutes to rest."

"Looks to me like you need more than a few minutes—" he dodged a car running a red light, and swore at the driver under his breath. *Dallas traffic gets more like a demolition derby every day.* "I'm gonna take you home with me whether you like it or not—we'll see if some sugar, protein, and aspirin can't straighten you out, huh?"

"Bananas," she replied from behind her hands.

"Is that a commentary or a request?"

"Request." Sounded like her words were coming through a strainer. "And Gatorade."

Supermarket—supermarket—where do I find a supermarket around here—ah! He spotted a lit sign and changed lanes so fast he probably left swearing drivers in *his* wake. He pulled into a vacant slot; fortunately it was too late for there to be much in the way of customer traffic. He had his booty and was back in the car so fast that Di nearly socked him one, evidently thinking he was a stranger.

"Jeez, some gratitude!" he complained, handing her the paper sack.

"Sorry." She rummaged in the bag at once, the paper popping and crackling, before he even had the car started. She emerged with the bottle and pried the top off like a wino with the shakes and a new bottle of Thunderbird.

He stared in awe as she downed nearly half the bottle before pausing for a breath.

"Good God, how can you drink that stuff *straight*? Yech! There's aspirin in there too."

"Don't ask." Without another word she finished the bottle, using the last gulp to wash down a couple of aspirin.

She sank back into the seat with a sigh, some of the pinched look gone from her face; put the empty bottle on the floorboards, and fished out the bananas.

"Monkey food?" she offered, handing him one.

"Don't mind if I do," he replied, accepting it. "Now, you mind telling me what happened out there?"

"I was stupid. I mean really stupid. I put myself in a situation where I had to use real live magic to get away—and I wasn't ready for it. Then to add insult to injury, I sprinted three blocks. Blew my electrolyte balance all to hell. Gave myself an instant morning-after without a night-before."

"Huh?" Mark replied, a little baffled.

"TANSTAAFL, my friend. 'There ain't no such thing as a free lunch.' Magical energy has to come from somewhere, just like physical energy. Guess I never told you that, huh? Well, I didn't have the right gear with me for self-defense against normals, only against paranormals. And if I'd been thinking I would have taken that gun with me, and taken the chance on Athena spooking. It's only the fact that I'm used to shooting from the hip that gave me *anything* to use in self-defense. So I squeaked out, but I paid for it. Give me an hour and a couple more bananas, I'll be okay. And I am *not* going to do that again."

He shook his head. "I hope the trip was worth the cost of the ticket."

"Hm. Well, it was worth it to me, personally, but not to the case—no, I lie. This contact was entrenched well enough in the neo-pagan community that she'd have known if our group was in that net—and they aren't. She couldn't identify them either."

"You said," Mark reminded her, "that we might have to go at this by process of elimination."

"I did. Okay, so tomorrow we go cruising. We're going to be talking to some more folks like my contact, more of the sensitives in the neo-pagan network; and while we're at it, we're going to be looking for two things—"

"Shoot."

"One—we'll be checking the Middle Eastern enclaves for 'protections'—amulets in windows, designs painted on alley walls, that kind of thing. If it's coming from there, the folks of those nationalities will know about it, and be actively warding against it. Like a Kali cult—neither devout Hindus nor Sihks are real fond of the cults that distorted the worship of Kali. These folks might not be willing to talk, but I'll know what to look for."

"And number two?"

"We're going trolling for gypsies. Noble told me that not *all* of them were gone—and as it happens, I have a hole-card. I did the Lowara Rom a big favor a while back. Big enough that it's an embarrassment to them, and they'd like the scales evened up. I think it's time I called it in."

EIGHT

It had been an exhausting several days, and mostly fruitless. More than once Mark had thought longingly of visiting Sherry—

But no. He contented himself with calling Robert—timed for an hour when he knew *damned* well Rob wouldn't be home—and gave her a vague sort of rundown on what was going on. And why he wouldn't be dropping by for a while. They'd talked for a lot longer than he'd planned, nearly two hours. Rob seemed to be burying himself in his work, and Mark frankly couldn't tell her if that was good or bad, or even if it was likely to last much longer. All he could do, really, was be an ear for her. The disappointment in her voice when he told her he wouldn't be by for at least a couple more weeks almost broke his resolve—

But work came first.

Chasing down the list of neo-pagans this "Athena" had given Di had proved more bewildering than anything else. They were a real odd lot—some about as ordinary as a dictionary; people Mark would never have guessed had odd tastes in religions. Certainly not the kind he would have picked as being psychic. Computer people, teachers, clerks—real suburban types, complete with station wagon and kids. But some—

Some were as weird as snake shoes, and as flakey as granola. Mark found himself wondering—if this was the "cream of the crop," what were the *rest* like?

There was the tiny, bespectacled lady with a house full of reptiles, including a twelve-foot python, which she fed while they were there—Mark would rather not have had that particular educational experience. He really had not seen the need to know how pythons ate. But that wasn't all—she *talked* to them. She kept a big lizard on her lap, petting it, the way anyone else would pet a cat. She had actively, *sadistically* enjoyed Mark's uneasiness, too.

There was the long-haired guy in the Grateful Dead shirt and hat who was composing music for whales—or so he said. Mark wasn't sure if he meant he was composing it for them to *hear* or that he was composing the music on their behalf, like some kind of cetacean dictation machine. The guy hadn't been real clear—his conversation tended to wander down strange little side paths. And even when he wasn't going on about the vibrations from the neighbors, he kept changing the subject back to his music, to the point of insisting on playing them bits of it. Thank God it had at least been easy to listen to—the guy may have been weird, but he was a decent musician. Mark had more than a suspicion that the guy was on something— acid maybe, or mushrooms; he sounded like it and looked like it. But what the hell, he was Homicide, not Narcotics, and the guy was looney, but he wasn't hurting anybody but himself with that stuff.

There was the couple in purple robes with little pyramids *every-where*—even suspended over the bathtub. Mark was ready to run for the car after five minutes in their presence. They were as bad as all the crazed maiden aunts in the world rolled up into two bodies. They *could* not be kept to the subject. They kept trying to get both of them to drink weird herb tea, stuff that smelled like a moldy meadow. And they had no interest in discussing the cult-killer. Instead they practically held the both of them down by force, and gave them long, rambling discourses about their own past lives, going all the way back to the caves.

Then there were the ones that looked like they'd just gotten off the set of a sci-fi movie—a group of five wearing identical silvery leotards; they looked and acted like clones, finishing each other's sentences—who said they were Atlantean ambassadors. Mark didn't have to deal much with them. They ignored him totally, as if he was invisible. If he wanted questions answered, he had to relay them through Di. It was a rather unnerving experience.

The *real* spooky ones were the ones—about a half a dozen altogether, all solitaries—who kept talking to their crystal pendants. It was hard to act normally when they were asking the crystals' opinions, and including the rocks in on the conversations.

But none of the weird ones bothered him down deep the way some of the "normal" ones did. The ones who wouldn't talk with him around at all; who seemed as frightened of him as if he were the representative of the Holy Inquisition. He felt uneasy, and obscurely ashamed, as if *he* was the one directly responsible for whatever had happened that made them so frightened of real-life authority. Living in fear like that—their fear almost made him nauseous.

And that fear seemed obscurely familiar. It was a while before he remembered where he'd seen a pathological fright equaling theirs in the past. It had been in the eyes of an old Jewish woman who'd survived the Holocaust.

Homicide had been wanting to question her about something she might have seen—but a uniform, *any* uniform, sent her into a state of panicked paralysis. He'd been in plainclothes, so he'd been yanked in to talk to her. *She'd* looked like that, before he took her away from the uniforms that called up old, bad memories of the SS and the concentration camps, and gotten her out into the open air and a park bench. He certainly had never expected to see that same fear in the eyes of people his age and younger, born and raised in the "land of the free."

That he *had*—that depressed him. And made him angry, though his anger had no target. And he wasn't sure how to deal with the situation, or the emotions it had raised. . . .

But while he wrestled with uncomfortable thoughts, Di questioned all of them, even the fruitcakes, with apparently unlimited patience.

Mark could understand her thoroughgoing care with the "normals," but not with the others. But when he asked her why she was bothering with a bunch of folk who obviously didn't have all of their ducks in a row, she just shrugged.

"You just happened to be *damned* lucky, Magnum," she'd told him. "Your particular sensitivity didn't show up until you were old enough to handle it. That isn't always the case. Think about what *you* might have grown up like if you'd gone mediumistic when you hit puberty—"

Mark gave that some thought. "I think I would have ended up in the school shrink's office," he said finally. "Or else—gotten a rep as a real looney."

"And when kids get a rep for being looney—frequently they decide subconsciously that it's easier to give in to the rep," she said sadly. "Then, if they're lucky—and usually around college age or later—some of these so-called 'looneys' find the neo-pagan movement. And they find out they really *aren't* crazed. Only—by now they *are*, just a little, as a result of living to that stereotype that they were stuck with as kids. But at least they're happier, and they've found somewhere where they're accepted. So if they live out a few gentle fantasies, where's the harm?"

"None," he admitted. "But—"

"No 'buts.' They may be odd—they may be living in a world that's half fantasy; that still doesn't make their talents any the less valid," she interrupted firmly. "If there's anyone who has *any* inkling of who's doing all this, I'm going to find that person. And there's only one way to do it."

He sighed. "Legwork; and among the whole lot of them."

"Roger." She smiled. "Just be glad Athena weeded out all the marginals and the ones with no psi at all. We could have been at this for months."

He shuddered.

Then there was search number two.

Mark had been in and out of more weird little stores in the past week and a half than he ever dreamed existed in Dallas. Thai groceries, Pakistani herb stores, Indian sari shops—it was fascinating, if tiring, but it hadn't been entirely pleasant. Not *unpleasant*, though he'd discovered the hard way that there were a number of spices and incenses he was allergic to. He was prepared now, but always a bit dozey from antihistamines.

Search three was getting nowhere; they had yet to find a single sign of the Romany.

He was ready to call this off; Di seemed inexhaustible.

"Not another Indian restaurant," he groaned, when Di gave him the address. He put the car in gear and sent it off down the back streets, the sun glaring off the pavement in front of them.

She sighed with a certain understanding. "Relax, you don't have to eat anything, you don't even have to go in this time. Just pull around through the alley in back. There—that'll do."

Mark echoed her sigh and obeyed, yet again grateful that the Ghia was tiny enough to squeeze through alleys lined with Dumpsters. They had the windows down; it was still damned hot. The odor of garbage was flavored with weird, spicy overtones. He felt a sneeze coming on, and suppressed it. The racket of the engine bounced off the brick walls and called up vibrations in the metal of the Dumpsters.

Di was scrutinizing the graffiti on the walls—but the scrutiny seemed almost automatic. Mark got the feeling her mind was elsewhere. So far *he* hadn't seen anything in any of these alleys that looked like protective signs. It was all the same; spray-painted filth and gang-signs, and the name of an occasional rock group.

"Penny," he said, finally, cutting around two Dumpsters jack-knifed across his path.

"It's been real quiet," she replied. "Three days of massacres—now nothing. Fits the pattern we established, but I still don't like it. And it makes me wonder—what do they do if they can't find any victims when they need them?"

He eased his foot off the gas for a moment, and took a look over at her; she was broody-eyed, a sign that she *was* worried and disturbed.

"Maybe they store them up, like mud-dauber wasps store spiders," Mark said jokingly. Then felt a cold chill as he realized that it *might not* be such a joke. *If I were raising power with blood-sacrifice, it's what I would do. You can't always be certain a wino or a punk is gonna be in the right place at the right time. And if they can block us from even knowing what rite they're practicing, surely they could hide a few drugged-out street people from us.*

Just then they pulled out of the darkness of the alley into the sunlight. The sun bounced off the hood of the car and into his eyes; Mark reached for the sunglasses on the dashboard with a little haste. *God, it might as well be summer.* It was still so *damned* unseasonably hot—with no sign that the weather was *ever* going to turn. The weathermen had been making vague explanations about the jet stream—which meant they didn't know why it was happening either.

I wonder if they have anything to do with the weather being like it is, too?

It was an idle thought; lost as Di turned and resettled herself in her seat.

"I wonder if we had ought to check out missing persons logs," he mused out loud, as he waited for a gap in the traffic passing by the Ghia's nose. "I wonder if they *are* stocking a larder."

"Me too," she replied grimly. "And I think maybe we'd better."

"This one—"

Rubbing her temple with her free hand, Di held out one picture—just one out of all the hundreds they'd looked at. Mark took it from her. It was a fairly bland color photo, obviously an enlarged copy of someone's driver's license picture. Some guy who looked like any other desk-jockey, except for a certain petulance around the mouth and a shiftiness about the eyes.

I wouldn't buy a used car from him, that's for sure.

"Why this one?" he asked, putting it flat on the table in front of him, propping his chin in both hands, and staring at it as she keyed up the file on the terminal next to her.

"I can't 'find' him. There's a blank where he should be; it isn't a 'dead' blank and it isn't a 'gone to Rio' feeling either—that wouldn't be a blank, it would be a 'not there,'" she replied absently. There was a crease between her eyebrows that told Mark she was on the verge of a headache. "And I *can't* get inside the blank; there's protections on it I don't want to chance springing. Ah—here's two more reasons for you in the files, reasons you can give the Chief. One, he didn't pull any cash out of the bank before he vanished—"

"Hm, yeah—" Mark agreed. "When a guy is dumping his family or running from trouble at work, he usually cleans out the bank accounts."

"Exactly—which bears out my feeling that he's not on some beach somewhere. Two, though—that's very interesting. The last place he was *seen* was at RemTech, by an employee who'd just quit. Athena told me that one of the places 'it' hunted was the industrial park where she worked. Guess where RemTech is—"

"Begins to add up," Mark replied soberly. "Adds up to a total I don't like. Now how the hell do we find him if they've got him? This isn't like an ordinary kidnapping—they don't *want* to contact anyone, they've *got* what they want. What are we gonna do?"

"Well, I'm pretty sure he's probably drugged—it would be the easiest way to keep him quiet and controlled. As I said, there seems to be a kind of blank where he should be, but I can't localize it at all and I'm afraid to trance out and try anything trickier for fear I'll be triggering something. We need a better clairvoyant than I am to do that."

Mark frowned, drumming his fingers on the table. "I have the sinking feeling we're going to go back to one of those fruitloops we've been talking to."

She glared at him—and there was some real anger and resentment in that glare. "If you insist on putting it in those terms, yes. But I would like to remind you that *they* are doing *us* a favor by even talking to us. And some of them will be putting their safety and maybe their lives on the line if they work with us. You *could* be a little more open-minded."

He flushed; she was annoyed with him, and was within her rights. None of these folk were under subpoena; none of them had insulted *him*—unless you counted the "Atlanteans'" studied refusal

to admit he existed. "Sorry," he mumbled. "I'm spoiled. The Spook
Squad was so—normal. I mean, we were *organized*. We may have
been a little bozo, but we were real careful about doing reality checks.
I keep thinking everybody that's a trained psychic should be that
professional."

"Welcome to the real world," she said. "Let's get to it." She stood
up, shoving her chair back, and taking the photograph back from
him. "We'll need this. I think our best bet might be Marion." She
picked up her jacket from the table, slung her purse over her shoulder
and was out the door of the Records room before he could react.

"Which one was that?" he asked, grabbing his jacket from the
back of the chair and running a few steps down the echoingly empty
hall to catch up with her.

"One of the ones that was scared to death of you," she answered,
lengthening her stride a little so that he actually had to stretch to
keep up with her. "The one with the thirteen cats and the boyfriend
that wouldn't come out while you were there."

He remembered that one after a little thought, a pale, washed-out
thing; no-color eyes and hair, and slightly overweight. A face so
round and bland only a cop would be likely to remember it—and
then only because it was *so* unlikely to be memorable. "Why her?"

"Because she and her boyfriend are much better clairvoyants
than I am—and I'm better at defense than anyone in this city," she
answered over her shoulder as they slipped out of the cool of the
building into the hot, white sunlight. The heat blasted up at them
from the baking asphalt of the parking lot and down from the cloudless sky. "We're going to need both."

Di made him go back to Aunt Nita's first; she ran inside and came
back out with the carry-on bag he remembered. The one she hadn't
unpacked. He got an involuntary chill, seeing it.

She was bringing out the Big Stuff then. Things were about to get
very serious.

She left Mark down in the car for a long time when they got to
the girl's apartment building—an old place; brick, four stories—too
old for central air, and heated with steam radiators, a structure probably built between the wars. When she came back, she looked deadly
serious—and asked him in a very quiet, almost toneless voice to follow her lead *exactly*.

He nodded agreement, and followed her up to the back apartment on the fourth floor.

There he was left in exile with the cats on the sun porch full of plants and candles and catboxes. They closed off the french doors into the living room and wouldn't let Mark in until the room had been—so Di told him—consecrated, cleansed, and warded.

He was just as happy. Warding he understood; he was fairly certain that *he* would not have been comfortable around a neo-pagan ceremony of "consecration and cleansing"; there was just too much Catholic still in him. In the past the few times Di had needed to do something like that she hadn't taken him along. The cats were all friendly enough company; they were overjoyed to find someone who'd drag a string around for them to chase. The windows were open and there was a really nice breeze coming through them. Each of the five catboxes had its own little wooden "house"—you hardly knew they were there except when one of the cats decided to use one. So the "exile" wasn't all that bad.

He played with the cats until his arm was tired. He was rather amazed to find how well they all got along together; he knew how Treemonisha would feel about sharing *her* space with any other cat! And she'd have taken her pique out on *him*.

Finally one of the curtained doors opened, and Di beckoned him inside.

He rose and obeyed; she shut the door behind him, the light filtering through the yellow muslin curtains on the doors was dim, but enough to see by. Marion and her nameless boyfriend were seated inside a small circle chalked on the rug. The boyfriend was dark, rather shaggy, and wearing just a pair of jeans—the girl had on a T-shirt and jeans, but nothing more. But *both* of them were scrubbed so clean they practically squeaked, and smelled faintly of herbs.

When he turned to Di, he could see that her long hair, usually free and flowing, was bound up into a knot at the nape of her neck and still damp—she smelled of the same herbal mixture.

He glanced back at the pair inside the chalked circle; they were holding hands now, and the photograph was on the floor between them.

Di was still armed; gun on the left hip, and the sheath of a knife on the other. She was wearing a heavy silver pendant with a large moonstone in the center; other than that, she looked pretty much as usual, which was a relief. He *still* kept expecting lurid lighting and bizarre costumes.

Di steered him wordlessly over to a floor pillow and shoved him down onto it. He seated himself obediently, cross-legged. The rest of the room's scant furniture had been shoved against the walls, all but a tiny table that had two knives, an incense burner, a cup, a little dish of what looked like salt, and a lighted candle on it.

Di sketched a circle in the air around him with her knife-blade, muttering under her breath as she did so. He *felt* something then; he hadn't expected to detect anything, not really—but there was something like a faint feeling of an invisible wall around him.

"*Don't* move," she told him in a fierce whisper. "No matter what happens. If you're tempted to break the circle, just sit tight and concentrate on the idea that you *aren't* there. If we're attacked, whatever comes after us is going to try to frighten us into bolting from our protections—because it won't be able to see us until we do. So *don't* break cover."

Then she left him, and knelt beside the other two. "All right, Marion—give it your best shot. If we can't find this guy I'm dead certain he's going to end up like the others—"

The girl just nodded; she and her boyfriend ignored Mark's presence completely. They let go of the hands nearest Mark; each rested the fingers of that hand on the edge of the photograph. They looked deeply into each other's eyes—and then closed them, almost as one.

And nothing happened. The dim light and stuffy, incense-scented air kept conspiring to put him to sleep. It was, frankly, boring. Mark kept looking at his watch, trying not to doze off, and trying not to fidget; Di hardly moved at all, and as for the two clairvoyants, Mark could scarcely tell that they were breathing.

Then, without any warning at all, the room was plunged into complete darkness.

Mark stifled a cry of alarm; a cold sweat broke out all over him, and he fought down the urge to jump up and head for the door.

It was a hot, stifling darkness, a darkness redolent with a metallic-sweet smell. It was nothing like the sharpness of the incense; after a moment Mark recognized it—in the small part of his mind that wasn't trying to flatten him to the floor in panic—as the odor of fresh blood.

He felt the building of a blind, unreasoning fear. It felt as if he was all alone in this endless night. Alone—

Not quite. There was something *in* that darkness, and it was trying to find him; Mark could feel the searching eyes peering blindly in his direction. Hot, hungry eyes. Eyes that wanted to find him; that *would* find him. And an intelligence behind those eyes that wanted him, wanted him badly.

I'm not here, he thought, his pulse roaring in his ears, the taste of blood in his mouth where he'd bitten his lip. *There's no one here. Nobody at all. No one here. . . .*

Anger was there, an ancient anger as sharp as broken glass. And that hunger kept searching for him.

From a thousand years and a million miles away, he could hear Di, singing something. He felt a pressure building—a *real*, physical pressure; he had to pop his ears when it began to get painful. The heat lessened just a little, and the smell; the angry hunger seemed to turn the hunt away from him.

Then it was gone, the heat and the odor with it, and the light came back to the room.

The two in the circle were huddled together; arms around each other and the picture lying forgotten and crushed under their knees. Di was on her feet beside them; with her hair come loose and flying about her, her hands over her head, palms together, the knife between them. She looked—like an outraged warrior-princess; angry, and tired, and frustrated all at once.

Mark realized at that moment that he *had* flattened himself to the carpet—still inside the invisible-but-not-unfelt boundaries of *his* circle. He slowly levered himself to a sitting position, feeling not in the least ashamed of himself. Whatever that thing had been—it had *not* been imagination, and he did *not* want to meet it again, not until he had some kind of weapon that would work against something like *that* in his hands.

Di took a deep breath and lowered her hands, slowly. She made a cutting motion beside the two next to her, and walked over to Mark and repeated it.

He felt the invisible "wall" vanish.

Di returned to the couple, who were untangling themselves from their fearful embrace.

"Anything?" she asked Marion. "Anything at all?"

The girl shook her head, tearfully. "Only th-th-the barrier, and that he's alive and in there," she stuttered. Her eyes were still dilated with fear, and she was shaking like a leaf. Her boyfriend was in the same shape, except that he couldn't even seem to speak. His back was shiny with the sweat of fear.

"I c-c-couldn't get anything else," Marion continued, unconsciously hugging herself. "Not where he is, or who has him. I got close, but—"

"He was guarded and we set off the alarm, so don't feel bad," Di replied, frustration giving an edge to her voice. "You did the best anyone could, love—you gave it all you had and there's no way anyone could fault you. Damn them anyway! Well, at least the Hunter didn't find you, or this place; I managed that much. Me, he knows about already; it'll be no big surprise that I'm still on his tail. You'll be safe enough, just like I promised."

The girl nodded; there were tears spilling now from those frightened eyes. "I tried—I-I-I r-r-really did—"

"I know you did," Di said, a little more gently. "It wasn't your fault—"

"You said 'he,' " Mark interrupted, getting clumsily to his feet.
"What?"

"You said," he repeated doggedly, trying to shake some feeling back into his benumbed legs, " 'he.' "

She sheathed the knife in her belt next to her gun, and began taking the jewelry off. "So I did—" she mused. "There *was* a masculine feel to that guardian."

"I got that, too," Marion offered timidly.

"If you picked up 'male' too—then it's a damned good bet. And—that thing had the same flavor as the strongest of the five signatures I picked up. Well—that gives us a little more than we had before." She looked a little less frustrated.

"One man, four women?" Mark hazarded.

She shook her head. "No, I can't be sure of that. The chief of this group is male; that much I'm certain of now, but the others—neuter feelings, could be male or female."

He sighed. It seemed like for every gain they made—

She nodded, her eyes bruised-looking, and rueful. "No kidding. Two steps forward—"

"One step back. And we still have no idea of where Ben Bronson is." He sighed. "Helluva haystack."

"And a damned small needle."

"Mark *stop!*"

Mark hit the Ghia's brakes; she squealed to a dead halt in the middle of the street. Di's shout, coming on top of the events of the last hour, had elicited from him a reaction even faster than normal. Fortunately there hadn't been anyone behind them—

"What—"

It was already too late.

She flung the passenger door open and was darting across the street across the Ghia's nose almost before the car stopped moving forward. This little area of fading and empty storefronts was nearly deserted under the late afternoon sun. There was only one thing Di could have been interested in—her goal could *only* be the brightly garbed woman wearing voluminous skirts who was standing in front of a little storefront. An odd storefront; it wasn't untenanted, but it had no sign, and curtains had been strung behind the empty display window.

Holy—that's a Rom—he had just enough time to think before Di reached her.

The woman suddenly seemed to notice the stranger sprinting toward her; she looked startled, then looked for one moment as if she would run away—then Di had her by the arm.

And then Di spoke a single word; spoke it too softly for Mark to hear.

But whatever that word was, it had an electrifying effect on the woman.

Her eyes went round. She stared, licked her lips nervously, and ventured a short question. Di shook her head. The woman scuffed her feet, fidgeted for a moment, and motioned to Di to enter the store—obviously a fortune-telling setup, now that Mark thought about it. Di shook her head again and pointed at Mark, still sitting stupidly in his car, blocking the (fortunately nonexistent) traffic. The woman frowned, gesticulated, argued with her for a moment. Di remained firm and stubborn, and gestured again at Mark. The woman then gave in, grudgingly.

Di sprinted back over to the car, and leaned in at Mark's window. "Find a place to park and meet me inside," she said hurriedly. "They've agreed to talk; at least the woman has. She'll have to check with her man, but I doubt it's going to be a problem. They're Lowara, and like I told you, the Lowara *owe* me in a major way."

"They know you?" Mark asked, amazed. "They really do?"

She nodded, and pushed a bit of hair out of her eyes. "Oh yes," she answered with grim satisfaction. "There isn't a Lowara Rom that doesn't know at least the name of the Starchild. That's what they called me—after."

Before he had a chance to ask "after *what?*" she turned and sprinted back to the faded shop. Mark perforce swallowed his mystification and looked for a parking place.

He found one about halfway down the block, fed the meter, and plodded back to the storefront. The door was unlocked—he'd halfway expected the woman to lock it against him, she'd glared at him so. A bell over the door tinkled as he opened it. It was dim, the red curtains filtered most of the light; it was like being inside a red-

dish tent. It was cooler in here; a relief from the heat of the street outside. When he peered through the red gloom of the tiny shop, he
could see that all of the walls had been draped with more fabric like
the curtains, increasing the tent-impression—there was probably a
door in the rear, but it was curtained off. There was just the standard
round table—covered by a red velvet tablecloth, of course—and four
chairs that looked fragile but proved to be wrought iron, or a good
imitation of it. Di was sitting at her ease in one of the spindly little
chairs beside the table. "Take a seat," she said, waving at an identical
chair. "She's gone for her man."

At almost the same moment, the curtain at the back of the shop
parted. A stocky, heavily mustached man with gold earrings and a
kerchief around his neck stepped through. He was as dark as gypsies
were popularly supposed to be; he was wearing a white, short-sleeved
shirt open at the neck, and dark, heavy trousers or jeans. His face—
and most particularly his eyes—looked wary and worried. He was
followed by the woman, who looked quite frightened.

The man began to say something; Di held up her hand to halt
him, replied, and turned to Mark.

"We're going to be speaking Romany," she said apologetically.
"I'm sorry, love, but there's a lot we'll be talking about that's secret, so
Yanfri wants to make sure you can't understand it. I'll translate what
it's all right for you to know."

He nodded reluctantly. He didn't like it—but these weren't *his* secrets, and it wasn't his territory. Di turned back to the gypsy and indicated that he should continue. They spoke for several minutes
before he nodded with reluctant satisfaction, said a few words to his
lady, and vanished back beyond the curtain again.

The woman, looking a little calmer, took a third chair and placed
it on the opposite side of the table from Di.

Di turned back to Mark. "What happened was that I established
my credentials. Yanfri is satisfied that I am who I claimed and that
what I get now will constitute a quit-claim on the Lowara; now he's
turned us back over to Dobra."

The woman seated herself and began to speak, nervously. Her
voice, though timid, was very musical. Mark found it quite easy to
listen to her and watch her. She was really quite attractive; as dark as
her man but more delicate, with a dancer's grace—though not a
dancer's figure—and expressive eyes. Di listened . . .

"She says," Di said finally, "that she is afraid; that they came here
last week before anyone could pass them warnings. I assume you
know that the Rom post special signs for other Rom to read—?"

Mark shook his head. "Not my department, but it doesn't surprise me."

The woman, who evidently *understood* English quite well, nodded and continued.

"She says that every Rom *kumpania*—that's a kind of extended family group—in this area is leaving; and they are *supposed* to be leaving signs and warnings on all roads out of town. She says that there is great danger."

Di turned back to the woman, and this time she spoke in English herself. "*Drabarni*, do you know from where the danger comes?" she asked. "Do you know its face, its land?"

The Rom licked her lips and spoke, softly, the words tumbling out over one another. Di listened carefully.

"She says that you and I should leave; that no one with sense will stay. She says that those of us with *draban*—that's 'magic'—are especially vulnerable, that this thing seeks those with it. It wants people like us—needless to say she's picked up on the fact that we're both psi. She says that this thing is evil, very *old* evil—"

"We already know that," Mark said. "And you know—surely *she* must know you and I can't leave. We have—"

He turned to the woman, and spoke directly to her for the first time. "We have a *duty*; if you know something of what this lady does, you must know she can't deny that duty. Please—anything you know—would be more than we have now. If we have to work crippled, it would be like sending a wounded dog to pull down a wolf."

Di broke in, her brows creased with concentration. "*Drabarni*, please—you know that what this man says is only the truth. If you know anything we don't, you must tell us!"

The Rom woman trembled at that; she clenched her hands on the table in front of her and spoke in a hurried whisper.

Di started. "*Drabarni*," she whispered in turn. "Tell me if I have misheard you—"

She turned back to Mark with a look of grim achievement. "She says that the evil is very strong because it *belongs* here. Mark, I think she's saying it's *native* to this continent!"

They both looked back at the gypsy woman who nodded, slowly. And shivered with an absolute and undeniable terror.

By day the building was just another warehouse; empty, deserted. The company that had used it was bankrupt, the company that owned it having no luck in renting the space. The building was just another victim of the boom that had gone bust . . .

By night—

The Jaguars had always met here; Jimi had an older brother who knew a guy who'd had a job and a key to the place—and had never turned the key in when the job went down the tubes with the company. Nobody bothered to check when he'd told them he'd lost it. After all, what was there to steal in an empty warehouse? So every Jaguar had a key; it was as secure a meeting place as a Moose Lodge.

But now, since Pablo had first met Burning Water—it was more than a meeting-place. It was a temple. And now and again—like tonight—their deity would deign to visit.

Pablo prostrated himself at the feet of the god. Burning Water was seated beneath the single overhead light that they had turned on, ensconced in a throne made of old packing crates and stolen fur coats. Under the one light, the throne had a certain rough splendor. Burning Water needed nothing special; he shone with his own power, a power that made itself felt all the way across to the door of the warehouse, where two or three new recruits were huddled in slack-jawed awe. The handsome face was transformed by that power into something clearly more than mortal.

Pablo was wearing his full regalia, the outfit that marked him as Burning Water's champion (embroidered loincloth, silver and jade pectoral, and feathered armbands and headpiece), with an almost overweening pride. Tonight was the first night that the god had permitted him to wear the regalia when not actually in ritual combat. Burning Water was pleased with his champion, and Pablo was ready to dance with joy.

The god was not alone tonight; he had brought all four of his handmaidens. That meant that certainly he intended to convey something especially important. They stood, garbed in *their* full regalia, two on either side of the throne. There was Quetzalpetatl, the eldest and most serious of the four, and vacant-eyed Coyolxauhqui on his left, and sexy little Coatlicue and the chief handmaiden, Chimalman, on his right. They were like princesses, all of them, in the headdresses of quetzal feathers, their gold and jade jewelry, and their brocaded skirts and blouses and feathered capes. Even Coyolxauhqui's pale skin and slightly glazed stare (brought on by a little too much mescaline, Pablo thought privately) could not detract from the dignity she wore as naturally as she wore her cape. They stood utterly silent, and utterly graceful; not even the slightest stirring of a feather showed that they moved. And the power of the god showed, ever so slightly, in *their* eyes as well.

The concrete was cold, but Pablo hardly felt it. His excitement was more than enough to keep him warm. He trembled, not with chill, but with anticipation. He kept his eyes fastened upon Burning Water's face.

"Tomorrow," the god said at last, the power of his voice making even the simplest words full of portent, "begins the feast of Xipe-Totec."

"Yes, lord," Pablo responded, struggling with the harsh syllables of the Old Tongue. He *was* learning it—but it was harder for him; the magic of putting the words into his mind didn't work quite as well for him as for some of the others, for some reason. He'd been severely depressed about it until the handmaiden called Chimalman told him it was only because he had been gifted with the strengths and skills of the warrior rather than the scholar. Hard-faced Quetzalpetatl had undertaken to tutor him the hard way then; she was the scholar of the four, not much of a magician, her beauty a little more brittle than theirs, but brilliant with words and facts. She would, undoubtedly, become the Lord's chief minister when they ruled this land again, as Chimalman would be his chief warrior, Coyolxauhqui the seer, and Coatlicue—she would do what she did best. "Lord, we are ready. We have the ones for the burning—and have found the place to trap the ones for the feasting—"

"And We shall deal with the other sacrifices of the third day," the god replied, frowning. Pablo shivered again, wondering what could have caused that frown. "But—there is, perhaps, a problem."

"Lord?" Pablo asked, bewildered. He didn't think that there could be *anything* that could cause the god a problem.

"There is a witch," the god said slowly, his eyes darkening with thought. "She seeks for Us. Already she has probed the edges of Our defenses. She is strong, and it would not be wise to rouse her to attack at this time. Therefore We desire you to warn her."

Now Pablo was truly bewildered. "Warn her, lord? How do you mean?"

"We wish you to follow her—then strike. Strike and kill. Strike close enough and in such a way that she knows it *could* have been she you took."

For the first time Chimalman moved. She leaned close to the god, her eyes blazing with emotions Pablo could not fathom. "The man, lord," the chief handmaiden said viciously. "It *should* be the man—he is a danger as long as you let him live. I, your right hand, say this to you!"

"We have said once—*the man is not to be harmed.*" The god's eyes flamed red with anger, and Pablo cringed. *He* would not have dared to anger the god that way.

"Come—" Burning Water beckoned imperiously, and Pablo inched forward until his head nearly touched the god's sandal. The god leaned forward a little; Pablo closed his eyes and felt the light touch of the god's hand upon his head, then felt the power of the god pour through him.

A picture formed against the darkness of his closed lids; a young *gringo* woman; tiny, big-eyed, long-haired. Pretty piece. For a *gringo*.

"The woman," said Burning Water.

Another picture took her place; a man, Hispanic, handsome, with more than a little Mestizo in him by the nose and cheekbones.

"The man that you are *not* to harm," said the god, forcefully. Chimalman sniffed a little; for her sake Pablo hoped that it was not in derision.

The god's hand lifted from Pablo's head, leaving behind a tingle of power that filled his whole body with a rush better than the best coke. "Do you understand what you are to do?"

Pablo lifted his head and his eyes to the face of his god. "Yes, lord," he said, filled with elation that Burning Water had chosen *him* for this important task.

The god settled back into his makeshift throne with a smile of satisfaction.

NINE

Mark pulled his diminishing attention away from the heavy, dusty book in his hands, sneezed, and rubbed his blurring eyes. He glanced up at the disgustingly cheerful clock on the kitchen wall, and felt even more tired when he saw what time it was.

Three ack emma. My God.

The harsh fluorescent light illuminated the mess in the kitchen and their own overtired faces without pity. The room was as deadly silent as a morgue; silent enough that the buzz of the fluorescent fixture was loud and very annoying. The only sign of life was the red light on the coffeemaker; Treemonisha had abandoned them to go curl up on Mark's bed, disgusted at the lack of attention they paid her. The sink was full of unwashed cups and plates, there was water puddled on the gray linoleum floor and coffee sprinkled over the white Formica counter. The white plastic trash can overflowed with pizza boxes and the wrappings from microwave sandwiches, some of which had missed the container and were piled around the foot of the can. The gray Formica table was crowded with the books piled between them and stained with spilled coffee and brown rings from the cups.

Di was still deep in *her* book, a frown of concentration on her face, one hand holding a forgotten cup of coffee. She looked bad; shadows under her eyes, a prominence to her cheekbones that spoke of too many meals missed at a time where she was using every energy reserve she had.

We've been living mostly on coffee, I guess—half the time I never get her back to Aunt Nita's in time for supper. Tonight included. She's got to be running on fumes, and I'll be damned if I know how she's con-

centrating. Especially on this stuff. I never realized the Plains Indian tribes had so many creative ways of killing people. . . .

They'd gone from the fortune-teller's storefront straight to the university library, using Mark's credentials to cart off as many books about local history and Indian lore as they could carry. Since then they'd been poring through the books, furiously taking notes on anything that seemed relevant, stopping only long enough to microwave a couple of sandwiches and fix more coffee.

Mark shut his book and leaned his head against his hands, closing his burning eyes. Things had been nagging at him—and not just this case.

Dammit, we're at a stalemate. And too tired to make any further headway tonight. So; I've got something else I'd like to talk about. Might as well bring this out into the open before it eats at me any more.

"Di—" he said, hesitantly, prying his eyes open to look at her.

She shut her book, noticed the cup, frowned, and put it to one side. *Then* she focused on him—and her frown deepened.

"Mark—*don't* tell me you're having a crisis of conscience—"

"Huh?" he responded cleverly, then continued with dogged persistence. "Di—tell me—give me a good reason *why* everybody in the case that's a good Christian seems to be a real asshole, and everybody that's *your* kind is a good guy—"

Her lips tightened, and her puffy eyes narrowed a little.

Uh-oh; looks like I hit a nerve—

"Just one minute there, fella," she said sharply. "Let's have some definition of terms, shall we? Just what do you mean by '*your kind*,' hm?"

"Hell—*you* know what I mean—"

"No, dammit, I *don't* know!" she snapped, her patience obviously exhausted. "I'm a *lot* of things, I'm female, short, a yank, a psychic, a martial artist, a writer—and I just *happen* to be a pagan along with everything else! I *do not like* that particular phrase, 'your kind.' Seems like every time it gets used it's meant to *exclude*. And I should bloody well think that somebody who's been on the receiving end of discrimination could be a little more sensitive!"

He flushed, first with anger, then with embarrassment.

Shit, she's right. That was a pretty crude way to put things.

"I'm—sorry," he faltered. "But—it just seems like—I just don't understand some of the things I've been picking up about people's attitudes while we've been tracking down what's been happening, and—Di, I don't like what the implications are."

Di cast her eyes toward the ceiling. "*Why?*" she asked. "Why are these things always at 3:00 A.M.? And why is it always *me*? Since when do I qualify as a teacher? Nobody ever handed *me* the credentials. I never *asked* for the job."

Then she looked back at Mark, no longer angry, just weary. "Mark, *why* did you have to be different? Why didn't you go through this in college like everyone else? I'd have been happy to tell you. I sure had a helluva lot more time for three ack emma discussions back then, and a lot more energy."

"Because—I guess because I always figured I knew what I was doing, then. Now—I'm not so sure," he said, admitting now through his tone of voice that he was profoundly troubled. "You never really took me around with you like this much back in the old days. You kept the fact that you were pagan so much in the background that I was able to forget about it. And back then, the few times you hauled me with you to deal with psis that weren't on the Spook Squad—I was one of your people. Now I'm not. Now I'm The Man, and it seems like I'm a potential enemy."

She sighed. "Didn't like what you saw, hm? Okay. *Use* that brain, Magnum. In A.D. 30, who were heroes, the martyrs, the saints? And *what* was the major religion in the civilized world? The positions are just reversed, and for the same reasons. Established religion gets stodgy, mired in laws and bureaucracy, and repressive. The 'new' religion attracts the free thinkers, the ones who aren't afraid to ask questions and challenge the so-called holy writ. And those *tend* to be the humanists, too. Okay so far?"

"I guess—"

"Established religion is like established anything else. It's *easy*." She looked off into space, and paused for a moment, seemingly gathering her thoughts. "It—offers answers you can get prepackaged and predigested; right off the shelf and the same for everybody. No thinking required, much less hard thinking. Like a board game; follow the rules, you go to heaven. *That's* why established religion gets the assholes. They *aren't* 'good' Christians, Magnum—do you think for a minute any of those yuppie middle-managers that ended up as victims ever sacrificed so much as their convenience for *any* cause? No—I rather doubt they ever gave up a thing they valued for any reason or anybody. People like that aren't good anything. What they believe, they believe because it's 'appropriate,' it's what everybody believes, because it's 'the right thing to do'—in short, it's easy. Our way isn't easy—oh, we get assholes too, but they usually give up and get out or get it knocked out of them."

"Huh. I guess that makes sense. Because somebody who's really a fat-cat jerk won't get into anything that is going to give him grief—"

"Right." She nodded slowly. "As to why those so-called good Christians ended up as the victims—my opinion is that it was simple enough. I would guess it was *because* they were idiots, just like that jerk on the highway. Accidents looking for a place to happen. They lived their lives thinking they were so wonderful and invulnerable that *nothing* could happen to them—unlike *my* people, who know damn good and well that most hands are against them—so they ignored dangerous situations *my* people knew better than to walk into. And finally the odds just caught up with them."

"Okay, I can get behind that. It makes sense—they're the same 'this can't happen to me' bunch that I've seen on cases before. But—"

"But that's not all. Spit it out before it chokes you."

"But why did *you* get into this? *Why?* You told me that you were raised Episcopalian—so why did you change? I trust your judgment, Di—what is it about this pagan thing that's got *you* doing it, instead of working within the C of E the way your great-grandmother did?"

"Lord and Lady. I swear, Mark, you pick the weirdest times to go into seeker mode," she groaned. "Damn, I *wish* you'd sprung this on me back when you were on the Spook Squad."

He just waited expectantly. She caved in.

"Look, I'll tell you what I told the folks who asked the same question back then," she replied, almost angrily, pushing hair out of her eyes. "You get no *answers* from *me*, buddy. I don't give answers, I'm *looking* for them. You want the Tregarde Creed? You *really* want it? It isn't comfortable and it isn't easy, and all it's going to do is raise more questions—"

He nodded anyway.

She sighed. "All right, you asked for it. First commandment. *There ain't no such thing as 'one true way,' and the way you find is only good for you, not anybody else, because* your *interpretation of what you see and feel and understand as the truth is never going to be the same as anyone else's.* Second commandment. *The only answers worth having are the ones you find for yourself.* Third commandment. *Leave the world better than you found it.* Fourth commandment. *If it isn't true, going to do some good, or spread a little love around, don't say it, do it or think it.* Fifth commandment. *There are only three things worth living for; love in all its manifestations, freedom, and the chance to keep humanity going a little while longer. They're the same things worth dying for. And if you aren't willing to die for the things worth living for, you might as well turn in your membership in the hu-*

man race. That's all there is, so far as I know or care. The rest is just ruffles and flourishes."

Her shoulders sagged, and she rested her chin on her hand. "Mark, I am not out to disturb anybody's faith. *I* happen to be happy and comfortable with a belief system that has a dual deity and operates on a lunar schedule. It suits my needs. If *you* happen to be happy and comfortable with a belief system that features a single masculine deity and operates on a solar schedule, *fine.* I don't give a fat damn. What matters, Magnum, is what you do, not whose name you do it in." She picked up the coffee and took a large swallow, evidently forgetting that it was cold.

She made a sour face, and Mark had to suppress a nervous chuckle. "Look," he asked, "what about changing established religion from within? From what I've seen of the C of E, it's not that hard to get them to accept new things—"

She snorted. "You're asking for *my* opinion. Kid, that's *all* this is—my opinion, which is that history proves that in general, people that try to do that fail and end up breaking off anyway. Look at the record. Start with Christ—move on to the Greek Orthodox schism, followed by the Albigensians, the Huguenots, the C of E, Luther, the Quakers—Lord and Lady, I could go on forever. They all tried to change from within, and ended up splitting off. This is the lesson history told *me*: when a religion gets so mired in bureaucracy that compassion takes second place to the *law,* and the law is iron-bound and iron-clad and has no room in it for exceptions, then it's no longer a religion for humans, it's a religion for paper-pushers, painted saints, and marble statues. So I didn't bother to try working from within; I looked until I found what worked for me. That's my way and my truth—you go find your own. End lecture. Happy now?"

"No. But I didn't expect to be happy, I just wanted information."

She nodded, and quirked her mouth in a half smile. "You're learning, Magnum."

He sighed, beginning to feel all the tension of the last couple of weeks knotting up his shoulders. "You know, we don't need any more caffeine. How about a nightcap instead? Scotch and soda? Then I'll take you home."

She managed a real smile. "I won't say no."

"Moutainhawk!" Mark called, spotting someone he'd been subconsciously watching for all morning. "Charlie!"

The uniformed patrolman with the carved-cliff profile stopped dead in the hallway and peered in Mark's direction. Mark waved; Charlie waved back, and waited for Mark to catch up to him.

Charles Mountainhawk had been one of Mark's fellow cadets at the police academy; when their stint as rookies was over, though, Charlie had elected to stay on the street while Mark grabbed his chance at Homicide. Charlie was a good guy—but more important than that, at least at the moment, he was a full-blooded Cherokee.

And he had a brother who was a political activist. So Charlie had ears in places where Mark had no hope of going.

"So, what's new—besides the rumor that the city is paying you to drive a pretty young lady all over town?" Charlie asked, grinning fiendishly as Mark got within easy conversational distance.

"Well, the rumor's true for once," Mark replied, returning the grin and the slap on the back. "How many scalps you lifted this week?"

"Three; got me a dope dealer this morning. How come you get all the luck?" Mountainhawk set off back down the corridor with an easy stride.

Mark kept pace with him. "Largely because she's on the big one, and I was the guy that suggested we bring her in on it. And I dunno about luck; remember that smack dealer Narco hauled out in a sack two, three weeks ago? We stumbled over him, and he just about ventilated us. But yeah, mainly you're right; you know good and well this sucker's gonna be mostly legwork, and it's no bad thing doing it in attractive company."

"Huh." That grunt and the sideways look Mountainhawk gave him were all that showed his surprise. "So that rumor's true too."

"Which one?" Mark asked.

"I just got off. Got time for coffee?"

Bingo—I think I just hit paydirt. Charlie wants to know something—which means I can trade favor for favor.

"Sure—"

"Outside?"

Ah ha. He doesn't want anybody to eavesdrop. Big bingo.

"Try again," Mark countered. "It's raining cats out there."

Mountainhawk made a sour face. "Been in here filling out reports for the past two hours. Hell, it figures. Where can we get some privacy?"

Mark thought for a moment. "Hey, about that back staircase over by the evidence room?"

Charlie shrugged. " 'Bout as good as any, I suppose."

A few moments later they were perched on the linoleum-covered stairs like a couple of kids, coffee cups in hand. Mark almost chuck-led; Charlie looked pretty odd sprawled over the stairs in his uni-form. At least he was wearing jeans—

The staircase hummed with machine sounds and the whisper of the air-conditioning plant, but this area was so seldom used that the landings had storage cabinets stacked on them. It would be a good bet that they wouldn't be disturbed here. Mark waited for Charlie to make the opening move.

It would take someone who knew him to tell, but Mark could see he was fidgety. "Okay," he said finally. "Rumor has it that this pretty thing you've been chauffeuring around is an expert on the occult."

"Cults?" he replied innocently.

"No, the *occult*. Ghosts, monsters—like—" he looked sheepish and embarrassed. "—she's a bigtime Medicine Woman."

"Where'd you dig *this* up?" he asked quietly.

Mountainhawk looked even more uneasy, as if he was trying to decide something. "Okay, it's *not* a rumor," he finally sighed. "It's—something I was figuring, and I asked Pancho Villa about it—you know, your buddy, Ramirez. The way he hemmed and hawed, I fig-ured I was right. Look, Mark, you can level with me, I believe in this stuff, my old granddad is a Medicine Man himself."

"You're right," Mark replied softly. "The Chief doesn't know it, but that's the *real* reason why I was pushing to call her in. She is kind of an occult expert, something like a Medicine Woman, I guess. Di and I go 'way back, and I used to help her out when we were both in college. When I knew this was something other than a Manson-type lunatic, I started pulling some strings to get her here however I could. She's tracked this sort of thing before—only by what we've hit so far, she says she's never dealt with anything this powerful before. This thing is a-one major bad news—"

"Yeah, I was wondering—" Mountainhawk replied unhappily. "See, my granddad back in Oklahoma's been writing me, telling me to cut out, take a leave of absence or something."

"Oddly enough, from what we've uncovered so far, you might be one of the safest—it seems to prefer WASP victims—"

"Huh-uh; that's not what Granddad meant. He thinks if I stay it's gonna get around to recruiting me." Mountainhawk's face twitched a little. "You gotta promise not to laugh—"

"Word of honor."

"I see things."

"Like what? Things happening at a distance, or things not visible to ordinary sight?" Mark asked seriously.

"The second—Granddad calls it 'spirit vision.' Hey, you—you know what I'm talking about!" Mountainhawk was clearly surprised.

Mark shrugged. "How the hell do you think I met Di in the first place? At a church picnic? Yeah, I know—I got a touch of that stuff myself, but don't spread it around. I get ribbed enough as it is." He thought for a moment. "Tell you what, Cochise, I'll trade you favor for favor. If you can get your brother to keep his ear to the ground for us, *I'll* get Di to fix it so this thing can't see you—or at least, can't get at you. She put what she calls 'shields' on me a long time ago, or I'd probably be taking a rest cure right now. What *I've* got can get you locked up if it gets out of hand."

Mountainhawk considered that for a moment, looking greatly tempted. "First, tell me why, and what you want to know."

"We've got a hot tip that this thing is a power native to this continent. The way I've got it figured, that won't stay secret for too much longer among the activists—if it's even a secret now, at all. So— maybe we can get at it through the native grapevine."

"Okay, Johnnie can go for that. He's into screwing the white-eyes with lawyers, not chopping 'em up on rocks." Charlie smiled mirthlessly. "Probably he'd say that they don't suffer long enough if you just chop 'em up."

"There are times when I'd agree with you," Mark replied wryly.

Charlie looked Mark over with a thoughtful eye. "Hey, Cisco Kid—you know, *you* could pass as one of us with the right person vouching for you. Johnnie just might be willing to do that, too—if you want."

Mark didn't even have to think about it. He was getting pretty weary of not being able to do anything on his own in this case. *This* would be right up his alley, if Johnnie Mountainhawk could be talked into it. "Hell yes, I want. I'm beginning to feel like nothing more than a driver or a bodyguard."

"Okay, I'll see if Johnnie will front for you."

"I'll pay off my half of the promise now; Di's at my place. I'll take you over right this minute, if you want."

Charlie stood, and dumped his plastic cup in the ashtray fastened to the wall as he did so. "The sooner the better. Grand-dad notwithstanding, I can't afford to take a leave. Too many car payments, and a new baby on the way."

Well—nice to have a piece of good *news for a change!* "Hey, you old so-and-so, why didn't you *say* something!" Mark exclaimed as they headed for the parking lot exit and the pouring rain.

Mark gave the recognition yell—which today was "Encyclopedia salesman!"—as he unlocked the door. Di had taken to keeping her piece close at hand, since they weren't feeling much like taking chances. Standing in the rain was like standing under a shower at full blast, and he didn't feel like waiting around for her to answer the bell. He and Charlie piled through as soon as he got the door opened, since his apartment was one without a sheltering overhang. Cops tended to choose places that didn't have anywhere for a would-be ambusher to lurk.

"My God, you look like somebody tried to drown you!" Di exclaimed from where she was crouched over five books spread open on the floor of the living room. "Who's your handsome friend?"

"Charlie Mountainhawk, and he's married," Mark replied, as Charlie blushed. "Charlie, this is Di Tregarde. Di, he wants to trade favors."

"Darn, the good ones are always taken." Di stood up, cheerfully dusting off the knees of her jeans. Charlie blushed again. "Name the favors; I'm easy, but I ain't cheap."

She grinned insolently at the both of them, as Charlie did his best to figure out if he should be embarrassed or amused.

"Charlie's going to get us some info from the activists if you shield him."

Di immediately went into "serious" mode. "Problems?" she asked. "I like to know what I'm dealing with."

"Nothing yet," Charlie said slowly. "But—I've gotten warning that this thing you're after may try and haul me in as a draftee. I figured the only thing that was going to stop it was distance, but Mark claims you've got a better solution."

Her eyes widened, but she asked nothing more; Mark suspected her reticence was something along the lines of "professional ethics." "I can see why you'd want shielding—but if what I do is going to run counter to your beliefs, the shields won't take," she warned, twisting a bit of hair around one finger. "Are you really *willing* to let me work white man's magic on you?"

"I don't think anything you do will conflict," Charlie replied, slowly. "I'd like you to try. The warning's been pretty pointed, and it's from a source I trust."

She nodded gravely. "Mark, why don't you two go dry off; I'll be ready by the time you get back to the living room."

Mark took his friend back into the bedroom and pulled out some dry clothes for the both of them. Charlie and Mark were pretty much of a size; he managed to squeeze into a pair of Mark's blue jeans without too much problem, and an old T-shirt stretched enough to get across his brawny shoulders, which had always inspired Mark with raw envy. By the time they'd toweled off and changed, Di had, indeed, gotten what little she needed ready.

She'd put her hair up in a knot again—she was wearing a plain silver choker and matching rings on each hand. "You sit there—on the floor in front of me, with your back to me," she directed, as she seated herself carefully in the chair just under the north window. "Just like I was going to massage your shoulders." Charlie obeyed her, sitting cross-legged at her feet with his back to her. "Mark, turn out the electric lights, would you? I don't want any other fields being generated while I do this."

He obeyed; now she was lit only from behind, by the gray, uncertain light that came through the window.

Huh—Mark thought with surprise, *Now that's peculiar. Very peculiar. They should look faded out—but they don't.* He looked closer. *If I didn't know better, I'd say she looks like she was sitting in sunshine—not in my living room!*

She held her hands about five inches away from Charlie's head, and her eyes went unfocused. Mark forgot the peculiar quality of the light around her, and watched all this with curiosity and interest—he'd been in Charlie's position the last time she'd done this.

There *did* seem to be a faint sort of light linking her two ring fingers—but when he tried to focus on it, it faded out.

"Okay, Charlie—" she said, after a moment. "Before I start, I would like to ask a question, and I promise you that it's relevant. Do you have what they call—uh—I think it's 'spirit vision'?"

Charlie started, and his eyes looked surprised. "I—uh—yeah," he admitted.

"There's a reason for my asking; since you do, you're going to see all of what I'm doing and you can actually tailor the shields to suit yourself. They'll 'take' better if you do. Poor Mark had to make do with what I made up for him." She smiled at Mark, and wrinkled her nose.

"Hey, they're okay, I've got no complaints," Mark countered.

"So what do you think of when I say I'm going to put protection on you?" she asked.

Charlie grinned sheepishly. "Promise not to laugh?"

"Promise."

"A force field, like *Star Trek*."

"Good image," she approved, nodding. "Easy to work with. Okay;

relax if you can, you're going to see just that kind of force field forming up around you in a minute. Um—it'll probably be blue; that's the
primary color in your aura. Once I've got it in place I'm going to
shrink it down so it's contiguous with your skin. Leaves less of a target that way. The way it'll work is to make magic slide around you,
rather than stopping it or absorbing it. Ready?"

Charlie nodded, and she held her hands out, one just above either
shoulder, and again, about five inches away from him.

Mark hadn't really expected to see anything of the shields going
up, so he was rather surprised to notice that Charlie seemed to be
blurring a bit. He blinked, thinking that it was tired eyes, but Di and
the furniture behind him remained in sharp focus—

Except those sections that were behind that five-inch distance;
those were blurry as well. It was a bit like the heat-distortions above
hot asphalt. And at the border of the distorted area was a thin line of
the faint light, only this time it was bluish.

Mark was fascinated.

Charlie was evidently seeing something a bit more elaborate, as
his eyes were wide with the greatest surprise Mark had seen him
show in a long time.

Just when Mark thought he *might* be seeing a bit of a glow running all through the distorted area, Di flexed her fingers slightly, and
the distortion seemed to sink into Charlie's body.

Charlie held out his hands in front of himself and stared at his
fingers, quite dumbfounded.

"Is that—it?" he asked, hesitantly.

"That's all there is," she replied, wriggling her fingers, then standing up and stretching for the ceiling. "End of dog and pony show."

"I didn't mean it that way," he told her, craning his head backward to look at her. "I meant—wow, that was pretty impressive from
in here!"

"Does it feel any different?" Mark asked. "It sure as hell did for
me."

"I'll say it does," Charlie exclaimed, getting to his feet. "Like—the
difference between driving my Bug and Johnnie's four-by-four. Or—
no, something heftier. A tank."

"Something like," Di grinned. "When I do a job, I don't do it
halfway, and I rather *like* armor-plating."

*One more crying baby or pass from that drunk in first and I think I'd
have killed someone,* Mary Johnson moaned to herself, loosening the

collar on her uniform and pressing her aching head against the glass of the window of the shuttle van. *Bad enough the hour delay on the ground in Frisco. Then we ride a roller coaster all the way here.* But then *to end up waiting two* more *hours on the ground because we can't get at a gate!*

The Amerine Airways shuttle van was crowded far past its intended capacity often. Mary and everyone else had their luggage on their laps. She was just lucky to have gotten a seat at all, much less a window seat, and knew it.

My God, it's almost 2:00 A.M. *Thank God I just went illegal, or I'll* bet *they'd call me in for the 5:00* A.M. *New York shuttle. I think I'd rather die.*

Thanks to three tornadoes on the ground near DFW this afternoon, virtually every flight in and out had been subject to a delay of at least an hour. DFW Airport was a madhouse; kids crying, babies screaming, weary, angry passengers in every terminal—and *of course* all the restaurants and concession stands had closed down at their normal hour of ten and *of course* the computer-driven terminal environmental controller had turned off the air-conditioning at the same hour and *of course* no one knew how to turn it back *on* again.

You could pretty much count on it—any craft that had hit the gate after midnight had left about half its passengers stranded for the night. The gate agents were equally divided between ready to commit suicide and ready to commit mass murder.

And there wasn't a hotel room to be had at any price. She and the rest of the crew were *so* tired they were just about ready to pool their cash to get one of the VIP suites—there were enough couches in one of those things to make sure everybody got some kind of bed, and there were the hot tubs and saunas—

But even those were gone.

So they were catching the shuttle out to the flight academy. Thank God for *that*. The rooms were all dorm-style and not exactly high-class, nor exactly cheap if you were just bunking down overnight and not there for training—but right now all Mary wanted was a shower, a flat space, and a pillow and blanket.

It was as black as the inside of a hat out there; the darkness had that peculiar quality it sometimes had down here after a rain when the sky was still overcast; it seemed to drink all the available light and give nothing back. Mary was glad she wasn't driving; it would be a bitch to see anything tonight.

"Anybody want off at the gate?" the shuttle driver called out. "You could probably walk to the dorm faster than I'm going to get there. I've got priority stuff for every building on the route."

Mary considered the amount of luggage she had—not much—and concluded that the walk might be just what she needed to settle her nerves.

"Me," she called, "and I'm right on the door."

Her seatmates sighed with gratitude and relief. "Don't use up all the hot water," Captain Forster said, from somewhere behind his carryons.

"Serve you right if I did," she answered. "You should have diverted to Houston—at least we could have gotten hotel rooms there."

"Bitch, bitch, bitch," the Captain retorted. "*I* got us a powercart so I could keep the A/C on. You *could* have been baking back there."

"More like steaming—and I was already," she replied, carefully working herself and her gear out of the van door. "If that jerk in First had put his hand up my skirt one more time—"

Her fellow attendants groaned in sympathy. "I'm black and blue where he kept pinching me when the beverage cart stuck," Lynn Jeffers seconded.

"Y'all had it easy," drawled someone in the front. "*We* had us a buncha drunk Shriners from Vegas—an' we was so low on fuel the cap'n had to kill the A/C *and* most of the lights while we was waitin' on a gate. Talk about your animals!"

The horror stories continued as Mary got herself out of the van and onto the roadway, and as the van rolled away she could *still* hear them at it.

Why did I ever think that being a flight attendant was glamorous?

She was right under the streetlight, so the first thing, the *very* first thing she did was to open her suitcase and extract her old, comfortable running shoes, changing them off for her pumps. Her feet stopped hurting for the first time in hours.

It was cool, but not too chilly—in fact, as overheated as she was, the cooler air felt wonderful. It smelled pretty nice too, all clean, the dust washed out by the rain. It was too bad that it was overcast; the stars would have been nice tonight.

She shut her pumps into her suitcase and stacked everything back onto her wheelie and strapped it all down, then peered around into the darkness beyond the cone of light from the streetlamp.

There's a jogging path around here somewhere, I know there is—hah! One thing you had to say for old Amerine; they'd put some really nice paved paths through the wooded grounds for runners. Bless their flinty hearts.

She headed off down the path for the dorm, feeling a little more like a human being and not so much like a sardine with sore feet.

One of the shadows beneath the trees on the right side of the asphalted pathway detached itself from the rest and moved off after her.

"Mark—" Di said, looking up from her book.

"Hm?" he replied, just as happy to set down his own. After sending Charlie home, they had elected to stay in the living room tonight; actually *reading* some of the books that seemed relevant, instead of just skimming through them. They'd moved two of the foam flip-couches over below the good reading lamp so they could share it, and Mark had some nice soothing space-music on the stereo rig. It was a pity the situation was so serious—this would have been an enjoyable evening if they weren't having to think about the guy that was going to become a corpse if they couldn't find him soon.

"Do you remember what Ramirez said when he was talking about trying to get that voudoun curse off him?"

He stretched, and shifted position on the couch. "About the girl in Dispatch?"

She shook her head, and chewed on the end of her finger. "No, before then."

"Huh. Give me a minute." He sat in silence for a moment, Treemonisha purring her approval of his choice of position from the pit of his stomach where she'd curled up. She was a lot better pleased that they were lounging in the living room instead of crunched up against the table in the kitchen. She hadn't been able to get into Mark's lap when they'd been using the kitchen.

"He said—" Mark replied after running the conversation through his mind, "that he had gone across the border trying to find an old-time *brujo* to try to take it off—"

"Yeah! Yeah, that's it! That's what I was trying to remember! That's the one set of practicing magicians we *haven't* checked out— *brujos* and *brujas*!"

He scratched the side of Treemonisha's nose, feeling a bit dubious. "Well, I guess it could be nasty enough. Aunt Nita used to tell stories that could curl a kid's toes. Is it *native* though?"

"According to this book it is—" She held up the heavy volume so he could see the title—*Superstitions and Folklore of the Southwest.* "Although this lot doesn't know as much about it as I'd like; they've got it mixed in with a lot of other traditions that I *know* are separate entities, like the mescaline ceremonies. At least they admitted they didn't know too much. But—that's what was nagging at the back of my mind. Now that you've jogged my memory, I'm remembering that someone in a position to know told me a long time ago that all the aspects of the Virgin that the *brujas* invoke are really Christianized versions of some of the traditional Amerindian goddesses."

"So that would qualify as native, all right," he agreed. "But I hate to tell you this—I know less about where to find a *brujo* or *bruja* than you do."

"*You* would not likely ever find a *bruja*," she replied, smiling a little. "They're rather down on men. And I'll have a hard time convincing one to talk to me—they're equally down on Anglos. But I'll have more luck than you will, I bet, especially since I can point out those three kids that were victims. And I bet I know who can get me pointed in the right direction."

"Who?" he asked.

"It's right under your nose, Magnum."

He shook his head, still baffled. She laughed.

"Your own Aunt Nita."

"This is as bad as when I was in high school." Julia pulled away a little and complained, as John fumbled with the buttons on her blouse. "Hell, we don't even have the backseat of a car—"

He pushed her back against the bark of the tree they were under. "You know why we can't rent a car—what if your husband or my wife found the rental record?" he said with exasperation. "And we couldn't *get* hotel rooms tonight to save our souls—"

Julia squirmed on the blanket she'd filched from the flight academy dorm room, trying to find a position where there weren't as many rocks under her rear. "We could have tried out in the boonies. Nobody else was bothering. We could have rented *two* cars."

"And have somebody turn up the fact that it was only the two of us out there and not the whole crew?" He had her half undressed now; the flight in had been a bad one—the plane had been hit twice by lightning on the way down. Bad flights, so Julia had learned, tended to make Captain John Powell horny as hell.

"Why are you so paranoid, O Captain?" she asked a little acidly. "I have just as much to lose as you do."

"Look I'm already paying out alimony to one ex—if Angie ever found out about us she'd take me to the cleaners. And I *think* she's got a PI checking up on me."

Julia would have asked some more specific questions at that point, but about then things were rapidly coming to a boil—and she didn't want answers any more. Bad flights frequently had the same effect on her as they had on the captain.

Beneath a stand of bushes was a clot of shadow. Within that shadow, a darker shadow watched them, and waited.

Tommy (his real name was William, but he hadn't gone by that in decades) Thomson was rather proud of himself. He thought he'd been real clever, sneaking on that Amerine shuttle van—

He, along with several hundred other passengers, had been stranded for the night when his flight from Florida missed the connecting flight into Chicago. The Amerine personnel refused to do anything for him, claiming that because the delays and missed connections were due to weather, they were free of obligations.

Hah. You can't get away with treating a vice-president of marketing that way. I know all the dodges.

He'd ranted and raved in his finest managerial style—but he'd only been one voice among hundreds—and nothing he'd tried had produced so much as an apology, much less the hotel room he was demanding.

They kept trying to claim that weather delays were "acts of God" and that they weren't liable for anything. Turkeys. I'll fix them.

Since trying to penetrate the bullshit of the underlings had gotten him nowhere, he'd decided to bypass the peons, and deal with the bosses directly.

The question was, how to get *at* them.

Then he'd overheard one of the stews talking about getting a bed at Headquarters, and had followed her. When the shuttle van with its inconspicuous Amerine Airways card in the corner of the windshield had arrived, he'd bullied and pushed his way on board, cutting out one of those uppity stews and leaving her to wait for the next van. He'd figured out a while back that if you acted like you were in a position of authority—if, in fact, *you* started making the demands—people tended to assume you had the right to push them around.

It had worked like a charm. Nobody had questioned him, challenged him, or even asked to see his employee ID.

He'd figured that in a bad situation like they had over at the airport, there were *bound* to be some honchos around. But they wouldn't be *at* the airport, they'd be at Headquarters, where they could monitor the situation, but nobody could get at them to confront them. It was easier and a lot more comfortable and convenient to work that way—it was the way *he* used to work.

So old Tommy was too clever for them; he knew all the end runs and the slick moves, and was ready with a counterplay.

He'd bitched and moaned about the van, the heat, and the driver all the way to the Amerine complex. After all, that's what an exec did. The rest of the van's occupants had gone silent after the first few minutes, and he figured he'd pulled a slick one on them all.

When the van driver had announced "Headquarters," he'd popped out of that van like a horse out of the starting gate. No one else got off, though—there had only been someone waiting at the stop for a package that the driver had handed him. By the time Tommy had gotten himself straightened out, that person had already vanished into the bowels of the building.

Tommy had found himself shivering in the cool damp air. He hadn't brought his coat with him; just left it stuffed in the locker where he'd shoved his suitcases. He was in front of a huge glass-and-chrome building, illuminated against the overcast darkness by floodlights all around it. The Amerine logo was carved into a stone monolith set into the sidewalk about ten yards from the front door.

And sure enough, just as Tommy had figured, there were lights on in some of the offices, and people-shadows moving between the lights and the glass.

Tommy strode confidently up to the front door—his every footstep echoing with authority—seized the chrome doorhandle, and yanked it open.

Or tried.

It was locked; nearly took his arm out of the socket when he pulled and nothing happened. He frowned, and tried again—rattling the door as hard as he could, but all to no effect. Then he tried all the other doors in the entryway.

No good.

It was only then that he noticed the magnetic keycard reader, and realized that *nobody* was going to get in or out of the building without a key.

Or the help of somebody already inside. If he could find someone with the right card, he could surely bully them into letting him in.

He pounded on the door, hoping to get the attention of at least a night watchman, but no one came.

Angry and frustrated, he turned on his heel and began the long hike to the nearest lighted building.

It was dark under the trees, dark and cold and damp—and the wind kept shaking showers of drops from the leaves down into his head. He was regretting his coat; almost regretting the whole idea. He needed to find some *people*; people he could deal with. Mag-card readers and closed buildings wouldn't yield to his skills.

The nearest building proved to be the flight academy dorm. There were lots of people there—and not a card reader in sight.

But he was also accosted immediately by a hatchet-faced old man in a rent-a-cop uniform who demanded to see his employee ID. He got downright surly when Tommy didn't produce one. He threatened to call the Dallas cops and have Tommy charged with trespassing on private property. He looked like he'd do it, too.

And in that mess of tired, irritable stews and crews, there wasn't a single *sign* of anyone likely to be able to give him satisfaction. Nobody was in the least sympathetic to *his* plight—he was invading *their* territory. He was the interloper here, and not at all welcome. They had no reason or desire to be polite or helpful to him.

Tommy beat a hasty retreat back out into the dark, mumbling about leaving his badge in the car. That seemed to satisfy the old man at least enough so that he was not pursued. . . .

But now he was lost somewhere on the grounds; he'd started following a path he *thought* would get him back to where the shuttle van had dropped him off, but instead it only took him deeper into the landscaped wooded area. By day this would have been no problem. But by night, on a moonless, starless night when he couldn't tell one building from another, he was baffled.

So baffled and preoccupied with his own predicament that he never noticed the footsteps that echoed his own along the path behind him.

TEN

Mark was hiding in the darkness, but the dark would not conceal him forever. Somewhere out there, somewhere past the boundaries of his tiny sphere of protection, was the Hunter.

The thick dark was stiflingly hot, and the very air seemed to cling to him, clogging his throat as if he was breathing wads of damp cotton. If he moved, he might be able to find someplace cooler, someplace where he could breathe freely.

But if he moved, the Hunter would find him.

He could sense it searching the realm outside his safe little bubble, piercing the darkness with eyes of fire. He was not sensitive, not an empath like Di, but he could feel its anger, its scorching hatred, its insatiable hunger.

Much blood had already been spilled to feed that hunger. More was fated to be shed, for the more the Hunter consumed, the more the Hunter hungered. But somehow Mark knew that if the Hunter found him, he would find himself meeting a destiny other than serving that hunger. The Hunter had another purpose in mind for Mark—

And if that purpose was fulfilled, there would be nothing left of "Mark Valdez"—at least, nothing recognizable.

The Hunter moved closer; now Mark could "see" it, a sullen red glow that did nothing to illuminate the darkness. His breath caught in his throat, for it was nearer to his hiding place than it had ever come before. Surely it could sense him, even through his thin walls of deception and protection. Surely it knew he was there.

It came closer still, and now he could see its eyes, its eyes like smoldering coals, and feel its hunger beating inside his head, keeping time with his pulse. Those hideous eyes swept the darkness like searchlights, *and he cringed as they passed over him; he expected at any second to be discovered.*

His instincts all screamed at him to run; his better judgment told him to remain where he was. But those eyes continued to probe the blackness all around him, coming nearer, nearer, until—

Something screamed in his ear.

He didn't so much jump as spasm, his heart pounding hard enough to tear out of his chest, his throat closing so that for one long moment he literally couldn't breathe. Then the sound came again, and this time he recognized it for the phone tucked into his headboard.

It was as dark in his bedroom as it had been in his dream, only the red eye of the digital clock glaring at him from a few inches away from his nose broke the blackness. He was still stuck in his nightmare, and the red numerals of the clock seemed to be extensions of the red eyes of the Hunter. For a moment he was paralyzed, unable to move or even think, completely frozen in fear at the sight of the strangely shaped red "eyes."

Then the phone shrilled again, and the spell was broken.

He groped for it, still almost in a state of shock. He shivered as the air hit his arm and realized vaguely that he was literally sodden with sweat, from his hair to his ankles.

"Valdez," he said into the receiver, trying to tell his heart that it would be a really good idea if it slowed down a little. *God, it's still night—this can't be Di! Or if it is—I'll kill her twice. Once wouldn't be enough.*

"Haul your li'l ass outa bed, boy." With another jolt, Mark recognized the Chief's voice—and it sounded grim. "Git that yankee gal and haul yerselves on over t' th' Amerine Airways headquarters. Our ol' buddies fin'lly woke up again, an' we got one *damn-all* mess."

Damn-all mess was an understatement.

There was blood everywhere, the first victim—there was more than one, though Mark didn't yet know the exact total—had been killed right on the pristine white sidewalk.

Maybe because they couldn't find a suitable rock? Mark wondered.

At any rate, it was pretty ghastly. No elaborate mutilations this time—they hadn't stripped the girl, either. Just torn the uniform open at the chest, and cut the heart out.

Lord, that was enough. The Amerine people were nowhere to be seen, which wasn't surprising. Likely the only time any of them saw blood was when they cut themselves. This must have messed their minds up for certain.

There was another difference in this kill. This time the girl's heart hadn't been left neatly beside the body. This time it was missing.

The sun still wasn't up; the site was lit by three floodlights, the poor girl sprawled faceup on the sidewalk, eyes open and staring sightlessly at the dark branches of the tree over her head, mouth frozen open in an eternally silent scream. Her face was distorted into a mask of absolute terror and pain. The trees continued to drip down all over everything and everyone, and directly over the corpse what they dripped wasn't always rainwater. There was blood splattered for several feet in every direction. In no way could the murderer have avoided getting it on him. In no way could he have gotten past anyone without their seeing the bloodstains that had to be all over him.

And no one had seen a thing that was suspicious—other than a businessman type who'd shown up over at the flight academy dorm, and who'd been found later when the hue-and-cry went up. Turned out *he'd* ended up as one of the victims.

The whole thing was giving Mark chills.

"This looks to me like it was done in a hurry," Di told him quietly; she was very pale, but very composed. "Like somebody was skimping on the rites for lack of time. Another thing—there's only *one* of those signature auras here; one of the weakest at that."

"Speculation?"

She rubbed eyes that had greenish circles beneath them, and suppressed a yawn. "That our five principals split up tonight, maybe because the four weak ones have finally accumulated enough power to cover their tracks for a limited time. My guess is that the stalking took longer than this one thought, and he or she had to finish up with a shorthand version of the proper sacrifice. Whatever power was lost by skimping was probably made up for by the number of victims."

"How many so far?" Mark asked Melanie Lee, who was in charge of the site nearest the gate.

"Six bodies, five sites," she said, distractedly. "We think that's all—it's not like anybody was trying to hide the bodies or anything. Amerine's had their people out checking the entire grounds since they realized that there was more than one victim. We think all this happened between eleven and one ack emma. We'll have to run some tests, but right now it looks like all six were offed within the same thirty-minute period."

"Which means it *had* to be more than one killer—just like we've been figuring," Mark said flatly. Melanie nodded, and turned back to her meticulous charting.

The Chief joined them at just that moment; it was fairly obvious that he was stressed—the cigar was lit, and he was sending up enough smoke to kill every mosquito within a mile.

"We got us a problem," he told Mark. "Them Amerine boys is raisin' holy hell about this. It's bad enough that four a' their stews an' a pilot bought it, but looks like the last stiff was some yuppie boy had no reason even *bein'* here—that's mighty bad publicity fer them, an' it don't look so good fer us, neither."

"We could *use* that, Chief," Mark replied, thinking furiously. "Look, half the department's had to deal with Amerine at one time or another—trying to get them to allow us on their sacred soil is like trying to get a bunch of old maids to look at a copy of *Hustler*. So— hit 'em back; it's *their* private property, as they've told us so often— it's *their* security that let these people on the grounds—killers and yuppies included. Since they tied our hands, let *them* take the rap."

"And even if the killers got in clandestinely, there's no way that businessman climbed over the wall—so *he*, at least, went right by their security. You might make sure the press *knows* that," Di chimed in. "Make sure they know exactly who was supposed to be in charge, here. You might drop a hint or two about how Amerine's thrown their weight around about sovereignty before this—and *now* they're trying to blame *us* for what *they* let in."

The Chief brightened a little. "That'll get 'em offen our backs, that's fer sure—"

"Chief!" Ramirez came pelting up, mostly out of breath from the long run to where the Chief's car was parked. "Chief, we got another one. White Rock Lake Park, burning car, unknown number of victims, but at least two. It's not a crash, the thing was set. They haven't been able to put it out yet, but it's homicide and no doubt about it."

"Aw shit—" the Chief spat. "Dammit, why *now*? Melanie, drop this 'un get yer team on over there. Valdez, go hunt up Fred, get his team split an' send half on 'em over here—"

"I'll help at this site," Di offered. "I can finish the preliminaries now that Melanie's started them."

"I'll take that," the Chief answered instantly. "Boys say y'all know what yer doin'. Okay, Ramirez, let's roll."

By the time Mark returned with Fred and a second tech, Di had completed the preliminary layout work and the body had been taken away. Fred sighed with relief when he saw how much she'd accom-

plished, and proceeded to wade into the tedious inch-by-inch comb-
ing of the site.

"I could use you," he told Di, "but why don't you check the other
four sites first, then come back here. By looking at all five you might
catch something in your field—"

"No bad thought," she replied. "No bad thought at all. It won't
take me long—"

"Go right ahead then; Valdez, you got a map, didn't you?" he
asked, craning his neck around so that he could see Mark from where
he was kneeling on the wet grass.

Mark nodded. "Yeah, no prob. We'll be back in—say half an
hour."

"Good, 'cause that's when I'll really start needing you, Di."

The second site—the one he'd pulled Fred away from—was
where they had found two victims together. And what the spouses of
the two would have to say, Mark didn't want to find out—for it had
been fairly evident that they'd been up to some serious fooling
around before their murderer found them. Their clothing had been
found tangled up with a couple of blankets nearby, and the various
items of apparel showed no signs of having been removed by force.

The pilot hadn't even fought—no sign that they were even surprised. They might as well have been asleep or drugged—and Mark
couldn't imagine two people being either out in the cold damp of the
park area. Again there were no mutilations, but there *were* signs that
the victims had been somehow rendered unconscious, dragged over
to a nearby boulder, given floral decorations, then favored with a
cardiectomy.

"Full ritual here, I think," Di mused. "But only one aura—this
time it was the number one, the one I know is male. Let's get to the
other three."

The third was like the second, except that the clothing *had* been
cut off the poor thing; the Forensics team had found what was left of
her uniform thrown under a nearby bush. The fifth site was exactly
like the third. But the fourth—

The fourth girl had either *not* been surprised so totally, or had
possessed a little more moxie than the others. She had fought back;
used her purse as a weapon until the strap broke, then had struggled
when seized and nearly torn herself loose. If her uniform had been a
little less well-constructed, she might have succeeded in getting away.
But the sleeve didn't *quite* tear off in her captor's hands, and she had
been clubbed into insensibility.

But she hadn't been stripped; once again, she'd been thrown to the sidewalk, her clothing had simply been torn open and the heart removed. No decorations, no evidence of elaborate ritual; just like the first murder tonight.

And for once, they'd been given a break. She hadn't been searched by her murderer, either.

"Well, lookee here—" one of the Forensics men had managed to pry the girl's clenched fist open.

She was holding a tiny scrap of elaborately brocaded cloth— most probably torn from the garment of her killer. The bright colors seemed alive in the harsh floodlights.

Mark sucked in his breath sharply. Di glanced over at him.

"I take it you recognize this stuff?" she said.

"It *looks* like some of the material Sherry's been working with," he replied slowly. "Robert's been ignoring her work, so she's been showing it off to me. . . ."

"It's pretty distinctive," Di agreed. "And it certainly doesn't look like any fabric I've ever seen before. How much of this stuff does she sell?"

"Not a lot; it takes a long time to weave, and it's real pricey. She got the technique from some Indians, though, so she isn't the only one that knows how to create it." He turned to the tech. "What's the chances I can have this some time tomorrow for about four hours? Or—maybe a good photograph would be better."

"Photo shouldn't be a problem," the tech replied, scratching his bald head. "Seein' as y'all are s'pposed t' get pretty much what y'all need, an' y' been pretty reasonable-like. Reckon we c'n get y'all a nice color print—enlarged, an' everything. Say, pick it up fr'm us round 'bout two? Reckon we'll be done with it by then."

"That would be perfect," Mark replied, knowing that Sherry was always home mid-afternoons—and so Robert usually wasn't. Right now he'd rather not talk to Robert around Sherry. And she was always less nervous and more herself when he wasn't around.

"You ready to head back?" he asked Di.

She nodded, and they began cutting across the landscaped area between the paths. The sun was coming up, and even though it was gray and still overcast, they had no trouble seeing where they were going. The wet grass squelched under their sneakers, and the cuffs of Mark's jeans were getting wet and kept wrapping around his ankles. The tree trunks were gray and ghostly in the ground fog that was rising, and the air smelled more like a tropical rainforest than dry-as-dust Texas. It was going to be another hot day, and after the rain of last night, a humid one as well.

"That last was the second-strongest of the signatures," Di told him, sniffling a bit in the cold air. "And I got a *definite* feeling of 'female' this time. I'll tell you something else, *this* one doesn't need Number One anymore; she's a power in her own right. If she fought that girl hand-to-hand, it was either because she was too startled to think of using her powers, the victim had some defense of her own, or because she *wanted* to fight that way. She ought to have been able to stun her with a psi-bolt, unless the girl had natural shields."

"What happened to the hearts this time?" Mark asked, having a sinking feeling that he'd already guessed the answer, and not looking forward to finding out that his guess was correct. "The last time we found them with the body."

Di looked a little sick. "I hate to tell you this—but—well, there's a lot of cultures that took hearts. And when they did—they generally— ate them."

The sun was well up by the time they finished at Amerine. They were both dead tired—but on a hunch, Mark headed, not for home, but for the White Rock Lake Park.

The park had guards at the entrance, chasing most people off. The site itself had been cordoned off, but their IDs got them past the blockades with no fuss. The site was in a very public place—even though the park was supposedly closed to the public after ten, it was patrolled; *someone* should have seen the car coming in, or found it before it was set afire. But, as at Bachmann Lake Park, no one had. That alone made Mark very nervous; it was beginning to sound to him as if this, too, was going to turn out to be another of "their" cases.

They found that the Chief had left Ramirez in charge of this site; it wasn't much to get excited about—just a blackened hulk of a late-model BMW near one of the picnic shelters.

Ramirez stumbled over to them, his face gray with fatigue, his chin shadowed with stubble. "I dunno what you're doin' out here when you could be grabbin' some sleep, Cisco," he told Mark, yawning and shaking his head. "This don't look like one of yours at all—"

"What *do* you have?" Mark asked, clenching his jaw on a yawn himself, and beginning to want a second shower almost as badly as he wanted his bed.

"Four males, two front, two back; race and identity unknown, all probably offed earlier tonight. Whoever offed 'em shoved 'em in the car, then the car was set on fire; we found the empty gas can in the shelter. Car belongs to a Missing name of Ben Bronson—"

"This is one of ours," Di interrupted, flatly. She looked like she was coming to the edge of her energy, and was operating on nerve and guts alone. "Is everything still in place?"

"Yeah, we've been waiting for the damn car to cool down; took the Fire Department boys nearly an hour to put the bastard out," Ramirez replied, looking somewhat taken aback. "You sure this is one of yours? Naw, forget I asked. Shit, you mean now they're settin' fire to 'em too?"

"Why not?" Di said wearily. "They drowned the last three."

Then she trudged off across to Melanie Lee, leaving the two men behind. Mark was not inclined to follow; first of all, he was too tired, and second, he'd been on a homicide by incineration once before. If he never saw—or smelled—another toasted corpse, it would be too soon.

It was less than a half hour, and Di was back, looking decidedly greenish.

"Well?" the two men asked simultaneously.

"Oh, it's ours; Melanie says they all got cardiectomy, and there were some little fried bits of flower wreaths on all of them. *I* would guess they had the full rites done on them; just like the man at Bachmann Lake—except for maybe the mutilations. I think the kills at Amerine were to raise power so that they could perform *this* sacrifice undisturbed. Ramirez, if I were you, I'd start looking for a big flat rock somewhere in the park with bloodstains all over it."

"I'm on it—" the detective shook his head wearily, and headed over to the picnic shelter, where a group of three uniformed cops were standing. He spoke with them for a few moments; they nodded, and started off into the park in three different directions.

"So this time they didn't clean up after themselves," Mark said, thinking out loud. "Probably figured on the fire taking care of the evidence—and either forgot, or didn't know that green plant stuff doesn't burn worth shit."

"Could be," Di replied, shaking her head and blinking hard, as if she was having trouble with blurring vision. "Could also be they're getting enough power that they don't care. And that scares me."

"I've got another guess—" Mark said, shifting from one, tired, aching foot to the other, and wishing he could sit down for a while. Or better yet, lie down for a while. "I bet that one of those four guys was our missing Bronson."

She nodded. "They won't know for sure until they match dental records, but *I'm* certain. The one on the passenger's side in the front seat was Bronson."

Mark cursed under his breath all the way home.

Mark was still feeling groggy as they pulled up to the gate at the Bear Creek apartment complex where Robert had moved his family in their newfound prosperity. *This* time (unlike the first time he'd come out here) he called ahead, so the guard had his name and waved him on—though not without the usual frown of disapproval at the battered, old Ghia.

"I wish you'd warned me," Di said with a completely deadpan expression. "I'd have dressed for the occasion."

Certainly they were going to look as out of place once they stepped out of the car as the little Ghia did among all the BMWs, Mercs, and Porsches. Mark pulled into a slot between a Corvette and an antique Triumph and replied defiantly. "Be damned if I'm going to cater to *this* lot's delusions—"

"Whoa there, Magnum, I was just putting you on!" she said hastily, swinging out of the passenger's seat. "Look at it this way—from the tensions around here, I can promise you that this bunch isn't enjoying themselves or their work half as much as you are—or at least the way you do when you haven't the kind of pressure on you have now."

"Yeah, well—"

"I know; there's times I get jealous, too," she said softly. "When I look at something that's selling off the bookshelves and think—'hell, I've thrown out better writing than that.' Stay cool; you do more good in half a year than these hedonists will do in a lifetime, and that's what counts."

He managed to grin at her as they headed up the sidewalk to Robert's townhouse. "Like they say, money may not buy happiness, but it sure makes misery comfortable."

"It does that," she answered, as they paused on the flagstoned doorstep and Mark rang the bronze-framed doorbell.

Sherry must have been waiting for them; the heavy oak-finished door was opened almost before the echoes of the chimes died away.

"Mark!" exclaimed the slender blond who pulled the door open—then practically flung herself at Mark. "Dammit, Mark we have *missed* you!"

Mark felt his temperature rise a notch, and told himself sternly to stay calm. He kind of wondered, with a twinge of worry, what Robert had been doing to make her so happy to see him. He also wondered what Di was picking up.

At that point Sherry noticed that Mark wasn't alone, and pulled away from him, flushing, and betrayed her nerves by tucking a flyaway strand of hair behind one ear.

"Sherry, this is Di; a colleague of mine," Mark said hastily.

The slight hint of wariness faded from Sherry's expression, and she extended her hand with nervous friendliness. "Hi," she answered, "I'm glad to meet one of Mark's co-workers, finally."

"Not quite a co-worker," Di answered serenely. "I'm more of a PI. Mark and I met back in college, and when all this mess started up, he remembered that I specialize in weird cults, and got Dallas PD to bring me in."

"Deprogramming?" Sherry asked, with a hint of interest. More, maybe, than the question warranted.

"Among other things, sometimes," Di replied, looking at her oddly. Sherry flushed a little, and looked uncomfortable.

At that moment they were interrupted by a blond-haired ball of energy that flung itself at Mark's legs. "Markmarkmark!" the boy crowed.

"Heya!" Mark was rather grateful for the interruption; Di was handling the situation, but Sherry was obviously uneasy and off balance. He grabbed the giggling child and tossed him into the air. "How's my favorite dragon-slayer?"

"*Miss* you!" the child said, completely without shame. "Da won't tell me stories, an' he won't play wif me neither."

Mark gave the little rug-rat a quick hug and put him down. "Now, kidlet, your Da's a busy man. He's—"

"He don't wanta play wif me; he wants to play wif the Mean Ladies," the child retorted.

"Bobby!" his mother exclaimed, blushing a full crimson.

"Well, he *does* an' they *are*," Bobby insisted. He turned his attention to the one stranger in the group. "Who're *you*?" he demanded.

Di was obviously struggling to keep from laughing. "My name is Di, and I'm a friend of Mark's."

"Are you a cop too?" he said with intense fascination. "Like on TV? Are you like Cagney and Lacey?"

"Kind of. I knew Mark from a long time ago, and when Mark asked me to come help him, I did. And if you'll promise not to embarrass your mum again by calling your father's models the Mean Ladies, I have something for you."

Bobby considered the offer thoughtfully. "Okay," he decided.

"Then hold out your hand—"

He did, and she put a lavender-toned, eight-sided crystal the size of a walnut in his palm.

"That keeps monsters away," she said, absolutely seriously.

He was enthralled, his blue-gray eyes big and round. "*Really?*"

She nodded. "Cross my heart. Put it by your bed and you won't even *dream* about monsters, unless you want to."

He cocked his head to the right and looked up at her, as if trying to measure her sincerity. "I *like* Godzilla."

"Then if you want to dream about Godzilla, you will. But only monsters you like. Okay?"

"Okay!" He ran back inside, clutching his prize.

Sherry looked at her with a very bemused expression. "How on earth did you know he's been having nightmares? And what was that you gave him?"

Di shrugged.

"Mark said something about it, and I've worked with kids a bit. At this age, nightmares are pretty common, especially when the family is under stress—moving to a new home is a lot of stress to a little one," she replied with delicate tact. "Frequently you can reprogram kids that age to eliminate their own nightmaring by giving them a talisman, and it works especially well if what you give them is unusual enough. That was just a common fluorite crystal, but I figured it wasn't likely he'd ever seen one. They aren't the kind being sold as pendants, mostly because they generally aren't as pretty as that one."

"Well, if it works—I am going to be in your debt. He's been waking up screaming about once a night and Robert has been getting pretty tired of it," Sherry replied, waving them in. "Not that he's blaming Bobby—" she added hastily, "but—"

"It's okay, Sherry, we dig," Mark replied. "After a while it gets old."

"Exactly," she said, leading the way to the sunken living room, a room utterly unlike Mark's apartment. It looked like a *House Beautiful* ad, all fashionable beiges and creams, from the soft carpet to the velvet upholstery of the pit-group. "Oh Mark, Robert's home for a change—he didn't like what the lab did to the last set so he swears he's going to do all the developing himself from here on in. We got the new darkroom finished *just* in time."

She waved at a door at the farther end of the room as they settled into the living room. Mark recalled that the last time he'd been here, that had been an extra-large bathroom. There was a kind of design of glyph in hand-forged brass mounted on the door. It matched the obviously handmade (and expensive) brass lamps and occasional tables.

"Like the logo?" Sherry asked, with a certain amount of pride. "It's Aztec, it means 'Fire and Water.' That's the official name of the company. I think that glyph is our good-luck charm; ever since we started using it, we can do no wrong."

"Nice," Di said. "Where on earth did you find someone to do that kind of metal work around here?"

Sherry shrugged. "Robert found an artist; he's good at getting things done nowadays. Well, what can *I* do for you?"

"We've got—" Mark began, when the door to the darkroom opened.

"I *thought* I heard your voice," Robert said genially, as Mark rose to meet him. His handsome, almost sculptured face was crossed with what seemed to be a genuine smile of welcome. Mark was gladder than ever that he hadn't given in to his longings and—

He'd have hated like hell to do anything that would have ruined that friendship. No matter how he felt about the way his friend was treating his wife, no matter how attracted *he* was to that wife, he still *liked* Robert.

"So, old buddy, what can we do for you?" Robert asked, when they'd finished exchanging greetings.

"This time it isn't your expertise we need, it's Sherry's," Mark said. "Got a fabric sample I want to see if she can identify. It's hand-made; we're hoping she can place it."

"Oh well," Robert replied, glancing (Mark thought) a little uncomfortably at Di. "I can tell when *I'm* superfluous."

"Don't give me that—"

"No seriously, I have a lot of work I need to do. I hate to say hi and run, but—"

"If you *don't* get back in that darkroom, you aren't gonna be able to keep up the payments on this heap," Mark teased.

"Don't I know! Okay Sher, be nice for me—"

"No problem," she replied, wrinkling her nose playfully at him. He waved vaguely at them and disappeared back into the darkroom.

"All right, let's see this fabric sample," she said, turning back to them as they all sat back down again. Mark thought he detected a certain haunted quality to her eyes, but if so, she closed it off before he could be certain.

"It isn't really a sample," he said apologetically, handing her the big envelope he'd picked up at the Forensics lab. "It's a photograph. The sample is the only piece we've got, so the lab's hanging onto it like it was the Holy Grail."

"Right, I understand," she answered absently, sliding the photograph out of the manila envelope. Her eyes went very wide with surprise.

"Recognize it?" Mark asked.

"I certainly do! It's Mestizo—only it's much finer work than I do. I work with bigger patterns and a coarser weave, but otherwise it's exactly the kind of thing I learned in Mexico. I'd say it was Chiapas, except that—see this line of figures, and this, and this?" She indicated the patterns as Di and Mark leaned over her shoulders. "Those aren't Chiapas patterns at all; in fact, I don't recognize them. But in general, well it's definitely Mex-Indian work. My bet would be that it's a renegade weaver; one using traditional techniques, but making up her own designs. That's supposed to make bad luck—but now and again somebody will say 'be damned to tradition' and chance it."

"What do you mean, that you use a coarser weave?" Mark asked.

"Well, come on into my workroom and I'll show you."

They followed her through the kitchen into what probably had been intended by the apartment designers as a third bedroom or a den. There was no carpet on the pale gold hardwood floor; the only furniture was a huge loom. But that loom was not in use; it wasn't even strung. Instead Sherry showed them a loom barely the size of a coffee table.

"You see?" she said. "This is a piece I'm doing for myself; a *huiple* and wrap-skirt with all the patterning in the weave instead of in the colors." She brightened as she stroked the finished fabric. "It was Robert's idea; it was the first time in a long time that he's shown any interest in my work. I've got the skirt done, the blouse is three-fourths finished. But look, this is the finest weave I've done yet, and you can see that my piece has only about half the number of threads per inch as the piece in the photograph."

Mark looked closer, and saw that she was absolutely correct. "So this couldn't have come from one of your outfits?"

She shook her head. "No, no way. I've only seen work like that once and that—" she faltered. "That was in Mexico," she finished flatly.

Her eyes flickered over to Di and back. Mark didn't miss the glance; neither did Di.

"If you don't mind, Mark," Di said then, "I'll get back to the car and start writing this up. It'll probably take me a while to put this into terms the Chief understands, so take your time."

"You don't have to leave—" Sherry began halfheartedly.

Di shook her head. "I'll think better in the car—and I mumble when I write. No problem, and it's a beautiful day."

"Then let me see you to the door," Sherry replied, obviously torn between relief and a desire to be the proper hostess.

Mark followed them as far as the living room, where he sank down into the luxuriously soft upholstery in one of corners of the pit. He couldn't help reflecting wryly on how out-of-place he looked, in his sneakers, jeans, and blue workshirt.

"So," he said, when Sherry returned alone. "Why don't you tell me a little about where you saw that kind of work."

Her face was closed and about as close to expressionless as Sherry ever got. "Well, it was on the trip where Robert met the girls. We were in Mexico City; Robert was working on spec for *TravelWorld*, and I was looking for examples of the kind of clothing I told you about. We were out at the pyramids when this young girl came up to us, trying to sell us silver jewelry."

Her brow wrinkled in puzzlement. "It was Lupe, of course; she's not the oldest of the girls, but she's the leader. She was wearing exactly that kind of weave, I think. The funny thing is that I *don't* remember much about that day, or the next. I think I might have gotten heat stroke, or something. I know that I was in a kind of fever; but I don't remember taking half the photographs or making a quarter of the charts that I obviously *did*. I do remember that Lupe loaned me more garments to copy while Robert took them out to pose in the ruins; that was what I was photographing and charting all day. But I really *don't* remember much about the things she was wearing, except that the figures in the weave were different from what she gave me."

"So—this stuff could, in fact probably *did*, come from Mexico City?"

To his surprise, she shook her head. "No, because I don't know where Lupe is originally from. She *could* be from up on the border around El Paso; her English is certainly good enough for that. It's really odd; I just don't know that much about the girls. It's that I really don't care that much, I guess. I—" She laughed, but it was obviously forced. "I resent them. And I just can't get past that. I guess I don't *want* to know more about them than I do; knowing about them would make them human, and I'd have to like them then."

"Sherry, why did you ask Di if she did deprogramming?"

Sherry blushed again, and bit her lip. "Just—I have these stupid ideas, sometimes. Like—sometimes it seems as if Lupe and the others have got some kind of strange hold on Rob that has nothing to do with sex. I can't help thinking that they've maybe gotten him tangled up in a peyote thing or something."

"He didn't look like or act like a druggie to me," Mark said, cautiously. "And I've seen more than my share."

"I know," she sighed. "I told you it was stupid. I think all kinds of nasty things about the girls; I'd like to think everything that's ker-whacky between us is *their* fault. But it isn't, and in my saner moments, I know it."

Mark was at a loss for words. He was saved from having to make a stupid reply by the sound of the front door opening and closing.

"That would be her highness now," Sherry said bitterly. "She never bothers to knock."

The rapid click of high heels on the tile of the entryway and hall preceded "her highness." Mark had no doubt who Sherry meant; his assumption was confirmed when one of Robert's four models prowled into view.

"Prowled" was the only appropriate word. Mark had seen women before who had been described as being graceful as a cat; this was the first one he'd ever seen who merited the description.

Lupe moved with all the lithe swiftness and controlled strength of one of the big hunting cats. Her black hair was confined at the nape of her neck in a simple knot; where Sherry was wearing little more than a bit of eye makeup and some lip-gloss, she was made up to within an inch of her life. And somehow Mark was irresistibly reminded of Indian warriors decorating themselves for combat. She had changed a great deal since she and her sisters had made those initial photographs—no simple folk costumes for *her*, not now. The skin-tight jeans she was wearing bore a top designer name over one hip; the sleeveless tee was silk, he'd bet on it. She was wearing a heavy silver necklace with odd designs incorporated into it; he rather wished he could see it a bit closer. It seemed to him that it looked a lot like the one Robert was wearing.

She was incredible, unbelievably sexy and attractive; skin so perfect it seemed almost poreless, vivid dark coloring, hair a thick fluid cascade of black silk. He could feel himself responding to her in spite of himself. She held herself with the poise of one born royal, and so aware of the fact that it had become unconscious awareness. Even that prominent nose was not a detraction—rather, it seemed that Sherry's nose (for example) was absurdly small by comparison.

The Queen of the Tigers, he thought, looking at her with mixed admiration and some emotion very like apprehension. *My God, poor*

Sherry! How can a lovely spirit compete with a body and face like that?
She looks absolutely washed out next to this girl.

"Sherry, señora, is Robert home?" the girl asked innocently. Her voice was low, and seemed to throb. Mark found his attraction to her increasing when he heard her speak, and he fought against it.

He managed to break the spell, at least in part—so he actually saw the split-second glance of hate she cast at him before turning a blandly sweet face toward Sherry.

He spared a second to catch a glance at Sherry himself. To his surprise, she was looking—bemused, was the only way he could put it. A little dazed. She showed not a hint of the resentment and anger she had expressed earlier. Instead she almost looked ensorcelled by the lovely model.

"He's in the darkroom," Sherry said slowly. "He asked me not to bother him."

"Ah well, in that case, we will wait for him at the studio, *si?*" She again cast a split-second glance of barely-curbed aggression at Mark. "*Buenos dias, señora.*"

And with that, she turned and glided back the way she had come.

"Now that was odd," Di said thoughtfully when they had left the apartment complex.

"What was odd?"

"First, *I* didn't see Lupe, but unless she made a really strange detour she'd have had to come right by me."

"Huh-uh, no mystery," Mark replied absently. "Sherry told me they live in the same complex; it's convenient for Robert."

"I bet it is," Di said flatly. "Still—I'm surprised I didn't at least see her at the front door. Well, the other odd thing was pretty minor—Robert is even more of a negative personality than you are."

"Gee thanks—"

"Sorry, that doesn't mean what it sounds like. A negative personality is one that attracts discarnate personalities and moves aside for them very easily. In other words, a medium. It has nothing to do with your strength of will, which is fine, thank you. It really doesn't have much to do with what makes you 'Mark Valdez'; it has everything to do with how strongly you and your physical body are linked in. In your case, not very. In Robert's case, even less so. That was why I put the shields on you in the first place right after we cleaned up the mess in Quasi's apartment; they prevent other personalities from forcing you out."

"Yeah I remember," he said, waiting for a light to change. "You told me I was about as defenseless as a baby. That if you hadn't come along, that thing we called up would have moved right in and set up housekeeping."

"It would have, too. Although I will admit to deliberately trying to scare you so you'd give me consent to shield you." She grinned thinly.

"Well I'm damned glad you did," he replied, returning the grin, and accelerating into traffic. "There's been a couple times since I've felt something tapping on the door that I was pretty sure I didn't want to let in."

"Then I'm doubly glad. I like *you*, Mark. I'd rather not find some-body else in your body. Well, the third odd thing is that Robert seems to have shields on him that are just as good as the ones I put on you. They *feel* like they were set up internally—so either he's been learning something other than photography these last few years, or he's a nat-ural."

"He must be a natural," Mark replied, thinking that she was right in saying that was odd. Robert was about the *least* mystical person he knew. "In all the years *I've* known him, he's never been interested in the occult."

"It's not impossible," Di said thoughtfully. "I've run into people shielded even tighter than he is that were doing the shielding uncon-sciously. Including a healer—which is *really* odd. So he isn't the weirdest natural I've run into, by a long shot. I just wish I could have gotten past those shields; it would have been useful to know how he *really* feels about Sherry. If he doesn't give a damn, we maybe could do something about the situation among the three of you—"

That cut a little too close to the quick. "Speaking of Sherry," Mark said hastily, "I've got a bit of a lead. She said she thinks she remem-bers that Lupe and the others were wearing brocades like that when they first met in Mexico City. So I'm going to take the pic to the Archeology and Anthropology Departments over at the university this afternoon."

"Sounds like we're splitting up, then," Di replied.

"Why?" he asked, surprised. "I thought you'd come with me—"

"If you can wait until tomorrow, fine. But this afternoon I have to get Aunt Nita talked into plugging me into the *brujiera* net. And like I told you, so far as the *brujas* are concerned, it's 'no men allowed.'"

"Oh." Mark thought about that for a while. "Okay, then I'll get hold of Charlie Mountainhawk and see if he's had a chance to get with his brother. We'll split up this afternoon, and get together tomorrow morning."

"If something doesn't happen first," Di replied, pessimistically. "This was just the first night; if the pattern holds, we've got two more to go."

ELEVEN

As it happened, Mark didn't have to go looking for Charlie Mountainhawk; Charlie was already looking for *him*.

There was a message in his locker: *If you can come by between noon and six, give me a buzz. Johnnie wants to talk.*

He checked his watch: it was only four. He stopped by the pay phone in the hall, plugged in a quarter, and punched Charlie's number.

"Hello?" said a familiar, female voice with more than a hint of wariness.

"Doreen?" Mark replied, holding his hand over his free ear to cut out the noise from the people in the hall behind him. "It's Mark Valdez. Charlie left a note—"

"Oh, Mark!" The tone warmed about twenty degrees. "Hi, sorry to sound unfriendly, but we've been getting crank calls. Charlie said you might be calling if you got a chance. He and Johnnie are down in the garage, so why don't you come on over?"

"I'll be there in about fifteen minutes, is that all right?"

"Silly man." Doreen Mountainhawk chuckled. "You know good and well you're welcome any time you choose to show your face. Bring your appetite and stay for dinner. I'll put some more water in the stew."

It was Mark's turn to chuckle. "Sure, okay—but only because I know you'll make me feel guilty if I don't. When are you going to stop trying to fatten me up?"

"About the same time I stop trying to find you a wife. Now hang up the phone and get your tail over here!"

"Yes'm," he said obediently, and replaced the receiver.

He stopped at Dispatch to leave his whereabouts with Lydia, the little girl from Baton Rouge. As he'd more than half expected she gave him a sobering stare, fixing him with eyes the color of the darkest brown velvet imaginable, but said only, "You-all be careful, Valdez. There's some folk out there got a serious anger wit' you."

He figured she would know. It was amazing how many sensitives were coming out of the headquarters woodwork since he began this case. "I am being careful," he replied. "But I've got a job to do, too— and damned if I'm going to let them keep me from doing it. Hear?"

She nodded, slowly. "I hear. Just be watchin' behind."

"And to all sides, and overhead," he responded. "I won't forget. I like my hide the way it is."

Charlie's apartment wasn't far, either as the crow flies or by road. It took him just about the fifteen minutes he'd told Doreen that it would—and then only because he'd checked his finances and stopped on the way for a baby gift.

"Hey, Cisco!" Charlie hailed him from the garage.

"Hey, Cochise!" he hailed back, pulling the Ghia in behind Charlie's orange VW bug.

"Better watch out," said a second voice from somewhere under the Beetle. "Don't park these two kraut cars too close together; it's springtime, and they might decide to mate. Then Charlie'll be stuck with a garageful of little orange safety cones."

As Mark got out, the owner of the second voice emerged from under the front end of the Bug; though he had grease smudges reminiscent of war paint on both cheekbones, there was no mistaking the family resemblance to Charlie. This young man, a bit thinner and a bit less muscular than Charlie, had to be Johnnie Mountainhawk.

Johnnie came around the car, wiping his hands on a rag. "Hi," he said, holding out his right, his expression cool and appraising. "I've heard a lot about you."

"Same here," Mark replied, taking the offered hand after shifting his package to his left.

Johnnie grinned. "If it was good, it was all the truth; if it was bad, it's all lies. Charlie, I think you're set for another year or so."

"My future offspring blesses you," Charlie laughed. "Because if I hadn't gotten those brake shoes replaced, Doreen was gonna kill me!"

"Speaking of Doreen—here," Mark said, handing Charlie his package. "Happy baby. It's an answering machine; best way I know of to discourage crank callers. For some reason they don't seem to take to the notion that they only have sixty seconds to make their point."

"Either that, or they don't like the idea that they're being recorded," Johnnie pointed out, visibly thawing a bit.

"Either, or. Doesn't much matter, so long as they quit," Charlie responded, obviously pleased. "Man, thanks. I hadn't even thought of using an answering machine, and those sickos are making Doreen real upset."

"Well I bet this discourages that," Mark answered. "*I* made the recording, my best 'I'm uh linebacker an' I like ta hear bones break' imitation. Anybody who gets past *that* really *wants* to talk to you."

Right after they hooked it up to the kitchen extension, the phone rang. Charlie checked his watch. "That just might be our spooks," he said. "They call about now—"

All four of them hovered over the machine expectantly. "This is the Mountainhawk residence," Mark's voice snarled after the third ring, pitched a good half an octave lower than he normally spoke, and sounding more as if he wanted to kill something than be answering the phone, even via recording. "They can't come to the phone right now, but if you'll leave your name, number, and brief message, they'll get back to you."

The machine emitted a tone; there was silence for a moment, then a high voice—either female, or young male—cursed briefly and softly, and the phone was hung up.

"That was them," Charlie said with satisfaction, as the machine rewound. "By damn, Cisco, it worked!"

Doreen threw her arms around Mark's neck and kissed his ear. He blushed.

"Aw, gosh, Sheriff, 'tweren't nuthin', " he drawled.

"Well, that makes two we owe you," Johnnie replied. "So let's see if what I can tell you makes a down payment, all right?"

"Sounds good to me," Mark nodded, as Doreen shooed them all into the living room.

"Okay, let me tell you *where* I am in the scheme of things," Johnnie said as they all arranged themselves on the brown tweed couch. "I tend to be a moderate, but I'm also fairly well known to be a peacemaker, good at building compromises. The gods themselves know that if you get two different *families* together you're likely to have fights, much less tribes. So I hear a lot that most moderates don't. I hope you don't mind, but I'd rather *not* help you infiltrate, okay? If anyone figured out you were a ringer, we'd both lose."

Mark shrugged. "I can live with that, so long as you're willing to keep talking to me."

It was hard to tell, but he thought Johnnie looked relieved. "I'm in a pretty good position of trust, and I don't want to blow it. Especially since, because Granddad is a Medicine Man, I sometimes hear more from the mystics than your average moderate would."

"I take it that you *have* heard something disturbing?" Mark said, with one eyebrow raised.

Johnnie leaned forward on the couch, hands clasped between his denim-clad knees. "From *both* the radicals and the mystics. From the radicals I've heard about a new militant who calls himself 'Burning Water.' They claim he's got the charisma *and the cash* to build a new Indian army and literally take this area away from the whites by force of arms. From the mystics I have been hearing about a new man-god—"

He seemed to be groping for the appropriate term, so Mark tried to supply it. "An avatar?"

"Yeah, that's it, an avatar. They say he's going to somehow reconcile all the tribes, purify their spirits, and build a new Indian stronghold right here in Dallas—a spiritual *and* physical stronghold. And if you guessed he's called Burning Water, you guessed right."

Mark sat back, whistling. "Damn. Now how much of this is smoke-talk and how much is real?"

Johnnie shrugged. "Your guess is as good as mine. I can't prove anything one way or the other, since so far it's just talk and rumor; nobody *I* know has actually met this Burning Water or been recruited by him. Thing is, about half of the mystics are scared spitless—they don't want any part of this 'savior.' The rest of them are falling all over each other in anticipation. The rest of the moderates other than yours truly are figuring the radicals have had a little too much peyote, if you know what I mean. But—this is the catch—none of them have the connections I do because of Charlie, and nobody's put the whole picture together with the sacrificial murders."

"You buy Di's speculation that this and the killings are tied in?"

Johnnie nodded. "Shit, yes. If those killings don't have all the marks of sacrifices, I'll eat your Ghia. I've *always* figured Medicine Magic was for real; took Charlie a while, but he came around to it too. There's *plenty* of traditions that involve blood-sacrifice; it was usually animal, but there's nothing against making it the blood of your enemy. I just wish I had some proof, is all. You wouldn't find many of us shedding any tears over those fat cats getting theirs, but not even the wildest of us go in for drowning kids. That's *not* the way you do it—you *kidnap* the kids and turn 'em into Indians. Anyway, if you get any proof that ties the name 'Burning Water' in to the murders, I want to know about it. If nothing else, this guy is liable to get a lot of *us* blamed for what he's doing, and a lot of us killed, and there aren't enough of us as it is."

"I'll do my best," Mark said. "And thanks for what you've given me. To change the subject, what *were* those phone calls that they got Doreen so upset? I remember the last time you got a porn caller, 'Reenie just laughed at him until he hung up."

"Unfortunately, that *isn't* changing the subject," Charlie said soberly. "They just started this week, and they're part of the reason Johnnie said he'd give you a hand. It was always the same voice, and the same words. 'Tell Mountainhawk that he can't hide behind white man's magic forever. When Burning Water comes, he will have to choose—or die.'"

"Aunt Nita," Di said from the kitchen doorway, "I have a real big favor to ask of you."

Juanita Valdez turned from her sink of dirty dishes and looked at her appraisingly. "From the look on your face, I would say you do," she said, "and the dishes can wait for a moment."

She walked over to Di, drying her hands on her apron, and pulled out two of the chairs around the kitchen table. "Sit; it's easier to talk sitting down."

Di did as she was told, trying to formulate her words in her mind. "I need to find a *bruja*," she said finally. "I figured that you would be the best one to get one to talk to me."

Aunt Nita pursed her lips. "I don't patronize that sort of thing," she said reluctantly. "I *do* believe in certain powers and so forth—but *brujiera*—it's so—I don't quite know how to say it. It seems so loaded down with peasant superstitions."

Di nodded. "I understand. But it's beginning to look like this case Mark and I are on could well be tied in with the darker sort of *brujiera*; the kind that keeps people living in fear of the sorcerers even to this day, and not always just in remote little villages."

"I don't know," Aunt Nita replied hesitantly. "I just *don't* know."

"Aunt Nita, we've been trying to keep this out of the papers, but do you know how many people have been killed by this bunch of lunatics just since I got here?"

She shook her head, dumbly.

"Sixteen," Di told her flatly. "Three of those were children—the three little ones they found in that cattle tank last month. And there were a half-dozen deaths before *that* murder that we know of."

The elderly woman straightened at that, and Di could sense the indecision leaving her.

"Well," she replied, after a long pause during which she was obviously thinking hard. "I personally don't believe in *brujiera*, but if I did, the first person *I'd* consult would be Marguerita, the woman that comes in to help me clean once a week. And it so happens that she's due tomorrow. I can have a word with her then."

Di fought down a feeling of triumph. They *still* had a long way to go before she could feel she'd accomplished anything.

Tom Beckerman usually went out running as soon as possible after dinner because he could lose himself and not have to think about the working day he'd just passed through. Unfortunately, right now *nothing* was going to drive his worries away, not even the endorphin-high of running.

No two ways about it; ever since they put me on project lead, I've been in a world of hurt.

He swung around the corner and into the parking lot of Five Banners Over Dallas, the big amusement theme-park. It was closed down for the winter, except on weekends, which was why he liked to run here. He couldn't get *in* the park, of course, but the landscaping around the fence was nice, there was a decent path worn there by the maintainance people, and there wasn't even a hint of traffic.

It wouldn't be so bad if those jerks supposed to be doing the programming had gotten off their thumbs and done some work *instead of deciding to prove it couldn't be done in the time schedule I set. So what if I'm not a programmer? No big deal to doing a decent project estimate.*

He ran through the parking lot and crossed the grass, heading for a little space between two big evergreen bushes. He got himself slotted into the path, and increased his pace a little, trying to drive the useless worries out of his mind.

But the worries wouldn't go.

Is it my fault the machine was down so much? Is it my fault we lost half the old crew? I hired in twice *as many new bodies—they should have been able to pick up the slack and then some! Programming is programming is programming.*

He recalled with shame the retirement party they'd thrown for George Herschal this afternoon. George had been with the company since—forever. Since before computers. And toward the end of the party he'd taken Tom aside—

"*Young'un,*" he'd said, in that good-ol'-boy accent of his, his arm lying heavily across Tom's shoulders, *"what you got is a people problem, he-ah. You don't know programmin', an' you don' know squat about how t' handle people. That wouldn't hurt you so much, I've seen leads manage with less'n you—but dammit, boy, you don't lissen t' them as* knows *what they're doin'! You done bit off more'n you c'n chew, an' the sooner you 'fess up an' let 'em put you back t' what you do good, the happier you're gonna be. You keep tryin' t' play boss-man when you ain't got what it takes, an' you gonna find you went an' painted yourself inta a corner fer sure."*

God, the humiliation.

The damp air was heavy, and seemed hard to breathe. He glanced up, noting that there weren't any stars visible. The sky was heavily overcast again tonight. Hopefully there wouldn't be a repetition of last night's monster storm. The path had dried out during the day, but another rain would make it a muddy mess and he'd have to use the street for a while. And if it began to rain now—Carole had told him not to go out running—

But shoot, that wasn't because of the weather, that was just because she was hysterical about all those people getting carved up. He snorted to himself. Women and their irrational fears. Nothing like that would ever happen to *him*. Most of that bunch had been bums, winos, street-gang punks. Probably the papers were making a big deal out of nothing. Probably the only two solid citizens that had gotten killed had been killed for their money. Nobody mugged a jogger. Everybody knew they never had any cash on them.

He rounded the first landmark that marked his halfway point, feeling the air weigh heavily in his chest, feeling none of the usual runner's euphoria. *Too bad one of those hadn't been my head programmer*, he thought wistfully. *Then I could have claimed that the entire team was too shaken up to work.*

He brooded on his problems as he continued to run, never noticing the shadows that were paralleling his course past the screening trees.

Mark had been forewarned, but it didn't make the scene any easier to handle. After one look, Di had turned pasty white, then headed straight for the nearest park ladies' room, and he didn't blame her.

The only good thing about this was that the Five Banners park was self-contained and more than adequately fenced. So there were no gawkers and journalists, and there had been no one at all in the park until the maintainance people had found the body.

If you could call it that. It was appalling.

The maintenance crew that had found the body had been carted off to the hospital to be treated for shock. So far as anyone could tell, they'd unlocked their entrance after checking the perimeter as they always did, and had found nothing out of the ordinary—certainly no signs of illegal entry. Then they'd gotten as far as the central plaza. . . .

As was getting to be routine (if such a thing could be called "routine"), there had been a cardiectomy. But not until after the victim had been flayed from his soles to his hairline. The heart was missing again; so was the skin.

The whole rite had been performed on a big flat rock right in the middle of the deserted park, next to the double-decker carousel. With the park closed for the winter and the maintainance people gone for the day, Mark figured you could have staged a sit-down orgy for five hundred and nobody would have noticed.

Of course, that didn't explain how the victim and his murderers got *inside* the park in the first place. The insurance company that covered the park was very unhappy; they had some pretty stiff rules regarding access to the place during off hours. Of course, the owners of the park were even less happy—this was supposed to be a place for fun, not mayhem. And since they ran their *own* security, they, like Amerine, had no one to blame but themselves.

To see the aftermaths of these things by floodlight had been bad enough—but to see it by the light of day made it somehow worse.

The coroner himself was on the scene, supervising the whole thing personally.

When Di got back, Mark came up behind him and tapped him on the shoulder, Di trailing along behind him, silent and still very pale.

"Got anything for me yet, Doc?" he asked.

The middle-aged, tough coroner looked more like a weathered old ranch hand than a doctor. It took a lot to rattle him—but by the pallor beneath his tan, this had rattled him good.

"A bit," he replied. "It ain't what you'd call pleasant hearing." He looked askance at Di.

"Fire away," Mark said, "I think I'm getting numb at this point."

"I'm part of the team, too," Di gulped. "I have to know eventually; it might as well be now."

"First thing is it looks like the poor bastard was gang-raped before he was skinned. Not what you're thinkin', not by men. By women."

Mark felt his jaw coming unhinged. "You have *got* to be kidding me!" he exclaimed. "A *guy?*"

The coroner nodded reluctantly. "Yeah, I know; it sounds impossible. But it can be done, and it leaves real distinct signs. It looks to me like it *was*. Second thing is it looks from the pattern of bloodstains and the condition of the corpse like they were real careful about how they got the skin off the poor SOB. What I'm saying is they literally skinned him alive. *Then* they cut his heart out."

Mark had thought he was numb, but his gorge rose at that. He was just as glad that they were taking the body away and he didn't have to look at it any more.

"And I got another update on the second lot of stiffs from night before last," the coroner added.

"Go ahead," Mark managed. Di nodded agreement.

"Ramirez found the rock, like you said he would. He found somethin' else; what was left of a bonfire, and we found bits of burned skin all over that rock. So it looks to us like they threw those four men into the fire, toasted 'em for a bit, pulled 'em out *still alive*. Then they tricked 'em out in their flowers and all, and cut the hearts out. Looks to us like throwin' 'em in the car and settin' it afire was just their way of cleanin' up afterward."

He grimaced, shrugged, and got back to his crew.

The atmosphere got a little easier after they took the gruesome corpse away. While Di worked with the Forensics group and did a little discreet "checking" with a different set of investigative "tools," Mark took the opportunity to talk with the Chief.

This was the first time he'd ever been put in charge of anything on a case this major, even if it was only a two-man team, and while he wasn't precisely nervous—

Well, he wasn't precisely at ease with the idea either. So he buttonholed the Chief—*outside* the "official" atmosphere of the office—and went over everything they'd checked out so far, including his own solo legwork. This wasn't a class, after all; this was a damned serious case. He wasn't being graded. And there were people dying out here. The Chief had told them all, time and time again, that they were a *team* and should act like one—and Mark was not too proud to ask for advice—ever. Especially not from the man who had solved more big cases than Mark and all his buddies combined.

There *were* a few things he had to leave out, of course, which was something of a pity, but he was surprised at the amount of ground they'd covered in the last four or five weeks.

"Have I missed anything?" he asked when he'd finished. "Left anything undone that you would have done?"

The Chief slowly shook his head. "Not by my reckonin', " he replied. "Yer doin' what I asked y'all t'do; m'nose tells me yer gettin' close. Closer'n we bin gettin', that's fer sure. Charlie's brother gonna git you in with them war-drummers?"

"We decided against it," Mark replied. "We don't want to flush *his* credibility; we might need somebody where he is again some day."

"Huh; yeah, could be. Jest keep in steady touch with him, okay? Otherwise play it as it lays, boy. Say, what was it Miz Di did t' rout that kraut t'other day? Heard somethin' 'bout that, but jest enough t' make me powerful curious."

Willing to change the topic of conversation now that he was fairly sure of the Chief's mind, Mark gave him a blow-by-blow account of Di and the German journalist. Before he was through, the Chief was laughing so hard his face was red and tears were squeezing out of his eyes.

"Oh *damn*!" he gasped. "*Damn*, I wish't I'd been there! That boy is one pain in the you-know; I bin prayin' fer an excuse t' bounce him out on his can, but he don't give me none. Lissen, you kin tell Miz Di fer me that I think she is one all-right gal. An' the next time she takes on Herr Fieber, I wanna be there. Front row seat, an' popcorn."

When Di returned to the house late that afternoon, Mark's aunt was waiting for her, and with her was a thin, sun-bronzed woman not too many years Juanita's junior.

"Diana, this is Marguerita Valdoza," Aunt Nita said quietly. "I took the liberty of telling her something about you, and something of what you need."

"I'm very pleased to meet you," Di replied with all the sincerity she could muster; not easy since she was about ready to drop. "Thanks, Aunt Nita; that makes things a lot simpler."

She held out her hand and the woman took it; her clasp was warm, firm, and dry. Di's immediate impression was of a woman who would brook no nonsense from anyone; and a woman of absolute and unwavering honesty.

Not an easy person to live with—but then, I don't have to live with her, she thought wryly.

The woman measured her with her eyes for a moment before replying. "Señorita Diana—I must tell you that I do not personally know anyone of the kind you wish to speak to."

"But you know someone who knows someone?" Di hazarded.

Marguerita shrugged. "So they claim. I have never seen the need for witchery—but there are those who believe. And those who believe are something shy of speaking to strangers. So I must send you through the maze; to my daughter-in-law, who has a friend, who—so I am told—knows a *bruja*."

Di nodded. "I understand," she said. "And I know it's going to take time. This kind of thing always does."

For the first time the woman smiled. "Less, perhaps, than you might think," she said. "I am not known for my patience."

Marguerita took Di in tow, a slender yacht being bossed out of the harbor by a very expert tug. They traveled to her home, just on the edge of an area near where Athena lived. They went by bus—a form of transportation Di was becoming depressingly familiar with. Once at Marguerita's home, a place scoured so fanatically clean that Di suspected her of Dutch blood rather than Spanish-American, there was coffee—and, at length, a phone call—and again after a wait, an introduction to the daughter-in-law, Consuela.

Consuela was another, younger version of Marguerita. There was more coffee, and questions by Marguerita while Consuela listened and passed a silent judgment. Eventually some signal passed between the two women, for Consuela became friendlier, and took her across the street to her own apartment.

There was *more* coffee (Di was rather glad she had a very high tolerance for caffeine) and another phone call, and at long last Di was passed into the hands of Maria Angelita Rosario.

This was not the end; like a pair of Inquisitors, both women plied her with questions, some of which seemed to have little or nothing to do with the problem she faced or the *bruja*. Di curbed her impatience, held her tongue, and answered them as clearly and with as much politeness as she could manage.

Finally the two women nodded to each other, rose from the table almost as one, and motioned to her to follow.

A walk of several blocks brought them all to the home of the *bruja*, a young widow, Theresa Montenegro. There the other two left her, after spending some time in a whispered discussion with the object of Di's search.

The widow was a tired-looking, faded slip of a woman, somewhat washed out by the black dress she wore. "You will come in, please, Miss Tregarde," she said, reluctantly, her voice as faded and tired as the rest of her. "I do not know that I can help you, but I will listen."

"Thank you," Di replied, preceding the *bruja* into the apartment, and finding herself in a room that had been intended as a living room and now was serving as a kind of place of worship.

Dominating one wall was an altar, thick with candles and statues of various saints, and surmounted by a statue of the Virgin. Despite the heat, every candle on the altar was lit, and the light reflecting from the gilded statues was a little dazzling. Beneath the altar was a padded kneeler, well worn.

There were a couple of benches at the end of the room opposite the altar; Theresa took a seat on one, and Di on the other.

Well, she's not as high-powered as Athena was, Di thought, after taking stock of the atmosphere, *but she knows what she's doing, and she's got the gift.* She took a moment to analyze the emotions emanating from the *bruja*, and was less pleased. *She's afraid. Dammit, I was hoping to avoid that. Is it me?*

She delved a little deeper, while the *bruja* appeared to be taking the same time to study *her*.

No, she decided. *It isn't me. But she is afraid. She doesn't want to talk to an outsider at all. There's some threat she perceives, and she thinks talking to me will draw its attention to her.*

"Señora Montenegro," she said, breaking the silence when it became apparent that the *bruja* would not do so, "I come to you in most urgent need of information. I have reason to believe that there is an evil *brujo*, a man of power, making blood-magic to give him strength. I think that only the power of *brujiera* or the knowledge held by the *brujas* will reveal him to me. I believe that it is *he* who has committed the murders that have the police so confused."

"You are working with the police, *si?*" the *bruja* asked in a thin voice.

"I am, yes," Di replied. "I am working with them as a favor to a friend, who is the nephew of the friend of Marguerita Valdoza and is himself a policeman."

"Ah." The *bruja* studied her for another moment. "I have no love for the police," she said, finally.

"Señora, it is not a matter of whether one loves the police," Di replied patiently. "It is a matter of whether or not one will allow this evil *brujo* to continue to kill. The police are only the means to remove him. It may become necessary to use other means, but for now, the police must be my means."

"Ah," the woman said again, and studied her worn, work-roughened hands. "I do not know, Miss Tregarde. I do not know that I can help you."

Substitute "can" for "will," and we're a lot closer to the truth, Di thought, curbing her anger at the woman's reluctance. *If I stay much longer—I am going to lose my temper; I know it. Damn. All right, I know where she lives—maybe I can find some leverage to use on her later.*

"I must go," she said, rising, the woman's eyes following her. "Whether or not you can help me, I must do what I can."

"I—" the woman began, then shut her lips firmly on whatever she was going to say, and led the way to the door.

"Will you just promise me this, Señora Montenegro?" Di asked as she paused halfway into the outer hall. "Will you promise me to *think* about what I have asked?"

The *bruja* bowed her head, as if taking on a heavy burden. "*Sí,*" she whispered. "That, I will promise."

Pablo had picked up the trail of the gringo witch as she passed near the *barrio*. He was elated that she had come to him; it would have been far more difficult to find her in her own territory.

Even better, she was taking the bus; that made it possible for him to follow her closely—if she had been traveling about with the man, in his car, Pablo would have had to borrow or steal a vehicle, and might well have been far more obvious. As it was, he was just one more Mestizo boy on the bus; a little quieter, more well-behaved than most, but just a face in the crowd.

He would have thought she would stand out in that crowd, but somehow she seemed to blur into it. He decided finally that it was because of her magic; she was blending in like the chameleons on a branch. That made him wary; he knew it took Burning Water a great effort and much power to keep their sacrifices hidden, yet this witch was casually hiding herself as if the effort was nothing. He understood the god's caution now in dealing with her; until Burning Water came into his complete power at the Great Sacrifice, it would be well to beware even of such a negligible thing as this witch.

Especially when it appeared that she was not insignificant at all.

But the witch seemed preoccupied, buried deeply within her own thoughts, as she sat hunched on her little sliver of bus bench. Her chin was tucked down into her jacket, and her collar up around her ears; her dark eyes stared ahead of her without truly *seeing* much of what was going on about her.

It came to Pablo then that she might well be working some of her magic; a thing not at all unlikely, now that he came to think about it.

His own magic was all borrowed, and he used it gingerly, as he would use an unfamiliar weapon. He feared to trigger something by coming too close, and so eased his borrowed magic only near enough to test the very edges of hers.

He recoiled at once, sensing powerful defenses, and alarms and traps behind the defenses.

So she *was* working magics. Best to leave her alone, then.

It was then, turning his vision from *within* to *without* that Pablo saw the strange blond man.

He certainly stood out on this bus, with his golden blond hair and his sunburned face. And there was no magic hiding *his* presence. Strangely enough the gringo witch did not seem aware of him—but he was certainly aware of *her*. He pretended to read a paper, but he never turned the pages, and Pablo knew within moments that this man was, as was Pablo, following the witch.

And that made Pablo very happy.

Helmut Fieber, journalist for *Der Tag*, was also very happy.

At first, after the strange madwoman had routed him with her maniacal speech and her supposed "fecal samples," he'd simply been relieved to escape from a potentially unpleasant situation. But after reflection, he had begun to wonder if he hadn't—as the Americans put it—"been had."

For he had seen this woman at or near the site of every murder since then—and yes, she *had* been working side by side with the coroner's Forensics team—

But she had never once departed with them. Rather, she left— and presumably arrived—with a young man. A young man who was never in uniform, but who Helmut had discovered was one "Mark Valdez." *Detective* Mark Valdez, to be precise.

And Helmut had more than once seen this woman in consultation with the Chief of Detectives, Samuel Grimes. He had watched as the unapproachable, surly Grimes listened to her every word, and seemed to accord those words some weight and importance.

In short, this was no coroner's assistant.

So he had attached himself to her at the Five Banners park, and spent the entire day following her.

That had *not* been an easy task—and it had been made more difficult by the fact that this woman (surely, surely she must be at least a *little* mad) had either walked or taken public transportation. He had nearly lost her any number of times today; he was hot and very tired, and did not in the least understand why she was not in possession of a car like every other American. The buses were all hot, crowded, and smelled of things best not thought of. And those who used the buses were not the sort that Fieber would have associated with by choice.

He was uncomfortably aware that his blond hair and light skin were (and had been all day) attracting surreptitious attention from a great many people; on this bus, on other buses, on the street. This obsession with public transportation of the madwoman—it seemed very dangerous to him.

Only now do I begin to understand that man in New York, who shot those boys on the subway, he thought, trying to make himself as inconspicuous as possible. *I felt safer in Nicaragua.*

He could not understand why *she* was ignored, either; she surely looked as out of place as he did.

Perhaps, in her worn jeans and jacket, she did not look prosperous enough.

He began to regret his clothing choice of the morning. He *did* look prosperous. At least more than most of the rest of the bus riders.

Perhaps she will get off, soon, he thought hopefully, seeing her rousing from the inward-turned concentration she had been showing and display some signs of taking note of her surroundings. *If I can get her alone—more important, if I can find out where it is that she lives— all of this will have been worthwhile.*

To his immense relief, at that moment she pulled the wire to signal the bus driver to stop, and rose gracefully to her feet, using the momentum of the bus to propel her down the aisle to the front door.

He lurched to his feet and took the rear exit, hopping quickly down to the pavement and trusting the darkness of near-midnight to conceal the fact that he was behind her.

But she did not look to see if she was followed, merely strode off at her normal (albeit unnervingly) brisk pace.

Fieber was right behind.

Juanita Valdez had known all her life that she was "sensitive"; the Gift (as her grandmother had called it) ran in her blood. That Gift had saved the family time and time again from fire, flood, Indian raid—

It didn't save us from the greed of politicians—but then, I'm not certain that anything would have—

Tonight her Gift was warning *her* of danger. Her nerves were as tight as guitar strings, and had been so ever since sundown. She circled the house repeatedly, checking locks, checking windows, peering out into the darkness and watching for the shadow that should not be there, the movement where nothing should move—

And all for nothing. The locks were sound, the windows secure, and all outside the house was serene.

You old fool, she scolded herself. *Nobody is going to get in except your girls. Nobody is going to get in without a key! And the girls are all safely in their beds. Except young Di, of course, and she should be able to take care of herself.*

Those thoughts did not comfort; instead the feeling of danger grew with every passing minute. It got so bad that she turned out all the lights, the better to see what was going on outside—*and* to avoid betraying her movements to anyone who might be lurking out there.

Finally she felt her way to the kitchen and armed herself with the biggest cleaver she owned. That gesture, as futile as it might be, at least made her feel a little better.

Certain that she was being terribly foolish, and yet unable to help herself, she set herself up as guard on the front door.

Great-grandmama must be grinning like a fox at me from her seat in Paradise, she told herself. *I am surely playing the senile old idiot. What's going to come at me anyway—bandidos? Pancho Villa? Renegades?*

Then she heard the rattle of a key in the lock, and froze.

Di wrenched the door open and closed it quickly behind her, double-locking it and throwing the security bolt. She was panting like a greyhound at the end of the race, and with good reason—she'd run the last six blocks to the boardinghouse.

From the moment she'd stepped off the bus she'd known she was in danger. At first she had simply acted normallyexcept for putting up full and battle-hardened shields. But nothing attacked—

Only the feeling of peril had grown, nearer and stronger with every minute, until she had found herself running as fast as she could for the relative safety of the boardinghouse and her tools. She'd hit the door and unlocked it so fast she hardly believed it, and had squirted inside as if she'd been oiled.

She heard a movement behind her and started to spin—then her empathic senses identified Aunt Nita, and she relaxed just a trifle; completing her turn, but without the urgency of self-defense.

Her eyes had already adjusted to the limited light in the hall. It did not surprise her to see that Aunt Nita had armed herself with a cleaver.

She cleared her throat. "So you feel it too—" she said; more of a statement than a question.

Aunt Nita nodded, slowly, the light from the streetlight outside glinting off the shiny blade of the cleaver. "Since sundown, and getting worse," she replied.

Di took a deep breath, willing her pulse to slow now that she was no longer running. "How about," she whispered, "if we make the rounds of the perimeter?"

Aunt Nita just nodded.

Although the feeling of danger had not faded, just having Diana with her made Juanita feel immeasurably better. *Somehow—anything I've missed she'll find. I'm not sure how, but—*

She followed in Diana's wake; the girl went first to the kitchen, to her faint surprise. She took a tumbler from the cabinet, filled it with water, then dumped the entire contents of the saltshaker on the kitchen table into it.

If I didn't know that she *knows what she's doing—*

Then Juanita almost voiced an objection, as the girl muttered something over the tumbler and traced little signs over it with fingers that moved more swiftly than the cloud-shadows racing across the moon outside. Then she remembered that the girl had promised *not* to compromise Juanita's beliefs—and that Di had weaponry that was—had to be—something other than purely physical. She bit the half-hearted protest back, and simply watched.

Starting with the kitchen, Diana began a circuit of the entire house, tracing little diagrams on each window and door with the salt-water mixture. She moved as surely as any cat in the darkness; moved as surely as if she had Juanita's own lifelong familiarity with the house and its contents.

Somehow Juanita was not terribly surprised to see those little diagrams glowing blue; nor that they continued to glow, very faintly, for a few seconds after they both passed.

When the circuit of the house was completed, Diana led the way, still in silence, to the darkened living room. There they sat, as quietly as it is possible for two living women to sit; Juanita clutching her cleaver so tightly her fingers hurt, Diana still holding that tumbler of saltwater as if it was both talisman and weapon.

It might well be both—Juanita thought—

Then the night was splintered by the shattering of glass.

"The back—" Diana cried grabbing a poker from the fireplace beside her and racing for the kitchen.

Juanita ran right along with her—until they both suddenly had an attack of good sense at the kitchen door and halted right there, listening for further sounds.

No sounds at all—

And—it's gone, Juanita realized suddenly. *The feeling of danger—it's gone.*

She steeled herself, transferred the cleaver to her left hand, and flung open the kitchen door with her right, flicking on the kitchen light as she did so.

There was a large blond man lying on his side across her kitchen table, sprawling half in, half out of the now-shattered west window.

He was staring at them both, from eyes that were nearly popping out of his head. He wasn't moving.

That was largely because he was very dead.

Juanita had not known until this moment that she was a brave woman. She put down the cleaver—noting, with a detached portion of her mind that her hand was not shaking at all—and followed Diana across an expanse of brown linoleum that now seemed as wide as the state of Texas itself.

The man was dripping blood all over her spotless kitchen table and floor, and another part of Juanita was outraged at the mess she was going to have to clean up. Now that they were closer, she could see that there was a gaping hole in his chest. Presumably his heart had been cut out—

It was a rational presumption, because she could easily see that a meaty lump of something vaguely heartlike and heart-shaped had been stuffed halfway into the man's mouth.

She jumped and nearly screamed as Diana cleared her throat.

"I think—" Diana said slowly "—that somebody is doing their best to scare me off this case." Her face hardened. "And it isn't going to work."

TWELVE

They had been expecting—and dreading—another massacre of some kind. It was practically inevitable, given the pattern that they had established.

But there was no way that they could have anticipated the scene they were called to in the early dawn hours at Possum Kingdom Park.

"Mark," Di choked, after one look, "I can't take any more of this."

Her face was so pale it was nearly transparent, and her eyes seemed to fill the upper half of it. Mark had a feeling that he was as green as she was pale. All of the horrors that had led up to this climax of the three-day cycle were totally eclipsed by the sheer *slaughter* that had been found this morning by the park-department employees whose duty it was to check the park over when they arrived for the day's work.

From the signs it appeared as though the park had been in use for some time as a transfer point for illegal aliens. There were half-a-dozen trucks parked in an orderly row, all cleverly set behind a screening of evergreens running as a windbreak on an island in the middle of the parking lot—evergreens that would just happen to hide them from patrols. Their painstaking arrangement argued for practice and much thought. All of the trucks were a mottled, dark green, further blending with the foliage, and all sported license plates from differing states. All of them were registered to families of migrant agricultural workers.

This didn't have the look of a "professional" people-smuggling job; it had more of the air of something that legal immigrants had concocted to get friends and family across the border.

It appeared that the illegals were taken across the border by some other means, then brought to the park and dropped off there, to be met by prearrangement. Probably each family (represented by a truck) took on three or four "new members," then headed on to another job. From there the new workers could slip into the migrant population almost invisibly.

It was a slick system; one that had probably been functioning for months, if not years, without detection.

Only—last night, the system had been used for someone else's purposes, and the migrants had walked into a trap. A death-trap.

There were nearly fifty bodies in the picnic area near the parking lot. Men, women—and children. Nearly *half* of the bodies were of children under twelve.

And there were parts missing. Hearts—and other things.

Di hadn't been able to bear more than a single glance. She took one look and buried her face in Mark's shoulder. He held her awkwardly, unable to give her any comfort at all. He attempted to deal with the scene, but he wasn't handling it much better than she was.

For that matter, neither was most of the rest of the Homicide team. They were somewhat used to death—but this went beyond their experience and worst nightmares.

The Forensics crew was coping, managing to do their job despite the horror that could be seen behind their deadpan expressions, but only with the help of the same emergency crew that had helped sort out the bodies after the last big air disaster at DFW. *That* lot was familiar with horror, and their steadiness helped to keep the Forensics folk from losing their own grip.

After several abortive attempts to face the carnage, all of which ended in her tears and failure, Mark sent Di back to the car; but he felt honor-bound to stay. She wasn't coherent enough for him to make out whether it was *just* the physical butchery that was getting to her, or something more. She looked on the verge of a breakdown—and he wouldn't let her risk one; he needed her too much.

But he also knew *he* must look like hell, because one of the parameds came over and patted his shoulder with clumsy encouragement.

"Hang in there, buddy," the stranger said, his own face stiff and his eyes dull, his blond hair lank with nervous sweat. "You get numb after about a half an hour, honest."

Something inside Mark winced at the idea. He didn't *want* to go numb—

And yet, at the same time, he did. It would almost be worth losing one's humanity to also lose the frustrated agony, the knife-edged guilt, the sheer revulsion caused by seeing human beings, *children*, reduced to so much butchered meat—

"How many?" he asked, his jaw clenched so hard it ached.

"Thirty-eight. And no sign that any of them fought, either. It's damned spooky, is all I can tell you. It's like they just laid themselves down for the knife—like another Jim Jones thing, you know?"

When Mark forced himself to go nearer to examine the bodies heaped in the center of the clearing behind the shelter, he discovered that the paramed was right. Even though every face he saw was a mask of terror, even though the expressions were distorted with a pain and fear he could only imagine, there were *no* signs of combat or attempts at flight on the part of any of the victims.

And that was more than just "spooky." That was unnatural, and it raised the hair on the back of his neck in a way that almost made him forget the blood and the mutilated bodies.

Now he was *drawn* to the actual sacrificial site by an urgency he could not deny. Behind the cement and wood shelter was a picnic table, the makeshift altarplace. There was thick, dry grass all about it, grass that was showing distinct signs of life after the rain of the night before. He knelt beside Jean in the grass and studied the site, studied the way the grass was trampled flat in places, studied the obvious trail—

Unable to believe what he thought he was seeing, he walked around to the opposite side of the site. It looked exactly the same—at least to his eyes—from there. He returned to Jean's side.

"No," he said flatly to her. "There is no way—"

"Tell me what *you* see," she replied. "I'm trying to decide if I've gone around the bend."

"It—no, it's too damned weird."

"Cough it out, dammit!" she snapped, a wild look of being near the edge herself stirring in the depths of her hazel eyes.

"It looks—it looks like they all lined up *here*—" He pointed to a nearly straight line of flattened grass at the edge of the parking lot. "—like they lined up like kids after recess. And then—then they came forward, one at a time—" He indicated the path that was clearly worn into the grass from the beginning of the flattened line, past the shelter, to end at the picnic table that had been used as the sacrificial altar. "—of their own free will—and—I *can't* believe it! Even if whoever it was had these people under guard, and the guards were armed with machine guns, *some* of them should have tried to break and run! But—"

"There's not a sign of it," Jean agreed, nodding, not losing a particle of that strange, fey expression as she turned to study the site once again. "I don't believe it either—but there isn't one single indication that anything else happened. They could have been zombies or robots—except that—those faces—"

She shuddered, and Mark shuddered in sympathy.

"They *knew* what was going to happen to them, and they marched up to their deaths anyway," she said. "Mark, it doesn't make any *sense*! Not even drugs or hypnosis could make people do that! It's like they were all under some kind of horrible, evil spell."

"It *was* a 'spell.' Of control," Di said flatly. "They were controlled, from first to last. Like robots—only these robots knew what was going to happen to them."

She had managed to come out of the car and face the site once the bodies were all carted off to the morgue. By then nearly everyone had gone except Mark and Ramirez.

She passed a trembling hand through her hair, and bit her lip. "That's not all, Mark. This time the cult leaders haven't bothered to wipe out the traces of what they did. It's like they've gotten powerful enough to be contemptuous of me. . . ."

"Maybe," he replied. "Maybe not. They *could* be counting on the idea that they've scared you off. Hm?"

"*I don't know!*" She looked at him with haunted eyes. "That's the problem—I *don't know!*"

"Easy kid—" he soothed her as he would have soothed Treemonisha in a thunderstorm. "Tell me how you know they were controlled."

She crossed her arms tightly across her chest and hunched her shoulders in misery. "I can feel it," she said. "It's still here. They were—like in a nightmare where you try to run and can't." Her nostrils flared, like a horse scenting smoke. "I—I know how to do it, too—I could control two, maybe three people myself if I had to. I'd be more subtle, though." She closed her eyes in a spasmodic grimace of pain. "And I wouldn't do it if there were any other way. But *I* couldn't control thirty-eight. Not if my life depended on it."

"There were *five* of them," he reminded her, "and half of those thirty-eight were kids, and not too bloody likely to run away from their parents. That's seventeen adults to control, and you can bet they only used psi-coercion on the ones that were *likely* to bolt. Say, half of the seventeen. What does that bring the total down to?"

"Nine-ish." She gave him a look that said she wanted to hope that he was right, but was afraid to.

"*Less* than two each," he persisted, laying a hand on her arm, with a gesture he hoped would steady her. "Whatcha think, Pancho?"

Ramirez nodded thoughtfully. "Makes sense to me," he agreed, rubbing his chin. "I mean, I don't know squat about this stuff, but stands to reason if they were good enough to put the whammy on thirty-eight people, Di, they'd have squashed you like a bug last night."

"And they didn't," Mark asserted. "Did they."

"No—they didn't even try to hurt me or someone connected with me. They got that kraut reporter instead." She was standing a little straighter, and losing some of that haunted expression. "What's more, they didn't cross my protections; they didn't even try. Maybe they couldn't. Maybe I am still their equal. I think—you might be right."

Mark heaved a mental sigh of relief. "How 'bout we get away from here—get somewhere you can think?"

She nodded, and unfolded her arms. He took the hand nearest him and gave it a brief squeeze before dropping it.

"Look on the bright side," he said, guiding her toward the car with one hand lightly on her forearm. "We're clear for another three weeks—"

"Sure," she agreed somberly, as Ramirez parted from them to trudge across the worn asphalt to his own vehicle. "And then it begins again—*worse* than this."

Di had never been one to use drugs as a crutch—but she was glad of the emergency one-pill stash of Valium in her purse. She needed more than herb tea to calm her nerves after the revelations of this morning. It was dangerous to be tranked—but far more dangerous to be on a hair trigger and ready to break if someone sneezed. When the pill took hold it steadied her enough to cope, but left her still pretty well in control of psi-senses and shielding.

I daren't try a levinbolt—but hopefully I won't need to use one until after the pill wears off. Okay—reality check. She took a careful accounting of herself. *I'll be okay. I'm wired enough that it isn't making me fuzzy or shutting me down, just getting me a little unwired. But no more after this one wears off.*

She parted from Mark at headquarters, but only after giving him

the address she was going to be seeking. If she didn't show up at the
university by the time his appointment with Professor Jermaine came
due—

Hopefully they wouldn't have to worry about that. But after last
night, she was taking no more stupid chances.

She was headed once again for the *barrio* and the home of the
bruja. And this time she was armed with more than mere words.

The bus was jammed full; noisy, hot, and full of diesel fumes. The
fumes gave her a headache, and she was literally squashed up against
the window. She leaned her forehead against the window-glass, unfo-
cusing her vision and shutting her ears, and delicately probed at the
minds around hers, looking for danger, for hidden enemies.

For there must have been one of those unknown enemies on the
bus last night, following her—and she had been too inward-turned
to pick him or her out of the crowd. She would not make that mistake
again.

There was nothing and no one to set off her internal alarms. Not
a hint of magic, not a trace of anything other than the normal flick-
ers of almost-psi encountered in any crowd.

But that did not mean she dared relax her vigilance.

*Ogoun told me to be wary; I didn't take the warning seriously
enough. Some "warrior" I am! Oh André—I wish you were here—*

She sighed, and rubbed the sweat-slick skin of her forehead between her eyebrows with her index finger. *If wishes were fishes we'd
eat for a year. Thank the gods—I get off at the next stop.*

She reached up for the signal cord and managed to yank it without disturbing the old lady dozing in the seat next to her. The woman
woke as she slid out, but only gave her a kind of half-smile, and settled back into her nap.

The driver glared at her as she passed him, as if he resented having to stop. She jumped down off the bus and the driver nearly closed
the door on her heels, taking off again with a surly and completely
unnecessary reving of the engine. She coughed and wrinkled her
nose in the resulting cloud of fumes; her eyes burned and watered in
the acrid smoke.

The *bruja's* apartment was not more than a few feet from the bus
stop; but this time Di climbed the linoleum-covered stairs to the
fourth floor alone. And found herself standing before the worn
wooden door for the second time in less than twenty-four hours.

But this time—this time I'm prepared.

She knocked softly and heard the approach of footsteps on the
other side of the door. Even if she hadn't heard the footsteps she'd

have known there was someone there; the feeling of *presence* was that strong. She waited then, waited for several minutes, *feeling* eyes upon her.

I am not *going away, señora*, she thought grimly. *I'll park out here all afternoon if I have to.*

At length the door creaked open, slowly, reluctantly.

"Señorita," the widow said, her tone as flat and expressionless as her face.

"Señora Montenegro—" Di replied firmly, "I would not have chosen to disturb you, but many things have happened since last night that I think you must learn of."

Once again the widow led the way to the two benches in the room that held her altar—and the feeling Di got from her was still one of fear, with a faint hint of hope that something about the room would make Di go away.

It isn't going to work, Di projected. *I need you and I need what you know.* She settled onto the unforgiving seat of one of the benches, and the widow perforce took the other, reluctantly.

Then Di pulled the photos taken at Possum Kingdom Park out of her purse.

It took only one—the pictures supplied by the Forensics team were in full color and merciless in their detail. Señora Montenegro folded within seconds. Just the one picture did it—the one of the six-year-old girl still twisted in her death-agonies. . . .

The *bruja* moaned with anguish after that one glance, and pushed Di's hand away.

"No more—*por favor*—" she begged, her eyes filling with tears. "Señorita, you are right, I am wrong. Please, show me no more."

Di took pity on her, and shoved the rest of the two-dozen photos she had yet to display back in her purse. She was quite willing not to have to look at them again herself.

"So?" she said, making the word a demand for information.

The widow looked about her, furtively, as if she suspected unfriendly ears in her own living room. "There *is* a *brujo*," she said, almost too softly to hear. "A most evil *brujo*. He is calling upon ancient magic, forbidden magic. He has been among us since the Feast of the Resurrection."

"Last spring, then," Di translated. The widow nodded, fearfully, her black eyes still scanning the room. And she was using more than her eyes to scan for enemies, Di sensed.

"He has not sought followers—not until very recently. He calls upon those of the *indios*, the Mestizo—always of the pure, or nearly pure blood. He promises much power, and the magic that only death and blood can fuel. And they answer him; more every day, especially the young *bravos*." She twisted her hands together on her lap, the beads of her ebony rosary tangled in her work-roughened fingers.

"Why?" Di asked, baffled. "I can't imagine gang members going in for *that*. Not magic—"

The *bruja* shook her head. "Indeed, no, not *brujiera*. Not *my* way, the uncertain and slow—no, no. Not the magic that does not always answer to the caller. But this one—it is said that *his* magic does not fail, not ever. And it is said that he promises great things, a new age for those who will follow him; he promises that a day will come *soon* when he will call forth an army and they shall slay the oppressors with their new powers of magic and take the land back from them."

Di felt her eyes widening. *Good gods—that sounds exactly like the line Johnnie Mountainhawk told Mark about—*

The woman was continuing. "This is the last that I know—I have felt his power calling me, and it is like a sickness in the blood, like the craving for drug or drink. At first he took only the eager, but now—it may be that he can claim all of the old blood. It may be that the Mestizo *must* answer now, his power grows so great."

"Who is he?" Di asked the obvious question.

The *bruja* shook her head. "I have not answered to his calling, so I do not know what this *brujo* names himself. I only know that *my* magic tells me that he is all that he claims, I can feel it in the part of me that wishes to answer the calling. And one thing more—"

Di waited, while the woman took a deep breath and whispered the last bit of information.

"He has caused the word to be sent forth that he is nearly ready, this one. And the word is that the rising shall be within the next pair of months."

"This is a *remarkable* photograph, young man," the professor said, staring at Mark over the top edge of it. His white mane stood out sharply against the dark bindings of the books crammed into the bookshelf that ran floor-to-ceiling on the wall behind his desk. "Rather *too* remarkable."

Mark sighed. It had taken him most of the afternoon to finally get in to see Professor Jermaine, and now the man was treating him like he was some kind of fraud.

"Professor, you've seen my credentials—"

The crusty old fart waved a dismissing hand at him, and the little breeze he raised stirred some of the nest of papers spread untidily all over his desk. "Really, young man, don't you think I've had pranks played on me before? Of course your credentials *look* genuine; so does your badge. The more elaborate the hoax, the better the props—"

There was a slight, hesitant tap, and the professor's secretary poked her mousy head in the door. "Professor, a Miss Tregarde is here," she said diffidently. "She says you were expecting her with Mr. Valdez."

"You might as well show her in too," the irascible old man grumbled, setting the photograph down and shoving it across the desk to Mark. "Might as well have all the jolly tricksters in one place."

The secretary vanished; Di opened the door wider and strode through it, wearing a certain air of confidence. Mark heaved a sigh of relief that he didn't bother to conceal. Now that Di was here—he saw that she'd donned her "successful professional" suit, and realized that she had probably dealt with characters like Jermaine before this. She'd know how to handle this old SOB. Mark had been feeling sorely out of his depth.

"Professor Jermaine?" she began—then took a long look at the professor's rather cynical expression.

"Doctor Jermaine is convinced we're trying to play an elaborate April Fool's joke on him a couple months too early," Mark said sourly, taking back the color photo of the swatch of brocade.

She cocked her head to one side and her face went unreadable. Her stance changed entirely, became challenging. "Oh, really?" Her tone was as dry as the professor's. "And just *why* would we be playing a prank on him when *neither* of us are students here?"

"Heavens, *I* don't know," Professor Jermaine replied, a little flustered that she had gone on the offensive. "For all I know you've been hired by—"

"The Dallas police?" she interrupted sarcastically, crossing her arms and giving him a cynical glare of her own. "If you were *really* interested in finding out if we were on the level, all you'd have to do would be to have your secretary call Homicide. Obviously you aren't interested in anything except saving some of your precious time. Obviously you have no intention of helping us. Come on, Mark." She crooked a finger at him. "I think I can possibly talk Carolyn Reseune into identifying this for us. The photo should fax all right—"

"Carolyn Reseune?" The professor reacted to *that* name the way a bull reacts to a matador's cape. He rose abruptly out of his chair; his voice rose as he did. "*Doctor* Carolyn Reseune? Of Yale?"

Mark had started to leave his own chair, now he settled back, re-pressing a smirk. Di had the professor well and truly hooked.

"I don't know of any other Carolyn Reseune," Di replied acidly. "I know she's busy, but she knows me; she knows I don't waste my time or anyone else's on stupid pranks. I suspect she'll make some time for me."

"But—" The professor's voice rose another octave, as he protested the wisdom of her decision. "—she specializes in *Incan* work—she couldn't *possibly*—dammit, *give* me that photograph!" He leaned over the desk and snatched it out of Mark's hand.

Di fixed the professor with a needle-like stare. "Do I take it that you've changed your mind?"

The professor just grumbled, and rummaged in the clutter on his desk for a magnifying glass. Di took the chair beside Mark's without invitation, settling herself into it and taking a position that said as much in body language as a book the size of any of the tomes on the archeologist's desk could have. Everything, from the way her legs were crossed to the way she held her head, was a challenge; her whole posture was saying, "All right, you old fraud—prove to me you aren't wasting *my* time now!"

After a few minutes' scrutiny, he looked up from the photo, stab-bing the both of them with a calculating glance of his own.

"Where's the garment this came from?" he asked, his voice full of sharp-edged overtones. "I need to see it!"

"I would say that only two people are likely to know that," Mark replied politely. *If Di is going to play "bad cop." I'm only too happy to play "good cop."* "The first is the owner, and the second is rather dead."

"And just why do you need to see it?" Di asked on the heels of Mark's statement, her tone still conveying impatience and annoyance.

"Young lady, the patterns woven into this scrap are patterns that have not been *seen* since the days of the Conquistadors!" he ex-claimed. "No one—certainly no modern weaver—knows how to produce them! Great good God, no modern weaver *would* produce them even if they knew how, it would be sacrilege bordering on in-sanity to reproduce the sacred garments reserved for Tezcatlipoca and his priestesses! It could *only* bring the weaver and the wearer the worst of misfortune!"

"Who?" Mark asked, bewildered by the strange name.

"Tezcatlipoca," the professor repeated impatiently. And at Mark's look of blank incomprehension, translated, even more impatiently, "Smoking Mirror."

Mark shook his head, still not understanding.

"The Aztec god of war and warriors," the professor explained with a sigh of exasperation.

Mark could literally *see* the light go on inside Di's head, but didn't want to wait for enlightenment. "Look, I'm just a dumb cop," he replied. "Can you tell me more about this Smoking Mirror?"

"He was the especial god of the Aztecs and of their capital city," Professor Jermaine began, and visibly thawed at the intense interest in Mark's face. "His symbol was the 'tiger'—actually, the jaguar; *'el tigre'* is a misnomer. His sacred time of day was the afternoon—the descending sun. His particular feast took place in April, nearly the same time as our own Easter, but he permeated the entire sacrificial year and presided as chief priest over many of the other sacrifices in the person of a young man, a kind of Chosen One or avatar. This Chosen One in his turn was sacrificed at Smoking Mirror's feast, and resurrected again immediately in the body of another Chosen One. It was really a very unusual ritual for the Aztecs in that the Chosen One was quite often a volunteer, and at this particular sacrifice, which was the culmination of their ritual year, there was only the *single individual* as sacrifice instead of the multitude of victims normally put to the knife."

"Why was that?" Mark asked.

"Because the Chosen One was *literally* Tezcatlipoca himself," the professor answered warmly. Mark's unwavering interest was obviously flattering to his ego. "He was treated all year long with all the honor and deference given the god—he was given four of the most beautiful virgins in the city to be his priestesses and handmaidens, and feasted and pleasured during his entire reign. So for the Aztecs, the man *was* the god, and the special god who had chosen them as his people."

"I thought the chief Aztec god was Quetzalcoatl," Di said slowly.

The professor shook his head vigorously. "A common misconception. Quetzalcoatl was the titular deity of the Toltecs, the people who preceded the Aztecs in the region. The Aztecs incorporated Quetzalcoatl into their pantheon, but as Smoking Mirror's brother and subordinate; in fact, in their mythology, the Smoking Mirror is the Feathered Serpent's implacable enemy and his ultimate destroyer."

This was beginning to make more and more sense. *This Burning Water—he must have set himself up as a priest of this Tezcat—whatsis, and he's using the old Aztec rites mixed up with* brujiera. *If we can*

*match the timing of these things, we'll have every correspondence we
need for a positive match.*

"What kind of calendar were the Aztecs on?" Mark asked carefully.

"Nothing like ours," Professor Jermaine said. "They had an eigh-
teen-month cycle, with each month being about three weeks long—
twenty days, if you want to be precise about it. There were major and
minor sacrifices at each month-end feast. Let's see, the last ones
would have been—" he reached behind him without seeming to look
and pulled a book down from the shelf and flipped it open. "—ah—
about three weeks ago would have been the Feast of Tlaloc. The major sacrifice would have been children, mostly. Following that—in
fact, it's only just over—was Xipe-Totec, the Flayed One."

"What *kind* of sacrifices are you talking about?" Mark asked. "I'd
like more than generalities, if you would."

The professor raised an eyebrow. "They *aren't* for the
squeamish—" For the first time, he smiled. "Foolish of me—you *did*
say you were from Homicide, didn't you. Well, the central sacrifice to
Tlaloc was designed to determine how long it would be before the
rains began; the priestess would paint the sacrificial children with
rubber-tree sap, and the priest would hold them underwater until
they drowned. How many breaths it took for them to die would tell
them how many weeks it would be until the rains."

Mark nearly exploded then and there—the details of the three
drowned children had *not* been released to the press. There was no
way the professor could have described their murders so accurately
unless he was detailing some rite that really *had* existed.

The professor continued. "The next one, the Feast of Xipe-Totec,
was one where the major sacrifice was flayed alive and the priest
donned the skin and danced in it at every other sacrifice during the
feast. Particularly grim, that one. Some sacrifices were half-burned
before being killed, and the whole thing culminated in a kind of can-
nibal feast."

As the professor continued, Mark could hear Di muttering under
her breath. "Aztecs!" she breathed angrily. "Why the *hell* didn't I think
of Aztecs?"

He was a little stunned.

The professor consulted his book further, oblivious to her mut-
terings. "The next would be the second most important rite in the
year, next to the sacrifice of Tezcatlipoca himself. And it's another one
where the man-god presides personally."

He looked up at Mark, obviously wanting to be coaxed into revealing his erudition. Mark obliged him by leaning forward with an

eagerness he did *not* have to feign, until he was sitting on the very edge of his hard chair.

"Yes?" he breathed encouragingly.

"Well, it's the Corn Goddess, and she bears several striking resemblances to John Barleycorn and the old Corn Kings," the professor said with unconcealed satisfaction. "She's a bit like Smoking Mirror in that she is supposed to die and be reborn. They would pick a woman who had borne at least one child—the fertility assured, as it were. Then they'd set her to weaving, making her own garments for her ultimate sacrifice. They had to be pure white, absolutely, no colored patterns at all, which for the Aztecs was practically unheard of. On the appropriate day Tezcatlipoca would present her to the multitude. Then with his own hand he would slay her—and he had to get as little blood as possible on the white of the garments. Then he would go into the temple and ceremonially flay the body—a little like the Xipe-Totec rite, except that the flaying was done after death, rather than before—then reappear clothed in her skin *and* her garments, denoting that the corn had gone into the earth and been reborn as the young corn plant. That it would be Tezcatlipoca that performed all this himself shows that it was considered almost as important a rite as Smoking Mirror's own."

Di shook her head. "All I ever knew about the Aztecs was the Feathered Serpent cult—"

"In the time of the Aztecs," the professor said firmly, "that's *all* it was; a cult. A very degraded and debased form of the Toltec rites. The Toltecs practiced a *kind* of blood-sacrifice, but it was their *own* blood they shed, like the priests of Cybele that castrated themselves, or the medieval monks who went in for flagellation until their backs bled. Shedding one's own blood was an act of will, of willingness to sacrifice one's own earthly self to one's higher self, and a kind of self-purification. When the Aztecs first arrived, they were *not* the powerful conquering army they later claimed to be; rather they were a rather barbarous, seminomadic tribe. Warlike, yes, but hardly capable of conquering the Toltecs."

"But—how could they take over?" Mark asked, now quite interested on his own.

"The simplest way of all; they insinuated themselves among the Toltec culture and conquered by subversion. You can trace that subversion by the gradual elimination of Quetzalcoatl as supreme deity and the substitution of Tezcatlipoca, and by the way in which self-sacrifice was replaced by the sacrificing of others."

He warmed to the subject; this was obviously his own pet theory.

"That was *why* the arrival of Cortez and his identification with Quetzalcoatl so alarmed and demoralized the Aztecs in general and the rulers in particular. The legends of Quetzalcoatl had always included a promise that he would return—and the Aztecs could *not* imagine him returning unless it was to conquer *them* as they had conquered the Toltecs. That might have been one reason why they never eradicated the Feathered Serpent cult—instead, they tried to *change* it so that it reflected *their* heritage. The writings, the records of the liturgy, had us puzzled for a long time; here were liturgical writings speaking of self-sacrifice and mercy, of self-abasement and peace—yet the actual rituals culminated in pain and agonizing death! *Then*, of course, we came upon the evidence that the Toltec had been absorbed into the Aztecs, that the Aztecs were *not* the first in the area, and everything became obvious."

"Professor," Di said when he paused for a breath, "are there *any* extant sources here at the university for the original *Toltec* rites?"

He pondered her question for a moment. "Well—*my* specialty is the Aztec culture, so I'm only peripherally interested in the Toltecs they replaced—but I think we have a fair collection of codex reproductions and translations in the library stacks."

"I *need* to get at them," she said, urgently, locking her eyes with his.

He looked at her with mild surprise. "Is it that important?"

She nodded, slowly, grimly. "We can't tell you everything, professor, but it is *very* important. The two of us are assigned to the 'Texas Ripper' case."

He was rather taken aback. "Well—I never thought I'd see the day when the police needed the advice of an old pot-hunter. Here—" he rummaged in his desk for two slips of pink paper, then scribbled his name on both. "—here are passes to the stacks for both of you. Am I right in assuming that madman the papers have been calling the 'Texas Ripper' has been using Aztec rites?"

It was Mark's turn to nod. "So closely that you inadvertently described things we didn't let out when you were talking about Tlaloc and—the one that sounded like 'Ziplock bag'—"

"Xipe-Totec," the professor answered, looking a bit stunned.

"And so far as we can tell, whoever this is has the timing down to correspond exactly to the Aztec calendar and no other."

Professor Jermaine could only shake his head. "If that is indeed the case—knowing what I know about the callousness and bloodthirst of the Aztecs themselves—I can only say, may God help you. Because you will need that help."

"Those bastards had me blocked but *good*," Di said as they left the building that held the professor's office. Her expression was still fairly neutral—but her eyes held a sullen, if suppressed, fury. "I never even thought of Aztecs, and it should have been obvious."

"Are you freed up now?" he asked anxiously.

She nodded. "Once I got shook loose, I shook everything off. I can see things now—it's like getting the keypiece of the jigsaw puzzle. Another thing, Mark, Johnnie Mountainhawk is right. The *bruja* told me about an Indian sorcerer that's calling for an Indian rebellion. *She* told me that she's felt his power, and she's something of a clairvoyant, enough to have identified the prime signature aura from the murders last night as *him*. She didn't know his name or what he calls himself—"

"Firm bet that it's Johnnie's Burning Water."

"That's a sucker bet if ever I heard one." She contemplated the stacks pass in her hand. "So what we have here looks like somebody setting himself up as the new priest of Tezcatlipoca; appropriate for a radical militant."

"Uh-huh, that's exactly what I thought," Mark agreed. "Probably originally a *brujo*, then began researching the origins of the rituals as he became more militant and radical."

"*Then*, once he tapped into the *original* rituals, discovered that he had the equivalent of a magical tactical nuke if he could build up enough power and believers." She chewed her lip a little. "From what we heard in there, and what the *bruja* told me—Mark, she says the word on the street is that the sorcerer is going to make his move some time within the next two months."

"We don't have much time—"

"No. And my guess is that he's probably planning on timing his uprising with an attempt to manifest Smoking Mirror. If he can actually pull it off—he'll have more than a tactical nuke at his disposal, he'll have enough power to play with to enable him to affect the physical world in very profound ways."

"Like what?"

"Like—think what could be done if the head of a guerilla force could call a storm *and direct the lightning*. Wherever, whenever he wanted."

"Like a direct hit on the main power station. Say, Friday night at about seven. The city would be paralyzed, helpless."

"And then—you felt the Hunter-in-the-dark. You know how

close it came to panicking *you*, and you were ready for it! Imagine all those helpless people trapped in the dark—then exposed to *that*. At a powerful enough level, he could make the Hunter physical enough so that even normals could perceive it and feel its hunger."

"Good God!" he exclaimed, stunned by the thought. "That would be like—yelling 'fire' at the circus!"

"Exactly so. Neither he nor the Hunter would have to *do* anything; people would kill each other in panic. By dawn the city would be depopulated." She shook her head. "Well, he's *not* there yet, and it's up to us to see he doesn't *get* there. I think we're going to have to split up again. To be brutally frank, love, you never were much of a scholar."

"No argument from me," he said agreeably, comfortably certain that she couldn't come to any harm in the university library—*especially* in the stacks, where entry was restricted. "Tell you what, why don't I see if I can get hold of Johnnie while you do your thing?"

"It's a deal," she nodded. "Come fetch me around seven?"

"Seven it is."

THIRTEEN

This week Charlie had been switched to first shift—which meant he was home now. Mark pulled the Ghia up to the first working pay phone he spotted, a booth nestled in to the side of the bus shelter, figuring he'd better call before he descended on his friends. He squinted into the setting sun while the answering machine played its recording at him. It was kind of unnerving to hear his own voice snarling at him from the handset.

"Guys?" he said when the thing beeped at him. "It's Mark Valdez. Can I—"

He heard the *click* of the receiver being lifted. "Mark?" It was Doreen, and she sounded quite definitely shaken up. "Mark, are you on your way over? Please tell me you're on your way over!"

"Yeah 'Reenie—" he replied, straightening from his slump, alarmed at the frantic tone of her voice. "What's wrong? Is Charlie—"

"No, it's not Charlie, it's Johnnie, and I can't explain it, you'll have to see for yourself. Only, please, Mark, hurry!"

She hung up; he hardly looked to see if the handset connected with the cradle—he just threw it in place, and sprinted back to the Ghia, heart in his throat.

It was almost dark when he got there; the Mountainhawk apartment was clear across town from the university, and he'd bent more than a few laws to get there as quickly as he had. Doreen answered the doorbell almost as soon as he pushed it; he rather suspected she must have been lurking at the front hall, waiting. A cop's wife learns to cover her negative expressions pretty quickly, but there was panic in Doreen's eyes, raw panic, and bewilderment.

Before he could say or do anything, she just grabbed his arm and pulled him down the dark hall into the back bedroom, in so much of a hurry that she didn't even bother to flip on the hall light as she passed the switch.

The only light there was back *here* was coming from the overhead fixture, and only one of the three bulbs it held was working. They didn't use this room very often, and there wasn't much in the room; Mark had figured all along that they were going to save it for a nursery. About the only furniture was a massive cast-iron bedstead, an antique that they used for guests. It weighed a ton; Mark knew that only too well, since he'd helped wrestle it up here when they moved in.

His back still hurt when he thought about it.

The light was dim, but there still wasn't much to look at—the bed was still about the only piece of furniture. Charlie was sitting on the edge of it; shoulders hunched, head in hands, looking drawn and exhausted.

Johnnie Mountainhawk was on the floor beside the headboard, looking twice as exhausted. He leaned against the mattress, his head pillowed in the crook of one elbow, the other arm draped clumsily over his head. He was *handcuffed* to the bedframe, sagging against the pull of the cuffs on his wrists.

"What the *hell*?" Mark exploded.

Somewhat to his surprise it was Johnnie who answered him, opening eyes that had purple circles beneath them. "I asked him to cuff me, Mark. It was the only way I could keep from following the thing that was calling me."

"*Huh?*"

"There's this—thing in my head. It wants me to go to it. Every so often it drives me crazy and I start to answer—"

Mark flashed then on some of what Di had told him about her second meeting with the *bruja*; about how the woman had told her that Burning Water was calling everyone of Indian or Mestizo blood. Presumably what she had *really* meant was that he was "calling"—using psychic coercion—those who could "hear" him, those with psychic gifts of their own. Charlie was one of those, but Di had put him under shielding, so he was safe—

Gifts *tended* to run in families, though. It looked like Johnnie shared Medicine Power with his brother and grandfather. And Johnnie was *not* shielded.

So Johnnie was right up this bastard's alley.

Mark clenched his jaw. *Like Hell! Not without a fight from* me! *But—*

Was there anything he *could* do? Mark knew warding—but that was meant for a *place*, not a person. And he didn't know if warding would work against something that was not an attack or an attempt to invade.

"How long have you been fighting this thing?" he asked.

"Since last night; it comes and goes," Johnnie replied wearily. "Just a damn good thing for me I was here when it hit. When I went zombie Charlie tackled me and Doreen knocked me out. When I came to, I told 'em to cuff me. It's better now, but when Charlie went off to work I nearly dislocated my shoulder trying to get loose."

"Mark," Charlie spoke for the first time, "you've been hanging around that psychic chick for a long time. Can you get hold of her? Can *you* do anything?"

"I probably can't get to Di right now—she's in the stacks at the university library, and she won't get any messages until she comes back to the desk. Which is going to be hours from now. The way you look—Johnnie, I don't think we have that much time."

Johnnie nodded unhappily. "I feel like I'm standing at the edge of a mental cliff; one or two more sessions and I may go bats permanently. But what about *you* doing something?"

"I'm thinking, I'm thinking." He tried to dredge up every fact he had picked up in the past few weeks since Di had started giving him theory-and-practice at his own request. "This—calling. I don't think it should be hitting you this hard. Di talked to a *bruja* this afternoon—*she* said Burning Water was calling in Indian and Mestizo psychics, but he wasn't getting to her *nearly* so strongly. Unless— unless they have a way of getting at you, specifically."

Okay; what laws could be applying here—Knowledge? Don't think so, nobody would know Johnnie that well, except maybe his own kin. That lets out the Law of Names too. And Words of Power; Cherokee is different enough from Aztec that the power words would differ. Synthesis and Identification are out; those are for acquiring power, not what's going on here. Balance; hardly. But—Association or Contagion—we might have an answer here.

"What's the chance somebody in that lunatic fringe that's been talking about the Great Red Hope could have gotten hold of something of yours or something that's been around you?" he asked Johnnie.

"Pretty good," he replied soberly. "I'm the original 'lose your head if it wasn't fastened on'; right, Charlie?"

"Worse, little brother—I see what Cisco's getting at. *You had a cold last week*. Remember?"

"Shit, yes! Scattering Kleenex behind me like snowflakes, and filling every wastebasket in town."

"I'd bet the Laws of Contagion and Association are in effect, here," Mark said. " 'What was part of you is always part of you.' And given how strong the pull is on you, I'd put money on the notion that while they are casting a general call-in spell, they've added a specific on top of it for anybody they could get artifacts for that they wanted to recruit."

"How come *I* don't feel it?" Charlie asked. "Given those phone calls and Granddad's warnings, they want me pretty bad. It would have been pretty easy to get something of *mine*."

"*You're* shielded," Mark pointed out. "Johnnie's not. Besides, get him and they're bound to get you. No?"

"Yeah," Charlie replied sourly. "And much as I hate to admit it, if they called me up saying they had him, I'd act like any moron on the tube and go charging in after him."

"Mark, can you do *anything*?" Doreen begged.

"I'm still thinking." He closed his eyes. *Even if I could shield, and I can't, it probably wouldn't do any good because shields don't necessarily block what's already there and they've got a line to his mind alr—*

—wait a minute; hold that thought—

They've got a line to his mind already. They've got a line to his mind. A line—

Di said those lines are psychically tangible; they can be seen and felt at both ends. I wonder; Aztec magic and Cherokee magic are both Indian magic. Maybe I could use Cherokee to force Aztec to release one of Cherokee magical lineage, 'cause Aztec wouldn't have a real claim. And to sever a line—

You cut it. You cut a line—with an edged weapon, like Di cut the line between me and the thing in Quasi's living room. But it would have to be a magically charged weapon. I don't have one, and I'll bet Charlie doesn't know how to fire one up—

—fire one up. Fire one up. Fire!

"Charlie, do your folk have some way of starting a kind of *sacred* fire?" he asked, hoping that the answer would be in the affirmative.

Charlie gave him a strange glance. "Yeah," he said slowly.

Good; holy things always *have identical arcane counterparts, Di said. The act of blessing creates the counterpart.* "Okay; the sixty-four-dollar question. Can *you*?"

"I—" He hesitated.

Mark could sympathize with the hesitation; he *was* an outsider. But this wasn't the time for secrecy. "Look, you want me to help, or don't you?"

Charlie sighed. "Yes. I can."

"All right then. I'm going to tell you what to do, but *you're* going to have to do it. I'd like to do this myself; I can't, my talent isn't going to do any good here. You said you've got 'spirit vision'; okay, use it. I'm betting you're going to see a kind of line, or rope, or something like that, leading off in the direction Johnnie's being pulled—"

Charlie sat a little straighter on the edge of the bed, and stared at the general area his brother occupied. His eyes went unfocused and blank; his brow creased and Mark held his breath, afraid to distract him even a little.

"I—see it," he said slowly, in what was very close to a whisper.

"Good," Mark replied just as softly. "Now, this is what you're going to have to do. Charlie, you have to start one of your sacred fires and *burn through* that tie. Johnnie—*you* have to totally disavow any connection with whatever's on the other end of that tie—otherwise they'll just be able to reestablish it. That sounds easy—I can promise you that it won't be. It's going to take tremendous concentration—and the tie is as much physical as it is mental."

"Which means?" Johnnie Mountainhawk asked, shaking sweat-damp hair out of his eyes.

"I can't predict what the effect of burning the tie will be—I only know that there *will* be a physical side to it. We're going to try something I'm still a sorcerer's apprentice with, and I don't know what the side effects are."

"We all ready?"

Charlie nodded nervously; he had a single stick in his hand; fire licked sluggishly at one end. It was a makeshift torch made of a piece of two-by-four wrapped with oily rags. Doreen had had to turn off the smoke detectors after they'd set them off twice trying to get it lit. Charlie had *not* allowed Mark to actually watch the lighting of the sacred fire—he was rather touchingly relieved that Mark hadn't been offended.

"Johnnie?" Mark made the name a question, turning to where the younger brother sat, held to the bedframe by only one cuff. He was seated in the middle of a warded circle chalked on the carpet of the room, a circle Mark hoped would protect him from some of the unknown "side effects."

"About as ready as I'll ever be."

"Okay—" Mark looked from one brother to the other, and hoped he knew what he was doing "—let's do it."

Mark got up from the bed and seated himself on the floor behind Johnnie, within the circle. Charlie advanced on the (to Mark) invisible line, with no sign that he might be feeling that this was ridiculous.

That was exactly what Mark was hoping for—as Di had told him at least a hundred times—in magic, *belief* was half the power. Both Charlie and his brother *believed* in this; and as long as they believed, it would work.

He hoped.

Within seconds, he had proof that it *was* working.

As Charlie reached out with the smoking torch, it suddenly flared up; now it was a clear, steady flame nearly a foot tall, and colored a bright blue-white, like an oxyacetylene torch—and Johnnie screamed in mortal agony.

Mark moved with the speed of a striking tiger; grabbing the younger Mountainhawk before he could begin fighting the cuff, gripping Johnnie's shoulders, and holding him steady. "It's *not you*. Johnnie—it's *not you*. Deny what hurts! Say it! Say it!" He continued to hold Johnnie's shoulders as the young man fought the pain that blocked his voice, fought to concentrate—he was *willing* Johnnie to regain control, to deny that what was being destroyed and what it led to was or had ever been a part of him.

"It's—not—me." Johnnie gasped out each word, fighting around the pain that made the muscles of his neck stand out like bridge cables, and forced his back and shoulders into an involuntarily arc. "It's—not—*mine!*"

With that last word, Johnnie threw his arms wide—and Charlie uttered a cry of triumph.

Charlie snuffed the torch in the bucket of water Doreen had brought from the bathroom, as Johnnie sagged back into Mark's hands and dropped his arms. Then Charlie was on his knees beside his brother, unlocking the cuffs.

And Mark knew that this time, in *this* battle, their side had won.

Di was startled entirely out of the book she was skimming by a sound—

—where no sound should be.

She suppressed the desire to sneeze; suppressed even the sniff she *almost* made. She was alone in the stacks; entirely alone, for the librarian had given her the only key. Therefore there *could* be no one else here.

Except that the sound came again, soft, but unmistakable. A footstep.

Internal alarms shrilled, even as she was closing the book, warning her of danger; deadly, and as near as the next breath.

And something brushed against the edges of her shields, testing them.

She set the book down on the metal shelf before her so softly that she did not even disturb the dust, and stilled even her breath, forcing her awareness and concentration into her senses and toughening her shields to one step below battle-ready.

This was no place to meet danger; all about her were the towering gray-metal bookshelves of the stacks, a veritable maze of them. There was no room for her to meet a physical attack, either close-in or a shooting match—there wasn't enough room to use karate, and all that metal made ricochets a dangerous probability.

But when she'd come in here, she'd followed one of her favorite mottos—"know where all the exits are"—almost without thinking about it. So she knew that to her left and two rows down from this, at the very end of the row, there *was* an exit. It wasn't one of those that led into the library, though—it was one of the fire exits that led to the roof.

She heard a soft whisper of sound, as if someone had inadvertently brushed against the spine of a protruding book; it sounded nearer than the footstep had. That decided her.

Cursing the necessity that had her wearing a suit instead of her usual jeans, she carefully slipped off her shoes and stowed them in her purse. Pulling the bag off her shoulder, she made a loop in the strap and slipped it over her wrist, closing her hand in a fist over the strap. Now she had a weapon of some reach; one that could, in fact, be slung with no little velocity into someone's face, if the need came. She eased her way along the bookshelf, stopping every time she came to a join and crouching to pass below line-of-sight, so that she wouldn't flicker the light that leaked between each bookcase. When she reached the end of the row, she crouched again to peer around it. She was *not* going to use her arcane abilities to probe ahead of her; not after that little brush by her shields. That would be as bad—and as stupid—as shouting her location. She had no illusions about avoiding a confrontation; she just wanted it to be on ground of *her* choosing.

The way was clear; she sprinted for the door, easing it open and shut again, then began the run up the staircase to the flat roof of the library.

The stairs were metal—and anyone in shoes was going to make a racket on them; even sneakers would make some kind of sound. She strained her ears behind her, but heard nothing by the time she reached the locked door that led to the roof.

The lock itself was no challenge; it wasn't even a deadbolt, it was the kind a kid could open with a credit card. Which was exactly what *she* did.

Unfortunately *this* door wasn't opened too often; its hinges shrieked in three separate keys, like three damned souls, and the screams echoed down the staircase and back up again with ear-piercing shrillness.

"Dammit!" she cursed, scooting through the door, then getting shoes and gun out of her purse and slamming the door behind her. *Well, he knows where I am now. Could have been worse, I guess. I could have set off an alarm, and gotten innocents into the line of fire.*

The tar-and-gravel-covered roof was *no* place for bare feet; she got her shoes back on and secured her purse around her waist by slipping it over her shoulders and cinching the strap like a belt. If it came to an arcane fight there were things she needed in there. . . .

It was a moonless night, but not dark; enough light was reflecting from the clouds and coming up from the streetlights for her to be able to see quite well once her eyes adjusted. She ran across the roof to a wind-turbine, one angled to the door, rather than straight ahead. Once there, she crouched in its slight shelter, and waited, gun in hand.

The door shrieked open; light poured from it. Something leapt out, almost too fast to make out—only that it was there one moment, and not there the next. It rolled into the shelter of another wind-turbine, and the door swung slowly shut of its own weight, seeming to scream even louder as it protested moving yet again.

Diana waited, gravel digging into her knee, but nothing happened.

Mexican standoff. In all senses, I suspect. Whose patience is better, buddy—yours, or mine?

She watched, and waited—and listened. There was no breeze tonight, so the only sound was coming from the air-conditioning plant behind the rooftop door and the elevator shaft behind them. Although *that* was enough; it covered just about any other sound anyone could produce, short of a gunshot or a shout.

After a considerable length of time had passed, a shadowy silhouette of a man rose from behind the structure, answering her question.

And as soon as he stood completely erect, his hands began to glow with a flickering orange light. He stood there for a moment, as the light strengthened and steadied, then drew a glyph in the air that flared redly and hung there for a full minute.

A challenge. One she dared not refuse.

She replaced the gun in her purse, and pulled out two rings and a necklace by feel, donning them even as she stood and moved away from the shelter of the wind-turbine. By the time she stood in the open, *her* hands were glowing as well—although the light was blue-violet, rather than orange. She answered his glyph with one of her own; green. It remained in the air a fraction of a second longer than his.

She couldn't *read* the meaning of his glyph, but she doubted that he could read hers, either. It was just the formal prelude to a duel arcane; challenge, acceptance.

This was *not* the chief *bruja*; she could sense it in the crude qualities of his shielding and the simplicity of the glyph he had drawn. *But he might well make up for lack of technique with sheer, raw power—*

She raised her shields to full just as he let fly a levinbolt that bid fair to prove her guess was right.

Glory—that one's so strong it's in the visible *range!* she thought, startled. The bolt hit her shield and actually penetrated a good bit before she could deflect it, splitting it up into a shower of harmless—and quite non-arcanely noticeable—sparks. She staggered back a little under the blow. *If he keeps that up, the normals are going to wonder who's shooting off fireworks up here!*

He evidently realized that himself, for the bolt that followed right behind it was apparent only to her Othersight. This one she did not deflect; she caught it and sent it hurtling back at him, following it with one of her own.

The first he captured and absorbed—

Damn. I was hoping he didn't know that trick.

The second staggered him, sent him stumbling back two or three steps before recovering.

He spread his hands wide, then clapped them together—and she had a split second to decide if the snarling thing with the head of a jaguar and the wings of a bird was an illusion or a real manifestation—

Because if she guessed wrong, the illusion could hurt her as much as the manifestation could, because she would *believe* it could.

But if she guessed that it was an illusion, and it was a

manifestation—it could penetrate her shielding and ravage her before she could turn it. *If* she could.

It was the complexity of the thing that convinced her that it was a manifestation—one who accidentally let fly a levinbolt that fluoresced in the visible range would never be able to control, much less build, an illusion that was so complex she could count the scales on its tail—

All this she decided in a fraction of a second, and reacted with a manifestation of her own; calling out of her left-hand jade-set ring the ally that wore the guise of a golden Imperial Dragon, and pulling on the power-pole on her right-hand amber ring to give it strength.

The two creatures met in the space between the two magicians. As the dragon fastened its claws into the serpentine body of the jaguar-bird-snake, Di felt a moment's rush of relief that her guess had been right.

But the jaguar opened its jaws in a soundless squall of fury, and sunk foot-long fangs into the dragon's neck. *Di* (as she knew she would) was the one who felt the pain.

She willed power to her ally, enduring what seemed to be the lacerating of her own throat; pain so real that the unwary would put a hand to the neck and expect it to come away red with blood.

And that was another trap; for if she allowed herself to believe *that*—it would happen.

For this was what was tested in a sorcerer's duel of manifestations: the testing of control, the testing of will, and the testing of concentration were as important as the manifestations themselves.

The dragon had wrestled the jaguar-creature to the ground, and was gaining the upper hand. The jaguar-creature responded with long, desperate rakes of its claws, trying to reach the dragon's belly.

But the belly of an Imperial Dragon is as well-armored as its back; the claws made no dent in the thick armor plates. The jaguar-creature bit at the dragon's legs, finding the weak place in the join of leg to body where there was no armor. Di bit back a cry of hurt and continued to will strength to her ally.

The jaguar twisted with the writhing of the dragon, trying to maintain its hold—and exposed its throat.

The dragon closed its jaws in a stranglehold on the jaguar's neck; and now the cat-snake-bird was no longer trying to attack, just escape.

Its struggles grew weaker—then ceased altogether.

The dragon threw back its head in a soundless roar of triumph, and vanished. The jaguar-creature faded out, dissolving slowly. Behind it, visible now, was the *brujo*, bent nearly double in pain and gasping for breath. Although he was scarcely more than a shadow, Di could *feel* his angry eyes on her. *Her* dragon would fight again, though the power she had expended to give it strength was gone until she could recharge the amber of her right-hand ring—but *he* had lost a valuable ally *and* a great deal of stored power.

In fact, he had lost enough so that the outcome of the duel was forgone, unless he had something extraordinary up his sleeve.

He did.

A gun.

Breaking the one and only rule of a duel arcane—*no physical weaponry*.

It was the glint of the streetlights on the blued metal of the barrel that warned Di, and just barely in time. She flung herself frantically back into the dubious shelter of her wind-turbine as his first shot rang out.

It ricocheted off the metal of the turbine, whining. Di fumbled in the purse at her waist for her own gun, and winced as a second shot rang out—

—and the magician crumpled to the asphalt of the roof.

Maybe Mark *wasn't* primarily a sensitive, but he figured he'd have had to be headblind altogether to miss the fireworks going on up on the roof of the library. A paranormal display like *that* could only mean one thing: Di had gotten cornered and forced into a magic duel.

Good God, that's the second *one this evening!* he thought in amazement, even as he whipped the Ghia into a parking space with a shriek of tires and a horrible stench of burned rubber. *Where are these guys coming from?*

Theoretically the fire escape that led from the roof couldn't be reached from the ground—but that was theory, and as any cop would, Mark knew better. Before too many minutes had passed, he was easing himself up the metal structure as noiselessly as he could.

Maybe she won't need me—he told himself—*but then again maybe she will. Might and right don't necessarily mean squat if the other guy decides to break the rules.*

The battle was mostly wasted on him; when he poked his nose over the edge of the low parapet surrounding the roof, all *he* saw were some amorphous swirls of colored light that were twining and twisting about each other in the space between the two magicians, and the back of a strange man. The guy near him was slowly doubling over in what looked like pain, though; and Di (at least he *thought* the shadow over on the other side of the roof was Di) wasn't, so he figured it must be going her way. Then the orange swirl sort of flattened out, the gold-colored one flared up, and vanished. And Mark saw the man before him reaching under his coat.

God damn! *I sure called that one!* he thought, as his own hand went for *his* piece, drew, and fired almost simultaneously with the stranger.

The man dropped like a stone—

And—that was wrong; Mark hopped up onto the roof and walked slowly toward the body, sorely puzzled.

I shot to wing *him, not ice him! My aim isn't* that *badly off!*

"Mark!" came a cry bright with relief and joy from the far side of the roof. He waved absently and advanced on the unmoving body.

Better be careful—he might be faking—

But no—

As Di came pelting up, he prodded the body—indisputably a body, there was *no* sign of life—with his toe.

"Damn—I didn't *mean* that," he said slowly, hardly aware that he was speaking.

Di was already on her knees beside the body. She did something then that she seldom *ever* did—she called up light—a ball of *visible* light—in the palm of her hand.

"You didn't *do* that," she said, finally. "Look for yourself."

And he did so, seeing with amazement what she had seen in the few moments before campus security came pounding up the staircase with a flashlight and she hurriedly extinguished the light.

There was *one* bullet-wound. In the gun-arm of the corpse.

And it showed no sign of blood whatsoever.

"Right," Mark said into the receiver, and hung up the phone.

He turned to Di, who was nursing a double Scotch, stretched out in one of his flip-chairs, which was half unflipped into a lounger.

"Seems I won't be facing a board in the morning after all," he said, not at all sure of what he was feeling, but quite sure that he wanted exactly what Di was drinking. He reached for the bottle on the stereo shelf and another glass, and poured himself one.

"Why?" she asked bluntly.

"Because I shot a corpse. Nothing in the rules covers that."

"You *what*?" she exclaimed, sitting bolt-upright—and not spilling a single drop of Scotch.

"I shot a corpse. The guy I shot—he wasn't American, he wasn't legal, and he wasn't alive when I shot him. Mexico City police say he was buried six months ago, Immigration says they have no records on him, and Forensics says he was cold meat when my bullet hit him. So I'm off the hook."

She stared at him, looked at her glass, took a *large* swallow, and stared at him again.

"Nobody's going to be saying anything about it," he continued. "It's too bizarre. The official word is that this one gets filed with the little green man cases and forgotten. The campus fuzz is former Fort Worth PD—he's agreed to keep his mouth shut. The Chief is *entirely* weirded out."

"That makes two of us," Di replied. "Zombies, I know; they're natural, and they're mindless. In no way would a zombie be able to handle magic on his own. This is a new one on me."

She settled back onto the backrest, crossing her arms—at least so much as holding the glass would permit—and took another large swallow.

"I'm still thinking," she said, finally. "I've been thinking ever since the professor shook my memories loose. You know the old phrase, 'What goes around, comes around'?"

"Yeah," he said, "I thought it was new, though."

She shook her head. "Old as the hills. Older. You know, arcane things, magic things, never just *stop*. They echo, sometimes for centuries. And—there's too much going on for all of this to be coincidence. Too damned many coincidences are piling up on top of each other. Like—was there any real reason for *you* to get interested in the Texas Ripper?"

"No," he replied, after taking a long moment to think. "Not really; I just felt like I needed to be in on it and I pushed real quietly until I got put on it."

"There's stuff going on here that has *got* to be echoes," she said. "And I would bet my hand that a lot of it ties in to you. It just feels that way."

Instead of denying that, Mark thought about it. "You know," he answered reluctantly, "I hate to say this, but I think you're right. It *does* feel that way."

"I have a proposition."

"Shoot."

"Your Prime is mediumism. There's a corollary to that—mediums very frequently are *quite* good at past-life regressions—"

"What, Bridey Murphy?" he laughed. "Come *on*—"

Diana Tregarde Investigates

She shook her head. "Let's leave poor Bridey out of this; it was a very *unscientifically* done study, and unfortunately it's thrown a pall over the whole notion. I've done some work along those lines that was a lot better, so I'm inclined to have it incorporated into *my* belief system. Thing is, I'll also keep an open mind on it—while I believe in recycling, I'm also willing to believe that what the regressed subjects are picking up is the memories of strong-minded individuals in the akashic record."

"The who?"

"Remember that I told you that there's another kind of collective memory—one that *does* go back to the caves?"

He nodded.

"That's the akashic record. You will also recall, I think, that I told you that *I* can't get at it without a whole elaborate song-and-dance act. And even then I'm not very good at it. Mediums, on the other hand, are—or else they're good at past-life regression. You pays your money, you takes your choice; the important thing is, it works the same no matter which you believe."

"So? Are you asking me—"

"To be the *victim*. I'm convinced this all dates back to the last days of the Aztec Empire. I'd like to regress *you* because I'm convinced you've got a former incarnation back then—or get you accessing the akashic record, whichever you prefer—and find out what the hell happened back then that links this all together."

He considered the proposition. It had a lot of merit.

"Any chance I could get—ah—*stuck* back there?"

"Not in my hands," she said. "I've done this too many times."

"Okay," he said, secretly a bit pleased that *she* was calling on *him* for help. "You're on."

The god was not pleased. Chimalman cowered beneath the lash of his anger. The metaphor was *not* figurative; although his anger would leave no *physical* signs, she felt the agony of one having the skin flayed from her back.

Finally his anger cooled enough to end the punishment.

"I told you to leave the witch *be*," he rumbled, sitting back into the furs of his throne. "I told you that if she drew too near, that you were to *kill* her, not challenge her!"

"Lord—"

"Five times a fool you are! Once—to be so proud as to leave your marks upon the last sacrifice. Twice—to decide that *you* were wiser than I, that the power of the sorcerers we have trained was greater than hers. Three times—to take the *best* of those *without my leave,* and goad him to challenge the witch. Four times—to *fail* to kill the witch when she began to win! And *five times*—to allow her to regain her memories and her mind!"

"Lord—"

"It was only by sheer good luck that I discovered what you had done and broke the spell that held him in life before they could question him!"

"Yes, Lord." Chimalman groveled a little more.

"Now it is too late; she is alerted, and we, *we,* are not strong enough to challenge her at her full strength." He brooded for another long moment, and his eyes glowed red with anger. Chimalman cowered, and awaited the descent of the sorcerous lash again.

"We must lie quietly; very, very quietly. In fifteen suns comes the sacrifice of the Corn Woman; that will bring us to full power, enough to defeat the witch. Until then there must be *nothing* to arouse her suspicion or her wrath." He stared down at the cowering handmaiden. *"Nothing!"*

"No lord," she quavered, trembling. "Nothing."

FOURTEEN

It took a week before they both felt ready to try the regression. Di needed to recharge after the duel arcane—badly. Although she hadn't let on, she'd been running on pure nervous energy until the moment Mark dropped her off at his Aunt Nita's.

She'd slept twenty-four hours straight, and so deeply that even her alarm clock going off in her ear hadn't awakened her.

After that she'd spent the next three days not only replacing the energy she had depleted, but bringing herself up to maximum energy charge. *Then* she'd spent three days in near-total isolation—"meditating," she'd said. Mark figured it was more complicated than that—but he also figured it was something along the line of religious secrets and had no wish to pry. One thing he did know: she'd spent at least part of those three days closeted with some of the Xeroxes she'd made at the university library.

Finally she'd gone over his apartment from top to bottom, first physically and non-arcanely cleaning the place (for which he was profoundly grateful), then purging it magically. She was taking no chances on *anything* going wrong—

And Mark wasn't feeling like arguing with her. After all, it was going to be *his* psyche on the line.

They decided that Mark's living room would be their "sanctuary" for the regression; it was where he felt the most comfortable and secure. Di could ward just about any place, so Mark's sensibilities took precedence.

"Scared?" Di asked Mark, easing herself down onto the carpet beside him.

"A little," he admitted, trying to find the most comfortable reclining position he could on the flip-chair which had been stretched out its entire length. Di had warned him that this was what he'd *better* do, since he might be spending a long time that way. "I've never been hypnotized before."

She half laughed. "That's what *you* think."

He twisted his head around so that he could see her; she was sitting in a very relaxed lotus position just behind the "pillow" of the chair. "What's that supposed to mean?"

"My turn at confession. I've had you under at least half a dozen times, my friend. Only I didn't tell you I was hypnotizing you; I told you I was putting you through a 'relaxation exercise.' You're such a good subject that after the first time all I had to do was use the trigger phrase on you, and *pop*"—she snapped her fingers, a rueful smile on her lips "—you were gone to na-na land."

He remembered those "relaxation exercises" quite vividly—they had all been times when she had needed his particular talent and he'd been spooked, too nervous (and, frankly, scared) to cooperate properly. "Spooked" was an appropriate term, since all six times they'd been checking out buildings Di had certified as genuinely haunted, and she had been unable to get the haunt to "move on," as she put it.

He felt a little betrayed. "Why didn't you tell me that was what you were doing?" he asked, hurt. It wasn't so much that she'd hypnotized him—because he could account for nearly every second of the time he'd been "under." It was that she had not told him the truth.

"Mark, you were the only reliable medium I had, and those weren't abstractions or Hollywood special-effects, those were *people* we were trying to help; trapped, unhappy *people*. Dead people, but still people. If I'd even mentioned the word 'hypnosis' back then, you'd have freaked on me. You still thought all hypnotists were children of Svengali. And you'd make a damned ugly Trilby."

"Okay, I'll admit I was a bit irrational. It still wasn't right," he complained, trying to read her eyes.

"I agree," she replied, and he had no doubt that she was feeling a certain amount of guilt. "And I'm sorry. I'm not immune to making mistakes, moral or otherwise. If I had it to do over, I wouldn't have pulled that trick on you; it wasn't fair at all. Will you accept my apology?"

"Yeah," he said, after a while. "You did what you thought you had to do, I guess."

"And there are times when my sense of proportion is a bit skewed. Still want to go through with this?"

"More than ever." He grinned up at her. "Now that I know you had me in your power before this, and didn't take advantage of me."

"Don't count on it," she grinned back. "The tapes will only cost you a small fortune. Okay, are you ready?"

"All systems go," he answered, getting himself back into his comfortable position.

"Meadowsweet, lycopodium, knotweed."

"Who are you?"

Cuauhtemoc heard the voice in his head without fear; it was odd—but he somehow knew that it meant him no harm, just as he somehow knew his name was also "Mark," although that was nothing like his name now, and that in that time-to-come he was not seven, but much older and a wise warrior. So he answered the voice without taking his attention from the spectacle before him.

"Cuauhtemoc, son of Nanautzin, a potter." Then, because that seemed too little to say about the kindest, bravest father in all of Tenochtitlan, he added, "Son of the best potter in all the world!"

The voice chuckled. "Well said, Cuauhtemoc. What is the year, and the place?"

"The year is Three House, in the Fifth Month, the Feast of Tez-catlipoca," he answered politely. The voice in his head gasped a little. "We are, I am, in Tenochtitlan, in the plaza before the Great Temple of Tezcatlipoca."

"What do you see before you?"

He described for the voice (poor, blind voice, not to be able to see the most beautiful place in all the wide world) the plaza in which he was standing. To both sides, and behind him was a throng of Azteca, brilliantly garbed in their very best. They had gathered, hoping with fading hope that the Great One would descend truly at the climax of this rite, descend and save his people. Their thin, sun-darkened faces were full of equal hope and fear. The bright colors of their festival costumes, red and yellow, blue and white and green, were dulled and smutched a bit by the smokes and fires that had plagued the city daily. Even now there was smoke on the wind, and beyond the chanting of the priests you could hear the screaming and the sound of fighting on the causeways to the city.

His mother's hand was warm on his shoulder as he told the voice of the immaculate stone-paved plaza, shining white in the blinding sun before him, the equally dazzling pile of the pyramid atop which rested the beautiful temple itself. "The temple of Tezcatlipoca is the most beautiful temple in the city—now," he concluded—and his voice faltered a little at the memory of the evil omen.

"Was there another that was more beautiful?" the voice prompted.

He began to nod; then, remembering that the voice was blind, answered, "Yes—the Great Temple, the twin temple of Huitzilopochtli and Tlaloc, the place called Tlacatecan. It burned, of itself. It was a terrible omen, though no one knew what it meant, then."

"What did it mean?"

"The coming of the Terrible Men, the ones led by the man who said he was Quetzalcoatl. He lied," the boy said defiantly, although he knew very well that his elders were divided on the subject. "There were other omens, too. There was a fire in the sky in the year Twelve House, then the temple burned. Then the sun struck a blow to the temple of Xiuhtechutli. That was all before I was even born. Then there was a fire that ran from sunset sky to sunrise sky, while the sun itself was still shining. Then in the year of my birth the lake boiled up and flooded the whole city, and there was a spirit-woman that ran through the streets, weeping and saying that all must flee. Then a bird with a mirror in its head, all covered with feathers the color of ashes, came to the emperor and showed him fearful things. Then there was a man in the city with two heads. I myself saw him," he added, self-importantly.

"I don't doubt you," the voice replied gravely. "Those are fearful omens."

"Then the Terrible Men came," he said, sadly. "That was why my brother—"

"Yes?" the voice prompted.

"That was why my brother became Tezcatlipoca. He said that if the Great Sacrifice was given by one who *chose* to become the god, that the god would *have* to answer and save us. My mama cried." *And so did I*, he added, without speaking the words aloud.

"That was very brave of him."

"Yes," he replied, secretly wishing that his brother had been a little less brave. There had been no shortage of volunteers. But his brother had said scornfully that most of *those* only wished to trade a probably painful death in combat for a year of pleasure and a quick, nearly painless death. "Even the emperor said so. The emperor is very afraid. He thinks the Most Terrible Man *is* Quetzalcoatl; but even if he *is*, and I know he cannot be, the Feathered Serpent is not as strong as Smoking Mirror. I know this, for are we not stronger than the El-der People? The Smoking Mirror is *our* god, and he is my brother, and when the Great Sacrifice is made, he will rise up from the altar and he will kill *all* the Terrible Men and their emperor who is *not* the Feathered Serpent!"

There were tears running down his cheeks now, tears of passion—and the loss he dared not confess, for was his brother not greater than the emperor? Was he not the savior of his people? Was such a sacrifice a reason for tears?

"Hush, hush—" the voice soothed. "Tell me what you know of the Terrible Men, what they have done to your people."

"They have taken Moctezuma; they hold him prisoner. They killed many, many people and they have burned up all the country beyond the lake," he told the voice, trying not to be afraid. "They tried to take the city, but we drove them out. I helped. I carried water and arrows to the soldiers."

"Where are they now?"

"All around the lake. They have demons that make a noise and throw round stones, and more demons, huge, with two heads and four legs and voices like trumpets, and they stop everybody who comes on the causeway from the city. They have tried to come back, but we have stopped them." The procession came into view just then, and the boy craned his neck, intent on being the first to catch sight of his brother.

"What are you seeing?"

"It is the procession!" he answered, excitedly. "I see the priests— now the handmaidens—there! There is my brother! He is playing his flutes, and he doesn't look the least, tiniest bit afraid! But—"

"Is something wrong?"

"He—" the distant figure seemed very pale, and not entirely steady. "He—nothing. He is going up the pyramid."

"Tell me."

"He is playing, he has a servant with all the clay flutes he has played this year, and he is climbing the pyramid and breaking each one after he has played it a little—"

There was no doubt about it, the distant youth staggered as if he was drunk.

"Go on."

"There is something wrong—" Panic edged the boy's voice.

"What?"

"I don't know!" The notes of the song quavered now, and it was not a deliberate trill. "I think—I don't know! He *can't* be sick! He's the god, gods don't get sick!"

"How, sick?"

"The Terrible Men—there was a sickness, with spots—"

"'Mission control to Mark,'" said the voice. "Mark, what is he talking about?"

"Measles," the boy heard his mouth saying, though he was too worried about his brother to find it strange that another spirit should use his mouth. "The Spanish brought measles with them; it wiped out hundreds, maybe thousands, and it's at epidemic levels right now."

Just then the youth, so small, so fragile on the great stone stairs, stopped halfway up the pyramid. He set his hand to his head, swaying, and dropped the flutes he was carrying. And as they shattered, he himself dropped to the stone, cried out—and stopped moving.

The boy screamed—echoing the screams of the thousands gathered around him, the screams of his mother as her fingers dug into his shoulder—

"'All systems, red alert!' Mark, take over!" the voice ordered; firmly, but calmly.

Mark found himself looking out of the eyes of the seven-year-old boy, observing, but unable to affect what was happening. Yet at the same time, he was in total control of *himself*. It was a very eerie feeling; like living in a movie.

"What's happening?"

"Looks like about half the people here are heading for the exits, screaming their heads off," he said, surveying the crowd about him as the boy stood in frozen paralysis. The boy's attention was still on his brother, but Mark found he could bend his own attention on whatever happened to be in the boy's field of vision. "The rest are just falling to the ground and having hysterics."

"Not surprising; that must be the worst of all possible omens. What are the priests doing?"

He looked toward the distant pyramid and distantly felt the boy's anguish. "They're dragging the body up to the altar, but I think the kid is already dead."

"Go forward a few weeks—"

He found himself kneeling in the dirt with a rope so tight around his neck that it nearly choked him, one of hundreds of young boys roped together in a chain of sheer misery. He was filthy, sore, and weary, and utterly without hope. There was a place on his shoulder that throbbed and felt burned; he *knew*, with the boy's knowledge, that the Spaniards had branded him there with the mark of a slave. He knew also that his father was dead, his mother a suicide rather than face a fate in Spanish hands. The once-great city was in smoking ruins; about a hundred feet away from him was one of the Spaniards. He wrinkled his nose in distaste; he could smell the filthy, greasy, un-washed mercenary from where he knelt.

Uppermost in the boy's mind was the hope that *this* man would not want *him*. The man was known to have a taste for young boys. And that was the only hope the boy had; all the rest was despair.

"What does the boy know about the aftermath of the sacrifice?"

"The priests and the sorcerer-priests were unable to take the liv-ing heart from the sacrifice, and right after that the Spaniards made their final assault on the city," he said, after scanning the memories. "But the priests swore that it wasn't the end; they cursed the Spanish and their faithless allies who had deserted them and gone over to the Spanish side; they said that since the cycle was left unfinished, it would hang over the invaders like a balanced stone, and that one day it would fall."

"Things left unfinished have a way of doing that," said the voice. "Okay, Mark—'there's no place like home.'"

He sat up, blinking. His mouth was dust-dry, and every muscle was stiff. "Wow—"

"Double wow," Di answered, handing him a glass of ice water. "That's one of the clearest regressions I've ever encountered."

"God, it was like watching a movie—when it wasn't like being there." He shook his head, trying to sort out the distracting double-memories.

"Now we know how *you're* tied into this," she said thoughtfully. "I *knew* it couldn't be coincidence. Did you pick up anything on your way out?"

He considered all the slowly fading impressions, and grabbed what he thought was the most important. "It seems like that Burning Water guy—I mean, the *brujo*-activist, here and now—and the guy that was my brother are the same person," he said, carefully. "I don't know, that's just what it feels like. Like, that was something *he* has to complete, too. But that's crazy! That would mean that he's going to let his own people sacrifice *him*!"

"Maybe crazy, maybe not," she answered slowly. "The original felt very strongly that a voluntary sacrifice would bring the god to save his people. Every tradition I've ever worked with agrees that a consensual sacrifice has enough power to work literal miracles—including your *own* tradition, my friend."

Days, weeks, even hours ago, that might have disturbed or even angered him, her lumping Calvary in with pagan traditions. Now, after having just spent several hours as someone who believed as passionately in the truth of *his* gods as any fervent Catholic, Mark could not find it possible to be offended.

"So, you think they're going to try to complete what was interrupted?"

She nodded. "Uh-huh. And going for the same results, I'd bet— given what he's been doing with the activists and the *brujos*. So; what's that tell us?"

"He's probably Mexican," Mark said, after thinking. "Or at least he *came* from Mexico; probably around April of last year, since that's when the first animal mutilations started."

"He probably *isn't* an illegal alien," Di frowned, thinking out loud. "That would hamper his movements too much, I think. Which means—"

"Customs will have a record on him!" Mark said in triumph. "Di, we've *got* him!"

"Next time I say the show's over before we've got it in the bag, shoot me, won't you?" Mark said in disgust, shoving a pile of papers away in complete frustration. "I mean, how long have we been at this?"

"Two weeks," Di replied wearily, reading another set of Customs records while she sipped her tenth cup of coffee for the day. "We're no closer than we were when I regressed you. And it's almost time for the next cycle. This is day one; you can bet there'll be blood tonight."

"What one was that?" Mark asked, wondering if there was some way they could pinpoint and stake out a probable victim.

"The—Corn Goddess thing. You know, mature woman, white outfit—"

"Right; pick a woman. Could be any female in the city over the age of thirteen. Shit." He glared at the pile of file folders. "Look at this—everybody and his brother was down there visiting Mexico about that time. Even Robert."

There was a crash of crockery, and Mark, spun, startled. "Di—are you—"

She was staring at him, the shards of the cup at her feet, sitting so rigid and straight it looked like somebody had jabbed her with a needle in the rear. "Robert—" she said slowly. "Before April—nothing. After April, the hottest photographer in Dallas. Before April, living in a roach-motel; after April, living like a *god*. A *god*, Mark. And those four gorgeous models of his—entirely at his beck and call, serving only *him*."

"My god—the four handmaidens? And—we've always been like brothers—my brother—"

She reached down beside her chair and dove into a satchel of Xeroxes from some of the university books, and began to dig frantically through them.

She pulled out the one she wanted, and skimmed it while Mark sat paralyzed. "Oh gods—" she moaned. "Mark, the other common name for Smoking Mirror is *Burning Water*—and look at this!"

She thrust a page with a sketch from one of the codexes at him. On it was a glyph he'd seen before, on the door to Rob's darkroom.

One of the simple hieroglyphs of Tezcatlipoca, the caption read, *the hieroglyph of Fire and Water, or Burning Water.*

"My god—" Mark choked out. "It all fits, god help me, it all fits!"

"Robert and Burning Water are the same—the channel for Tezcatlipoca. That would account for those shields I sensed on him, and why he didn't much want to stick around me. *And* why his model avoided me; the deity could probably keep me off the scent, but there'd have been no way I wouldn't have sensed what *she* was. Mark, there's no other answer at this point."

"My god." He *thought* his mind was going in circles; it wasn't—it was putting facts together too fast for him to follow. He only knew what was happening when it presented him with the answer to his earlier question.

"Oh my god—Sherry—"

She didn't need prompting.

"Oh *gods*—" she groaned. "The Corn Goddess—"

Sherry set the last stitch into the snowy *huiple*, knotted the thread and cut it. Her hands fell away from the completed work. The blouse lay on her lap, finished at last, and she could only stare at it, dull-eyed.

Okay, it's done. It's beautiful, no doubt about it; my best work to date. Now what? God, talk about all dressed up and nowhere to go—

The thing had come to completely dominate her life over the past couple of weeks, an obsession that strengthened every time Rob asked about it. She even had dreams of weaving. This last week she'd put off all her commissioned work, put off her clients, just so she could work on *this*—

And for what? Why had she *done* this? What on earth had possessed her?

"Sherry?"

The voice startled her out of her wits. She jumped and let out a little yip, half scream and half gasp, despite the fact that the voice was achingly familiar.

"Rob!" she snapped, twisting in her straight-backed chair to face the door, "I've *asked* you a million times not to sneak up on me tha—"

She bit the rest of the sentence back when she saw that Robert wasn't alone. That he'd brought all four of his models with him, ranged behind him like acolytes with a priest, faces expectant.

"Is it done?" he asked, ignoring what she had said completely, and nodding at the *huiple* in her lap.

"Uh-huh," she replied, listening for the sounds of Bobby rattling around in the kitchen, and not hearing him. "Where's Bobby? He should be home from school by now."

"I told him to go to his grandmother's after school today," Robert said softly. "You and I need to—talk."

Before she could react to that statement, he turned to Lupe and said—*something*—to her. It wasn't Spanish, that was for sure. Whatever he said, it was in some guttural language *Sherry* had never heard before, and it sounded like an order.

It *was* an order. Lupe smiled, threw a glance of veiled triumph at Sherry, bowed to Robert—and turned to lock the door of the workroom just behind her.

That tore it. Now *they* were taking over *her* territory, *her* space. That was *it*, she wasn't going to stand this charade another moment!

Sherry leapt to her feet, hot with anger. "Now just one *damn* minute here! What the hell do you think you're do—"

"*Be still.*"

Sherry blinked—and found herself sitting meekly back in her chair, clutching the *huiple*.

She took a good look at him—and realized that *this* wasn't the Robert she knew and loved anymore.

She looked at the girls, and they were looking at her the way Bobby looked at an ice-cream cone.

"Robert—" she faltered.

Their expressions didn't change, and she felt her throat choke with fear at the sight.

She had had nightmares about this. This was obviously her worst fear come home to roost. Whatever those girls had gotten Robert into had him good now—and for some reason they wanted *her* as well. Or else they wanted her dead.

And she'd just thought she was being jealous and irrational!

Her head reeled, but she managed to hold to just enough calm to think a little. Without a single backward glance she abandoned seven years of marriage and all her new-won prosperity. If she could get out with Bobby and her life—

"Look, Robert," she pled shamelessly, "whatever you want, you can have. Anything but Bobby. You can have a clean divorce, I won't contest, just leave me my workroom stuff and a little furniture, and a college trust fund for Bobby. No alimony, no child support, we can do fine—"

"I don't want a divorce, Sherry," he said in that deadly, gentle tone. "I want something far more from you."

She had a sudden, panicked vision of herself as the center of some kind of weird, orgiastic ceremony, and then flashed on Lupe holding a knife over her—and stood up so abruptly that the chair overturned. She backed away from them, stumbling over the chair, moving slowly, whimpering a little with fear. "Please, Robert, you know I never hurt you, no matter what you did to me!"

"Sherry—" He followed her.

She ran right up against the wall and flattened herself to it.

"Sherry—*look at me!*" he ordered, seizing both her arms.

She did, completely unable to disobey the command in his voice.

She felt dizzy—almost as if she were being drugged. His eyes were—strange. Depthless. Glowing? It felt as if she was falling into them. And she couldn't—didn't want to—look away. Or escape. Her knees went weak, and she couldn't move.

"Listen to me Sherry—" he slid his hands down her arms, took both her wrists in his hands, and pulled her back into the center of the room, where Lupe was setting her chair back upright. Some tiny corner of her mind screamed at her to resist, to fight—but her body wouldn't obey her, and the rest of her mind was drowning in Robert's eyes.

He pushed her down into the chair; once there, she couldn't move.

"This is true, what I'm going to tell you," he said, with a power Sherry could almost touch behind his words. "When the Spanish came to Mexico, the greatest nation, the greatest *empire*, in the New World was the Aztec empire. They *could* have stopped him, but he lied to them, and told him that he was a god that was supposed to return, Quetzalcoatl. By the time they found out differently it was almost too late."

"But—" she heard herself saying, as if in a dream, "they lost—the Aztecs—"

"There was one rite, the Tezcatlipoca sacrifice, that *would* have saved them if they had been able to complete it. It would have brought Burning Water down on the heads of the defilers and He would have crushed them like the insects they were!"

There was no doubt about it. Robert's eyes *were* glowing, down in the depths of them. A sullen, smoldering red.

"But those bastards brought more than guns with them; they brought disease, diseases the Azteca had no defenses against. The intended sacrifice died of that disease on the very steps of the temple pyramid. The cycle could not be completed; the door was closed to Smoking Mirror, and he could not save his people. Until now."

She shook her head, not understanding his words.

"I am Robert. But since last April, I am also Tezcatlipoca. We, my handmaidens and I, have begun the cycle again—but *this* time, it will be completed. When it is complete, Tezcatlipoca will be freed to enter this world in full power, and we will drive the interlopers back into the sea, giving the land back to the ones to whom it belongs!"

She believed him. She *had* to believe him; his will overwhelmed hers and crushed it to dust.

"But you don't need *me*—"

"I *do* need you, Sherry. I am asking you to agree to what I, Robert, have already sworn to: to sacrifice this pitiful shell so that Tezcatlipoca can return and liberate his people." His voice was still gentle, but now it was persuasive. Very persuasive. "The sacrifice tonight must be a woman, a mature woman in the fullness of her beauty who has borne a child. And she must have made the garments she will wear at the rite with her own hands—and they must be completely white, without ornamentation."

Lupe laid the *huiple* and wrap-skirt she had just finished on her lap. She felt her hands clutching the fabric involuntarily.

"Yes," Robert/Tezcatlipoca said. "Yes. Think, Sherry. Think what a little thing it is. Such a small thing, one life, in the light of all the suffering it would end. For the good of the people. Sherry. Think how much it would mean to those who suffer, who *have* suffered for so very long . . . fated to be the lowest of the low ever since the cursed Spaniards came. Everything was taken from them, they've been made hardly better than slaves. *You* can give it all back to them, Sherry."

He was *so* persuasive, and his eyes were so compelling. She felt herself nodding.

The Ghia screamed into a parking place just outside the apartment complex; they were *not* going to warn Robert by pulling up to the townhouse. Instead, they pulled into the *unguarded* subdivision that abutted it, then found a place where houses screened the thick adobe wall that divided the subdivision from the complex. They weren't worried about being spotted; it was almost rush-hour time and this was yuppie territory. Both spouses were about to hit the Twenty-Mile Parking Lot, aka the Dallas-Fort Worth freeway, any kids were in after-school care, and that held for both sides of the fence.

The whole of the way here Di had been muttering something under her breath, eyes closed in complete concentration—words like nothing Mark had ever heard before, yet which had a tantalizing air of familiarity. But he'd been too busy breaking every traffic law on the books to get to the townhouse—if Di was going to call something up, he wasn't about to stop her, but he also wasn't going to be much help either. So he'd stuck to his driving, and let her do her thing—

The wall around the complex was of fake adobe, a good twelve feet tall and a foot thick—daunting to punks, maybe, but not to Mark, who regularly worked out on the Academy obstacle course. Nor did it provide any barrier to Di—for when he pulled himself up onto the top, and turned to offer her a hand up—he found that she was already beside him.

He nodded, then, and they dropped down together with similarly soft *thumps*, finding themselves on the service road behind the complex.

Together they slipped onto one of the sidewalks threading the complex, headed toward Robert's townhouse, strolling casually as if they belonged here, until they reached the last townhouse block before his. *Then* they took to the bushes planted all along the walls, sprinting across any open spaces one at a time like commandos, ending up at the outer rear corner of Robert's place.

"Let me check the front to see if Rob's car is there," he said, as they eyeballed the back for signs of life in the privacy-fenced patio.

Di grabbed his arm before he could slip off. "Mark—I want to take the shields off you. Now."

"Why?"

"Because—I'm going to try something, to bring in help—but it's going to need a physical body if it comes. It can't be mine; I'll have to handle the girls."

"Which leaves me." Mark didn't entirely like the notion. "What if Tezli-whatsis decides he likes me better than Rob?"

"He can't switch; not until Robert is dead."

"You think. Are you sure you *have* to do this?" he asked, still not happy. He *liked* being under shields; he didn't want to give them up, not now, not under fire.

"Shit, *I'm* not sure it's even going to do any good!" she replied, looking just as unhappy as he felt. "It's an outside chance at best; I'm not sure I read the rite correctly, I'm not sure I *did* it correctly a week ago, I'm not sure I recited the right invocation in the car, and I'm not sure it's going to work at all even if I did everything perfectly. But we're dealing with powerful stuff here; one hell of a lot more powerful than *I* can handle—go ahead, test the water; even *you* ought to be able to feel it—"

He closed his eyes and imagined himself extending a cautious mental "hand" toward the townhouse—and pulled it back a lot faster than he'd extended it.

"Something—there, and not there." He shivered. "Weird, even by your standards. And *strong*."

"Exactly. *He's* up there, and manifesting through Robert. The only way he could be stronger would be if he didn't need a vehicle. In no way am I going to be able to hold off a god! Mark—please—"

"Okay," he sighed. "Take 'em off."

Mark had been shielded for so long, he'd forgotten what it "felt" like to be unshielded.

It felt naked, was what it felt like. Open to every little thing that blew by. A house with all the doors and windows standing wide. *Come on in, sit right down, make yourself at home, help yourself to the family silver—*

"Okay," Di told him. "Go—"

He slipped around the corner, bending low to stay under the windows; he peeked around the next corner at the assigned parking slots. The car *was* there, and so was Sherry's. He sprinted back.

"We're go."

They kept to the shrubbery, edging their way behind its concealment, until they made the edge of the privacy fence itself. A quick eye to the cracks showed there was no one on the patio, and there didn't seem to be anyone in the kitchen beyond. This fence was a mere six feet tall, but it did not have the wide top that the exterior adobe fence had. Di took one look and shook her head at him. Mark got himself over; then, with a cautionary glance at the patio door, slid over to the gate and let Di inside.

The patio door led into the kitchen—and it was not locked. Which was just as well; if it had been, Mark had been quite prepared to pick it, or if that took too much time, shoot the damn thing open.

They eased it open enough to squeeze through, and froze as they heard voices.

Di looked to Mark for guidance.

"We'd better rush them," he whispered. "It sounds like they're moving toward the front door. Anything I should do to kick off this 'help' you said you've called?"

"Pray," she said, grimly. "Just—pray. It doesn't matter to who; it'll get where it needs to go."

With his shielding off he could *feel* the weirdness and the strength of it, and he was coldly afraid. He couldn't think of anything—just as on that long-ago Halloween night. Not so much as a "Hail Mary."

So he did now what he'd done then—as he charged through the kitchen and dining room and on into the living room (grateful for all the times he'd been here, so that he knew the layout of the place), he put everything he could spare into a single, simple cry for help.

He hit the carpet of the living room in a roll, and came up behind the back of the sectional sofa with his gun drawn and trained on the astonished group headed for the outer hallway.

Sherry was toward the front of the group, dressed (Mark's heart plummeted) in the white outfit she'd been working on all this time. He'd been hoping that he and Di weren't right in their guess.

Behind her were the four priestesses, two on either side, wearing perfectly ordinary clothing. Bringing up the rear was Robert.

But when the man turned, and Mark saw his eyes, he knew there wasn't much of Robert there anymore.

"Freeze!" Mark barked. "Rob, don't try me. You know I never aim at what I don't intend to hit."

Behind him, he could hear Di gliding into the room—without shielding he could *feel* her too; like a bright flame at his back. Before him, Robert laughed softly.

"Go ahead," he mocked. "Shoot. You won't get very far."

Then he made a short rush toward Mark—and reflex took over. He fired three times.

And he heard the bullets hit something with an audible *clang*— and saw them hang in midair a foot in front of Robert's chest for a moment, then fall to the carpet.

Robert laughed again, and gestured, and Mark discovered that *he* couldn't move.

"You won't manage that trick with *me*, Burning Water," Di's voice rang out behind him, high and clear. Then, before any of them could react, she vaulted the sofa—into, then out of the pit group—then leapt for the group of five women, tearing an unresisting Sherry out of their hands and shoving her out of the way behind her. The moment Di's hands were free of Sherry, she had both of them raised before her, and Mark could not only sense the shields she'd raised about her and Sherry, he could *see* them—like some kind of special effects force-field in a sci-fi movie.

The girls recovered quickly, and raised shields of their own. Within a heartbeat the living room began to resemble the kind of battle a special effects man would sell his soul to reproduce—fiery balls and lances of colored light licking out and exploding against the shields in showers of sparks, an occasional weirdly shaped and half-seen critter tearing into one side or the other before one of those blasts of light could take it out. Only two things would the effects man have to complain about. First, that there was nothing visible happening when the weaponry connected; just a gasp of pain from the recipient, or the momentary weakening and dimming of the shield. Second, that the entire battle was soundless except for grunts of effort or gasps of pain.

After a few moments during which he was too confused to make out much, Mark began to get a clearer idea of what was happening. Robert had not yet joined in—and Di was holding her own, but just barely.

If Robert decided to pitch in—

He glanced at Robert as the fight began to work away from Robert and back nearer to where Sherry sat dull-eyed and unseeing beside the couch. He saw Robert frown; he saw Robert start to raise *his* hands.

If Rob joined in, Di was doomed. And so were Sherry and himself.

And Mark again remembered Di's admonition to pray.

This time he wasn't distracted by having to make a dive for cover; he sent every bit of what he had winging outward in that inarticulate call for help.

If he could have fallen, he would have; dizziness made the room spin and start to go black. This was a replay of the strange, disorienting vertigo he'd begun to feel that Halloween when the *thing* had set eyes on him, only *much* stronger, much more intense. Once a private plane he'd been in had gotten caught in turbulence and began to spin out of control; this was like that, only the plane was *him* and he didn't have the controls—

Suddenly everything steadied, as if a giant, gentle hand had caught him and was supporting him. He still couldn't see—but he felt a—a *presence*. Like the bright flame that was Di, only *more* so.

Your pardon for the intrusion, little brother, the presence said/felt/thought in his mind. *But you called; is it permitted?*

What the hell am I supposed to say? he thought, confused. All Mark could think of was old vampire movies. *Uh—enter freely and of your own will?*

My thanks.

Now he could see and hear—but when he tried to raise his gun, he discovered that he could not act. It was uncannily like what had happened when he was doing the regression with Di; he was an observer in his own body.

As his hands holstered the gun, Mark saw with relief that Robert had not yet completed whatever action it was that he had intended to take.

"Brother—" said his mouth—

But it was not *his* voice coming from that mouth.

Robert started, and pivoted to face him, a look of utter incredulity on his face. Mark's body rose, and stood facing him, completely relaxed, completely confident, radiating serenity.

Mark managed to notice that the battle with the four priestesses had now gone from pyrotechnics to a battle of wills: the four grouped together, holding each other's hands; Di alone, feet slightly apart, hands clenched at her sides—both sides staring silently at each other with eyes locked.

He turned his attention back to Robert. The man's expression was one of surprise, disbelief, and something Mark couldn't identify.

"Your time is past, my brother," the voice said gently.

Robert flushed with anger. "And yours is not?" he spat.

"Both yes and no."

Robert was gone now. There was no trace of Mark's old friend in the figure that faced him/them.

Burning Water sneered. "I see you haven't given up ambiguity. Still the philosopher—"

"As *you* still seek war and conflict, and turn your back on other solutions. Brother, this man you hold, you have some right to—he is yours by consent, and twice. And the four priestesses. But *this* man—the other women—no. No. Choose another Corn Woman, brother. Or choose another way."

Burning Water snarled, and his face twisted into something very like a cat's snarling mask. "Your way? *Never*. I destroyed you once, *brother*—"

"Yet I continue to return." Mark felt his lips smiling.

Then he felt the presence within him turn a fraction of its attention back on him, as if it had forgotten that he was still there and only just now remembered the fact. He could feel its regard; it was a great deal like being caught in the tropical sun at high noon. It was warming, and dazzling, but too bright and intense to bear for long.

Then he heard himself speaking again, but his lips were shaping strange, guttural words that sounded faintly familiar, but not familiar enough for him to guess what was being said.

If he could have flushed, he would have. It was frustrating and a little shaming; he felt as if he was a kid again, and the adults in the room had just switched to a code so he wouldn't be able to eavesdrop!

Whatever was going on, both entities were still arguing. The argument finally ended when Mark's controller suddenly gestured peremptorily toward the group still engaged in their psychic duel in the far corner of the living room.

The four priestesses went glaze-eyed, and froze. Di blinked, shook her head; then swiveled, hands in the guard position, to face Mark.

He had no notion of what she saw there, but she relaxed completely.

She shook herself all over, gave a great sigh of evident relief, then made a strange little bow and said something hesitantly in that odd guttural tongue, of which Mark only understood the word "Quetzalcoatl."

That was enough for him to figure out just who he was sharing his body with. He didn't feel *quite* so badly then at being left out. . . .

The entity sharing his mind replied to her salutation, but not with voice. Mark could actually feel the thoughts reaching toward Di, although he could not touch them, nor read them himself.

She made a sour face, but didn't protest, although he could tell from her expression that she would have liked to. Instead she stepped reluctantly away from the four handmaidens.

Robert beckoned, anger written in every muscle-twitch. The four women seemed to wake partially from their trance, and answered his summons, gathering around him with bewilderment, confusion, and a little fear in their eyes.

Robert snapped something at them, and they headed for the door, still acting a bit glazed. Then Robert stalked toward the couch, and Sherry—

Mark fought the entity controlling him, then; fought in sheer rage and panic.

Dammit, no! he shouted at the entity. *You said he has no right to her! I won't let you give her away, damn you! Not Sherry—*

But Robert only seized his wife by the arm, yanked her to her feet, and shoved the half-conscious woman straight at Mark. "Take her and be damned to both of you," Robert snarled in English, as Mark's arms caught and held her gently.

He realized then that it was *his* arms catching her; the entity Quetzalcoatl had relinquished most of the control to him, only remaining watchfully in the back of his mind.

Robert snarled something else, then—and Quetzalcoatl took back just enough control to reply—

Then Robert was striding angrily out of the room, into the hall, slamming the front door behind him so hard that the whole apartment shook.

And like an omen, the bronze glyph of "Burning Water" fell from the darkroom door and shattered on the tiles of the doorstep where the carpet ended.

For a few moments more, Mark was held by the entity within him; able to support the now completely unconscious Sherry, but unable to do anything else.

Then, with a rush very like great wings of light sweeping all about him, it was gone, leaving only a sense of deep peace behind.

But with it went ninety percent of his energy.

He sagged against the couch, the weight of Sherry in his arms now more than he could cope with. He managed to haul her ungracefully over the back of it and down onto the couch cushions where she curled up on her own into a sleeping position, and then did not move again except for her steady breathing.

That done, he suddenly remembered that his quarry was getting away.

He stumbled toward the front door; Di intercepted him before he could get there and caught his arm. Weakened as he was, she was more than a match for him.

"What the *hell* do you think you're doing?" he cried, too damned tired to muster anger, and trying to pull out of her grasp. "Those— those *things* have murdered nearly a hundred people, and they're getting away!"

She collapsed to the floor—looking just as exhausted as he was— and let go of his arm. "That's the price Tezcatlipoca demanded for letting us go," she said, wearily. "Enough time to get away. When Sherry wakes, we can set the dogs on him, but not before."

He stared at her, totally aghast.

"Mark, I don't *like* it any better than you do," she snapped. "It sure as hell wasn't the way I figured things would turn out. I thought we'd either win or lose—and win *or* lose, I thought we'd get this stopped for good. I told you once that if I went, I'd take this thing with me—I felt Burning Water beginning to make his move, and I was getting ready to do a really spectacular kamikaze act when your visitor arrived. And I never expected him to work this thing out to a damned draw!"

"Well, the hell with that!" he growled, and headed for the door—

And literally bounced off an invisible barrier at the entrance to the hallway, landing flat on his rump.

"What I figured," he heard Di sigh from across the room, and saw that she was pushing at what was probably a similar barrier, trying to get at the designer phone on the table next to the dining room door.

"*Shit!*" he cursed, seeing no way out of it.

She looked over at him, and favored him with another of her rueful smiles.

"Gods," she told him, "have a habit of enforcing their bargains."

". . . so I guess they figured we'd finally fingered them," Mark concluded. "Since by the time we got there, they were gone and Sherry was just coming around after they'd knocked her out."

Sherry hadn't remembered a thing, so that was the story he and Di had concocted between them, claiming their arrival time at Robert's apartment for a good six hours after the actual confrontation.

"Aw *hail*," the Chief swore. "We got an APB on 'em, but ah doubt it'll do much good." As always, when angry, his accent had thickened. "They're prob'ly halfway t' Tee-ah-joo-wana by now."

"Probably, since Rob had more than enough cash to *buy* his own plane, and there's more little private airports around here than fleas on a hound," Mark agreed. "Well, at least we've seen the last of them—and you *have* got a perp. They practically confessed by heading out."

"Yeah, they did, an' that's how ah'm gonna handle it," the Chief replied, still mad as hops. "But they got two more afore they went. Gawddammittall!"

"Oh *hell*," Mark groaned.

"At least we *think* they got 'em; ain't found no bodies yet, but the husband and the ex are hollerin' up a storm. Two broads," the Chief said, totally disgusted. "An' both of 'em pokin' their noses inta places ain't nobody with the sense God gave a mosquito would go." He

threw down two pictures that looked to have been cropped and enlarged from vacation photos; one of a post-middle-aged woman with
dead-white skin and overly black (obviously dyed) hair, the other of
a younger woman with round glasses and brownish hair the length of
Di's, tied back with a scarf. "*That* 'un, that one's fr'm Frisco," he said,
pointing his cigar at the second. "She was cruisin' th' *barrio* fer
Godssake! Her ol' man says she was looking fer *folk music.*" The
Chief's expression spoke volumes about what he thought of that.
"T'other idiot's a touristo too—fr'm KC. She was—you ain't gonna
believe this, boy—lookin' fer a *gay bar.* Th' ex says she was suppose'ta
meet a friend'uv hers, what useta be a tenant. Gawdawlmighty! How
th' *hell* are we suppose'ta keep damnfools from gettin' killed by their
own damnfoolishness?"

"I dunno, Chief," Mark sighed. "I dunno. Sometimes I think it's a
losing battle."

He looked over the makesheets, and suppressed an hysterical desire to laugh.

Living with Sherry had certainly given Robert a very distorted
view of women. And Tezcatlipoca wouldn't know any better, either.

Robert was used to having a wife *with child*, and one who hand-
made all her own clothing. That, naturally, had made her perfect for
the sacrifice. And there was no reason for him to suppose all women
were less domestic than Sherry, *despite* the fact that Robert had
worked for the fashion industry.

Both of the women abducted had disappeared while wearing all-
white outfits—and since neither of them were the least virginal, he
figured Tezcatlipoca expected that *one* of them, at least, should have
had a child.

In point of fact, neither had.

And neither was at all likely to have *made* her clothing, since the
younger one was wearing a bargain-basement ripoff of one of
Sherry's designs, made in Mexico and bought just that afternoon—
and the other had been gowned by Calvin Klein. . . .

DFW; it all begins and ends here, Mark thought, as he and Di scouted
for empty seats in the waiting area.

"Well, did you get *any* research done?" Mark asked Di, while the
gate agent announced the delay of her flight.

"Believe it or not, yes," she said with a certain weary content. "Between all that Mexican and Indian stuff we waded through and your
darling aunt, plus spending all that time hauling around Dallas and

Fort Worth, I have plenty for a linked family series. Just a matter of getting it organized and doing the outlines—I have most of what I need in my head."

"Thank God for small favors," he replied, giving up on finding a seat; he fed the paper-vending machine next to them with the last of his coins and extracted the afternoon newspaper from its bowels.

"Which one?" she asked impishly. "God, I mean."

"Jehovah, the Almighty," he replied serenely. "I've decided I'm perfectly happy with a masculine deity that operates on a solar schedule, Catholic style. And I'm equally happy to let anyone else choose differently."

"*Good,*" she replied with a sincerity no one could doubt. "That's all I've ever hoped for. Quick—two chairs!"

They scrambled for them before anyone else could grab them, and settled in. Beyond them, a cold winter rain lashed at the window and the tarmac beyond.

"Look at that beautiful rain," she said, nodding at the drippy gray sky beyond the glass.

"Never thought *I'd* be happy to see cold rain again," Mark confessed. "Now—every time it gets warm in midwinter I'm going to have nightmares."

"Don't blame you; the heat wave sure moved out when Burning Water and company did, didn't it?"

"You figure they were causing it?"

"Uh-huh. No doubt in my mind. Can I have some of that?" she asked, setting her carryons down.

He handed her most of the paper, reserving to himself the only two important sections—the sports and comics.

They slumped into the hard plastic chairs that no one could be comfortable in, and perused quietly—until Di made a choking noise.

Mark looked up, startled. "What—"

She pointed to a tiny article on the bottom of page five.

Mexico City. Associated Press. American photographer Robert Fernandez was found murdered today on the tip of the Pyramid of Tlaloc, it read. *Fernandez, who was known throughout the fashion world for his photographs of four young Mexican models recently was named as a suspect in the mass slayings in Dallas and Fort Worth attributed to the "Texas Ripper." He fled the country with his models, and until now his whereabouts have been unknown. He is also suspected of having ties to the radical Indian movements and to a cult that he apparently founded among the radicals. This cult apparently advocated terrorist-type activities, which may have been the goal of the murders, and his death has been attributed to those activities. The whereabouts of his four models are still unknown. Fernandez is survived by his wife, Sherry, and a son, Robert Junior.*

"So they went through with it anyway," Mark said softly. "I wondered—when we found both those women skinned—"

"They must have been hoping that a flawed sacrifice would do anyway." Her face was very quiet. "I could almost feel sorry for him; he was trapped in so many ways by the past. . . ."

"Yeah," Mark said softly, sadly; remembering a friend, and a brother.

"Mark, don't you think you'd better go to Sherry? She's *got* to have been notified; surely she needs at least a shoulder."

"She's gotten a lot stronger and a lot more mature in the last six weeks. And besides, I'm playing that very cool," Mark replied. "If she needs me, she'll call me. It's touchy enough, what with me being the cop that fingered him."

"Hm. If this were one of my novels, there'd be an instant happy ending. It would turn out not to be as touchy as you think," Di replied thoughtfully, her eyes shuttered. "Let's see, how would I plot this—maybe I'd give you a quicky reading, a surface scan of Sherry's psyche—"

"I—" he hesitated.

"Then—then I'd tell you something comfortable—like—that a good part of her standoffishness was guilt on *her* part; half of her feeling like she still should be loyal to Robert, half wanting desperately to go to you. Then I'd point out that now she won't have to deal with that—now she can get her mourning over with, and come to you without the guilt. And I'd tell you that's what she'll do. Bingo, all better, everybody in love, or at least in bed."

"Right—" He snorted. "Too damned easy—and too damned convenient."

"Love, you're learning. No free lunch, and the happy endings aren't guaranteed."

"I don't suppose you have any deathless wisdom at all?"

She sighed. "Not a bit; I have no more idea what's in her mind than you do, and if I did, I probably still wouldn't tell you, because the information wasn't mine to give. We may be the good guys, but we don't get to ride off into the sunset with the significant other of our choice. You go back to try to deal with a lady as fragile as a glass unicorn right now, and I go home—"

"To what?"

She grimaced. "A hatful of work, a man who can't understand

why I won't make a commitment to him when he knows I care for him, and a good friend who's dying by inches."

"No happy endings."

"No happy endings. Does Sherry remember anything?"

He shook his head. "Not a damned thing. Her memory is that the girls roped Robert into a weird pro-Indian cult, probably involving drugs, and *that* was the reason for his personality change, and the things he did."

Di shrugged. "I won't swear to you that Quetzalcoatl didn't play some tricks with her memory to make it easier for her to cope. How's she *really* been doing these past few weeks?"

"Better than I expected, all things considered. You said one thing that *was* true, this makes an end to it for her. And I suppose that's the end of it for us, too."

"Huh," she said thoughtfully, looking out of the window in front of her, but obviously not seeing the plane pulling into the gate. "They failed this time, or I'd feel it. So now—"

"So now, what?"

"Now I only wonder who the *next* one is."

AFTERWORD

I apologize to any true devotee of Aztec culture for taking some liberties (sometimes extreme) with the Quetzalcoatl/Tezcatlipoca mythic cycles for the sake of the story. I plead poetic license. For the curious, it is likely that the sacrifice to Tezcatlipoca was *indeed* interrupted in exactly the way I quote—it *is* known that the sacrifice was aborted, and it happened in such a way that it was a terrible omen, and that there was a measles epidemic raging in Tenochtitlan at the time.

The omens that I quote preceding the invasion of the Spaniards are also noted in the chronicles of the times.

For those interested in Aztec mythology, I offer the following as excellent sources:

Burland, Cottie. *The Gods of Mexico.*
———. *Montezuma, Lord of the Aztecs.*
Carrasco, David. *Quetzalcoatl and the Ironies of Empire.*
Davies, Nigel. *The Aztecs, A History.*
Duran, Diego. *Book of the Gods and Rites and the Ancient Calendar.*
Lafaya, Jacques. *Quetzalcoatl and Guadalupe: The Formation of Mexican National Consciousness.*
Radin, Paul. *Sources and Authenticity of the History of the Ancient Mexicans.*
Sejourne, Laurette. *Burning Water: Thought and Religion in Ancient Mexico.*
Vaillant, George. *The Aztecs of Mexico.*

Weaver, Muriel Porter. *The Aztecs, Mayas, and Their Predecessors.*
Wolf, Eric. *The Valley of Mexico.*

And finally, please, *please* do not ask me to actually *pronounce* any of the Aztec names! I had a hard enough time keeping them spelled right!

—Mercedes Lackey
January 1988

JINX HIGH

Dedicated to
Melissa Ann Singer
for helping to bail!

ONE

uffie Gentry pounded the steering wheel of her brand-new Miata, and cursed—though what she really felt like doing was crying her eyes out like a little kid. It *couldn't* have stalled. Daddy had *just* picked it up today. There was nothing wrong with anything, it had a full tank of gas—

But it had died way out here on 101st, and now it wasn't responding at all.

And this was a spooky place to get stranded past midnight. You might as well be in West Texas instead of less than twenty miles from downtown Tulsa. There wasn't anything out here but cows and cicadas, mysterious shadows, and an awful lot of dark.

Visions of the Rainy-day Rapist and the Southside Strangler kept popping into her head, making her look over her shoulder as she tried to get the *damn* car started one more time.

No luck. And now the tears did come; she sobbed in what she told herself was frustration but felt more like fear. *God, this is like the classic slasher-movie setup, girl stuck out on a deserted road at three* A.M.—*next thing I'll see is a guy in a hockey mask*—

She shivered and told herself not to be stupid. There was a gas station not a half mile behind her—it was closed, but there *was* a phone there. She could call the auto club. That was why Daddy had a gold card with them.

Resolutely—though it took every bit of courage she had—she left the protection of the car and started the long trudge back toward the Kerr/McGee station. But she kept seeing things out of the corner of her eye, things that vanished when she looked straight at them, and before long she wasn't walking, she was running.

She'd never been so grateful to see a gas station in her life.

She fumbled the last quarter out of her purse—this was one of those phones where you couldn't use a charge card, and you had to put a quarter into it even to call 911. She was just glad she hadn't dumped all her change, back at the mall, when Fay Harper had sneered at her for putting cash in the liver-transplant box. Fay had made her so damn mad—just because she'd beaten the senior out on the Teenage America finals, that was no reason for Fay to imply she'd gotten that far by sleeping with one of the judges—

Well, neither of them made it to the regionals, so there.

Buffie just wished Fay hadn't said what she did, when Buffie had retorted with the truth nobody ever said out loud.

"You should know, Fay Harper. You get everything you want by sleeping around and passing out nose candy."

And Fay had said something horrible, whispered it in Buffie's ear. So horrible Buffie couldn't remember exactly what it was—just some kind of threat.

Or promise. Because it had ended with—*"And when you see what's coming for you, remember I sent it."*

Buffie shoved her coin into the slot with hands that shook so hard she could hardly dial the number, and prayed for a quick answer.

"God damn it." Sharon LeeMar looked at the phone resentfully. It *would* ring, now, when she'd just gotten a new coat of polish on her nails. It was probably nothing; some drunk, like last night, wanting the auto club to pull the car out of the ditch where *he'd* put it. Or some stupid kid who'd missed her ride home from some rich-bitch party, and wanted *them* to provide her with one.

Well, there was a way around that. It wasn't like she hadn't done it before. She hit the button with her elbow. "Big A Auto Club," she said. "Will you hold?"

And before the caller could say a word, she hit the hang-up button.

Buffie stared at the phone in gut-wrenching shock, unable to believe she was hearing a dial tone. "No—" she whispered, a panic that she knew was irrational starting to take over. "No, you can't—"

She scrabbled desperately in her purse, hoping for one more quarter. Nothing. With a sob, she upended the whole thing on the pavement, pawing through a tangled mess of makeup, jewelry, credit cards, and odd bits of paper, praying for a quarter, a dime, anything—

Then she heard the sound; a kind of growl. And looked up.
And the scream died in her throat before she could utter it.

"What?"

Derek Kestrel half closed his lids against the wind that was drying his eyes, and gathered breath for another bellow. "I *said*," Deke
yelled, trying to make himself audible over the bellow of the
TransAm's engine and the painfully howling guitars of Motley Crüe,
"I can't *hear* you!"

Fay Harper shook her head, her blond shag whipping wildly
about her cheekbones. Her hair looked like spun frost under the fluorescent streetlamps, her pale skin glowed in the moonlight, and her
eyes were turned to crimson embers by the reflections from the panel
lights. "I can't hear you!" she screamed back, turning the volume up
another notch until the TransAm's floor panels shook from the bass.

Deke sighed and gave up, leaning back into the padded headrest
of his seat. It was custom-leather upholstered, of course, in deep bur-
gundy to match the rest of the car; Fay Harper was never seen in less
than the very best. Nothing was going to compete with *those* speakers. Nothing natural, anyway. A B-52 at full throttle, maybe.

Hanging out with Fay was hazardous to the eardrums. He wished
now he'd brought earplugs or something. First had been the concert,
front-row seats, now it was Fay's ass-kicking stereo; he was going to
be deaf before the night was over.

Then again, hanging out with Fay Harper was hazardous to a lot
more than the eardrums.

The TransAm tore down Memorial, Fay daring anything to pull
into her path. Deke squinted against the headlights of the oncoming
cars, assessed his blood-alcohol level by how fuzzy they looked, and
came up with an answer the Parental Unit wouldn't like. It was a
good thing his dad couldn't see him now. Hell, it was a good thing his
dad hadn't seen the concert! While Deke hadn't shared anything but
the bottle Fay'd brought, grass had been the mildest of the recre-
ational pharmaceuticals making the rounds tonight. Funny. Dad may
have been a wild-eyed hippie back when he was Deke's age, but he
didn't know the half of what went on these days. Deke said the word
"concert," and he could almost see nostalgic visions of Woodstock
drifting through his dad's mind in a sunshine-golden, artistically
backlit haze. *The Summer of Love. Peace, pop. Like, it's a happening.
Oh, wow.*

He laughed out loud, and Fay gave him a funny look, then

cranked the stereo up the last notch. His whole body throbbed and vibrated with the song. He could feel the amplifier overheating—

Or maybe the heat he felt was the effect of her hand sliding up his leg.

There was a drunken howl from the back seat, and Sandy Foster, football bohunk extraordinaire, leaned forward and handed them both cold beers, after throwing his own empty through the open T-top.

"Kick ass, Fay!" he shouted, as Fay gave him a smile that dazzled in the hellfire glow from the instrument panel, and a long, wet kiss in exchange for the beer. She never once took her foot off the gas, but she never swerved, and she hadn't missed a light yet.

There was a flash of headlights in the left lane as a couple of hopped-up metal-heads in a chop-top Cougar pulled alongside. The driver shouted something, lost in the howl of engines and the screech of feedback. Fay tossed back her head in laughter, rapped on the horn once, contemptuously. Then she gave them the finger, and blew the doors off their pitiful poser-custom.

Deke wondered if his spine was going to have a close encounter with the back seat. The speedometer was in three digits by the time his stomach caught up with the rest of him.

Sandy howled again, and another bottle hit the pavement behind them.

Deke looked back at the Cougar eating their dust. For a minute, the guy on the passenger's side looked a little like his buddy Alan.

He bit his lip, and wondered what Alan was doing tonight—then looked at the bottle in his hand. His conscience awoke, and sanity reared its cold, ugly head.

What in the hell am I doing here? How did I ever get mixed up with Fay's crowd?

Sandy was screaming along with the Crüe; the simpleminded lyrics of any popular song were all he needed to cover *his* questions.

Yeah, but Sandy's got three answers to deal with everything he runs up against—drink it, screw it, or tackle it. Every Bud's for him.

Jillian McIver, Fay's best friend, was nuzzling Sandy's neck like a toothless vampire. *The rest of them pretty much match Sandy. Jill's got no life outside the mall. Fay's got anything she wants. I'm the oddball here. So what the hell do they want with me?*

He glanced over at Fay; she smiled and licked her lips, and her hand reached the Promised Land. Questions began to seem pretty immaterial. . . .

However, Fay's luck with the lights ran out at just that moment. She pulled her hand away as the light changed from yellow to red. She *might* have tried to run it—but there was a little something bearing down on the intersection.

Deke wasn't so gone that he couldn't see the semi—and his reactions weren't too blown to grab for the "aw-shit" bar on the door as Fay cursed, locked all four wheels, and put the TransAm into a sideways drift, stopping just short of the intersection.

And as the front swung around, the headlights glared right into the eyes of the metal-brains still trying to race them. They *didn't* see the semi, or the red light—and if their music was as loud as Fay's, they couldn't hear the air horn blasting at them, either. They headed straight into the free-fire zone.

The Cougar dragged against the side of the semi's cab in a slo-mo shower of glass and plastic, fiberglass pelting down like candy-apple-red hail—the impact inaudible over the hellish guitar.

Fay wasn't fazed in the least. She bared her teeth, mouthed something, and down-shifted; gunned the car, and fled the scene in a cloud of tire smoke.

Smiling.

Jill and Sandy were in a heap somewhere on the floorboard, mingling with what was left of the cold case Fay had brought to finish off the concert.

All that Deke could think of for the first, shell-shocked minutes, was—*Sandy's probably enjoying the hell out of himself.*

Deke pried his fingers off the bar, one at a time. Fay's hands were on the wheel and the shifter, giving him a moment of thought unclouded by raging hormones.

He looked back at the wreck, and in a break between songs yelled, "What about *them*? Aren't you gonna—"

"They weren't fast enough," Fay shouted back, interrupting him. "They got what they were asking for. They weren't good enough, and they weren't fast enough."

She gave him a long, sideways look, measuring him against some unknown standard. Her eyes narrowed, and she licked her lips, the barest hint of her tongue showing between them. "So how about it, Deke? Are *you* fast enough?"

Shit. He looked back at the wreck; Fay shoved the stick up into fifth and slid her hand over to his leg. Again.

Christ. She's crazy! I think that wreck made her horny! Or— hornier— Deke suppressed a wince.

"*Fay!*"

Jillian McIver had a voice like a ripsaw, but the harsh whine was music to Deke's ears about now. Fay pulled her hand away.

"What?" she snarled over her shoulder.

"What the *hell* were you doing?"

Jill's disheveled head rose over the seat back, her dark curls falling over one eye; her lower lip was swollen and cut a little, and she sucked at it petulantly. Deke watched as Sandy's hand came up and made a grab for her, and she elbowed him away. "I about broke my *neck*, Fay," she complained, raking her hair out of her eyes with talonlike finger-nails. "An' I cut my *lip*. It's gonna be a mess for a *week*. What d'you think you're doing, anyway?"

My God. The guys in that Cougar could be dead, and all she's wor-ried about is her lip!

"Livin' life in the fast lane, girl," Fay replied with poisonous sweetness. "'Smatter? Can't you take the pace?"

"But my *lip*—"

"Sandy'll kiss it, and make it all better," Fay cooed. "Won't you, honey?"

"You bet," Sandy said thickly, from somewhere below the level of the seat back, and Jill vanished in the direction of his voice with a muffled yelp.

Deke hunched his shoulders and tried to become part of the upholstery. *Yeah. Life in the fast lane. And me a Yugo. Neep, neep. Oh well; the wreck wasn't that bad. At least those guys walked away from it.*

Fay had just hit a bad stretch of road on the winding back way into Jenks, and she needed to keep one hand on the shifter, one on the wheel, and both eyes in front of her. Fay was a foot-to-the-wall driver, but she wasn't suicidal. Even this late at night, you never knew when some drunk cowboy was going to pull out in front of you from one of the kicker bars around here.

Trees and bushes blurred past, sparked with the occasional flick-ers of fire that were animal eyes staring, mesmerized by their speed-ing headlights. Deke blinked.

So Fay caused a bumper-bender. Big deal.

As he watched the shadows blur past, the memory slowly faded from his mind. All he was thinking about was the speed, the night, and Fay.

Seems like there was something I should remember. . . . Aw, hell. Forget it. It's a damn good thing I'm not the one driving, he thought muzzily. *This road's right out of* Grapes of Wrath. *God only knows why*

Fay's using it. Your county taxes at work. What was it Alan said? The difference between Chicago and Tulsa County is that Chicago politicians steal the money after the roadwork's paid for? Yeah. Then Dad laughed and said that was why we live in Jenks. Good ol' Jenks, Oklahoma. All the benefits of Tulsa, none of the drawbacks.

Twenty years ago, Jenks had been Hicksville, and Tulsa wouldn't give the residents of Jenks the time of day—now it was the bedroom community that Tulsa would *love* to incorporate, and Jenks wasn't having any part of the idea.

Now Jenks was the haven for some of the area's wealthiest professionals—doctors, lawyers, top management—who didn't want to give up their well-maintained roads or their autonomously funded school district, thank you. Jenks money stayed in Jenks. Because of that money, the Jenks schools were as good as the private academies over in Tulsa, and a far cry from the Tulsa public school system. That was a big selling point; yuppie parents believed in expensive education. From computers in the classroom to Olympic pools, what Jenks High *didn't* have wasn't *worth* having.

And a mere fifteen minutes up the interstate from your job. Shit, I sound like a real-estate ad.

A yuppie paradise. Every acquisitive dream come true, and no slums to mar the landscaping; no low-income housing, no porno rows, no bag ladies, no "undesirables."

It harbored those who lived a sheltered, pampered life. The kids who went to Jenks were used to living their parents' fine lifestyle to the hilt, used to the goodies that came without asking.

Like Fay, Sandy, Jill. More money than they knew what to do with, and parents too busy clawing their way to the top to pay *too* much attention to what their kids did with that money. They'd had expert nannies as babies—the finest shrinks money could buy to get them through their early teens—and once they reached sixteen or seventeen, most Jenks parents figured their kids could take care of themselves. Sort of the ultimate latchkey children. So long as they didn't bring the law down on them, so long as they kept their grades up and *looked* like they were straight, everything was cool.

Parents seemed to rely a lot on appearances in Jenks.

In Fay's case, there were no parents at all. Daddy was long gone to wherever dead oilmen went; Mummy was sucking up tranks in the loony bin at Vinita. All Fay had was some guy in a bank making Mummy and Daddy's trust-fund dollars produce baby trust-fund dollars, and a "guardian" who spent all her time watching the soaps, making herself invisible whenever Fay wanted to party.

Deke felt more than a twinge of guilt about that. Dad knew Aunt Emily existed—and assumed she was keeping an eye on the proceedings every time Deke was over at Fay's. Tonight was no exception; he'd said something about it being nice that this aunt didn't mind hanging out with the kids.

When all the time Aunt Emily was not only letting them do damn near anything they pleased short of burning the place down, *she* was the one who'd bought the booze.

It's a good thing Mom's in Japan. She's got radar, I swear she does, she knows every damn time I get shit-faced. I bet she's the one that put Dad up to giving me that grass and making a video of me making an ass out of myself. He blushed, glad that it wouldn't be visible in the scarlet lighting from the dash. *I've never been so embarrassed in my life. God. I wanted to die.*

He couldn't even imagine Aunt Emily doing what Dad had done. *No way anybody's ever done that to Fay. No way anybody'd* dare *do that to her. She gets what she wants, and that's it. What the hell am I doing with her, anyway?*

Back to the same old question. It didn't make any sense. It hadn't made any sense when she asked him if he wanted to go with her. Fay Harper, head cheerleader, a senior, the prom queen, and the hottest roll in the sheets in Tulsa County—and *she* wanted *him*? Derek Kestrel, a junior, a guy who wasn't even on the basketball team for Chrissake, a guy who didn't even have a *sports car*, just a Chevy Citation. It didn't make any sense at all. And that she'd stuck with him for two whole months was way outside probability.

He couldn't figure out what Fay wanted, what kind of prestige she was getting in going with him. It couldn't be his family—Dad was a pretty high-fee architect, but no Frank Lloyd Wright. Mom was as far up in the hierarchy as she was ever going to get—or wanted to get—with Telex. Fay had more money *now* than Mom and Dad put together, and when she hit eighteen—it was no contest.

And it wasn't like his parents gave him *any* extra on his leash, either. Fay didn't need him to do whatever she wanted; she just did it, and got away with it, just like tonight. The concert party had been her idea; the whole evening was *her* little treat. She'd wanted to raise some hell, and nothing was going to get in her way. She'd bought the tickets from a scalper, prices that had made Deke blanch; now she'd haul them all home with her, there'd be more booze, and she'd hinted she had some really hot videotapes.

All without a single word of opposition from anybody. Anytime Fay wanted anything, good old Aunt Emily okayed the credit card charges, bought the damn booze, and wouldn't poke her nose out of her room from the moment they all came in through the front door.

Aunt Emily doesn't give squat what Fay does. So long as she's got her soaps and Fay's trust fund keeps her life cushy, she's happy. She sends so many excuse notes to the principal's office you'd think Fay cranked 'em out on the Xerox. Shit, sometimes I think Fay only shows up at school 'cause cutting is more boring than going to class. Damn if I know how she stays head cheerleader. Or how she keeps from getting flunked out. Not that Aunt Emily would care.

God, how am I going to stay out of the doghouse? Derek suddenly realized that his dad would probably still be up when he came home—Mom and Dad were both night owls, given the chance—and he began trying very hard to think of a way to sneak in without Dad finding out he'd been putting a few down. It wasn't like Dad would *say* anything, or even *do* anything. He'd just give Deke that look—

The one that says, "I thought you had more brains than that." The one that says, "I still have that video, remember?" Christ. Good old straight-edge Dad. You'd think he never got fucked-up in his life. You'd think giving me that dope and letting me get shit-faced and making that tape was legal. So I put down a few, so what?

So I figure I'm making an ass out of myself, that's what. Worse; I'm being a shithead. We should have stopped at that wreck—Fay caused the wreck. I let her get away with running out. I was too blown—or too scared—to stop her. And Dad doesn't have to tell me what a chicken-shit I am.

He sighed. He really didn't belong in Fay's crowd; *they* didn't care what their parents thought of them. He really kind of wanted his folks to—to respect him.

He just didn't fit in, no matter how hard he tried.

But Fay wanted him anyway.

I like the way the other kids look at me. Like I'm some kind of—of—superstar, to get Fay. I want to keep her—but what's the attraction? he asked himself, sneaking a look at the devastating blond out of the corner of his eye. *I don't think I'm that good in bed.*

She seemed to sense his eyes on her, and gave him a sideways glance of her own, a proprietary look that made him feel very uncomfortable, even though he grinned back at her.

One of those stoned cowboys pulled out right in front of them, and Fay cursed, pulled her attention away from Deke, and skidded around him. Warm, wet wind slapped Deke in the face as they rolled past the jacked-up pickup so fast it might just as well have been parked.

Deke slumped down in his seat, his hands clenched around the warming bottle of beer. For a moment, he'd been mesmerized by those eyes, but the minute she took her gaze off him, his mood sank again. *When she looks at me like that, I feel like a boy-toy, some kind of prize she can show off in front of everybody. Like a piece of meat. And I still don't understand why* me. *Why not Bob Williams? Shit, Mr. Touchdown, big-time quarterback, Senior All-Star. He's more like her speed. More than a match for her in the looks, too. Muscles all over, including between his ears, blond—shit, guy looks like a recruiting poster for the Hitler Youth.*

He turned away, brooding out the window at the shadows in the fields and the vague hints of outbuildings going by. They were past the Jenks "downtown" now, all two blocks of it, and everything but the bars locked up tight; out in the country, heading for Fay's place. Warp Factor Four, Mr. Sulu.

It ought to be Bob sitting here. No, that's backward—it'd be Bob in the driver's seat, Fay over here; in his Porsche, not her TransAm. Bob doesn't take the back seat for anyone.

Bob's old man was the basketball coach—one reason why Deke had never even bothered to try out for the team. He got all the exposure he wanted to the Williams family just avoiding Bobby-Boy and his idea of what constituted a joke. Bob had a way of finding exactly the most humiliating thing to say or do to you, and he liked picking on what he called "brains." Deke had gotten dumped on a couple of times by Bobby-Boy. He didn't need to put up with Coach and the Gestapo Method of Basketball Training.

He runs that team like a concentration camp. Hell for the outcasts, paradise for the Chosen. And a raise every year, even when the teachers don't get one. Not that Coach Big Bob needs the job, or the money. Mrs. Bob has enough loot for twelve. And Bobby-Boy spends it like it's Argentinian pesos, throws it around, makes like hundred-dollar bills were pocket change; just the kind of guy you'd think Fay would dig.

More than that, Bob's parental leash was as long as Deke's was short. Big Bob let him get away with literally everything, with rule-breaking that would get any other kid bounced from the team for the rest of his school career. In fact, Bobby had gotten a girl from Union pregnant last year—Big Bob got the pregnancy hushed up, then got the family lawyer to scare the girl into an abortion.

Then had the balls to sit front-row center at the Mabee Chapel over at ORU every Sunday, and campaign for Right-to-Life.

Deke had overheard his parents talking about the story one night—Mom had been ready to fry nails, she was so hot. Seems that

Big Bob had been boasting about his boy's "prowess" over at the club bar, and Mom had overheard. *And* given him a piece of her mind, right in front of his cronies in the bar.

Which makes for another good reason not to try out for the team. Thanks, Mom.

Deke rubbed his thumb along the wet side of the beer bottle. Bobby-Boy's mom would never have *dared* do anything like that. Deke kind of admired his mom's guts, but he wished she'd found some other way to take Big Bob down. One that wasn't so—public.

No, that would never have happened to Bobby-Boy. Not good old Bobby Williams, apple of his mother's eye, pride of his daddy's stable, master of all he surveyed.

Maybe that's why Fay didn't move in on him. She doesn't like to take second seat to anybody, any more than Bobby-Boy does.

Still . . . sometimes, it seemed like it would be nice to have a dad a little like Big Bob. Deke would lay odds that when Bobby-Boy came home shit-faced, not only would his dad hand him a beer, he'd want to know how many notches Bobby'd carved on his gearshift that night.

Fay was taking the long way home tonight. Deke stared up at the full moon pouring pale light down through the T-top, and wondered why she'd decided to tour the county. Not that it mattered. The end of tonight's ride was as predictable as the full moon. Fay's house, Fay's living room, Fay's movies; then Fay's bedroom, Fay's bed.

Life in the fast lane.

And somehow, some way, he was going to have to figure out how to cope with it all—Fay, money, lifestyle. Before he said or did something that would make it all fall apart and turn her against him. Because if she turned on him—he might as well try to talk his parents into getting a transfer for him, because life at Jenks would be unbearable. Fay would see to that.

You can't go back, isn't that what they say? I sure can't, not now. I'm doing stuff now I never even dreamed about.

Used to be, though, weekends would be over at one of the guys' houses, often as not. Either George Louvis's place, or Alan's. If George's, they'd listen critically to the band; give George their two cents' worth. Sometimes he'd even take their advice, like when he got rid of the third Fender and picked up a Gibson. If Alan's, they'd do some computer stuff—Alan was too together to be a nerd, but he knew his micro like most guys knew their cars. Some of the games he'd come up with were pretty incredible.

Used to be, when he went out with a chick, the farthest he got was some really heavy petting.

Used to be, he knew who his friends were.

Now—well, since he'd taken up with Fay, George wouldn't even talk to him. George hated Fay, though he'd never say why, exactly. But he didn't let that show—he just avoided her like she was contagious. And since now Deke was constantly in her company, he avoided Deke, too. The only time Deke ever saw him anymore was at dances.

Alan was still his good buddy—except—

Except he figures Fay is Trouble. Keeps bugging me to drop her. Even when he doesn't say anything, it's like with Dad, like I can hear what he's thinking. That she's gonna get me in deep. And that when she does, she'll bail out on me, leaving me stuck up to my ass.

Deke grimaced. *Hell with it. They don't have a clue.* Because, God, it was worth it—Alan couldn't even guess. His life was so exciting. . . . Fay'd done things with him he hadn't even fantasized before he got involved with her. Some things he hadn't even known were anatomically possible! She was incredible, insatiable, a real sexual athlete—

Takes the gold in the water-bed races, not to mention the pole vault. . . .

In short, so far as Deke understood the meaning of the word, Fay was a genuine nympho.

There was only one problem. He was beginning to have trouble keeping up with her.

—as 'twere—

The real problem was, when he failed to come through with the goods, she really knew where to put the knife, and how to twist it to make it hurt the most. Her standards, and her expectations, were high. *All* the time. No coffee breaks, no vacations, no sick leave.

And when Fay didn't get what Fay wanted, there was hell to pay. *Oh hell. No pain, no gain. Right? Maybe more vitamins.*

Deke could see the lights of the cars on the interstate beading the horizon; that meant the turnoff to Fay's driveway wasn't too far away. He began to hope, desperately, that Fay *did* have some video-porn planned. Between the bottle that made the rounds at the concert and the beer he'd drunk in the car, there wasn't much rising tonight except hope.

I'm going to need all the help I can get, he thought unhappily.

A sudden lurch threw him against the door and broke into his preoccupied thoughts. Fay was weaving pretty badly, though she hadn't slacked up at all, speed-wise. Deke knew that the steering on her car was touchy, but this wasn't touchy steering, this was DWI. Her foot was *still* right down against the firewall, and she was taking up every inch of her lane, and then some.

Fay was pounding out the tempo on the steering wheel, just a hair off the beat, nodding her head in time to the music. She never did that except when she was well and truly polluted.

Deke closed his eyes and hoped that the driveway wasn't too far away.

"*Fay!*" Jill shrieked, five inches away from his ear, startling him so badly that he lost his grip on the beer and dropped it.

Oh, great, he thought, groping for it. *Terrific. In the morning, when she smells beer all over the car, she's going to have my ass for a rug.*

Fay just laughed at nothing, and took another swig from her brew.

"*Fay!*" Jill howled, her hair blowing into her wide, alarm-filled eyes as she leaned forward over the back of the seat.

"What?" Fay shrieked back, still laughing wildly.

Jill waited until the pause between songs. "I think you've had too much, Harper," she screamed, gesturing at the beer in Fay's hand. "You oughta let somebody else drive before we—"

Fay flung the empty out the top of the car, her face twisted with an anger Deke knew only too well.

Oh, shit. She's going to have a tantrum, right here and now, at warp speed.

She'd had a few of those tantrums at *him,* when he didn't bow to whatever whim of the hour she was embracing. They were not among his most cherished moments.

He usually wound up feeling like he'd been skinned and dipped in boiling lead. He'd *rather* have been skinned and dipped in boiling lead. It would have hurt less.

"It's *my* goddamn car," Fay screamed, twisting the wheel viciously as they rounded a curve, throwing both Jill and Deke against the right-hand side. "I'll drive it any way I fuckin' want!"

Jill clawed her way back up to her position between Deke and Fay. "Yeah," she wailed, "but we're gonna get stopped!"

Fay's teeth were bared in a snarl. "I never get stopped!" she countered.

"Yeah, but—"

"You callin' me a liar, McIver?" Her eyes glittered, hard and cold, and it seemed to Deke that not all the red in them was due to reflections from the dash lights.

"No, but—"

That was one "but" too many. Fay whipped around to face the girl, her expression a distorted mask.

"*All right!*" she screamed. "*You* drive!"

And suddenly—there was no one behind the steering wheel.

Derek couldn't move. He *tried*; tried to grab for the wheel, tried to vault the shift into the driver's seat. He *could not* move; something outside of him was holding him in place.

Jill screamed and bailed over the back of the seat, grabbing desperately for the wheel. The wheel wrenched to the left, just as she got her hands on it.

By itself.

It was enough to make his breath stop and the hair to rise on the back of his neck. Derek watched the wheel actually fighting her, like the car was steering itself.

The last obstacle on the way to Fay's place loomed up in front of them—an overpass with a little county road running underneath. The motor roared as the car impossibly accelerated.

Jill screamed, still clawing at the wheel.

The tires echoed her screams, in terrifying harmony.

Deke tried to break the paralysis holding his body as he realized they weren't going to make it past the overpass—

The left side of the car dropped sickeningly as the wheels left the road.

"*Fu*—" was the only sound from the rear seat, indicating that Sandy had at least noticed they were all about to die.

It was the phone call every parent is afraid he'll get anytime his kid goes out.

"Mr. Kestrel? This is Officer Ridell of the Tulsa County Police. There's been an accident—"

Larry Kestrel's hand spasmed on the handset; his heart stopped beating. He stared at a single pale-beige Art Deco rose on the kitchen wallpaper. And in his mind only one thought was clear. *Not Deke. Dear God, not Deke*—

"—your son's all right," the stranger's voice continued. "But you'd better come on down to Hillcrest and pick him up. He's cut up and bruised, and—real shook up. It was a pretty bad wreck, and one of the other kids was killed, one of the girls in the car."

His heart started again, leaping with relief and something shamefully like joy. His eyes blurred; his knees went to jelly. He wanted to laugh and cry at the same time. One of the other kids. *Not* Deke. Not *his* son.

He stammered something to the police officer on the other end of the line; it must have been all right, or else the cop was used to incoherent parents. Probably the latter. Whatever, the cop told him he'd get all the details when he got Deke from the emergency room, but no, the kids weren't in trouble and there weren't any charges being filed; it was just a hideous accident.

Somehow he got out to the car; he didn't notice that he was driving until he was already rolling past the Jenks downtown district. It was a damned good thing that the bars hadn't closed yet; if he'd had to play dodge-'em with a bunch of drunks, he'd have been wiped out before he got past Seventy-first Street. Shook up as he was, the drive to Hillcrest passed in a blur. He began to notice, but only after he'd passed them, that at least half the lights he hit were red. He slowed down a little, tried to relax by telling himself that the cop *had* to have been telling the truth—if Deke was at Hillcrest he couldn't be *too* badly hurt. He'd have to have been coherent enough to tell someone to take him there; otherwise he'd be someplace closer to Jenks rather than the hospital Larry had told him to ask for if he had a choice.

The parking lot was nearly empty, but lit up like a tennis court; Larry pulled the BMW across two spaces, flung the driver's door open, and raced for the emergency room without bothering to lock it—

He hadn't expected an automatic door; it had been years since he'd been to an emergency room. The double glass panels suddenly gaped wide for him, like the doors of the Starship Enterprise. He found himself in the anteroom, people turning to stare at him, most of them dressed in white, while he stood there blinking stupidly in the fluorescent lights.

Movement to his left; a dark tan-and-brown shape. He blinked again. A portly security guard approached him, a man obviously past retirement age, moving slowly, cautiously. Larry wondered what it was in his expression that made the man walk toward him so carefully, as if *he* was dangerous.

"I'm—" He coughed. His throat was too dry to talk easily. He swallowed, and tried again. "I'm Larry Kestrel. The county police called, an Officer Ridell. My son—"

The guard's anxious expression cleared. He nodded a balding, age-spotted head. "No problem, Mr. Kestrel," he said. "Your kid's okay; he's all patched up and ready to go home. We've got him over here." He gestured that Larry should follow him down the blindingly white corridor to his right, a corridor lined with closed and open doors. Larry glanced inside one of the open doors, looking for some sign of Deke. There were curtains on ceiling runners, some open, some making little partitions around waiting gurneys, some entirely closing off little alcoves. Examination areas?

Probably; from beyond one of those curtained-off alcoves he

could hear voices, fragments of conversation. One, female, young but tired sounding: ". . . Christ, they oughta call it *Jinx* High, there's been so many accidents. That's the second one tonight, and three DOA. . . ."

Not my boy. Thank you, God. Not my boy.

There was a cop—a *real* cop, in a real Tulsa County uniform— waiting outside one of those closed doors.

"This's the boy's father," the paunchy old man said, and shoved him slightly in the cop's direction when he didn't move.

The cop took his elbow—this was a middle-aged man, maybe a little younger than Larry, but as lean as the rent-a-cop was paunchy. And he knew his business. Larry dazedly discovered himself being gently steered toward a bench and pushed down on it. The cop eased down next to Larry with a weary groan. Larry looked at him anxiously, and found himself staring right into a pair of tired, but friendly, brown eyes.

"Okay, here's the scoop," the cop said, the weariness that showed plainly in his eyes making his voice a little dull. "I'm the guy that called you; I'm the guy that got called to the scene. I'm the guy who's writing this up. I've stayed with these kids the whole time. First of all, your kid is fine. He had a scalp cut that took about three stitches, and he might be concussed. What he *is*, he's scared, he's shocky, and he's pretty well shook up. One of the two girls took a header through the windshield, practically in his lap, and—well, that's the one I told you about on the phone. The doctors are with her folks."

The man shrugged, but the look in his eyes told Larry everything he needed to know. It hadn't been pretty. And the girl's parents wouldn't want to see the father of one of the survivors.

"The other girl, the driver, she says the steering went out on her. Right now we don't see any reason to call her a liar. Things are a real mess under what's left of that sumbitch." He shook his head. "Things pretty well tally with what she told us. You can figure we ran blood and Breathalyzer tests on all of the kids, anyway. That's SOP for a case like this, that's part of why we couldn't call you right away. We were waiting for the results. All three kids came out straight. Nobody was doin' anything, no drugs, no booze. So, no charges. Not like the other one—two private-school kids out drag racing on Memorial, stoned to the gills. Glad the town boys got that one, I hear there wasn't much left."

Larry let out the breath he had been unconsciously holding in, and inhaled a lungful of harsh antiseptic. He hardly noticed as it burned his throat.

So Deke's not only okay, he wasn't fucked-up. "Then—what happened?"

The cop sighed, and rubbed his eyes with the back of his hand. "I don't know; the kids weren't real coherent. The other boy, Sandy, he can't remember anything after they left the concert—doc says it's traumatic amnesia, and he probably won't ever get that memory back. The other gal says her girlfriend was probably unbelted; she was leaning up between the front buckets to talk, anyway. You know kids—all over the damn car, yakking, and no way to convince 'em to stay belted. The other three were buckled up, but not the McIver kid. My guess is she was half over the front seat when the steering went out. Odds are they were probably speeding some, but since there's no skid marks, there's no way to tell for sure, and after this—hell, I may file a report, but *I'm* not gonna book 'em."

"But Deke's all right?" Larry wanted that reassurance again, though a part of him reflected on the irony of a former flower child begging for reassurance from The Man.

"As all right as he's going to be," the cop said, then hesitated. "Look, I'm no psychologist, and it's none of my business, but your kid just had a friend die, about as ugly a death as you can think of, and within inches of him. It was real messy. I don't think you want to know *how* messy. Go easy on him, okay? Give the kid some space."

"What I'm going to give him," Larry said slowly, "is the most convincing hug I've *ever* given him; I'm going to tell him I love him, and that I'm thanking God he's okay, and that anything else doesn't matter squat."

The cop grinned, his tired face wrinkling with smile lines for a moment, and he slapped Larry on the back lightly. "You're a good dad, Mr. Kestrel," he replied with sincerity. "You go in there and take your kid home."

They both rose and started for the examining room, the cop reaching the door a little ahead of him and opening it for him.

Larry stepped inside; Deke was sitting on the edge of a green plastic chair, slumped over. For the thousandth time since his son hit puberty, Larry was struck by the incredible likeness he and Deke shared. Same bone structure, same wavy hair—only the green eyes were Miri's. For Larry, looking at Deke was like looking into a time-reversing mirror. He wondered if Deke realized.

The boy looked up quickly at the sound of the door opening, his face white, his eyes like a pair of hollows in a snowbank. His clothing was torn, mud and blood splattered, and there were bruises on his forehead and neck. Under the harsh fluorescent light the kid looked like a corpse himself.

Then the blank, strained look Deke wore vanished as he realized who was there. "D-dad?" he faltered.

And threw himself into Larry's arms.

Legacy of the sixties; Larry and Miri Kestrel had taken no small amount of pride in the fact that they'd raised a boy who thought it no sin to show how he felt. Now Larry was deeply grateful they'd been able to do that. As the cop closed the door of the tiny cubicle to give them some privacy, the two of them shivered and cried together, and held each other tightly.

Deke couldn't speak at all for a long time, and Larry wasn't in much better shape. His throat was knotted with conflicting emotions, and he was trembling just as much as his son. Finally the tears seemed to ease something inside his boy, and the young body began to relax. "Dad—" Deke sobbed. "Dad, I'm sorry, I'm sorry—"

What it was he thought he had to be sorry for, Larry had no idea. At the moment it didn't matter. All that really mattered was that Deke was safe—

—for the moment.

The thought came out of nowhere, unbidden. As if it wasn't his.

A chill threaded Larry's spine at that alien, unguarded thought. A chill he hadn't felt for years.

Until now.

He held Deke a little tighter, and he stared over the boy's shoulder at the cold, blank, antiseptic wall. There was nothing there. Nothing that could be detected by the five senses.

But Larry Kestrel was not necessarily limited to five senses. He closed his eyes, and let his mind open, just a little.

Danger.

The feeling was unmistakable; as clear and acrid as the metallic, chemical scent of disinfectant permeating the room.

Something was threatening his boy. He let himself relax a little further, hoping to identify it.

Hunger.

A deep, insatiable hunger; an old hunger.

Something *wanted* his boy. Something that did not operate by the laws and rules of the so-called normal world, the world Larry had lived and moved in exclusively for the past seventeen years.

But not always. Before that—before he and Miri had moved to Tulsa—he'd had no few encounters with another world altogether. And that feather-light brush of cold down his back that had just alerted him had always been the signal that he was about to have another such meeting. The other feeling, the feeling of danger—that wasn't exactly new, either. But he hadn't felt it in years, and it had never been this strong before.

It had never been aimed at anyone but *himself* before.

He stiffened—and the feeling faded, leaving behind it only bone-deep weariness, and the even deeper relief of a parent whose child is safe.

For now, said something, a certainty deeper than thought. *For now.*

"Come on, son," he said, quietly. "Let's go home."

TWO

A nn Greeley surveyed the twenty-four pupils of her Honors English class and grimaced. And not because they were wearing clothing *she* couldn't afford unless she won the Publisher's Clearing House Sweepstakes—which they were. Not because in general they spent more on one haircut than she spent in twelve months; she'd gotten used to that over the past three years. Not because she knew that the "allowance" most of them got from their parents every week equaled or bettered her salary.

It was because she felt as if she was facing a class full of trendoid zombies.

One and all, with very few exceptions, they hung over their reading assignments listlessly. They were not acting as if they were distracted, but as if they were too emotionally burned-out to care about the assignment or comprehend it. And that was *not* the norm for this class, a class that a kid had to *earn* his way into.

The empty desk in the third row was the reason; Jillian McIver's seat. Oh, it didn't have her name on it, but it might as well have. That had been her favorite desk for most of the year—she'd even come to class a minute or so before everyone else just to secure it. Now it shouted her absence, the rest of the kids so studiously averting their eyes from it that they might just as well have stared and gotten it over with.

The funeral had been on Wednesday, but the kids were still in mourning, and Ann was desperate for a way to wake them up. She'd tried anything and everything—she'd taken a risk that the principal might find out and object to her playing anything more controversial than *Bambi*, and brought in her own videotapes, showing them *The*

Breakfast Club and asking them for reviews and analysis. She'd tried asking for reports on their favorite Judy Blume novel. She'd had absolutely no results, and no luck. Response was automatic and dead. Jillian's seat was empty, and that emptiness ate at the whole class like a cancer.

It was ironic that Ann hadn't wanted the girl in her class; despite high grades in English (though never anywhere else), to her way of thinking Jill had been just another mindless mall bunny. The principal and Jill's counselor had both prevailed against Ann's better judgment. "She needs to be motivated and challenged," they'd said. "She's not getting any challenge that she recognizes as such anywhere else."

The latest buzzwords, had been Ann's disgusted thought. *The latest excuse for why a spoiled kid doesn't give squat about school, when her parents don't care what happens so long as she graduates* or *gets married, whichever comes first.*

But for once her superiors had been right. Much as Ann hated to admit it. She was of the cynical, if unvoiced, opinion that guidance counselors were failed teachers who were too inflexible to find a job outside the school system. And that principals were inept teachers who'd been bumped upstairs to keep them from ruining any more kids.

The fall term traditionally began with drama, working in no particular order, anything from modern to classic to Greek. Ann confidently expected Jill to wither under the onslaught of *The Lady's Not for Burning*, and capitulate with *The Seagull*. But that scenario never developed.

Jillian McIver encountered classic literature and freedom of thought, and blossomed. Much to Ann's astonishment (since she hadn't expected that the girl would even be able to read without moving her lips) Jill devoured Jonson, raced through Chekhov. And then she went on to gobble Molière, Ibsen, and Schiller.

Then they'd hit the section on comedy, and Jill had *really* shown what she was made of. She'd done a synopsis of Aristophanes' *The Wasps* in ValSpeak that had even Ann rolling in the aisles. The girl was a natural comedian, which may have accounted for her popularity. Despite a voice like a whining saw, she could convulse either a listener *or* a reader. And Ann had cherished hopes of nurturing that gift. There was no reason why the girl couldn't become a *real* comic, or a comedic writer. She had the wit, and the talent.

But not the drive.

Gradually Ann had become aware of a curious metamorphosis. Inside the class Jill was one of the shining stars, bright, articulate, witty. Outside that classroom door, Jill was the same vapor-brain she'd always appeared to be.

Inside, she held her own with the Brain Trust.

Outside, she trailed around with the Trend Set, and never opened her mouth except to second someone else's ideas.

It had been, all things considered, rather like watching a multiple-personality case switch personas. It had also been maddening to witness, because the girl was only interested in using her comedic sense to amuse her classmates. She had no ambitions otherwise.

It was the waste of intellect that had troubled Ann the most. That, and the switch to airhead she pulled whenever she hit the door on the way out of Ann's classroom.

Dear God, it was like watching Segovia pump out guitar backups for Muzak tapes.

The kids in the class didn't seem to be bothered by the fact that Jill was one person to them and another to the social crowd. In fact, they seemed to have expected it, and there was a kind of unspoken accord among them not to approach Jill in any way outside the class, unless she approached them first. As if they were all obeying some kind of tribal law of conduct Ann hadn't been made aware of.

It had annoyed the hell out of Ann; among other things, Jill *could* have been a bridge between the academic and the social cliques. If she'd chosen to do so . . .

But she wasn't interested in being a bridge to anything. Once that kid passed the threshold, she had no life outside of shopping and parties. As far as Ann could tell, she never even opened a book outside of school.

Ann could not imagine a life without books, especially for someone as bright as Jill proved she could be.

A life without books . . . There was a book locked up in Ann's desk right now that was Jill's—*I, Claudius*. She'd brought it in under her notebooks and asked Ann to keep it for her so she could read it between assignments.

Presumably because if she'd been seen with it, she'd have had the stigma of being a Brain.

Well, it was all an academic question now; the girl was as dead as last year's leaves, and all her ambitions—or rather, lack of them— were dead with her.

And the kids, ranging from freshman to senior, were taking it much harder than she would have dreamed. The life was gone from the class.

She wasn't just the star pupil with a gift for comedy, Ann thought, watching Derek Kestrel turn over the last page of the assignment, then brood out the window. *She was their passport into the In Crowd, if only by proxy. And it isn't just that she's dead, it's the way she died.*

The accident had not only been freakish, but there were some strange rumors circulating about it, rumors that had reached even the teacher's lounge, that things weren't the way the official story had them.

According to the police reports, Jill was the only one of the four kids in the car *not* wearing her seat belt. And that, given that Ann had personally heard Fay Harper boast of having no less than twenty-three warning tickets for *not* wearing her belt ("It scrunches my clothes"), was very odd indeed. So was the way Jill had died. She'd been catapulted over the front seat and partially through the windshield. But not completely through—and it wasn't the impact that had killed her.

She'd bled to death, her throat slashed open to the spine by the broken windshield. When Jill's head went through the windshield, the glass had fragmented into knife-edged shards that had closed around her throat like a collar of razors.

Yet none of the blood had fountained into the interior of the car. Neither Deke nor Fay had so much as a single drop on them.

There were rumors that Fay had been moving in on Jill's steady; that Fay had told Jill not to object *or* tell Deke Kestrel, or Fay would "take care of" her.

Yet Fay wasn't acting like a teenager who'd gotten her way over a rival; and Ann hadn't met a kid yet who could convincingly cloak gloating triumph or fake grief. Fay was acting "normally," just as distraught as anyone would expect. She hadn't been overly hysterical, nor cold and distant. She'd wept *exactly* as much as one would predict for a girl whose best friend had just died.

Even more telling, to Ann's mind, she wasn't zeroing in on Sandy that Ann could see, which would have been the next move for a girl whose rival was out of the way. At least, she wasn't going after the boy publicly, and teenagers, in Ann's experience, were just not good at subtlety or strategy.

There were other contradictions, though. There were rumors and eyewitness accounts that the quartet had been drinking heavily at the concert and afterward.

According to the doctors' reports and a dozen lab tests, there hadn't been a trace of alcohol or drugs in the kids' systems. Even Jill, who'd been the first tested. Of course, it had been pretty easy to get a blood sample from what was left of Jill. . . .

The official story was that Jill had unbuckled her seat belt to talk to Fay, because the music on the car stereo was too loud for her to be heard from the backseat. That would certainly account for *why* the girl went headfirst through the windshield when the others were only cut by flying glass, or bruised. Fay's story was that the steering went out, cause unknown. According to the police, there was no way of telling what had happened, because the undercarriage had been destroyed when the car went off the road. . . .

Enough already, Ann told herself sternly. *You aren't Miss Marple, and there's no way any of this could be anything except a particularly bizarre accident. Life goes on. You have a class to teach, and they've already lost a week to this. You have to get them motivated again. That's your job. Not trying to make an episode of* The Twilight Zone *out of this.*

She watched the kids finishing their assignment, one by one. Finally the last one turned over the final page, and Ann stood up. Twenty-four pairs of eyes turned listlessly toward her.

"You've all finished C. J. Cherryh's essay," she said. "It might interest you to know that Ms. Cherryh is a very prominent science fiction writer and lives here in Oklahoma."

And used to teach in Oklahoma City, poor thing, Ann thought wryly. *No wonder she went into writing. They ought to issue machetes and Uzis, and award combat pay over there.*

Some of the kids *did* look interested, as if they hadn't imagined that a *real writer* could come from anywhere they recognized. Ann smiled in satisfaction.

Now that they've got that idea in their heads, maybe I can install the notion that they could really become writers. Then I get them to deal with what happened to Jill through fiction. If I can get these kids to put their trauma in writing, it'll help them a lot. That's what all the teaching magazines say, anyway.

"I'm telling you this," she continued, "because I want to prove something to you. I want to prove to you that the people who write books are just like you and me. I want to prove to you that any of *you* could be one of those people, with enough work and talent. And believe me, the work is more important than the talent."

She paced back and forth, slowly, in the little Demilitarized Zone between her desk and theirs. She watched their expressions as she spoke, hoping for the spark of interest that would tell her that she was motivating them again.

Because this class was her reason for continuing to teach. Without it, she'd have gone slowly crazy, like so many other teachers she knew. And if she couldn't get this class going again, she'd lose *her* motivation, for this year, and maybe for good.

If that happened, she might as well take that job over at that advertising agency. The pay was *much* better and the grief factor bound to be less.

"So, what you're going to be doing for the rest of this quarter is this: you are going to learn how to write fiction yourselves. First you're going to see *how* to write, which is why I chose 'Arms and the Writer' as your first reading assignment, so you can understand the importance of choosing the right words." She smiled at them, noting that the new girl in the back, the transferee from Colorado, was looking particularly bright and eager.

Ann had high hopes for that one. Normally she didn't warm much to the pretty girls—they tended to be as bad as Jill, if not worse. And this girl was spectacular—creamy-brown, perfect skin, green eyes, bronze hair, and petite face and figure. But she had been genuinely interested *and* talented, and Ann found herself directing at least half her remarks to the newcomer.

Maybe she'll replace Jill. . . . "Mark Twain also said something of the same thing: 'The difference between the right word and the almost-right word is the difference between lightning and a lightning bug.' Here's your homework assignment: I'm going to give you each a different picture. I want you to write one paragraph about it; choose *exactly* the right words to describe it. Make it not just a description of the scene, but try to describe what seems to be happening, as if you were writing a tiny story. You are absolutely forbidden to use the words 'almost' and 'nearly.'"

She began passing out the pictures, culled from a dozen different magazines she'd gotten at the Salvation Army, carefully matched to her students' individual interests. The only things the pictures had in common were that each contained two people, one old man, one young woman—and it appeared that the old man might be teaching her or offering advice.

"While I'm distributing these pictures, I'd like to ask your help."

Derek Kestrel took his picture listlessly. Ann was particularly worried about him. He'd gone as uncommunicative as a mute.

Not that she blamed him. It couldn't be easy to have a friend beheaded, particularly not when it was virtually impossible to have saved her.

"I need to know," she continued, passing the glossy bits of paper down the row of desks, "if any of you or your parents know a real, professional writer who would be willing to come in and help me show you what you need to do to become a writer." She smiled encouragingly. "The only ones that *I* know have full-time jobs too; they can't take several weeks off just to come in and teach a class."

A couple of the kids roused up enough to look surprised. Ann responded to that surprise as the first genuine reaction she'd gotten from them in a week. "That—having to hold down a 'real job,' or as those writers call it, a 'day job'—is part of becoming a professional writer. Some people *never* make it to full-time, self-supporting authordom. I'd like to have someone here who *has*, who can tell you what it takes and give you a taste of what his nuts-and-bolts world is all about."

She looked around the classroom; to her surprise it was Derek who raised his hand.

"My dad knows someone," he offered tentatively. "There's a lady he used to go to college with. She's a full-time writer; she writes romances."

Two of the boys snickered; half a dozen of the girls looked truly interested, though, and the little girl from Colorado positively came alive. Her green eyes glowed and her cheeks flushed with excitement.

"That's *exactly* the kind of thing I was hoping for," Ann said quickly, to counter the snickers. "Romance writers are very business-oriented people, and there are quite a few men writing in that genre under female pseudonyms. I'm not interested in someone who's been spending the last twenty years trying to write the Great American Novel. I want to bring in someone who can tell you and *show* you what it's like to work at the craft."

"Okay," Derek replied, looking a little more in tune with the rest of the universe than he had a few minutes ago. "I'll ask my dad tonight."

Derek slumped over the leather-wrapped steering wheel, with the engine running and KTHK blaring from the radio. There was no use in trying to move until the last of the aspiring Indy drivers had cleared the school parking lot. He wasn't in the mood to fight their flashy muscle cars with a Chevy Citation; it was sort of like taking on a bunch of F-15s with a Piper Cub.

With a lot of imagination, balls, and skill it *could* be done—in fact, he'd bet Jackie Stewart could do it in a Yugo; he'd heard a story about him trashing Porsche drivers in a rented Lincoln—but Deke wasn't feeling that magical. Magic seemed to be in pretty short supply, lately.

Gray clouds bulked lethargically overhead; the air smelled like rain, but so far nothing had fallen.

It would be just my luck to have it start pouring the minute I pull out of the parking lot.

He was beginning to wonder if he'd used up his entire lifetime quota of luck the night of the accident.

Nobody'd been wearing a belt, but only Jill had taken a header. The car hadn't rolled, though by all the laws of nature and physics, it damn well *should* have.

But that had only been the beginning of the weirdness.

Because Fay had *vanished* from the front seat before the steering went crazy. Deke remembered that, with all the clarity of something that had happened a few minutes ago.

It gave him a queasy feeling just to think about it; made him feel a little dizzy. Or maybe that was because of the concussion. *Sometimes I wonder if that hit on the head made me see things. . . .*

But no, he hadn't been concussed then, *or* even all that drunk. He was remembering right. One minute Fay had been cussing Jill out. The next, she'd *disappeared.*

But when the car came to a stop, hitting the abutment of the overpass with enough force to throw Deke against the dashboard and total the front end of the TransAm, she was back. She was cut up a little, bruised a little, and totally hysterical—but back in the front seat.

And she was buckled in.

And so were Deke and Sandy.

He fingered the buckle of his own seat belt now, and eased the shoulder strap away from the side of his throat. *I* wasn't *belted, I* know *I* wasn't. *So how did I get fastened in?*

The cops had appeared out of nowhere—on a road they never patrolled, since there was a dispute on between the County Mounties and the Jenks Police as to who "owned" it. Somewhere in the back of his skull, in a part that wasn't gibbering about Jill's twitching body right in his lap, a little piece of his mind figured that they were doomed. The cops were going to see all the bottles, and they'd end up in the Juvenile Home for the night, then up in front of the court in the morning, and they'd get it in the teeth for drinking underage— even if he and Sandy hadn't been the one in the driver's seat, they'd still be lucky if any of them got their licenses again before they were twenty-one, and Dad—

Dad would hit the roof. Probably send him to military school.

But there wasn't so much as a single beer bottle anywhere in the car. Not even a shard of glass.

The back of his neck crawled. The whole night was right out of *Twilight Zone*.

The cops had *searched*, too, and hadn't found a thing. What was more, when the doctors pulled blood samples at the hospital, there wasn't anything in *them*, either.

That had totally weirded him out. Though at that point he'd felt as sober as a Baptist preacher, Derek couldn't believe what they told him. But they'd run the tests twice, and every single one of the doctors insisted. All four of them, including what was left of Jill, were clean.

So when the cops and the docs tried to ask him what happened, he stopped himself before he could blurt out the truth. Truth that the evidence denied. He'd just sat there with his mouth open, unable to think of *any* story at all.

The doctors put down his stunned inability to answer their questions to shock. Well, that was okay. He figured he'd just let Fay give her version and keep quiet. And when Sandy woke up, they'd probably figure he was hallucinating. After all, what good would telling the truth do now? It wouldn't unmake the accident, or bring Jill back, or even make Jill's parents feel any better. All it would do would be to get *him* in trouble, maybe ending up with having to see a shrink.

But things got even stranger. When Sandy came to, his uncoached, unprompted version of the night's ride tallied exactly with Fay's—and ran completely counter to what Deke remembered.

Fay admitted, tearfully, to speeding "just a little. There wasn't anybody else on the road. I kind of forgot to watch the speedometer. I can't believe the steering and the brakes went out; my God, I *just* had my car inspected and worked on!"

Then she coughed up a real fairy tale, the sanitized Walt Disney version of the night's outing; *sans* booze, racing, and sex.

And there was something else he felt he should have remembered, but couldn't. Something about a drag-race?

If it hadn't been that he *knew* Fay, and *knew* that the innocent, playful joyride she described was about as typical of her as finding the president of Exotic Furriers in a Greenpeace meeting, he'd have figured he was going nuts.

Maybe I am *going nuts, anyway*, he thought, watching the last of the losers in the exit race rev their engines to make up for their poor showing. *I could believe that he was just covering everything up* really well, *but Sandy still doesn't remember what actually happened.*

He pondered that a while longer, staring at his hands on the steering wheel and wondering just what the signs were of someone going bonkers. Was it really true that if you wondered about your sanity you were probably still sane?

A spatter of rain hit the windshield; Deke looked up, startled, and realized that the lot was empty. He looked at his watch, swore, and threw the Citation into reverse. He backed out of his slot with a shriek of abused tires, threw her into drive, and burned as much rubber as *any* of the other rocket jockeys getting out of the lot.

Once out on the street, though, he cooled his jets. Be pretty damn stupid to get a ticket after all he'd just been through.

The rain was just drooling down; barely enough to make him put on his wipers. He knew better than to trust these streets, though—some of those muscle-cars leaked oil pretty fierce. Add oil buildup to enough rain to float it above the asphalt, and you had more trouble than he wanted to take at speed. Hydroplaning was no fun, and he didn't need another wreck right now. So he took his time getting home, watching for slick spots.

And remembered, suddenly, about the English class, and what he'd promised Ms. Greeley.

That was something he hadn't much thought about when he'd volunteered—how he was going to approach his dad about this business with that writer friend.

He began to feel a bit more cheerful with the change of mental track. He flicked on the headlights; it was getting pretty gloomy and it didn't look like this storm was going to die out anytime soon.

When Ms. Greeley had made her pitch, he'd just shot his hand up, because he'd been wanting to meet this Diana Tregarde for ages. Mostly because of the funny way his folks acted whenever they talked about her.

First of all, they *didn't* talk about her when they knew Deke was around, and then it was like by accident. He'd gathered that his mom had met her when Mom was going to college in New York, at about the same time that Di Tregarde and Dad were Yale classmates. Which was odd, because you wouldn't think that somebody would know people at Yale and NYCU, much less get them together. The other hint he'd gotten was that there was something really funny about the way that his parents had met and that the meeting involved Di Tregarde.

But they wouldn't *talk* about it. Or not much.

"Di introduced us," Dad had said once, with a funny, sly sort of grin at Mom. "I thought I was seeing things—"

"No doubt," she'd retorted—then they'd both broken up, for no reason that *Deke* could see.

Granted, they were probably all hippies together back in the sixties; he'd seen a couple of pictures of them and their friends. They'd looked like the cast of *Hair*; beads, headbands, Indian-print shirts and granny dresses, wire-rimmed glasses. He'd hardly recognized his mom; she'd had crinkly Art Nouveau hair down to her waist, a flower behind one ear, and was wearing a miniskirt so short he wondered how she ever sat down. Hell, her *hair* was longer than her dress!

He grinned, thinking about it. *Mom didn't look bad in that mini, either. Don't blame the old man for jumping her.*

His mom had taken one look at the photo, blushed beet red, and asked him if he didn't have better things to do than look at a bunch of old pictures of people he didn't even know.

That's when he'd *tried* to get them to talk about when they were his age. And they avoided his questions as neatly as a diplomat. Now that was crazy; when his friends asked *their* folks to talk, you couldn't get them to shut up, especially about when they were in college.

But Dad wouldn't talk about college, and neither would Mom. It was like there was this four-year gap in their lives that they didn't want anyone to know about. A gap that was somehow tied in with this Diana Tregarde.

Probably it was something along the lines of the wild stuff Alan said *his* parents used to do—psychedelics, Mazola-oil parties, that kind of thing. And they didn't want him to know the kind of trouble they used to get into.

Deke had always been pretty good at deciphering Parental Codes. Spelling hadn't held him for long, pig Latin baffled him for less than four months, and when they used French it only forced him to become bilingual at ten. But the cryptic references the folks used when they *did* talk about Diana completely threw him. And the way they acted about her—like they didn't want him to talk about her to anyone—you'd have thought she was a CIA agent, or a rock star incognito, or something.

He was thinking so hard that he was startled to notice that he was on his own street, and practically in his own driveway. He thumbed the garage door opener hastily, and pulled the Citation into his side of the garage, just clearing the slowly rising door.

He checked the answering machine for messages, but the only ones on it were the disconnects of "robot calls" and one intrepid siding salesman.

He hunted through the refrigerator for something to eat, but nothing looked good, so he settled for some microwave popcorn to tide him over until his dad got back from the downtown office.

When the corn was popped, though, he suddenly didn't want it. The first bite was fine, but after that it was dry and tasteless.

Because he kept seeing Jill—

Deke dumped his snack down the garbage disposal and plodded up the stairs to his bedroom, where he threw himself down on his bed and beat his pillow into submission with angry fists.

"I'm *not* going crazy," he said aloud, fighting back fear and tears. "I'm *not*. Somebody's lying, and it isn't me!"

Finally he rolled over on his back and stared at the ceiling, at the little constellations of glow-in-the-dark stars his folks had put up there when he was eight.

He wanted, with a desperation he couldn't admit aloud, for his mom to come back from Japan. Things never seemed right when she was gone, this time especially.

But—well, when she was gone, Dad was a bit more talkative. *And* he'd been moping around a lot himself. Maybe if this old college buddy came out, it'd pick Dad up.

And I can see if I can't figure out what the big deal is about her, Deke promised himself. *That'll give me something to think about besides seeing Jill lying across the dash—*

He shuddered, and turned over on his side, burying his face in his pillow.

Dinner was Kentucky Fried—Mom would have had a cat. No veggies, no salad, just chicken and double potatoes and biscuits. Deke and his dad grinned at each other in delicious guilt over the bones. It seemed an auspicious moment to broach the Question.

"Dad—" Deke said as they cleaned up after themselves and disposed of the evidence, lest Mom find it. "You know that writer you used to hang out with? The romance lady?"

Larry Kestrel stopped shoving bones down the garbage disposal and looked at his son with a very strange expression. "Di Tregarde? Funny, I was just thinking—why? What about her?"

Deke plunged straight in. "Ms. Greeley wants us to try writing and she wanted one of us to find a real writer to come in and help for a couple of weeks and I said you knew a writer and she said to ask you if you could get her."

It all came out in one sentence, without a pause for breath. Larry pondered him with a puzzled frown for a moment; then his face cleared. "Is *that* all?" He was so relieved that Deke wondered what on earth he *had* been thinking. "Well, I can't promise anything, but . . . come on back with me to the office; I'll make a few phone calls and we'll see what happens."

Deke followed his father into the inner sanctum—the "den of iniquity" was what his dad called it. Actually it was just a home office where Dad worked on his private projects. It held nothing more sinister than the usual office furnishings and a drafting table and a microcomputer, and the all-important speakerphone. Larry picked up the handset, though, flipped through the Rolodex, and lifted an eyebrow at his son, who was hovering at the threshold.

"Let me talk to your teacher a minute, kiddo."

There was a low-voiced exchange on the telephone, while Deke stood uncertainly beside the door. Finally Larry hung up and nodded to his son, who edged over into the pool of light around the desk.

"Ann seems to like the idea—now I'll see if Di is free. Have a seat; this is going to take some time."

Deke picked a comfortable-looking chair, then sat on the edge of it while his father thumbed the Rolodex again, and punched buttons. A long-distance call from the sound of it.

"Mark?" Dad said, the sound of his voice very loud in the quiet of the office. Deke jumped in startlement. The phone on the other end couldn't have rung more than twice. "It's Larry Kestrel." He listened, then chuckled. "Yeah, I know, long time, no hear. How's the job treating you? Oh, really? Sonuva—"

He flushed, and glanced belatedly at Deke. "—ah—gun," he finished, ears flushing. "Listen, I've got a favor to ask. I've got DT's address, but not her phone, and I know she keeps her number unlisted. Could you—?"

He grabbed a pen and scribbled something down on the blotter of the desk set. "Great, old buddy! Thanks! I owe you one—" He listened for a moment more, then laughed out loud. "Okay, so we're even, have it your way. I gotta go, they're an hour ahead of us on the Coast."

He hung up and dialed again. This time when the phone was answered, he frowned for a moment. "Excuse me, but I was trying to reach a Miss Diana Tregarde—is this the right number?"

Deke ran his thumbnail nervously along the seam of his jeans, while his father listened cautiously to the reply.

"Well, I'm an old friend of Diana's, from college. Larry Kestrel." Larry's face brightened then. "So *you're* André. Great, Mark Valdez told me a little about you. I don't suppose the Lady ever told you about the Squad, did she?"

The Squad? What the hell is that? Dad wasn't in ROTC; he'd rather have died! If there's anything more frustrating than listening to one side of a phone conversation, Deke thought, squirming in the chair, trying to find a comfortable position, *I can't think of it.*

His father seemed to be taking an awfully long time, just listening. But finally his face lightened. "Terrific—I'm really glad to hear *that.* Carte blanche, huh? Well, I'd say we all earned it at one time or another."

He listened again for a minute, and laughed. "No, no, I promise, this is mundane. My kid's English class is looking for a writer to come talk to them and I wondered if there was anyway I could lure her out. . . ."

While Deke watched, an expression of incredulous joy flickered briefly over his father's face; then, after his eyes met Deke's, the expression vanished, replaced by casual cheerfulness so quickly that Deke figured he must have misread it.

"Kansas?" Larry said, and chuckled. "No, really? I'll be darned. That's practically next door! Listen, let me ask you something, has she got anything urgent she needs to take care of back there? Do you suppose she'd be willing to take a detour and a little vacation?"

Suddenly Deke's father lost all the cheer he'd been projecting; he looked as if what he was hearing was entirely unexpected.

"Oh," he said faintly. "Oh, God. God, I am really sorry to hear about that, I really am. I never met Lenny, but she used to write about him so much it feels like I know him. He sure was a good friend to her when she first moved to New York, I remember that. The last time she wrote, she said he was sick, but I had no idea—"

Deke bit his lip to keep from interrupting.

"—yeah, it might be a real good thing for her to have a break, I agree. And I'll do my best to keep her distracted. Listen, I can pull some strings, I know a few people; I could get him into one of those experimental programs, the ones that *aren't* giving out a placebo run. . . . Oh. He is. No improvement. Shit."

Larry's expression was angry and frustrated, and the tone of his voice was bitter. It wasn't the first time Deke had ever heard his father swear—but it was the first time he'd ever heard him put quite so much feeling into it. He wondered what it was that was making him feel so strongly.

"Yeah, give me the number, please."

Larry reached for one of his drafting pens, and jotted down a number in careful, neat little numerals.

He repeated it back to the other person, and nodded. "Thanks,

André. Yeah, you too. Do you want me to say anything about—okay,
I won't mention him unless she does. And if there's anything I can
do, you let me know. And I mean *right away*. I'm not just making
noises, I'll help if I can. You know our crowd—we tend to make some
oddball contacts—I could even get him some of that Mexican stuff if
he really wants to try it. I don't advise it, but I'm not in his shoes.
Thanks again. I'm only sorry I'll be stealing her away from you for a
month." He listened again, and smiled at the reply. "Yeah, I suppose
so. You take care."

Deke slouched back in the chair as his father dialed this new
number; he couldn't help wondering if this was *ever* going to get anywhere.

His father's face lit up again. "Di? Larry Kestrel. Yeah, the real
thing! Same to you, Spooky—"

There was something really odd about the way his dad looked as
he listened to his old friend on the other end of the line—something
that made Deke feel strange and uneasy. He wasn't sure he understood the sparkle his dad's eyes were taking on, or the way he seemed
to be getting younger with every minute.

"Whoa there, milady," he interrupted at last, laughing. "Let me
put you on speakerphone. I've been on the horn half the night trying
to track you down, and my ear's getting tired. Besides, I want my son
to hear this; he's the one that got me to track you down in the first
place."

He laughed again at something she said, and thumbed the
speaker switch.

"—and your yuppie techie toys!" said a young-sounding female
voice. "Honest to gods, Larry, I swear you've been hanging around
in bad company! Weren't you the one who refused to own more
than two pairs of jeans, because anything more was conspicuous
consumption?"

"I got corrupted by easy living." Larry chuckled, looking far more
amused than the comment warranted, or so Deke thought. "Besides,
the more I buy, the more jobs I create. So what in hell are you doing
in Kansas?"

"Oh ye suffering *gods*," she groaned feelingly. "Signings. That's
'autograph parties' to you. Bee-lyuns and bee-lyuns of them, or it
sure seems that way. If I never see a mall again, it'll be too soon."

"In Kansas?" Larry said incredulously.

"In Kansas," she replied. "Believe it or not, they can *read* in
Kansas. My publisher found out that I was going back to Dallas to
pick up a car Mark Valdez found for me, and he decided that since I

was going to be driving it back to New Haven, I might just as well stop at every godforsaken shopping mall between Dallas and Kansas City and sign a few thousand books. After all, I don't have anything better to do, right?"

"Do what Nancy Reagan says. Just say no," Larry replied, his mouth twitching as he tried to keep from laughing. Deke was grinning himself.

"He *bribed* me, the skunk," Diana protested. "He bribed me with something I could never afford on my own—a state-of-the-art laptop. With more software than *anyone* has a right to own. And a built-in modem. So I didn't even have the excuse that I couldn't work on the road. How could anyone say no to that?"

"Jeez, Spook, you have no room to twit me about *my* techie toys!"

If he grins any harder, Deke thought, *he's going to split his head in half.*

"So why did you have to go halfway across the country just to get a car? And why from Mark? Don't they have cars in New England?"

"Not ex-highway-patrol interceptors, they don't," she replied, her tone no longer light. "Not with less than ten thousand miles on the engine and tranny; not with both the engine and the tranny rebuilt and retuned until they sing the 'Halleluia Chorus.' And not with most of the goodies still *on* it—and you did *not* hear that from me, laddy-buck."

"I hear you," Larry replied.

"Good. Mark pulled some real strings to get it for me, KK. I've needed something like this a long time, and the offer was too good to pass up. You know why—"

"Yeah," Larry interrupted her. "Yeah, I know—listen, like I said, my kid's here, and we've got a big favor to ask you. Can I talk you into backtracking a little? If you'd be willing to come on back down here, I'll treat you to a month's vacation as my houseguest. I just talked to André, and he thinks you need the break. Granted, Tulsa isn't exactly the pleasure capital of the universe, but as I recall, you were into culture, right? We've got a couple of decent museums, and a pretty good opera and ballet company—"

"I know about the ballet company," she interrupted. "I saw them do that Ballanchine revival in New York. You're damning them with faint praise if you think they're only 'pretty good.' I'd do a lot to get a chance to see them again—" she continued, sounding wistful. "And not just because they're good; they're also darned scenic. It's too bad Jasinsky Junior's married, he's *really* slurpy. But I don't know, Kosmic. It's going to take a lot of convincing to get me to drive back down through Kansas again. What's this got to do with your kid?"

Deke was back on the edge of his chair and bouncing. For some reason—for some reason he couldn't even define—getting this lady to come visit was *important*. He didn't know why; he just knew that it was.

His dad seemed to feel exactly the same way; he was talking to Diana as if he'd forgotten Deke was still in the room. It felt like eavesdropping—and Deke *wanted* to eavesdrop. He tried very hard to think like a leather armchair.

"Ann Greeley—that's Deke's teacher—is doing a section with her Honors English classes on creative writing, and she wants a real full-time author to come in and show them the ropes. Not just critique, but the day-to-day stuff. Watching the markets, revisions, tailoring to suit a particular editor, that kind of thing. Thing is, there's more to it than that. It's not just that she wants the kids to get an idea of what it's like to write for a living, she wants 'em—I don't know—distracted, I guess. Deke and three of his buddies were in an accident this weekend, and one of them—well, she didn't make it."

"Ah. So the kids are taking it pretty hard?"

"Yeah," Larry replied. "She was pretty popular, with this class in particular. Ann's hoping bringing you in will be enough of a novelty to get them all going again. Right now they're all pretty much in shock."

That was news to Deke, who tried not to move, for fear his dad would remember he was there.

"Yeah, I can see that. You say Deke was one of the kids in the accident? Am I thinking what you're thinking?"

"Probably," Larry replied cryptically. "So what's it going to take to lure you down to glorious Oklahoma?"

"Just that you need me—and clean air. Right now—definitely clean air," she moaned. "You don't have any stockyards down there, do you? I think they park a stockyard next to every damn motel in Kansas. I am *never* going to get the smell out of the back of my throat!"

"No stockyards," Larry promised. "You—you don't want to arrange any more of those signing things down here, do you?"

"*No!*" she exclaimed. "Great Jesus Cluny Frog! These women are *crazy*! They think I'm like one of my damned heroines—they think I write this stuff from experience!"

Larry bent over in a spluttering, choking, laughing fit. The laughter was infectious—and besides, Deke didn't think he'd get to overhear any more stuff about what Ms. Greeley had told his dad. So Deke joined in.

"Oh, right, Kosmic Kid. Go ahead and laugh! *You* aren't the one they're descending on, with their books clutched to their all-too-ample bosoms. *You* aren't the one they're asking for advice on their love lives. *You* aren't the one with the groupies—"

"Groupies?" Larry chortled. "You have *groupies?*"

"Every romance writer has groupies, laddy-buck. Most of 'em thirty-nine going on thirteen. And they want *me* to solve all their personality problems with a wave of my magic wand. Kee-rist. If I could do *that*, I wouldn't be hacking out bodice rippers, I'd be making a fortune as a Hollywood shrink."

"I'll buy that. Okay, no signings, and to sweeten the pot, we just put in a six-man Jacuzzi."

"Uncle!" she cried. "For a Jacuzzi, I'd emeritus a class full of gorillas! And since I just did my last spot in the barrel, I'll be there by late afternoon tomorrow."

Deke and his dad exchanged triumphant grins. "Okay, sport," Larry said. "Looks like this is a done deal. I'll call your teacher as soon as I get off the phone with Di. How about if you go take care of that homework, hmm?"

Obviously he was *not* going to be allowed to eavesdrop anymore. He capitulated. "Okay. I guess I'd better."

He slid out of the chair, while his dad switched back to the handset and began talking too quietly for Deke to make out what he was saying without making it plain he was trying to listen.

Very obviously he wasn't going to be allowed to eavesdrop.

But he couldn't help wonder, as he headed back up to his room and a dismayingly long history assignment, what it was that a romance writer did that would call for owning a former police car. . . .

THREE

Deke pretended to read his history text, and peered through the half-closed door of his room at his father. Larry Kestrel was pacing again, and Deke was beginning to wonder if this business of having Diana Tregarde come out here was such a good idea after all.

Ever since she'd agreed, his dad had been acting like—like Deke, with a hot date coming up. Diana had told them that she expected to be there "late afternoon," which Deke interpreted as between four and seven tonight. Larry had hardly eaten his supper; he'd parked himself in the family room, and when he wasn't pacing, he was pretending to read a book. This after rushing Deke through his own meal and up to his room "to work on homework." But Deke could see him easily enough from his desk—and he didn't like what he saw.

Larry flung himself back down in the corner of the beige velvet pit-group, and reached for the book again. Deke wasn't fooled. For one thing, Deke could tell his dad was only pretending to read. He hadn't turned a page in the last ten minutes.

Besides, somehow I don't think Dad's the Danielle Steel type. . . .

And he spent more time pacing than staring at the book, anyway. Miss Tregarde was due any minute now, and Larry was getting increasingly fretful.

So was Deke.

I don't know, he thought worriedly, drawing aimless little scribbles on the blotter. *Maybe I made a big mistake. I mean, there's all kinds of "old friends." Maybe this lady used to be a real hot item with Dad, and Mom didn't know. And Mom's clear the hell over in Japan.*

*And it's not like Dad's taken a vow of celibacy or anything. As far as I
know, he's still got all his hormones and everything. . . .*

Deke chewed on the end of his pencil and wished he'd thought
about this a little more before he'd gone and opened his big mouth.

*But maybe I'm getting all worked up over nothing. Yeah, I probably
am. Miss Tregarde's a year older than Mom, at least that's what Dad
said; there's got to be a good reason why she hasn't gotten married. Besides, all she does is write—I bet she never goes anywhere. Probably
she's still stuck in the sixties, no makeup, straight hair, granny glasses,
patched-up bell-bottoms, and Earth Shoes. Either that or she's about
twenty pounds overweight, maybe getting a little gray in the hair. Sort
of like Ms. Greeley. Even if Dad is kind of expecting something to happen, I bet he's thinking she looks the way she did in college. I mean, he
told me himself he hasn't seen her since he and Mom got married.*

Deke chewed his lip a little, feeling a bit better when he pictured
this Tregarde lady as looking a lot like his English teacher—a little
matronly, certainly nobody's idea of a sex fantasy.

Just as he reached this conclusion, he heard the sound of a car
pulling into the driveway—a car with a big, powerful engine. Of
course it *could* be someone using the drive to turn around—

But the engine stopped, and Deke saw his dad leap up from his
seat on the couch and head for the door.

Deke abandoned his own pretense at study and bounded out of
his room, taking the stairs two at a time and winding up right at his
father's heels.

Larry Kestrel pulled open the front door of the house before the
driver of the car now taking up a good portion of the driveway in
front of their garage could even make a move to get out.

The vehicle had had its driver's and passengers' doors primed,
but it was going to be hard for even the gaudiest Earl Scheib paint job
to hide the fact that this used to be a cop car. Brake-vented hubcaps,
extra heavy sway bars, and most especially the skid plates underneath
gave its history away to anyone as car-crazy as Deke. You just didn't
see Crown Vics out on the street with mods like those. Like all cop
cars, the beast was a four-door, and Deke had the shrewd suspicion
that there was a roll bar still in the door pillar.

Sunset painted the sky behind the car in exotic shades of purple
and gold, and the interior of the vehicle was so shrouded in shadows
that Deke couldn't make out what the occupant looked like. For a
moment, while the driver was still involved in getting extricated from
the seat harness, Deke's attention was on the car. He itched for a

chance to get under that hood and poke around. He had no doubt, given the way the engine had sounded, that this thing was exactly what Diana had claimed—a police interceptor, capable of catching just about any commercial vehicle on the road.

And even more than getting under the hood, he wanted a chance to *drive* it.

But then Diana Tregarde opened the car door and slid out into the last light—and Deke's worst fears were realized.

Jee-zus, he thought in dismay. *She's a babe!*

She was willowy and supple, and looked athletic without looking like an athlete. In fact, Deke had the startling impression that she was in better physical shape than Fay. About five feet tall, she had an over-all build like a dancer, and she moved like a dancer, too. Instead of the holdover hippie outfit of peasant skirt and baggy blouse, or patched jeans and ratty T-shirt he'd been picturing her in, she was wearing a leotard that might as well have been a second skin and chic designer jeans nearly as tight as the leotard. She *was* wearing makeup; subtle, just enough to make her look model-like and a touch exotic. Her waist-length chestnut hair was caught in a pony-tail, and hadn't even a trace of gray.

She sure doesn't look Dad's age, Deke thought unhappily. *She looks more like a college student.*

She bounded over to his dad (she *ran* like a dancer; she hardly touched the ground) and flung her arms around him, an embrace that Larry reciprocated, much to Deke's discomfort. And the warm and enthusiastic kiss she gave and got didn't make Deke any happier.

She finally let go and backed off a pace, looking Larry up and down with a strange smile. The sunset glow haloed her as if Ridley Scott were directing the entire scene. Deke wanted to be sick; this was a setup, and it was all his fault. The next thing she'd say was "Oh God, Larry, I never realized how much I missed you. . . ." And they'd clinch again, and then they'd hustle him out of the way, and then—

"Why, Kosmic Kid," she said, laughing, "you look positively bourgeois! Where's the wild-eyed revolutionary I used to know and love?"

Well, *that* certainly wasn't in the script! *Kosmic . . . Kid? Wait a minute, she called him that before. What is this, a comic book?*

"Know, I'll admit, Fearless Leader," Dad replied, shoving his hands into his pockets and grinning back. "But love? Hardly. Not from the way you used to abuse me. Oh, I'm doing what you told me I should do, way back when. I got tired of beating my head against monoliths. It's guerrilla warfare now; real subversion. I'm being the thorn in the foot."

"You mean 'pain in the ass,' don't you?" She chuckled, her grin spreading still wider. Deke couldn't help but notice that she stood, not like a dancer, but like a martial artist, balanced and a little wary. And that those designer jeans had the special little inset piece that would let you do a sidekick without tearing the crotch out.

This is a romance writer?

Larry clapped the back of his hand to his forehead theatrically. "Crushed! How *could* you?"

"I couldn't crush you with a bulldozer," she retorted, tossing her tail of hair over her shoulder. "So answer the question already— what's with the yuppie rig, and where'd the rebel go?"

"Undercover." Larry put his arm around her shoulders and pushed her gently back toward the car, leaving Deke to trail along behind them, sneakers stubbing along on the concrete of the driveway. Next to this "old lady," he felt as awkward and ungainly as a bull calf. Larry continued, oblivious to his son's reactions. "When I'm not separating the wealthy from their ill-gotten gains by translating their vague notions of one-upmanship into their homes and buildings, I'm designing low-income housing, and doing it for a lot less than anyone else will." They exchanged conspiratorial looks. Deke bit his lip. "It drives my accountant crazy."

She raised one eyebrow, like Mr. Spock. Deke wondered how she did it. He'd practiced that for hours in front of the mirror without getting it right.

"I'll bet," she said sardonically.

"I keep *trying* to tell him that money isn't everything, but he keeps tearing his hair out."

"Did it ever occur to you that an accountant is probably *not* the kind of person who is going to believe that little platitude?" They all reached the car, and Diana freed herself from Larry's arm and turned to give Deke a very penetrating once-over, quite unlike the examination she'd given his father. It gave Deke a very funny feeling, uncomfortable and a little scary. It felt like he was being tested in some way, but it wasn't any test he recognized.

Finally she held out her hand with a cheerful smile, one that somehow didn't seem superior, the way most adults smiled at kids. "Hi. You're obviously Derek. I'm Diana Tregarde, as you've probably figured out on your own. Di, to you. I can't say I know a lot about you, but what I do know, I like."

Derek shook her hand gingerly, a bit taken aback by her forth-rightness and frankness.

Her smile turned into a grin full of mischief; the corners of her enormous, velvety-brown eyes crinkled up. That was the first sign he'd seen that she was anywhere near Dad's age. Mom took pains to hide *her* crow's-feet and never smiled that broadly as a consequence; Diana Tregarde didn't seem to care.

"I should warn you now," she told Derek in a confidential tone. "You're going to have to put up with a lot of nonsense while I'm here. We're likely to start reminiscing about our romantic, wild youth at the drop of a poncho."

"Hey, man," Larry drawled—the accent he was using sounded vaguely Valley, but not *quite*. Derek couldn't place it. "Is that, like, a real poncho, or is that a Sears poncho?"

It sounded as though he was quoting something, but Deke didn't recognize what. Then, as they started to giggle, for Chrissake, he identified it as a quote from one of Dad's Frank Zappa records. "Ca-marillo Brillo," whatever the hell *that* meant.

Jeez, he thought, half in dismay and half in disgust, as they both looked at his expression and went from giggling into gales of laugh-ter, *am I going to be sitting through reruns of* The Wonder Years *and* Hair *every night?*

They finally calmed down, Di leaning against the fender of her car and wiping her eyes with the back of her hand. "Lord," she said weakly. "I'd honestly forgotten how dumb we all were. At one point that really *meant* something, Deke. If you didn't wear a real, honest-to-gods poncho, handwoven either by some poor Guatemalan peas-ant or somebody named Moonflower—if you had some kind of polyester fake, you were what we called a 'day-tripper' or a 'plastic hippie.'"

Gods? Plural? This is a romance writer? But she was looking at him expectantly, waiting for a response. He tried to sound intelligent. "Like a poser?" Derek hazarded.

"Yeah." She nodded vigorously. "A real nowhere man, a plastic flower child. Some suit who came out to the campus on the weekends to get high and get his brains balled out by hippie chicks so he could boast about it to his suit buddies during coffee breaks. Or some deb who came looking for Sexual Liberation in easy, one-screw doses."

"Di!" Larry exclaimed, looking shocked.

She gave him a wry *look*. "Come off it, Kosmic. Kids these days have twice the sex education we did by the time they're Deke's age. I'll lay you odds eighty percent of his female friends are on The Pill."

"More like ninety-five," Deke admitted, deciding, however reluctantly, that he was beginning to like Di Tregarde. She didn't talk down to him, and she didn't pretend to be a buddy, either.

"See?" she said. "You can't shelter 'em, KK. Not any more than our parents could shelter us, or Yale could. I've told you before; if they've got brains and a drop of sense, your best bet is to give kids all the facts. Then when they've had a chance to absorb the facts, throw 'em my theory of Teenage Evolution, and ask them the One Big Question."

"What's that?" Deke asked, curious against his will. "The question, I mean."

Di leaned back against the hood of her car, a dark silhouette against the fading sunset. "I know your mom and dad, and they're no hung-up born-agains, so I'm going to assume you *do* know all the facts, including the ones about AIDS—"

"That you only get it with exchange of mucus and semen and blood, and that it isn't just a gay disease," he offered. "That anybody can get it; that the only known protection is a rubber."

She nodded soberly. "Right on; that sums it up." Deke sneaked a look at his dad; he looked like somebody'd hit him in the middle of the forehead with a two-by-four. Stunned. *I can't tell if it's 'cause of what Di's talking about, or because I already know what she's talking about. We had the Big Talk years ago, but we never got around to AIDS.*

"Okay, here's my theory of Teenage Evolution. You know why we—human beings, I mean—start to fall apart when we hit forty?"

He shook his head.

"Because, evolutionarily speaking, we aren't meant to last beyond our reproductive years. I mean, that's what evolution really means— survival of the fittest means *reproductive* survival; the one that spawns the most wins, not the one that lives the longest. Nature favors quantity of life, not quality."

Deke scratched his head. He'd never quite thought of it that way. *I guess that sure explains cockroaches, mosquitoes, and linebackers.*

Di nodded, and smiled a little, as if she had heard his thoughts. "So—given that, the *best* years for the human being to reproduce are its youngest fertile years, so that you've got a chance to raise and teach the young. Basically, in these days of improved nutrition, that's thirteen to twenty-four, or so. Which means, kiddo, that right now your hormones are screaming at you to get out there, establish a territory of your own, grab you some wimmen, and raise you some babies. Like, *now. Lots* of wimmen, and lots of babies. Have you figured out what that means to you, personally?"

"Uh—" he replied brightly.

She *didn't* laugh at him, though he'd half expected her to. "Okay. One, establishing your own territory means aggravating the hell out of your old man, so he'll throw you out of the cave and force you to go fend for yourself. Two, grabbing you some wimmen means just that, which is why all the peacock stuff everybody does as soon as they figure out the opposite sex is pretty neat—from fancy cars to fancy clothes. *And* that's the whole rival thing too, so that all you young bucks start locking antlers to figure out who's top dog. I mean, you're supposed to have a harem of about two or three—that means knocking off some of the excess competition. Establishing your territory kind of goes along with that. Three, raising you lots of babies means your hormones are going to have you screwing anything that'll let you. Now the Big Question, Deke."

At some point during this astonishing discussion, Di had scooted up on the hood of the car, where she now perched with her legs neatly crossed. She didn't look like an adult, or even, oddly enough, like a kid. What she *did* look like was ageless, as if she was some kind of modern incarnation of the Delphic oracle, perched on a weird substitute for a tripod.

The Fordic Oracle?

Larry looked more than stunned, he looked paralyzed, with his mouth hanging half open.

This is a romance writer?

"Which is?" Deke managed.

"You aren't a mindless tomcat surrounded by queens in heat, and you aren't a caveman, kiddo." The "kiddo" didn't even come out sounding patronizing, just earnest. "You're a human being, and you have brains as well as glands. So tell me, what are you going to let run your life—your head, or your hormones?"

Now it was Deke's turn to stand there with his mouth hanging open. He'd never heard—things—put quite that way, or that bluntly, before.

"Well," Larry managed to choke out, before the silence drowned them all. "You sure know how to get a kid's attention. I hope you aren't planning on delivering this same lecture to Deke's class."

She grinned, and blinked innocently. "I might. If the situation calls for it."

"In that case, I may have to protect you from a lynch mob." Larry swallowed twice, and managed to get his jaw back in place.

"My brains," Deke said, at the same time.

"Good choice, Deke," Di replied, sliding down off the hood of the car. "Keep that in mind next time your libido goes into overdrive. Your kid is smarter than you were, KK."

"Before or after I met you?" he retorted. "I have the feeling some of those escapades you got us into cost me more than a few brain cells, milady."

She just snorted, but reached for Larry's shoulders and gave him a hug. It looked to Deke like an apology for the teasing. "Listen, I've been thinking about that Jacuzzi you promised me for the last hundred miles. My shoulders are killing me."

"The boiling pot is ready and waiting, Spooky, and if it can't cure your shoulders, nothing will." Larry seemed to have gotten over his previous shock.

"So what are we waiting for?" she asked, skipping around to the rear of the car, popping the trunk just as the automatic floodlights over the driveway came on. "Let's get this junk into the house and get cooking!"

Deke's dad grinned. "Your wish is my command, milady," he said mockingly—but he reached into the trunk and pulled out a trio of purple ripstop nylon bags. Deke grimaced. *Prince had a yard sale?* She looked at him, grinned, and shrugged, as if to say, "It was cheap, what can I say?" Buried in the sea of purple were a black ripstop case and a corner of a briefcase. Di took the former out gently.

"My new toy," she explained to both of them. "Sorry, Deke, no games. The IRS won't let me deduct it if I put games on it."

"The things we do for taxes." Larry sighed, looking just as disappointed as Deke felt.

Deke found himself loaded down with gear, all of it purple nylon. *Now this, I'd expect from a romance writer. This, or rose pink.* His dad got his fair share, though, and to her credit, so did Di, including a beat-up leather briefcase; that case looked heavy. *Very* heavy. Deke had avoided reaching for it on principle; it looked like it held an entire IBM mainframe. Di hefted it easily; another surprise. Larry led the way into the house and up the stairs to the guest room. Di was close behind, leaving Deke to trail forlornly in their wake. His dad and their guest were chattering away at high speed now; their conversation was full of cryptic little references to things he couldn't even guess at.

That was quite enough to make him feel like the one on the outside, but besides that, they kept making sidelong glances at Deke.

I'm not that *dense,* he thought. *I know when I'm a third wheel.* He dropped the luggage beside the bed and started to leave.

Di touched his arm as he passed her; he stopped, startled.

"Deke," she said quietly, "I had a reason for the lecture. I don't want you to think that *I* think you're some kind of idiot. I—I'm trying to save people. I'm losing somebody I really care about. To AIDS. I don't want to lose anybody else, okay?"

Suddenly that entire conversation Larry had held with the mysterious André made sense.

"Okay," he said weakly, blushing. "Really, it's okay. I understand. And—thanks."

She smiled faintly in reply, and he escaped before he could make a fool out of himself.

But he still wasn't comfortable leaving them—Di and his dad—alone together. He *really* wished his mom was back from Japan.

Diana Tregarde was entirely too attractive to trust with his father. Especially alone.

Di didn't even bother to hide her sigh of relief when the kid finally left. *Nice kid, but—Jesus Cluny Frog!* She just shook her head, strolled over to the bedroom door, shoved it shut with her toe, and gave Larry a look she *knew* he could read.

He grimaced apologetically.

"Ye gods, Kosmic," she groaned, lacing her hands across the top of her head. "How in hell did you and Miri manage to give birth to such a—a—" Words failed her, and she shrugged.

"Square?" Larry suggested, sitting astraddle a chair, after turning it wrong way around. "Three-piecer? Young Republican? Budding IBM rep? Corporate Clone?" He tilted his head sideways and waited for a reply, blinking with mild expectation.

There was a little gray in that lovely, wavy hair, and he was wearing it shorter these days, but otherwise he was about the same as when she last saw him, and definitely in good shape.

Like all the kids in the Squad. Makes me feel like I did something right, anyway—they're fabulous as adults. Mind and body alert and sharp. And damn fine role models.

"Something like 'all of the above,'" she replied. She dropped her hands, headed for the dresser, and began transferring neat stacks of clothing from suitcase to dresser drawers.

The guest room was just as impressive as the rest of the house—which was saying something. If this was an example of Larry's handiwork, he'd fulfilled his promise of talent. If it was an example of his income, it was in the high six figures. This room had a skylight, its own bath, and dry sauna, was paneled in what looked like white birch (and probably was), and was furnished with some truly lovely pieces finished in white lacquer. The gray rug was thick enough to lose change in. But the effect was warm and airy, not sterile; by day it would be like living in the sky. On a practical note, there were *lots* of dresser drawers, and a very generous walk-in closet. Evidently Miri was over the box-and-milk-crate phase.

"Except the Corporate Clone," she amended. "If we can just get your boy's spine a bit stiffer, he *can* think for himself. The hard part is going to be getting him to want to. Which brings me back to the question; how'd a pair of bone-deep rebels like you produce a kid like that?"

Silence. A pregnant silence. She stowed the last of her leotards and turned back to face him, leaning against the edge of the dressing table on one hand.

"I have *no* idea," he said, as she took in his expression of bafflement. "Maybe it's karmic, much as I hate to put any stock in that. It sure would serve me right, given my misspent youth."

"More like it's Jenks," she observed. "Gad. More top-shelf European cars than in Europe. This town looks like Yuppie Central. Capital of expensive bland—no guts, no passion—Jeez, Lar, even the damn *houses* are pastel. And the *people*—cut 'em and they'll bleed tofu."

He shrugged. "The choice was here, or subject him to the Tulsa school system. He'd have come out of there being able to find the nearest muscle car, count to first-and-ten, and figure out exactly how much cash or coke would keep him from getting beaten up *this* time, but that's about it. Di, we average *forty* kids to a classroom over in Union— even if Deke *wasn't* psi, that'd have driven him nuts, and he'd never have gotten the kind of attention a kid with his brains deserves. He does here—they have a special course load for the bright kids, and he's on it. And over in Union, his life expectancy wouldn't be too high in some crowds. The car-crazy kids in Jenks tend to hover over basket cases in the garage. Kids from Union drag-race into the sides of semis."

She paid scant attention to the last sentence. It was the remark about Deke being psychic that caught her attention. "So he *is* psi? I thought so, since you had shields all over him, but that could have just meant Miri's paranoia was acting up. What's his Talent?"

Larry draped his arms over the back of the chair, then rested his chin on them. "No real idea," he admitted. "We bottled him up too fast. We had to shield him back when he was nine—he was picking up everything within a five-foot range. I was kind of hoping he'd grow out of it at puberty, but he didn't."

Di considered that in the light of what she knew about early-developing psychic gifts. "A five-foot range, huh? Not bad," she said thoughtfully. "Not a superkid, but not bad. So why didn't you do more than bottle him up? Or were you trying to keep him out of *your* business—"

"None to keep him out of."

Di looked at him measuringly. "Are you still into hot-and-cold-running esoterica at all?"

Larry shook his head slowly. "No, not since we moved here. Tulsa is about the most psychically null spot you'd ever want to see. Didn't see any reason to keep up the old skills; there was no use for them. Besides"—he nodded in the general direction of Di's shoulder—"this is the home of Oral Roberts University; the Prare Tar is right behind you."

"The *what?*"

"The Prare Tar. That's 'Prayer Tower' to you non-Okies."

"I saw the supposed-to-be-hospital, I didn't see that."

"You have to be on the campus to see it; it only looms subjectively. Anyway, Miri and I figured we'd be better off keeping our heads down and our profiles low."

Di licked her lips, stowing that data away for further examination. "Good move," she said finally. "Probably what I'd do in the same situation. Dear gods, I wish I didn't have to cart all these signing clothes. . . ." She shoved away from the dressing table, and stood hip-shot halfway between the bed and Larry's chair. Watching him, his face in particular. She was, after all, still an empath—and she hadn't lost her knack of reading him.

There's more here that he's not telling me. It's got to do with the kid.

She hooked her thumbs through her belt loops and rested her knuckles on her hips. "So," she said, after waiting fruitlessly for *him* to broach the subject. "Talk. You really didn't bring me out here just to lecture for a month to a bunch of rich-brat pseudointellectuals. Or to reminisce about old times and keep you company while Miri's gone. You know better than to detour me for no better reason than that."

"You needed a vacation," he ventured. "That's what André said, anyway."

"Uh-huh." She continued to stare him down, and eventually he capitulated.

"I've—got a bad feeling. Just a kind of hunch." He looked sheepish.

She gave him the patented look of Exasperation. "Kosmic, back in the Squad days your hunches were better than most people's certainties. So what's this so-called bad feeling centered around? Deke?"

"Yeah." She waited. "This could just be normal parent stuff. Parents are supposed to worry about their kids; it's part of the job description."

"Uh-huh. And I'm the Pope. Cough it up, Kosmic."

Problem is, his precognition was always vague, she thought, waiting for him to find the right words. *And he used to be pretty sensitive about that. As if it was* his *fault that he couldn't pin things down.* After watching him grope around for what he wanted to say, she decided to prompt him a little.

"So how long has this feeling of yours been going on?" she asked. "Days? Weeks?"

"Really strong—about a week. Before that, vague, a couple of months. Before that, everything was fine."

He chewed on his lower lip and looked up at her, his expression worried and absurdly young-looking.

"Could all this be normal paranoia?" she asked, knowing that it *wasn't* but wanting to get him to admit the fact. "Or could it be because of that accident you told me about on the phone? If you were picking *that* up, but not that Deke would come through it all right, you'd have been itchy."

"No . . ." he replied, slowly but firmly. "No, it was going on before that, and it's worse since. If what I had been picking up was a premonition of the accident, I wouldn't be feeling anything anymore. And—"

"And?" she prompted. *Now we're getting somewhere.*

"It's not a mundane threat," he said firmly. "I realized that right after the accident, when I got him at the emergency room. I don't know why I didn't figure it out before, but now that you're here, I'm sure of it. But that's as specific as I can get. And *damn* if I can figure out what it is, or even where it's coming from."

She shifted her weight from her left to her right foot, but otherwise didn't move.

"It's like—" he began, then stopped.

"Go on."

He grimaced. "It's not like anything we ran into as the Squad, okay? So I'm just getting little hints around the edges."

Di kept her mouth shut this time; she could sense desperation and fear.

"Di," he said in a near-whisper, "Di, it's like there's something really hungry out there, and it wants my boy. And Miri isn't here to help me protect him."

He never was any good at combative magics, she recalled. *That was Miri's specialty. I remember he had precog, but Larry's biggie was the Sight and clairvoyance. Hell, that's why we named him Kosmic Kid—he was always Seeing things. Things I had to strain to even get a hint of.*

"Do you suppose that's a coincidence?" she asked.

He shook his head. "No, I'm beginning to think it wasn't. Whatever this thing is, it seems like it was waiting for Miri to leave for Japan before it went after Deke. I don't dare contact her; this is very hush-hush negotiations with the Japanese, they're paranoid as hell, and she isn't allowed to talk to *anybody* in the States except superiors in the company. They're so paranoid she told me before she left that the only way I could get to her would be a *real* emergency, because the Japanese would be checking, and she could lose her job. There's no doubt in my mind why it waited for this trip—she's secluded, and half a day away at the very best, and twenty-four hours is more like it."

Di nodded. This was beginning to make very nasty sense. "In our line of work, twelve hours can be all it takes. . . ."

"Exactly." He sighed, and massaged his temples. "You know the other factor here—Deke's age. He's never going to be stronger than right now, when he's got youth *and* energy *and* a fluid mind *and* all that burgeoning sexuality just looking for a place to go."

Di nodded, her lips compressed. "And I'll wager that it wasn't too long ago that he lost the protection of innocence, too. He's got that look—like he's started *knowingly* violating laws and rules, and doing it in a way he knows is going to hurt people if they find out."

Larry nodded *his* head unhappily. "Yeah. And that makes him a legal target, doesn't it?"

"It does. We'll just have to hope he hasn't hurt anybody badly by what he's done—and we'll have to hope he's feeling appropriately guilty about it," Di sighed. "If he's getting his kicks—"

"Not Deke," Larry told her. "I'd stake my life that he's not happy about breaking the rules. He knows we don't lay down the law arbitrarily. And I'm equally sure that he wouldn't hurt anyone on purpose, much less enjoy doing it."

She sagged down onto the edge of the bed. "I hope you're right, Lar. I just hope you're right . . . because you know as well as I do what could happen if you're wrong."

For unmentioned, but not unremembered, was the reason she had answered his call so promptly. The reason she *owed* him, beyond friendship and the help any teacher owed a student.

Melinda Dayton. Unchildlike child, who'd done more than break the rules—

Di did not even need to close her eyes to see Melinda; the one and only time they'd come face-to-face was all too vivid in memory.

Melinda, cowering against the wall of the kitchen of the abandoned shack. Not pretty; Di would have suspected a child that was too pretty, too clean, in that situation. Melinda was plain, a tattered little brown sparrow, with big frightened eyes. Vulnerable, and helpless.

She'd put on a very convincing little act.

Melinda Dayton, who looked so pathetic, had been dismembering kittens at seven, torturing and intimidating her playmates at eight, and at nine had learned how to bring in outside allies to help her do the same to adults.

She'd very nearly gotten Di.

Melinda Dayton, demon-child, who even before puberty had learned the pleasures of cruelty and pain.

Willingly, with full knowledge of what she was doing. Enjoying it. Granny had claimed that there were kids like that, born absolutely evil, wrong, twisted. Who knew the dark and chose it. Di had been skeptical. After Melinda, she believed.

If it hadn't been for Larry, who'd seen past the little-girl-lost eyes to the alien mind behind the eyes—who had spotted the things Melinda had brought in through the gate she'd constructed into the world of nightmares—

I might not have been toast, but I sure would have been hurting.

Some of the traditions she had worked in claimed that once there was a life between two people, they were karmically linked for all time.

Maybe that's true, she thought soberly. *Maybe it isn't. But Melinda or no Melinda, Lar was one of mine, and I take care of my own.*

He was watching her closely, as if trying to follow her thoughts. He looked worried to Di; well, that wasn't too surprising. He tended to think in terms of debts and balances—and maybe she owed him one by those terms. But he'd owed her just as big a debt; maybe bigger, in his eyes.

She'd kept him from killing himself.

That memory was nowhere near as immediate—she remembered more of what she'd picked up from him, and what she'd done; she really couldn't remember exactly what she'd said to him that dark, windy night. Not the way she recalled every second of that nightmare encounter with Melinda.

Not that it really mattered.

The bleak, hopeless despair, that's what had caught her attention; the kind of despair that saw no way out. The kind of hopelessness that drove home to her why *the Catholic Church considered despair to be a mortal sin. Emotional trauma that profound could not be ignored—especially not when it carried the overtones of someone with a strong psi-talent.*

She'd looked wildly around, using all her senses. The roof of the math building—

She remembered dropping her Coke and sprinting for the door, thanking all the gods that the math building wasn't one of the ones kept locked at night.

She'd caught him ready to throw himself off the top of the building, convinced that he was going crazy because he was "seeing things."

Except that *she* could See what he'd been Seeing.

Poor, pathetic thing, it had been trying to hold him off the edge with hands that could no longer grasp anything material. It was a ghost, of course, the ghost of a classmate who had managed to get some bad acid and take a header out the window the week before. The poor guy didn't even know he was dead.

All he knew was that no one seemed to be able to see him except Larry. He didn't understand what was going on; his mental processes were still scrambled from the bad trip. All he understood was that Larry represented his only hold on the reality that he'd known, and he wasn't about to let him get away.

The revenant had been haunting Larry for two days, turning up anytime, whether he was alone or not. Larry had thought his mind had finally snapped, that the pressures of school and political activism had gotten to him. After all, he was a rational, modern guy, who didn't believe in spirits.

Which meant that he had to be going crazy.

The thing hadn't let him sleep, hadn't left him in peace for most of those two days—and an hour before he'd run up the stairs of the math building, his roomie had quietly dialed the medical center to get them to come haul him away. Larry'd overheard that, and was at the end of his rope. He'd often said he'd rather die than go nuts—just the idea of being locked up in a little white room was enough to make him shake.

Di kept her smile strictly mental. Poor Lar had his share of quirky phobias back then—well, they all did; phobias kind of came with the territory of being psychic.

So when Di had pounded up those stairs, Larry was seconds away from proving he'd meant that statement.

Except that she didn't let him. And before the night was over, she'd put both spirits to rest.

"Well," she said finally, "I'm here now. Anything that wants Deke is going to have to go through me to get him."

Larry grinned with real relief. "God, Di, I was hoping you'd say that. I didn't want to ask—"

She crossed her arms over her chest. "No kidding. You never did. If you had a failing by the time I got through with you, it was that."

"—but I was hoping. So I'm not overreacting?"

She put out mental feelers. *All quiet on the Western Front, but that doesn't mean a damn thing.*

"The truth is, I don't pick up anything now, but that doesn't prove a thing. You know that as well as I do. No, I don't think you're overreacting. I think there's something going on. And one more thing—I think your kid is overdue for an evaluation and maybe some lessons in psi, before *he* winds up doing a soft-shoe on a ledge."

Larry grimaced, but nodded. "I was hoping he'd never have to deal with it."

She snorted. "Fat effin' chance, as you well know. If you don't deal with power, it deals with you. Now about that Jacuzzi you promised me . . ."

"With or without bathing suits?" he asked puckishly. "It doesn't look to me like you've got anything to be afraid to show, even at our age."

Di chuckled. "Lecher. Wouldn't you just like to know—and what would Miri say?"

"She'd say, 'I've always wanted to reenact the murder of Agamemnon.'"

Di laughed. "She probably would. Well, much as I hate wet spandex, in the interests of saving your life, and to avoid traumatizing your child, I guess we'd better use suits. I wouldn't want to shock poor Deke."

"I hate to say this, love," Larry said mockingly, "but I'm afraid you already have."

FOUR

The kitchen was hot, and smelled like fresh garlic. "Keep grating that cheese," Rhonda Carlin told her daughter. "Your hands and mouth can work at the same time."

Monica made a little wiggle of impatience, but picked the grater and ball of mozzarella back up, and resumed her assigned task. It was better than setting the table, anyway; she *hated* setting the table—she couldn't talk to her mom while she was setting the table.

Let *Dan* set the table.

"*So*, anyway, I saw Deke out in the court and he was sort of sitting kind of slumped over, so I went over to him and asked, like, what was wrong." She grated away vigorously so that Rhonda wouldn't interrupt her again, and picked a curl of the cheese out of the bowl to nibble on.

"And? What was wrong?" Rhonda frowned at the lasagne noodles, and Monica immediately felt guilty about asking her mother to make dinner tonight. After all, Rhonda was putting in a lot of overtime at her new computer programming job, and it wasn't really fair to ask her to do something that required more effort than setting the microwave.

"It was, you know, the accident." Monica felt a little chill go up her back when she mentioned it. Everybody at the school seemed to be affected that way—like if they talked about it, they might be next. "He's really down about it."

Rhonda nodded, her black hair curling in the steam from the noodles. "I'm not surprised. So, he was down. And?"

"Well, I said I didn't think he ought to be alone if he was that unhappy, because all he'd do would be to keep thinking about it and getting unhappier." The cheese was done, and Monica handed the white glass bowl to her mother. "And then I said, why didn't he talk about it, because that might help him feel better, and he said with who? And I said, with me. So he did. Or he started to, anyway." She giggled, and her mother raised a sardonic eyebrow at her as she drained the noodles.

"And then what happened?" Rhonda asked, deftly putting the lasagne together, layer by layer. Her sable-brown hands moved like a dancer's, graceful even in performing such a simple household task.

"Well, he started asking me questions, like about Colorado, and what did I like to do, and what did I think of Tulsa." Monica giggled again; she couldn't help it, it just bubbled up out of her. "I told him some stuff, and then I told him I thought the guys in Tulsa were pretty lame, 'cause I've been here a month and nobody's asked me out *yet*."

Rhonda laughed. "Why didn't you just hit him with a brick with your phone number on it?"

"*Mom,*" Monica protested indignantly. "Anyway, he had to go to class, but he said the guys in Tulsa are just slow, and that maybe somebody'll get the idea. And he said I was the sweetest girl he'd ever met, and he kissed my cheek."

"But did he ask for your phone number?" Rhonda asked shrewdly, putting the pan of lasagne carefully into the oven.

"Well," Monica admitted with reluctance, "no."

Rhonda shook her head. "Lame. Just like the others. And what about Alan? Yesterday you were all excited because he'd asked you if you had a boyfriend yet!"

"He's still okay," Monica replied coyly, following her mother into the living room. "He wrote me a note in class today. He's a hunk, too. They're *both* hunks. Besides, Deke knows all about that writer lady that's going to teach us on Monday. She's a friend of his dad's, and she's staying at his house." *That* was almost as exciting as having Deke notice her. "He says she's real nice."

"Did he say anything about whether he thinks she'd be willing to help you?" Rhonda asked, as Monica flung herself down on the couch, upside down, her legs draped over the back, her head dangling down the front.

"He says she might," Monica said happily, examining her nails. "He says I should ask her after class."

Not even her father knew how much Monica wanted to be a writer—not, she reckoned cynically, that he'd care. He was too busy with his new girlfriend to worry about his ex-wife and the two kids he'd gladly shed. Rhonda was the only person who knew; who knew about the boxes full of stories she'd written and never shown to anyone else. Not even her teachers knew.

But she had no idea how you became a real writer; did you just send things to magazines and book companies and see what happened? The writers' magazines, with their articles on marketing and agents and equally bewildering topics, only confused her.

And anyway, she had no idea if she was any good. Certainly Rhonda seemed to think she was, but that was her mother—the same person who'd framed her crayon drawings and hung them on the wall. She'd long ago decided that what she needed was the opinion of a real writer, a stranger, someone with no prejudices on her behalf.

And now it seemed that she was going to be able to get just that. And maybe, if this lady said she *was* any good . . .

I'll worry about that when—if—she does, Monica told herself, then chuckled. *Besides, wanting to know about her makes a good excuse to talk to Deke some more.*

"So what are you going to do this weekend?" Rhonda asked, breaking into her thoughts.

"I don't know," she admitted. "Rent a movie, I guess. And I've got a lot of homework."

Her mother shook her head, but didn't say anything. Monica knew she worried about her kids—she'd been pretty reluctant to transfer to Tulsa in the first place; she hadn't been too thrilled about being a divorced black woman *anywhere* in the South, and she was even more uneasy for the sake of Monica and Dan. "Being black in a mostly lily-white profession can cause enough problems just for me," Rhonda had confided to her daughter. "But you kids—going to a place like Jenks, and not only being black but having a dad who's white—I don't know."

Still, there hadn't been any problems so far, except the ones Monica usually had—jealousy from the other girls because she was pretty. The same thing had happened in Colorado. Monica couldn't help her looks, and she didn't intend to act like a nun or a Brain just because other people felt threatened. The only difference between Colorado and here, so far, was that the guys just couldn't seem to get their acts together. That, and Tulsa was pretty boring most of the time.

Privately, Monica thought her mother worried too much.

"I wish you'd get some friends, honey," Rhonda said, in that *concerned* tone of voice Monica was hearing a lot lately.

"It's okay, Mom," she said quickly. "It's just, you know, coming in like in the middle of the semester. Everybody's got their friends and it takes a while. But Harper was even nice to me today; she told me I ought to try out for pom-poms in the fall. If Harper's nice to me, everybody else will start being nice."

Rhonda's eyebrows climbed halfway up her forehead. "What brought *that* on?" she asked. "I thought she was trying to freeze you out."

"So did I. I don't know; all I know is she's not anymore." Monica went back to checking her nail polish for chips, examining it minutely. "Maybe she changed her mind. Maybe she's figured, you know, people are going to think she's racist if she keeps getting on my case. Maybe now that I've been here for a month she figures I'm not a threat."

"How could you be a threat?" Rhonda asked sardonically. "The guys around here are too *lame* to bother with!"

Monica snorted her agreement delicately. "Anyway, she's going to be graduating in a couple of months; maybe she figures that she doesn't have to worry about competition at this point. She should, though." She grinned at her mother. "It isn't prom time *yet*. I could still end up going with Deke. Or anybody else, if I decided to work at it."

Her mother laughed at her. "Girl, you are so *vain!*"

Monica made a face at her. Rhonda *still* got plenty of looks from guys; more than enough to make her daughter a little jealous. And maybe Dad was a jerk, but he was also a studly hunk. Monica had a mirror; as far as she could see, she'd gotten the best of both sets of genes. Daddy's hair and eyes, Mom's face and build, a blend of both for complexion. *I don't even need to work at a tan,* she thought smugly. *I've got one built in.*

And she didn't see where there was anything wrong with being aware of the fact that she was hot.

"Deke was being *real* nice to me," she told Rhonda, playing with the fringe on one of the sofa pillows. "When he figured out I wanted to know, he told me *lots* about that writer. And he didn't have to, either. He could have gone off with some of his buddies, but he stayed to talk to me. I think he just *wanted* to talk to me, that's what I think. And I think he likes me, so Harper better watch out, or she *will* have to get somebody else to take her to the prom."

The oven timer chimed, and Rhonda pulled herself up out of her chair to go take care of the lasagne. Dan appeared out of nowhere, sort of materializing in his chair.

He's as bad as Garfield, Monica thought in disgust. *All he does is eat. And he* never *gains any weight. It's just not fair!*

She followed her mother into the kitchen, and Rhonda glanced at her with a funny expression as she got the big bowl of salad to carry out to the table.

"You know, *you'd* better watch out," Rhonda warned her. "Harper could be a lot bigger threat than you think she is. She's got money, she's the most popular kid in the school, she's a pretty big frog in that pond."

Monica shrugged. "What could she do to me, really? She can't get me in trouble, and she can't put me on the outs with people who don't even know me."

Rhonda lifted the lasagne pan out of the oven and shook her head. "Sometimes it isn't a matter of what somebody can do on her own, and more a matter of what and who you know. It sounds to me like this Harper chick has more than her fair share of both."

It's show time—

Ann Greeley finished her introduction, making Di sound like the next Pulitzer Prize winner. Di had been waiting inconspicuously at the rear of the class, using just a touch of magic to make sure no one noticed her lurking back there. Now she chuckled to herself, and while Ann took her place at the rear of the class, Di strolled to the front of the uncrowded classroom to face the first of the two Honors English classes she would be teaching. She'd gone over her pitch very carefully with Ann first. She was wearing her usual working togs: blue jeans, boots, and leotard, with her long hair knotted into a bun at the nape of her neck.

She very nearly laughed at the surprised expressions most of the kids wore.

"Hi," she said, half sitting on the edge of the teacher's desk, leaning back a little on her hands. "I'm Diana Tregarde, and I write romances for a living." She smiled, surveying the young, astonished faces around her. "It's a tough job, but somebody has to do it."

The eighteen assorted pairs of eyes stared at her, and she stared back. They looked absolutely incredulous, and Di knew why. She waited, and finally one of the girls, a trendy little redhead, blurted out, "But—you don't *look* like a romance writer!"

Di did laugh this time. "What did you expect?" she asked them all, spreading her hands as she met each set of eyes in turn. "Lace and ribbons? Silk negligee? Torn bodice, with handsome hunk clinging to my ankle?"

She turned back to the redhead. The girl shook her head word-lessly.

"These," Di told them, taking in the ensemble with a gesture, "are my working clothes, mostly because they're comfortable. When I have meetings with my agent or publishers, I do the 'dress for success' thing, gray suit and all, but when I'm working I need to wear some-thing that won't distract me—because I may be sitting at my desk and pounding away at the keyboard for eight to twelve hours at a stretch. Sometimes more. It's never, ever less than eight."

One of the boys raised his hand. "Why never less than eight?" he asked. "I thought writers could do whatever they wanted to."

She leaned forward a little to emphasize her earnestness. "Be-cause this is a job, and I treat it as such. My office may be another room of my apartment, but I go there to work, and I give that work the attention it deserves, just as if I were working for a bank, an oil company, or anywhere else."

Now was the time to be a little more casual. She scooted up on the desk, and crossed her legs. "So, let me tell you what it's really like to be a writer—the way I live my life. It starts out around nine in the morning, because I'm a late sleeper. . . ."

She had them now, and she gave them a précis of what her work-ing day was like.

They seemed fascinated, not the least because her life was so *or-dinary*.

Once she started in on this part of the lecture, she had more than enough attention to spare for other things. And now that she had Deke out from under the shields Larry and Miri had put on their house, she could see if there was anything targeting him.

There wasn't, no matter how carefully she looked. Not that the absence of anything malevolent meant that he was safe—in fact, quite the opposite. If there was something after Deke, but it was will-ing to take its time and use a long-term plan, the smartest move would be to leave no telltales behind. After all, the kid was hardly in-visible; he had a set schedule to keep whether he liked it or not. And he was quite visible from a psychic point of view; the shields on him were anything but subtle.

So the absence of telltales only meant that anything after Deke was smart.

She did notice one other thing out of the ordinary about the class, though. There was one other kid with psi, one of the girls in the back row. Unshielded, she glowed with it, though not nearly as brightly as

Deke did through the shields. So it wouldn't be enough to give her any trouble, unless there was something out hunting kids with psi-potential, or unless there was a lot of activity in the area.

Now that's worth checking out—Di made a quick scan of the immediate vicinity. And came up with nothing. Absolutely nothing; like dead air. Exactly as Larry had told her, the immediate area was psychically null.

And that *was* strange.

But she really didn't have time to explore that at the moment; she was getting into the part of her lecture where she might start getting some questions.

She turned all of her attention back to the kids, and pointed out that she spent more actual time working than most of their parents, because there was never a break in her work, and in a "regular job" there would be times when there was nothing to do. At that point Deke asked, "What do you do when you've got writer's block? Sit there and stare out the window?"

She laced her hands around her knee and leaned back a little. "This is probably going to sound like heresy—but I don't believe in writer's block. And neither does any other genre writer I know. And you know why?"

Deke shook his head.

"Because we can't *afford* to be blocked. We have bills to pay, and deadlines to meet. We can't afford to be prima donnas, we can't take the time to nurse neuroses. I do one of several things if I'm having trouble with a book. I can go work on another project, because I generally have one book in outline, one being written, and one being revised at any one time. Or I can talk the problem over with one or two friends—and usually, just the act of discussing the problem gives me the solution for it. Or I can go back to the outline, see where I started having trouble, and see if there's an alternate way the plot could go. All sounds terribly businesslike, doesn't it?"

Heads nodded all over the classroom. This was not the way any of them had pictured the craft of writing—and having taught this kind of class before, Di was quite well aware of that. They'd all pictured the inspiration, then the jump to finished product, without a single thought for all the work in between.

She was slowly destroying that illusion.

"That's because it *is*," she said. "This is a business. I have a product—stories. And like any other product, what goes into it is far more work than creativity. That's why I laugh when people come up to me and say, 'I've got this great idea for a book—all you have to do is write it and we'll split it fifty-fifty.' I mean, just think about it. Think about the simple act of typing one hundred thousand words—that's about 400 pages. Not composing them, not revising them—just typing them. It takes me five minutes to get an idea, about a month to outline the book, and then another three *just to write it.* And some fool wants me to do all that work and split fifty-fifty with him? Five minutes against four months? Give me a break!"

The kids chuckled; some of them looked sheepish.

And there go about half a dozen more offers for so-called collaborations, no doubt.

"I'll tell you what I really think writer's block is—it's reluctance to sit down and do the damn work. When you tell people, 'I'm not writing right now because I don't feel like it,' you're not going to get any sympathy. But tell them you've got writer's block—you get plied with wine and cheese and all the 'poor babies' you can handle. Okay, since Deke started it, anybody have any more questions?"

"Yeah," one of the kids in the back said. "If ideas are so easy to get, where do *you* find them?"

She was tired of sitting, so she shoved herself off the desk and moved into the space between her desk and theirs, a kind of no-man's-land. "If I were being really snide, I'd tell you that I belong to the Idea of the Month Club; it's run out of Poughkeepsie, New York, and you get the regular idea, the alternate idea, and a selection of six featured ideas—"

The kids were all smart enough to see through that, and laughed.

"The truest answer would be that it's easier to tell you where I don't get ideas from. Life is full of them, especially for a romance writer. I can go downtown and people-watch, and see a dozen possible stories go by me. All you have to do is start noticing things around you, and then ask the really important questions—'what if,' followed by 'what then.' What if that model that passed you was in love with some photographer but thought he was gay? What if that worried-looking businessman thinks his wife is cheating on him—and why would she be, if she was? The ideas are there; you just have to open yourself to them."

"Do you ever try and write something the way you think an editor will like it?"

That was the young girl in the back of the room, and Di blinked in surprise. That was one question she hadn't expected.

"Of course I do," she replied. "And I'm sorry if that disappoints you, but it's true. I'd be a fool not to. They're expecting a certain kind of product from me, and I've signed a contract promising to deliver it. Once again, a genre writer can't afford to have feelings of sensitivity about his deathless prose. It's *not* deathless. It may—hell, probably will—be changed before it hits the bookshelves. So when you're a genre writer, you develop a very thick skin, and you learn to be flexible. Not that my editors haven't, on occasion, driven me up the wall with stupid revisions"—she grinned wryly at all of them—"because they have. But that's life. They pay me for the things, and besides, I usually manage to give them what they asked for, but the way *I* want it done."

"So why do you do this?" another girl wanted to know. "I mean, if it's like that much work, and people drive you nuts with what they want, why don't you go do something else for a living?"

"Mostly because I love writing," she answered. "Truthfully. I like telling stories, I like doing it well. In any other job you get people who drive you nuts, too—just ask your parents, or Ann Greeley, here. And I'll tell you something else—most people find themselves in the position of working at a job they're good at, but that they don't enjoy. It isn't too often that a person gets to work at something they really love. And I promise you all, from my own personal experience, if you *ever* find a job that you love to do, go do it, and damn the consequences. You'll live longer—but more than that, you'll be happy. And what you don't spend on ulcer medication and psychiatrists will more than make up for a pay difference."

She could see by the expressions on the faces in front of her that she'd gotten about half the kids in the class to think with that last statement. *Good. In five or six years they're going to be out there making a living—and the more people in the world there are that like what they're doing, the better off the world is going to be.*

She checked her watch; she had just enough time left to give them their first assignment.

"All right, now let's get down to business." She hooked her thumbs into her belt loops and moved over so that she stood directly behind the desk. "The reason I'm here is to give you all a start on learning to write. I say 'a start' because if you're any good, you never stop learning. Some of you will decide that you don't like it; some won't be much good at it. That doesn't matter, and what's more, you won't be graded down for it. As long as you *try*, that's all I care about. But believe me, I *will* be able to tell whether or not you're trying. So. Right now, everyone starts out with a B and you won't go any lower."

There were stifled gasps all over the class. She'd just violated every precedent for classwork they'd ever heard of, and most of them weren't sure how to handle it.

"What does matter in this course," she said, following up on her advantage, "is that you'll have gotten a chance to try your hand at this stuff. And you'll know whether or not you've got the particular combination of skill and persistence this takes. You'll never have to say 'if I'd only' . . . because you *will* have tried. And that is the single most important thing I'll be able to give you."

While they were still in shock, she gave them their assignment. "Now, I want one page of dialogue and description from you tomorrow. A simple scene; a girl and a boy having a fight. *You* choose what it's about. Don't allow them to make up at the end of the page. That's basically it. We'll read them all aloud and see how they work tomorrow."

The bell rang less than ten seconds after she finished speaking, and she congratulated herself not only for completing the lecture on time, but for keeping them so engrossed that none of them had been watching the clock just over her shoulder.

The kids filed out slowly, in clumps of two and three, all of them talking animatedly.

And that's one more gold star in my bunny book. I've got 'em going again.

The bell that had just rung was the one for lunch, so Di was a bit surprised when one of the girls lingered behind the others, hovering right near the door. She'd thought the lot of them would vanish.

It was the girl that had asked several of the better questions, a pretty, delicate child with a café-au-lait complexion and blond hair. Obviously a mixed-race girl, and Di envied anyone who'd been handed such a perfect combination of genes. *Model material if ever I saw it . . . especially in Europe.*

"Miss Tregarde?" the girl said shyly. "I wonder if I could bother you for a minute?"

"Sure," Di replied automatically, "though it isn't a bother. What can I do for you?"

Ann had moved unobtrusively to the front of the classroom. "This is Monica," she offered quietly. "She just transferred in from Colorado."

"I wondered if you'd look at some things I wrote, and tell me if they're any good or not." The girl wouldn't look at her; kept her head down and her eyes on the floor between them.

Now Di understood the intensity, and the look on the girl's face. This was one who wanted, badly, to be a writer.

The question was, did this girl have it in her to *do* what she had to, or was she just a "wannabe"?

"Sure," she replied. "I'll take a look, provided you're ready to handle criticism."

"I—" the girl began.

Di interrupted her. "The fact is—Monica?—the fact is that I can be kind, or I can be honest. I can't be both." That usually deterred the wannabes. "I'm not going to be nice, because an editor wouldn't be nice. It's an editor's job to pick the good stuff out of the crud, and to do that she—or he, my editor's male, though a lot of them aren't—can't afford to waste his time being nice to every poor soul that sends in an unsolicited manuscript. And I'll do one thing that she won't; I'll tell you what's wrong and why. She'll just send you the standard 'This does not suit our purposes at this time' rejection notice."

"That's great, Miss Tregarde," the girl replied earnestly. "It really is. I *want* you to tell me if it isn't any good, really I do. I—I just finished reading *Heart of the Wolf* last night, and I thought it was really terrific. I think I could learn an awful lot from you."

Di gave her two mental points. *Bright girl; read up on me to know who she was going to be dealing with. Okay, she says she's tough. Now we'll just have to see if she really is.* "Fine, if you're really sure. Would you like to take care of this tonight? I don't have anything I need to do."

"If you could—I mean, you know, it would be really great!" The girl looked about ready to kiss her feet.

Di thought quickly. *I'd better pick a public spot to meet her, public enough that if it turns out she can't take criticism, it'll be too embarrassing for her to make a scene. The last thing I need is a hysterical teenager—*

She did a quick take, and recognized the girl from her scan of the class earlier, looking for clues to Deke's hunter.

—make that hysterical, psychic teenager having an emotional tantrum at me.

"I could meet you at the library," she suggested. "The one next to Woodland Hills mall. That could be at about seven if you're up to it."

"I've got a lot of things all ready—I really do. That would be fine—that would be great!" the girl exclaimed breathlessly. She didn't even wait for Di's reply; she just clutched her books to her chest and ran for the door.

Di chuckled and shook her head, looking at Ann with a raised eyebrow. Ann shrugged, and smiled, and began pulling out the next class's assignment from her desk. "Kids," Di said to no one in particular, and followed the girl out.

She couldn't help but notice that Monica seemed to have picked up an escort once she hit the hall. And there was no mistaking who it was, either.

Well. Well, well. Dear me, Mr. Kestrel, I do seem to remember your father saying that you had a steady—and I also recall that it wasn't Monica.

Still, it might just be that Deke was discussing the assignment with the girl. Or that she was asking *him* about Di. It might be innocent.

Then again—they weren't holding hands, or even touching, but there was no mistaking the way they were leaning toward each other, oblivious to everything else.

Partially that's psi-attraction. And partially hormones. Derek, you're flirting with trouble if your steady finds out.... Di stayed behind them all the way to the outside door, trying not to grin at the romantic glow Deke was emitting. Once outside the door, they headed for one of the concrete benches surrounding the front entrance, presumably to share confidences and lunch.

Di, on the other hand, was not a student—so she wasn't stuck on school property. She also wasn't a teacher, so she wasn't limited to a half-hour lunch. With Lunch Monitor duty. That was the benefit of doing this without pay. Ann simply arranged for her to be a "guest speaker," and since she wasn't contracted to anything, she wasn't obliged to follow rules. The principal and school board had been so flabbergasted at having her run her "seminar" for nothing that they hadn't balked at any of her conditions.

She could go have a leisurely lunch in a restaurant, far away from babbling kids.

She took a quick look back at Deke and Monica, who were being very attentive to each other, and chuckled again. "Young love," she said aloud, "or is it young lust? What the hell, at that age they can't tell the difference!"

As she turned back toward the parking lot, though, she caught sight of someone else, someone in a fancy red sports car, pulled up at the foot of the sidewalk, very obviously staring in her direction.

At her?

No—behind her. And the only people directly behind her were Deke and Monica—

At that point, whoever was driving the car pulled out in a splatter of gravel and a shriek of tires; the car had been too far away from Di for her to even see what sex the driver was.

Peculiar, she thought, making a mental note to find out who drove a car like that. *Very peculiar.*

Barbecue—pronounced, or so Larry had told her, "bobby-cue"—
seemed a good option. It was one of Tulsa's three specialties, the other
two being chili and "deep-fried everything."

Since the latter choice sounded pretty vile, she opted for
"bobby-cue."

Tulsans, it seemed, barbecued everything, too. She blinked in
amazement at the barbecued baloney, and wondered what her old
friend Paul Lazinski would say about the unholy concept of barbecued kielbasa.

He'd probably call the Pope and get them excommunicated, she decided, and opted for something a bit less—exotic.

And just a touch of caloric sin. "And cold potato salad," she told
the waiter.

"Y'all want that Easterner potato salad?" he asked, making it
sound as if it were toxic waste. "Or good Oklahomey potato salad?"

"What's the difference?" she asked, just a little apprehensively.

"That Easterner potato salad, they put in the mayo, an' the mustard, an' the relish," he told her, "but them potatoes, they's cut up in
chunks."

"Okay," she responded. "So?"

"In good Oklahomey potato salad, they's *mashed!*"

He grinned as if he had just revealed that their cook was a Cor-
don Bleu chef in disguise.

Di swallowed. "I'll settle for french fries," she told him faintly.

She took the moment of peace before her "feast" arrived to
arrange her facts in order.

*One, Larry thinks his son is being stalked. Nothing to support that
at the moment, but nothing to contradict it, either.*

She played with the edge of her napkin. *Assume he's right; whatever is after him is leaving no fingerprints. Okay, that's not a problem,
particularly if it's noticed he's shielded and has decided to move in on
him slowly. What that means is that he, she, or it is probably more than
just adult age—probably fifty at least. It takes age and experience to be
that subtle.*

Which left out any of Deke's classmates playing at magick. Unless
one of them happened to be an apprentice to somebody older and
wiser. Even then, it was a virtual certainty that an apprentice would
have blundered somewhere along the way. And that would leave
traces.

*One way to be sure; call Fred and ask him if there's anybody that he
knows of operating in Tulsa. Anyone working darkside that has taken*

apprentices usually devours or ruins them, and that would show up in Guardian telltales.

She stared at the water beading up on the side of her glass. *Two, Tulsa is absolutely psychically null. Frankly, I wouldn't want to operate here. I'm going to have to figure out the boundaries, and figure out why. And how long it's been this way. It may or may not have any bearing on this case.*

Rolls arrived; warm, but obviously mass-produced. She ignored them. *Three, Deke is a legal target. He's obviously flirting with that little black girl, and that means he's knowingly violating the implicit promise made to the chick he's going steady with. That makes him an oathbreaker, and puts him on the negative side of the karmic ledger, which in turn makes him open to subversion, or even attack. Even if he'd been protected up until now, he isn't anymore. Which leads me to number four—he's hiding something. It's something he's afraid to tell anyone else. And I don't know him well enough to judge whether it's mundane or psi-related. It might even be both.* She bit her lip. *With teenagers, nothing's ever simple.*

Her order arrived, and she ate it quickly, without tasting it. As soon as she was finished, she headed for the bank of pay phones near the rest rooms, and dialed a Kansas City number from memory.

"Guardian Plumbing and Heating," said a tinny voice, faint Eastern Seaboard accent tingeing the words. "Fred Hunter here."

"Fred, it's Di," she said, laughing in spite of herself. "You know, one of these days that name is going to get you in trouble!"

"What, 'Fred'? How could that get me in trouble? When are you going to let me fix that furnace of yours?"

"Fred, you moved to Kansas six months ago. Is business so bad that you're willing to make house calls to Connecticut? Besides, there are perfectly good heating contractors in New Haven—"

"The boys in New Haven are a bunch of crooks," Fred interrupted, as she bit her lip to keep from laughing anymore. "They wouldn't tell you if you had a transdimensional portal to hell in your humidifier."

"Why would I want a transdimensional portal to hell in my humidifier?" she asked. "It's easier to take the Greyhound down to Newark. Listen, I've got a serious question. I'm on a personal case. Is there anybody operating in the Tulsa area that I should know about?"

"There's nobody operating in the Tulsa area at all worth talking about," Fred replied. "At least, not according to my sources. Never has been, likely never will be. Even the Indians won't work there. Can't tell you why, it's out of my territory. Let sleeping dogs lie, I always say. No news is good news. Curiosity killed the cat—"

"Okay, okay, I get the idea," she said hastily. "But I'm the one that's down here. I could sure use some local information."

"Sorry," Fred said, sounding sincere. "Wish I had some. But you know how thin we're spread. Hell, we didn't have *anybody* down in these parts till I moved here after that Dallas mess you got yourself into. Good thing you were able to handle it alone. Now about that furnace of yours—"

If I'd had anybody available, I wouldn't have tried. "Fred, you're incorrigible. But thanks."

"No problem," he said. "Call me if you need a hand."

"I'll try to stick to smaller guns," she told him. "I don't intend to pull you out of your territory unless it's a screaming emergency."

"I don't know what you'd call a screaming emergency, Di, but I do gotta admit I got a tricky little problem of my own up here. I'd kind of prefer taking things in order, if you know what I mean."

"Is this the disappearing kids?" she asked. "That sounded pretty mundane in the papers."

"Yeah. I think it was supposed to. Not sure I'd have picked up on it if I hadn't been doing a furnace installation in the neighborhood. Bad feel, Di. Bad feel. Think I got a handle on it, though. Just gonna take a little more time."

Just what I need. Working two juggling acts a state apart. Still— "Are *you* going to need *me*?"

"No; just think it's a job for a professional. I can handle it."

She closed her eyes and tried to invoke her own limited precog. The little she got said he'd be all right.

And after all, he was, indeed, a professional. "All right, Fred. Good luck. Thanks again."

"Same to you, Di." She started to hang up, and thought she heard him say something else. But by the time she'd gotten the receiver back to her ear, he was already gone, and all she got was a dial tone.

Had she heard him say, "You'll need it"?

FIVE

Fay Harper clutched the steering wheel of her brand-new Dodge Shelby and lifted her lip in a delicate snarl. Even as she did so, Deke leaned across the concrete bench and oh-so-casually brushed the black girl's cheek with his hand.

If she'd had the energy to spare, Fay would have called down a lightning bolt to fry them both then and there.

And it would *take* a purely physical attack to get through those damned shields Deke had on him—at least given the energy level Fay was at right now.

Miserable bitch! Double-timing twit!

In complete disregard of school rules that stated no student was to leave the school grounds until classes were over, Fay pulled her car out of the parking lot in a gravel-scattering, tire-smoking show of anger.

How could she have so misjudged that new girl? After the little bitch had failed to get a single date in the first month since she'd moved from Colorado, it seemed as if, despite the undoubted fact that she was disgustingly cute, she wasn't going to be any kind of threat. Fay's ascendancy at Jenks High was going to remain unchallenged.

So Fay had turned her attention elsewhere, to taking care of other competition, to beginning the tiniest moves toward ensnaring Sandy and parting him from Jill—and as soon as she turned her back, disaster had struck.

A stray dog started across the street in front of her, and Fay hit the accelerator, hoping to ease some of her anger by killing something. Unfortunately, the cur saw her coming, and managed to dive out of the way before she could run him down. It hid between two parked vans, completely protected.

This was *not* her day.

And it was all Derek Raymond Kestrel's fault.

He was letting that sugar-sweet little bit of fluff haul him in like a hooked fish; he was falling for her just as quickly as he'd fallen under Fay's carefully controlled fascination.

It just wasn't *fair*.

She pulled the Shelby into one of the local Sonic drive-ins; this one was franchised and run by a bunch of born-again bigots, and it always gave her a little thrill to eat there. After all, here she was, the Scarlet Woman, the Enemy, smiling and feeding her face right under their noses. They took her money, and never guessed what she was. And she would use the money to carry misfortune to them, making certain that something went wrong after she was ready to leave.

It was too pathetically easy, really, but it was such fun—they were opening themselves to her so thoroughly that she *always* had an opportunity to make them miserable. Their karmic balance sheets would be constantly in the red if only for the way they treated their employees. That they cheated on their taxes and quietly hated their fellow man (in the form of anyone who didn't belong to *their* little fundamentalist sect), all the while professing to love their neighbors—that only made it easier. Hypocritical liars that they were, they were ripe for her tampering. And then there was *his* mistress, and *her* secret alcohol binges—

Lovely. They played right into their hands.

She ordered from a harried-looking middle-aged woman whose red-rimmed eyes testified that Mrs. Bigot had been brow-beating the staff again and threatening cuts in hours.

That was wonderful; that alone would justify something satisfyingly expensive. Perhaps an invasion of cockroaches and a surprise inspection from the Health Department?

It had occurred to her, as she'd watched and ground her teeth in frustration, that Deke was playing into her hands exactly the same way, by taking up with little Rosey Tush. Unfortunately, it wasn't something she could take advantage of; that kind of leverage didn't fit in with the plans she had for him.

Her plans were more complicated than that, because the little twit was exactly what she'd been looking for over the last two years. Perfect, in fact; callow as hell, easily manipulated, good-looking, amusing in bed, and a walking power plant of magickal potential.

And she did *not* intend to turn him loose,

"I have thee, Derek Kestrel," she muttered, "and yet I cannot take thee."

"Pardon?" said the startled carhop, tray in hand.

"Nothing," Fay said, smiling sweetly. "That was how much? And take the tray, dear. I won't need it."

She paid the woman, including a big tip—half of which Mrs. Bigot would confiscate, thus increasing the feelings of rancor the staff had for her.

The woman retreated; Fay contemplated her problems with Derek. There didn't seem to be any simple solution, and she bit savagely into her hamburger. There was no hope for it; she couldn't counter his shields and haul him back to the fold. She just didn't have the time or the resources to deal with Deke and his little Juliet right now. Not with the current project she had going.

In a few more days the rivalry between Sandy and Bob would be finally out in the open; ripe and ready to harvest. She'd been playing one against the other for some time now, working them both into a fine froth of jealousy over school status. Now it was time to add sex to the picture. It wouldn't be too long until the lust-spells she'd cast on both of them had them literally at each other's throats. She'd have added Deke to that emotional stew, except that his parents had shielded him too well, and too long ago, to make the shields easy to subvert.

Ah, well. She licked ketchup off her fingers daintily. Red, and thick, it could have been blood. A hundred years ago, it likely *would* have been blood. The rivalry between the two football heroes would have been resolved at gunpoint, in a duel of some kind, or in an ambush. A case of winner-takes-all, where Fay was the only true winner.

She'd instigated more than a few duels in her time. Death and spilled blood were such *fine* sources of power.

Fine, and satisfying. She finished her fries and sighed with nostalgic resignation; it was too bad, but she'd just have to make do with the power surge she'd accumulate when Sandy and Bob finally confronted each other, fought—and hopefully beat the pulp out of each other.

Time to go. And time to visit retribution upon the Sonic drive-in. She considered and discarded several minor disasters, and finally settled on an irreparable leak in the hot water heater, and several more in the plumbing in the Bigots' house. She set the spells on the money Mrs. Bigot had taken from the carhop; they would activate as soon as the old bat touched the handle of a faucet.

That accomplished, she started the car and threw it into reverse, not being too careful about whether there was anyone in the way. There *were* compensations for living in this age. This vehicle was certainly one of them. She'd considered replacing the TransAm with a Firebird, but the salesman had put her off; he'd acted as if he was immune to her looks, and he himself had been far too ordinary to bother with. In contrast, there had been the young man who'd sold her this T-top Dodge Shelby—*he'd* been more to her taste . . . and a tasty little morsel indeed, once she got him home.

Vehicles like this one meant no more dealing with horses, stupid, smelly beasts that they were. She never could abide animals, and the feeling was mutual.

She pulled out into traffic, cutting off a senile old lady who nearly had a heart attack on the spot. The old biddy slammed on her brakes, and was rear-ended by some nerd in a metallic gold VW Beetle. Fay smiled and continued smoothly on her way, casting a glamour on her own license plate so that, should anyone think to note the number, it would in no way match the one registered to her.

As she passed Sooner Federal, she noted that the bank sign said 1:47. She was already late for class—but the sun was shining and it was much too nice a day to spend further indoors. And besides, that last little pair of indulgences had cost her; she felt a little weak, and was starting a moderate headache. Suddenly she had no wish to return to school; basking on the sun deck, with a strawberry daiquiri in hand, was much more attractive.

This business of "school" was such a bother, anyway. Not like in the old days. . . .

As Fay roared into her immaculate driveway, the garage door opened silently without her having to raise a finger. This was, of course, as it should be; it meant her Servant was properly anticipating her needs. As usual, she parked across two spaces; she hated having her car too close to another to get the door open completely, and hence having to squirm to extricate herself from her vehicle. It was undignified; it rumpled her clothing and her temper. Besides, there was plenty of room; this was a four-car garage and there were only two cars in it, hers and the Mercedes.

The Merc reminded her, as always, of Wes. Wes, who'd chosen the stodgy little Merc over the Ferrari he could easily have afforded. Who had never understood why *she* drove the Porsche. Dear, stupid Wes, no taste, no zest for living, who had asked her plaintively *why* she needed a garage big enough for four cars when they only had two.

"But what about Fay, dear?" she'd said sweetly. "She'll be old enough to drive soon, and she'll surely want her own car."

She certainly did, Wesley. She certainly did.

She waxed nostalgic over the Porsche for a moment. It *had* been a lovely car until she'd wrapped it around a tree. And, matters being what they were, she'd had to walk back home and have Aunt Emily report it as stolen. Too bad; no car since had possessed quite the élan of the Porsche.

The garage door closed. The Servant was waiting silently for her, holding open the door to the house, as always. As it *should* be. Fay had returned to her kingdom, where she alone ruled.

As she passed the Servant, Fay took a moment to give it a minute inspection, and was satisfied that it was holding up. If anyone had bothered to examine it closely—which nobody ever did—they'd have been struck by how closely it resembled her.

Well, it was supposed to be her aunt, after all, and so close a resemblance wasn't unusual in near relations. And there was no reason for anyone to take that second look and see that "Aunt Emily" was Fay's double—if you aged Fay fifty years or so.

Not that anyone would *ever* see her aged sixty-eight.

"The doctor called," the Servant said, when Fay had finished her examination of it. "He wants to know when you plan on visiting your mother. He'd like you to come by as soon as you can."

Fay laughed, throwing her head back and baring her teeth in a feral smile. "Why? The last time I showed up, she had to be tranked afterward. He surely doesn't want that to happen again. It looks bad on his record."

The Servant bared its teeth in an identical smile; it tended to mimic her expressions when she was around, since it was an extension of herself. Of minimal intelligence, of course; enough to answer questions and direct the other, flesh-and-blood servants. Building it had taken all the power Fay had left after the transfer. But she'd discovered some time ago that having a Servant during her minority was well worth the cost, especially these days. Modern laws did not permit thirteen-year-old children to govern themselves and a sizable fortune; did not even permit them to live without adult supervision.

"The doctor said that your mother is asking to see you," the Servant replied. "He believes his new therapy is working, and he wishes to put it to the test. He feels that if your mother remains calm when confronting you, it will be a sign that her recovery is near."

"He's an old fool," Fay said scornfully, starting up the rust-colored, wool-carpeted, oaken staircase to her room.

"You pay him very well to be a fool," the Servant replied from the base of the stairs behind her.

That was so unexpected and so intelligent a response that Fay stopped, and turned to look at her simulacrum thoughtfully.

It occurred to her that the thing had been saying some clever things lately. Perhaps . . . too clever. And it had been acting as if it disapproved of some of her recreations, especially the pharmaceutical ones. The problem with a Servant was that if you left it alone too much, forcing it into a position of making too many decisions, it *could* develop an independent intelligence. And when that happened, you could lose control over it.

That would be a disaster, for other than life, Fay had no hold over the thing. It was oblivious to the pain of psi- or levin-bolts, and she dared not injure it in a way that would show. And, like Fay, because it was a part of Fay, it was convinced of its own immortality.

Fay tightened her lips; another annoyance in a day of annoyances. If that was what was happening, she'd have to destroy this Servant and make another. She could reuse the raw materials, of course, which would make the energy expense minimal, but it would still *take* energy, and time—and she could ill afford either at the moment.

"I'll go in the morning," she told the Servant. "Call and make the appointment, then call the school and tell them that I'm going out there. And while you're at it, tell them I went home with a migraine at noon."

The Servant bowed slightly, and moved on silent feet to Wes's den and the nearest phone. Fay continued up the staircase to the master bedroom.

Something was going to have to be done about Monica Carlin. Something to keep that obnoxious little creature occupied with something other than hauling in Deke.

She stopped again on the top step, and smiled as a thought occurred to her. By *knowingly* encouraging Deke, who was going steady with Fay, Monica had opened *herself* to retribution.

She was poaching, in short. And poachers deserved punishment. After all, as far as that little tart Monica knew, Fay was truly in love with the twit. If this were an ordinary affair, Fay would be devastated by his loss.

Now what would throw her off balance—yet be so bizarre that she would be unwilling to tell anyone about it?

Fay bit her lip, and continued on her way to her room. This was going to call for some careful planning. The poolside and that daiquiri were definitely in order.

Deke wasn't paying much attention to his homework; not with Alan on the phone, with one of the best pieces of news he'd heard in a month.

"—so Coach gets the guy in his office, and before he even gets a chance to start name-dropping, the guy tells him he's the DA, and the old crow Bobby-Boy rear-ended is his grandmother!" Alan gloated.

Deke cradled the handset between his chin and shoulder, and typed a few more words on his micro. "Jesus, I bet *that* took him down!"

"The best is yet to come, my man," Alan chortled. "Seems like she had two of the professors from ORU with her. Bobby-Boy didn't see 'em, I guess, or else he didn't think they were important."

Deke stared at the screen, but wasn't really paying any attention to the words on it. "Or else he was too drunk to care," Deke put in.

"Could be. Basically, she had two witnesses to the way he cussed her out, and then cut and ran. One of 'em was taking down the license; that's how they caught him."

Deke chuckled heartlessly, and took a pull off his can of Coke. "Kind of makes you believe in God, doesn't it?"

Alan laughed. "Amen, brethren and sistern. Dork should never have taken off like that; they're gonna have his license for sure. Of course, if he hadn't cut and run, he'd have had a DWI underage."

"Probably," Deke agreed. "I've never heard of Bobby out dragging when he wasn't stoned. So then what happened?"

"I don't know. About then Coach saw that the door was open and closed it. I cut out before anybody could see me lingering and tell Coach I was dropping eaves. God, I'd love to know what's going to happen to Bobby-Boy, though."

That hint's about as subtle as a lead brick, Deke thought. *He knows damn well that Fay's gonna find out, and she'll tell me when she calls tonight.*

"I'll probably be able to tell you tomorrow," he began, when the "call waiting" signal beeped at him.

"I heard that," Alan told him. "I'll catch you later."

"Okay." He let the incoming call through as Alan hung up from his end.

"Deke?" The coyly seductive voice turned his knees to jelly.

"Uh, hi, Fay." He gulped. "Whatcha doing?"

Boy, is that ever a dumb question. She's calling me, of course. Wake up, Kestrel, and start sounding like you know what day it is.

"Did you hear about Bobby yet?"

"No," he lied. "What's up?"

She was only too happy to tell him. Funny, though, although she *sounded* upset about it, there was a faint undertone of something else in her voice. Like she was kind of gloating about it.

"He and Sandy were like, you know, racing a little. And this senile old lady pulled right out in front of him. He kind of tapped the back end of her car. I guess he yelled at her for being such an asshole, and then he pulled around her. But I guess she's the DA's mother or something, and besides, she had two of the religion professors from ORU with her—anyway, he's in a hell of a lot of trouble."

He scribbled a couple of notes while she talked. Alan was going to want to know about this—and how Fay's story differed from the one he'd overheard. "Like how much?"

"Reckless driving, leaving the scene of an accident; the insurance company is gonna nail his ass to the wall, I guess, and the DA came up with some law about cussing out old ladies, because they got him with that, too."

Deke managed to keep from laughing. "Gee, that's too bad. What's Coach doing?"

"It's pretty awful. They already took Bob's license; Coach took the car away from him, and he's grounded for a month."

We'll see how long that lasts, Deke thought cynically, saving down his homework. *Bet he's out partying Saturday.*

"Is this gonna make any difference to those recruiters?" He already *knew* the answer to that one. They weren't calling the UO athletic dorm the "Knife and Gun Club" for nothing.

"I don't think so. Bob says not."

Which meant she'd been getting her information straight from Bobby-Boy. If *that* didn't figure . . .

He flopped down on his bed and stared up at the ceiling. "Well, he's pretty lucky, I guess. What about Sandy?"

"I guess nobody saw him, so Bob didn't squeal on him."

Besides, it wouldn't have made any difference. What could Coach do, drop him from the team? The season's over, and he's graduating. Deke bit his cheek to keep from chuckling. *Bet that really scralled Bobby's nurd!*

"What were *you* doing?" she asked.

"Homework. And thinking about you." *Good touch, Deke.* "I'm *always* thinking about you." *Even better.*

"You're so *sweet.*" How come she made that sound like something she'd have said about a cocker spaniel? "You *know* how much I love you."

"Me too," he said awkwardly, feeling his mind start to go to jelly along with his knees. How did she *do* that to him, anyway?

"Why don't you come on over here, hm? You could do your homework over here."

"I can't," he said hastily. "I've got this assignment for English and I can't get a handle on it. It's a creative writing thing, and . . . I just can't work on it and be around you, you know? You're too *distracting*, lover. And it's due tomorrow."

And we go through this every night, a small part of his mind that hadn't gone to guacamole thought. *Every night you want me to come over there.* What was she trying to do, get him to flunk out?

"You're no fun." Again, it was like he was hearing two conflicting things in her voice. On top—that she was pouting. But underneath was something else. And he just couldn't make up his mind what it was, or even if he'd heard it at all.

"I can't help it, you know what my dad'll do if I mess up my homework and he finds out about it. And I can't get away with saying I forgot; it's for that writer that's staying here."

"Well, okay. This time. Better not make a habit of it, though. I *might* get tired of you." Definitely a hint of threat there.

"I won't," he replied hastily. And spent the next five minutes placating her, without really understanding *why* he suddenly felt like he was in the wrong.

Monica flipped on the headlights and pulled carefully out of the parking space; her mother waved good-bye from the door of the apartment, then turned and went back inside, closing the door behind her. There was at least one thing Monica liked about living in Tulsa—the apartment complex they'd moved into. The complex itself had anything you could want; *two* swimming pools, a sauna, an enormous Jacuzzi, an exercise room, a clubroom. The apartment was bigger than the house they'd rented in Denver, and it was cheaper—

Rhonda said that was because the Tulsa economy was depressed and rental places were cheap. Monica had no idea; she was perfectly willing to believe whatever her mother said.

She waved at the guard at the gate and pulled out onto the main street. They'd never lived in a place that had a guarded entrance before. It was pretty intimidating at first. In fact, once she'd *seen* the situation and had figured out the kind of lifestyle they'd be having, Monica had been all for the move. Between the lower cost of living out here and the substantial raise Rhonda had gotten to come here,

the family was living higher on the hog than Monica had ever
dreamed they would—

—until she'd seen her fellow classmates.

And at that point, she realized that these luxury apartments were
Jenks's version of low-income housing, and far from being the envy
of her classmates, she was going to be considered strictly middle-
class.

These were kids who routinely got foreign sports cars for their
sixteenth birthdays. Kids who thought nothing of dropping five or
six hundred dollars on a date. Who spent more on clothing in a
weekend than she did all year. Who flew down to Dallas for a day the
way she used to drive over to Colorado Springs—and who flew out
to New York, or London, or San Francisco to do their Christmas
shopping.

It was not at all what she'd expected.

She headed the car in the direction of Memorial and Woodland
Hills Mall. Kind of funny name; no hills, and no woods—but then
again, right down the street was "Shadow Mountain," all one hundred feet of it. There were rocks in Colorado taller than that.

It was all pretty much in keeping with the way people thought of
themselves around here; like the whole world was centered in Tulsa.
Or at least, that was the impression Monica had gotten.

That alone was a good enough reason to want to show the rest of
the kids up, at least a little. *If Miss Tregarde says I'm good enough—
they can't look down their noses at me anymore. And it won't matter
how much money they've got. Money won't buy talent. Money won't
make them writers. I'll have something they can never have.*

Rhonda understood; when Monica told her the root of her problems and why school was making her kind of unhappy, she'd been
both concerned and relieved. Concerned because she didn't want her
kids unhappy—but relieved because the problems *could* have had
other causes.

"We could move," she'd suggested that very night. "I'd rather not;
Jenks is so much better than the Tulsa school system it's pathetic, but
we could move—"

Monica was not inclined to take her up on that offer. "I'm not going to let them beat me, Mom," she'd said stubbornly. "I'm not. I'm
going to have something that's going to make them want to be my
friends."

In the back of her mind she had no doubt what would happen if
she actually got published. She'd be a celebrity, like the prom queen,
only better. The kids would be impressed because the money she got

for a book would be *hers*, and they'd all want to be in her next book. . . .

And, practically speaking—it sure would help pay for college.

Rhonda was the one who'd mentioned that, when Monica had come bursting in with the news that Miss Tregarde was willing to look at her work. And it had been Rhonda's idea that the girl should take the car herself over to the library. They'd have two hours before the library closed at nine. That ought to be enough time for Miss Tregarde to get a good look at her work and critique it, too.

Monica squinted a little; the headlights of the cars in the opposite lane were bothering her, and she was cold. She'd just gotten her license a month ago, and she hadn't driven much at night. And her mom's old 280-Z might not be a Porsche, but it was a bit more to handle than the Pontiac Bonnevilles the driver's-ed class used.

So she was nervous; nervous enough that when she turned off onto a side street rather than fight the mall traffic anymore, she was going about five miles *under* the speed limit. Since most of the other cars on the road were trying to do ten miles over the limit, she'd been getting a lot of tailgaters and horn-blowers. It was a real relief to get away from them.

"Jerks," she muttered, as she took the right-hand turn too slowly to please the last of them, and he roared past her, nearly taking her tail off in the process. "Jenks jerks." She turned the car heater on and rolled her window up, wishing she'd brought a jacket.

The street she chose wound through a half-built subdivision, with empty fields stretching for several hundred yards on both sides of the asphalted road. There was no traffic at all here, which was fine, but there weren't any streetlights, either. After the dazzle of the sodium-vapor lights and the car headlights out on the main drag, Monica felt like she was half blind. The nearest sources of illumination were the lights of the houses hundreds of yards away. She slowed still further, fumbling for the high beams.

She couldn't find them. Wherever they were, they weren't in the same place as on the Pontiacs. She looked down for a moment at the steering column.

That was when the *thing* hit the windshield.

It was only there for a moment, but that was more than long enough.

She got a fleeting glimpse of something horrible, twisted, wrong—

The eyes were what she saw first—evil, yellow eyes, eyes that *glowed*. Then, under the eyes, a round mouth full of sharply pointed teeth.

She tried to scream, but the sound was stuck somewhere in her throat.

The awful thing flattened itself against the windshield. She could see long spindly arms and legs now; the thing seemed to be all head with the arms and legs just attached wherever there was room. It slavered, pressed its face into the glass, and the talons at the ends of those skinny arms clawed and clutched hungrily at her.

She *did* scream then, and jerked the steering wheel sideways, try- ing to shake it off. It grinned at her and mockingly ran a tongue that was at least two feet long all around its fur-covered face. It clawed once more at the glass.

Then it was gone, leaping off the hood of the car, into the dark- ness. At that moment the car ran off the road.

She shrieked again, this time in surprise, when the car jolted over the concrete curb. It wound up with its nose buried in the weeds. If she'd been going any faster, she *could* have had a serious accident.

She took her foot off the clutch, the car jumped, and the engine coughed and stalled.

There was dead silence except for the ticking of cooling metal un- der the hood. After a while, Monica could hear the sounds of traffic off in the distance, even though the windows were closed, but other than that she couldn't hear anything. Certainly nothing—strange. In the glare of the headlights she could see the bank of weeds immedi- ately in front of her; when she looked away and gave her eyes time to adjust to the dark, she could also see that there was nothing in those fields except more dead, weather-flattened weeds.

There was no sign, *absolutely* no sign, that what she thought she had seen had ever existed—outside of her own mind.

She put the gear in neutral and tried to start the car, her hands shaking so hard she had trouble turning the key—and her knees were so weak she had trouble keeping the clutch down. Once the engine caught, she found she couldn't move; she just huddled in the front seat, trembling all over.

It took a while before she was able to think. When thought came, it was a denial of what she thought she'd seen. *I didn't see that. It wasn't real. It was never there. It can't have been there. Things like that don't exist.*

But if it didn't exist, what made her think she saw it?

I'm going nuts. I'm going nuts, just like Gramma. I'm seeing things just like she did before she died.

That was a thought almost as horrible as the notion that she *had* seen something.

The wind blew a piece of newspaper into and out of the cone of light from her headlights. She jumped and screamed—and then laughed, when she realized what it was. And that gave her a rational answer.

It was just an old movie poster or something. Yeah, that's what it was; somebody's poster, the wind blew it into the windshield.

She kept telling herself that, over and over, until she stopped shaking. Until she began to laugh at herself.

Stupid! she told herself. *Getting all shook up over a dumb piece of paper.* She was sure now that she hadn't seen the thing move or make faces at her, that it had all just been her overactive imagination.

I'm not going crazy like Gramma; Mom told me that was senile dementia, and you can't catch it, and you can't get it unless you're real old, like forty at least.

She even managed to get up enough courage to get out of the car and check it over for damage. There wasn't any, to her immense relief.

Like, what would I tell Mom? Gee, I'm sorry, I wrecked the car 'cause I thought I saw the bogeyman?

She climbed back into the driver's seat and carefully backed the car up; she would have preferred to pull forward and around, but she was afraid of something more normal than the bogeyman—what might be hidden under those flattened weeds. Gaping holes that could break an axle, concrete blocks to take out the undercarriage, or sharp pieces of metal that would slash up the tires.

Mom would really kill me if I messed up the car just being stupid. She could forgive an accident, but stupidity would get me grounded for the rest of my life.

The car lurched sideways as first one rear tire, then the other, went over the concrete curbing and hit the asphalt. She held her breath and inched it the rest of the way out, hoping that ridge of cement wasn't high enough to scrape the bottom of the car.

It wasn't, and she let out the breath she'd been holding as the front tires met the curb, and she had to gun the engine a little to get them over it.

She sat there for a minute, with the car heater drying the sweat on her face and scalp. Then, trying not to feel nervous, she took a deep breath, put the car in first, and took her foot slowly off the clutch.

At *exactly* that moment, the thing came back.

This time it landed with a *splat* on the driver's side door, and Monica screamed at the top of her lungs.

There was a second *splat*, and another of the things landed on the hood. It sat there for a fraction of a second, then leapt at her and was stopped only by the windshield.

She and the things stared at each other for a paralyzed eternity. Then *they* moved.

She screamed again, as the things rocked the car, gnashed their teeth at her through the fragile protection of the windows, and tried to claw their way through the glass to get at the front seat and her.

The car hit the curb again, but this time only lurched halfway over it before the engine died. She kept shrieking and waved her hands uselessly at the things, and they grinned and slavered at her. They seemed to be enjoying her fright.

She was still screaming a moment later, when they vanished as abruptly as they'd appeared. She couldn't *stop* screaming, not until her voice was gone.

Then she started crying.

She curled up in a tight little ball on the front seat; unable to move, unable to do *anything*, except to cry, and to think the same thought, over and over.

I'm going crazy. Oh, God, I'm going insane. . . .

SIX

There's something about a library. . . .
      Hey, that's a good line.
      Di paged back in the scene to the point where Claire first entered Lord Burton's library, and inserted the new text. *"There's something about a library, the masculine scent of leather bindings. . . ."* She grinned. *Oooo, I just looove leather. Don't look now, Claire, but Lord Burton's about to insert something other than text. How did I ever manage before I got a computer?* She paged back to the end of the chapter. *Never mind, I know the answer to that. I did a helluva lot of retyping.*

      She contemplated the screen, and decided that this was a good place to close the chapter down. Claire was just about to be ravished. *Little does Lord Burton know what he's in for. Heh, heh. Very good place to stop. Make the reader anticipate what's next.*

      I wonder if I should get a little kinky in the next chapter? Yeah, I think Claire ought to get out the honey and brandy. . . . Surprise, Burty-baby. You—ahem—bit off more than you could chew. I'm going to have a hard—you should excuse the expression—time convincing people you're up to Claire. So much for macho bullshit.

      She chuckled. *My mind's right in the gutter tonight. Not even the gutter, the sewer. Less than a week of vacation, and already I'm feeling better. And feistier. More feisty? Whatever. Boy, is André going to be in trouble when I get back home.*

      Still, there is something about a library.

      Di saved down the chapter, and stretched, easing that ache just under the shoulder blades that every writer she'd ever met complained about.

I must have spent half my life in libraries. Granny's library in the old place, the reading library and the stacks in college—those wonderful libraries in New York— She stretched again and settled back in her chair. *This is an unusually good branch library, though. Tulsa County must have a pretty decent library system. Glad I picked this one, and not the one in Jenks proper.*

She'd found a quiet corner where the steady clicking of keys wouldn't bother anyone, but close enough to the door that she'd be able to see Monica as soon as she arrived. There weren't too many people here to bother, which was a plus. One woman and a set of three kids, all of them loading up and probably about to reach the max limit on their cards, if not their arms—*that* was an immensely cheering sight. There was one old man over in the corner; he looked like part of the furniture. And there were four teenagers scattered at tables, stacks of reference books beside them, three with notebooks, one with a laptop identical to Di's. From the hot outfit and hair that cried out "mousse abuse," Di figured him for a denizen of Jenks, out slumming.

Well, maybe not. There were a couple of very pricey sections in Tulsa proper; the Shadow Mountain condos weren't that far from here. Within—perish the thought!—walking distance, in fact.

The kid looked up, saw her, and smiled before turning back to his book. *I'm being snide,* she thought, a little ashamed of herself. *There are an awful lot of really nice people in this town. Like that cop outside.*

When she'd turned off into the library parking lot, she noticed that there was a car following her. When she got out of the car, it pulled up beside her—

An unmarked fuzzmobile, with a uniformed cop at the wheel. *Oh shit,* she'd thought, *what'd I do?*

"Hi," she'd said, trying not to sound resigned. "What can I do for you?"

" 'Scuse me, ma'am." The cop opened *his* door, and rose—

—and rose.

"My God," she'd said involuntarily, stepping back a pace. "There certainly is a *lot* of you!"

"Yes ma'am," the cop had answered. "I've been told that before. Ma'am, I'd like to ask you—that an interceptor?"

"Well, it *was,*" she'd replied, very glad that it was too dark for him to see some of the things that were still installed in the dash. "I got it from a friend on the Dallas PD. I have to drive in New York City a lot, and he thought I needed something with more acceleration and protection that the Hyundai I was going to buy. So Mark got this for me from the Texas Highway Patrol when they surplused her."

The cop's long face lit up. "Gee, ma'am—that's kinda what I thought. Can I—look under the hood?"

"Sure," she'd told him. "There's *something* under there. I'm not sure what, but Mark Valdez said it was legal. Barely, but legal. Big, mean, and nasty, and it makes a lot of noise. Mark called it a 'rat.' With a temper, he said."

Evidently that meant something profound to him. "If you don't mind, ma'am, I know a tad bit about engines. Dad useta run Pontiacs at Kaney Valley Speedway. I could kinda make sure you're street-legal. And if you aren't, well, I don't see how just givin' you a verbal warning would hurt. Not like a lady like you is gonna go out drag-racin.'"

He was dying to get under that hood; it didn't take an empath to figure that out. "Be my guest," she'd said.

She'd moved the car under the light, so he could see better; he wasted no time in popping the hood and diving in.

From time to time appreciative noises echoed out of there. *She* was baffled; while she was a damn fine driver (even Mark said so), the innards of cars were a mystery deeper than the Quabala to her. Only one recognizable comment emerged: "Ma'am," the fellow had said in tones she normally associated only with worship, "I cannot believe they surplused this baby."

"Mark said he had someone work on it for me," she'd said diplomatically.

Afterward, he'd been kind enough not only to tell her that the car was, indeed, street-legal—"barely," he'd grinned—but to give her a rundown on *good* restaurants within fifteen minutes of Jenks—and his dad's garage.

Praise be, there was even an Uno's Pizzeria and a sushi place.

"Yes ma'am," he'd teased. "They got your barbecue sushi, your deep-fried sushi, your okra sushi—you know what most people call sushi 'round these parts?"

"Besides 'ick'?"

"Bait." And they'd both laughed.

I don't think I could stand to live here, but Tulsa has its moments.

She glanced down at her watch; it was past seven. Funny, as eager as Monica had seemed at school, Di would have expected to see her coming through that door by seven at the very latest.

What on earth could be keeping the child?

Di was a Guardian; she had resources most occultists couldn't imagine. Her alarms were sensitive to the brush of power passing by, even if she wasn't the target.

The alarms went off.

What the hell?

There were certain habits she did not break, no matter how safe she thought she was; full shields and alarms went up and stayed up at all times unless she was deliberately taking them down.

In the time it took to frame that startled thought, she had already determined that she wasn't the target, and was tracing the passing surge of power back to its source.

Whoa! She juggled shields, cataloged the overtones, and searched for telltales, all at the same time. She felt like an F-15 pilot with a hundred things to do and a MIG on his tail. *I thought Larry said this whole area was psychically null—hell, I didn't find anything either!*

She wasn't fast enough.

Like the opening and closing of a portal, an arcane "door" in the void that was the Tulsa area; one moment the sullen scarlet beam of magic was there, the next, gone.

It couldn't have been more than a couple of minutes at most. Just not long enough to do anything, especially not when taken so completely by surprise. She blinked and stared at the bookcase on the opposite wall, not really seeing it. *Damn. I wonder what that was all about.*

It hadn't felt good, whatever it was. It *had* been familiar, though; old-fashioned, Western-style sorcery. As opposed to witchcraft, of course. A witch worked with natural balances, rather like a t'ai chi master in that way. If you attacked a witch, if the odds, power levels, and skills were equal, chances were you'd find your own attack turned back against you.

Maybe it's too bad it wasn't *me that it was after. Like* sensei *keeps telling me, there are times when the first to attack has already lost the battle. And I've assisted a few people into a wall in my time.*

A sorcerer ignored those balances. A sorcerer worked with or against the grain; it didn't much matter. Partially that was because an awful lot of the kind of people who became sorcerers were pretty weak in the psionics department. They couldn't sense the natural flows in the first place.

And the kind of person who became a sorcerer also tended to be a manipulator. That wasn't in and of itself a bad thing, provided your motives were reasonably unselfish. Sorcery was a matter of dominances; your will over the material world, your mind over the wills of others, and ultimately, if the sorcerer was skilled enough, the dominance of the master over slaves created or invoked. Again, that wasn't of itself a bad thing; some magickal critters were only under control when they *were* enslaved, and the sorcerer in question did not need to be the one who had invoked them to be the one who controlled them.

You could—as Di *had*—control them right back to where they came from.

Di, as a Guardian, was both a witch and a sorcerer; although by preference, she tended to favor the former. But she *knew* sorcery in all its various forms and flavors; knew it well enough to recognize even when she only "saw" it for a fleeting instant.

She stared hard at the blank screen of her laptop, using it as a focal point of concentration. *Works as well as a crystal ball . . . huh. That's a hoot. A techie witch. Cyberwitch? I'll have to pass that one on.* Since she couldn't trace the power back to its source, she began delicately questing for the signs that would lead her to the target.

She wasn't expecting the second power surge, any more than she had been expecting the first.

She managed to stay with it long enough this time to get the "signature," the characteristic shape and flavoring of the power that was individual to every mage. It *wasn't* anyone she'd every encountered before; that much she knew before she was cut off again.

It *was* stolen power; there was no mistaking that. Though incorporated into a skilled and controlled whole, the individual threads of the work could be identified, and they were all from sources other than the signature. Each had the faint traces of the personality that it had been reft from, and the strong coloring of the emotions that had invoked the energy in the first place.

Nasty emotions, for the most part; fear, pain, loveless lust, anger, hate, envy, and jealousy. Which told Di quite a bit about the sorcerer.

Okay, you, she told the unknown. *Third time's the charm. Poke your nose out again, and I'll have you.*

She waited, ready to pounce the moment that portal opened and the sorcerer used his power—

Nothing.

Until the library door swung open and shut again, letting in a blast of cold air that scattered the papers of the students behind her. And the echoes, the traces, of that same power Di had been waiting for (faint, but near at hand) made her look up sharply.

Monica.

Shaking, green, with all the signs that *she* had been the sorcerer's target.

What in—Monica? She's just a kid! Why would . . . There is something very weird going on around here. . . .

Di shut the laptop down and shoved her chair away from the table. Monica jumped at the sound of the chair bumping across the carpet, and turned white-rimmed, fear-glazed eyes in her direction.

The girl blinked several times, and finally seemed to see her.

"M-m-miss Tregarde?" she quavered.

A few feet to Monica's right, the librarian looked up sharply at the sound of her voice and evidently recognized the same symptoms of fear and shock that Di had. She emerged from behind her microfiche reader and the massive desk, and headed straight for the girl.

Shit, I hope she isn't going to cause me a problem. Di took her attention off Monica for a fleeting instant, just enough time to "read" what the librarian was projecting. And felt with relief a solid grounding of worry, with overtones of protectiveness and desire to help. *No wonder there's all these kids studying in here. She must be mother-confessor and trusted adviser to half the neighborhood. Bet she bakes a mean chocolate-chip cookie, too.*

Di and the librarian converged on Monica wearing nearly identical looks of unprofessional concern. The girl reached involuntarily toward Di as the other woman said, in unmistakably maternal tones, "Honey, it isn't any of my business, but y'all look like you're gonna pass out. Looks to me like something just shook you up pretty bad. Why don't you come back to my office and sit yourself down."

The woman gave Di a sidelong glance of inquiry. "I'm one of Monica's teachers; I was waiting for her," Di explained. "Let me get my things, and I'll be right with you."

This is weirder than snake shoes. Why would anyone target a kid like this for a sorcerous attack? Jesus Cluny Frog, she's not even high-psi!

Di gathered up her laptop and her notes, stowed them all in her briefcase with practiced efficiency, and followed in the wake of the librarian and her temporary charge.

The librarian was just as efficient as Di; within two minutes she had Monica ensconced in a comfortable chair, her feet up and half a glass of cold water and two aspirin inside her. At that point, she gracefully bowed out of the picture, telling Di that if they needed anything, she would be at the front desk.

"What happened?" Di asked quietly.

"I—I almost wrecked the car," Monica stammered, twisting the paper cup nervously in her hands.

"How?"

Monica just stared at her, her lower lip quivering, the tears in her eyes starting to spill over.

Di took a firmer tone of voice. "Monica, there's something wrong—and you 'almost wrecking the car' is just the smallest part of it. Tell me. People don't look the way you did when you walked in the door unless something really horrible has happened to them."

The paper cup was a shapeless wad, and two tears were tracking down Monica's cheeks.

Di sighed, and patted her clenched hands. "Monica, when I said 'really horrible,' I meant it. From the way you're acting, you'd rather die than go back outside right now—and I somehow don't have the feeling that you'd react that way to a simple accident, much less a near-accident."

She leaned forward, projecting sympathy as subtly as she could. She had to be careful around this one; as wired as Monica was, even though she wasn't a psychic powerhouse like Deke, she'd be much more sensitive than she usually was. If she picked up on what Di was doing, after being attacked once tonight by magic, she might assume the worst, and panic.

"You—" the girl began, then shook her head and scrubbed the back of her hand across her cheek.

"You can tell me, Monica. I've seen some pretty bizarre and nasty things in my time."

"You—no, you won't believe me!" Monica cried—then burst into hysterical tears.

Di thought about hugging the kid for a split second, and then rejected the notion. She was pretty much a stranger to this girl. She could try to convince Monica to trust her, but this was not the time to use physical contact.

"How do you know I won't believe you?" she asked. "All you know about me is that I'm a writer. But writers see and hear more strange stories than you'd ever imagine. I'm always getting people telling me their life history in the grocery store. If there's one thing I've learned over the years, it's that the strange and *true* stuff is a lot odder than what's in the supermarket tabloids, but it never shows up there; mostly because it *is* true and the people it happened to are like you—they figure that either other folks will think they're crazy, or that they *are* crazy."

There was a tremor of stronger emotion from the girl when she said that. Di followed up on her advantage.

"This may sound like I'm spitting platitudes at you, but it's been my experience that the old saying is true; people who think they're nuts usually aren't. It's the ones who are convinced that they're sane and the rest of the world *isn't* that you have to watch out for."

Monica buried her face in her hands. "What about people who think they've—seen something?" she replied, her words interrupted by strangled sobs.

"Well, if you think you've seen something, there's usually a cause. Like drugs. Some folks are allergic to drugs in odd ways; some prescription drugs have side effects doctors don't always know about. I have a friend who hallucinates on penicillin, and another who talks to God whenever she's given something with caffeine in it."

Monica peeked out from behind her hand. "You aren't BSing me?"

Di shook her head. "Straight up. I could even give you their numbers and you could talk to them if you wanted. Have you been taking *anything* you don't normally?"

Monica shook her head woefully. "N-no," she stammered. "Not even an aspirin until just now."

"Okay, that shoots that one. I have more. There's the weather angle; under the right conditions you can get reflections of things that may be hundreds of feet or even miles away, often very distorted."

She pretended to think for a moment, waiting for the girl to say something.

Monica shook her head. "It wasn't anything like that. It wasn't a reflection."

She nodded. "It's just as well. I didn't think that would fly; you have to get a combination of fog and hot and cold spots and pressure changes to get really convincing fata morgana in the middle of a city, and it's chilly and damp, but not foggy, tonight. So, there's always the idea that you were set up. Have you got any enemies at school, or friends that like to play nasty jokes?" She smiled grimly. "I had *that* one played on me. I made the mistake of letting it be known I believed in ghosts. Some kids in my high school thought they'd haunt my house for me. Trouble is, even then I knew more angles on faking those things than a stage magician, and I caught them at it. Then *I* scared *them*—and afterward, I made sure everybody else at school knew I'd made fools of them by turning the tables on them."

Amazing what anger will do for your ability to project. I wonder if they ever figured out why *they ran out of my place screaming at the tops of their lungs?*

Monica gave that one careful consideration. Finally she answered slowly. "I—don't think so. It would take a real techie to—do what I saw. The Brains aren't like that at Jenks. I mean, they wouldn't go after anybody who hadn't gone after them first. I like all the techie kids, and I think they like me."

Di leaned back in her chair. Making her *think* had forced the kid to calm down. Good. Now for the move. "All right, then. That just leaves one other possibility. You *did* see what you thought you saw."

Monica's lower lip started to quiver, and her eyes brightened with tears about to spill. Di pointed a warning finger at her. "Hey—that's enough. You were doing fine a minute ago. I told you, I've seen a lot of bizarre things in my time. Remember what Sherlock Holmes told Watson: if we've eliminated everything else and all we've got left is the impossible, then the impossible is the only answer."

"But—"

Di interrupted her ruthlessly. "All that the word 'impossible' means is that nobody's been able to prove something yet. Hell, Monica, there are people in this town convinced that men never walked on the moon, that it was all faked in a movie studio!"

"But—"

"So why don't you tell me what happened? Maybe I can help."

"But—"

"I sure know I want to try." Di let her expression harden a little. "If there's one thing I can't stand, it's somebody that gets his kicks by scaring the shit out of people."

Come on, kiddo. I'm not allowed to stick my nose into your problems unless you ask me to. And I can't help but wonder if this has something to do with what Larry thinks is after Deke.

Di held her breath as the girl visibly wavered between mistrust and a desperate need to confide in *someone.*

Desperation, and the aura of sympathy and trustworthiness Di was projecting, won out.

"I—saw—these *things,*" Monica began, and then the words spilled from her the way her hysterical tears had a few moments before. There were a few more of those tears, too, before she was finished.

Di kept a tight hold on her anger, aided in part by bewilderment. Whoever that sorcerer was, he'd played one of the nastiest little mind games Di had ever seen pulled on a kid. For an imaginative kid like Monica, one who *knew* she had active imagination, this must have been a nightmarish experience.

And why Monica? That was the part that made no sense at all. There was no sign that she understood or recognized any of what had happened to her. She wasn't even marginally involved in the occult.

Who it was had to be inextricably tied in with that question of "why."

But "what"? That was no problem.

"Wait here a minute," she said, as Monica sniffled into a fist-sized wad of Kleenex from the box on the librarian's desk. The girl started to say something, but Di was already out the door.

There was something to be said for a lifetime spent in libraries. Di knew the Dewey decimal system the way most people knew the streets of their own neighborhoods. Of course, there were some categories that held special interest for her. . . .

She came back in that promised minute with a history book, a colonial history of New England, lavishly illustrated. She was flipping through the section on witch-hunts as she came through the office door and shut it behind her, looking for a particular woodcut. Most histories that covered witch-hunts and trials other than the ones in Salem used that particular picture.

Sure enough, there it was; good old sanctimonious "Barryman Deaton, Witchfinder." Crude though the picture was, Di always thought she could tell a lot about the man from it—the self-satisfied, smug set of his mouth, the cruel enjoyment in his eyes, the stiff spine showing certain knowledge of the righteousness of his cause.

Of course, she could just be reading into the picture what she knew already about the man from family tradition.

Idiot never actually caught a single real witch, she thought cynically. *Only poor fools with bad taste in neighbors. Harmony Tregarde even managed to get the midwives and herb doctors out of Newton before he could accuse them.*

The thing about this picture was that in this one case (as she also knew from family tradition), for the *only* time in his career as a witchfinder, Deaton had caught someone who'd deserved to be caught.

Not a "witch," though, or at least not when Hardesty was caught; Dimwit had caught a magician of another ilk altogether. The Pennsylvania Dutch would have called Hardesty a *Hexenmeister;* the not-altogether-Episcopalian Tregardes of the time had called him a warlock. That did *not* mean "male witch," the way current popular literature had it, but "oathbreaker." Hardesty had been both a sorcerer and the Green Man for another coven, but he had broken the Prime Law of the Wiccans. *Harm none.* His first victims (before he moved to Newton) had been his old associates. . . .

None of that concerned Di at the moment; she was more interested in the creatures surrounding old "Dimwit Deaton" and his victim. "Familiars," the caption called them. Each of them had a little scroll apparently coming out of an ear or a mouth, each scroll ornately lettered with some bizarre name or other: "Thrudsnifter," "Lemdoodle," "Fryestappen."

I suppose Dimwit made those names up himself; they sound about like his speed.

She flopped the book down on the desk in front of Monica, and pointed to the critter crouched down in the far left-hand corner of the illustration. *The only supernatural manifestation Dimwit ever saw in his life. What a jerk. And he had no idea what it was he had seen.*

"Does that look like something you've seen before?" she asked Monica.

The kid's eyes were like saucers. Di wasn't much surprised. The depiction was incredibly accurate. Dimwit had gotten an eyeful when he'd come to take Black Hardesty, and he'd made sure to relate the tale in grand and glorious detail to anyone who'd listen. He'd been more than happy to spend several days with the author of this particular treatise on "The Foule and Unnattural Practices of Witches," telling the story several times, with special emphasis on his own bravery in "facing the demon and conquering it."

And a five-year-old with a stick in his hand and courage in his heart could face an imp down. They live on fear, but any show of guts sends 'em screaming back to Mommy.

It scared the bejesus out of Dimwit, though, and sent him *back to Mommy; it took sixty-two-year-old Glory Fenwick to "disperse the demon and subdue the heretic." Poor old Glory-Be-To-God; at least he was sincere. Good thing Harmony managed to get a psi-bolt through Hardesty's shield and knock him out before poor old Glory came storming in there with nothing but a Bible for protection.*

Well, nobody ever knew about Deaton chickening out but the Tregardes and Dimwit, and Glory. Glory was too modest, Harmony wasn't about to blow his cover, and Dimwit sure wasn't telling. Gods. What a jerk; what an appropriate way for him to go, too; getting drunk two days after he talked to the chronicler, falling down the stairs of the local alehouse, and breaking his stupid neck.

"Come on," she said finally, "let's get out of here. I'd like a burger, and we need to talk."

She picked up her briefcase, and reached across the desk to close the book. Monica stared at the cover, then looked back up at her.

"That—" she said faintly, "that's what I saw."

"I know," Di replied. "I'm *hungry*. Let's get going."

She took Monica's wrist and tugged her to her feet. The girl followed her obediently out to the car—

—which, not so incidentally, was *very* heavily shielded. Not a bad notion at the moment.

There was a burger joint less than a block away; while the kid sat in stunned silence on the passenger's side Di ordered food for both of them from the drive-through window and drove them back to the library parking lot.

"French fries and chocolate," she told Monica, who was still staring at nothing. "I don't have a lot of vices anymore, but I'm keeping those two. I *love* french fries. Combine them with a chocolate shake, and I'm a contented woman." She handed Monica the paper bag full of burger, fries, and Coke.

"That thing in the picture—" Monica stammered, staring at the bag in her hands as if she'd never seen anything like it before. "That thing—that was what I saw. Exactly what I saw."

"Well, that's not *too* surprising, all things considered," Di replied, examining the burger to make sure nobody'd put any mayo on it. Tulsans seemed to put mayo on *everything*, the way midwesterners put ketchup on everything. "If you've done something to piss a sorcerer off, he's going to use the smallest guns he has on you, and those little guys are barely popguns. They make a really good burger here in Tulsa, have you noticed that?"

She was keeping her tone deliberately light. After just proving to the kid that she'd been attacked by a supernatural agency, it would be a good idea to remind her that the mundane world of hamburger joints was still the greater part of her life. There was absolutely no use in letting the girl know how worried Di really was. It wouldn't do Monica any good.

"How can you sit there and eat a hamburger and talk about—*things* like that monster?" Monica cried, clenching her hands on the paper sack.

"Really easy," Di replied matter-of-factly. "First, I'm hungry. Second, I've seen those things before, and they're small potatoes. Thirdly, I'm not just a romance writer, I'm also a practicing witch."

Monica's eyes got big again, and she started to wriggle away; she was stopped by the car door. The locks were all controlled from Di's side. That was one of the police modifications that Mark had left on; pretty useful at a time like this.

Di put her hamburger down and sighed dramatically. "Jesus Cluny Frog, Monica, do I look like one of the bad guys to you? I thought you had a little more sense than these Oklahoma hicks. 'Witch' is just a religion, okay? No baby-sacrificing, no Black Masses, no sending imps out to scare the dog-snot out of kids, trying to make them think they're crazy. We don't *do* things like that. Our number-one law is 'Have fun in this lifetime, but don't hurt anybody.' "

Nice little paraphrase of "An it harm none, do as ye will," if I do say so myself.

She deliberately picked up her burger and took another bite. Monica stopped trying to find the door lock.

"But if you didn't—"

"Who did?" She stirred the shake on the dashboard with her straw. "I don't know. I'm psychic—you don't have to be, to be a witch, but a lot of us are. I picked up on the fact that something was going on just before you came in, but I couldn't tell who or what, and I didn't know you were the target until you came in." She met Monica's eyes; they weren't quite so big anymore. "I'm pretty good, kiddo, but I'm not as good as I'd like. You feeling better?"

Monica licked her lips nervously. "I don't know," she admitted. "I don't understand what's happening. . . ."

"Neither do I," Di said bluntly. "I came here to teach creative writing and I find myself in the middle of a magickal attack. I promise you, you aren't crazy, what you saw was real. Those critters really couldn't have hurt you, no matter how impressive they looked; they're all bluff. The worst they could have done was give you a few bruises. If you'd yelled at them, they'd have split. Remember that if they show up again. What worries me is that this means that *somebody* in this town is practicing traditional sorcery, and that person wants you to be upset. I don't know why. You're not involved in the occult; I could tell if you were. So this is a very bizarre situation. I *would* like to help you, if you'll let me."

The kid straightened up. "How do I know I can trust you?" she asked.

Good girl. Keep that skepticism; that's sound sense if there's somebody with a grudge on gunning for you. "You don't," she replied. "You don't know me—hell, you never even had any hint of trouble before I showed up in town. All you can go by—*if* you decide to trust me—is who my friends are."

She fished in her purse and hauled out her wallet. "Look here," she said, flipping it open and holding it under the light from the parking-lot lamp. In the first pocket was the photo-ID that the New Haven police had given her, with "SPECIAL INVESTIGATOR" printed in red beside the picture.

"This *could* be a fake," Di said. "It isn't, but I'll be happy to drive over to the nearest cop shop and prove it. I've worked for the New Haven cops a bunch of times—here's my permit to carry a concealed weapon in Connecticut. Here's another one for Texas; last year I did some work down in Dallas. This car is something I was able to get because of some friends down there. It used to be a high-speed police car—"

She flipped the switch Mark had hidden under the dash, and the police scanner came on with a squawk and a crackle of static. "If you know anything about police scanners, you'll know it's not legal to have them in your car. Mark's making sure I get the right permissions to keep this one." She turned it off again.

Monica bit her lip; she still didn't look quite convinced, although she did look as though she *wanted* to be convinced.

"You need something closer to home? Deke's dad and I have been real good friends since we were in college together, and his mom and I go back almost that far. They *both* know what I am—in fact, they used to help me a little. So, I've got friends in two different police departments, and some solid citizens right here in Tulsa. Can you trust somebody with friends like that?"

Monica nodded, slowly but not reluctantly.

"Great. You want me to help you?"

"Yes," Monica said. "Please. With the writing too—"

Di laughed. "Right on! Okay, kiddo, start in on that ham-burger, and while you're eating, take it from the top. You were over on that side street, and it was dark. Tell me everything that you can remember, and I mean *everything*—"

Deke finished reading Alan's assigned story fragment, and put the last page down on the desk. He restacked the papers neatly, then swiveled his desk chair around to face his friend, handing them back to him.

"So," Alan said, fidgeting a little in Deke's armchair. "What do you think?"

"I think," Deke replied, shaking his head sadly, "that you'd better stick with what you know, like computers. It's pretty lame, Al. Pretty lame."

Alan sighed. "That's what I was afraid of."

Ms. Greeley had two sessions of the Honors class this year, one in the morning, one in the afternoon. Alan was in the afternoon session; they'd tried to get in the same class, but it hadn't worked out. Although Alan was primarily a techie whiz—he'd told Deke that he identified strongly with the Val Kilmer part in *Real Genius*—he generally breezed through all his classes. And Deke knew he'd figured on doing the same with this one.

He'd done just fine as long as they were analyzing someone else's work—but he'd lost it as soon as they started this creative stuff.

The one-page argument scene had been bad enough, but now Ms. Tregarde had upped the ante.

Deke had been expecting a totally new assignment. He'd been a little surprised by what Di had told the class.

"Okay," she'd said, after all the pages were read aloud and picked over. "Now we're going to do what a professional writer would do with that scene. We're going to pretend that this is the climax of a story or even a book. That means that you're going to revise and expand on what you wrote."

She'd turned to the blackboard and begun making a list. "I want a lead-in to the argument; how the fight starts in the first place, maybe even how the two protagonists meet before the fight. If you haven't got a root cause of the fight, I want that in there, too. Lastly, I want a conclusion to the fight."

"How long?" Jennifer wanted to know.

"Minimum of three pages, maximum of ten. Oh, and some of you were swapping viewpoint even in the one-pager; that means you kept getting inside both protagonists' heads so that the reader could see what *both* of them were thinking at all times. Don't do that; there's a way to handle it, but you're not ready for that yet. Pick your viewpoint character and stay with him—the boy or the girl, I don't care which. Remember you can only *show* what's in that character's head; your reader will have to guess what's going on in the other character's head from the way you describe his or her expressions. Got that?"

Well, Deke had gotten that all right, but it sure didn't look like Alan had. His two characters just walked up to each other and started fighting for no apparent reason, then shook hands and walked off, also for no apparent reason. And the fight, predictably enough, was about the girl claiming the boy had stood her up.

"It's a yawner, Al," Deke said honestly. "Like, they're bored actors in a bad existential play; they're just walking on, reciting lines they don't understand and don't care about, and walking off. It was bad before, but it's worse now."

Alan sprawled across the arms of the overstuffed beige chair, and picked at his thumbnail glumly. "Yeah. Man, I don't know what I'm gonna do about this quarter, this 'creative' shit." He leaned back and stared at the ceiling. "I'm acing everything else. I *gotta* ace this; I gotta get into MIT or Cal Tech or Rose Poly—I can't do that unless I ace everything. What am I gonna do?"

"Hey," Deke objected, "I don't know what you're so worried about. It's not like you're going to flunk out. Di gave us a B to start with, and she said she wasn't going to grade anybody down unless they didn't try—"

"But a B just isn't good enough," Alan insisted stubbornly. "And I don't want her giving me an A just 'cause she feels sorry for the poor computer nerd."

Deke threw his hands up, conceding defeat. "Okay, okay, have it your way."

"So what am I gonna do? You gotta help me, man. You're doing okay at this stuff—what am I doing wrong?"

Deke thought about the problem for a minute. "Look, let's take this thing from the top. Remember what Di said? About how if something doesn't work, she goes back and changes things until it does?"

"Yeah," Alan replied. "So?"

"So this isn't working for you. Try something else, from scratch. Write what you know. Like when Tracy came after you in the hall and just about took your ass off for what you did to her computer in lab? Di said an argument—she didn't say about *what*. You're just assuming that since she's a romance writer, it has to be like what she does."

"Isn't that, like, cheating?" Alan said doubtfully. "I mean, that stuff with Tracy really happened."

Deke shrugged. "I don't see how it could be cheating. I dunno about *your* class, but most of the guys in *mine* pretty much rewrote the last breakup fight they had."

"Good point." Alan mulled it over for a while. "Real good point. Okay, I'll do it. Can I leave out the part where Tracy dumped her Coke down my pants?"

"Hey, it's creative, right?" Deke grinned. "Make it come out any damn way you want to. Make the Tracy character come out looking like a fool. Make her start the fight 'cause she really wants to screw your brains out and can't think of any other way to get at you. Whatever."

Alan's answering grin was bright enough to light up the whole room. "Yeah," he said, in a contented sigh. "Yeah. Hey, can I see yours?"

"Sure, I printed it before you came over." Deke took the little stack of paper off the printer. "Haven't even had a chance to strip it."

"That's okay." Alan left the papers in their virgin, fanfold state, and began flipping through them. Deke was rather pleased with his version of the assignment. It started out calmly enough, with his two characters meeting in the hall between classes—but then the girl started cross-examining the guy, and making like the Spanish Inquisition when he didn't give her immediate answers. Before long the guy had taken about all he was willing to, and the last two pages was him getting pretty hot about how possessive his girl had been getting. It ended with him telling her he'd had just about enough, and leaving her open-mouthed and shocked speechless in the middle of the hallway when the bell rang.

"A little more of Art replicates Life, huh?" Alan said archly, as he turned over the last page.

"Say what?" Deke said, startled by his response.

"Well, this shit about Danny here being Marcia's boy-toy—strikes me like that's awful close to the way Fay treats you, ol' buddy."

"What would *you* know about it?" Deke retorted; stung, but determined not to let Alan know.

"I've got eyes, Deke. I've got ears. She does some pretty cold things to you, and you just sit there like a dog and take it." Alan put the stack of paper down on the coffee table, and swung his legs back down to the floor. "I'll tell you, man, you could do a lot worse than what old Dan here did. Tell the bitch off. Give her a little hell right back the next time she gives it to you."

Deke found himself in the uncomfortable position of having nothing he could say. If he said Alan was right, he'd look like a wimp. If he said Alan was full of shit, he'd be lying through his teeth. If he told Alan it wasn't any of his business and to butt out, he might lose the last of his old friends.

Maybe if I just tell him I'm in love with Fay . . .

"I suppose," Alan said sarcastically at that very moment, "that you're going to try and tell me that it doesn't matter because you're in love."

What actually jumped into his head at the moment Alan said that wasn't Fay, but Monica. How sweet she was, how gutsy, standing right up and not letting any of the moneyed kids shove her around.

It's too bad I didn't meet her before I started going with Fay. I'd probably be going with her instead. . . .

But he couldn't let Alan sit there and get away with that last remark.

"A lot *you* know," he retorted, throttling down his feelings of guilt. "Half the time, I don't think you even know women exist! If they had hard drives or monitors, maybe. As it is, there's no way you could relate to a guy with normal hassles—"

Alan arched an eyebrow. "Yeah, well, maybe you haven't been paying too much attention to what I've been up to lately. It doesn't take an engineer to figure out female couplers. And *I* never forget I'm the one with the hard drive."

Oh, you poser—"Oh, yeah, right," Deke retorted. "Sure. And when have *you* ever been with a girl? Have you *ever* been with a girl? Third base? Home plate? All the way?"

"Maybe," Alan replied, looking unreasonably smug. "At least I've got a girl that thinks with something besides her—"

"Hey—" Deke said warningly.

Alan shrugged. "Have it your way. But *I've* got a chick with more than two brain cells."

"Oh yeah?" Deke replied, suspicion heavy in his voice. "So who is it?"

"Nobody you know. Now that you're flying with Fay's crowd, you don't notice lesser mortals much." Then Alan grinned, and laced his hands behind his head, leaning back in the armchair. "Your loss, old buddy. She's a hot little number."

"So who is she?" Deke persisted.

"She's in my math class," Alan taunted, "which should tell you something about her brains."

"So who *is* she?"

Alan wouldn't say, which just left him frustrated and annoyed when his old friend left to rewrite his homework.

And it didn't help matters when he called Fay, and she proceeded to get on his case for doing homework with Alan instead of coming over to her place.

Shit, he thought in disgust—at himself, at Fay, at Alan, at the whole damn world. He held the receiver a couple of inches away from his ear and let her rant on until she wound down.

Finally she seemed to sense he was on the verge of finding an excuse to hang up, and her voice softened. She even apologized.

"I'm sorry, lover, I know how your dad is. I guess I'm just jealous of everything that takes you away from me," she cooed, the honeyed words pouring over his bruised ego and taking the sting out of Alan's taunts. "And it's *really* nice of you to help Alan out. You know, I think it's real nice of you to keep him around. *Somebody* ought to find him a social life, or he's going to wind up chained in some cubicle someplace, drooling over computer parts."

Yeah, he thought, basking in the warm glow she was casting over him. *Yeah, what does Alan know, anyway? He probably wrote this chick up on his micro.*

But . . . I wish we didn't have to go through this every time I call. If I'd been calling Monica, she wouldn't have started out by ragging on me. . . .

SEVEN

Diana closed her eyes for a moment, and sent a tentative probe around the house. Not a full probe; she wasn't going to expose herself like that, not even in friendly territory. Nor did she take her shields down. Not after last night.

She touched three presences in the building besides herself. Immediately below her, which meant in his office, was Larry, easily identified by virtue of long familiarity. Two more together, one heavily shielded—Deke—one very bright, simple, and young. A stranger, about Deke's age.

Deke must have a friend over again. Probably Alan; the poor boy is having some real problems with phase three of the argument assignment. Good. That'll keep him occupied. I need to talk to Larry, and I don't want to be interrupted.

She slipped out of her room, moving like an assassin; closed the door of the guest room behind her without a sound. Every time she'd tried to closet herself with Larry, the kid had found some reason to be there or to interrupt. Not this time; it was mildly funny before, but not now, not when she figured she needed to have a serious talk with his dad.

I'm not sure yet what he thinks we're up to, but I may be able to take a good guess. . . .

Thank the gods for thick, expensive carpeting; that made it a lot easier to move quietly.

The bitch is that the kid's room is right at the head of the stairs. If he comes out at the wrong moment, I've got no reason for being out in the hall. If I say something like that I'm hungry, he'll go all helpful and follow me.

She froze for a moment, right outside Deke's door. She could hear Deke's voice, and that of his friend, fairly clearly. They were talking about their homework assignment. Her own name had just come up in the conversation. They were talking about how different her style was from Ann's. It seemed to surprise them that Ann was backing her—giving advice, but not direct help, nor offering any sympathy for the perplexed who couldn't figure out what combination of gimmicks would glean them an A. Alan in particular was looking for gimmicks—well, it worked in other classes. . . .

Lord and Lady—they're not going to come pounding on my door looking for help with their work, are they? I don't even have the excuse of looking for the bathroom, not with the Tulsa Water Festival attached to my room.

But Deke was well trained; the idea evidently didn't even occur to him. Di was a guest, and besides, she was (supposedly) working. You didn't disturb guests in the Kestrel household; you especially didn't disturb *working* guests.

She slipped down the staircase as quickly as she could, and headed down the back hallway to Larry's office.

She found the door closed; evidently *he* didn't want to be disturbed, either. Too bad. She placed her palm lightly against the door and sent out the probe again, just to be sure.

Nobody home but Larry. Good.

She opened the door silently, slipped inside, and closed it behind her just as silently. She waited for a moment with her back against the wood of the door, letting her eyes adjust to the darkened room.

The track lighting was dimmed way down. The only bright illumination was from the light-table; Larry was bent over it with his back to her, hard at work, the warm orange of his aura showing her that he was concentrating.

In that case, better not startle him. I'd hate to ruin several hours' worth of work by making him jump. She reached out with a mental "hand" and gently stroked the edge of his shields.

Funny; he still has the habits I drove into him, even though Tulsa is apparently a null zone, and he's inside his own house shields. She examined the edges of his shielding critically; he might *need* those habits, now. The edges were a little ragged, a bit uneven; heavier around the head, hands, and heart, weak in the back and around the feet. *A little sloppy, but no holes. Good.*

When his aura began to lighten to yellow, indicating that he'd noticed her subconsciously, she tapped lightly on the doorframe.

He looked up, squinting, waiting for his eyes to adjust to the dif-

ference between the brightness of the light-table and the dimmer
light of the rest of the room. In a few moments, his expression
changed from minor irritation at being interrupted to surprise and
concern.

Evidently I look like a bearer of bad tidings.

He reached for the left-hand side of the light-table and snapped
the switch off. Di blinked; the loss of light was as startling to her eyes
as the sudden flood of it would have been if he'd snapped a bright
light on.

With a second smooth motion, he reached for a remote control
on the table, and dialed the rest of the lights back up to a comfortable
level. Not bright, but bright enough to see everything without straining.

"What's up?" he asked quietly.

She made certain that the door was closed. "I've been trying to
get you alone ever since last night," she told him, "and your offspring
hasn't been cooperating."

He grinned. "Why, Di, I'm a married man—" Then, when her expression didn't lighten, he sobered again quickly. "Not funny?"

"Not relevant." She crossed to his corner of the office and helped
herself to a chair. "Got a surprise for you. Tulsa may be a null zone,
but it *isn't* empty. I got brushed by some high-level activity last night.
Maybe related to Deke, maybe not; definitely from someone experienced. I wanted to tell you last night, but you were working late."

"What?" he asked quickly.

"Sorcery. Good old-fashioned High Magick." If the situation had
been a bit less serious, she'd have laughed at his expression of flatfooted surprise. "Somebody tried to throw a good scare into one of
the kids from the school—the one I was meeting at the library. Sent a
couple of imps to shake her up, make her think she was hallucinating
or something."

She leaned back into the embrace of the chair, and found herself
surrounded by the aroma of old leather. Larry, bless him, didn't waste
any time trying to contradict her; if she said the girl had been attacked by imps, so be it, he accepted it.

He chewed on his bottom lip, his eyes shadowed with thought.

*Now I know where Deke gets that habit. Or maybe it's the other
way around; Larry didn't used to do that.*

"Based on the experiences I had when I was working with you,"
he said finally, "if the scare tactics don't work, the sorcerer usually
ups the ante."

She "fired" her finger at him. "Bull's-eye. Give that man a prize."

He snorted. "Sorcerers and high-powered executives have a lot in common. Arrogance, belief in their own infallibility, and a tendency to run right over anything and anyone in their way."

She stretched, and shifted sideways a little. "I've got a load of questions that we need to find answers to."

Larry, efficient as always, grabbed a legal pad and pencil. "Fire away," he said.

She'd already organized her thoughts; she knew how he worked. He'd always wanted things in order, organized and succinct. The trait had made him an asset both to the peace movement and the Spook Squad, both of which seemed to operate on the Heisenberg Uncertainty Principle. "One, who is the sorcerer? Two, why stay silent so long as to make everyone think there's nobody operating here? Three, why break silence now? Four, why target *this* kid? What's so special about her? *I* sure didn't pick up anything remarkable about her. Deke's high-psi; she's only moderately psychic."

"Good points, all of them," Larry agreed, printing the questions neatly. "By all rights there's no way a teenybopper could have done something to collect an enemy like that. The ability to conjure imps, target them, and control them at a distance suggests a lot of other abilities I'd rather not think about. My only suggestion is that the kid's in the way of something. Money makes a pretty good motive, and there's a lot of money in this area. Any chance she's an heiress?"

He looked up, pencil poised.

She shook her head, little wisps of hair coming loose from the knot at the nape of her neck. "No. Not poor, by any means, but not anywhere near the league of most of the kids in Jenks."

Larry sighed regretfully. "So much for that theory. Okay, I'll add my questions to the ones you came up with. This sorcerer seems to be targeting one kid—any chance the same guy is after *my* kid? What do the two kids have in common that could make them both targets?"

"Not much," she said. "I've been thinking about that myself. High-psi, both very bright, they both go to Jenks, they're both in the same English class. Ann Greeley's, the Honors class I'm teaching. That's it, so far as I can tell."

He pondered that a moment, then shook his head. "The first probable that occurs to me is their English teacher, and I don't think it'll wash. I can't picture Ann Greeley as a sorcerer. Not ruthless enough."

"Unless she's putting on a good act and she's skilled enough to hide what she is from me—no, I agree." It was Di's turn to sigh. "I'm in the same room with her for two hours every day, and *she* doesn't know what *I* am. If she was ever going to work on the kids, it would be right then, when they're concentrating on something else and under her thumb. Pity, that would have wrapped things up very neatly. But even if it *was* Ann, what would her motive be?"

"Search me." He shrugged. "The only motive I can think of would be that the kids are driving her loony, and if that were the case I think both of us would have picked it up. What about it being one of the other kids?"

Di shook her head emphatically. "Not bloody likely; it takes power *and* experience to control an imp. No kid could do it, however precocious. My best guess would be that the motive ties in with the targets being high-psi kids. Not a lot of them in Jenks so far as I can tell. Last question: Why are we in a null zone? Is that tied in? My sources couldn't tell me."

Larry wrote that down. "The more I see, the older I get, the more I'm convinced that there are no coincidences," he stated flatly.

She nodded, the loose ends of hair tickling her temples. "Not when magic and those who use it are involved."

"Right." He shoved the pad away and leaned back into his chair. "I may have an answer to your next-to-last question, if my hearsay has any grain of truth in it. According to at least a dozen people I've talked to over the years, Indian legend, most notably Cherokee, says that there's a goddess buried under what they call 'old Tulsa'; that's the city limits as of about the nineteen-twenties or so. They say that's why that area of Tulsa never gets hit by tornadoes."

Jesus Cluny Frog. Not another demideity . . . I had more than enough of that *in Texas.* "Good or bad goddess?" she asked resignedly.

Somewhat to her surprise, Larry didn't have an answer. "I don't know," he said, shrugging. "I haven't been able to get anyone to tell me. Could be it depends on which tribe you belong to."

"Yeah, I've run across that before. Like if you're an Aztec, Quetzalcoatl isn't the good guy he is if you're pre-Aztec." She tucked her hair back behind her ears absently. "Okay, I'll buy that, just for the sake of the hypothesis. Is she dead, or asleep?"

"Again, no consensus," he replied. "I've got a logical guess, though."

She yawned, though hardly from boredom; it had been a long two days. "Say on."

"Since the legends say that the reason tornadoes don't hit the ground around here is that even the sky gods don't want to wake her up, I'd say that the logical deduction is that she's sleeping." He grinned. "She sounds just like somebody I know, a real bitch before she gets her first cup of coffee."

She made a face at him. "Thanks a bunch."

He contrived to look innocent. "Did I name names? If the foo shits . . . Anyway, the legends say that nobody, nohow, wants to wake her up, so they all cooperate to very carefully steer storms around her. Interesting 'coincidence,' if you like though. The null area quits at just about the same place as the tornado-free zone. The 'old Tulsa' border."

She frowned. "So this goddess—or whatever—has a high probability of being the cause of both the null area and the no-tornado area."

"Looks that way. I can tell you something else," Larry continued. "I checked, and there's never been a tornado touchdown within those bounds in all the time that there's been record-keeping in the area. I'm talking about going all the way back in the newspaper and military records as well."

"Interesting . . ." She played with a strand of hair, twisting it around her finger while she thought. "I think I'm going to have to stick my neck out. I think I'm going to have to check as deep as I can in this area—find out if I can see below the null and figure out if there's anything more involved than just a psychic anomaly, or a critical mass of Fundamentalists. Now, the big question, Kosmic. Mind if I do that here?"

Larry shook his head after a moment of thought. "No reason why you shouldn't, so far as I know. You know what you're doing, you won't breach the house shields, and I trust you. I'll ask you a big question: What's the odds of this null stuff being tied in with the attack on the girl and the thing after Deke?"

Too many red herrings. "I don't even want to hazard a guess," she said truthfully. "There's no way of telling. What I tracked was a real sorcerer. You don't know what's after Deke. The Indians as a whole weren't much into sorcery, but there were individual exceptions to that. Besides that, a lot of colonial sorcerers picked up on their lore, so the American version of sorcery has a lot of commonalities with Amerind magic."

"You're so helpful."

She made a face. "I'm truthful. And this is not to say that it couldn't be something else entirely. A lot of even the ultra-Christian Spiritualists picked up on Indian medicine, or at least the *appearance* of having something to do with Indian medicine. Ever go back in the old records? An amazing number of the 'spirit guides' the old crowd used to call on were supposedly Amerind. All chiefs, too, or shamans. It runs to about eighty percent."

"What about the rest?"

"Divided about equally between Wise Buddhist philosophers—which gives you an idea of how much most of them knew about Buddhism—and Druids."

"Which gives me an idea of how much any of them knew about Druidic stuff." He half smiled. "Okay, what about this goddess, whatever she is, being the thing that's tapped onto D—"

The door opened, without anyone knocking on it first. Both of them jumped and turned toward the door.

Deke blinked at them suspiciously.

Speak of the devil. If I look as guilty as he does, Deke is going to be damn sure that we're up to something.

"Alan's going home now," Deke said, eyeing both of them dubiously. "Do you mind if I follow him and hang out at his place for a while?"

Di had no problem picking up what was bothering him. If it hadn't been for his shields, the kid would have been projecting so hard Fred in Kansas City would have "heard" him. *He figures Larry and I are either in the midst of an affair or about to start one. With Miri gone he's got me pegged for the Old Flame Returns. And the boy is not happy about this. I can't say as I blame him. I'll bet the divorce stats for this area are phenomenal. I'll bet the stats on philandering are even more impressive.*

"That's fine, Deke," Larry replied. Di could tell he was trying to hide his irritation. To her eyes, at least, he was unsuccessful.

He hasn't figured out what his kid is thinking, she suddenly realized. *He's so used to thinking of us as working partners—and me as essentially neuter, despite the teasing—that he can't imagine anyone else thinking otherwise.*

"Well, I guess—I guess I'd better get going." Deke shuffled back and forth a little; not wanting to leave them alone behind a closed door, but unable to think of a reason that would allow him to remain.

"Fine," Larry sighed. "That's fine. And Deke—knock next time, okay? You have better manners than that."

"Okay," the kid said unhappily.

He closed the door slowly. Di waited until she could "feel" his presence moving down the hall before continuing.

Larry and me. No thanks. Not my type, Deke, trust me. If I didn't have André—Mark Valdez, maybe, but not anyone else who was ever on the Squad. It's not a good idea to mix business and pleasure, especially this kind of business.

"Whatever is on to Deke," she said, continuing the conversation as if Deke hadn't interrupted it, "is not leaving psychic fingerprints. That means it hasn't done more than try to act *around* him; it hasn't actually touched *him* yet. It could be the sorcerer, it could be this power native to Tulsa, whatever it is. It could be a third entity, something entirely different. It is just barely possible that we have three different things acting here—one after Deke, one after Monica Carlin, and the power that's been here all along. I'm not counting that out."

"It could also be that all three, or any two of the three, are acting together," Larry reminded her. "I wouldn't count that out, either."

"I'm not." She wedged her elbow against the back of her chair and leaned her head against her hand. "Basically, I decided to tell you what I'd gotten so far, and warn you that I need to do some serious probing of the area. New territory, love. I need some maps. I *also* need to put a telltale on both kids, so that if anything comes after them, I'll have a chance to protect them. I've already got Monica's permission. I'd rather not ask Deke since you don't want him involved, but since he's a minor, your permission will do."

"All right." Larry grimaced. "If that's what you have to do, then that's what you have to do. Are you going to need *my* help on any of this?"

"Eventually."

I wonder if I should tell him just what it is that his only-begotten thinks that Daddy and the Dragon Lady are up to. The kid could make things awfully difficult for Di, especially if she, or she and Larry, had to do anything of a serious magical nature. This attempt at chaperoning them for instance—

No, she decided reluctantly. *No, I don't think it will help. If Larry comes down on Deke like a load of rocks, it'll make him go uncommunicative. If he tries to give him the "there there, baby, everything's okay" routine without being specific, Deke will resent it, and figure we have to be up to something. On top of that, Larry won't be able to tell the kid how he figured out what Deke's thinking. It's pretty obvious that Larry doesn't want to tell Deke the truth about me or what we're really up to, and anything less than the truth will be an evasion Deke will recognize as such. And if anything is going to be the wrong move with Deke, it would be evasion or outright lying.*

In spite of everything, she had to grin at the sour expression Larry was wearing. He had *never* much liked having a psychic gift;

he'd only used it because people needed it. She figured he'd been rather pleased to discover how null the Tulsa area was.

"I think you ought to seriously consider giving Deke lessons," she said slowly. "The shields you have on him are all right—but what if something busts through them? You can't be there all the time. And eventually he's going to leave the nest, KK. He's got the Gift—"

"But he's not comfortable with it," Larry replied quickly. "I know, I know—in theory I agree with you. But not now. Not while he still has unbalanced hormones and he might be tempted to *use* what he's got. And not while Miri's half the world away."

She shook her head, but only replied, "He's your kid. I think you're making a mistake, but he is your kid, not mine. Now about what I plan to do—"

"Ritual, or what?" he said finally.

Her grin widened a little. Besides being reluctant to use his powers, the Larry she knew had been very uncomfortable with ritual of all kinds, from Catholic mass to her own. In fact, her Wiccan magics were among the few rituals he found barely tolerable, and that, she suspected, was because they were considerably cut down from the originals that Granny had taught her. She preferred to travel light, arcanely as well as otherwise.

"Or what," she replied. "Pretty basic stuff. It's just that I'm going to have to go real deep, and real far, and that makes it a bit more dangerous. How's your Earth magic these days? If there's such a thing as 'easy' in this business, it'll be tracing the sorcery. Assuming there's traces to read—if the sorcerer has cleaned up after himself, I'll be on a cold trail. The tricky part is going to be reading this goddess. I don't know what it is, and I'm going to be *very* careful. If the business about not wanting her awakened is true, there's probably a damned good reason, and I don't want to be the one to find it out."

Larry growled a little. "Caught me, didn't you?"

"Huh?" she replied, startled.

"I *am* still doing a little magic now and then, and it's all Earth magic. That's why I'm such a good architect, and why I've got the rep I do. My buildings all fit their surroundings, and I make sure nobody pulls a fast one while they're going up. I've caught more than a few subcontractors trying to skimp on me, and weakening the building in the process."

"Oh really?" She gave him a wide-eyed look of respect. "That's one application I never thought of. Good thinking, Kosmic."

He shrugged uncomfortably.

"So—since you're still sharp in that department, let's figure out when it's going to be safest to do this—"

Sometime when Deke is off with his friends again. Safe from interference from outside—and from your nervous and ever-vigilant kid, old friend.

Fay stretched luxuriously, smoothed down her silk negligee, and sipped at her fresh-brewed gourmet coffee. She had decided on a leisurely breakfast in bed this morning, since she wouldn't be going in to school. Across the room from her, the Servant was on the telephone to the principal, making excuses.

"—well, Dr. Powell told us last night that her mother started asking for her. He thinks that she really should come out to Vinita now, before Rowena moves out of this phase or slides back to the old one." Aunt Emily's face was an absolute blank; unnerving when you heard the whining anxiety in her voice.

Fay nibbled a croissant, hot and dripping with butter.

"Yes, sir, he thinks it should be today." The Servant sounded completely sincere and entirely human. The performance was truly a marvel.

If I do say so myself.

"Yes, sir, she's getting ready to go right now, but I can put her on. She's very anxious to see her poor mother."

Fay finished the last bite of croissant, and licked the butter from her fingers. Then she put her coffee cup down on the breakfast tray with a sigh of regret, and picked up the radio extension.

Now, let's make this convincing. "Mr. Daniels?" she said, pitching her voice a little higher, so that it sounded strained and anxious. "I'm really awfully sorry about missing a day of class like this, but Dr. Powell was, like, really *insistent*. He said if I came out right away, it might make Momma a lot better—and if I didn't it might"—she broke her voice a little, in a convincing imitation of a suppressed sob—"it might make her a lot worse."

She heard Roger Daniels, the principal of Jenks High, clear his throat awkwardly. She'd just put him on the spot, in an indefensible position. The best he could manage now would be some appropriate posturing. "I realize this is very important, Fay, but you've been missing a lot of classes this year."

And last year, and the year before that, you old fool. "I know, Mr. Daniels," she replied, pitching her voice a tiny bit higher and adding a breathy quality to it. "I really do know. But I've been sick an awful lot. Every time Momma gets worse, I get these, like, migraines. It gets so bad sometimes I, like, throw up."

And I've been very careful that nobody credible ever caught me at playing hooky, Roger. I've been careful that no one has caught me at anything the teachers or you would really disapprove of. And I've been oh-so-repentant whenever someone tagged me with so much as a minor slip, like not doing homework or skipping a test.

"I know that, Fay. For the most part you're a model student, a credit to Jenks. But all these absences aren't doing much for your grades." She could hear him leafing through papers; probably checking her records.

If one quarter of what I've done the last three years showed up in those records, she thought with a little smile and a repressed giggle, *I'd have been turned over to the juvenile courts by now.*

"Frankly, Fay," he continued, "I'm rather amazed that UO accepted you. They don't usually accept anyone with grades this low."

You'd be amazed what a quarter-mil grant would make them swallow. They'd have taken me with an IQ of sixty.

"I know, sir," she said, speaking so low that she was a short step away from whispering. "Believe me, I really appreciate it. They talked to Dr. Powell, and he explained everything, and I'm really not going into a terribly hard course, anyway."

Crocheting and Creative Swimming. Which is exactly what you, you old fool, think that all girls should do. You really never have approved of higher education for women. You think we should all become wifies and mommies right out of high school. You aren't fooled, are you? You know this is just a smoke screen so I can catch a husband, about like half the other little tarts in my class.

"I can understand that," he said paternally. "And I'm sure they do, too. And I'm sure that once the excitement of senior year is behind you, you'll settle down."

"And once Momma is well—" she prompted, to keep him reminded of why she needed this excused absence.

"I hope she'll be recovering very soon," he said, sounding sincere. "Well, I'll write this in as an excused absence, Fay. But please, do try and keep these to a minimum for the rest of the year, will you? There isn't that much of it left."

"Oh *thank* you, sir," she bubbled, trying *not* to laugh at the transparent old goat. "Thank you *so* much! I really can't tell you how grateful I am—"

"That's quite all right, Fay," he said hastily. "Now if you're going to reach Vinita before noon, I expect you'd better get on your way. Don't forget to bring me a note from Dr. Powell."

"Yes, sir, I will," she said. "I won't forget. Thank you, sir. Good-bye, sir."

She hung up. "And fuck you very much, sir," she said mockingly to the handset as she put it down on the tray.

The coffee was cold, though, and so were the croissants. She surveyed the remains of her breakfast with disapproval. "Idiot kept me talking longer than I intended," she said, half to the Servant, half to herself. She looked up; the Servant was still where it was supposed to be, perched on the edge of the couch across from her bed.

"Take this away, and bring me a fresh cup of coffee," she ordered. "I suppose I'd better get ready. When is the appointment?"

"One o'clock," the Servant replied, picking up the tray so that Fay could slide out of the king-sized bed. "You have plenty of time."

"Good." Fay pulled the straps of her negligee off her shoulders and let the garment fall to the carpet. She strolled nude into the bathroom, thinking about a nice hot shower with sensual anticipation.

And the only flaw of this entire day is that I couldn't convince Deke to come over last night. The little ninny really is taking his training well. He's becoming quite a skilled lover. Much better than Wes was. But then, I did get Wes rather late in life. Thank God I didn't have to put up with him for more than four years. Thank God the gardener was adequate, even if Wes wasn't. I'd have lost my mind within the year.

The shower was preset; she turned it on with little more effort than a flick of the finger, and stood under the pounding of the massage setting.

This business of school is such a damned nuisance. Such a boring waste of time. I can certainly think of better ways to spend my afternoons and evenings. . . .

The Servant was waiting with a towel when she emerged, and handed her a hot, fresh cup of coffee to drink while the Servant styled her hair and applied her makeup for her.

The outfit awaiting her approval was a disgustingly demure and girlish knitted sweater and skirt. Fay frowned at it, but waved to the Servant to assist her in putting it on. Awful as it was, the clothing *was* the appropriate sort of dress for a seventeen-year-old visiting her mother in the hospital.

Even if the seventeen-year-old was the one really in control of the situation. And even if the hospital was Vinita, institution for the criminally insane.

And the mother had tried to kill her own, dear daughter.

A couple of years ago, Fay would have had to stop just outside Vinita to switch places with her bogus Aunt. The law did not permit fifteen-year-old drivers to handle sports cars, particularly without a license. Now she no longer had to engage in that little touch of farce; she was able to pull her Shelby-Z right into the parking lot without anyone thinking twice.

If they thought twice about why a woman with as much wealth as Fay's mother was in the state loony bin rather than an expensive, discreet, private hospital, they never voiced the question.

Fay swung her long legs out of the car and emerged to the appreciative glances of several of the guards and attendants. One or two even dared to whistle, and her mood was good enough that she flirted her hips at them and gave one a come-hither wink.

The fact was, she reflected, as she led the way up the cracked cement walkway, that this situation was as nearly perfect for *her* as was possible in this day and age.

It's too bad they don't lock loonies up to rot like they used to, she thought wistfully, waiting as one of the guards scurried to hold the glass door open for her. *That would have been perfect. And it's too bad this isn't back in the fifties, when they used to use the criminally insane as experimental subjects. I could have gotten a lot of mileage out of shock treatments, if I could have convinced the doctor to try them on Rowena with me there.* She sighed. *Oh, well. This will certainly do.*

The staff at Vinita, as at any state-run facility, was overworked and underpaid. Most patients never saw a therapist more often than once a week unless they had families that could pay extra for it. And therapy was a joke even for those who could pay. The doctors, besides being years behind the times, were working from inaccurate information, and treatments were based on speculation at best.

The staff, including the doctors, tended to be shell-shocked and incurious; aides and nurses were frequently the dregs of their professions.

For those under state-paid care, there was only one question—if they hadn't committed an act of physical violence, could they be bullied into a simulacrum of health so that they could feed, clean, and clothe themselves? Because as soon as they could, they went out the door, to be "mainstreamed," or "normalized into society," as Dr. Powell liked to put it. If they *had* committed a crime of violence, the question was, could they be coached or bullied into a state in which they could convince a probations board that they were recovered and wouldn't do it again? In that case, it was out the door as soon as the ink was dry on their release papers. Only a few, notorious criminals were the exceptions.

And for those whose care was being paid for privately—

"You get what you pay for," Fay murmured to herself, smiling, as she chose the least damaged of the plastic chairs in the institutional-green waiting room. "Exactly what you pay for."

Dr. Powell emerged from the door at the end of the dingy room after she and Aunt Emily had been waiting for about five minutes.

Looks like he's halfway together this time, Fay observed, noting the key to Rowena's room in his hand. *It's just as well. I don't feel like sitting around for an hour while he tries to remember where he left the damn thing.*

She noted with amusement that his hands were shaking.

Silly man, can't you even get your own scheduling right? Must be time for your snootful, or you wouldn't be so wired. You should have snorted up in your office and made us wait a little longer. If I didn't want you incapacitated, I'd be very suspicious of you right now.

She made a mental note to check with Powell's pusher. If he was getting too heavily into coke, it might be time to think about replacing him.

If he gets caught, it'll be an inconvenience at best, because I'll have to find another incompetent in a hurry. At worst—all his patients and treatments are going to come under examination, and someone may put Rowena in the hands of a real doctor for a while. What a pain that would be. . . .

"She's a lot more lucid," Powell said, blinking his bloodshot eyes rapidly. "I think we're on the right track with the lithium therapy."

Fay hid a smile, and contrived to look awed and overwhelmed.

What an idiot! Even I know that lithium is for manic-depressives, and does nothing for anyone else. Whatever they're calling Rowena now, it's not manic-depressive!

"Oh, Dr. Powell," Fay breathed, looking up at him with sweet, round eyes. "That's *wonderful*! How much longer do you think it will take? I'd *so* love to have Momma back with me!"

She could see the calculations going on behind Powell's eyes; cocaine was an expensive habit to maintain, and Fay's trust fund was paying him very, very well. If he lost Rowena Harper as a patient, his income would drop by a fourth. She was the only private client he had.

"Now, Miss Harper," he said soothingly. "Your mother's problem isn't like pneumonia, where we can tell exactly when she'll get better. The treatment of mental illness is a science, but it isn't an exact one, yet."

Here comes the platitude.

"She has to understand that she's sick, and truly want to get better." He turned to Aunt Emily; telegraphing desperation, if he only knew it. *She* was the other—supposed—beneficiary of the Harper largess. If Rowena Harper was "cured," theoretically Aunt Emily would be out the door, too. "You understand, don't you, Miss Baker?"

"Of course, Doctor," the Servant replied, showing all the submission any doctor could ask of a lay person. "Fay, dear, you mustn't get your hopes up. The doctor isn't going to be able to make your mother better in a single afternoon, not when she's been ill for five years."

Fay allowed her face to fall. *Same song, new verse,* she thought smugly. *Same game we play every time I visit. I really did pick you well, didn't I, Dr. Powell?*

"But that doesn't mean that your being here isn't important," he added hastily. "She really has made some significant progress, and if we can just cement that progress today, it will make an enormous difference in her prognosis."

Buzz, buzz, buzz. "Sound and fury, signifying nothing." All empty prattle and platitudes. You're a marvel, Dr. Powell.

"As I told you on the phone, she has been asking about you for the past few weeks now. It was my judgment that this would be a good time to bring you in. I'm hoping it will give her the boost of reality she needs."

Time for inflating his ego. Fay gave him the same look of submissive adoration that Aunt Emily was wearing. "Anything you say, Doctor," she cooed. "Aunt Emily and I have faith in you."

And if by some chance the authorities ever turned her loose, I'd probably take her over to the faith healers at ORU. She'd have as much chance of "getting well" as she does with you. The only reason I haven't suggested that is because they might believe her. I can't risk that.

Dr. Powell stood a tiny bit straighter and preened under that look. Fay had it down to an art; it was, after all, the same look that had ensnared Wes Harper—and others before and since him.

He led the way past an attendant who did not even bother putting his girlie magazine away or taking his feet off the desk, down the institutional-beige corridor lined with closed and locked doors, all solid, with little viewing hatches at eye level. Fay knew that the attendants were supposed to check on the occupants of these little cells about once an hour. She wondered if they ever got around to it more often than once a day.

Dr. Powell stopped at one of those doors, one Fay knew by heart by now. He opened the viewing hatch, and took a quick look.

"She's fine," he said with satisfaction. "I'll let you in now. This time I'll stay outside. Don't forget, though, I'll be right here the whole time. If you need me, I can have that door open in a minute."

"Thank you, Dr. Powell," Fay replied, managing a credible imitation of someone subdued and a little frightened. "I—I hope you won't need to."

"So do I, Miss Harper," he replied, and unlocked and opened the door.

Rowena Harper sat on her iron-framed cot, staring out the mesh-covered window. Unlike a good many of the inmates here—and unlike the first two years of her tenancy of this cell—she was neat, clean, well groomed; her hair trimmed tidily, her hospital-issue dress clean and unwrinkled. She ignored the opening and closing of the door, continuing to stare out at the clouds.

Fay frowned. This was a new development, one she wasn't sure she liked.

"Mother?" she said tentatively.

Rowena ignored her.

"Mother," she repeated, sharply now. No reaction. "Rowena, Dr. Powell said you've been asking for me."

Rowena turned slowly. Her face was fairly expressionless, but her eyes showed her hostility. She still did not speak.

"Rowena, I had to take time off from school for this. You might at least tell me why you wanted me to come."

The eyes blazed and the hands crooked involuntarily into claws.

"Why do I *always* ask you to come?" she hissed. "I won't give up, Mother. Damn you, *I want my body back!*"

EIGHT

O h, *Mother*," Fay cried in mock dismay, clenching her hands at
chest level to add verity to the performance. "Dr. Powell said
you were so much better—"

She bit her lip as Rowena's face spasmed; Rowena could guess
what she was thinking; probably fairly accurately at the moment. *But
can you realize how relieved I am to discover you haven't gotten any
wiser since last time I was here?*

"*Better?*" Rowena exclaimed, laughing bitterly, holding tightly to
the edge of her thin institutional mattress. "He's giving me *lithium*. I
can read, I see TV programs—even *I* know how stupid that is! I
wouldn't send my dog to a quack like him!"

"Mother, that's *not* nice," Fay replied, pursing her lips in disapproval and keeping clear of the door so that the doctor could open it
if Rowena rushed for her. The woman seemed to have learned that
much since last time, though; she stayed where she was, seated on the
edge of the bed. Fay smiled tremulously for the benefit of the camera
in the corner. "Dr. Powell has been doing what's best for you; I'm sure
you realize that. And he said you'd been doing so well—"

"I don't fight him anymore. That way he can't have me tranked,"
Rowena retorted. "God damn you, I want my own body back!"

Fay shrank in on herself, and clasped her arms across her chest.
You can't have it, dear. I'm enjoying it very much, thank you.

"Mother, this is stupid. You know what Dr. Powell says," she
replied for the sake of the doctor and any other listening ears—and
recording tapes. "He says that's just a fantasy. He says you couldn't
face getting older, so you made up this story about my stealing your
body."

She smoothed her skirt over her hips, in what could be taken for an ordinary gesture of adolescent nervousness—unless you knew what Fay and Rowena knew. "It's all in your mind. And you're going to have to face facts, Mother. You're in that body, and I'm in this one, and nothing is going to change that."

Rowena's eyes narrowed, and her fingers bit into the mattress. "You bitch," she whispered.

Fay pouted a little, and tossed her head. "And it isn't very nice to call your daughter a bitch."

"You—aren't—my—daughter." Rowena ground the words out from between her clenched teeth.

"There you go again," Fay sighed dramatically, and sniffed. "Mother, I don't understand you! Don't you realize that if you'd just face the facts you could be out of here anytime you wanted to leave?"

Rowena loosened her grip of the mattress and clasped her hands on her lap. "And what?" She turned away again to look out the window. "Go home so you could find some way to kill me?"

For a moment Fay was taken aback. *So she's figured that out, has she? I'm impressed. I hadn't expected her to be thinking that clearly yet.* "Mother," she whispered, pretending shock. "How could you say such a thing?"

"Very easily," Rowena said, turning back and lifting her chin in defiance. "I've had a lot of time to think since that phony started me on lithium. I'm talking to the woman who murdered my father. Why should you worry about getting rid of me?"

"Grandfather Harper died in a factory accident," Fay said with the patience one displays with a retarded child. "And Grandfather Baker died in Korea. When you were two."

It wasn't too hard to engineer the accident, Fay chuckled to herself, *given the miserable conditions at all of Harper's plants. Maybe if he'd paid a little closer attention to the rate at which his workers were getting hurt and a little less to the bottom line, he might have survived a little longer. It was a tad harder to arrange Gary's death; but I'd gotten back up to full ability by then. It's amazing what can be hidden in a combat zone.*

"You know who I mean," Rowena growled. "Your husband. Wesley Harper. Remember him?"

"Daddy—" Fay quivered her lower lip, just a little. It wouldn't do to overact on this one. Fay had only been three when she'd gotten rid of Wesley. "Daddy was killed when he ran off the road. You *know* that, Mother."

That was even easier to set up. When you're driving a dark country highway, late at night, and a thing out of your worst nightmares pops up in the seat next to you, it's somewhat difficult to keep your mind on the road. Another benefit cars have over horses. Horses have a habit of trying to save themselves and their driver—but a car is mindless, and a collision with a tree at seventy miles per hour never leaves a survivor.

"You killed him, Mother," Rowena replied stubbornly. "I don't know how you did it, but you killed him. I bet you killed Granny Baker, too."

She freaked when she found herself in Maria's body. It was so convenient that we happened to be on the yacht at the time. "Granny Baker drowned when you were thirteen, Mother. You know that, too—you were there." Fay was increasingly pleased with the way this interview was working; Rowena was beginning to look like a classic case of paranoid delusion.

"Did you do to her what you did to me?" Rowena cried, pounding on the bed with both fists. "Is thirteen the magic age? Can't you steal their bodies until then? Did you think I'd kill myself the way she did?"

It's partially because sexual maturity makes you corruptible, dear. I have had to wait as long as sixteen years. "Mother, please—" Fay held out her hands coaxingly. "Please, stop saying that. It's only going to make Dr. Powell want to keep you here longer."

She was thinking over the ramifications of this interview even as she spoke. *I'd just as soon she stayed here for another three years. And if I can get her as hysterical as she was when she woke up in that old hulk, Powell will probably go for that. In three years I'll be legally adult; plus by then I should have all my power back. At that point I can arrange for her to drop dead some night when the attendant is drunk or stoned.*

But Rowena didn't look as if she was going to oblige Fay this time. She sagged back, slumped over her knees, hair hanging down limply over her face. "There's no point in even trying to fight you," she said. "I can't win." She sobbed hopelessly. "Why do you do this? How long has this been going on, Mother? How long have you been stealing other people's bodies?"

Longer than you imagine, child. "Mother, I don't know what you're talking about."

"It's got to be great," Rowena said dully, ignoring her protest. "I've been thinking about it a lot, at night. I mean, you party down for a while, till you're maybe thirty and you're wearing the old bod out—then you go find some poor little girl, and get her stoned, and you're all set to party down for another twenty years." She looked up, her eyes glaring at Fay through the curtain of hair and angry tears. "Does it have to be your daughter, Mom? Or can it be anybody?"

"Mother," Fay replied, putting just a little scorn behind her words, "you sound like a bad horror movie."

It has to be my blood-daughter; I've tried others, and all I did was kill them. But you can't know that, can you?

God. It's still so clear; most of the others have blurred in my memories, but not the first.

The first transfer—it had been totally by accident.

She'd settled in Virginia only the year before, she and her very nubile, attractive—and quite corrupt—daughter. There had been one too many close encounters with church officials in London, officials who had been suspicious of her simply on the grounds that she was a wealthy widow with no interest in remarrying. They'd suspected her of immoral behavior, no doubt; they had no idea *how* immoral. The colonies had seemed like an attractive venue—she could buy herself a remote homestead, staff it with slaves, and practice the Arte free from interference. Purity had been equally eager for the move, sensing, doubtless, that she would be trading the jaded and soft deminobles for virile and eminently seduceable men of the frontier. Unpolished perhaps, but also unspoiled. . . .

All started well. She found exactly the kind of place she had been looking for, and at an attractive price. The owner had been eager to sell and return to England. Too eager. She'd assumed he was one of those gentleman-adventurers, more fop than man, who had thought to find gold in the colonies, and discovered that the only fortunes to be made required distasteful hard work.

But it hadn't been hard work that had frightened the man off. It had been the Indians. They survived one attack, but at the cost of half the slaves. Fay (she'd been "Cordelia" then) had been determined she would not be driven off.

Up until that moment, Purity had no notion of what it was her mother did, not really. Cordelia had carefully kept that part of her life from her daughter; there was always the chance that she would need a bargaining chip, and if Purity had known just how choice a counter she was . . .

My dear, debauched daughter. It was so easy. All I needed to do was wait until you were finished with that young farmer, and sleeping the sleep of the sodden. Your cooperation was not essential to my plans. Your body was.

She'd tried a most ambitious sorcery, the invocation of one of the

Greater Abyssals, using her unconscious daughter as the proffered sacrifice.

Then a mouse ran across one of the lines of protection surrounding her and erased a fraction of an inch of it.

The Prince of Darkness being notoriously ill-tempered about being summoned and coerced, the creature had gone for *her*—

She could still feel the fear of that moment, as she scrambled backwards and flung all the power she'd gathered over the years in a single frantic attempt—not at defense, for she had sensed somehow that defense would be futile—but escape.

There had been a moment of pain and disorientation.

When I could see again, I watched the Prince devouring myself— and I was my daughter. She shook her head; she hadn't thought of that in years . . . decades.

Rowena was watching her with her eyes narrowed, as if she could see something of Fay's thoughts. "How long?" she insisted. "How long have you been doing this?"

"Mother, don't be a drag." *Three hundred years and more, child. If you knew that, you'd know you have no hope at all, and only such life as I feel like granting you.*

Rowena must have seen something in Fay's expression that frightened her. She scooted back to the center of the bed, tucked up her knees, and hugged them to her chest like a small child. "You know," she said, her voice quavering, "I've been wondering, ever since Powell stopped tranking me. Like, if you have to do this to a daughter—that's pretty cold, Mother. That's, like, pretty heartless. I mean, you get yourself married, and then you have a kid, and then you do *this* to her. That's, like, worse than a Nazi."

"Mother," Fay said, carefully aghast, "that's—that's sick!"

Actually, you haven't even guessed most of it. I choose my husbands very carefully; rich and handsome—and not overly bright. Not necessarily young, either—just so they were handsome in their youth and are fertile now. It's easier if they aren't *young; that way I don't have to go to the trouble of getting rid of bothersome parents. And occasionally I've been able to drive one to death without resorting to arcane aid.*

"You probably *built* Aunt Emily in the cellar or something," Rowena continued, a little sob catching in her throat. "That's why I never heard of her until she showed up with you."

"Mother . . ." Fay shook her head with sorrowful disbelief. "I just don't know what to say to you. I can't believe you're making these things up! Are you"—she let her own voice quaver a little—"are you *trying* to hurt me? Why do you hate me so much?"

You're a lot smarter than I imagined, child. I'd like to know how much else you've figured out. Did you guess that the transfer and the creation of a Servant takes all the power I have? Do you know how weak I am now?

"Trying to hurt *you*?" Rowena laughed wildly, tossing her head back and leaning it against the wall behind her. "Christ, Mother, you're a hoot! Me, hurt *you*? You haven't got a heart; you've got nothing inside you but stone!"

So you don't know. Time to end the farce. "Mother—" She backed into the wall and hid her face in her hands. "Mother, I can't believe you're saying things like this. Nobody's going to believe you, nobody will *ever* believe you! You're never going to get out of here, never! I'm going to spend the rest of my life knowing my own mother is locked up in a loony bin! You're going to *rot* in here—"

Rowena snarled, going into a crouch, hands and lips twitching—

Because when Fay parted her hands, very carefully, Rowena could see what the camera and the doctor couldn't.

That Fay wasn't sobbing, she was laughing.

"You're never, ever going to get out of here, Mother! They're going to keep you so tranked you won't even know what day it is! And there's nothing you can do about it—"

That last was too much for Rowena—she screamed and lunged at Fay—

But Fay and Dr. Powell were ready; the door snapped open, admitting two burly attendants who, if they'd been less Neanderthal-like, could have taken top prizes in body-building contests. The two of them pushed Rowena back down onto the bed, ignoring her screams and her attempts to wrestle free of them. Dr. Powell entered a few moments later; he was sniffing a little, and his hands were no longer shaking.

Finally got your toot while you were waiting out in the hall, hm, Doctor? I wondered why you hadn't interfered by now. It's because you didn't know; you were off snorting your nose candy.

He was carrying a syringe; Gorilla Number One held Rowena's arm still long enough for him to give her the injection. Within a few moments she was so sedated she couldn't even mumble a protest when they put her to bed.

"I'm very sorry about that, Fay," the doctor said insincerely. "I really thought she was making progress. But it's partially your fault. I wish you hadn't said those things to her. You practically drove her into relapsing. I'm going to have to keep her sedated for the next three months at the absolute minimum."

He glared at her as if he suspected her of engineering the "relapse."

He probably did, Fay reflected. Coke tended to make people paranoid.

She decided she'd had enough for one day, and burst into a flood of orchestrated tears.

"My God," Fay said, stretching to relieve the kinks in her shoulders. "What a farce. It seems now like such a waste of time." She'd turned the wheel over to the Servant; for once she felt like being the passenger.

"Hardly a waste," the Servant replied from the driver's side, parroting what Fay had already said half an hour ago. "There's no chance she'll convince anyone that she's cured if she keeps *that* up."

There were times when talking to the Servant felt like talking to a mirror. Or a tape recorder. "But I can think of a lot better ways to spend my afternoons than on a fiasco like that one," Fay said petulantly, watching the eternally boring landscape of Oklahoma rolling by. "In fact, I can think of any number of ways I'd rather be spending my time than wasting it the way I am now. School, for instance. Bloody nuisance, that's what it is. Having to dance around the asinine laws they have hedging in so-called minors—like compulsory schooling. And if that wasn't bad enough, having to waste *more* time in college just to find a suitable man if Deke doesn't work out—" She gritted her teeth. "Up until *this* transfer I could get away with having my own governess to teach me. I didn't have to cool my heels in a classroom. I *could* be spending the time getting my power back. I *could* be spending the time enjoying myself. Instead I spend most of my time being utterly bored, and the rest trying to get around that old fart of a trustee *just* so I can get some use out of *my* money! I don't dare use magick on half the people I need to—if they act out of character, other people will notice."

"You should be thinking about your demons," the Servant reminded her. "They need feeding."

"I know, I know," she snarled, having forgotten. "You don't have to keep telling me!"

"As you wish," it replied passively. Fay looked at its bland face and wondered what, if anything, was going on in its mind. Was she imagining things, or had it really seemed earlier as if it was beginning to act on its own?

She turned away and stared moodily out the side window of the Shelby. Finding inconspicuous victims had been getting harder lately. She'd already taken as many of the kids from Jenks as she'd dared.

The ones she'd fed to her allies had been punks or druggies, mostly. Kids nobody would miss—

And nobody was surprised when they turned up dead. But it's starting to get noticed. I heard that a couple of people are saying that there are more problems than usual this year at Jenks.

So that left the kids out. Which meant that she was going to have to go hunting.

"Downtown?" she said aloud.

The Servant shook its head. "You hunted downtown three months ago. You told me to remind you that you might be recognized if you went there again."

She tried to think of other well-stocked hunting grounds. "How about the Fifteenth Street Bridge?"

"The police cleared it out last week." One of the Servant's jobs was to keep up with the news, which was why it spent so much time watching TV.

"Shit," she said in disgust. "The campground?"

The Servant shook its head. "The rangers aren't letting anyone camp there for more than a week anymore; too many vagrants were living there. And the abandoned house at the airport burned down a month ago."

"What does that leave me?" she asked it.

The Servant was silent as it checked its memory for her. "Across the river, or out near Sand Springs," it offered. "One of the other high schools. Or serendipity."

She didn't like any of the choices. All offered hazards she didn't want to deal with, not as low on energy as she was. "Next time you see a place to eat, pull in," she ordered. "I want to think about this a while."

She hadn't had time to blink before the Servant was slowing the car and pulling into the parking lot of a Ken's Pizza right on the edge of the Tulsa city limits.

There was actually a city limits sign right on the weed-covered verge. The pizza parlor was so close to the edge, Fay realized, that while the restaurant itself was within the city boundaries, the line stopped at the edge of the parking lot.

The Servant parked the car smoothly, and as Fay emerged from the air-conditioned interior, she could hear voices, angry voices, from the trash area behind the building.

Her interest piqued, she turned and shaded her eyes against the last rays of the sunset.

Two uniformed Tulsa police, both female, were giving a young teenager on motorbike an unnecessarily hard time. One was examining his license so carefully Fay wondered if she was checking it for wear or flyspecks; the other was reading him a lecture on traffic safety at the top of her lungs, to the vast amusement of a group of his peers in the next block.

Both of them looked distastefully butch, so far as Fay was concerned. She might have passed them by altogether, except for the look of sly self-satisfaction on the face of the one delivering the lecture.

Fay prided herself on being unusually deft at reading people. As she followed the Servant into the restaurant, the reason for that self-satisfaction dawned on her.

They're bullies, both of them, she decided with a surge of delight. *Bullies who put on badges just because it gives them an excuse to push people around. Which means they're not likely to do things by the book. Which also means that they're very likely to actually break the law they're supposed to be enforcing just for the sake of their own ego-tripping.*

Which makes them fair prey.

How marvelous! I begin to believe that my Servant is prescient!

While they ordered, Fay was watching to see if the pair entered the restaurant. They did. A few moments later, the manager came over and spoke with them in a low, urgent voice. The second of the two, the one with dark, curly hair, responded in tones that could be heard all over the dining room.

"Look, I don't give a fart if my jurisdiction ends at the edge of the lot. If I want to bust somebody's ass, I'll bust his ass, and they can argue about it in court."

Good, Fay thought with satisfaction. *So they know. That will make it all the easier.*

The manager left, his ears and neck flushed, and glanced at her out of the corner of his eye as he passed.

Probably hoping we didn't notice, she thought, and yawned, pretending that she hadn't overheard the woman.

When their meal arrived, Fay ate quickly, which forced the Servant to do the same. By the time she was finished, the policewomen were just being served.

Good. Being interrupted at dinner will make them irritated. They'll want someone to pay for their irritation.

"I'm going to the rest room," she said quietly to the Servant as she toyed with the remains of her meal. "When I'm inside, go without paying for our dinner. Take the car, drive about two blocks back the way we came, and wait for me. Keep the engine and the lights off."

The Servant's eyes flickered to the police and back, and it nodded.

Fay got up and flounced off to the women's room, swaying her hips aggressively. She wanted the women to get a good look at her, and to get the impression that she was a spoiled, rich-kid punk. She gave the Servant just long enough to move the car, then emerged, going straight out the door without stopping to pay for the meal either, making sure to choose a moment when the manager's back was turned so that he wouldn't stop her before she left.

Darkness had already descended. She walked quickly in order to be beyond the edge of the lot by the time the two police came out of the restaurant. She noted as she watched for them out of the corner of her eye that the area was half developed at best. That was in her favor. In fact, at the moment everything seemed to be in her favor.

Once she was one step beyond the city line, she slowed, sauntering along, waiting.

She heard them coming; they walked so noisily she could have heard them half a mile away.

"Excuse me, miss." There was a heavy emphasis on the word "miss" that made a mockery of the apparent politeness.

Fay smiled slyly as she turned. *Right on time. And we're all standing on county property.* "Yes?" she replied snidely. "Just what's *your* problem?"

"Did you just leave without paying?" the blond woman said.

"I don't think so," Fay said, in tones that implied she knew very well that she had. She started to turn away, and the first one reached out and grabbed her arm.

"Where do you think you're going?" the woman snapped.

Fay looked at the hand on her arm with a lifted eyebrow. "To my car, of course. Would you mind removing that? You're getting grease on my sweater."

Oh, you fools. You played right into my hands. If you'd just stopped the minute I crossed the line, you'd have been safe. Now, by knowingly violating the law, you've given me carte blanche to do anything I want with you.

"I think you're going to hustle your expensive little rear end back into that restaurant and take care of your bill," the dark-haired woman said nastily.

"I doubt it," Fay answered, with a sneer that was more than a match for hers. "I'll take care of it after I get to my car. I'm in a hurry. Of course, I don't imagine anyone like *you* would understand that, would you? After all, the only thing you types do is sit around in pizza joints and hassle kids."

They weren't expecting a show of defiance from anyone as young as she was. The woman's grasp loosened for a moment, and Fay pulled her arm away and started walking toward the car. She allowed them to catch up with her just beyond a stand of overgrown bushes and young trees, growth that would effectively conceal what was about to occur—

The dark-haired one caught up first and grabbed her arm again, yanking her around with completely unnecessary violence. "All right, you little tart," the woman snarled, "that's about enough crap out of you! Let's see how you like your ass being thrown in jail!"

Come to me, my friends, my companions. . . . She twitched the magick in her mind, the spell that called her allies in to feed. *Here is proper meat for you.*

Fay smiled as the Abyssal Creatures rose up behind each of the officers. They materialized silently, giving no hint of their presence.

I do so enjoy a good farce.

"I really don't think you're going to have time for that," she said gently. At about that moment, the blond evidently noticed that Fay's eyes were going to something considerably *above* her head, and turned.

The Creature smiled as she started to scream.

I do so enjoy a good farce.

Fay leaned back against the trunk of a tree, folded her arms, and prepared to enjoy the show.

They took an artistically long time about things.

Fay could not "feel" the power flow, but she knew from experience that it was there in abundance. She cast the small magick that enabled her to gather it in, and waited, watching her allies at their task with detached curiosity.

This is going to be quite profitable, she thought, moving a little deeper into the gloom beside the trees. *These two were better than I thought. They truly enjoyed exercising their petty authority on the least provocation; it was probably their only pleasure. That kind of petty tyrant always produces a gratifying amount of energy when trapped and helpless. There's going to be enough for my allies and plenty left over for me. Delightful.*

The demonics had the women reduced to quivering rags just as her feet began to hurt a little. *Stupid shoes,* she thought in irritation. *This was getting rather entertaining. I suppose I'd better get them to finish up. A pity. I love watching someone that enjoys his work.*

"I think that's enough, children," she interrupted them gently. "It's time to put your toys away."

The larger of the two looked over at her with sulfurously glowing eyes, and grunted.

"And don't forget to clean up after yourselves," she reminded them as she walked back toward the restaurant.

The spring breeze was comfortably cool, and touched her cheeks like a caress. She savored the sensation, and the faint hint of peony scent carried with it. She noticed with a feeling of gratification that the squad car was still where she'd last seen it, parked unobtrusively behind the restaurant, where no one would notice it for an hour or two at least.

Lovely; no one will wonder where they went until after I'm long gone. And by the time my friends finish, there won't be a single trace that they ever existed. It's quite likely they won't even be missed until shift change. The department may well spend weeks looking for them. I wonder what they'll finally decide?

Her grin widened as a thought occurred to her. *I could see that someone gives the authorities a story about seeing them in that little porn store on Eleventh, buying little toys together. And then see that someone else reports seeing them abandoning the squad, getting into a car and driving off west. What fun! Especially if I see that the press gets the same stories. . . .*

The Tulsa Police Department won't be in quite such a hurry to find out what happened to them, once those rumors start flying. They'll be very happy to let the mystery fade into obscurity.

But it wouldn't do at all for the people at the restaurant to remember the unpaid dinner, or the fact that they'd sent the police off after her.

Or, really, for them to remember the police at all.

Always tidy your loose ends, she reminded herself. *That's why you're the success you are today.*

She arranged her expression in a carefully calculated mix of chagrin and distress, and entered the restaurant, rushing up to the fake-wood counter and the girl behind the cash register.

"Oh gosh, I'm so sorry," she gushed to the startled cashier. "I had to visit the—you know—and I thought my aunt had taken care of dinner, and she left, thinking *I* was going to take care of it—I'm *really* sorry. We were halfway home when we both realized—"

She extracted a pair of twenties from her wallet, babbling the entire time and carefully weaving a spell of forgetfulness as she did so.

All she needed was the key phrase to get into their minds. . . .

The manager obligingly gave it. "Didn't you see the cops?" he said.

There was the briefest moment of hesitation; an instant in which everyone who was involved froze while the magick flashed into their minds and worked Fay's will.

"Cops?" she said innocently. "What cops? Oh no, heavens, keep the change, I owe you that much, at least."

The manager blinked uncertainly. "I could have sworn—"

He glanced over at the table where the policewomen had been sitting, but there was nothing there to show who or what the customers had been; just the clutter of half-eaten pizza and used utensils.

"Never mind," he said, shaking his head. "I don't know what I was thinking about. Thank you, miss, it's a pleasure to run across somebody as honest as you."

"Oh, I have my moments," she replied, laughing, and exited the door he held open for her.

The Servant was waiting just as she'd told it to, in the dark and silent Shelby. In the passenger's side, which pleased Fay. Now she was in the mood to drive again.

"You did well?" the Servant asked.

"Very well," she replied, gunning the motor and pulling away with a satisfying screech of tires.

Very well indeed. Now I have a bit of power to spare. Enough to throw a better fright into that Carlin bitch.

NINE

Monica took her time stowing her books away in her locker, eavesdropping shamelessly on the conversation a few feet down the hallway.

"So anyway, from what I heard from Janet, Harper's mom said she was like, a witch, and had put some kind of curse on her. In front of the shrink and everything."

A bitch is more like it, Monica thought acidly.

"God, I'd *die*. So then what?" the walking Bloomingdale's advertisement standing next to the speaker asked.

"Well, *then* Mrs. Harper, like, jumped her. Janet says it took three guys to get her off." The speaker, a tribute to tanning machines, shuddered dramatically. "I mean, can you *imagine* it? Your own mom going after you like that?"

"She's a nut-case," the Bloomie's display said laconically. "You never know what a nut-case is going to do."

"Well, yeah, but still . . . You'd think she'd be embarrassed or something, you know? I mean, even a nut-case ought to have some *pride*. And I'm surprised Harper told Janet."

That's Jenks, Monica thought. *Never mind your poor mother is so crazy she attacks you. Imagine what people will say.*

"She didn't. Jan was on the switchboard when Harper's aunt called her in sick. *Any*way, Fay's got a migraine from it. So no practice tonight."

"Not much point to it right now; what are we doing cheers for? The wrestling team? Tennis? Golf?" The third member of the little group, a chick Monica suspected of wearing glasses only because they made her look like Molly Ringwald, emitted a high-pitched cackle that made Monica's teeth ache. "Shit, give me a break!"

"Oh, right," the bronzed one laughed. "I can just, like, hear the golf cheers. They'd probably make us do 'em in mime!"

That set the Ringwald clone off on a series of gestures that started like boy-scout flag signals and ended obscene. The other two went into gales of laughter and all three migrated in the direction of their next class.

So that's why Harper wasn't here today or yesterday, Monica thought smugly. *Her loss. She's not gonna keep Deke much longer at this rate.*

She grabbed her notebook for the English class and started down the hall herself, feeling very much in tune with the universe. Because in the inside pocket of her purse were three notes from Alan and *five* from Deke.

Just ahead of her she caught sight of Joy Harris, one of the Brains, a skinny, long-legged kid who devoured science and science fiction with equal enthusiasm and wore glasses because she *needed* them. "Hey, Harris!" she called. "Wait up!"

Joy looked back over her bony shoulder, spotted her waving from behind a bulwark of freshmen just getting out of French 2, and grinned, showing braces like a Chrysler grille. She stopped and got over to the side to let the crowd move around her, and ignored the push and shove until Monica reached her.

"Hey, I'm glad you caught me before I forgot," Joy said without preamble. "Carri said to tell you that if you're really interested she'll sell you the Cabri for four. She wants that Firebird real bad, and they'll only give her three on the Cabri."

"Okay," Monica said happily. "I'll tell Mom, and she'll tell Dad that she thinks it's a bad idea, and that'll make *him* cough up some cash just to make her look like a jerk. So what's the verdict on contacts?" she finished.

Joy sighed. "No way. My eyes are changing too fast. The optometrist says to wait another year. And besides, I wanted extended-wears and he won't give them to kids. He says we don't follow instructions."

Monica made a face. "He ought to talk to your chemistry teacher. Like, Alan says you're the only one in the class that *always* gets the results like in the book."

"Yeah, I know, but he's an old fart. Mom got a little disgusted with him this time, though—he wanted to know why she wanted a pair in every color, and what did she think she was, a movie star? I might be able to get her talked into going to the guy at the mall—you know, the one you went to—just taking the 'scrip from our regular guy but getting 'em made up over there. If she does that I bet I can get her talked into 'em for me." Joy gave Monica a wistful sideways glance. "I'd really *die* to have green eyes. Although why I bother, with all this barbed wire in my mouth—"

"I think you'd look cute with green eyes," Monica reassured her, "and the braces aren't as bad as you think. Lots of the kids have 'em."

"Yeah, but not with enough metal to make a DC-10 on their fangs." Joy fished a mirror out of her purse, grimaced at herself, put it back, and kept walking. Monica ignored the gesture; Joy complained about her braces at least twenty times a day.

"So what's this about Harper's mom?" Monica brought up her *real* reason for catching up with Joy. "I heard some kid talking about her. I didn't know she was, like, locked up." Joy Harris was the unofficial school historian. Not a gossip; she didn't indulge in speculation or rumors—but if it had happened in Jenks in the last ten years, Joy knew about it, every last detail.

"What, the nut-case? Oh, right, I keep forgetting you don't know." Joy shifted her books over—a huge volume on the Etruscans (whoever they were), topped by three fantasy books with dragons on the covers, and her English Lit stuff. "Harper's mom's in Vinita."

"Isn't that the nuthouse for murderers and stuff?" Monica said doubtfully.

"Yeah, except that it used to be, like, just the state loony bin, and that's what it was when the shit happened and they put Harper's mom in there. When the Bitch-Queen turned thirteen something really weird happened over at this cottage where they kept Harper's horse." Joy's notebook slithered off the top of the pile, and she caught it just before it hit the floor.

"Like what?" Monica asked, taking the notebook away from her.

"Thanks. Like her mom went—*blam!*—off the deep end. Real sudden, for no reason. It was a good thing this aunt of Harper's had shown up for a visit, or God only knows what would have happened." She paused dramatically. "It was bad *enough,* you know? She, like, passed out or something, and when she came to, she ran all the way down to 169 and tried to flag cars down, yelling about how Fay was a witch and had stolen her body."

"Oh, *God.*" Monica managed to feel a flicker of sympathy for the bitch. "I bet she wanted to *die.*"

"Well, that's not the worst, either—right after that, when they were making Vinita into the max-security loony bin, and they had to move all the regular patients out, they were, like, making all the relatives show up to take 'em away. Well, Fay and her aunt showed up, okay, with her mom's shrink? And her mom started in again, about how Fay was a witch, only this time she'd gotten hold of a knife and she went after Fay with it and cut her up. So they left her there, 'cause she'd just proved she was violent, you know?"

"Wow." Monica was awed. "That's pretty gross. I mean, there's that, and there's the way Jill croaked—like Harper sort of attracts disaster, doesn't she?"

"Makes you kind of feel sorry for her. She's almost got a reason to be such a pain. It's like *she's* the one with the curse on her. Even if she *wasn't* the Bitch-Queen, *I* wouldn't want to be her friend," Joy said emphatically as they reached the door of the English class. "Around Harper, seems like if you don't go crazy, you get hit by lightning or something."

"Or else Harper gets tired of you," Monica whispered nastily. "And then you wish you *were* dead or crazy."

They both took their seats, choking on giggles.

Deke passed her another note halfway through the class. She smiled sweetly at him, but Diana was watching, and while Monica didn't think Ms. Tregarde would be mean enough to make her read it out loud, she didn't want to make any trouble, either. So she tucked it inside her notebook for later.

Alan had already given her a note earlier, so that made two today, and it wasn't even noon yet. *This is getting kind of fun*, Monica thought, enjoying just a little snicker at their expense. *Deke doesn't have any classes with me* and *Alan and I bet they don't know I've got classes with both of them. I bet neither of them knows that the other one's been coming on to me.* The idea was rather exciting, really; her own little secret.

I think maybe I'll just keep it that way as long as I can. I don't think they know that I know that they're best friends. So when they find out, I can just act surprised that they know each other. It's a whole lot more fun this way.

She tried to pay attention to Bart Young reading his assignment aloud, but his scene wasn't very good. The original argument itself was pretty stupid, with one character saying nothing but "Oh yeah? Prove it!" And poor Bart, a gawky guy who looked like a hockey stick with hair, hadn't improved it any since the last time.

Her attention wandered. *I can think of one good reason* not *to tell them about each other—they'd be ready to kill each other, the way Bob and Sandy are. I wonder if that's over football, or over Harper? Probably Harper, from what Joy says. Bob's been playing footsie with her forever, and I know I saw her making kissy-face with Sandy in the hall after school a couple of days ago. God, Deke must be the only person in the whole school who doesn't know about the way she sleeps around on him. He still thinks Harper's playing by the rules.*

She wondered if she should tell him. Or did he really know, and was just pretending not to?

It occurred to her for a brief, guilty moment that *she* wasn't exactly playing by the rules either, but she shrugged it off. *I'll tell Alan and Deke as soon as one of them makes up his mind. I can't tell Deke about Fay—he'd think I was just being bitchy.* It was too bad he didn't spend more time with his friends—the ones Alan hung out with. Instead, from what he'd told her, he spent most of his time either hanging out with Fay's crowd, or at home. Alan was about the only one he saw anymore.

And I bet Fay has a lot to do with that, too.

Her writing assignment was the confrontation she'd imagined between Deke and Harper if he ever *did* find out that Harper was fooling around.

But when she'd read it aloud, he didn't seem to make the connection—although a couple of gasps and snickers told her that everyone else in class had. And maybe it was a good thing Jill wasn't around anymore; she'd have gone straight to Harper with the dirt.

He just didn't see what I was trying to say. Unless he was pretending not to. I mean, it's gotta look pretty lame, her running around on him all over town. Maybe he figures it doesn't look so bad if he doesn't act like he knows. Boy, that's dumb. Everybody has him figured for a real dope this way. But maybe he'd rather look like a dope than a wimp.

But he had to know *something* was wrong; she'd recognized the subjects of *his* assignment right away, and from the way everybody else looked, the rest of the class did, too.

Him and Harper having it out, except that he wins and walks out on her, which he never does in real life. Come on, Deke you only wish!

Yeah, and I wish he would, too.

Bart finished droning, and she woke up to the fact that he was the last one to read his piece as Diana nodded and hitched herself up onto the top of the desk. She seemed to like to sit up there.

Maybe it's because she used to be a hippie.

The writer scooted herself back and folded her legs up, lotus-style. "Okay, remember I said I wasn't going to grade anybody down as long as it was clear that you were trying. You all have been, and if there's any reason why some of you guys that aren't comfortable with this need something higher than a B come talk to me and I'll see what we can arrange, okay? Because by now it's pretty obvious that some of you were better than others, am I right?"

Monica could see a couple of the other kids, Bart among them, nodding vigorously.

Diana grinned. "It's also pretty obvious that the two best were Monica and Deke. Now what stands out in your minds about those two scenes that make them good?"

Diana led them all in a spirited discussion of what made the scenes work, and what was lacking in the ones the rest of them had done. "And just to keep you two from getting swelled heads," she finished, just before the bell rang, "Monica, you repeated yourself too much and I got the feeling you were padding the thing out to make it ten pages—and you had some *really* choppy sentences. A sentence needs to be more than three words long, folks; if you have a lot of three-word sentences, it's more than time to think about combining them. Deke, your protagonist was pretty unrealistic. There's no indication to *me* of why he ever started dating this chick in the first place. There's no *way* you'd catch *me* going with a bitch like her if I was a guy."

Monica saw him flush beet red out of the corner of her eye, but Diana had turned back to the blackboard and missed it.

"Okay, gang, here's the next phase. It's time to put in some action and a third character." She was writing all this down in a series of two- and three-word notes. Monica thought her eccentric style of printing was kind of neat, like calligraphy. "Follow your viewpoint character right after the fight; bring in that third character and make him or her an ally. After all, some of you just trashed your v.p. character; now it's time to give him somebody sympathetic. But not *too* sympathetic; this is an ally, not a yes-man. And for those of you whose viewpoint character won—what if he's really in the wrong? He needs to get taken down a peg. Even if he's right, there's two sides to every argument, and somebody should point out the other side. For the sake of making things interesting, let's *not* make it the v.p. character's best friend, okay? Somebody who's maybe a friend, maybe a teacher, but somebody who can give him a little grief along with the sympathy."

Diana turned away from the blackboard, and by then Deke had gotten his blushing under control. "Have fun with this, gang. That's what we're all about in this business."

At that moment the lunch bell rang. "See you tomorrow, kids. Monica, can I talk to you a minute? I got a chance to read your stuff last night."

"Sure." Monica gathered up her things; her stomach felt fluttery and uncertain. She was no longer quite so certain about the quality of her work. Sure it was all right for class, but—Diana was a real writer, and she'd asked for a real writer's kind of critique.

"Monica," Di said, pulling a manila envelope out of her briefcase and handing it to her, "I'm pleased and surprised, on the whole. I won't kid you. You've got real, honest-to-God potential. You have a genuine flair for characterization and a solid grasp of the way conversation works. But—"

All through this Monica's heart had been lifting—now it plummeted into her shoes. "But?" she replied doubtfully. "You might as well tell me the worst."

"Your plots are weak," Diana said, with a touch of reluctance. "You make things entirely too easy for your characters. Think about it; a story where everything goes right and your character is perfect from the beginning is boring! Even in fairy tales things start out rotten for the heroine, get worse, and only at the very end does she 'live happily ever after.' You've got to make your character *work* for her happy ending. And making her wonderful, sweet, understanding, no faults at all—what is she, Mother Teresa? If she's that fabulous, she should be a saint. You've got to make her interesting; give her warts, make her human."

"Like how?" Monica asked weakly. "I mean, what should I do?"

"Give her faults; make her impulsive, oversensitive, something. Give her PMS, for heaven's sake. And every time your heroine thinks she's got a clear path, throw something in her way and make her trip over it." Diana shook her head, and lifted one eyebrow at her. "You're taking this very well, Monica. I've got to say I'm relieved—and that I'll be happy to work with you."

"You will?" Visions of book covers with her name on them danced before Monica's eyes. "You really will?"

"Now don't get too excited," Diana cautioned her, a trace of a smile lurking at the corners of her mouth. "You may decide this is a hell of a lot more work than you want to get into. You also have some viewpoint problems, and you have nowhere near enough description, but I'd like to handle all that in the next draft—*after* you straighten out your plot problems."

"The next draft?" Monica couldn't hide the tremor in her voice. "That—sounds like a lot of work."

"It is," Diana replied soberly. "My guess is that once you get a good plot going, you'll have another five or six drafts after that before it's submittable. We're talking a year or more of work here. Just be glad you're writing on a computer; *my* first books were all done on a typewriter, and each draft had to be retyped from the beginning."

"Oh," Monica said faintly.

"I didn't promise you it would be easy," Di reminded her. "But I did say that I would tell you if I didn't think you had it in you to be a writer. And I think you can do it, if you're willing to put the work in." She sighed, and looked a little sad. "So far I *have* had to give bad news to six of your schoolmates—each of whom came to me clasping what they obviously thought was the best story of the year to their hope-filled bosoms."

She heaved a larger, more melodramatic sigh, and clutched a notebook to her chest with one hand while sending the other hand fluttering to her forehead.

Monica giggled. The fact that Diana had turned the others away—but had just said she'd help *her*—cheered Monica up immensely.

Diana grinned back, but sobered again in the next instant. "Now, about your other problem—have you told anyone else what happened. Even your mother?"

Monica shook her head. She'd *wanted* to tell her mom, and she somehow knew that Rhonda would believe her—but she also knew what Rhonda would say about Diana. The family had some cousins in Jamaica—and Rhonda had come a bit too close to some of the nastier aspects of voundoun to ever trust anyone who *admitted* she was a witch.

And no matter what her mother would think, Monica was certain she could trust Diana Tregarde.

"Nothing else has happened to me," she told Diana. "Nothing at all. Maybe it was all a mistake or something."

To Monica's dismay, Diana shook her head. "Not a chance, kiddo," she said regretfully. "I wish there was, but magic has to be targeted very specifically to get *that* kind of result. Nope, somebody out there wanted to send you screaming into next week. Have you come up with *any* idea who that somebody might be? It's *got* to be someone you know, or who at least knows you."

Monica shook her head. "Everybody I know is pretty normal," she said slowly. "There's supposed to be some heavy-metal dudes that are into Satanism in my class and in the senior class, but I've never met any of them and I wouldn't know who they were unless somebody pointed them out to me. Most of the kids that like metal look pretty much alike, you know? There's even a Christian heavy-metal band."

"Heavy-metal Satanists?" Diana said incredulously, and snorted. "Posers. Bush league. The Dan Quayles of High Magick. Not even close to whoever was after you. The kind of knowledge and practice it takes just to call one of those imps is a hell of a lot more than any kid is going to have. And the kind of *control* it takes is something most of them would never even dream of. It takes the same kind of discipline and patience it's going to take *you* to get that book into publishable form, if that's making any sense to you."

Oddly enough—or perhaps not so oddly—it was. "You're right," she agreed. "From what I've heard they aren't into anything more complicated than lighting candles, getting stoned, and running around naked while they play Judas Priest on the CD."

"Pretty much what I figured." Diana nodded. "It looks to me like whoever sent those critters after you is an adult. Call me a kind of magic-tracker; I can read the footprints that power leaves behind, and everything I saw suggested a mature mind. Can you think of *any* adult you've pissed off lately?"

The last time somebody yelled at me, it was for passing a note to Alan—and before that, it was Ms. Greeley giving me a hard time for daydreaming.

"I—no," she said. "Not anybody, not an adult, anyway."

Diana gave her a long, hard look, then nodded reluctantly. "I think you'd tell me if you could. I think you've got the good sense not to go playing games with me. All right, then, we're stymied for the moment. And *maybe* nothing more will happen to you."

Monica noticed that she was clutching that manila envelope so hard her fingers were starting to ache. "Do you really think so?" she asked hopefully.

"No," Diana replied. "No, I certainly don't. I think whoever it is will keep coming at you until you do whatever it is he wants you to. And I'd feel a hell of a lot better if you'd let me put a stronger kind of protection on you. I know you said I could help you, but every time I do something else, ethically, I have to ask first. Think of what I gave you the first time as burglar alarms—well, this is an electric fence."

The deserted classroom suddenly seemed very quiet—and a world away from the student-filled corridor outside.

"Would it—would it hurt?" Monica asked in a whisper.

Diana shook her head and reached out to pat her clenched hand. "No chance. I doubt you'll even notice it's there. But anything that comes after you *will* know it's there, big-time. They'll see it, and that should be enough to make them go away. If not—anything that touches it is going to get its little paw fried."

"And nobody else is going to notice it?" Monica persisted. "I mean, I don't want anybody to think I'm looking weird or something."

"Not unless they're *very* psychic—in which case whoever notices is going to be used to seeing odd things and keeping his or her mouth shut about it." Diana's little smile had a bitter cast to it, and barely stretched her lips. "Think about it. What would *you* say if somebody started telling people he saw glowing lights around one of the other kids?"

"Yeah." Monica could see Diana's point. "Okay, then, I guess it wouldn't hurt. . . ."

"Fine. I had it ready, just in case you were willing. Take this a minute—" Diana handed her a piece of rock, not even a crystal, just a polished black pebble. Funny, though, it felt warm—and instead of cooling as she held it gingerly between her thumb and first two fingers, it seemed like it was getting warmer.

"It's all ready," Diana said, her eyes a little unfocused—or maybe focusing on something Monica couldn't see. "Just—call it. With your mind," she added as Monica started to open her mouth. "Think of wanting to be protected from those things. Want it very, very badly."

Monica squeezed her eyes shut, after a hasty look toward the corridor. She started this feeling foolish, but as she remembered those horrible *things* that had come after her, she stopped feeling like an idiot. In fact, she was able to do as Diana had asked without any difficulty whatsoever.

"Very good." Diana's voice broke her concentration, and she opened her eyes, startled.

"I don't *feel* any different—" she started to say.

Then she noticed a faint glow just out of the corner of her eye. She turned her head to look at it directly, but it seemed to keep moving, staying just within the barest limits of her vision.

"There's—something there," she said, waving her hand vaguely. "But it's only sort of there."

"That's because you're not really looking at it with your physical eyes, you're looking at it with your mind," Diana replied, nodding in a satisfied way. "You're a bit more sensitive than I gave you credit for. When all this is over, if you want some training in how to use it, let me know. I think you should get some kind of instruction, okay? If not from me, there are a couple of books that should suit you fine."

"What is this thing, anyway?" Monica peered at it sideways, but the more she concentrated, the more ephemeral it seemed. But there *was* something there; she was certain of it.

It was scary. Because this meant there was something to all this magic stuff. Monica would have been perfectly happy if Diana had only been cultivating a very peculiar delusion.

Or would I? she wondered suddenly. *Because those things—they're real. And even if Diana claims they can be scared away, I don't want to have to try it.*

"It's like a 'Star Trek' force field," Diana told her. "It'll keep most nasties off your back, and protect you long enough for me to get there if what hits you is more than the shield can handle. Listen, it's gone really gloomy out there, and you don't live that far from Deke. Do you want to meet me after classes this afternoon? I could drive you home."

Monica was tempted, but then she remembered that Alan had asked her what route she usually took to get home. If she walked, she just might "run into" him.

"No, thanks," she said. "Mom doesn't like me to get rides from people she doesn't know—and I'm not sure I want you two to meet. If she figures out what you are, she might freak."

Diana raised an eyebrow, and gathered up her purse and briefcase. "I take it Mom is where you get your psychic abilities."

Monica shrugged, and flushed. "I don't know. Just we've got some relatives in Jamaica that do some pretty gross things, and Mom doesn't want to even talk about it."

"If your relatives are doing what I think they're doing, I don't blame her." Diana held the door open for Monica, and the two of them stepped out into the deserted hallway as the door shut and locked behind them. "Okay, kiddo; how about working on the very first story in the bunch you gave me—turn your heroine into a human being, screw up her life, and put some of the guts into it that you put in that fight scene. When you've got about thirty pages, come show it to me, okay?"

"Okay," Monica said, already thinking ahead to this afternoon, and trying to remember if the Computer Club met after school today, or tomorrow.

It was today. In a way that was good, because it meant she had a better chance of intercepting him alone.

Maybe. If the club members all got started on something and

stayed more than the hour the meeting was supposed to take, she'd
have to start for home on foot and hope he'd drive her route.

She loitered for a while in the empty hall outside the computer
lab, but it didn't sound like anybody was ready to go home in there. It
was kind of funny how those Brains were; real quiet even in class, although they could pull some real rude tricks if they were pushed to it.
But get a bunch of them together, and it was worse than a pajama
party.

She paced up and down the hallway; the janitor came by, pushing
the big stainless-steel floor waxer toward the cafeteria. He looked at
her curiously, but didn't say anything or even stop; he just kept right
on going, leaving the heavy scent of floor cleaner in his wake. Once
he was gone, she heard her own footsteps echoing up and down the
corridor every time she moved, and the faint murmur of voices and
occasional laughter from behind the heavy computer-lab door.

It was getting dark, darker than she expected. The corridor had
windows high up, right near the ceiling, and when she looked up she
saw heavy, charcoal-gray clouds bulging overhead. There weren't any
storms predicted when she'd gone to school this morning, so she
hadn't brought a raincoat. If it started to rain, as evil as those clouds
looked, she'd be drenched before she got a block.

She eyed the clouds dubiously, then went over to listen at the lab
door. This time she could hear one of the machines beeping, and the
muffled exclamations of the kids when it made that *blat* sound that
meant something had gone wrong.

They're running something, she decided finally. *They could be in
there until their sponsor kicks them out. I'd better head home now.
Maybe Alan will catch up with me.*

Once outside, the gloom seemed even thicker, even though it
didn't *smell* like rain. March had been gorgeous, with balmy temper-
atures in the seventies and even eighties during the day, and no
storms at all. April was turning into a stone drag. Monica shivered inside her windbreaker. The air felt thick and heavy, and even though
there wasn't a bit of wind, she was cold. It might not smell like rain,
but it felt like it; damp and oppressive.

It could be worse, she told herself. *In Colorado there's still snow on
the ground.*

But snow, even the dirty, gritty snow of April, seemed preferable
to this.

Alan was *not* worth loitering around for.

I wish I'd called Mom at work and had her pick me up, she thought
wistfully, as the damp penetrated her light jacket and chilled her

right down to her bones. *It would have given her an excuse to get out of some of that overtime and she wouldn't have minded. I don't think.*

The street she usually took home wasn't much like Colorado. There weren't any sidewalks, for one thing. Joy had explained cynically that this was because Tulsa was an oil town; people were expected to drive half a block to get a carton of milk. Houses sat in the middle of absolutely huge lawns, acres of lawn. Monica supposed they'd be pretty once things started growing, but right now they were a sort of dirty brown-green. Except for the people who had a lawn service come out. You could always tell those; the lawn was a bright emerald.

When Joy told me how they dye their lawns for the winter, I about fell out, she thought, giggling at the very idea. *And how they have* contests *for "Lawn of the Week." Not garden, lawn—God, these people are crazy out here. Maybe it's the Prayer Tower. Maybe it attracts cosmic rays or something.*

She walked another block, the clouds getting thicker and darker overhead, everything getting dimmer and gloomier.

They may be crazy, she thought forlornly, *but I wish I had some company out here. God, it's dark. I don't blame everybody for being inside, but I wish it didn't feel so deserted around here.*

For the past month whenever she'd walked home those huge lawns had been full of people: yard crews or dads taking care of their own gardening work, little kids playing, guys from school running or having a game of frisbee, girls working on their tans. Now, tonight, she could have been the only person left alive in the universe.

Like that old movie Joy rented, about how everybody dies while this scientist is down in a cave, and when he comes up he's all alone.

Even the lights on in the windows of the houses seemed cold and distant, like there really hadn't been anybody in there to turn them on, just a bunch of timers in empty dwellings, faking the signs of life.

And it's so dark it might just as well be dusk. God. This is creepy. She glanced back over her shoulder, but there wasn't anything, not even a stray cat.

So why does it feel like somebody's watching me?

It materialized, just as she turned back.

This time she saw it arrive—or rather, she *didn't* see it; there was nothing but empty street one minute, and the next minute it was *there*, all teeth and claws and sulfur-yellow eyeballs. There wasn't even a special-effects-type shimmer, like in a movie—just nothing, then the thing was *there*.

She jumped back a foot, and tried to scream, but all that came

out was a squeak. The thing growled and drooled at her; she remembered Diana telling her that these monsters were cowards and easy to
scare off—

No. *Oh* no. This thing didn't look like it was going to scare too
easily. And *she* didn't want to try. Those teeth were each as long as her
little finger, and the talons were even longer. And this time there
wasn't the dubious safety of the windshield between her and it.

She backed up another step. Another.

And the thing *giggled*, a high-pitched titter, like a dumb blond on
a sitcom. Then, before she had time to react, it jumped for her.

She squeaked again, a panicked-mouse sound; it leapt high into
the air, twice its own height, and it was coming straight at her—

But before she could move, before she could even do more than
raise her hands in a pathetic attempt to fend the thing off, it hit something about a foot from her body. It landed, spread-eagled, in midair,
and hung there for a moment, like a bug squashed against a windshield.

She felt her heart stop, and had just enough time to register that
the thing looked very, very surprised.

Then there was a sizzling sound, the same sound a bug-zapper
made when it caught something big, like a moth or a horsefly. The
thing's eyes bugged out, and it looked like *it* wanted to scream, but
when it opened its mouth, nothing happened.

Then it was gone, exactly the same way it had come. One minute,
defying gravity. The next, gone without a trace. Not even drool marks
on the sidewalk.

Monica dropped her books because her hands were so paralyzed
and shaking they could no longer hold them. She stared at the spot
where the thing had been, and whimpered in the back of her throat.

Then she turned and ran blindly into the middle of the street. She
didn't know where she was going, and she didn't much care. There
was only one thought in her mind at the moment, and that was to get
out of there.

She sensed, rather than saw, the approaching vehicle. Sensed it
far too late to evade it. There was a shriek of brakes practically on top
of her; and *now* she screamed.

The car swerved wildly around her, somehow, and came to a sliding, sideways halt fifteen feet away. At just that moment her knees
gave and she dropped to the pavement, crying hysterically, her face
buried in her hands.

"Fuckin' Jesus Christ, Monica! I almost killed you! What in hell were you doing, running out into the street in front of me like that?"

The voice was familiar. After a moment her numb, fright-dazed mind put a name to the voice, just as his hands pulled hers away from her face.

Alan.

"Hey, hey, it's okay. I didn't hit you, did I?" He stroked her hair tentatively. "Are you hurt? Are you all right? Talk to me, Monica. Say something!"

Alan. Familiar. Normal.

She flung her arms around his neck and hung on to him, afraid that he, too, would disappear.

He hauled her clumsily to her feet, and coaxed her into the front seat of his car, where she sat shivering from head to foot, hugging her arms to her chest. After a moment, she noticed that *he* wasn't there, and panicked, only to have her heart slow again when he returned carrying her books and notebooks.

"Hang on," he said. "Let me get this parked somewhere, and we can talk."

"O-okay," she stammered, the first coherent word she'd been able to speak.

To her immense relief, he pulled immediately into the parking lot of a nearby church.

Oh, God, thank you. Thank you. Those things can't come near a church. At least I don't think they can come near a church. . . . They can't in movies.

But this isn't a movie.

Well, the movie people had to get their stuff from somewhere. *So they probably can't come near a church.*

But what if it has to be a special kind of church? She tried to re-member every horror movie she'd ever watched. *It's always priests and things in the movies,* she realized. *Maybe it has to be a Catholic church. . . .*

She craned her neck around to see the lawn sign. *I don't know. Does Methodist count?*

Either it did or the frying the thing had gotten had made it change its mind about coming back. Although she waited for what seemed like forever, with Alan way over on his side of the car, staring at her, nothing else happened.

"Monica?" he said tentatively. "Monica, you still haven't said any-thing. Are you okay?"

"Oh, *God*," she wailed, finally feeling safe, safe enough to let everything go. "Oh *God*, Alan—"

And that was about all she managed to get out before she started crying and babbling hysterically.

Alan reached awkwardly for her over the gear shift, and held her against his shoulder. Before she had a chance to stop herself, she'd spilled the entire story to him.

Then she started crying harder. "You're going to think I'm crazy," she wailed. "You are, I know you are, but it's true, I swear it, there are these *things* after me and Miss Tregarde believes me, and she put, like, this force field on me and—"

"Whoa, Monica, hey, it's okay." He held her a little more tightly and patted her hair. She closed her eyes and started shivering again. "It's okay. *I* believe you, too."

She gulped, and began to throttle down the flood of tears. "You— you do?" she said, doubtfully. "You really do?"

She felt him nod. "I really do. I mean, shit, people don't go running out in front of moving cars just for fun! And I don't know what the hell you'd have to gain from lying, either, or making all this up. You tell the wrong person, and they just might get you locked up, you know? Now why'd you tell Miss Tregarde, anyway?"

"Because she was there, I mean, I was going to meet her at the library the first time this happened. . . ." She told him the entire story, feeling a heavy weight fall away just because she could finally tell *somebody* about it. "So today just before lunch Diana asked me if I could think of anybody who'd want to do this to me, and I said no. And then she asked me if I'd let her put this thing on me to keep them away, and I said yes. So she did." The image of the thing, spread-eagled in midair just at her eye level, seemed burned into her brain. "Alan, the thing tried to *get* me! I don't know what would have happened if Miss Tregarde hadn't—"

"Did it ever cross your mind that *she* could be the one who's doing this?" Alan interrupted. "I mean, none of this started happening until *after* she got here. None of it started happening to *you* until after you met her. And both times these things have come after you when you'd either just met with her, or were going to."

She pulled away from him, and stared at him in shock. "I can't believe you're saying that! Diana's been really, really nice to me! She's helping me with my writing and everything."

"And if she wanted something out of you, that's *exactly* what she'd do," Alan retorted. "What if she needs a virgin sacrifice or something?"

"Then she isn't going to look for one in Jenks," Monica snapped angrily, flushing. "And if this is a sneaky way to find out if I'm— well—I don't think it's very funny, Alan!"

Alan blushed, starting with the tips of his ears and working down past his collar. "Monica, I didn't—I mean—hell, I'm just trying to think about you. I think you're putting too much trust in somebody you don't know anything about!"

"I know enough." She set her chin stubbornly. "She's got a special investigator's card from the Hartford police; she showed it to me. And she—"

She had *started* to say "she's known Deke's dad for ages," but she stopped herself just in time. "—she's staying with somebody in my class," she said instead. *Better not let Alan know I know who Deke is. At least not yet.* "So she isn't exactly some kind of mass murderer."

"Yeah, well, I know the guy she's staying with," Alan replied with a sulky frown. "*He* thinks Miss Tregarde and his dad are having an affair."

Monica burst into peals of laughter, which obviously discomfited Alan. "So because she's hopping into bed with this guy's dad, she's got to be Charles Manson? Come *on,* Alan, that's dumb!"

He glowered.

"And I don't care what you say," she continued, just as stubborn as he was. "I trust her. And I'm going to keep on trusting her."

"Then I guess I'd better get you home," he replied, starting the car and refusing to look at her.

Two can play that game. She turned away from him and stared out the passenger's-side window.

"Yeah," she replied tightly. "I guess you'd better."

TEN

A sharp pain caught Di right between the eyes. The screen of the laptop blurred and vanished as her eyes unfocused; then her vision blanked.

*Jesus Cluny Frog—what—*She grabbed the edge of the desk to steady herself and give her a reminder of where "reality" was. She exerted control; the smoothness of the cool, lacquered wood beneath her palms gave her something to concentrate on. Her vision came back, but she ignored the now-blank screen in favor of vision of another sort.

A fraction of a second later, she knew *what* had happened, and to *whom*, as well. *Monica. Power pulse right in her lap. Hot damn—first shunt some of that off into* my *shields—*

The pain vanished as she took the overflow of energy and gave it somewhere to go.

Now, let's see what's going on out there.

She closed her eyes and focused, following the tie from herself back to Monica. *Something just bamphed in on top of her. That's what caused the pulse. Now what is it, anyway?* She "read" the energy signature just as eddies in the power flows told her that the creature was bracing itself to attack the girl. *You little—no you don't, you twisted bastard!*

She shunted all the energy she'd drained off and plenty of her own besides into the shield around the girl, just at the moment it impacted against the barrier. She felt it "scream" in her mind. Then she felt it "die."

Good riddance to bad rubbish. Ye gods, I hate those things. Bloody little sadists. Now, let's just follow the shock wave back to your daddy, and find out what kind of magician it was that gave an imp that much power to play with. Normally the little creep would never have dared *take on a shield, no matter how weak it looked.*

She stretched her probe out, very carefully, very cautiously. The very last thing she wanted to do was alert this magician to her presence. Better to take things slowly; undoubtedly she'd miss out on some information, but it wasn't worth the risk of having this guy decide to rush the job on Monica. *There's time. I can afford to stick around until I've got this guy taken care of. Nothing worse has happened than Monica getting scared out of her shorts. But if I rush him, he may up the ante before I'm ready, and I can't be everywhere. And if the Guardian stuff decides* not *to kick in, all I've got to depend on is little old me, and maybe Larry.* Her probe met resistance; a shield. A shield with the boundaries roughened with pain. *Aha. The plot sickens. So you felt that, did you? Good. About time the threefold retribution clause kicked in.*

An *old* shield; layered and reinforced with decades of spell casting. It had the slightly "artificial" feel that she had come to associate with High Magick. It also had the "constructed," crystalline matrix that told her that the sorcerer had no sensitivity to energy flows at all.

Her shields, her magic, were a lot more organic. Like her psisenses, they were a part of her, and carefully shaped themselves to her environment without Di's needing to think about it. That harmony with surroundings tended to be a hallmark of neopagans in general and Wiccans in particular. Although a lot of the New Age types were building constructs that integrated the crystalline properties of High Magick with some of the organic properties of Wiccan traditions.

Di tended to baffle folks of all traditions; her "base" was organic, but she built some pretty impressive High Magick constructs when she needed to—and then there was the Guardian touch. The impression that there was enormous power around her, but not necessarily available to her.

Which is pretty much the case, actually, she thought ruefully. *And not something anybody but another Guardian even recognizes. Not even the folks on the Squad ever knew. André's the only non-Guardian that ever ID'd me . . . but then André's different.*

But although this shield was strong, it had the brittle taste of something put together by rote.

Exactly what I was thinking. Uh-huh. And there's no hint, nothing at all, that it's ever been in contact with worship-centered magic or group magic. Which means that whoever this is has either never been exposed to Wicca or any of the other neopagan movements, or simply decided never to have anything to do with them. V-e-r-y interesting. A pure sorcerer. I didn't think there were any around.

The edges of the shield prickled a little, like the hair rising on the back of an animal's neck, telling her that her probe had been detected. She withdrew quickly.

If I'm lucky, he'll think it was just some random brush-by; maybe even an echo of what Monica did to his imp. I hope he figures Monica did this on her own. The potential is there, if she was scared enough to focus it. It would have been crude—but the way I fried the imp would look the same as if it had been blasted, which is something Monica could do. This could be a lot worse. I'm dealing with somebody who's essentially tone-deaf and color-blind. And if I can't use that to my advantage, I'm going to turn in my union card.

But one thing was absolutely clear now; this was no youngster playing at sorcery. Not with a shield like that. This was someone Di's age, or older. Most likely the latter.

And I would dearly love to know where he—or she, actually, there's no way I can tell through that protection, and High Magick tends not to have sex signatures—has been learning pure sorcery. I suppose it's possible to get it from books, if you've managed to get hold of someone's private notebooks. You'd almost have to inherit them, though, or you wouldn't have the keys to uncode them.

She opened her eyes slowly; they still weren't focusing quite right, but that wasn't too surprising. Magic was always twice as hard to work when you hadn't prepared yourself for it in advance.

She began taking deep, slow breaths, concentrating on physical sensations—the sweet scent of the bouquet of freesia on the bureau, the cool desk under her hands, the warm current of air across her face as the furnace activated. When her focus suddenly sharpened, and she could see clearly again, she let out the last of those breaths in a long sigh, and stretched.

"Oh, my ears and whiskers," she said to the empty room. "This gets more interesting all the time. I think it's time to ambush Larry again. Between doing that research last night, and this, I've got an earful."

She checked the house for Deke automatically; this was becoming second nature, watching for the kid. No muted glow surmounted by her unobtrusive telltale, though; the kid must be over at a friend's place, or staying late after school for something.

Thank the gods for any favors. She chuckled and popped the door to her suite open with no attempt at silence.

"Hey, Kosmic!" she shouted down the hall. "Are you in the kitchen?"

A muffled "yes" from down the stairs and to the right was all the direction she needed. She took the stairs slowly, still not entirely certain of her equilibrium. That was one of the less pleasant aspects of working magic on a regular basis; you sometimes felt as if your body were an ill-fitting garment.

Once she reached the bottom of the staircase, her nose told her that Larry was in the kitchen, and she followed the marvelous aroma she'd encountered through the formal dining room, into an informal breakfast bar, and from there into the kitchen itself.

"Will you marry me?" she asked Larry, who was watching the progress of a truly impressive pizza through the glass window of an eye-level oven.

"Sorry, already taken," he replied. "Besides, you only love me for my cooking."

"Too true, Kosmic. You certainly haven't lost your delicate touch with spices." She inhaled again, blissfully. "Is this for supper? Do I get to make a pig out of myself?"

"As much as you want, and in about fifteen minutes; I timed this to be ready when Deke gets home—this is club night." He cracked open the oven door about an inch and eyed the pizza with a frown of concentration. "I hope this thing isn't going to scorch around the edges again. . . . What brought you down here?"

"Monica got hit," she said shortly. "Same source as last time. *Definitely* High Magick."

"Does that extra *k* on the end seem as pretentious to you as it does to me?" he asked. "Seems like you ought to enunciate it. *Magick.* Sounds like a speech defect."

She chuckled a little. "As a matter of fact, yes, it always has seemed a little pretentious. But then I've always figured that half of what sorcerers did was just for show."

"Really?" Larry dug a couple of Cokes out of the fridge and handed her one. "But you're a sorcerer, aren't you?"

She shook her head. "Only by necessity. I'm more comfortable with Wicca. I'm a kitchen magician, Larry. If I have to do something, my choice of tools is pure psionics first, witchcraft second, and sorcery as a definite third."

"So what happened?" He sat down at the kitchen table, and waited for her to do the same. "I'm going to assume, since you trotted down here looking for dinner and not reinforcements, that whatever it was the girl ran into, it wasn't serious."

"Not very," she replied, staring out the kitchen window at the sunset. There was something odd about it. "Oh, it was probably pretty scary, but at least now she knows it wasn't an accident the first time, or something she only thought she'd seen. She's going to be more likely to trust me now, I hope."

"Or else," Larry pointed out, "she's going to notice that none of this happened to her until you showed up in town."

Di grinned. "Too late; she already gave her permission for the shield and telltales. She won't be rid of me until I'm ready. She can avoid me all she wants; I'll still know where she is and what's happening to her. Thanks for stealing Deke's worry stone for me last night, by the way. *His* shield's nicely in place. Now, let me bring you up to date."

After years of briefing sessions, Larry knew better than to interrupt her at this point. He just leaned his arms on the table and listened until she finished describing everything she'd picked up.

"And I've just noticed something else," she concluded as an afterthought. "Look out there—the weather's cleared up."

She waved her hand at the kitchen window; he looked, and frowned a little. "So?" he replied. "Happens all the time in Tulsa. Oklahoma is the state that Will Rogers made the original joke about—you know, 'If you don't like the weather here, wait an hour.' We're a prairie state; weather systems can sweep in and out in a matter of half a day because there's nothing to stop them."

"That may be true—but remember that this goddess thing is somehow tied in to the weather, and I find it a real odd coincidence that threatening rain cleared up as soon as the attack on Monica broke off." She looked outside again; there wasn't even enough cloud cover now to make a decent sunset. "Now I will admit that there's another possibility; weather-wise, this area may be naturally so unstable that the least little upset in the energy patterns around here changes the weather for good or ill. And the insensitive way that sorcerer was wrenching energy around was making some interesting little eddies and back-flows. But—" She held up her index finger in warning as he started to say something. "But—I don't *know* that the area is that sensitive. Do you?"

He shrugged.

"So, where does that leave us?"

"That we don't know if this is tied in with the goddess, whatever it is, but that the circumstances sure make it look suspicious." One corner of his mouth twitched. "I assume that you're more determined than ever to investigate."

"Believe it," she said firmly.

He sighed.

Larry slipped through the door to the guest suite as quietly as he could. Di looked up as her host closed and locked the door behind him. She hadn't needed to shove the furniture against the wall the way they had back in college; the room was more than big enough for her to cast her circle without moving anything out of place. She was holding a small throwing knife about an inch above the pale-gray carpet. Larry concentrated a moment, letting his Sight kick in, and he Saw the faint line of blue light it left behind.

"I told Deke you were too wrapped up right now to eat," Larry told her. "That you were on a hot love scene, and you didn't want to stop."

"That's as good an excuse as any," she said as she finished inscribing the last of the protective circle with a frown of concentration. "That'll cover why I didn't come down for dinner, and why I'll go down and eat like a spring bear when we're done. But I hope Deke didn't catch you sneaking up here."

"I told him I was going for a walk," Larry replied. Di drew the knife point up to meet the end of the circle she'd inscribed. There was a moment when the thin line brightened; at that point she held out her hands, and then there was a kind of half-dome of fainter light, too faint to make out the color, where the circle had been.

"Do you ever do that?" she asked, sheathing the knife at her side and picking up a candle from the dresser. "Go out for a walk, I mean."

It seemed an odd question. "Sure, sometimes. Why?"

She made a face. "Because, m'love, I think young Master Derek has figured out something is going on, and I don't want him to try and bust in on it."

Larry thought about that for a moment, and nodded reluctantly. "He's been acting kind of funny lately, hasn't he? Shit, he *is* sensitive. I don't suppose even shielded I could reasonably have expected him not to notice the kind of things you've been doing."

Di gave him an ironic look, but went on with her preparations, first driving anything that had been inside that protected area out, then sealing it off, using salt and water, the candle, and incense. Larry tried not to let his uneasiness show, but Di knew him too well. When she finished, she wrinkled her nose at him.

"It's all right, Kosmic; that's as fancy as it gets. The floor show is officially over."

He laughed self-consciously. "That obvious, huh?"

"Yeah." She "cut" a door in the dome for him to enter by, and re-sealed it behind him. "You still remember how to do this? All I need is for you to anchor, nothing fancy. I *don't* intend to kick any confrontations off."

"I think I can handle that." She toed a pillow toward him. He dropped down onto it and took a lotus position with an ease that probably would have surprised the socks off his kid. She took a similar pose—without the pillow—across from him, then picked up the candle she'd used earlier, set it in a plain wooden holder between them, and lit it.

Good, Larry thought. *I need a focus, even if she doesn't. I haven't done anything like this in years. Rusty is not the word.*

He stared at the flame, letting it fill his field of vision, and *letting* himself relax. This wasn't so much a matter of concentrating as it was of changing his focus, ignoring everything except the flame. Shutting the senses out of his conscious awareness, one by one, sight the last of all.

This wasn't precisely a trance, although it was quite close to trance-state. As Di's anchor, he didn't dare be in trance (a state of passivity), or he wouldn't be able to haul her in if she got into trouble. The crude EEGs of the psych lab at the university back in the early seventies had shown his brain-wave activity in this state to be very like the patterns when he was creating something at the drawing table.

Definitely not a trance. Refined and directed concentration, perhaps. Except he wasn't concentrating on anything anyone else could see.

He let his eyelids close slowly. Now that he *knew* how to shut his Sight off, it mostly stayed off, and he rarely thought about what he could sense when he did use it.

For him it worked a lot like real vision, which was what had confused him so much when it had first decided to manifest itself.

A late bloomer, Di had called him. He remembered her words clearly, coming as they had with relief so profound he'd cried and hadn't been ashamed to. "Gifts usually show up when you hit puberty," she'd told him, keeping it all very light, very offhand, as if it were the most natural thing in the world to see things that "weren't there." "You're a real oddball, waiting this late."

He really had no idea *when* he'd started to See things, because what he Saw had the same solidity and reality as what he only saw with his eyes. He'd had no real way of telling which was which until Di came along.

Like now; with his eyes closed, he could still see—or rather, See—her. She looked just about the same, except that she was very faintly haloed with a spectral iridescence. And there wasn't anything else "visible" except her.

Most people didn't Look like that to him; most were fairly faint ghosts of their outer selves. Only the rest of the gang in the Squad—and a couple of the people they'd made it their business to shut down—had been more substantial than that.

If he really opened up, he'd be able to See that spectral radiance around anything alive. Now, however, was not the time to do *that*.

Di stretched out her "hand"—he took it in both of his. Then she was "gone," leaving him holding the end of a glowing cord. Through that cord he could feel things; not much, but enough. If she was in trouble, he'd know. If she needed to be hauled back, he could do that too. As long as nothing cut the cord.

Let's not think about that, shall we? Besides, she's got defenses against anyone trying.

He settled himself patiently. Waiting. Something he was used to doing, one way or another, all of his life.

Wait for clients to make up their minds, wait for them to decide what changes they want, wait for contractors to put in their bids. . . . And before that, waiting in ambush, waiting for clues, waiting while Di and Miri went off and did things while I just held the fort.

Waiting for Mom and Dad to get back from their latest emergency call. Waiting for vacations, when we could all be together without phone calls hauling them off somewhere. That's why I decided not to be an engineer. I wonder if they know that? I wonder if they ever knew how terrified I was that they wouldn't come back? All those trips to South America—and when the Texas Towers collapsed, and all I knew was that they happened to be in Texas. . . .

I probably ought to tell them.

This, he realized, was one reason why he hadn't done this in a long time. The state of passive hyperawareness made for a bad case of introspection. Every time he went under, he wound up confronting truths he would rather not have known about.

"He thinks too much; such men are dangerous." Boy, Julius, you sure got that in one.

The "line" he held thinned, and thinned again—Di was going a lot "farther" than she ever had back in the Squad days. It wasn't getting any weaker, though, so he decided it wasn't worth worrying about.

Finally the cord of light stopped growing thinner; it remained as it was for several minutes (insofar as anyone could judge time in a near-trance), then began thickening again. At that point Larry knew she wouldn't need him, and set about waking himself up and shutting that extra "eye" down.

He began paying attention to his other five senses in reverse order: first sight, concentrating on that candle flame, then bringing the rest of the room back into view, then body awareness, then the rest. By the time everything was back to normal and he was ready to stretch the kinks out of his joints, a movement across the circle caught his eye. Di blinked once or twice, took a very deep breath, and let it out slowly, then sagged forward, touching her forehead to her crossed ankles.

"So, what's the scoop?" he asked. "You get anything?"

"I'll tell you in a minute," she replied, her voice muffled. "Let me clean up my toys first."

She straightened slowly, turned that movement into a stretch, then turned the stretch into an extension that gracefully pulled her to her feet.

Larry found himself a little resentful—*his* feet were still tingling because they'd fallen asleep.

"You must be made of rubber," he said disgustedly. She threw him an amused little glance.

"You've said that before," she told him, and held out her hands, pushing with them palm-down against the air, as if she was lowering some invisible barrier.

The half-dome of the protective circle shrank down into a glowing trail above the floor.

She took her knife and "uncast" the circle; Larry shivered, looked down at his feet, and concentrated on getting *himself* all locked down. There was something about the way that the light was pulled back into the blade of the knife that made his head ache and his stomach queasy.

When he looked up again, she had finished, and there was no sign in the room that anything out of the ordinary had gone on.

He rose, and forced his stiffened joints to take him over to the plush, charcoal-gray couch. She flung herself carelessly into an armchair, draping herself across the arms of it in a way that reminded him very much of Deke and his friends. She rested her head against the back of it, but was not looking at him.

"So?" he said, when the silence had stretched on too long.

"So, I found *something*," she replied vaguely, her eyes focusing on some point past his shoulder. "Something quite impressive."

"What is it?" he asked, feeling the first stirrings of unease. This vagueness wasn't like her; she generally didn't have to be prompted for information.

"I'm not certain," she answered. "I'm really not certain. It's very big, very old, and not really aware of much. That's all I can tell you."

Something about the way she said that made him certain she was being evasive. He'd seen her in this mood once or twice before. Like Sherlock Holmes, unwilling to say *anything* until he was certain, she would keep what she knew to herself as much as possible. She probably wouldn't lie if he asked her a direct question, but she'd certainly do her best to distract him, and she probably wouldn't tell all of the truth.

And anyway, he didn't know the right questions to ask in the first place.

"Does this thing have anything to do with Deke?" he prompted.

"No," she answered. Too quickly? "No, nor anything to do with Monica. Though it's been aware of the magic currents and the power flows going on around here lately. Vaguely aware, but it's noticed." She sat in silence for a moment, head tilted back, staring at the moon through the skylight. "This isn't finished yet, Larry. It isn't even close to being finished. I just don't have all the pieces." She pulled her gaze down from the moon to stare at him, and he felt a little chill run up his spine. "Look, you'd better get, before your kid wonders if you fell in a hole or something. Do me a favor and go nuke the leftover pizza. I'll be down in a minute."

He got slowly and reluctantly to his feet. "Are you okay?" he asked. "Are you going to be all right up here?" He didn't like the hint of a green glow in the back of her eyes, he didn't like the way she was evading his questions, and he most especially didn't like the odd, masklike quality of her expression—or lack of one.

"I'll be fine," she said, then suddenly shook her head hard, and gave him a gaminlike grin. "You worry too much, Kosmic. It's okay; I just need to sort some things out."

He left, shutting the door quietly behind him, and slipped down the hall and the stairs past his kid's room as if he were some kind of intruder.

But the more he thought about this, the less he liked it. He reached the kitchen, put the pizza in the microwave, and stared at the food through the glass door, frowning.

If this thing she ran into is all that powerful, he thought, *it could be suckering her. She always told us you couldn't lie mind-to-mind, but that a stronger mind can conceal things from a weaker one. This thing could be hiding almost anything from her.*

He closed his eyes and tried to recall exactly what she'd said. And came up with an even nastier thought.

It could even have sucked her in. Power calls to power. Greater power can dominate lesser. It could have her on a string I can't even detect. I couldn't See anything while she was searching, and I should have been able to. Point of fact, I wasn't even aware that anything was there. So it's strong enough to conceal itself. Which means it's a lot more powerful than anything I've ever dealt with before.

As in, orders of magnitude more powerful.

The more he thought about *that*, the unhappier he became.

Especially since he wasn't sure he could trust Di anymore.

"C'mon, Fay," Bob slurred, leaning drunkenly over the back of the black leather couch. He pawed at her shoulder. "Le's go upstairs."

Fay was beginning to regret she'd invited him over tonight after the fiasco with Monica had put her short of energy again. She was regretting even more that she'd given him free run of the liquor cabinet. Bob had been dry since his father had taken his license away, and that had not set well with him.

He's a borderline alcoholic, Fay thought in disgust, *and if he wasn't so good in bed—and so easy to put in a rage—I would never have bothered with him, captain of the football team or not.*

"Not right now, honey," she told him, pushing his groping hands away. "Why don't you watch that tape for a while? I bought it just for you."

That was a patent lie, but he was too drunk to question her assertion or even care if she told him the truth. He turned his wavering attention back to the screen, where several impossibly blond girls, decked out in spike-heeled, black-vinyl thigh boots and imitation Nazi officer's caps, and not much else, were "interrogating" a "prisoner."

Maybe not so impossibly blond, Fay thought, taking a second look as one of the girls achieved an amazingly athletic pose. *I don't think you can dye that.*

The title of this classic was *Sex Secrets of the SS*. Fay had bought it, not for Bob (although he looked—when he was still capable of focusing—as if he was enjoying it), but for Deke. And not for the mundane sex. There were a couple of remarkably accurate depictions of the rites of Sex Magick in this piece of tripe, and she wanted to see his reaction to them. Would he recognize them for what they were? Would he be revolted, or attracted? A few of her spouses in the past had become willing participants in her rituals; as a reward she had allowed them to live until the time of transfer. On one or two occasions she'd even delayed her daughter's menses until the girl in question was eighteen, in order to enjoy the benefits of having a helper that much longer.

She'd set the tape up in the VCR this morning, anticipating that she would be able to coax Deke over after dinner. But she hadn't reckoned on that little Carlin bitch being able to successfully defend herself.

When the imp's here-and-now body fried, releasing the essence of it back to where it came from and out of her power, the energy she'd given it was also released. Like an elastic band now held only at one end, it had backlashed into her, knocking her to the ground before she managed to absorb it. Then it had drained maddeningly away.

So now she was in dire need of replacement energy—and that meant Sex Magick, and that meant Bob, since she couldn't get Deke drunk enough not to notice what she was doing to him.

Bob had lost interest in the pseudo-Nazis again. He was out of his own shirt, and was working his hands up her legs, trying to come at her from the bottom instead of the top this time. *It isn't worth it,* she thought angrily, pushing his hands away from under her skirt. *I should have called Sandy instead. But it was Bob's turn . . . If I'd called Sandy, he'd have figured I want him more than Bob, and he'd have lost that edge of jealousy. Damn. This is not working out right.*

Bob slouched back on the couch, defeated for the moment. Fay curled her legs up underneath her, out of his reach, and considered the afternoon's events. The imp had impacted on a shield, then been blasted. It *couldn't* have been Monica's doing, could it? Fay nibbled her fingernail, peeling all the nail polish off it in tiny bites. But if it wasn't Monica, *where* was she getting her help? Who could it possibly be?

It had to be Monica.

Bob reached for her again, and nuzzled at her like a toothless vampire. She decided to let him; at least he wasn't trying to undress her at the moment. *I had that kind of power the first time I was her age, in my first body,* Fay thought, while Bob ran a thick tongue over her neck and shoulder. *She doesn't seem to be trained, but she could be faking it. Even if she's not trained, I've seen natural shields that strong, and if she was frightened enough, fear would give her the means to blast something. . . .*

No. No, she has to be trained. The imps didn't shock her at all; she didn't run around school the next day babbling about them or make a run for lights and people at the time. It's too bad. She'd have found her-self either in a little padded room or in a drug rehab program. In either case she'd be out of my hair.

Bob's hands were suddenly under her sweater, kneading her breasts like they were pieces of dough. "C'mon, Fay," he said, breathing fumes into her face. "Let's go upstairs."

At that moment certain internal alarms stirred, but did not quite go off. Fay herself couldn't sense the stirring of power, but her allies could, and she'd had them set up protections and detection systems for her over the decades. As a man could not actually *see* radar waves, but could view them and their reflections indirectly, so she could track power.

Damn—I've got a line on something here.

She tried to shrug Bob's hands off, then gave in and let him feel her up. As long as he kept his attention on her breasts, she might be able to ignore him.

The power she was tracking was very subtle, and moving cautiously. The origin was in a Magick Fay wasn't familiar with, so it was pretty surprising she'd detected it at all. Only the fact that it was strong made it possible for her to "see" it; it was *damned* hard to track.

Then she lost the trace entirely as Bob began pulling at her sweater, trying to get it off over her head. He'd been taking steroids lately, really strong ones he'd been getting on the street. Fay hadn't minded at first; they gave him energy and a potency he hadn't had before. But now they were making him aggressive, as well. *Too* aggressive, she realized, trying to fend him off and having no luck. She couldn't handle him anymore. He laughed at the surprise on her face at the moment she came to that conclusion. It was not a pleasant laugh.

"Don't be such a cold bitch, Fay, baby," he growled, snaking one hand under her skirt and groping for her panties. "That's what they call you, did you know that? The Bitch-Queen. The Bitch-Queen of Jenks High."

The way he pronounced it made it sound like "Jinx" High, and it startled her. "What else do they say?" she asked without thinking.

"Plenty. They say you're a teaser—I don't take to bein' teased. I'm ready *now,* girl, and you'd better be, too."

He laughed again, perhaps mistaking the look in her eyes for fear.

Enough is enough, she decided abruptly. *He's not worth the game anymore. I can play Sandy off against Deke; I don't need Bob.*

She wrapped the reins of the spells she had cast on him around her mental hands and pulled hard.

He froze, unable to move unless she willed it, and unaware of the passage of time.

She paused for a moment, just long enough to consider exactly what she was going to do with him.

He was of no further use to her in the context of Sex Magick, but there was another even more potent—the combination of Sex and Blood Magicks.

And it was time for the Servant to eat, too.

She loosed her grip on his mind, just a little. "Wait a minute, honey," she said, disengaging his hands and pulling her sweater down. "You know I don't like to be rushed. Let me get into something comfortable. Come on up in about five minutes."

She slid off the couch before he could grab her (the slick leather was good for that), and twitched her hips flirtatiously at him. "You *know* it's more fun with the stuff in my room," she said. "And we've got all night."

He looked as though he might lunge up off that couch in a few moments if she gave him the chance. She didn't. She laughed lightly, and ran up the stairs.

And planted a compulsion to stay where he was until she was ready for him.

She called the Servant the moment she'd crossed the threshold of her room.

This wasn't the first time the Servant had substituted for her; nor, probably, would it be the last. The trick was extremely useful at parties, or on those occasions when she'd forgotten whom she was supposed to be going out with and accepted two dates. But this would be the first time she'd fed her Servant this way. If the experiment worked, it might be well worth repeating.

She clothed the "old woman" in one of her sheerest negligees. It hung ludicrously on the stringy body, making a mockery of the withered breasts. Fay smiled; no one would ever see *her* that way.

I'll be young forever, she thought, the assertion bringing with it the taste of triumph. *Whatever else happens, I'll be young and beautiful forever. I'll never have to look in a mirror and see myself like that.*

Then she held her hands pressed to the Servant's face and breastbone, and began a high, keening chant.

When she did hands-on sorcery like this, she *could* feel the power; she could feel it flowing from her, taking strength with it, as if she were bleeding from two huge wounds in the palms of her hands.

She was weak-kneed and shaky when she took her hands away, but the effort had been worth the result. There, standing before her in her own silk negligee was—herself.

With one important detail differing.

She gave the spell-born command of release, heard Bob stumbling up the staircase, and directed the Servant to go meet him at the door. She forced her own knees into a semblance of steadiness and headed for her workroom. When the power began to flow, she would have to be ready. And she needed this power badly.

"Take your time, you have all night," she said over her shoulder, as she opened the door of a small cedar-lined closet in one corner of her bedroom and tripped the switch that released the second door at the back of it. "When you're done with him, put him in his car and crash it."

She pushed the few hanging wool coats and sweaters aside and eased the door at the back of the closet open. *How convenient that he put himself in my hands by defying his parents and driving over here anyway, without his license, breaking his curfew.*

"Where?" the Servant asked. "It should be far enough away that you are not associated with his death."

She thought about it. "Over in Catoosa, I think. There are a couple of long, deserted roads out there. And a liquor store that isn't too careful about checking IDs. You might as well make a really hideous wreck of it. Oh, and elevate his blood-steroid level, and make sure he has a stash with him. And don't let the car burn. I want his parents to react properly; I should be able to get a line into them to siphon some of that energy off. If all they have is an unrecognizable cinder, they won't give me half the power they will otherwise."

The Servant nodded. Fay slipped past the soft, heather-toned sweaters, through the redolent closet and across the threshold of the workroom door. She closed it behind her just as Bob shoved open the door to the bedroom.

The light came on automatically as soon as the closet door was closed. She surveyed her lesser Place of Power with a satisfied smile on her lips. From black-velvet-covered walls, to black marble floor, to the permanent altar on the north side of the room, it was perfect. Its proportions were exact, the materials the finest, the workmanship exquisite. Nothing but the best for Fay Harper. Of course, she hadn't been Fay Harper then—she'd been Rowena. And this was supposed to have been an extension to the closet. The workmen who'd installed the marble had wondered, until she'd erased their memories. She'd *rather* have fed them to her allies, but they would have been missed, and as Rowena she could afford the energy expense.

Wes had never known it was there.

She crossed quickly to the pentangle she (as Rowena) had inscribed by expensive use of Magick permanently in the black marble floor of the room; it was cut deeply into the stone and filled with white marble. Had anyone with her training in High Magick been with her, the hypothetical observer would have noticed immediately that it was incomplete, lacking one side. She removed her skirt, sweater, and panties quickly and tossed it all into the corner in an untidy heap, then pulled off Deke's class ring and added it to the pile. The Servant would fetch it all later when she was finished. Waiting within the heart of the diagram were her sword and a piece of simple white chalk. She used the latter to close the incomplete side, and waited.

And listened. Bob was wasting no time in preliminaries; she heard him pulling his clothing off so quickly she heard his shirt tear. Then she heard the impact of bodies falling heavily onto the bed. Then silence for a moment.

Then the bedsprings began to creak. At first she could hear only Bob's grunts, then moans, as the Servant brought him with hands and lips to a complete state of readiness.

Then—

Thrashing; another grunt of deep satisfaction, one she knew well.

Then a scream that spiraled up into the soprano range.

She loosed her spell and sank to her knees within the confines of the inscription. Her strength returned, flowing into her as it had flowed out, and she smiled as the screams continued.

What a wonderful idea that was, she mused. *How clever of the Vietnamese to have thought of it. Of course, I improved on it. It was so ingenious to put the Servant's real mouth down there. And I do think the three rows of shark teeth were a nice touch.*

She raised her head and laughed, as the screaming from the other room devolved into whimpers.

ELEVEN

George Louvis doodled a few notes on the back cover of his chem workbook and tried *not* to listen to the ghouls behind him. Like everyone else today, they were rehashing the accident that had wiped out Bob Williams.

It had been pretty gory; five miles outside of Catoosa on one of the back roads, a dirt road, no less. That Bob had taken his Porsche down it was a pretty good indicator of how blitzed he was just before he crashed. Stupid. It looked like he'd careened off the road at high speed, and bounced nose-first into a ditch. The car stayed where it was; he'd gone through the windshield and bled to death. The wreck hadn't even been found until this morning, by some kids on their way to the bus stop. George wasn't comfortable thinking about the number of times he'd wished Bob into his grave. Not that the bastard hadn't *deserved* wiping out—

Hell, he didn't deserve the Big One, George thought, a little disgusted at himself. *He deserved to get trashed, yeah; he deserved to get what he was used to dishing out, but he didn't deserve what he got.*

Not that he didn't go asking for it often enough. If there was ever anybody out cruising for a headstone . . .

It had taken some work to get blood, but when the coroner did, it turned out that the fool's blood-alcohol level was through the roof. So, rumor had it, was the level of steroids and THC. George shook his head in disgust.

Man, the guy had anything he wanted in the whole damn world, and he blew it; threw it all away on fast living and cheap thrills. What a jerk. Wonder if any of the other rich jocks are thinking twice about their lifestyles today?

Realistically speaking, he wasn't much mourned, not by anybody in George's crowd. He'd had the habit of throwing his weight around a little too much, of bullying people a little too often, for anyone to even *pretend* that they missed him.

And George could think of one little bird over at Union that might well find the news right welcome. She might well decide to go dancing on Bobby-Boy's grave.

And if she did, George would be plenty pleased to play her the tune to dance to. They had a lot of friends in common, Jannette and him. He didn't know *her*, but he knew about the treatment she'd gotten at the hands of Big Bob's lawyer. When they were through with her, she hadn't a shred of rep left that wasn't bad.

His pencil point snapped as he dug it into the cardboard of the notebook without realizing what he was doing. He started, looked at his broken pencil in vague surprise, and traded it off for a sharp one.

No, nobody's mourning Bobby Williams, except his folks and maybe Fay. And if you ask me, I'd say she carried on just so she could get another so-called migraine and split from class. It's not like he was nice to anybody even on his best days. On his worst, I'd say the only reason nobody ever had him up on assault charges was because his dad bought 'em off.

Still, George was getting pretty tired of hearing about the wreck. It made him feel guilty for hating Bobby. You weren't supposed to hate the dead. And that wreck—God, he hated thinking about it. He wouldn't have put Manson through *that*. Didn't those vampires ever get sick of it?

He tried to concentrate on what the chem teacher was saying, but it wasn't easy, with the whispering going on behind him.

"Yeah, well, I still say he got what was coming to him," one of the Brains, a thin, beaky kid, said aggressively. "The time he came after me, the only thing that saved me was that I was faster than he was."

"Yeah," said one of the others, a guy so quiet George didn't even know his name. "And I hear that the only thing that saved Carol the time he caught her alone in the team bus was that she knew karate. She threatened to break his passing hand if he touched her. *I* think he got exactly what he deserved! *I* think he should have had his d—"

"Shhh!" the Brain cautioned. "You're getting loud."

"I think somebody should have cut it off a long time ago," the other kid replied angrily, though in a much softer tone of voice. "Only I think they should have kept him alive afterward."

"But that's a pretty awful way to die," said Alan quietly. "I wouldn't wish that on anybody. Bob wasn't that bad. He was a real jerkoff, but he didn't deserve that."

George had the feeling that Alan's comment had been mostly for *his* benefit. *Yeah*, he thought sourly, *but Bobby-Boy didn't make a habit of going after* you, *old buddy. You didn't spend half your schooltime trying to dodge the bastard. Not like some of the rest of us.*

Shit, I may go dance on the goddamn grave!

"George?"

He jumped, and looked up at the teacher with startled eyes.

The teacher was looking at *him* expectantly.

"Uh, sir, I, uh—I didn't hear the question."

The teacher looked pained and impatient, and George had the sinking feeling that he was going to pay for his uncharitable thoughts four or five times over in the next hour. . . .

The last chord died away, and Alan was staring at George and the rest of the band with a look of such profound disbelief that George felt a grin taking over his face.

The astonishment didn't fade, either. Alan seemed to be frozen in his seat, an old recliner that had been relegated to the Louvis garage.

"So?" George said nonchalantly, taking an arrogant, hipshot stance, in half-conscious imitation of every rocker he'd ever seen on MTV. "*Now* what do you think?"

Alan's mouth worked for a moment before he got a word out of it. "I—uh—wow!"

George grinned and raised his chin. "That all you can say? You, Mr. Music Critic?"

Alan shook his head. "I don't believe it, man! You guys were okay before, but now you're *great*! What'd you do, find a fairy godmother?"

George snorted. "Fairy godmother my ass. We've been working at this, and it paid off. We just hit, that's all. We just finally started to hit on all eight cylinders, you know? You play together enough, and you either hit or you fall apart, and we hit. It had to be this year or next one, buddy, 'cause if we didn't get good enough to start the circuit before we graduated . . ."

He shrugged. He wasn't about to let on about the feeling of panic he'd had when he realized that a couple months ago. Nor the feelings of despair before the band finally began to sound like something more than another garage band.

It seemed like we had all the time in the world—and then all of a sudden there wasn't any time left. And that was when I knew I didn't ever want to do anything but the band. Not college, not music school— classical guitar was okay, but not for me. But if I couldn't get it together, and do it fast, I'd spend the rest of my life working some dumb job and wondering why I didn't go for it when I had the chance.

George suddenly realized that in a way, he had Bobby-Boy to thank for that. The bully had been at every single one of the guys, for one thing or another; at some point they'd all decided, separately, that each of them was going to *show him*, somehow. And at that point, they'd all started to buckle down at the one thing they were good at—music.

That had helped, that and the lecture he'd given the rest of the band. About how this was it—and if they couldn't make it, with parents willing to back 'em, and parents with the money to get them the kind of equipment other garage bands could only *drool* over, then they were all just a bunch of posers.

Good old Bobby-Boy, he thought. *And good old Dad. The ridiculous and the sublime. Now, let's see if Lady Luck is really jamming with us, or jiving us.*

"So, what about your brother?" he said, not really hoping Alan would have anything but bad news. He hadn't even told the other guys about Alan's plan, because he didn't want them brought down if it didn't happen.

But Alan settled back in the chair and started grinning, and George suddenly found his own hopes soaring.

"It's a go," he said gleefully. "Doug's prof is all for it; he says it's a whole new art form. KOET said it's okay, so long as we pay for the tapes. Doug's got permission to take the really *good* Minicam, the one they used for the land-rush documentary. And the portable recording system that goes with it. He's going to show Steve how to run the boards, but he says it isn't much different from the mixing he's already doing for you, so everything should be fine. Just two rules. Don't tell him what to shoot, and *nobody* touches the Minicam but Doug."

George had a flash of Steve wanting to play techie and messing up several hundred thousand dollars' worth of camcorder and shuddered. "No problem," he said hastily.

Steve hadn't a clue yet as to what was going on, but he raised his white-blond head at the words "Minicam" and "sound system." "But—" Steve said. "I—"

"I *said*," George repeated, fixing Steve with a nasty glare, "no problem."

"Hey, would somebody mind letting us in on the big secret?" Paul Bellman asked plaintively.

George turned back to his band—*his* band!—and let himself

gloat for a minute. They might not make it. There was luck involved with making it in rock, as much luck and connections as talent. It might not ever get any better than this moment. But right now, he had the world by the tail and everything was going right.

"Alan's brother works at the PBS station," he said. "He's there on a theater internship. He's specializing in video right now."

"So?" Paul said. "What's that got to do with us?"

"Only that he's got to do a kind of TV term paper. And the station manager likes his prof and his prof likes rock. And the station manager told him he could borrow the best Minicam and recording gear they've got, and shoot his term paper with us."

"Wait a minute—" Steve was the first to put two and two together. "We're gonna make that basement tape we've been talking about?"

George laughed; he couldn't help himself. "Exactly so, my man," he crowed. "Except—*except*—this is going to be a live concert, with a live audience. I haven't seen a single basement tape yet that was done with an audience. I *know* we're good, but we all know you've gotta have a gimmick. Well, maybe having an audience'll be enough of a gimmick that MTV will take a chance. Who knows? Weirder things have happened."

He gave them a moment to let it all sink in—then without warning plunged into the intro to the song they'd planned on opening the open dance part of the gig with. His enthusiasm was infectious, so much so that the rehearsal was the best they'd had, ever, and he called it a session when they ran out of energy, though not out of interest.

"That's a wrap," he said firmly, when Paul protested. "We all have school in the morning; we aren't ZZ Top yet, guys. I dunno about you, but if *I* flunk out 'cause I was rock 'n' rollin' all night, my old man would strangle me with my amp cord."

"Are you still gonna take everything over to Bob Long tomorrow?" Steve asked.

George checked his watch. "Tonight; he's still open for lessons. If we get it all loaded into the car in the next fifteen minutes, I can make it over there before he closes."

"But what am I gonna do without my axe?" Paul complained. "How are we gonna rehearse between now and Friday?"

"You've got your backup, don't you?" George replied, fixing him with a stern eye. "Look, we can't afford any screw-ups. This gig is either gonna make us or break us. The *least* we can do is make sure the instruments are in top shape."

"But I'll sound lousy—"

"Come on, man, chill out," Steve drawled. "Better you sound lousy to us than that you sound lousy up there on stage. Bob Long's an okay guy; he'll do right by us."

"And he promised he'd have everything working so well our stuff'll practically play itself," George pledged. "Look, I've been going to Guitar House for *years.* They've never done me wrong yet. Bob knows what the stakes are, and if Bob says he'll have our stuff in top shape by Friday, you can believe it." He grinned, thinking about how it had been Bob who'd taken the unpromising, battered Gibson George had found in a pawn shop and turned it into the crown jewel of the band. "I swear, I think that man can work magic, sometimes."

Fay stared at the ceiling of her room, tracing the subtle patterns she'd had the Servant paint above the bed, ivory on cream. Patterns so subtle only *she* knew they were there; patterns meant to collect power.

But not enough, she brooded. *Not even with that fool's blood and death added to the Sex Magick. Not if I have an enemy. I don't even have the resources to discover who that enemy is, much less defeat him—or her. Shit.*

She played with a strand of hair, and attempted to put her thoughts in order. It was more difficult than she'd expected.

I should never have indulged in the hashish, she thought, resisting the urge to simply not worry about the problem. *But I needed it. Between the frustration of not* knowing, *and the cramps . . . There are times I devoutly wish I had been born male.*

At least in these modern times one can make the Curse a bit easier to endure.

The phone rang, and she reached out to the bedside table for the extension.

It was Deke. Dear, faithful, stupid Deke. She listened to him babble with half an ear, thinking that perhaps she should abandon him as a project. . . . Was he really *worth* the effort she'd been putting into him? Would he be worth cracking those obdurate shields to get at?

Surely there would be more promising material in college—and easier to acquire. If she really *wanted* the child, she was going to have to break through his shielding in order to take him over. *Then* she'd have to get rid of his parents, somehow.

The mere thought of the work it was going to take made her head swim.

Deke continued to rattle on about the Louvis boy and his band.

Fay smiled; if anyone had any notion of what *she* had planned for the dance, they'd have had a coronary.

And old Oral would have the Prare Tar spinning like a high-speed lathe.

Maybe I'd better give up on Deke. He's so damned dull, he'd make a saint weep with boredom.

". . . like Monica."

The hair went up on the back of her neck, her lip lifted in a silent snarl, and she curled the fingers of her left hand into claws. For a moment, for one critical moment, she had allowed herself to forget about Monica. No, she *didn't* know who her enemy was, but the Carlin brat was on the top of the list of suspects. And that she had almost forgotten that fact was in itself a telling piece of evidence.

That she had been considering abandoning Deke was another.

I wonder—could it possibly be that I am not the only sorceress to have uncovered the secret of eternal youth and life? Could the Carlin girl be another? After all, we have only her word for it that her mother works for a living—that her mother is her mother. Her life-style may simply be a form of camouflage. She certainly is not poor; she simply does not seem to command the wealth that I do.

Does not seem . . . She could be new at this. Or she could be keeping a lower profile than I. If she knew she was entering the territory of another sorceress . . .

She could have been stalking me all this time, and I dozed on in blissful ignorance!

Deke was back on the topic of the band again; she made non-committal sounds to keep him happy, and thought furiously.

I need more power. The dance itself won't give me that. And I need to be rid of the Carlin girl; she may be just what she seems, but I dare not chance the risk that she is not. But how? And where to get the power?

". . . so George took everything over to Guitar House last night," Deke said, as she tuned back in on him for a moment.

"Well, I'm really looking forward to hearing the band," she replied, when silence on his part seemed to indicate that he expected a response out of her.

"Even with the old stuff, they sounded great this afternoon," he enthused. "Listen Fay, I really appreciate you putting a word in for them. I can't tell you how much it means right now. I mean, it's all going to come together for the guys, I just feel it."

And maybe you do, she thought suddenly. *Maybe you're what brought that little tart here. If she's been able to get past your shields a little further than I have—if she's seen more potential in you than I've already seen—*

No wonder a few imps didn't frighten her off!

Fay's jaw tightened with a surge of rage. *I will be damned if I will let her have a free hand with you!*

"Oh, Deke," she cooed. "It really wasn't any trouble, not when I was already on the dance committee. You *know* I'd do anything for you, lover."

She spent a little of her carefully hoarded energy on strengthening the spells she had on him. Since they were nonthreatening, simple sex spells, the shields couldn't interfere. She could work on his mind and memories later.

She frowned a little, realizing that she would have to go back to school to do that. *What a bore.* But those spells required at least eye contact.

He went into the predictable routine, verbally strutting for her like a bantam rooster for a hen. She played him out for a little while longer, then let him hang up when she'd exercised her hold over him to her own satisfaction.

As she returned the phone to the bedside table, though, she was frowning. She turned over on her stomach and stared at the headboard, hugging her pillow against her chest and thinking furiously.

I have to do something about that tart. And I have to have the power to crack Deke's shields and see if he's worth my while. The dance in and of itself is not *going to accomplish what I need.*

An old memory surfaced, of the May Day festivals she had sponsored in the early days. How she, the Lady of the estate, had presided over the licentious revels of her indentured servants, revels that would have had the prudish authorities in an uproar, had they but known about them; revelries imported from the English, Irish, and Welsh countryside and homes these displaced peasants no longer had. There was a tacit understanding between her and her peasants; they called her "my lady," and did not ask what went on in the House. She let them serve out their time in relative comfort, and provided the wherewithal for their celebrations four times a year.

That *she* acquired a considerable amount of power from those celebrations of the earth and the flesh probably never occurred to them.

Most especially in those times when smoldering rivalries broke into open flame under the influence of a butt of brandy shared 'round.

The dance, as she had planned it (with Jill's entirely ignorant help), would only be a pale imitation of those long-ago potent festivities.

Unless . . . unless I can do something to stir things up. I can't feed them brandy—but a good half of them will be drinking or stoned by the time they get to the dance. But how to manipulate them? In the old days I'd supply the music by way of one of my allies disguised as a fiddler—

The music. Yes—yes, I think that will do. Not the musicians in my influence—but the instruments.

She rolled over and reached into the drawer of her bedside table—the one *without* the "toy chest" in it—for the phone book. A few moments of leafing through the yellow pages told her exactly what she needed to know, the location of Guitar House.

It was dark enough behind the building that a casual observer shouldn't notice the Shelby nestled in under the shelter of the dumpster.

She hadn't brought the Servant; she was going to have more than enough to keep her occupied without trying to watch *that* creature as well. It was a bit restless since its feeding; better to keep it at home, playing mindless video games to purge it of excess energy. It was unfortunate that this restless energy was not something she could use. The Servant was, sadly, an energy sink. Anything that went in never came out again.

Too bad Bob didn't know that, she thought, smiling.

She looked carefully about for any signs of another soul before slipping out of the car, slinging her heavy bag over her shoulder, and closing and locking the door behind her as quietly as she could. She found herself smiling in spite of tension and threatening cramps; this was rather exciting, recalling her days of riding to the hunt.

And the days of her unchallenged rule on her own lands, when the quarry hadn't always been a fox.

She slipped over to the back door and placed both her hands over the lock and latch mechanism, whispering the words of the Cantrip of Unbinding. She felt the tiny outflowing of power—it wasn't, thank heavens, a very complicated bit of Magick; mere beginner's work. Then there was a *click* that she felt more than heard, what with the traffic noise just on the other side of the building. And when she tugged at the heavy metal door, it swung open. She paused for a moment before stepping inside, and set the second spell in motion, the one to short-circuit any alarm systems the owner had in place.

Then she crossed the threshold, savoring the moment. *Breaking and entering is such a special thrill . . . even though the only danger is from some passerby or too-curious police officer. I suppose I could elim-*

inate that as well, except that it would alert my foe to my abilities. And I can't spare the energy. A nonspecific glamour like that is terribly expensive. . . . Ah, well, what's life without a little *uncertainty? There's a certain perverse enjoyment in taking risks.*

She found herself in a narrow back hallway; it was too dark to see, and she felt her way along one wall until she came to a half-open doorway. She inched her way into the room beyond, closed the door behind her, and conjured herself a light.

As she had hoped, it was a practice room.

She shoved all the chairs and music stands over to one side, then opened the shoulder bag she had brought with her. The first item, folded carefully on top, was a heavy square of virgin canvas; underneath it were a bottle of ink made with her own blood and a brush made with the hair from her head. She unfolded the canvas and spread it out to cover the floor. In a few moments it had been inscribed with the duplicate of the pentangle she had carved into the floor of her workroom.

Only this one was meant to contain, rather than protect.

She spared a fleeting regret, as always, for the fact that she would be unable to see, or even *feel*, most of what she was about to do. She had been told by another Magick practitioner, a member of the Hellfire Club, who had the Gifts of Sight and Sensing, that it was rather spectacular. That was the reason so many aspired to sorcery and so few succeeded; without the Gifts there was only the will and infinite patience, the patience of one blind and deaf learning to pick locks, embroider, and dance. It could be done—she was the living proof of it—but it took so long, so much trial and error, even when one had begun at an age when other children were just beginning to walk about and prattle.

And this would be a much more difficult proposition than when she had called the Abyssal Creatures, the vessels used by her allies to feed by proxy. She needed some new servants for this task; her allies were too powerful to constrain to anything this petty, and besides, she was young in this body and had yet to prove herself worthy of their full aid.

Sometimes she tired of this continual bargaining and rebargaining, lifetime after lifetime—but when she was at her full powers again, it always seemed, in retrospect, that the game was more than worth the candle.

So; the night wasn't getting any younger.

She spread her arms wide, her fingers twisted into the first of the Signs of Power, and began to chant, holding her pitch to a perfect

440-cycle "A." With each new line of the chant, she raised her pitch exactly one half step, until she had covered a full octave. Then she dropped back to the beginning "A" for the second Sign, the second chant.

Three Signs; three incantations.

On the last note of the last chant, she reached for the little bag of prepared powders she had put in the pocket of her robe, and cast it into the center of the pentangle.

There was a flash of sullen green flame; the lights dimmed for a moment.

She was no longer alone in the room.

There was the inevitable struggle of wills as the demon she had called attempted to wrest control from her. *This* was something she could feel, as their eyes locked and she fought the urge to look away from it; first because it tried to make her fear it, then because of an overwhelming sensation of there being something lurking *behind* her.

She did not succumb to either, staring the creature down— literally; it slouched lower and lower as she kept her eyes locked with its, until at last it pulled *its* eyes away and groveled.

"Very good," she said aloud. "You can get up."

It glared at her for a moment, then subsided sullenly.

It really hadn't had a chance. It *was* a demon, but a very minor one. Nothing like the ones she would be calling on later; this one was hardly a challenge.

She smiled at it to remind it of which one was the master, then laid a strip of canvas across one of the lines of the pentangle to release it.

It crossed the line slowly; one of her allies had told her that crossing out of the gateway of the pentangle was painful to creatures of its type. She waited until it had abased itself at her feet, then gave it careful instructions on how to find the three guitars belonging to George's band. "Quickly," she told it. "You need not be overly careful with any of the other instruments, so long as you are quick to find the ones I need. When you have them, bring them here to me."

It rose and bowed to her, snarling silently, and passed through the wall of the room. In a moment or two she could hear it thrashing about, knocking instruments over in its efforts to accomplish the task she had set it.

It was a bit noisier than she had anticipated, but at least she had ordered it to confine its efforts to the back of the store. Between the muffling effect of the cinder blocks and the traffic noise out on Admiral, the commotion should go unnoticed.

She didn't have time to waste worrying about it, anyway.

She shook the cloth out and relaid it, adding the strip of canvas across the line so that the demon would be able to cross back into the center for dismissal. Then she prepared herself.

She emptied the carryall on the floor, picking out her Wand, tipped with obsidian from Mount Vesuvius, then slipped her Robe over her head and tied her Girdle (braided from the hair of as many of her victims as she could manage) around her waist. She picked out another pouch of prepared powder and the brush and a bottle of thinned white glue.

Carefully she went over all the lines of the pentangle with the glue, then the powder. In the old days sorcerers had only used the powder, and no few of them became the prey of the demons they had called because of an errant breeze or a scurrying insect. Fay had discovered that the addition of the glue made no difference in the efficacy of the spell—and all the difference in the world to her personal safety. It made cleanup a little more difficult, but she'd be burning this cloth anyway, and at home there was always the Servant to take care of cleanup problems.

She would leave the line with the canvas strip across it unpainted until after she had dismissed the first demon.

The noise in the farther rooms ceased at that moment; she straightened just as the demon, burdened with three instruments, kicked open the door. It could make itself ethereal, but not the guitars; though not of a class with the next creatures she would summon, it was bright enough to realize that. Brighter than the Abyssal Creatures, which probably would have tried.

She accepted the instruments one at a time; sure enough, each of them bore tags saying "Louvis" and "reconditioned." Two Fender Stratocasters and an old Gibson with a quarter-moon pearl inlay on the head. The Gibson rather surprised her; it was very nearly an antique and hardly the sort of instrument she'd expect a hard-edged group like the Persuaders to use.

Well, it didn't much matter; the instruments themselves were only the vehicles for her power and her plans.

The demon stood beside her, its face expressionless, but she could tell by the sly glances it gave her from time to time that it was considering testing her hold on it again.

"There," she ordered, pointing to the pentangle. It snarled a little, but complied, taking its place in the center. She didn't need to finish that side just yet—and didn't want to take her attention from this obviously restive creature for even the few moments it would take to paint on the glue and sprinkle the powders—

A judgment that was reinforced when she noticed it inching toward the scrap of canvas crossing the line that would otherwise hold it pent inside the diagram.

She pulled the canvas out of the pentangle while the demon hissed with frustration, and stuffed it into the pocket of her Robe.

The ceremony of dismissal was mercifully short; one line of chanting, one Sign of Uncasting. The thing was gone, leaving behind only a faint scent of scorched cloth and a slightly burned patch on the canvas.

She arranged the three guitars carefully in the center of the pentangle; this was a tricky proposition since there wasn't a lot of room to work with, and she did not want to stack them in any way—and most especially she didn't want to have any part of them cross the lines of protection bounding the center.

Finally she had them arranged to her satisfaction, and completed the new pentangle with glue and powder.

Now for the possession.

For the guitars were to become demon-possessed, an idea that had occurred to her after remembering she'd seen a horror movie recently that had featured a demon-invested object. While a possessed lamp was a fairly ludicrous proposition for her purposes, calling in demons to take the guitars was actually an inspired notion. Once possessed, the quality of music they played would be under her control—and loaded with psychic and subsonic influences. Just as her demonic fiddlers had played her peasants into a state of aggression guaranteed to cause trouble among them, so the possessed guitars would do the same.

Who needs Satanic lyrics, or messages you can only hear when you play the tape backward? she thought with a cynical smile. *By the time I'm done with them, the kids at the dance will have adrenaline and sex hormones giving them such a rush that the ones that don't start a riot will probably go out to their cars and screw each other's brains out! And the beauty of it is, the* only *people who might suspect it was the music that did it will be born-again fanatics that no one sane would believe in the first place!*

In some ways it was much easier to operate as a sorceress in this age; who would believe that there really *was* such a thing, other than a handful of paranoids, assorted religious crazies, and the odd real psychic or magician? And so far, none of those had proved much of a threat. She seemed to recall some vampire movie where the bloodsucker had told his hunter that the strength of the vampire lay in modern man's persistent disbelief that he existed. The same was certainly true in her case; faced with the "impossibility" of seeing her vanish out of the front seat of the TransAm, Deke had chosen to consider the entire episode a postaccident hallucination. The community in general had chosen to consider the rash of "accidents" that had plagued her to be a series of unfortunate coincidences, and the deaths of students at Jenks to be sheer bad luck (with a liberal helping of too much money and too little supervision). No one had gone looking for an outside cause, much less a supernatural one.

So long as she kept her creatures under control, her profile relatively low, and her involvement with the supernatural a secret, she could operate with impunity.

Keeping her profile relatively low was harder than it could have seemed. She needed to feed her allies; that was part of the bargain. They needed blood and pain and the energy released with violent death, and they needed it at regular intervals. And these days she couldn't just lure an unsuspecting peddler or trapper into the house. For one thing, there *weren't* any such equivalents; for another, these days they'd be missed. An opportunity like the one that had occurred with the two policewomen came along once in a year at best. The street people who lived under bridges and in dumpsters were a danger-free source, but even they became alarmed when too many of their kind started going missing. As Rowena she had been able to select single, uncommitted men and even women at the various pickup bars, take them home, and allow her allies to take them after enjoying them herself. She had learned over the years exactly how to choose the ones with indifferent families, the ones who were living beyond their means, who would be missed only by their creditors when they vanished. But as Fay, that entire segment of society was closed to her. She had learned only too quickly after a couple of really narrow escapes that the kind of person likely to pick up an underage prostitute had, more often than not, a wife and family who would raise the most incredible fuss when he didn't return from his "late night at the office." She had gone out hunting from time to time, looking for would-be molesters and rapists—but that put *her* at physical risk, not something she courted willingly.

Although it was a little ironic . . . the police never *would* find out who had killed and buried all those hitchhiking kids along old Route Sixty-six, nor discover why the "Rainy-day Rapist" just stopped taking victims.

Well, none of that mattered at the moment, except that she was out of options right now for the means of acquiring power, and this was the safest way she could think of to get it.

She completed the diagram, stepped back as far as the wall would permit, and raised her arms over her head. Her sleeves slid silkily down along her arms as she began the first of the chants and Signs.

There were nine of them this time, not three, and all of them increased in complexity from one to the next. Halfway through the diagram began to take on a dim, greenish glow even to *her* eyes. Three quarters through, and the diagram burned with a fierce green flame that consumed nothing and gave off neither heat nor smoke. As she began the last chant, her arms trembled with the effort of holding them above her head with the fingers contorted into the Sign; she was drenched with sweat, and shivering with exhaustion.

And if she stopped there, the backlash of pent-up power would very likely kill her—if her allies didn't find a way to do it first. There was no safe exit from *this* casting; the only safety lay in perfect performance and flawless completion.

As the final word of the chant left her lips, the diagram blazed up, creating a curtain of dark-green light that rippled like the aurora and prevented her from seeing the center of the pentangle. From the center came a sound—an electronic wail, an amplified snarl that sounded as if the three instruments inside were being tortured.

She lowered her arms slowly, and waited. Waited until the light died down, then died out, leaving behind only the diagram, the lines now covered with a kind of phosphorescent slime. And the guitars, strings still quivering slightly.

And no sign of whether or not her Magick had worked.

Fortunately she had another means of finding *that* out.

She pointed at the first of the two Strats, and intoned a harsh series of guttural syllables; the spell dated back to the spell that the ancient priests had used to make the statues of their gods speak.

"Who are you?" she demanded hoarsely, as the strings quivered.

The voice of the guitar sounded like one of those novelty records from the late fifties and early sixties, the so-called Talking Guitar— using an early precursor of the synthesizer to combine a vocalist with a guitar track.

"Sehkandar," it snarled sullenly. "What do you want of me, oh woman?"

Trapped in the guitar as it was, it didn't have any eyes to lock with hers, but she felt its anger and hatred in its words, and she used her voice as she had earlier used her gaze as the vehicle of her will.

Shortly and succinctly she explained what she expected of her prisoner. And, as she had anticipated, when the demon heard her plan, it lost some of its surliness. It, too, would share in the power the violence she planned to release would bring—and the more violent the kids' reactions, the more the power. It had its own interests to consider here.

Finally it said the words that bound it to her will. "I will obey," it grated; she smiled, and repeated the procedure with the second Strat, with equal success.

Then she turned to the Gibson—

But before she could intone the ritual question of "who are you," the spirit in the instrument spoke up for itself.

"Oh, wow," it said, in tones of complaint. "Oh, wow. What a *bummer*, man! You didn't have to go through all that jive—"

She stood speechless for a moment, then snapped angrily, "Who *are* you?"

"Moonbeam's the name, and music's the game, and what's a nice chick like you doin' in a place like this? Like, what's your sign?"

"*I'll* ask the questions here," she snarled, feeling the situation slipping out of her control. "What are you doing in that guitar?"

"Like, I was about to ask you the same question. I don' much like this gig that you've got goin', and I don't much like the one you've got planned. This's the Age of Aquarius, lady. Peace an' harmony, make love, not war, you dig?"

Fay felt her head reeling. *What* had she gotten herself into? Or rather, what had she put into that instrument?

But as she glanced down at her watch she realized it was too late to do anything about it now. In another five minutes the regular police patrol would be by, and they might notice the Shelby. It was time to go.

"I don't care what you like," she spat, breaking the spell that permitted the guitars to speak and reaching across the lines of the pentangle to take the Gibson by the neck. She shook it a little to emphasize her point. "I don't care what you want, or what you think. You'll do what I ordered, or you'll find yourself inside that instrument forever!"

She picked up the other two instruments and removed them from the canvas; now that they'd given her their pledge, she was safe from them. As for this "Moonbeam," she didn't know what it *was*, but it wasn't a demon. It should be no threat to her.

She stuffed the stained cloth back into her carryall, and left the guitars in the middle of the practice room. After the mess that the minor demon had left in the rest of the store, the owner would probably just be pleased to find them there, and wouldn't worry about why they were there.

She slipped out the door, and out into the hall, taking her witch-light with her. She only extinguished it when she reached the back door. She took a quick look around before dashing across to her Shelby, unlocking it, and slipping in behind the steering wheel.

So far, so good.

She pulled off a little down the street, then turned and made three gestures and spoke five words. With that bit of Magick, she not only canceled the spell that was holding the alarm systems inactive, she *activated* them.

It wouldn't do for the owner to wonder why the alarm hadn't gone off in the shop.

But as she pulled off onto Admiral at a sedate thirty-five miles per hour, she wondered, with an increasing sense of frustration, what could *possibly* have gone wrong with that third guitar.

TWELVE

The history teacher droned on about the Korean War, a dreary subject that made little or no sense to most of the class, Monica included. Monica chewed a nail in complete frustration, contemplated the back of Deke's head, and wondered why in hell she was wasting her time on anybody that dense.

He spends half his time with me on the phone, she thought, copying down the history teacher's notes in an absentminded sort of way. *He spends* tons *of time hanging around me at school. He knows I like him. He still doesn't know Alan's after me. So why doesn't he do* something?

It made her want to scream. She hadn't been at all backward about telling him what she thought he should do, either. She'd told him right out just two days ago that she thought he should break up with Fay. This, of course, right after he'd finished complaining about something or other Fay had done to him. It had made an excellent opening.

But, as always, he'd had some excuse. This time it was that he'd promised to be Fay's escort to the spring dance.

"It means a lot to her," he'd said lamely, a glazed look coming into his eyes as soon as she mentioned Fay's name. "I can't just dump her like that. What would it look like? Besides, I still like her a lot."

It would look like you'd finally caught on to the bitch, she thought angrily at the back of Deke's head. *It would look like you'd finally gotten tired of getting walked on. But no—And God, I even showed you how much I trusted you by telling you what Diana's been saying about you and your dad, so you'd know she probably* wasn't *after your old man. And you still keep acting like all I'm good for is to be your crying towel.*

This whole school was getting to be a royal pain. The kids were mostly pretty stuck on themselves and all their money, and not even Alan had managed to get up enough guts to ask her out. About the only good thing she had going was Diana T's interest in her writing.

And on top of it all, there were those two—attacks. She still hadn't told anyone about them but Alan. *He* believed her; but he was still suspicious of Diana.

The things themselves, thank God, hadn't come back again. Diana had finally told her that she didn't think *they* would, but that it wasn't likely that whoever it was that had gone after her was going to give up. This, of course, had been wonderful news. And Alan had insisted that *this* meant that Diana was planning something awful.

Monica was getting pretty tired of Oklahoma, all things considered.

I miss the mountains, she realized. *I didn't think I would, but I do. And I miss having places to go, things to do. The only things to do around here are—well—go to the mall, go to parties, except I never get invited to them, or go to movies at the mall.*

She sighed and rested her chin on her hand. It was going to be a very long day.

It got longer as soon as the class let out. Harper was waiting for Deke, standing right opposite the door, wearing a *hot* outfit that Monica would have died to have, every hair perfect, with a sickeningly sweet smile on her face.

I think I hate her, Monica thought grimly, watching her greet Deke as enthusiastically as if he had been away from her for a year. And watching Deke return the favor, just as if he hadn't spent the ten minutes before class complaining about her. *Scratch that, I know I hate her.*

Deke strolled off arm-in-arm with the bitch, completely oblivious to Monica's presence. Grimly she reversed her course and took the long way back to her locker—then, because she had lost so much time, she had to run for her next class, sliding into her seat behind Carri Duval just seconds before the bell rang.

It was algebra, which she hated, because she was only getting a B in it, and she must not have been concentrating because half her homework was wrong. Fortunately this wasn't a graded assignment, but it was humiliating all the same. Even George Louvis's grimace of sympathy when she botched her problem on the board didn't help.

The bell rang for class change; next, thank God, was English. Maybe she could get Deke to notice her there.

Then again, maybe not. *Maybe I ought to see if Mom was really se-*

rious about moving back to Colorado, like she said over breakfast. I know she's getting tired of all the overtime. And this shit is getting old.

Then, just when it seemed as if everything was conspiring to go wrong today, things started to go right.

Sandy's locker was right around the corner from hers, and the acoustics in the hall were such that she could usually hear everything he and his buddies said. Nine times out of ten, this was basically pretty boring and not worth straining her ears over, since Sandy never had anything more on his mind than his next beer or his next lay.

This time, however, his "next lay" proved to be pretty interesting.

She almost dropped her books when she heard Fay's voice coming from around the corner.

The girl's voice was pitched too low for her to be able to pick out exactly what she was saying, but Sandy's reply was clear enough. "Shit, babe, I can't, not tonight. My grandma's coming in for Julie's recital, and we've all gotta go pick her up at the airport. You know, the whole 'Brady Bunch' thing. *Then* we all get to go out for ice cream together. Then Grandma is gonna tell us all about her latest operation, or her trip to Las Vegas, I forget which."

"Sounds like a thrill a minute," Fay drawled. "I think you're just trying to avoid seeing me."

"Give me a break, will you? Grandma's the one with the money in the family, and she's a Reagan-mom-and-apple-pie-nuclear-family pusher. She's *still* not sure she approves of Mom. I'm tellin' you, we have to do this perfect-family shit every time she comes, otherwise she'll leave all the cash to the Salvation Army Girls' Home. If I try an' sneak out on any of it, I'll catch hell. They might even ground me."

"Well, I guess it's okay," Fay said sullenly, while Monica tried simultaneously to look busy and *not* to make any noise. "But baby, I *want* you. I want you *now.*"

Sandy snorted. "What about Deke? You're *supposed* to be going with him, aren't you?"

"He's a kid." There was silence for a moment, and Monica's imagination ran riot. "You're a man."

Sandy cleared his throat; it sounded like he was having a hard time doing so. "Listen," he said thickly. "My car's in the shop, and they let me take the van today. You want to, like, meet me in the parking lot at noon?"

"Van?" Fay replied doubtfully. "I don't know. . . ."

"It's an RV. It's Dad's Boomer Sooner wagon; he takes it to all the UO games. It's like a little living room, you know? Stereo, TV, wet bar, carpeting, miniblinds . . . and the couch at the back folds down."

"Oh," Fay breathed. "Does it?"

"Yeah. Think that'll do?" Sandy sounded very cocky; Monica had the feeling that he might have engineered this little coincidence, especially if he knew that he was going to have to do this Grandma gig but didn't want to miss a shot at Fay. It was true that Sandy never thought much beyond his next beer or his next roll in the sack, but from what she'd seen, he could be very persistent in making sure he *got* them.

"Oh yes," Fay replied, her voice so sugary that Monica wanted to throw up. "That will do. See you at noon?"

"At the parking lot door."

Monica closed her locker and hurried off toward her English class. If Fay knew she'd been overheard—it wouldn't be pretty, and Monica would most likely end up getting the short end. Somehow it always seemed that no matter who was in the right, when Fay tangled with anyone, the principal always backed Fay Harper.

Now how am I going to get Deke out there to catch them? She wracked her brains for an answer all the way to class. *I've got no reason to ask him to meet me out there. He's got no reason to be out there.*

She beat the bell by less than a second; fortunately Diana was inclined to be generous about things like that. She scooted into her seat with an awkward little nod; Diana replied to her half-apology with a shrug and a grin. Then she brought the class down to business. And ironically enough, it was Deke himself who gave Monica the answer she needed.

They were into character development; Diana had told them all that there was no point in trying to re-create "reality" for their main characters.

"First of all, writing exactly what you know will be boring for all of you; second, when have any of you *ever* seen a best seller about a kid from Oklahoma who does all his homework, never gets into much trouble, and basically minds his own business?" The class had laughed, and Diana had spread her hands. "See what I mean? So let your imagination go; so what if whatever you produce isn't what I'd call salable? You'll have fun, and maybe, just maybe, with more experience under your belt and a good editor, someday it *might* be salable."

So Deke's viewpoint character was turning into a race car driver; exactly what *kind* of driver, Monica wasn't sure—his prose was full of things like "group B," "cracked transaxles," and "oversteer." In fact, today's pages were so jargon-intensive that it was pretty clear he was writing for himself and no one else.

That didn't matter. What *did* matter was that he knew about cars. And Monica had been talking to Carri about buying *her* old VW Cabri, but she really wanted somebody who knew about cars to look at it first.

And Carri's car was out in the parking lot just a couple of rows away from Sandy's van. . . .

When discussion time came, they broke up into groups of three and four to dissect each other's pages. Monica waited until the other two kids had given Deke a hard time for sounding like a columnist for *Car and Driver* ("only without the humor," said Mark). Then she put in *her* oar when he turned to her for help.

"Well, it *was* a little too much," she said as gently as she could. "I mean, like, we're not *all* lifetime subscribers to *Auto Week*, you know? Half of what you had in there sounded like rocket-scientist stuff. The other half sounded like Swahili."

His face fell. "I thought I was just making it sound like it was real."

Mark Shepherd snorted. "You know what *I* think race drivers talk about when they sit around? Taxes. And broads. And maybe airline food. Not 'transaxle overcooked megafarts,' or whatever the hell you had in there."

"But I had no idea you knew so much about cars, Deke," Monica said, grabbing her opening with both hands. "Do you suppose you could do me a favor?"

"Yeah, I guess," Deke said, looking a little uneasy. "Depends on what the favor is."

She leaned over her desk so she could look right into his eyes—and tried to look helpless, not sexy. "I need a car. It's a real drag having to ask my mom to drive me all over—and besides, she's putting in a lot of overtime and she can't always. Carri says she'll sell me her Cabri for four grand, and Mom says that sounds okay to her, and Dad says he'll go half if Mom goes half, and they *both* say it sounds like a good birthday present, but I don't know if the car's any good. Could you like, you know, look at it at lunch?"

"How about right after class?" Deke said promptly, perking right up. "I know what the car looks like; I could meet you over there. Do you know where it's parked?"

"Carri said it's about a row down from a big RV at the edge of the lot." Monica smiled sweetly at him, unable to believe how easy this had been. "I can find Carri in the cafeteria and get her to come on out so you can start it and whatever. If that's okay."

"Sure," Deke said cheerfully.

"If you two are *quite* finished—there's a little matter of our assignment," Mark said, giving them both *looks*.

Deke blushed, and Monica gave Mark the evil eye before returning to more mundane matters.

To lend authenticity to her ploy, Monica intercepted Carri in the hall on the way to her locker. Rather than going out, once she heard what Monica wanted, Carri just turned the keys over to her. "Bring 'em back after lunch, and don't take it out of the lot," Carri told her. "Otherwise I could get in trouble, 'cause we're not supposed to leave the campus and it's my car. Okay?"

"No problem," Monica said. "This shouldn't take long."

She *thought* she managed to keep most of the glee out of her voice, but Carri gave her kind of a funny look before she handed her the keys.

Monica waited what she thought might be a reasonable length of time for her to have taken to look for Carri, then waited five minutes longer than that before heading out to the lot.

Her timing was impeccable. The fight was already in full flower when she pushed the door open. As she squinted against the dust, she saw Sandy slam the door of the van and make tracks back toward the building; then she saw Deke's back. He was gesturing wildly. She heard Fay long before she saw her; her shrill voice cut across the rising wind.

That wind made it hard to get the door open; she had to really fight the door, and even then only got it open enough to squeeze through.

Do I go over there? she debated. *Yeah, I said I'd meet Deke; I'm not supposed to know about the thing with Sandy and Fay. But I'd better just look curious.*

"You were *spying* on me, you little geek!" Fay shrieked, as Monica made her way slowly between the rows of parked cars.

After a moment of thought, Monica decided, given the look of rage on Fay's face, that she'd better not head directly for Deke. Instead, she loitered out of Fay's line of sight, pretending great interest in a brand-new Miata.

"I was not!" Deke spat back. "I have more right to be out here than you do! I was coming out here to look at a car, not to climb into a rolling bedroom and screw my brains out with some oversexed jock!"

Monica leaned down and peered into the car's interior.

Fay's expression darkened. "Since when do you tell me what to do, Kestrel?"

"Since we're supposed to be *going* together, Harper! How long have you been doing this, anyway? Ever since I gave you my ring?" Deke sounded sick and disgusted. "Boy, I must look like a real jerk. I'll bet the whole school knows about what's going on. Who *else* have you been messing around with? Bob? Jim Glisson? The entire goddamn athletic department?"

The wind was rising more by the minute; it whipped Monica's hair around and blew dust into her face so hard that it stung. She shielded her eyes with her hand and stayed right where she was. This was too good to miss.

"What's it to you?" Harper sneered. "You don't own me!"

"Well, you've been fuckin' well acting like you own *me*! And I got news for you, babe, I like to know where something's been before I mess with it! Seems to me the only place you *haven't* been is peddling your ass down on Denver!" Monica took a quick glance at Deke. He was white; his eyes were wide and the whites showed all around the irises. His hands were clenched into fists but held rigidly down at his sides, as if he might be afraid that he would hit her if she took one step closer.

Fay spluttered for a moment, unable to get a single coherent word out. Then she ripped Deke's ring off her finger and held it up. "Listen, asshole, I don't have to put up with this! I can give this thing back to you anytime I want—and have somebody else's ring on this finger in thirty seconds flat!"

Deke drew himself up to his full height and looked down his nose at her. The wind was howling now, making it hard to hear what his reply was. Monica moved closer; to hell with the risk if Harper saw her and put two and two together. She didn't want to miss this. As it was, she missed the first couple of words, though the rest was plain enough. "—I'm not sure I want it back—unless you get it disinfected first."

Fay snarled like an enraged beast—and threw the ring in his face. Deke ducked, and simultaneously his right hand shot up.

And somehow he *caught* the thing.

Fay stared at him, then at his hand.

"You're not even a whore, Harper," he said. "You have to give it away, 'cause nobody'd pay for what you spread around. It's too easy to get. It's a damn good thing you're a rich bitch, 'cause you sure couldn't make a living—"

Her hand shot out; there was a *crack* like a rifle shot as her palm connected with his face.

His right hand was already in a fist clenching the ring. He started to draw back to deck her—and then their eyes locked.

Deke froze.

And Monica felt—*something*—poised to strike him. She couldn't see it, she couldn't hear it, but she knew it was there all the same. And she knew that Fay Harper had something to do with it.

"No!" she cried, a tiny sound, lost in the howl of the wind; but she reached out her hand as if to protect Deke, and—

Some force stretched between them; some force reached between her and him, and interposed itself like an invisible barrier between him and Fay Harper. Like the thing poised to strike Deke, she couldn't see it, but she could feel it. And she remembered some of what Diana had told her about how magic worked for the people with the Talent for it if they just believed hard enough. She *believed* with all her strength.

Fay's head snapped around; her angry gaze swept the lot and came to rest on Monica. Monica stepped back an involuntary pace or two before the red, unthinking rage in those eyes. Fay Harper didn't even look human at this moment.

She held up her hand to ward—whatever—off. The menace had transferred itself from Deke to *her*.

Oh, shit. Now *what have I done*?

The wind hit her like a middle-linebacker; she staggered and braced herself against it. There was some force besides the wind trying to get at her, the same one that had been targeted for Deke. She felt that instinctively; the only thing she could think of to do was to stand and refuse to give way to it. . . .

She heard what sounded like a frustrated growl, only it was all inside her head.

Then the wind whirled around her in a vortex, some kind of magnified dust devil, and pulled at the notebook she was clutching at a velocity of about fifty miles per hour. Her fingers slipped and the cover tore; the loose pages of her writing assignment flew out, and the wind grabbed them and sent them halfway to Kansas before she could even blink.

She made an ineffectual grab after them, then turned to face Fay Harper with suppressed fury in her own eyes.

You did that, you bitch! I don't know how, but you did that!

But Fay's own expression was not one of triumph, but of thwarted anger. She stared at Monica for one moment more; then, as the wind shoved at Monica so hard she had to brace herself against the car next to her just to stay on her feet, Fay whirled and flounced off to her Shelby-Z.

She yanked the door open, flung herself inside, and slammed it shut. And in direct defiance of school rules, pulled out of the parking slot and onto the street in a cloud of burning rubber from the front tires. She gunned the engine and tore out of the lot, leaving a long streak of black rubber on the pavement and another at the entrance to the school. In seconds she was out of sight, leaving Monica and Deke staring at each other; Deke accusingly, Monica with a feeling of shock.

Deke was the first to move; he strode up to her and grabbed her by the elbow. "Inside," he shouted above the wind. "I want to talk to you."

As soon as they got inside the foyer door, he wrenched her around to face him. She didn't recognize him. His face was contorted with anger, his eyes glazed. She'd never seen him look like this, not even when Bobby-Boy had been at him. He did not look like the Deke she knew.

"You set this up," he snarled. "You set this whole thing up. You *knew* she was going to be out there with Sandy. You *knew* what was going to happen when I found them. Didn't you?"

Monica looked down at her feet, feeling a combination of guilt and anger. Since she *had* set Deke up, she could hardly deny his accusation with any real feeling. But she *hadn't* tricked Sandy and Fay into sneaking out there!

"You little bitch," Deke spat, the strange light outside making his eyes look as if they were glowing red. "You jealous little bitch! I thought you were my friend! I thought I could talk to you! I thought I could *trust* you!"

"I am!" she cried, stung. "You can! I—"

"I can't believe a single word you say," he interrupted, voice dripping with disgust. "You're just like every other girl; you can't just be a friend, you've got to have everything your way, you've got to have some kind of collar on me, like your little puppy. You've just been making up all these fairy tales about what a good friend you are. Just like you made up all that stupid shit about how you want to be a writer and what Ms. Tregarde's been telling you; you just did it so I'd pay more attention to you, so that I'd think you were better than Fay or something! I *knew* you were just making that shit up, but I thought, okay, she wants to be a writer, she just daydreams a lot. But I guess you wouldn't know the truth if it walked up and hit you one! Probably *everything* you've ever told me is a lie!"

She clutched her hand at her throat; that *hurt*. It had taken a lot of soul-searching and guts to tell him those secrets. The only reason she'd told *him* was because he'd been agonizing over finding out that Diana and his dad had been spending hours to-gether in Diana's room with the door locked. And she just wanted to give him the real reason for them spending all that time together. Not that they were having an affair—that they were working, helping her. She *couldn't* tell him what they were really doing, but she did let him think they were critiquing Monica's own book. . . .

She had been thinking all this time that he believed her. After all, *Alan* did, even about the magic attacks on *her* and that there was somebody after her, which was a helluva lot harder to believe!

But Deke didn't. He'd been stringing her along.

She tried to think of something to say, and couldn't. She tried to think of some scathing put-down and failed. And anger at his treachery just built up to where she couldn't stand it any longer.

So she pulled back her hand and belted him a good one. No stupid little slap, either; a solid blow to the chin that rocked him back, forced him to windmill his arms to keep from falling down, and made his eyes water.

Before he could even *start* to recover, she wrenched the door open against the wind and stalked back out; back straight, eyes stinging, throat tight.

If that bitch Harper can leave in the middle of the day, so can I, dammit!

She didn't hear running footsteps behind her; she just sensed someone back there, someone too small to be Deke. She kept right on going, at a fast, stiff-legged walk.

"Monica," Ann Greeley shouted above the wind. "Monica, wait!"

She stopped right at the edge of the parking lot and turned reluctantly.

"What?" she asked, pouting, *knowing* she was pouting, and unable to keep herself from pouting. *I can't talk to anybody right now. I just can't.*

"Monica, where do you think you're going?" Ann asked reasonably, catching her by the elbow and keeping her from going anywhere, at least temporarily.

She'd had just about enough of being grabbed for one day. "Home," Monica said tightly. "I'm going home. I don't feel good." Belatedly she remembered Carri's keys, still in her hand. They'd bruised her palm when she'd hit Deke. . . .

"You can't do that," Ann pointed out; it was hard to sound gentle when you were shouting over a windstorm, but somehow Ann managed. "You can't leave during the day. You have to get a nurse's excuse, and then your mother has to—"

"My mom's working," Monica interrupted. "And I don't feel good. Harper left—"

"She did?" Ann said, wrinkling her brow in puzzlement. "Are you sure?"

That was too much. "You don't believe me!" Monica cried, bursting into hot tears of anger. "*Nobody* in this whole school believes me! You believe *Harper* when she tells you *anything*, but not me! It doesn't matter what I say, I could have the Pope backing me up and you'd all still say I was lying!"

Ann stared at her with the wind blowing her hair into her eyes and practically ripping her clothing right off her body. She let go of Monica's arm and grabbed her skirt in a futile attempt to keep it under control as it blew up toward her waist; Monica didn't even bother.

"Here," Monica wept, grabbing Ann's wrist and shoving the keys into Ann's limp hand. "You probably won't believe *this* either, but Carri Duval loaned me her keys so I could look at her car. Ask her yourself. Of course, you *probably* think I stole them. I don't care *what* you all think anymore, and I don't care what you do to me. You can all go to hell! I feel awful, and I'm going *home!*"

She threw the tattered remains of her notebook at Ann's feet, and turned on her heel, leaving Ann staring after her with her mouth hanging open in dumbfounded amazement at her outburst.

I don't care, she told herself, hugging her arms to her chest to keep the tears inside. It didn't work very well. Angry tears kept escaping anyway, burning their way down her cheeks. *They're all a bunch of phonies and posers. They all hate me, and I don't care what they think.*

She walked fast, as fast as she could, trying to outdistance her troubles.

She kept her head down, as much to keep the dust out of her eyes as to keep anyone that might be passing by from seeing that she was crying. It occurred to her, in some isolated corner of her mind, that she hadn't really believed in those Oklahoma dust-bowl stories before. Now she had to. It was as dark as twilight out here; she had to lean at a forty-five-degree angle to keep the wind from blowing her over, and the sun was little more than a vague disk in the sky, about as bright as the full moon on a cloudless night. The sky itself was a dirty yellow-brown, about the same color as a cardboard box.

I hope I can make it home—

She was getting tired quickly; finally she had to shelter for a moment in the lee of somebody's house. Her anger and her unhappiness were long since put into the back of her mind. As bad as the weather had turned, they'd probably send everybody home right after lunch. So she not only wouldn't be missed, unless Ann snitched on her—which she probably wouldn't—she wouldn't even get into trouble.

Of course, she thought, tightening her lips with anger, that meant that neither would Harper.

Her legs burned with fatigue, and she wasn't at all surprised to see that her clothes were getting to be the same dirty brown color as the sky.

I'm gonna have to wash these about twenty times just to get all the dust out, she thought unhappily. She was afraid she was going to cry some more, so she concentrated on her anger instead. And how everything, *everything,* was Harper's fault. *I'm gonna have to reprint everything in my notebook. I'm gonna have to somehow remember everything everybody said about the story and fix it. Goddammit. It's not fair! Harper's the one that's been cheating on Deke; she's the one that started all this shit in the first place. She drove off and she'll have her aunt phone in some phony excuse for her, she got to drive home and I have to walk through this shitty storm, I'm gonna be filthy, and she probably won't even have dust in her hair.*

She sounded bitchy, even to herself, and she didn't care. After a rest, she steeled herself and walked back out into the wind. If anything, it was worse than ever. She saw cars being rocked by it as she stumbled past them, and massive limbs were creaking and thrashing and snapping off every tree in sight. She finally decided to move into the center of the street; it was safer.

And on top of everything else, she couldn't help but remember, *Harper can basically get anybody she wants as her date for the spring dance tomorrow night. She wasn't lying about that. And I still don't have a date. Alan's too damn lame to ask me, and Deke's a bastard. Damn it, it's not fair!*

Ahead of her, a phone line snapped and went down, lashing the ground like a whip. She sidestepped the whole area gingerly.

I hate this school, I hate this town, I hate this state!

She made a kind of chant out of all the things she hated, using it to give herself the impetus to get through the storm, to cut through the wind.

I hate the kids, I hate this weather. . . .

Three more blocks to go, and another line snapped, practically on top of her. *This* one was a power line, and it came down in a shower of sparks, missing her by a few feet at most.

She screamed and jumped out of the way, her heart pounding with fear.

Then, from somewhere, found the unexpected strength to start running.

She only slowed when the wall around the complex was in sight. When she reached the guard shack at the entrance to the apartment complex, she was halfway afraid the power would be off. It wasn't, but the guard at the gate cautioned her against using anything that might have problems if there was a surge, like a computer or a VCR. "I'd stick to the radio and electric lights, if I was you, miss," the guard said. "And keep some candles and matches handy. Weatherman says this isn't going to let up until about midnight."

"Midnight?" She swallowed. "Does this happen a lot?"

Because if it does, she thought with a kind of forlorn hope, *Mom isn't gonna want to stay in this state much longer. Tornadoes are bad enough; she's gonna have a fit about this.*

"About once every five or six years," the guard replied, squinting against the dust. "One of those oddball things the weather does in the springtime."

Not often enough for Mom to get mad about it. Damn. She nodded, and forced her tired legs to get her as far as her own door and into it before she collapsed on the couch in the living room. Her brother popped out of the kitchen, his mouth (as usual) full.

"We lost power at school, and a buncha windows got broken by stuff, so they sent us home," he informed her. "Mom called and said they're expecting to lose the lines over there any minute, so she might get off early, too. And she said if you wanted something hot for supper, you'd better either cook it now or we're probably gonna have to do hot dogs in the fireplace. Okay?"

"Okay," Monica replied wearily. She tried to think if the hot water heater was gas or electric. The one in Colorado had been electric. . . .

"Is the hot water gas, or what?" she called out.

"Gas," her brother replied promptly.

Good, that means I don't have to hurry up and get a shower.

She let herself sink into the couch cushions; every muscle in her body was twitching with exhaustion, even the little muscles in her hands and feet. Every time she moved, she could feel the gritty dust that had somehow gotten inside her clothes. It was pretty gross. And in about a minute more she'd go get that shower. In a minute. When she wasn't so tired . . .

I wish this was tomorrow. If it was tomorrow, they'd cancel the dance until next week. Then I'd have a whole week to get a date. Even if I had to ask Alan to go myself!

She clenched her jaw angrily. *Dammit, I'll show them all! I'll go without a date! They can all go to hell, I don't need them, I don't need anybody—*

The phone rang. Figuring it was her mother, Monica stretched out a weary hand to the extension on the end table, and caught it before the answering machine got it.

"Carlin residence," she said automatically, continuing with her standard anti-burglar response, "Monica Carlin. Mom's in the shower right now, can I take a message?"

But the voice on the other end was young and male—and familiar. "Monica? Uh—this is Alan."

A quick glance at the clock showed it was only one-thirty. *They did let everybody out,* was her first thought after a moment of blankness. *Alan? What does he want?* was the second.

She sat up and bit back an exclamation of pain as several muscles in her back and neck protested the sudden movement.

"Monica? Are you okay?"

"Yeah. Uh—hi, Alan. Yeah, I'm fine, I just had to walk home. Gee, I was just thinking of you."

"You were?" His voice rose in surprise. "Monica, I know it's kind of late, but—I'd like to ask you something."

"You would?" *If there's a God . . . oh, please. Please let him ask about the dance, please, please. . . .*

"Yeah. Uh—do you think—I mean, you don't—uh—could you possibly be free for the dance tomorrow night?"

There is a God. Suddenly the world was a wonderful place.

"Gee, Alan," she said flirtatiously. "I don't know. I'd *love* to go with you, but I don't know what the kids at Jenks wear for these things, and I don't know if I've got anything really hot, you know?" She lowered her voice coyly. "I wouldn't want you to be ashamed to be with me."

As he stammered something about being proud to be with her even if she was wearing a garbage sack, she thought about Deke. And what his face would look like when he saw her there with Alan.

Revenge was sweet. There *was* a God.

"How in hell did I let you rope me into this?" Di muttered at Ann Greeley in the sanctuary of the cramped, two-stall ladies' room in the teachers' lounge. She scowled at her reflection; it scowled back. Her agent Morrie might have recognized her in her current getup from all the writers' teas and publishers' cocktail parties he'd dragged her to, but none of her friends would. The normally straight brown mane of her hair had been twisted into a fashionable creation reminiscent of an Art Nouveau print. Her dress continued the theme; flowing cream-colored silk and heavy lace insets at the throat and shoulders, in a Pre-Raphaelite style that made her appear fragile and seductive at the same time.

"I look like one of my damn heroines," she complained to the mirror. "*How* did I let you rope me into this? I hate chaperoning!"

"But the kids think you're fabulous." Ann chuckled. "Did you hear what Alan said to those friends of his?"

"What, the band kids?" Di turned away from the mirror and leaned against the sink. "By the way, they look pretty pro. I was impressed. No, I didn't hear what he told them. What was it?"

" 'See, I *told* you she looked just like Stevie Nicks.' "

"Christ on a crutch," Di groaned, covering her eyes with her hand. "Oh, that's *just* what I need, a room full of adolescent males with the hots for me because I look like Stevie Nicks. Terrific. Ann, I am *not* the type to enjoy the role of Mrs. Robinson!"

"Which is why you'll make a good chaperone," Ann had the chutzpah to point out. "You're as hip as any of these kids, but you never forget you're twenty years their senior—"

"Thanks for reminding me," Di muttered. "I really needed that. Should I have brought my knitting?"

"They figure you understand them; they respect you. They'll listen to you."

"You think." Ann started to remonstrate; Di held up her hand. "All right, I'm here, aren't I? Just remember what I told you. I don't break up clinches, I don't arbitrate in lovers' quarrels, and I don't keep kids from smoking in the john. And I don't care whether or not what they're smoking is legal. Unless it's heavier shit than grass. What I *will* do is break up fights, keep kids from *driving* out of here if they're drunk or stoned, try and put the fear of God into anybody doing heavier drugs than grass, and keep anybody from raping or getting raped. And that, my dear, is the extent of my involvement."

"You have a far more realistic view of our student body than most of their parents do," Ann said dryly. "Or the teachers, for that matter."

"I can afford to," Di replied just as dryly. "They aren't my kids. I don't live here. I'm not dependent on their parents' goodwill for my salary and continued employment. I can be just as blunt as I want to, and just as realistic as the situation calls for."

"You also must be a lot tougher than you look, if you're planning on restraining high-flying adolescent males." Ann gave her an interesting look; not at all doubtful, just speculative.

"Karate. Second *dan* black belt," Di said modestly. "I'd be higher, except for two things. I don't compete, and my *sensei* teaches cross-discipline stuff so we'll know how to handle martial artists from other schools. So we don't exactly have what you'd call perfect forms, and you have to have perfect forms to compete."

Ann laughed a little. "You're going to play Bruce Lee in that dress?"

"That's the reason why it's so full. And silk has another advantage; it doesn't tear easily." Di eyeballed the paper towel dispenser, and spun into a *kata*, with the dispenser as a target. Front kick, side kick, back kick, and finishing with a second side kick; hitting the dispenser very lightly, the kind of pulled blows that showed truer skill than full-contact karate. She wasn't even breathing heavily, and she'd only lost one hairpin. "My jeans are all karate cut, with the extra gusset in the inseam. Last but not least, you'll notice I always wear flats." She grinned.

Ann nodded. "You'll do, my dear. You'll do. If you ever want a teaching job—"

"Bite your tongue!" Di laughed. "I'm not that tough. You couldn't pay me enough."

"That's what I say every spring—and every fall I'm right back here." Ann said over her shoulder as they left the teachers' lounge, "You take the punch bowl; see if you can keep the little psychotic darlings from spiking it, will you? I'll take the stage corner and try and keep them out of the curtains."

Di sighed, smiled sweetly at one of her erstwhile pupils who seemed to have been struck dumb by the sight of her in a dress, and tried to keep a weather eye out for Monica. Fortunately the canned music wasn't bad. She hoped the band played half as good as they looked.

But Monica, and the threatening ruin of her reputation among the teachers, was foremost in her mind. *If I can just talk to her alone for a little, maybe I can repair some of the damage she did to herself.*

She's just damn lucky the principal sent everybody home halfway through lunch period because of the storm, or she'd be in even deeper kimchee than she is now. As it is, nobody knows she left the campus; they're assuming she stayed until everyone was turned loose.

Teachers are well known to have detection systems that rival Stealth bombers and spy satellites. Within five minutes of the moment Monica had stormed off in her cream-colored huff, half the teachers in Jenks had heard some version of the blowup. By the time school was canceled, it was the talk of the faculty lounge.

The way the current (and most popular) version had it, Monica was a first-class troublemaker. According to *that* version, Fay and Sandy were set up by Monica; Deke caught them together and came to some unwarranted conclusions—thanks to Monica making a lot of little innuendos beforehand.

But Di had heard part of the story from Deke himself—and the version of intercourse Sandy and Fay had been about to engage in when he caught them *wasn't* "talking." Yes, Monica had all but pushed him at the van during the critical time period—but she hadn't set the pair up. They'd arranged their little tête-à-tête all on their own.

And everyone seemed to have forgotten that.

Yeah, well, Fay is teacher's pet for everybody except Ann and me; Ann just basically could care less about the little bitch because she never even tries in class, and I haven't done more then see her at a distance since I got here. Di leaned back against a column, trying to ignore the half-dozen moonstruck adolescent males who were lurking in her vicinity. *Jesus Cluny Frog, guys—where the hell were you back when I was in high school? Back when I needed you?* Three of the six weren't at all bad looking, if a trifle nerdy.

They were all on edge, though, and it wasn't just because of the dance. But before she could figure it out, she saw someone else standing a little apart from the crowd.

There was a seventh kid who wasn't giving her puppy-dog eyes; he was just watching her. She couldn't help but notice him; he had an aura of vitality that practically glowed in the dark. He was something really special—not classically handsome, not even close, but so cutting-edge he'd stand out in New York, with wicked good humor gleaming out of those big green eyes.

You're going to be a real lady-killer, my lad, she thought with amusement. *And it won't be long, either. These provincial posers don't appreciate you. Just you wait until you get out in the world—*

He lifted an eyebrow at her—then headed straight for her.

Lady Bright. He can't possibly have the audacity—
He did.

"Care to trip the night fantastic, my lady of the camellias?" he asked, offering his arm. "You'd make Alphonse Mucha swoon with rapture."

"I'm a chaperone," she said sharply.

"Does this mean your legs are broken?" he retorted. "Come on, you're dying to dance, I can tell. And it's too early for anybody to get the guts to dump anything in the punch bowl. That won't happen until the lights are down for one of the couples' dances."

She looked at him; at the mostly empty dance floor; at the wistful expression his broad grin wasn't quite hiding.

"Oh, come on," he whispered. "Half the guys here want to dance with you, but they're too chicken to ask. You'll do wonders for my rep."

That did it. *What the hell. There's no law about the chaperone not having a little fun.*

She allowed him to sweep her out into the middle of the floor, where she proceeded to do both her t'ai chi instructor *and* all her professional-dancer friends proud.

And the boy wasn't half bad himself.

They cleared the floor, drawing impromptu applause from the kids that gathered on the edge.

"I feel like I'm in a music video," she laughed, after the third song. "Enough, I'm out of breath, and I've got to get back to my job"—she leaned close so she could whisper—"and I don't think there's too many girls who'd turn you down tonight, not after *this* little exhibition."

The wicked sparkle in his eyes told her that she'd hit the mark, but he escorted her demurely enough back to her station.

The kid—whatever his name was—was the only light spot in the evening, though. Yesterday's windstorm had died down some, but it wasn't over. The sky was the color of a grocery sack all day; Di had decided that it wasn't quite so hard to believe the old dust-bowl stories of the sky being black at high noon. She was just glad that her silk dress was washable, and that she'd changed here instead of back at Larry's.

And that she'd brought a can of antistatic spray. There was an incredible amount of static electricity in the air. She was wearing rubber-soled flats and had liberally sprayed her dress, but nearly everyone else was getting shocks when they accidentally touched something metallic. The kids were nervy and restless; even the adults were on edge. Di had seen just this kind of nervous tension in Cali-

fornia once, when she'd been around Orange County while the Santa
Ana was blowing. The experts claimed that the hysteria generated by
the Santa Ana was caused by the static and the positively charged ions
caused by the constant high wind. Whatever the reason, it set everyone jumping like cats in a dog pound.

And there was a sense of something stirring, ever so slightly, elsewhere. *She doesn't like it either,* Di thought suddenly. *She's still
sleeping—but this wind is disturbing the surface of Her dreams. Whatever She is. Definitely female, but nothing I've ever crossed before.*

Ever since Di had communed with the edges of the dreams of the
One Below, she'd been vaguely aware of what She was sensing. Di
hadn't wanted to get too close; it would be only too easy to get pulled
into those dreams, and damn hard to get out again.

She *was* the reason for the psychically null area here. She tended
to influence psis; either She made them uncomfortable and they
moved as soon as they possibly could—

*—or they get sucked in and never come out again. Wonder why no-
body's ever noticed that an unusually high number of catatonics come
out of the Old Tulsa area?*

Di shook her head; she tried *not* to think about the One Below
too much. Just thinking about Her brought you in closer contact. The
dreams of the One Below were *not* the kind of thing Di preferred to
have loose inside her skull.

This storm, though—it had nothing to do with Her. The legends
were right; *nobody* wanted Her to wake up. She was dangerous and
touchy, and Di hoped profoundly that this anomalous weather didn't
disturb Her even a little.

*It would take an awfully long time to brew five thousand gallons of
coffee. I don't think She'd wait.*

At that point there was a *squawk* from one of the stage amps the
band was setting up, and Di jumped, then grinned sheepishly at some
of the kids nearest her, who'd reacted the same way.

"Static," said one kid. "Gremlins," said another. There was a nervous giggle—

The amp squawked again; one of the mikes was on and did a
feedback squeal that set Di's teeth on edge.

"Shit—" said the kid on stage, the one Alan had introduced as the
bass player, unaware that the mike was live. There was a nervous
laugh at that and the rest of the chaperones glared; the kid blushed the
most spectacular shade of firecracker red Di'd ever seen in her life.

"Uh—sorry—" the kid mumbled into the mike; it began to
squeal and he turned it off before it could pierce their eardrums.

Some things never change, Di thought, looking around at the decorated auditorium. *The only difference between what we've got here and* my *high school dances is the cost of the trimmings.*

The theme of the dance—there was evidently a law somewhere that high school dances had to have a theme—was "Spring Fling."

I hated themed dances when I was a kid, and that hasn't changed, thank you.

Someone in his or her infinite wisdom had decided that "Spring Fling" meant some sort of bizarre connection to medieval Scottish May Day celebrations. There was an abundance of tartan, all inappropriate and in ghastly colors, and an overabundance of inappropriate paper flowers and garlands. And the Major Decoration (*where is it written that "there shalt be a papier-mâché Monument?"*) was a Maypole. Complete with crown and streamers.

Dear gods, does anybody here really *know what a Maypole means?*

No. Not possible. Unless . . . there's a couple of teachers here that are the right age to have been flower children. Including Miz Greeley over there—

She caught Ann's eye and nodded toward the—ahem—erection. And raised an ironic eyebrow. Ann started to grin and covered the grin quickly with her hand.

But the shaking of her shoulders told Di everything she needed to know. Ann Greeley, at least, knew *exactly* what Maypoles meant, and found it hilariously funny.

I wonder if it could have been her *idea in the first place?*

But at that moment, Fay Harper, the Spring Queen, made her appearance on stage surrounded by her court.

And suddenly nothing was quite so funny anymore.

THIRTEEN

There's something very strange going on up there, Di thought, staring at the crowded stage. *Somebody up on that stage is doing a shield that's as good as Deke's. And I can't tell who. Or, most importantly, why.*

And it was impossible to tell *where* that shield originated. The four members of the Persuaders were already up there, plus the assistant principal, the Queen and King, the escorts for the six Princesses, and the Princesses themselves.

Like trying to pick out one goldfish in a tankful.

The stage wasn't exactly crowded, even with twenty people standing on it; as with everything else, Jenks had superior facilities for their would-be thespians. Although no amount of bunting and tissue-flower garlands was going to conceal the fact that this was the cafeteria by day, and Di was just as glad she wasn't on the cleanup committee; this place was going to be hard to get in shape after the dance was over. In Di's time dances were held in the school gym—but apparently the pristine condition of the precious hardwood basketball court took precedence over convenience of cleanup.

According to Ann, that Fay would be Spring Queen was as predictable as the coming of spring itself; there was no surprise there. But standing on the right as her escort—though *not* as the Spring King—was Deke.

Now that *was* a surprise. As late as just before dinner, Deke had been swearing that Fay was a bitch and he'd rather die than take her to the dance.

So something changed his mind in the last two hours. I wonder what?

He didn't look too happy up there, though. He was hunched up a little, face sullen, and he oozed Bad Attitude. The latter was hardly surprising, since at Fay's other hand was the Spring King, Sandy, who was doing an Attitude number right back at Deke. On the other hand, this sulky brat didn't look much like the Deke that Di knew; *something* had certainly been playing with his mind and his hormones. Deke could be awfully easy to manipulate.

That something was undoubtedly his date. Di took an instant dislike to Fay Harper. She was blond and gorgeous, and at the moment looked like the proverbial cat that ate the canary. Exactly the kind of chick that used to make *Di's* life miserable back when she was in school. It was pretty obvious to Di what was going on here; Fay was playing Deke against Sandy, and neither one of the boys was bright enough to catch on to what she was doing.

There was more to it than that, though. Di had gotten a peculiar feeling the moment she laid eyes on Fay Harper—a feeling as though there was something very wrong about her. It was an uneasiness that ran deeper than the animosity Di would have felt *anyway,* given that the girl was obviously a manipulative little tart.

Di didn't get much of a chance to analyze her. The vice-principal took over the mike to announce the crowning of the Queen, and Fay moved, with false and simpering modesty, behind him, out of Di's line of sight.

The static discharge from his clothing was playing merry hell with the sound system. Every time he touched the mike, it squealed. It didn't help that he was wearing what Di thought of as the Plastic Teacher Suit (Ann called it the Sears Sucker Suit; "whole herds of polyesters died to make Sears great.") The static he was creating could have powered Tulsa for a week.

Finally he gave up, and gestured to one of the band members to try to make the introductions and announcements. The boy (Di remembered he'd been introduced to her as George) did his best, but the mike kept interrupting with howls and shrieks so often that the kid just threw up his hands in frustration, took the tinsel crowns from the vice-principal, and did the whole ceremony in mime.

And still that uneasy feeling persisted. *There's something in the air, and it isn't static. Something's going down.*

Sandy marched up to the mike and turned it back on, and Di braced herself for another shriek from the tortured electronics.

He cleared his throat self-consciously, and the mike popped threateningly, but didn't quite act up.

"I guess all of you know that the Spring King was supposed to be Bob Williams." His face looked like a plastic mask in the harsh stage lights, and his words sounded stilted, as if he'd memorized them.

He probably did. I bet I can predict the rest of this little speech. "Bob isn't with us anymore; he's gone to that big football field in the sky."

"Bob isn't with us anymore. I guess somebody up there must have needed a good team captain." The microphone popped again. It sounded, oddly enough, like laughter.

Give me strength. Who wrote this piece of tripe, I wonder? Just about then Sandy hesitated, and Di saw the vice-principal's lips moving in an attempt to prompt him.

Aha, I might have known.

"Bob always gave everything he had for Jenks, one hundred and ten percent. He never missed a game, no matter what. He was the best football player Jenks ever produced." Feedback through the amp made the speakers whine petulantly.

And the less said about his academic achievements, the better.

"We'll all miss Bob. He had a heck of a future ahead of him. It's going to be real tough to fill his cleats."

The vice-principal leaned forward, and Di got a good look at Fay Harper's expression. She wasn't quite sure how she'd been expecting the girl to look—at least a little moved, maybe. But whatever she'd been anticipating, however vaguely, it *wasn't* the deadpan Fay was wearing. Sandy cleared his throat again and prepared to continue with his recitation, but the sound system chose that moment to break into a screech that probably vibrated the fillings out of people's teeth.

Sandy just shrugged (looking relieved) and retired to his spot beside Fay to the equally relieved applause of the audience. Then Fay stepped forward.

It was only at that moment that Di saw how odd her gown was. If it hadn't been that the thing was a very modern shade of baby blue, it *could* have come straight out of a costume exhibition of the Revolutionary War. Beribboned, ruffled, and panniered, with a neckline that was just short of pornographic, all it lacked to make it perfect was a powdered wig. Di wondered what on earth had possessed her to buy it—and where on earth she'd *found* it.

Most girls Fay's age would have looked awkward in a dress like that. Ninety-nine percent wouldn't have known how to handle the wide skirts and panniers.

Fay carried herself as gracefully as if she were Marie Antoinette. Di had to admit to grudging admiration for the girl. It took a certain amount of chutzpah to wear a dress so entirely out of step with the

neon lamé and hot-pastel organdy currently in fashion. And it took
native grace to be able to *move* in something like that.

Fay's little gratitude speech was as clear as the proverbial bell. The
sound system didn't misbehave once during the entire proceedings.

Given Fay's reputation, Di couldn't help thinking, *it's probably
afraid to. So, what's next?* She looked around, trying to find a source
for her feeling of impending disaster, and couldn't spot a thing. As
she scanned the crowd, identifying and dismissing every marginally
psychic kid she could spot, the six Princesses and their escorts picked
their way gingerly down the slippery wooden stairs to the stage,
heading straight for the Maypole.

That was enough to distract Di from her search. *They can't be—*
she thought, incredulously. *They* can't *be. Good gods. They are.*

Sure enough, each one of the twelve grabbed a streamer, and began to sort themselves into a ring of facing pairs. Boys facing girls,
boys to be circling clockwise, girls widdershins.

*Does anybody out here know what that Maypole dance really
stands for?* Di spotted Ann at the edge of the crowd, trying to bury
her giggles behind a cup of punch. The fact that the cup was empty
was a dead giveaway.

*Yeah, she knows what's going on, all right. Yeah. Let's hear it for
Fertility Rites in the Modern High School. Coital Rituals 101, first door
on the left.* Di bit her lip to keep from giggling herself. *I wonder if Ann
even bothered to try to keep them from going through with this when
she heard about it?*

From the way Ann's shoulders were quivering, she probably
hadn't. And it was an odds-on bet she hadn't even tried to tell *anyone*
what she knew.

*And the rest of the teachers are all seeing innocent little flowers of
romance performing a quaint little Victorian custom.* She double-
checked the Maypole; straw crown, green ribbons, phallic knob on
top . . . completely authentic. *Oh, my ears and whiskers, it's about as
Victorian as I am!*

One of the guitarists up on stage fingered an opening passage,
and the twelve kids raised their streamers in unison, preparatory to
going into their dance.

—and suddenly Di sensed the stirring of power, and the scene
didn't seem quite so funny anymore.

The rest of the band joined the first guitar, playing something
slow and fairly low-key, while the twelve kids began weaving in and
out with their ribbons, moving at a slow walk.

Twelve . . . and the pole makes thirteen. It's the Sex Magick ver-

sion. Lord and Lady, somebody *out there knows what he's doing! Now if the band starts speeding up . . .*

The band did.

. . . I've got potential trouble on my hands. Scratch that; I have real trouble on my hands.

Ann Greeley? Despite having dismissed her before, Di was forced to consider her the prime suspect now. She fit all the parameters— adult, in contact with the kids, and demonstrably knowledgeable. She didn't have an apparent motive, but that didn't matter; the motive could be something Di just hadn't spotted yet. She didn't have the "feel" of a magick-worker, but Di suddenly realized that if she wasn't at all psi, Di would never know she was a sorcerer until she actually cast some sort of spell in Di's presence.

Di tore her gaze away from the Maypole dancers, who were skipping around their circuits without a single flaw in the weaving, faces set in the blank masks of entrancement. Even more ominously, the rest of the students had begun to crowd onto the dance floor and by *their* dancing were raising more power to feed into the Maypole ritual.

Di finally saw Ann making a lateral for the punch bowl, and threw a full probe on her, a probe which included Di's own rather limited ability at mind reading.

And got nothing. Ann wasn't interested in power, she didn't even realize there was anything unusual going on; Ann was making sure nobody'd dumped anything into the punch besides sherbet and fruit juice.

But the power was going *somewhere*. And there was a lot of it. Maybe, she realized with a feeling of dread, enough to wake up the One Below. . . .

She was going to have to ground it, and fast. The way the ritual was *meant* to go, with the power going right back into the fertility of the earth.

She couldn't scan for the culprit, make sure the One Below *didn't* wake up, and drain off the power harmlessly at the same time. She hesitated for a moment, then sensed the unknown sorcerer pulling the energy as fast as the dancers could generate it.

Not this time, bozo, she thought grimly. *You just ran up against an expert in Sex Magick. You should have tried something other than a pagan ritual, mister. We're on* my *home turf here.*

She tapped straight into the spell casting, taking the power and grounding it the way her granny had taught her. She could tell that the other was surprised when the energy stopped feeding into him; felt him groping around for some way to stop her. But he didn't have any feeling for the power flows, and he had found a way to use the pagan ceremony either completely by accident or through a lot of study. He couldn't tell where she was tapping in, and he didn't know how to block her. And he didn't have time to figure out how to get around what she was doing.

I just love being made default High Priestess with no advance warning.

But despite the fact that she could feel her enemy nearby—was probably close enough to touch him, in fact—she was just too busy to try to single out which of the people on or near the stage was the sorcerer. Sweat trickled down the back of her neck as she struggled with the reins of power. Like controlling a horse that wanted to bolt; she dared not take her concentration off her task or it would escape from her. If she'd had a chance to prepare for this, it would have been different; she'd have been in a trance of her own, and not fighting to hold the power, stay conscious, and ward the sleeping Leviathan. The muscles of her shoulders began to cramp with strain, and she put her back against a pillar to keep herself upright.

The kids continued to dance, and the band continued to play, all oblivious to the arcane fencing going on under their noses. All except for the green-eyed kid, who had his back to the wall, his eyes frantically scanning the crowd, his face set and a little frightened.

He feels it too—and he doesn't know where it's coming from or going to, either. Shit, I'm scaring the hell out of a budding psi. Sorry about this, kid. I've got my hands full at the moment.

That was when things took a turn for the worse. The music the band was playing started to change.

Strange undertones crept into the sounds two of the guitars were putting out. The music made the hair rise on the back of Di's neck; the only thing she could think to compare it to was the stuff Dave's band had done—

But this wasn't music meant to generate psychic energy. *This* music carried undercurrents of hatred and anger. This was music designed to incite violence. None of the band members appeared to notice what was going on with their own music—

In fact, they looked oblivious to everything around them, completely caught up in what they were doing, paying no attention to the audience. Up on stage, only Deke and the vice-principal were left besides the band; Sandy and Fay were already gone.

Two of the kids to Di's left collided accidentally on the dance floor. Five minutes ago, they'd have ignored the collision, or at worst, grinned and gone on dancing.

Not now.

They rounded on each other, snarling, fists clenched, every muscle tensed to attack.

One just happened to be black; the other, white.

The stage was set for disaster, the curtain was about to ascend, and she had her hands full. Too full to even try to stop it.

Lord and Lady, I've got too many balls in the air, and if I drop any of them—Come on, *I need some help here!*

She felt that little something extra that made her a Guardian finally kick in, giving her the equivalent of one more hand—

—and with it, instructions.

She sent a surge of power at the band without knowing why she was doing so, knowing only that she had to.

The third guitar cut across the music of the first two. *Literally* cut across it; what the third one played canceled the undercurrents of the others completely. Peace and harmony and sheer good fun caroled out, Woodstock and a sixties Beach Boys concert combined.

The expression of pure hatred on the white kid's face faded. Between the music and the crowd noise, Di was too far away to hear what he said, but it was evidently an apology. The black one looked down at his clenched fists as if he was surprised to see them attached to his wrists, and sheepishly nodded and backed off.

I don't know what's going on here, but I sure as hell know which side I'm *picking!* She stopped grounding out the energy she'd been taking from the Maypole spell casting and instead of feeding it back into the earth, sent it straight at that third guitar.

Whoever that other magician was, he figured out what Di was doing immediately. He stopped trying to find a way to pull control away from Di, and began feeding the other two guitars from whatever stores he had already, and whatever he could glean from the other dancing kids.

The two enemy guitars—Di recognized them, absently, as Stratocasters—howled like a pair of demented Sirens, and threw out their song of destruction. And Di's ally, a Gibson probably older than most of the kids here, reacted like a t'ai chi master, taking their music and transmuting it. Picking up their riffs and purifying them; turning their own force against them.

It *was* recognizably music; anything that wasn't might have attracted attention and broken the spell the Strats were trying to weave. Everything depended on their being able to keep the kids in that kind of half-trance the first notes had sent them into—and keep them dancing. The Gibson couldn't break the spell, but it could change it, and that was exactly what the instrument—or whatever was inhabiting the instrument—was doing.

The kids were the rope in a tug-of-war conducted by a trio of latter-day Pied Pipers. All they heard was the music and the beat; they were deaf and blind to the subtle manipulations of their emotions. It wasn't fair, but there wasn't much Di could do about it. All she could do was support the side that intended to set them free when the fight was over.

The Gibson was going strong, but Di wasn't sure how long *she* could keep this up. She wasn't sweating anymore; she was shivering with reaction and weariness. Her knees felt so weak that it was only the pillar at her back that was keeping her on her feet.

I need some way to end this. I need some way to overwhelm them.

Then she saw her opening. And so, she sensed, did the Gibson. It pulled back a little, preparatory to giving its all. Desperate for a way to finish the battle, she dropped everything she was doing and sent her ally one last, frantic burst of concentrated power.

The Strats felt it coming, and tried to rear a wall of sound to deflect it.

But the amps had taken enough for one night.

Between the static charge in the air and the dueling magics, they couldn't take any more.

There was a final note from the Gibson that stopped the kids in their tracks, froze the band cold, and made even the Maypole dancers drop their ribbons and clap their hands over their ears. And at that point, two of the three stage amps died.

But they went out in a blaze of glory; shooting flames and smoke everywhere, in a pyrotechnic display that rivaled anything Di had seen name bands do on purpose.

The Gibson wasn't done yet—it still had a partially live amp, and it was moving in for the kill. Di fed her ally one last burst, and together they blew the circuits on the Strats—

Which was calculated to send whatever was *in* them back to whatever hell they came from.

The Strats wailed as their circuits fried. The two Strat players cursed, yelped, and dropped their instruments, frantically hauling the straps off over their heads. The amps were still burning. For some reason the fire alarm hadn't gone off; Di suspected it had been turned off at the office to prevent kids turning in false alarms during the dance. She also suspected that there would be heads rolling over that in the morning. But for now, it was just as well.

The vice-principal and another teacher jumped up on the stage with a pair of carbon-dioxide fire extinguishers and began spraying everything and everyone indiscriminately.

The first of the two Strats gave a last dying shriek as the thing inhabiting it lost its grip on the guitar. There was a power surge that flickered the lights. Then the *guitar* went up in a shower of sparks, and the resulting short circuit blew every fuse in the building.

There were a few screams as the lights went out but not much more than that. Di dropped her shields enough to ascertain that the kids were all mostly dazed. There would be no lasting harm, but the shock of being put *into* a trance state and then blown out of it again was going to keep most of them a bit confused for the next few minutes.

Most of them, but not all.

"Oh, man," came a mournful voice from the stage. "Oh, *man.* If we're gonna blow amps and guitars every night, we *gotta* get better-paying gigs. . . ."

Deke headed straight for the can the minute the lights came back on. He felt like he was going to be sick, even though he hadn't had much to eat and not a thing to drink that wasn't perfectly harmless.

It had been a long day, and it didn't look like it was over yet.

First the vice-principal had called him on the carpet for fighting with Fay in public. Then Fay had been all over him every chance she got, pouting and trying to make up to him. And Monica had *avoided* him all day, even going so far as to sit on the opposite side of the English class from him.

And somehow, some way, Fay had managed to get him talked into first coming over before the dance, then giving her his ring back. He still wasn't sure how she'd done it; the entire afternoon and early evening were lost in a kind of tired haze. When he got to the dance, he wasn't mad at her anymore; he was mad at Sandy for making it look like he and Fay were going to—

Going to—

Now he didn't remember what it was. But it was all Sandy's fault.

Then he'd taken Fay to the dance—in *her* car, not his—and all this weird shit started happening.

First off, there was Sandy, acting like Deke was poaching on *his* turf.

Then there was that stuff with the sound equipment; George *never* had trouble with his equipment before.

That was when he started feeling sick. He had gotten down off the stage without Fay, who managed to vanish at some point during the Maypole dance. He remembered her looking startled, then angry, then completely enraged—then she was gone, about the time the music started to go thermonuclear.

He'd had a pretty good idea where she'd gone, because Sandy disappeared a few moments later. But he was feeling too dizzy and lightheaded to care.

Then the band blew up.

When the lights came back on, it turned out that the damage was a lot less than it had looked like. Basically two of the three guitars were totaled, and two of the three amps. The sound system itself was okay, so the vice-principal grabbed George's sound guy to play DJ and told everyone to take five; they'd start the dance back up once the stage was cleaned off.

Deke had about had it. He'd decided he was going to confront Fay about vanishing on him and head home; *walk* home if he had to. But every time he started to track down Fay and demand an explanation, he felt sicker.

He went to the sinks and started throwing cold water on his face. *God, it's hot in here,* he thought. *When the band was playing it was so hot I thought I was going to smother. Shit. Like I couldn't breathe—no, more like somebody was sucking the breath out of me.*

The door to the johns creaked and Deke glanced up at the mirror reflexively to see who it was. "Hi, Alan," he said wearily.

Alan was looking pretty smug. "Hey, what's wrong?" he asked, giving Deke a look of concern mixed with condescension. "It's pretty early in the evening to tie one on, buddy."

"I didn't 'tie one on,'" Deke replied with as much heat as he could manage to dredge up. "I haven't had a damn thing to drink except a Coke. I think I must be catching something."

"Too bad," Alan replied, messing unnecessarily with his hair. "Don't give it to me, okay? I finally got together with that girl I was telling you about. We just *might* go somewhere private. Depends on if they can really get the sound system working again or not."

Deke's stomach turned over, and he clutched at the sink until his knuckles were white. "Yeah, fine," he mumbled. "Great, nice going. Hope you finally manage to get laid. It'll do you good."

He looked up at Alan's reflection.

Oh shit. Boy, I really put my foot in it this time.

His friend bristled with anger and pulled himself up as tall as he could without standing on his toes. "This is for those who don't deserve the very best," Alan said, holding up his fist with his little finger sticking out of it.

Then he stalked out, leaving behind the scent of bruised dignity.

Now why in hell did I say that? Deke asked himself. *God, what kind of a jerk am I? Alan didn't deserve to be insulted. What in hell is wrong with me?*

He finally went into one of the stalls and sat with his head between his legs until he felt a little steadier. *First I take Fay back, then I dump on Alan. It's like I'm my own evil twin or something. Maybe I am catching something. Maybe that's what the problem is.*

One of the teachers came in, making the rounds, and took pity on him when it was obvious that he wasn't drunk or stoned. The teachers' lounge wasn't far away; it was cool, and dim, and stocked with everything a teacher might need to face a class full of bored adolescents—everything short of Valium, anyway. Two Maalox later, and his stomach settled at last, he felt ready to face the rest of the school, and to deal with Fay. He straightened himself up as best he could, and headed out into the hall.

And ran straight into Monica.

"Monica!" he exclaimed. "Hi! I—uh—"

"Hello, Derek," she said coldly, in a tone so chill he could feel ice forming on his eyebrows.

She turned away from him without another word, and started to walk off down the hall toward the cafeteria. He looked around quickly; there was no one else around. This was a good chance to try and apologize.

"Monica, wait!" he called desperately. "Look, I—uh—about yesterday, I—"

She stopped, and looked back over her shoulder at him. "Yes?" she said, in tones of complete indifference.

"I—uh—I was a little hot." He flushed, and his stomach did another flip-flop. "I lost my temper, you know?"

"Oh, really?" she replied. "Is that what you call it?"

She turned away and started to walk off again, her back stiff and straight. "Monica, wait!" he cried desperately. "Can I talk to you later? Please?"

"No, you can't," she said frostily, without turning around. "I've got plans. For the *whole evening.*"

She stalked off with all the pride of an outraged dowager, trailing disdain behind her like a cloak.

Shit, he thought glumly, staring after her. *Shit, I really screwed that one up, too. Good job, Kestrel. Now you've got Monica and Alan pissed at you.*

Then, suddenly, he remembered something. When he'd been up on the stage with Fay, he'd noticed Monica in the crowd below. And Alan had been next to her. What if that hadn't been coincidence? What if they'd been together?

But how could she have met him? She—oh shit. That math class. He's in it, too.

He started to hurry after her, to find out who she'd come with, but Fay intercepted him just as he got to the cafeteria door.

"There you are," she said playfully. "Sandy and I were wondering if you'd fallen in."

From just behind her, Sandy glowered at him.

"They've gotten the sound system put back together," she told him. "They're just waiting for me to get the dance started. Sandy thought I should do the first dance with him, but *you're* my escort, and I think I ought to do it with you."

It was all in the open now; she was playing Sandy against him and vice versa, and loving every minute of it. And he couldn't help himself; he took Fay's arm like some macho cowboy grabbing his dance-hall girl in an old western. And she was as desirable now as she'd been distasteful half an hour ago. "Yeah," he said aggressively. "Yeah, I think so, too. You *did* come with me. And you *are* my steady."

Before Sandy could say anything, he hustled Fay out into the center of the floor. That seemed to be the signal everyone was waiting for; somebody started a Stevie Nicks tape, and he put his arms around Fay like he owned her. . . .

But out of the corner of his eye he saw Monica. Dancing with Alan.

Aw hell—

How dare *she move in on my territory! How* dare *she steal my power! When I get home, and I'm alone, I'm going to break something.* Fay relaxed bonelessly—outwardly, at least—into Deke's arms and turned up the sexual heat. She'd managed to get Deke back under her control; and now he was so worked up tonight that his face was white and his stomach must be churning.

Poor little boy. So easy to manipulate. But I'm still going to kill something before the night's over.

She moved her hips in tight against his, reminding him of everything she'd done to him on all the nights before this; reminding him of all the things he *could* have from her. Promising things with her hands under his jacket. It was hard to maintain this pose of calm, when inwardly she was screaming with rage at the loss of all that power. Only the coke and grass she'd done right after the demons were exorcised enabled her to stay in control.

Body language is so eloquent. And if it could say what I felt, you'd be short a body part or two, Deke dear.

She'd made up her mind last night, after she'd cooled down from the fight. Deke had done the unthinkable; he'd broken free of her control. So there *was* something worth digging for under that shield of his. He was the best prospect she'd seen yet; the signs were all right. If she let him get away, there might never be another target as easy, or as tasty.

So she set herself to winning him back. Because as soon as graduation was over, she intended to move on him. First she'd have to get rid of those inconvenient parents of his; then she could get him to marry her. Deke would have a tidy little fortune by inheritance, especially if she made certain his parents died in some kind of double-indemnity accident. Added to her own wealth, Deke would never actually have to work a day in his life. In his *short* life . . .

But the parents were going to have to go. Absolutely. There was no doubt that his father had brought in that witchy female, that Tregarde woman—and Fay had no doubts whatsoever that it *hadn't* been primarily to give Deke's English class a creative writing teacher.

She was probably the one responsible for the shield over the boy in the first place. If it hadn't been for the lines she had on him before he was shielded, Fay would never have been able to work Deke at all tonight. The hooks were set, though, and with Deke's tacit consent, when he'd given her his ring right after the accident. Not even an Adept could work a passive shield against something like that.

But this writer was a wild card Fay didn't like. A rival, a competitor, on *her* carefully staked-out ground. *She* was certainly the one responsible for foiling the attacks on the Carlin brat. She'd suspected the Kestrels at first, but no more. If Deke's parents had the Gifts or the Power, they would have used it by now for more than simply shielding their son. They hadn't, therefore they didn't have it. But they knew it existed; they may have even guessed the threat Fay was to their child. That was undoubtedly why Larry Kestrel had brought the witch to Tulsa. And once here, the potentials were obvious. . . .

And it's why your life is going to be cut much shorter, old man, she thought maliciously, leaning on the son's shoulder, and swaying in place to the gentle song that was playing. *Then I'll produce the next vehicle, and dear little Derek will have a fatal accident, too.*

She was rather looking forward to that. Derek had cost her dearly in the past month or so. Her nerves were fried; as scorched as the remains of the amps now being carted away by the members of the band.

All that power—right in my hands, and she took it away from me. That bitch. I should have known what she was when she started draining the Maypole. I planned that ceremony, and the power I was to get from it. I planned everything, right down to the costume, the copy of the one I used to wear, and that was a bitch to have sewn. That power was mine, I earned it, I set it up, and she stole it. And I lost even more fighting her. Fay's jaw clenched. *Then she nearly gave me a stroke with backlash. If I hadn't had shunts set up into the Servant, I'd be unconscious. I want that power back, and I want it back now! And I want her gone!*

Her hands caressed Deke's back automatically. Her mind seethed with anger. *Sandy. He was useful as a smoke screen during the confrontation, but not as useful as I hoped. Someone just might tell Deke we were off necking, and I don't need that. I hadn't intended to get rid of him quite so soon, but he's a nuisance, and he's been worked up to the proper pitch. And I've got everything I need right here with me.*

Then home, and I drain Deke, then some coke, bennies—that's another thing modern times are good for. Drugs. I'd have had to make do without the boost. Coke was the only stimulant I could get back then.

Right. A new plan. I should have set one up beforehand. Never mind, it doesn't matter. This will probably work out better in the long run.

The dance came to an end, and Deke pulled reluctantly away from her. She smiled up into his glazed eyes. "I've done my little duty," she whispered. "I'm not in the mood for dancing, or for putting up with Sandy anymore. He acts like he's high, or something. I think we should go home." She licked her lips sensuously. "I can think of other things to do tonight besides dance. You still have the keys, don't you?"

"Right here," he said, blinking owlishly at her.

"Then why don't you go get the car. I'll meet you at the front entrance."

He blinked again, then turned away from her and wound his way through the crowd. She'd had him park at the back of the lot, in a place she knew would be hard to get out of once the lot started to fill. And *he* knew if he so much as scratched the paint on the Shelby, he'd never hear the last of it.

So that would keep him occupied for a good fifteen or twenty minutes. Long enough to deal with Sandy.

The Servant was also here, having driven the Merc over, playing the doting relative right down to bringing the camera and taking pictures of her being crowned. She sidled through the crowd until she came to its side.

"I need the drug," she said softly.

The Servant handed her the packet, but didn't let go of it.

"I believe this is a mistake," the Servant replied, just as quietly. "I do not think this is a wise decision on your part."

Fay resisted the urge to tear the tiny packet of PCP out of the Servant's hand. "You aren't *supposed* to think," she told it coldly. "You're supposed to do as I order you."

"You created me to see to your well-being." The Servant's expression was calm and serene. "I am attempting to perform that function. You have not been acting in a wise or thoughtful manner of late. You have been impulsive, irrational; you have been acting, if I may say so, like a child. This unreasoning insistence on ridding your path of that girl-chit, for instance. She is no threat to you, except that you make her one. Perhaps it is because of the stresses on this body you wear, perhaps the transfer was more of a strain than you had guessed, or perhaps you have indulged too much in spirits and drugs—"

"I've lived over three hundred years, and I've made the transfer more times than I remember," Fay whispered angrily. "I know what I'm doing now! And *you* are nothing but a puppet I created to serve me!"

"Very well." The Servant released its hold on the packet. "I exist but to serve you."

"And you would do well to remember that." Fay palmed the packet of PCP and shook her hair back. "Wait until you see Sandy going after that little Carlin bitch, then follow him. I want to make sure nothing goes wrong."

The Servant looked as if it would like to say something, but then shrugged slightly and nodded. Fay bit her lip angrily, and only the sweet taste of blood made her wake up to what she was doing. *I think it's time, and more than time, to be rid of that thing. It's outlived its usefulness. Damn. It couldn't have picked a worse moment to go independent on me. I'll have to create a new one at a time when my reserves are a lot lower than they should be. Then again . . . I did want to kill something tonight. . . .*

She turned her back on the Servant, letting it see how angry she was with it, and regretfully abandoned the idea of destroying it tonight. *No, I'd better be a little more careful than that. It's possible I'll have to keep the thing around longer than I would like. Unless . . .*

Unless I can persuade Sandy to extreme excess.

She licked her lips thoughtfully, as she spotted Sandy spiking the punch bowl with Everclear.

Perhaps I can, she thought, fingering the little packet in her hand. *Perhaps, with the help of this, I can. And rid myself of Monica as well.*

FOURTEEN

Fay threaded her way through the crowd, smiling and nodding at those who made eye contact with her, but not devoting a great deal of attention to anyone except Sandy. She reached his side just as he poured the last of the bottle into the punch bowl and slipped the bottle up his sleeve.

"Hey, lover," she murmured, slipping up behind him and sliding her arms around him from the back. He turned, a little clumsily; she avoided his elbow and snuggled up against him again before he'd even noticed that she'd pulled away.

"I've got something better than *that* with me," she whispered. He grinned and nuzzled her neck; the booze on his breath was enough to get her high just by contact.

"Well, why don't you just work a little magic and produce it, hm?" he mumbled, working his tongue into her ear.

"Not *here*," she protested, with a little giggle. "I've only got enough for the two of us. Let's go out back, okay?"

She wriggled neatly out of his grasp, and caught up his hand before he could protest. She tugged impatiently when he blinked dully at her, and he finally followed her, like the fool he was, through the crowd, past the double glass exit doors and the Servant, out to the second parking lot behind the cafeteria.

Once there, his instincts took over, and he pulled *her* into the shadows beyond the lighted doorway. She allowed him to back her into a corner, encouraging him with hands and lips and tongue. The stiffened, low-cut bodice of her dress allowed him nearly as much access as if she'd been bare-chested, a fact no few of the ladies of Fay's acquaintance back in her youth were very familiar with.

When she thought he was sufficiently engrossed, she extracted the packet of PCP from the pannier of her dress, palmed it, and placed it against the side of his neck. Once it was in place, she used some of the last of her magic to dissolve the gel of the packet and leach the drug directly into the major vein in his neck.

He started a little when it first began to seep in and pulled away, sensing that something was out of the ordinary, perhaps. He made as though he was about to say something; she drew his head down with her free hand and opened her mouth under his.

He took the hint.

She kept him occupied and under control until the drug had a chance to get into his brain; then, when she could tell by his increasing aggressiveness that it was hitting him, she let loose her second spell.

It was a hypnotic, and one she'd used on him before, though never in tandem with PCP. He stiffened and stood up rigidly straight as the spell took effect.

"Relax," she ordered, and he did so. She pulled his head down against her shoulder and stared off into the bright-and-dark patterns of shadow and parking lot lights as she whispered her orders into his ear. . . .

At length he pulled away from her and went back into the cafeteria. She waited a moment, then strolled casually around the outside of the building until she reached the front portico, where she waited for Deke.

It was pleasant enough out here; a little chilly, but not bad. The wind had died down sometime during the duel she'd had with that witch. There was dust all over everything, but she sat down on one of the concrete benches under the portico anyway. She wouldn't be wearing this dress again, so it didn't much matter if it got soiled. Having it made and wearing it had been a purely symbolic act, to accent her differences from the rest of the world and to evoke the mood of bygone times when it had been her indentured peasants performing the Maypole rite.

Well, that gets Sandy and *that little nuisance Monica out of my life,* she thought with angry satisfaction. *Even if the Tregarde woman is protecting her arcanely, she won't be looking for a physical attack. And when Sandy gets done with the little tart, at the very least she'll be ready for a nice, long stay in a hospital. He might even kill her; I'm not sure how far he'd go if she fought back. And even if all he does is damage her, they'll put Sandy away in the juvenile home so fast he won't even know what's happened. Even all his daddy's money and influence won't buy him out from under a charge of rape and assault under the influence of an illegal drug.*

The Servant was presumably following him to make certain nothing interfered until the Carlin bitch had learned her lesson. Fay folded her hands in her lap, and nodded to herself. This was as foolproof a plan as she'd ever come up with. Even though her primary plan had failed, she was still able to come up with backups on an instant—and the power released by the pain and fear of a budding mage was worth that of all the ordinary children at the dance put together. Now all she needed was a way to negate the Tregarde woman.

Retrench and cool off. Plan ahead. Don't let a little failure throw you into confusion. . . .

Yes—the Tregarde woman could wait. If she'd known what Fay was, she'd have attacked directly, instead of working through the guitar. So she hadn't figured out who her enemy was. She had no notion of Fay's resources, nor would she ever be able to learn where Fay's major Power Place was. She would probably think tonight's failure would set Fay back enough that she wouldn't be able to counterattack for days.

Little do you know. First Monica, then you, witch. I wonder what it is you want? Maybe I ought to let you make your offer before I shut you down. How long were you going to string Monica along before you used her? And I wonder what on earth the Kestrels offered you to protect their brat. . . .

Deke was pulling up next to the portico in her Shelby; the night was young, and she had more plans for insinuating herself even more deeply into his emotions.

She smiled sweetly at him as he leapt out of the car and ran to hold the passenger-side door open for her.

She rose, and he looked at her uncertainly. "Do you—" he said awkwardly, holding out the keys.

"Oh no, not tonight," she murmured, caressing his arm lingeringly as she passed him. "No, tonight *you* drive, lover. I'll just sit here and—relax."

And she snuggled up against his shoulder as he pulled the car out onto the street.

When I get done with you tonight, little boy, you'll never even think about anyone else ever again.

The kids swirled past the eastern corner of the cafeteria, avoiding it, and not at all aware that they were doing so. Di had managed to

track down the young psi who'd inadvertently found himself stuck in
the cross fire, and she didn't want to be disturbed while she talked to
him.

"... so there was just some real heavy shit going down, and you
got caught in the middle," Di told the green-eyed youngster, feeling
quite apologetic and a little defensive. "I'm sorry, but sometimes
these things just happen."

The boy who was Spring Thing, or King, or whatever, drifted by
them. Di didn't much care for his glazed eyes and rigidly set expression, but he wasn't doing anything out of line, so she ignored him for
the moment.

"Yeah, I guess." The kid rubbed the back of his neck and looked
around uneasily. "Weird things kind of happen around me, always
have, but I can't say I like it."

"I can't say I blame you." Di shrugged. "It could be worse, trust
me. You could have my job."

"What, writing romances? Ooo, pretty scary." The kid seemed to
be recovering his aplomb fairly quickly. "Or did you mean cruising
high schools for wicked witches?"

She gave him a raised eyebrow. "I'm the only witch around here
that I've been able to spot—" *Wait a minute, did he pick up something
I missed? Could the sorcerer be a female? Hell, why not? I'd been thinking "he," but there wasn't a sex signature on the spell casting.* "—and
last time I looked I was on the side of the angels," she finished without missing a beat. "Unless you know something I don't."

He spread his hands in a gesture of denial. "Hey, not me, lady! I
like to keep my profile low, if you know what I mean." He glanced
significantly down past his feet. "I wouldn't want to wake anybody
up, you know? I hang around the art classes so I don't stand out . . .
much."

"Not much more than an anthurium in a bouquet of daisies," she
replied dryly.

"Tasteful comparison." He smiled wickedly.

She was about to make a scathing retort, when every alarm she'd
put on Monica went off at once.

Lady Bright! She didn't even stop to excuse herself; she just
whirled and set off at a dead run for the opposite entrance to the
cafeteria. Somewhere outside that door Monica was in deep, deep
trouble, something no shield could handle—and even if Di *hadn't*
put those alarms on her, the emotional distress she was giving off
would have alerted Di to the emergency. She ignored exclamations

and protests as she ducked through the crowd, shoving people out of the way if necessary. She was vaguely aware that the kid was following her; she hoped he had the sense to know when to stay out of the way.

All her training told her that there was some serious mayhem going on outside. And now that she wasn't juggling magic, she could and would do something about it.

She stiff-armed the doors at top speed; they flew open and she dove through them, then stopped dead. She peered through the dust-laden air, trying to spot her quarry in the crowded expanse of the back parking lot. The wind had stopped after her duel with the sorcerer, but the dust that had been kicked up was still sifting down, making a haze that was hard to see through when the lights from the parking lot shone on it.

But then she spotted movement and heard an angry shriek; the combatants reeled into the pool of brightness under one of the parking lot lights. She took off like a sprinter, trying to identify them as she ran. The aggressor was the Spring King, and he was making chutney out of Deke's hacker-buddy.

Gods—what the hell is going on here? Who started what?

She noticed that Monica was not doing the expected—she *wasn't* standing out of the way and screaming like a ninny. She was trying to pull the jock off, dragging at his collar and beating on his head with her shoe.

Good Lord . . .

It wasn't doing a lot of good; he was paying about as much attention to her as he would have to a mosquito.

In fact, in the next second, he shrugged Monica off. She went tumbling across the pavement. The hacker flung himself at the jock, and took one on the chin that sent him down—so for the moment, the fighters were separated by about three feet. That would be enough. Di put on an extra burst of speed and blindsided the jock with her shoulder, knocking him off balance and sending him staggering into a car. She bounced off him in a more controlled manner, and used the momentum of her bounce to position herself between him and the other two kids.

Before he had even begun to recover, she was in a balanced, "ready" stance, and—

—dropped back an involuntary step as he focused on her and the sheer force of his rage carried the blind emotion and some of his thoughts past her shielding.

It felt like a blow to the temple. But more startling were the images she got. The hacker hadn't been his primary target; *Monica* was. The hacker just got in the way when he went after her, and scrambled neurons took over.

Now Di was the one in the way. And the glazed look in his eyes wasn't from spiked punch, either. The yellowish sodium-vapor light glared down on both of them as she tried to figure out what he was on. It was something that was making him oblivious to pain, something kicking his adrenaline into "high" and shutting off his reasoning processes entirely.

He seemed paralyzed for a moment, and she took her opportunity to drop shields and "read" him quickly.

Holy— There were the magical fingerprints she'd been searching for in vain all over his psyche.

"Lady!" She recognized the voice of the green-eyed kid. He was yelling from behind the shelter of a parked car to her left. "Lady, watch it! I think he's dusted!"

Now everything made some sense. *Angel dust, PCP, yeah, that would explain it. But not the tampering with his mind. Somebody was finally a little careless, and as soon as I get a minute, I'm going to find out exactly who . . . if I get that minute.*

So *that* was the picture; the unknown had decided to go after Monica mundanely. Sending someone else to do his dirty work.

"I'm getting the principal!" the kid shouted from the darkness, as she heard him take to his heels. "Don't let him grab you!"

Great advice, kid. Now tell me how *to keep him from grabbing me!*

She concentrated on the jock, and saw the tensing of his muscles that meant he was going to rush her; she stood her ground until the very last minute, then danced out of the way.

And tried to remember what she knew about angel dust. *PCP is going to sharpen his reflexes; he's already a trained athlete and he outweighs me by a bunch, and right now I could break both his arms and he wouldn't even notice.*

He bounced off the car and spun, faster than she would have given him credit for; he spotted her again and lunged for her. She escaped by a hair, and only by kicking the back of his knee and following that with a punch to his kidneys. And although the contact was solid and would probably leave a bruise the size of her head, it just barely staggered him.

She sensed his attention wavering for a moment, as if something was trying to "reset" him. *Oh hell. Monica is over there playing Florence Nightingale to her boyfriend. Great, just great. I'd better make sure I keep myself between him and them, or he may go for them instead of me.*

In fact, at that same moment he spotted them, and his attention was split between Monica and Di for a second.

Then it centered on Monica, and he took one step in the girl's direction.

Oh bloody hell. Better get him back . . .

She pulled a flying side kick just to wake him up a little. She connected better than she'd had any reason to hope; he went reeling into the trunk of a Caddy, and hit it with both forearms, with enough force to dent the trunk lid. She came down much too close to him for her own comfort and skipped out of his reach with adrenaline sending little electric chills down her back.

When he turned around and spotted her again, his attention wasn't divided at all.

His face twisted into a snarl of completely unthinking rage. *Great, Tregarde. Now he wants to kill you. Smooth move.* His anger clawed at the outside of her shields and she winced at the impact of it.

Then something occurred to her, and she took a closer "look" as she skipped sideways to avoid his lunges at her.

Wait a minute. He's wide open. If he can affect me, even though he's a normal, I'll be able to hit him! Maybe that's why his buddy used it on him; dust must leave normals open to magic and suggestion.

"Hey!" she yelled, wanting to make sure he focused on her entirely. She waved her arms at him, as if he was an animal she was trying to herd. "Hey!"

He focused *entirely* on her; his whole world narrowed to just her, and he lunged for her.

She backpedaled, gathered her strength, then let him have it with a full-force psi-bolt; if it worked on him the way it would work on a psychic . . .

It hit him just as he lurched forward.

The result was spectacular; his eyes suddenly rolled up into his head, and he plowed face-first into the asphalt at her feet, like a stunned ox.

She stopped backpedaling, and heaved a sigh of relief. *Well, that was—*

"*Look out!*" Monica screamed.

She glimpsed movement out of the corner of her eye, and she spun to one side, narrowly avoiding the attack of—something.

It was human-shaped, but its aura said that it wasn't any such thing; it was mage-created. An artificial construct.

Which didn't matter except that it was likely to be faster than she was—and as impervious to pain as the dusted jock.

It had leapt out of the shadows and back into them so quickly she didn't have a chance to see or sense more than that. It snarled, hidden deeply in the shadows between two cars; a hoarse rasp that didn't sound like anything human. Di sensed that it was going to attack again.

All this registered in the time it took her to jump away and orient herself.

If it's made by magic, magic will take it down. And I've been playing High Priestess all night. I may be tired, but I've got a full charge, and I'll bet it doesn't know that.

Before the thing had a chance to move a second time, she got ready to hit it, this time with a levin-bolt, a torpedo of pure magical energy.

She caught it just as it sprang at her and entered the pool of light; it spread-eagled there, caught by the force of the blast, shrieking. It stood there for just a moment, arms thrown wildly over its head, face twisted and contorted. Then it was gone.

Entirely.

But in that moment before it winked out, Di had a chance to scan it briefly, and the unknown's fingerprints were all over it, too.

Gotcha. By the gods. She slumped against the trunk of a car, her knees going weak with reaction. *As soon as I deal with the wounded, friend, I'm going to have you dead to rights.*

She looked down and to her right, at the prone body of the dusted jock. Amazingly enough, the jock was moving, groaning; starting to come to and actually trying to lever himself off the ground.

"Jesus Cluny Frog," Di muttered. "I don't believe this! What's it take to stop this guy, a tank?"

She stalked over to his side, and stared down at him. He was definitely trying to struggle to his feet and to full consciousness.

Hang if I'm going to waste another psi-bolt on him.

She removed one of her flats, weighed it thoughtfully in her hand and gave him a scientifically placed tap on the head with the heel— one well weighted with another psi-bolt. He gave a grunt, and collapsed back onto the pavement.

She slipped her shoe back on, and walked slowly over to the other two just as the vice-principal came puffing up in the wake of the green-eyed kid.

She ignored both of the new arrivals for the moment; she wanted to assess the damage to the two victims.

Though the sodium-vapor lights didn't do much for either kids' looks, the hacker was obviously the most damaged, so Di concentrated on him.

In contrast, Monica looked a little disheveled, and one sleeve of her dress was torn, but she was mostly radiating anger, not shock or pain.

Honey, you were lucky. You don't know how lucky.

Di hunched down next to the two of them; Monica was helping support the boy in a sitting position, and holding a handkerchief to his bleeding nose.

"I don't think anything's broken," the girl said hesitantly, looking up at her. "He can move everything, and he's not dizzy; he said he just hurts a lot."

"I'll bet he does," Di said absently. She tilted the boy's head up so she could see his eyes. Both pupils reacted equally, and though his nose was bleeding, it didn't look too badly damaged. "I don't think you're concussed," she said. "Although I think a real doctor ought to look at you. You're going to have a lot of bruises and a pair of black eyes that are going to make you look like a raccoon in the morning, but other than that, I think you're going to be okay. How are *you* feeling?" she asked, turning to Monica.

The girl scowled. "I'd like to rip Sandy's head off and shove it up his—" She caught herself, and took a deep breath to calm herself. "I'm sorry. I'm mad, that's how I feel."

"Good. You should be." Di stood up slowly.

She had gotten a pretty good chance to assess the vice-principal earlier, and she had a fair idea of what his notion of "handling the situation" would be. Basically, he'd try to cover it up. *CYA, you officious little bastard. Well, not this time.*

She scowled at the vice-principal, putting everything she'd ever learned in dealing with overweening idiots into her glare. "Well," she said. "You certainly have a *fine* school system here."

The vice-principal was taken rather by surprise. He'd obviously been preparing to bluster right over her, intimidate her into keeping her mouth shut, forgetting that she *wasn't* one of his teachers.

"Wh-what?" he stammered.

"Just a *fine* school system," she repeated acidly, "where some lame-brained jock stoned to his eyebrows on PCP can attack two perfectly harmless kids and *then* try to beat up a helpless woman. Wonderful. Just *wonderful.* I really admire the level of control you have over these kids."

"I—uh—"

"You—" she continued, turning to the green-eyed boy, who was obviously enjoying all this to the hilt. "Go call an ambulance. *That* idiot over there should be under restraints when he wakes up. And *this* poor child should see a doctor. A real doctor, in a real emergency room."

"Yes *ma'am*," the kid said with relish.

"Don't you—uh—think it would be better if we called the students' parents and let them handle it?" the vice-principal said weakly.

She gave him a look that made him shrink at least two inches. "No," she replied, venom dripping from each word. "I don't." She turned to raise an eyebrow at the young psychic. "What are you waiting for?"

"Not a thing, ma'am," he said quickly, and trotted off toward the school.

Twice more the vice-principal tried to convince Di to let him call the parents and cancel the ambulance. Each time she withered him with a glance. She knew damned well what he was up to; when the hospital got hold of Sandy they'd run a blood test, and there would be no covering up what he was on. And that would make local headlines, for certain.

The kid was quick. The ambulance arrived before Sandy came to again, and before the vice-principal could make up his mind to push any harder.

Di made quite certain that the paramedics knew what she knew. "Listen," she said quietly as the first of them bailed out of the emergency vehicle and grabbed his kit. "The only reason the cops aren't here is because nobody got seriously hurt."

That stopped him in his tracks. He took a good look at the vice-principal hovering in the background, at the hacker, and at the unconscious jock.

"So?" He took his time about setting up. "Why don't you tell me more?"

Di did.

He had a quiet little consultation with his partner when she got finished giving him the facts. She couldn't help but notice that afterward they were very gentle with the young hacker—and *very* careful about securing the jock to the gurney with some heavy restraining belts. . . .

She leaned against one of the cars, feeling every bruise, mental and physical. *Ye gods. This is more than enough for one night. And I still have to use those little traces I picked up to figure out who's behind this.*

She blanked for a minute, lost in weariness. She shook herself awake as the vehicle pulled away, with the jock in the back guarded by one of the paramedics, and the hacker in the front with the other.

Monica refused treatment, and Di wasn't going to force her. The girl stood staring after the flashing lights of the ambulance, dark shadows under her eyes.

"Okay, kiddo," Di said, coming up behind her. "Now what do you want to do? You could go talk to the cops if you want to press charges. *I'm* certainly thinking about it."

Out of the corner of her eye she saw the vice-principal wince and pale.

"I just want to go home," Monica said tiredly. "I just want to forget this ever happened."

"If that's what you want, I'll take you," Di offered, before the vice-principal could say anything. "I've about had enough for one night." She leveled one last icy stare at the man. "Tell Ann Greeley I'm giving up, please. I'm just about chaperoned out."

The green-eyed kid had vanished somewhere after calling the ambulance. *Just as well,* she thought. *I'm not up to much more tonight.* "Come on, Monica, my car's over in the front lot."

"But—" the vice principal protested weakly. They both ignored him, and walked off together into the darkness, shoes clicking in unison on the pavement.

"How awful do I look?" Monica asked mournfully, when they were out of hearing distance.

Di smothered a chuckle. "Not bad, really. I don't think that sleeve's going to be repairable, though. If I were you, I'd just cut the other one off, too. Might make a nice little sleeveless number with some careful tailoring."

"I don't think I ever want to wear it again," the girl said in a subdued voice. "Not ever." She glanced at Di out of the corner of her eye. "Diana—what—really happened back there?"

Di pulled the last of the pins out of her hair and shook it loose. "Whoever was after you went after you again," she replied, checking her dress for damage. There wasn't much that a good dry cleaner couldn't handle—the one advantage of expensive materials and tailoring. "This time he—or she, I'm not sure which—went after you physically, probably thinking I wouldn't be guarding you against that kind of attack. He got that meathead stoned on PCP and sent him out to beat you up. Your boyfriend just got in the way."

"Oh," Monica said, in a small and frightened voice. "I thought it was just—I mean, everybody knows Sandy does drugs, I thought—"

"Trust me. It was deliberate, and aimed at you," Di said firmly. "Monica, you can't keep telling yourself that this is all just something that isn't really happening. It *is* happening, and denying it isn't going to make you any safer. Wasn't it you who warned me about that other thing?"

Monica shuddered, and shrank in on herself. "I thought it was just one of Sandy's buddies."

They had reached the car, and Di unlocked the passenger's door for her. "Did you?" she asked, holding the door open so that Monica could get in.

"No," the girl said unhappily. "I guess I didn't."

"Good," Di said, climbing into the driver's side and sighing as her tired body sank into the upholstery. "Now we're finally getting somewhere. . . ."

Monica's mother—blessings on the fates—had been so worried about Monica that she hadn't asked too many personal questions of Di, and she hadn't wasted any time getting the child into the apartment.

That gets one child safely home. And I don't think I want to be Sandy's parents when Rhonda Carlin gets hold of them. Assuming she doesn't call the cops first. Thank the gods it isn't much farther to my own bed.

Di drove up into Larry's driveway feeling weary to the bone, and all she really wanted to do was go have a hot shower and go to bed.

Fat chance. There was still work to do.

Deke's car wasn't in the garage, which meant he wasn't home yet; well, it wasn't even midnight, so that wasn't too surprising.

If I'm going to try tracking down this bastard—or bitch—I don't want anyone untrained around anyway. Not even one of the targets.

She let herself in with her key. Larry wasn't obviously around, which meant he was either buried in his office or watching a videotape in his bedroom. She doubted he would have Felt the ruckus; that wasn't one of his abilities. Just the Sight, and a little bit of other things. That was just as well; she didn't want to tell him what had happened just yet. Not until she had all the information in her possession.

So, first things first; the hot shower. She emptied her mind and let the needle-spray wash all her weariness down the drain with the dirt and perspiration from the fight. That was a little mental trick that usually worked for her, at least for the short term, and it did this time, too. As she'd thought, her dress, amazingly enough, was in perfect shape, except for a couple of stains that would wash out. Well,

perhaps not so amazing; it was heavy silk and cost a small fortune—
but was worth it, seeing the amount of abuse it could take and
bounce back from.

*Think next time I make a ritual robe it'll be silk. It'll probably out-
last me.*

She braided her wet hair and coiled it in a knot at the back of her
neck, slipped on a leotard and jeans, and laid out four candles in the
middle of the rug. This was the "quickie" version of a protective circle; she lit each of the candles in turn, evoking the powers of the four
compass quarters, and then sank to the floor in a cross-legged position and picked up the threads of magic she'd detected on the jock,
and on the construct.

She let herself drift into a light trance. *Now to follow the traces
back to where and when they were created. That should keep my quarry
from sensing what I'm doing; if I invoke retro-cognition he won't send
up any alerts in the here and now.*

Unless of course he's laid a trap back there for me. She acknowledged the possibility, then dismissed it. *That's the chance I'll have to
take, I guess.*

She allowed all the identifying factors to sink into her mind, the
way a bloodhound would memorize a scent. Then, like the bloodhound, she began "sniffing" for that same scent.

But this time she was sniffing about in the recent past; about two
hours ago, to be precise. Just *after* the duel, when the sorcerer presumably set his compulsion on jock Sandy.

Ha! She found the "scent"; followed it back to the moment
when it was strongest, then invoked that rather wayward Talent of
retro-cognition—the ability to "see" things happening at some time
in the past.

That involved putting herself another layer deeper in trance, then
disconnecting her "self" from the here-and-now; when it worked, she
generally got a little lurch of dislocation and disorientation.

Even though her eyes were closed, she felt that identifying surge
of dizziness—and suddenly she was "there," right outside the cafeteria door, getting a camera's-eye view of the entire scene.

Sure enough, there was good old Sandy, putting the make on the
Spring Queen—

Or was he?

He *wasn't,* she realized. He was just standing there, not moving at
all. And the spell casting that was swirling around like a blood-
colored haze about Sandy and the girl was centered on the girl.

And there were webs of power tying the girl to a woman Ann had said was her aunt, when the chaperons were introduced to each other. She was standing just inside the cafeteria door.

Aunt? Well, the woman *looked* just fine, but not to Di's enhanced senses. The so-called aunt was the construct who'd attacked Di earlier tonight.

And yes, constructed by that little adolescent brat.

It didn't make any *sense*! No eighteen-year-old girl should have that kind of power!

Her own surprise was enough to tip the delicate balance of powers in her own magic, and Di felt her grasp on the scene slipping. She *could* try to get the vision back, but—the Talent was unpredictable. And it didn't feel as if it was likely to cooperate again tonight.

She drifted back up out of trance, and finally opened her eyes on her perfectly mundane bedroom, feeling stunned and a little confused.

This is crazy! No kid that age is going to have the kind of acquired skill and patience it takes to work spells like that!

She blinked, and thought about it again. *Okay, I could be wrong. Look at Olympic athletes; at eighteen they've got that kind of skill and patience. It's obviously a fact; I can't change it. Fay Harper is the sorcerer.*

Which explains the attack on Monica; she's a rival. She may even be moving in on Deke for all I know. And it explains the feeling of threat Larry had concerning Deke. That gal is a man-eater if ever I saw one, and if she's a magician, there's more ways than one she can take to use a guy up.

Oh, shit. They arrived together; by now they've probably left together. Deke's with her now!

She didn't need to be in trance to check on him. All she had to do was close her eyes and relax; the shields and alarms she put on top of Larry's protections were easy enough for her to track. Usually.

But when she finally picked them up, they were very faint.

She's got the kid on her territory, she realized. *Under her shields and her protections. Hell. I can't go in after him. I don't even know exactly where her territory is. It might be her house; it might not. And five'll get you ten she got her hooks into him before I even set the shields.*

She opened her eyes again and ground her teeth in frustration. *I've got no choice,* she decided. *It's going to have to wait until after Deke gets home. I don't think she'll try anything tonight. Even if she does, he's got Larry and Miri's stuff on him. She can't kill him; consensual hooks won't allow that. She can't even drain him dry. And I think she's planning on something for him. Hell, she's only seventeen, eighteen—if she was finished with her toy, she wouldn't have taken his escort at the dance.*

I hope I was a good teacher. Larry and Miri's shields have held so far. I hope they still do.

And he's got my stuff on him. At least I know that line of work better than she does. I don't think she can do anything to him I can't counter. I don't think she can work any permanent damage through those old hooks.

I hope it'll be enough.

Scratch that; I just hope she doesn't *try anything. That's* my *best hope at the moment. I hope she isn't thinking beyond the moment and the Sex Magick she plans to do to him. I hope destroying her construct gives her a migraine and she sends him home! I don't think she could have ID'd me in all that mess, so at least I'm in the clear on that. That should buy us the time we need.*

She pulled both her knees up to her chest and hugged them, staring at the northern candle.

And I'll have to go dig up Larry and tell him the truth. Then we're going to have to figure out what we're going to do about her. Shut her down, obviously. If she keeps playing around recklessly with magical energy the way she has, she'll wake up the One Below.

Good night, I don't even want to think about that.

No, this is going to take more than just me, or even just me and Larry. I need a third set of hands. It can't be Bill, he's busy—

Mark. Mark Valdez.

She pulled herself up off the floor, blew out the four candles, uncast the circle, then plodded wearily over to the bed and the bedside table that held the phone.

Looked like the night had just started.

She dialed Mark's number after consulting her phone list in her purse. It rang twice, then—thank the Lord and Lady—was picked up.

"Valdez," said a familiar voice.

"Mark?" she said hesitantly. "I'm not interrupting anything, am I?"

A quiet chuckle. "Di. No, though if it had been last night you might have. Sherry's out of town doing a trade show; she won't be back until Thursday. The grandparents have the munchkin. Aunt Nita offered to take him, but Sherry wouldn't hear of it."

"Sounds like things are progressing—" She made the statement into a question.

He chuckled again. "With patience. And fortunately, most of the designers she meets seem to be either married or gay. Or both. So, what can I do for you?"

"You working this weekend?"

"No," he replied. "I'm collecting some comp time and catching up on my sleep. Or I *was*. I take it you have other plans?"

She sighed with relief. "I do. How soon this morning can you catch a plane up to Tulsa? I'll make a reservation for you by phone and have the ticket waiting at the airport. . . ."

It was going to be a very long night.

FIFTEEN

It was three a.m. by Deke's watch when he pulled his car into the garage. It felt later than that; *days* later.

He'd barely managed to get home. He'd been tempted to stay with Fay, and only the nagging of his conscience telling him that his dad would worry if he didn't come home by dawn got him out and moving. He felt as if he were running on fumes, and three quarts low to boot. It had been one strange night.

He managed to get the car in beside his dad's Z without damaging anything, although he did run the tires into one of the concrete parking bumpers Larry had installed. He'd put them in all three slots to keep the family from inadvertently shoving their vehicles into first instead of reverse and totaling both car and insurance rates. Tonight Deke was glad of the things; he might well have put his car's nose right through the garage wall and never have noticed, as tired as he felt.

He was almost tempted just to fall asleep in the front seat.

Then I'll wake up with a stiff neck. Nope. Not worth it. I want my bed.

He dragged himself out of the car, wincing a bit as some of the muscles he'd strained complained at him.

Keep this up, and I'll be a damned sexual athlete too. Or dead of exhaustion. Whichever comes first.

Fay had vanished for a moment, pleading a sudden migraine, just as they got to her house. He thought she was going to let him cool his heels to humiliate him, but when she'd come back, pale and wan looking, she'd been all over him. Somehow, some way, he'd managed to give her everything she asked for. He still wasn't quite certain how. And he'd come real close to believing in vampires tonight, what with the way she leeched onto him, and because he felt absolutely drained when she finally turned him loose to go home.

He didn't expect the house lights to still be on when he opened the garage door. And he doubly didn't expect his dad's voice to call out to him from the living room.

"Deke—would you please come in here a minute?"

Oh shit. Now what have I done? I don't have a curfew on the weekend, and I didn't drink anything. Thank God. And I didn't do anything out of line at the dance.

"Dad, I'm *really* beat," he called back. "Can't it wait until tomorrow?"

"I'm afraid not." His dad actually sounded apologetic. "Please, we really need to talk to you."

Oh shit. His heart suddenly sank as the fact that his dad had said "*we* need to talk to you" sunk in. There was only one other person in the house this late at night.

Diana Tregarde.

Oh shit. I was right. They've been having an affair. He's going to tell me he wants a divorce from Mom . . . and that he's in love with that Tregarde lady.

Sure enough, when he reached the entrance to the living room, they *both* were there, Diana and his father. It sure looked like a setup for the "D" word.

But they weren't sitting together. In fact, his dad was sprawled out over the couch, while Diana, looking as dragged-out as Deke felt, was curled up in one of the overstuffed chairs.

They weren't dressed up, either, and that was the way his friends at school had said It Was Done.

"They always pick some weird time when you aren't expecting anything. First one of 'em, your dad or your mom, asks you to come talk about something. When you get there, the Significant Other's sitting real close, and they're both dressed up, like they want to impress you with how serious they are. Basically they look like they're going to a funeral. Then you get the Big Speech about how people change, and sometimes things don't last. . . ." That had been part of Jill's sarcastic little stand-up routine on "the 'D' word."

He waited hesitantly in the entrance for a moment, until his father gestured for him to come in.

"Come on and sit down, Deke," he said. "This is going to take a while, and you're going to be wanting to sit down for most of it."

That was one of "the lines" his friends had warned him about. *Oh holy shit. He is going to tell me he's getting a divorce.*

"Deke, this has been a very strange evening," his dad began awkwardly.

Deke sat gingerly on the edge of the sofa, positioned exactly between the two adults, thinking, *Yeah. I'll bet it has.*

"I think you know that Di volunteered to chaperone for the dance. . . ."

"Not exactly 'volunteered,' " Di muttered. "It was more like I was drafted."

Deke nodded, puzzled. This wasn't exactly what he'd been expecting.

"And before dinner you were swearing that you weren't going to take Fay—that you'd go alone."

He nodded. *Where the hell is* this *going?*

"Deke," Di said, "I saw you up on the stage as Fay's escort, and you left with her early in the dance. I figure that means you've been with her for most of the evening. So what changed your mind about her?"

Huh? He'd been all set for the big divorce speech; this took him totally off guard. "I—I don't know," he faltered. "I mean, I met Fay by accident at the gas station. I guess it was an accident; she couldn't have known I was going to go there. And we started talking and I just followed her over to her house, and—and I guess she talked me out of breaking up," he finished lamely. "It seemed a pretty cold thing to do to her, break up just before the prom, you know? I figured we could at least, like, keep up appearances until we graduated. And, I don't know, I started to like her all over again. I think she's changing. . . ."

"Judging by the way you look, I'd venture to say that you were keeping up more than 'appearances,' " Larry commented dryly.

Deke felt himself blushing.

"Larry, stop it," Diana said sharply. "Deke, think about it; that's important. When you *weren't* with her, you were thinking for yourself. But once you *were*, you were doing exactly what she wanted. Right?"

"Uh—I guess—" He couldn't think of a better response. "I mean, I sort of wanted it, too—"

"That's not what you said at four o'clock this afternoon," his father reminded him. "Wait a minute, don't say anything yet. Di's got some stuff she wants to tell you that is going to sound right out of Vinita, but I'll back her on it, one hundred percent."

Diana pushed a strand of hair out of her eyes with a tired little sigh. "Okay, here goes. First off, magic is real, and I'm a practicing witch."

Deke started to laugh; he couldn't help himself. "Oh come *on*," he said. "You're trying to weird me out, right? Or else you're saying this shit to see if I'm on something."

Di shook her head. "Larry-love, you pull your shields off him and I'll pull mine. Then we'll give him a demo. Don't worry, I've barricaded the house already; nothing less than a deity is going to break in."

"Christ, *that's* comforting," Larry replied sarcastically. "Considering what *you've* dealt with in the recent past."

"Give me a break," she retorted. "We're just dealing with something human where Deke is concerned. Just *do* it, okay?"

Deke looked from one to the other of them, seriously alarmed. *They've gone off the deep end. Or else* she *was already there, and she took Dad with her. Jesus Christ—*

But just about then was when he felt something leave him, something he hadn't noticed was there until it was gone, like when his ears cleared after being deadened when he had that case of flu and all of a sudden he could hear right again. He felt oddly naked, like his clothing had been stripped off without him noticing.

And *then,* when he looked up in startlement, he saw Diana—

Well, he saw *someone* in the chair she'd been sitting in.

But that someone looked a lot taller. And she glowed with a bright, hazy purple aura that haloed her entire body. Crackling blue energy crawled over both of her hands and arced across the space between them.

Maybe, if it had been daylight and he'd been rested, he *might* have handled it better. Maybe he'd even have been able to come up with a snappy comeback, like "Ever think about working for Steven Spielberg?" But it was late, and he was exhausted, and he *was not* prepared for any of this. Especially when the vision raised one of its hands and pointed at him.

He yelped, and lurched violently away from the apparition, and found himself tumbling over the back of the couch. He hit his head going over, and saw stars for a second.

When they cleared, his dad and Diana were bending over him, helping him to his feet, and they both looked perfectly normal. And that "clothed" feeling was back. He was *very* glad.

"How in hell did you do that?" he squeaked, his voice breaking like a kid's.

He sat down heavily on the couch as Diana and his father exchanged a look of weary amusement. "Magic," she said, shrugging.

He scowled. "That's not funny."

"No. But it's true." She went back to her chair and flung herself down into it. "Your dad and your mom and I used to work together in college. You know the movie *Ghostbusters*? Something like that, only we mostly used ourselves rather than gadgets. When we had the money for gadgets—which wasn't often, may I add—we used those to catch the phonies and expose them. *We,* with the Talents we were born with, did all the real ghostbusting."

He felt his jaw sagging open and closed it with a snap. "You? *Dad*? Jesus Christ—*Mom*?"

"Deke, do you remember that scrapbook your mother doesn't like to talk about?" his dad said, leaning his head on his hand. "That was us. The 'Spook Squad,' we called ourselves. The reason we haven't wanted to talk about our little adventures back then isn't that your mother and I have bad vibes about those days—we had a blast, actually. It's that—"

"It's that *you're* a psychic, kiddo," Diana interrupted, her head on the arm of the chair, her long hair brushing the floor beside it. "You have psis on both sides of the family, so that's hardly surprising. You showed real early that you have some kind of psychic Talents, and your folks didn't want you to freak when you were little. So they didn't talk about it, and they shielded you, so you wouldn't know. That 'shield' thing is what your dad and I just pulled *off* you, so you can figure the kinds of things you might have seen without it. And later on, well, no kid likes to be different from the other kids; it looked to them like you were no exception. And on top of that, since you didn't seem to want to believe in the stuff, they figured you didn't *need* to know about your abilities, at least until you were older, and maybe better able to handle having them."

"I—I'm a psychic?" he said weakly. "I am?"

"Sure," the writer said matter-of-factly. "Why do you think you saw me the way you did? That's *one* of your Talents. It's called the 'Sight,' or 'Second Sight.' You know, your dad has it, too; you can probably do other things, but we don't know what they are yet."

"I'm a psychic?" He gulped. "Does that mean I'm crazy?"

Diana gave a long-suffering sigh. "Am I crazy?"

"Well . . . let me get back to you on that."

"Thanks, kid." She grimaced, and her mouth tightened. "Now listen up; this is deadly serious, and I mean that quite literally. There's big danger in being psi, and you in particular have a problem right now. That's why your dad asked me to show up here. *He's* been getting the feeling that you were in danger for a couple of months now, but he couldn't tell where it was coming from. Your mom might have been able to, but she was in Japan. He started to really panic when you had that accident, and the feeling only got worse instead of going away. So when you came up with that business with your English class, it seemed to him like the perfect opening to see if I'd come on down and give him a hand in figuring out what the hell was going on. You know the rest."

This was all coming at Deke too fast. "I'm a psychic. And I'm in *danger*? From what?" He looked imploringly at his dad.

"She told you, I couldn't tell." His father shook his head. "That's not my area of expertise. All I knew was there was something out here that wanted *you*, that endangered you."

"Oh." He couldn't think of anything else to say.

"Okay, so I got down here, and from all the info I got, I figured your dad was right. But the first person that *I* saw attacked magically wasn't you. It was Monica Carlin." Diana looked at him expectantly. She probably wasn't disappointed by his reaction.

"Monica?" His voice broke again. "But—Monica?"

"Believe it," Di replied grimly. "And tonight I have the bruises to prove it. Because tonight it happened again, at the dance. And *tonight* I was in place to find out exactly who was after her, and why."

Then she proceeded to tell him a story about Monica and Alan that he *never* would have believed if his dad hadn't been sitting right there, nodding his head in agreement.

"And you can call Monica or Alan in the morning and ask them yourself," she concluded. "They *both* have physical injuries to prove that Sandy went after them, and they *both* saw the thing that attacked me after I put Sandy out. And they saw it vanish after I hit it with magic. But don't try calling Sandy, because you won't be able to reach him."

"Why not?" he asked dazedly.

"Monica's mother called the cops after Di took her home, and pressed charges," his father said, with grim satisfaction. "So did Alan's folks. The cops went over to the hospital, and as soon as the blood test came back positive for PCP, they hauled Sandy over to the juvenile detention wing."

"But—" Deke protested, bewildered. "Sandy wouldn't do dust. He's an athlete, they'd bust him off the team—and you *know* they're going to cancel the scholarship offer they made him for UO after this. He drinks like a fuckin' fish, but he'd never do anything that'd show up on a blood test!"

He was a little too tired to be careful of his language, but his dad didn't seem to notice.

"Exactly," Diana agreed. "That's the point. The person that

wanted Monica out of the way *got* him stoned to the gills on PCP, and did it in such a way that he wouldn't know she was slipping it to him. And that very same person is the one who created the creature that attacked me, and is the one that is posing a danger to you. Fay Harper."

"*What?*" he yelped.

"You heard her," his dad replied. "And I'm backing Di on this. It makes everything fall into place."

"She was after Monica because you were attracted to Monica, and she wanted the competition out of the way," Diana continued remorselessly. "She used Sandy probably because she'd used him up and he wasn't useful to her anymore, so she didn't care what happened to him. I went over there to the hospital after I figured out who our enemy was, and checked Sandy out. Honey, even without the dust, there isn't much left of him but some basic reactions and emotions. The boy's a burnout case if ever I saw one."

For the next hour or so, until the sky outside the picture windows began to lighten with the dawn, they alternated lucid, reasoned arguments about Fay. And the worst part of it was, the crazier the arguments were, the more they made sense.

Like the way I feel whenever I'm with her—like I can't think about anything except her, he thought, when Diana described how fascination spells ("the *real* meaning of the word 'enchantment'") worked on a guy's brains and hormones. *Like how when I'm with her, and I get bored or sick of the scene, and then she just turns and smiles at me and all of a sudden it's okay.*

And when she described, with the clinical detail of a Dr. Ruth, the way Sex Magick worked—well, that *really* hit him where he lived. Except he didn't want to talk about it. Not with his *dad,* for Chrissake.

And he really didn't want to admit just how deep Fay had gotten her hooks into him. So he just sat there and listened, and felt sicker and sicker. Then they asked him questions about Fay, a lot of which didn't make any sense. Like whether she had a little room with just a table in it, or owned a cabin somewhere. He answered them as best he could, but he realized with every question they asked how little he really knew about Fay. It was as if he never, ever saw anything of her outside of school, parties, and her bedroom.

When they finally finished with him, and he still hadn't said anything, they just sat and stared at him for a while, like they expected him to explode, or turn into a frog, or something.

His head hurt, his stomach hurt; he basically felt like hell. And he didn't even want to *think* about this anymore. Maybe in the morning it would all turn out to be a bad dream. And even if it didn't—

Well, he'd deal with it later.

Right now, *he* felt like a burnout case. And he wanted a chance to talk things over with Alan. And Monica.

And apologize, for real. Maybe they'd accept the excuse that Fay was messing with his head, after tonight.

"This's all too much for *me*," he said, throwing his hands up in the air. "I'm going to bed. And after that—I'm going to stay clear of Fay."

He waited for their reaction, wondering if they were going to jump him and tie him up or something. At the moment, anything seemed possible.

Instead, they just looked at each other, then at their empty coffee cups, then at the brightening sky outside. And shrugged.

"That's probably the smartest thing you've said in a week," Diana opined. "I think it's time we adjourned this little session."

"Sounds good to me," his dad replied, climbing up out of the depths of the couch. "Come on, old buddy." He held out his hand to his son.

Deke took it, and his dad hauled him to his feet while Diana extracted herself from the chair.

"After you, Alphonse," she said, gesturing to the two of them to proceed her up the stairs. They did; Deke's dad first, then Deke, then Di following after she'd turned out all the lights.

Deke pulled open the door to his room and started stripping off his clothes on the way to the bed, just leaving everything where he'd dropped it. He had just enough strength left to pull the covers over his head and turn out the light, but not one ounce more.

And just enough consciousness to think, before sleep descended like a lead curtain, *And to think I was afraid Dad and Diana were having an affair.*

Christ. Now I wish they were.

The alarm went off in Di's ear. She groaned, but hauled herself out of the tangle of blankets she'd created. It was too damn early in the morning, and she'd gotten less than three hours of sleep—

But Mark's plane was due within the next forty-five minutes, and she was going to have to be there to meet it. And she'd gotten by with less sleep before this.

She turned on the light, and headed for the bathroom to put herself into some semblance of order.

There were certain things she could do to kick her metabolism up and stave off weariness; certain disciplines she could invoke that would enable her to replace some lost sleep with food. They were temporary, and she'd pay for them later, but that would be *after* this whole mess was over with.

I need to move on this, and move on it fast, she thought grimly, telling her body what she would be requiring of it while she pulled on her clothing and brushed her teeth and hair. *Before too much longer, Fay is going to know who I am and that I'm the Enemy; she has to. I wasn't making any pretense at hiding, and besides, I'm the only new game in town. She's going to want my innards on a hook for destroying her Servant last night. If I'm lucky, she'll be at low power for the next few days and I can shut her down at a reasonable cost.*

Lady Bright, she's just a kid. . . . She was just using her power like any other kid would if you gave them that kind of—

Hell with that. I'm not a social worker, I'm a Guardian. I don't want to take her out, but if I can't reason with her, I'll have to. She's screwed up at least three kids that I know of, and who the hell knows what else she's been up to? And even if she really didn't think about what she was doing, or hasn't figured how wrong it is, she's putting too much strain on the local environment. Even without the One Below to think of, she's playing merry hell with the weather systems every time she does something major. Lady bless. These spoiled Jenks yuppie brats are all alike; don't think past their own noses and their own wants. Even Monica has a touch of bitch in her, and Deke's been trampling all over his own friends.

I hope this teaches them a lesson. I hope she's not as psychotic as some I've had to take down.

She was dressed, clean, and out the door with her keys in her hands within ten minutes of the alarm clock ringing. *I'm going to have to do this absolutely right, because I may not get a second chance,* she thought, as she pulled her car out of the driveway. *I want this confrontation on my terms, with me on the high ground and with my allies around me, and while I'm at full strength. So I'd better prioritize things before I pick Mark up, so I can give him a decent ops plan.*

There wasn't a great deal of traffic around on Saturday morning at seven a.m. She even accelerated onto the 169 on-ramp without the usual hassles of dealing with the local drivers, who didn't seem to understand the meaning of the word "merge." She cranked down her window to get some fresh, cold air on her face. It was almost as good as a cup of black coffee.

Number one priority has got to be to find the physical spot that this girl is using for her major ceremonies. I've never seen a sorcerer yet who put that *where he lived. She might be the exception, but I doubt it.*

High Magick was incredibly ritualized; most sorcerers had a small workroom where they could do simple spell casting and summoning, like Sex Magicks and simple Blood Magicks, but for the really major rituals, a huge room and some very specific trappings were required. In the old days of witchfinders, it was simply too dangerous to keep that sort of setup where you lived. And in modern times, it was too damned inconvenient. If you lived in an apartment building, had parents, nosy neighbors, or human servants—well, people tended to get really curious about cries and screams, strange people coming and going at odd hours, really awful stenches and clouds of smoke. . . . And Di didn't even want to think about the havoc that could result if somebody stumbled over even an innocent spell in progress. And with High Magick, that was increasingly likely the more skilled you were at it. The more elaborate rituals of High Magick tended to require a series of spells that would be cast over a period of days, or even weeks.

It was much safer to have a little vacation cabin somewhere, or a second place out in the country, out where there weren't a lot of people. And if you had the kind of money that Fay had, acquiring that sort of property was as simple as calling up a real-estate agent.

So she'll have her secret sanctum, and it will be someplace that she thinks is safe, but will be within about an hour's drive. She won't be willing to be farther away than that. It'll be some place that isn't public, that she can secure from interlopers and snoops.

She passed a slow-moving pickup and told her growling stomach that she'd give it a real good breakfast in about half an hour.

It didn't believe her, having heard this promise before.

I wish I could use Deke, but without training he's probably useless. So that leaves me and Larry to trance out and triangulate, and Mark to bodyguard and drive.

That place—wherever it was—would be the gate to Fay's main reserves of power. When they found it, they could do two things. Di could safely disrupt any major rituals that were in progress—and it was a pretty good bet that there *would* be one, and maybe more—and Mark and Larry could drain the power reserve while Di went off to confront Fay while she was at her weakest.

But it would all have to be done today. Before *she* realized that Di knew what she was doing. Before she had any idea that Di might go on the offensive.

That was the one advantage in dealing with a bad apple like Fay:

she'd probably assume Di was another like her and could be bought off. Once she knew who her "rival" was, she'd be waiting to hear the challenge and the price Di would ask to go away. She'd never figure Di wouldn't stand around to hear the counteroffer.

They never figure someone would have any interest but his own at heart.

The Tulsa airport was gratifyingly easy to get to—and Mark's plane must have been right on time. She pulled up the "arrivals" ramp to see him waiting at curbside for her, waving.

She stopped the car right in front of him and popped the door. He slung an overnight bag into the back and slid into the passenger's side without a single word; she pulled the car out again so quickly that they couldn't have spent more than thirty seconds stopped at curbside.

"Well?" he asked, as she took the on-ramp back onto the highway.

"Mark, m'love," she replied, "there's only one thing that could make me happier than seeing you right now."

"Oh?" he said, raising a thick, raven-wing eyebrow at her.

"And since archangels don't make house calls," she continued, "I don't think you're going to have to worry about competition. Did they feed you on that plane?"

"Feed me? On Cattle-Car Airways? Are you serious?" He laughed. "I was lucky to get a seat that had a working belt!"

"You know," she mused out loud, "I should have suspected something when they told me they'd give me a discount if you could bring a giant rubber band with you. . . ."

"That was for the motor," he told her. "They had holes in the floor for the guys in back of me to stick their feet through. They got their seats at ten percent off for being the landing gear. You know, you should never buy a ticket for a plane that has a smiley-face painted on the nose."

"I'll remember that," she laughed. "And listen, big guy, thanks for coming. Now, how about some breakfast? I'm starved, and you should be."

He gave her a closer look. "You're starved? You look more like you're running on empty. Writing IOUs to your body again, hm? It must be worse then you told me."

"Well, it gets complicated." She pulled off at the Twenty-first Street exit. She'd discovered a great place with a breakfast buffet, and at this time of the morning it wouldn't be crowded. "I hate to tell you this, but there's a maybe-deity involved."

She saw his swarthy complexion go paler out of the corner of her eye. "Tell me I didn't hear you say that."

"So far it's okay," she told him. "The thing's asleep. The kicker is, we *don't* want her to wake up. . . ."

"Okay, so what am I looking for?" Larry asked. This was feeling just like the old days—

Except I'm a little stiffer, a little slower, but a lot *smarter. Let's hope if it comes to a showdown, smart turns out to be the most important.*

"He wasn't in on the Madam Mysteria thing, Di," Mark reminded her, as he lounged back in one of the living room chairs. "That was about two months before we hooked him in, remember? Mysteria was doing her thing right at the beginning of the fall term, and we got Larry at midterms."

"Thanks, I'd forgotten that," she said with a touch of chagrin. "So who was the other sensitive? Jake?"

"Yeah. Remember, he bailed out of school and went back to Montana. He just couldn't take all the people. Can't blame him. Heard from him a week ago; he's still working that Forest Service fire-watch job, and happy as a clam." Mark didn't look as if he'd aged much more than Di. *Working as a cop must be keeping him in pretty good shape.*

"So what am I looking for?" Larry asked again, before they could get off on a reminiscence kick.

"A negative spot," Di said. "A great big energy sink. Fay's major workplace is going to be shielded against detection, but because it's a place where energy goes in but doesn't come back out again, we're going to have a kind of magical black hole out there. Not a place where there *isn't* anything going on, but a place where every available bit of energy that walks by goes in and stays there. You'll have to be in trance to do that, with your set of Talents. That's what makes these things a little hard to find."

"Great," Larry groaned. "The Zen of Magic; looking for the place that isn't there."

"Exactly." She managed half a grin. "It's kind of too bad you aren't like Jake; all we had to do was move him around until we found a place where he was suddenly comfortable. Now the reason we need two of us is that we're going to act as checks on each other. Partially we'll triangulate, partially we'll just make sure that one or the other of us isn't getting thrown off. It's easier to double-check when there's two of you working." Di was meticulously packing a small bag with all manner of odds and ends that she'd brought down to the living room. Some she'd just swiped from the kitchen, with the wry comment that it was a good thing Miri loved him. . . .

After seeing the bottle of asafetida in with the rest of the herbs, Larry was inclined to agree. And that had been *before* they found the hemlock.

He couldn't help but wonder if Miri'd been keeping her hand in, now and again, all these years. She *was* the one of all of the Squad who had been the most interested in witchcraft, as in the practical, spell-casting side of Wicca.

And when he recalled the way certain chauvinistic, abusive executives Miri had worked under had come to grief—well, it certainly gave him food for thought.

Pleasant thought, actually. It meant that while he'd always known instinctively that he would never have to guard his back or sleep with one metaphysical eye open while Miri was around, he now had evidence to prove his belief wasn't misplaced.

Di packed the last of the little bundles away and zipped the bag shut—then looked up at him as if she had read those last thoughts.

And smiled, a brief flicker across her otherwise solemn face. "I wish she was here, too. The gods know we could use her. But Mark and I managed all by ourselves down in Texas, and this isn't anywhere near as nasty an opponent."

Always provided that "goddess" hasn't suckered you, Larry thought worriedly. *There's always that chance. And there's the chance that Fay Harper could be working for the goddess.*

"Okay, are we ready?" she asked, getting to her feet.

Mark rose unhurriedly, and looked up the stairway. "What about that kid of yours?" he asked.

"Di put even stronger shields on him last night," Larry said. "I renewed mine, and we doubled the house shields. Besides, when I looked in on him he was sleeping like two logs. He won't be going anywhere for a while."

"Good," Mark replied, and ran his hand through his thick, black hair. "Let's lock and load."

Larry's range wasn't anything near Di's, which slowed progress down considerably. They were hampered in the fact that it was Saturday and the county offices were all closed. If they'd been open, a simple check of the property tax rolls would have shown them what property (other than the house and surrounding grounds) Fay and Fay's family owned. That would have narrowed their initial search down by quite a bit.

So it was plain grunt-work; starting at the far south end of town and moving north and east, stopping every four or five blocks to "look" for what was essentially a black hole, something which would be revealed only because of the distortion it left around it.

They stopped for lunch at the sushi bar Di thought so highly of. Both Larry and Mark opted for *cooked* teriyaki and tempura, and watched with awe and a little trepidation as Di devoured a small mountain of raw fish and rice.

She took a great deal of delight in eating her raw octopus and squid with gusto while Mark looked away and Larry winced.

Lunch over, they went back to business. The roads were getting crowded, and the interference from all those living, active bodies cut down on Larry's optimal range. It wasn't until late afternoon that he finally got a "hit," clear over on the north side of town past the airport.

He came up out of his trance to see Mark and Di staring at him from the front seat with expectation.

"Me, too," he said, as soon as he could talk. "I got it. That-a- way." He pointed east and a little north of where they were now.

"Pretty much what I got," Di agreed, pulling open the map of Tulsa they'd brought along. "Look, Mark, let's try this route." She pointed at a little county road that intersected with Mingo, the street they were currently on. "Go about half a mile and stop, and we'll try again."

"Okay." Mark put the car in gear and whipped it around in a tight U-turn, picking up the county road at the intersection a few hundred feet back in the direction they had come. Almost exactly half a mile later, he pulled over onto the verge beside some sorely puzzled cattle, and Di and Larry went back into trance.

And came back up immediately. "That way," they said in chorus, pointing ahead and slightly to the left.

"I don't think it's more than half a mile," Di added. "I've got a feel for distance now, and I don't think it can be more than that."

Mark consulted the map, smoothing it over the steering wheel and squinting at the fine print as Di and Larry looked over his shoulder. "If that's the case, this would be a good candidate," he said, pointing. "It looks like there's a gravel access road that intersects with this one in about another half a mile. There's probably farms all along here, and a farm would be a good place to put something like a sorcerer's work base. You could bring animals out there and nobody would notice, and if it's the first farm after the turnoff, your neighbors wouldn't see cars going by at odd hours."

"Let's try it," Di agreed. "We won't lose anything by going

straight there, and let's stop and check out the very first farm along
that gravel road. We may end up saving ourselves a lot of time."

It didn't take that long to get there; this was rural farming country, with grazing cattle and freshly plowed fields on either side of the
county road, so there wasn't any traffic to contend with. And when
they turned off on the gravel road Mark had indicated, they found
themselves driving through a tunnel of cottonwood trees.

"This road isn't that bad," Mark shouted over the crunching of
gravel under their tires. "What kind of cars did you say this chick
drives?"

"Mostly sports cars," Larry offered. "This one's a Shelby, the last
one was a TransAm, I think; the one before that was foreign."

Mark drove around a washout, the first bad hole they'd seen in
this road. "None of those would have any problem getting in here,"
he observed. "And if you turned off your lights as soon as you pulled
onto the road, the only way anyone would know you were here would
be if they heard you. Whoa!"

He slammed on his brakes and they skidded to a halt beside a
cattle gate that barred another graveled road, this one a one-lane
drive.

"Okay, gang," he said, turning the engine off. "Do your thing."

Larry didn't need to drop all the way into trance; he could feel the
place pulling at him the minute he closed his eyes and dropped his
shields. "This is it," he said, reshielding immediately and opening
both eyes wide. "Jesus. You mean to tell me a kid my son's age is responsible for that?"

Di shook her head. "I know it seems impossible, but there it is.
For the record, I agree, we just hit pay dirt. Okay, Magnum, now that
we're here, how do we get in?"

"That's the other reason why you asked me to come on up, isn't
it?" Mark grinned. "Just leave it to me."

He popped the door and strolled up to the cattle gate, taking
something out of the back pocket of his jeans, a small, hard case a little bigger than a wallet.

He reached for the padlock, then interposed his body between it
and the road—which also blocked *their* view of what he was doing.
He stood there a moment, then pushed the gate open wide, and came
back to the car.

"Haven't lost your deft touch, have you?" Di said, as he slid into
the driver's seat and backed the car up a little.

"It's a useful skill for somebody in my position," he agreed.
"Nothing like being able to go where you need to. Some of the other

guys like that high-tech lock-gun, but hey, this little kit doesn't need batteries, you know? Boy, I'll tell you, it's amazing how careless people are, leaving their gates unlocked like that."

"Amazing," she agreed. "Let me get out; I'll get the gate closed behind us."

She hopped out, and Mark pulled the car into the graveled drive, stopping just past the gate. Di swung the gate shut behind them, but did not relock it; she just secured it with a broken branch, then ran back to the car and jumped in.

Mark continued onward, through more huge cottonwoods, this time several deep on either side of the drive. The gravel drive took a dip and a sharp left just past the gate—and abruptly became an expanse of asphalt, as smooth as anything in Tulsa County.

"Even if I hadn't trusted you two, *this* would have told me we hit pay dirt," Mark said after a moment. "Either that or I would have started looking for a big, flat, mowed field, the kind you can land a private plane on."

"As in drug runners?" Di asked.

Mark nodded. "Look at this, it's a perfect setup. The first part of that county road is in great shape, but since it's graveled, you're not going to get too many curiosity-seekers coming down it. Then the drive; also graveled, and looks like it could get bad, until you go around that curve and out of sight of the county road. And *this* won't even be visible from the air because of the trees overhanging it."

"I can't believe this is the work of a kid," Larry said, puzzled. "I'm not sure that I'd be able to think of things like that."

"Let's wait until we see the house," Di cautioned.

And at just that moment they came around another cluster of trees, and saw it.

A falling-down, tilting derelict of a place.

It hadn't been anything spectacular to begin with; a basic two-story farmhouse, tall and narrow, the kind of simple wood-frame dwelling you saw all over rural Oklahoma. But now, it was a total wreck. Every window had been broken out; the doors flapped open in the breeze, and the right-hand porch support pillar had given way, leaving the porch roof drooping without any support on the right-hand side. Any vestige of paint had long since peeled away; the house was the shabby dead-gray color of unpainted, weathered wood.

Larry stared; he couldn't believe it. Nobody had been inside that heap for years; if they *tried* to get inside, the floor would probably collapse on them. How could he have been so wrong?

"Are you seeing what I'm seeing?" Di said quietly from the front seat.

"Uh-huh," Mark replied calmly. "What's a brand-new pole barn doing out here, where the house isn't fit to live in?"

"Yep." Di tilted her head to one side, and Larry finally looked past the wreck of a house to what lay, partially concealed by its bulk, behind it. A relatively new barn of corrugated metal. Freshly painted, too.

"And why are the electric lines running to a barn?" she continued calmly. "Looks like two-twenty service along with the regular line. And unless I miss my guess, a phone line. First time I've ever heard that hay had to make phone calls."

"Good question," Mark replied. "Want to go find out?"

"Yeah," she said. "Larry?"

He was already opening his door. "You couldn't keep me away," he told her, staring at the building. "*I'd* like to know why it needs a chimney. I always was too curious for my own good."

"Sweet Mother of God," Mark muttered for the fourth or fifth time, as they stared at the interior of the pole barn.

The big double doors had never been intended to be opened; they found when they approached the front of the building that the doors had been welded shut, all along the edges as well as in the middle. On the side they found a smaller, padlocked door—and an air-conditioning unit.

Mark had quickly picked the lock on this door, too; and when they opened it, Di had pulled a flashlight out of the bag she'd brought, and found a light switch.

But what they saw when the lights came on was nothing like they'd imagined.

The original metal of the walls and roof was paneled over; the building seemed a little shorter inside than out; probably the small door at the far end led into a partitioned-off utility and storage room. Certainly if the place had an air-conditioning system it also had a furnace, and there was no sign of one in this room.

The air was stuffy, and held a faint, sickly-sweet hint of incense. And the work on the interior must have cost the owner several hundred thousand dollars.

The floor was covered with a mosaic design of geometric figures; one large, central figure, and four others in each of the corners. The

central figure was composed of several circles nested within each
other. Each circle had inscriptions of some kind around the perimeter. And within the innermost circle was, not a pentagram alone, but
a pentagram within a hexagram.

At the heart of the pentagram was a huge slab of stone; probably
native limestone. The rough block was topped with black marble,
and there were manacles set into each corner of the slab.

Beside the altar was a reading stand, with a huge book still on it.
Beside the reading stand was a smaller table with an assortment of
objects on it, ranging from a single crystal goblet to a supple, brightly
gleaming rapier. In each of the points of the pentagram stood a man-
high, wrought-iron candle holder, with a half-burned black candle as
thick as Larry's wrist in it.

The walls had been paneled and then finished with black lacquer,
and they gleamed wetly in the subdued electric light. Lighting came
from three massive chandeliers depending from black wrought-iron
chains.

And there was a veritable forest of more candlesticks, ranging
from a foot tall to man-high. All the candles were either dead black
or blazing scarlet.

"So what's going on in here?" Mark asked, having recovered from
his shock while Larry continued to stare. "Anything current?"

Di tilted her head to one side and narrowed her eyes. "Yes," she
said finally. "An appeasement ceremony. It's due to complete in about
two months. And she wouldn't be able to build another construct
here until that's over with."

"Anything you want us to do?" he asked.

"Not at the moment. Just stand there and let me go pull some
fuses." She opened her bag and pulled out a jar of water and a blue
cardboard cylinder of prosaic Morton salt. "Just call me a one-
woman UXB squad."

She pulled the spout loose and made her way carefully around
the edge of the largest circle until she came to the side opposite the
entrance. Then she stepped over the first of the perimeters, and began
walking around it in a clockwise direction, sprinkling salt before her
and muttering something under her breath.

When she got to the place where she had entered, she stepped
into the second circle and repeated her actions.

When she reached the circle containing the hexagram, pentagram and altar, she replaced the salt in her bag and took out some of
the herbs she'd taken from her own supplies and the kitchen. These

she crushed in one hand and broadcast over the figures, then opened the jar of water and threw it on the altar.

Both Mark and Larry jumped as something shrieked, and the altar hissed and steamed where the water hit it.

Di didn't even flinch. She took the heavy book, threw it on the steaming altar, and removed a square can from her bag. As she squirted something all over the book, Larry caught the distinct odor of lighter fluid. She emptied the entire can onto the open book, saturating the pages, then tossed the can to one side and pulled out a Bic.

There was a second scream as the book went up in blue and green flames. Di watched it for a moment, then turned and took the nearest of the heavy, four-foot-high wrought-iron candlesticks from the point of the pentacle nearest her. She weighed it experimentally in her hands, then smashed it down onto the mosaic pattern at her feet.

After two or three blows, the tiles powdered.

"Okay, guys, it's safe to come in here," she called softly. "You want to give me a hand? Grab one of these and make sure all the lines of all the figures are broken in some way."

Mark strode over to her and took another of the candlesticks. Larry moved a bit slower; even with his shielding he was seeing things out of the corner of his eye that he didn't much care for.

But he noticed after a few moments that they didn't seem to be able to move; that, in fact, they seemed to be frozen in place.

At that point Di came up beside him, still methodically hacking away at the lines of the diagrams. She noticed him staring at one of the things, a particularly ugly little blob of filth. Or not-staring, since he could only view them by looking at them sideways.

"Don't worry about them," she said reassuringly. "That's what the routine with the salt was all about. They're stuck; I froze them halfway between this world and theirs. They can't get out and they can't get back. This way they can't warn Fay about what I'm doing."

"Oh," he said weakly. *God, it has been a long time. I am* really *out of practice. . . .*

And out of the habit of taking this sort of thing in stride.

"I'm taking this all very well, aren't I?" he said to Di.

She laughed. "Don't kid yourself; this is *not* the kind of thing I do every day. This gal is using some *powerful* stuff, and there's only one advantage that I have over her—it's all old. Real old, like three hundred years or more. I know some shortcuts she evidently doesn't, and some ways to nullify what she did that she evidently didn't know to guard against. And I will be damned if I can figure out *where* she learned all this."

Just the thing to make me feel at ease. Thanks, Di.

"Are you going to just stand there?" she asked finally. "Or are you going to help us?" Behind her the last flames were dying on the altar. They were still blue and green.

"Oh, shit."

Larry stared out at the setting sun, frozen by the realization of how much time had passed.

"What's the matter?" Di came up beside him, emptying out the last of the stuff in her carryall—more herbs—and strewing handfuls at random.

"We've got a problem," he said grimly. "There's a big birthday party tonight for one of Deke's friends, a kid named Brad Sinor. All of Deke's friends are going to be there—and Deke's probably left for it already. We didn't tell him not to leave the house—we just told him to avoid Fay."

"So what?" Mark asked.

"So Fay *has* to know about it. I don't know if she was invited, but you can bet she'll be there."

"Oh, shit," the other two said in chorus. Di looked from one to the other of them, her face set and blank.

"I deliberately destroyed this stuff in such a way that she *won't* know it's happened until she actually shows up here or tries to call something tied in to what she was doing here," Di said finally. "But there was something else I needed you two to do—drain out her power reserves. You both know how, right?"

Larry nodded reluctantly, as Mark said, "Yeah. Haven't done it for a while, but I think I can handle it."

"Good. Neither one of you is up to handling a sorcerer, even a young one. I think she may try to blow through Deke's shields; I think she's getting desperate enough to try whatever she wanted him for." She took a deep breath. "Larry, this is it. You're going to have to trust me. I need you to do what you can here, and let me handle Fay. Otherwise we're *all* going to lose on this one. Will you do that?"

Larry struggled with his paternal instincts, which were screaming at him to go rush to his son's rescue, and finally won. "Go," he said thickly. "Do it. We'll hold the fort here. Brad's address is in my Rolodex. Brad Sinor."

She didn't wait for another second; she spun around and tore out of the building at a dead run. And in a few seconds more, they heard the car start up and the screeching of tires as she peeled out back down the road.

Larry looked at Mark, who just grimaced. "Okay, old buddy, looks like we're on our own. Let's do it."

They walked to the ruined center of the diagrams, and stood back-to-back, preparing to tap into the stored energy and let it drain harmlessly away.

"Hey," Larry said suddenly, "she took the car!"

"I noticed," Mark replied, "but there's a working phone in that storage area. I know, I checked it. When we're finished here, I vote we call a cab."

Larry sighed. "I'm really taking this all very well, aren't I? So who pays for this cab?"

"Who do you think?" Mark retorted, bracing himself in a wide-legged stance.

Larry found himself grinning weakly in spite of the seriousness of the situation. "She does?"

"Right. So let's get this over and blow this pop stand."

"Right on," Larry replied, and prepared to tap in.

SIXTEEN

"Honey," Rhonda Carlin said worriedly from the living room, for about the fifth time, "are you *sure* you want to go to this party?"

Monica looked away from the mirror, sighed, and hunched her shoulders stubbornly. "Yes, Mom, I'm *sure*. I'm okay. There's gonna be a lot of rumors about what Sandy did to me—"

"He didn't do anything to you," Rhonda interrupted, sounding even more worried, "did he?" She pushed the door to Monica's room open slightly, and their eyes met in the mirror.

"No, Mom, he didn't. Honest. But he probably would have if Alan and Miss Tregarde hadn't been there."

Rhonda still had that somebody's-hurt-my-baby-and-she-won't-tell-me-about-it look on her face, so Monica figured she'd better reassure her. Again.

For about the fifth time. You'd think she *was the one Sandy went after.*

"Alan was right with me; Sandy just sort of came up behind us and grabbed me, and that's when my dress tore—then Alan jumped him. He didn't wait around to see what the hell Sandy wanted." Monica slipped her dress over her head and continued, though her voice was a little muffled. "Sandy beat up on him a little bit; then Miss Tregarde came out and saw what was going on, and waded right in. She's a black belt in karate, did she tell you that?"

She thought it was probably a good idea to leave Rhonda with the impression that Diana had taken Sandy out with martial arts instead of magical. Monica still wasn't quite sure what Diana had used to knock Sandy out—she'd just stood there and pointed at him—but it sure had been effective.

Probably more effective than karate would have been. Monica had heard stories of kids on dust—how they'd broken and dislocated bones and hadn't even noticed until they came down off the high. Sandy hadn't even *noticed* when she'd beaten on his thick head with her shoe.

Too bad it wasn't a spike heel, she thought vindictively.

"Well, all I can say is that it certainly is a good thing Miss Tregarde took an interest in you," Rhonda replied. "And if you think it'll kill some nasty rumors to go to the party, then I guess you should do that."

Monica straightened the seams of her dress, and fussed with her hair a little. "Alan's taking me," she said. "Black eyes and all. So no matter *what* anybody thinks, they're going to *see* both of us, and they can ask us about what happened for themselves if they really want to know."

"All right, honey," Rhonda replied reluctantly. "If that's what you want."

What I want is a chance at whoever put Sandy up to this, Monica thought grimly. *And I can't wait to find out who that is from Diana. And when I do . . . they're gonna find out that Monica Carlin learned a few nasty tricks from her daddy before he decided Mom didn't fit his career image.*

"You *do* look like a raccoon," Monica said to Alan as they strolled up the walk to Brad's house. They'd had to leave the car a block away; Brad's driveway was full, and so were both sides of the street right by the house. "Miss Tregarde said you would, and you do."

"Thanks," he said sourly. "And everybody's gonna know I got bailed out by a lady. Sandy was waxing my ass before she showed up, and everybody in the world is gonna know that."

"I don't see how," she objected. "Sandy can't talk to anybody except his parents, I haven't said anything, and neither has Miss Tregarde. And old Soames didn't get there until after Miss Tregarde put Sandy out."

"What about what's-his-name, the car nut? Tannim?" Alan wanted to know.

"He never talks to anybody," she replied, dismissing him with a toss of her head. "Except about cars. And art. And rock 'n' roll. *He'll* probably talk about the size of the dents Sandy put in that Caddy. Besides, he doesn't hang out with the same people you do."

"I guess," Alan acknowledged grudgingly. "Maybe I won't look like such a wimp."

"Alan, you jumped on *Sandy Foster*," Monica said in exasperation. "He's a *football player*. And he was *dusted*. And you took him on all by yourself! People aren't going to think you were a wimp, they're going to think you were crazy!"

"Well, I didn't know he was dusted, did I?" Alan replied, beginning to sound a little more pleased with himself. "Yeah, I guess that was kind of crazy, wasn't it?"

"Yeah," she said, grabbing his arm and snuggling up to him. "It was."

At precisely that moment they came into view of the front entry to Brad's house; it was a big, sprawling, Spanish hacienda-type place, and had a front courtyard full of red pottery and plants, enclosed by a wall pierced by a wrought-iron gate. You couldn't see if there was anyone standing around in there until you were practically on top of the gate, but whoever was inside the gate had a terrific view of people coming up the walk.

Monica cursed her wretched timing, because there was Deke, along with half a dozen other kids, watching her snuggle up to Alan.

He had a really pained expression on his face, and he grabbed Monica's arm as soon as they passed the gate. "Listen, Monica, I have to talk to you right now—" he began.

Then Alan pushed him off.

"Just you watch who you're grabbing, *old buddy*," Alan said angrily.

"Just who do you think you're pushing around?" Deke snarled back. "I know Monica a hell of a lot better than *you* do!"

"Oh yeah?" Alan retorted cleverly. "You want to make a bet on that?"

They stared at each other with the same fixed stare and stiff-legged stance as a pair of rival tomcats. Monica braced herself for the explosion. They kept looking over at her out of the corners of their eyes, and there was suspicion beginning to dawn there, as well as the antagonism.

I think Deke just figured out I've been playing up to Alan, she thought guiltily. *And Alan just figured out I've been playing up to Deke. Oh, God. And here I am in the middle. . . .*

"Hi, everybody!" The brittle, sharp-edged laughter and too-familiar voice made all three of them start.

Fay Harper swept in the gate with a blithe smile for everyone. "Deke, dearest, *there* you are! Let's go find something to drink, I'm *dying* of thirst—"

She touched Deke on the arm as the boy started to recoil, a look of—fear?—on his face.

Monica stared numbly. Because the minute, the very *second* she touched Deke, his expression changed, just went blank, and so did his eyes. Fay laughed at nothing, and whisked Deke off before anyone had a chance to say a word. Monica felt sick to her stomach over how Deke's expression turned puppylike with bemused adoration.

Why did I ever bother *with him?* she thought in disgust—when Fay turned back to the group at the door and finally spotted *her.*

Fay's smile turned icy and poisonous, her eyes narrowed, and she clutched Deke's arm possessively. Monica didn't need to know body language to read the message written for her there.

I'm going to get you, you little bitch. He's mine, you tried to split us up, and I'm going to get you for it if it's the last thing I ever do.

Fay turned away and hustled Deke out of sight inside the house. Monica wanted to scream. *She either figured out or found out I was the one who set Deke up to find her and Sandy out in the van. That must be what Deke wanted to talk to me about. No wonder he was mad. And when he figured out about Alan, he was even madder.*

Her heart was somewhere down in her shoes. *Jesus, I just ruined the rest of the school year. Deke probably hates me, and I know Fay hates me—and if Fay hates me everybody in school except the Brains and the Nerds and the Crazies is going to avoid me just to keep off Fay's shit-list. The only* good *thing is that there isn't more than a month of school left.*

And at least Alan still wants me.

She let Alan lead the way into the house; let him find a place for them to sit, over in the big rec room by the pool, where everyone was dancing. It was too cold to swim, but the pool cover was off and somebody had thrown dry ice into it so it was bubbling and steaming like something out of a George Lucas movie. It looked kind of neat, and it gave her something to watch while Alan went off after a Coke for her.

But Alan never came back, and after waiting for him for at least ten minutes, Monica swallowed her pride and went looking for him.

She pushed her way through the dancers and checked all the public rooms; the family room where four guys were playing Nintendo and had collected an excited audience, the living room where a bunch of people were watching a bootleg copy of *Rocky Horror Pic-*

ture Show on the big-screen TV, the den where the Brains had all gathered around Brad's father's computer—he wasn't even in the dining room where the food was laid out.

But that was where she ran into Laura, the Saks queen; she was talking shopping with Joy, who was going to Dallas next weekend and wanted to know what was hot. Monica signaled Joy frantically, and her friend broke the conversation off to wave her over.

"Hi!" Joy said, her eyes gleaming with excitement behind her glasses. "What's this I hear about Sandy beating up on Alan? I heard they were *fighting* over you!"

"Not exactly," Monica said, her eyes searching the room for Alan's red jersey. "Sandy was dusted, and I guess he was just looking for something to hit. Listen, have you *seen* Alan? He was supposed to get me a Coke, and he just, like, disappeared."

"Gosh, no," Joy said sincerely. "I wish I had. Mark told me he had *two* black eyes—"

"Oh, was that Alan?" Laura said, with an artificial giggle. "No wonder I didn't recognize him! He was here just before Joy got here."

"He was?" Monica turned to see the girl looking at her with a touch of malicious enjoyment. "Did you see where he went?"

"Oh, yeah, I sure did," Laura replied with relish. "He went off to the back of the house with one of Fay's buddies from Union, one of the cheerleaders—you know, that real fox, the one with blond hair down to her ass."

Brad's parents are gone for the weekend—and the back of the house is where the bedrooms are. And if Laura doesn't *know that, I'll eat my shoes.* She noticed Joy giving her a sympathetic look, and schooled her face into what she hoped was a mask of amused indifference. "Oh, did he finally catch up with her? He said he was supposed to meet her here. Well, good, that means I don't have to keep watching for her."

Laura's face fell, though she covered it up pretty well. *So Fay set me up to get humiliated, did she? Oh, fine. Just fine. Maybe I'll see if Mom can get me transferred over to Union. Shit, I'd better see if Joy can get me home, too—right after I go find someplace to have a good cry.* "I'll see you later, okay, Joy?" She winked, and swallowed down a painful lump in her throat, smiling brightly. "I'll give you the *whole* story about Sandy jumping us last night. Did you know the cops arrested him?"

Both Joy and Laura looked surprised.

"I thought maybe you hadn't heard." Monica smiled again, even though it hurt. *I'll fix him. I'll teach him to go off with some bitch-*

friend of Fay's and leave me out here alone. "If it hadn't been for Miss Tregarde, Sandy would have cleaned the parking lot with Alan's face. Anyway, I'll tell you all about it later. I've got somebody waiting for me."

She swept off before either of the two of them could stop her, and made her way out into the garden. Brad's parents had landscaped the place in a major way, with all kinds of neat little gazebos and benches with trees and things over them; there were even a couple of ponds, one with a fountain, one with a waterfall. Monica had hoped to find someplace out here to have her good cry, but every place she looked there was another couple necking. She finally found a spot by one of the ponds, right near the edge by the blue-lit waterfall; there was only enough room for one person to sit, which was probably why no-body'd taken it over for a petting session.

She stared into the water, keeping her face carefully averted so that no one coming up behind her would be able to see her crying.

But she didn't even get a chance to start before she heard Alan calling her.

He can't possibly have had time to do anything with that bimbo, she thought, frozen with surprise. *It hasn't been that long, not more than fifteen or twenty minutes. So either he struck out—or he likes me better.*

Oh hell, it doesn't matter. I'll get even . . . later.

She heard footsteps behind her and turned, ready to fling herself into his arms, relieved and grateful to the point of being ready to cry again.

Only what stood behind her wasn't Alan.

It was too dark out in the garden to see very much—only that the thing was taller than any basketball player, wider than any weight lifter, and very, very black. There was a little reflected light coming off the waterfall, and what Monica could see of the thing's face in that light made her squeak with terror.

It grabbed hold of both her arms, and not all the squirming in the world would tear her loose. Her knees went numb and gave out; but she didn't fall. The horrible thing held her up with hands like a pair of cold vises, as if she weighed nothing at all.

"Hello, Monica," it said caressingly in Alan's voice. "I'm very pleased to find you. My mistress wants you to come to *her* party now."

She squeaked again; tried to breathe, and found that she couldn't. All she could do was stare into those horrible, sulfur-yellow eyes, too numb to even *think*. Then the thing *smiled at her*.

And she fainted dead away.

Fay Harper wanted some heads. And she wanted them *now*.

That Tregarde woman's by first choice, followed closely by Monica Carlin's and Alan's. Then Sandy's, for screwing up.

Then that goddamn Gibson guitar. I don't even know where it went. The band did a better vanishing act than I could have, and I don't have the resources to track it down.

Her head pounded with the backlash from the destruction of her Servant. She ground her teeth and paced her room, occasionally picking up a small, fragile ornament and hurling it against the wall. It didn't do a great deal of good, actually. What she *wanted* was to hurt something.

But she didn't have any pets, the Servant had been obliterated, and the human servants had all vanished the moment the first signs of temper appeared. And *she* didn't have the authority to fire the bastards. Only "Aunt Emily" could do that; that was the way her trust fund and guardianship were set up. And there wouldn't *be* another Aunt Emily for another few days at the very best.

She didn't even dare call up an imp to abuse. Not with the low state of her resources and the fact that she'd have to tax her powers heavily to create another Servant.

Oh, she wanted to *hurt* something!

It was bad enough that the Tregarde bitch had completely *ruined* the Maypole spell. It was evident now that this little piece of sabotage was meant to challenge Fay—the destruction of the Servant had been the assurance of that. That spell would have given her enough power to make up for any losses over the past few months and "pay" for a new Servant—or several Servants. It was worse that the bitch helped whatever was in the Gibson overpower her demons, costing her not only the two allies but the added power that would have enabled her to break through Deke's shielding and eliminate his bothersome parents.

Right at the moment when Fay was about to get to Deke in a major way, the backlash had hit her. She'd drained him the best she could, and reinforced her controls on him, but she'd had to send him home, and everything else she'd planned for that night was a lost cause.

And the bitch had kept Sandy from getting rid of that *damned* obnoxious Carlin tart!

That was insult on top of injury; it was almost worse than the injury itself. The more Fay thought about it, the more enraged she became. She stopped her pacing just long enough to do another line or two of coke, and somehow all her anger at the Tregarde woman transferred to Monica.

It's all her fault, she snarled, hurling a crystal dragon against the wall. *It's all that little whore Monica's fault. If she hadn't gotten in the way, that woman would never have found out about me until it was too late to stop me!*

There were no more breakables in the room; she forced herself to stop pacing and sit, hands clenched in her lap, trying to think of an alternate plan, the coke making her mind come alive. At least there was no Servant here to chide her. . . .

I've made a mistake. The little tart must *be the Tregarde witch's protégée,* she decided. *That must be why she's been so diligent in protecting her. That must be why Monica showed up here* before *the woman did. The Master invests a certain amount of his power in his apprentice—if I destroy the one, I'll cripple the other.*

Her lips curled away from her teeth in a savage smile.

I haven't met anyone in the last three hundred years who could best me in an open fight. I doubt I'm going to now. All right, Tregarde. It's war. And the first act in war is to hit the opposition where it will hurt the most. I'm going to take out your precious little negress, your dear little darkie apprentice.

But first—I need a clearer head.

She rose and went back to the bathroom, to the special little concealed drawer in the vanity. It wouldn't do for the servants to find her personal stash, after all; they'd probably give way to temptation and help themselves.

She cut herself two more lines of coke—*moderation in all things my ass*—and sniffed them delicately. The rush cleared her head and gave her a burst of energy that left her overcharged and buzzing at the same time.

The Servant hadn't approved of the drugs—but then, the Servant hadn't approved of most of what she'd done, not lately.

Why should it matter? she thought dreamily. *I'll be discarding this body in twenty years, at most. The last time I was this young, I was stuck in Traverse City, Michigan—where I didn't dare enjoy myself, or the entire town would know. Which was precisely why I got married as soon as I found someone wealthy and stupid enough. And then I had to play proper society wife until I could get rid of the idiot. And when I finally got loose, what did I discover? That I was living in the backwoods of a hick oil town, and all my contacts to the pleasures of life were up north. So why shouldn't I enjoy myself? I've earned it!*

· She suddenly remembered just where both of her targets—

Monica *and* Deke—would undoubtedly be tonight. Brad Sinor's party. She hadn't been invited—but that hardly mattered; he wouldn't dare throw *her* out.

Ephemeris, ephemeris, where did I put it? She also realized belatedly that tonight was the night of the dark of the moon. And if it was astrologically as good as she *thought* it might be—

She found the ephemeris under a pile of romance novels, and leafed through it. *Well, it's not perfect—but it's not bad. And it's better than it's likely to be for the next couple of weeks. . . .*

Without any conscious decision on her part, she began dressing for the party, choosing an outfit she'd invested with a very powerful enchantment keyed to Deke.

Red for lust. You lucky boy, you. Lust. And blood. But we won't talk about that. It won't be yours, anyway.

She hadn't intended to use this just yet, but it was time to strike, while the Tregarde bitch thought she was off guard.

They'd never know what hit them.

Let's see. I can buy off my allies by giving them Monica to play with. The moon phase is certainly right for that. She giggled, sliding the smooth silk of her blouse over her head. *That should give me all the extra energy I need to deal with the Tregarde woman. But to do that, I'll have to build up enough extra power to pay off a fiend to do the snatch for me. And I'll have to get Alan out of the way. . . .*

She smoothed the blouse over her hips and admired her reflection in the mirror. *Wouldn't dear little Alan love to get a taste of this! I'll bet he's never been laid in his life.*

The perfect solution to her dilemma appeared like a burst of light, and she spun on her toe in front of the mirror, laughing.

Of course! I can call up a succubus with hardly more effort than it takes to snap my fingers! They'll perform just for the sex, which means the energy is all mine. I'll take her with me, and get her to seduce Alan. Then while she's screwing Alan's brains out, I can be concentrating on keeping Deke under my thumb. Then I give Deke to it. That'll keep him busy long enough for me to get away with the tart trussed up in the trunk. And I can call the fiend with the energy the succubus takes from Alan, and pay it with what I have it take from Deke! It's brilliant!

She turned to face the mirror again, as elated now as she had been enraged before. *It's perfect. While she's draining Deke down to nothing, my ally will be locking the little bitch in the back of my car. Talk about poetic justice! It can't miss.*

And they'll never know what hit them.

If it had been anyone but Di at the wheel, the car would have been pulled over half a dozen times. But somehow the cops never seemed to see her roaring past, bending traffic laws to the breaking point.

But there was an even more reckless driver pulling out of Brad's block as Di came screaming in. Someone in a red sports car, driving like they owned the entire universe. Di didn't pay it a great deal of attention; the driver was alone at the wheel, and Di had more urgent matters to attend to.

She pulled the car right up over the curb and parked it on the lawn; bailed out and barged straight into the house and the party without a single "excuse me." In the living room she grabbed the first person she recognized, one of the kids from her class, Terry—literally grabbed him; seized him by the collar and dragged him down to her level. "Urk—" he said, his eyes bulging. "Uh—Miss Tregarde, what are you doing—"

"Alan," she said. "Deke, Monica. Are they here? Have you seen them?"

She inadvertently tightened her grip. He made a choking sound and waved wildly at the room behind her. Since he didn't seem to be signaling for help, she let him go and turned quickly.

Alan was just staggering into the room, disheveled, glaze-eyed, and absolutely drained. And reeking of Sex Magick and the unmistakable overtone of succubus.

There was absolutely no mistaking what *he'd* been up to. And if *he* was off getting his brains turned into mush, that left Monica alone.

She muttered a curse at the general stupidity of teenage boys—and men!—who thought with their gonads, and stalked across the room, giving him the same treatment she'd just given Terry—except that she grabbed his shoulder instead of his throat.

"Come on," she said forcefully, as he goggled at her. "We've got to find Deke and Monica."

"Uh, yeah," he replied, following her because he'd lose his arm if he didn't. "Sure, anything you say, Miss Tregarde."

They hadn't gone much further than a deserted little office before they ran into Deke. Who looked even more drained than Alan.

Jesus Cluny Frog! Isn't there one *kid in this world that thinks above his beltline?*

But if Deke was *here,* that meant he wasn't with Fay. Di sighed with relief—

But Deke stared at both of them, and the first words out of his mouth were a blurted "Where's Monica?"

Oh, shit.

"How should I know?" Alan snapped back. "Janice said she'd gone off with *you!*"

"Janice who?" Deke and Di asked simultaneously.

Alan ignored Di. "Fay's trendoid friend from Union!" he shouted at Deke. "She said Fay was ripped and you left her and took off with Monica!"

Oh, double shit. Di grabbed Alan's shoulders and shook him violently. He stared at her stupidly, evidently not expecting that much strength in someone so tiny. "Who's this Janice?" she growled.

"Fay's buddy. The girl I was—" Alan blushed bright red.

Di shook him even harder. "You little cretin! You left Monica alone on the say-so of something that came with Fay? That *wasn't* a—"

"Hi, guys!" chirped a bright, seductive voice. "Want to party somewhere in private?"

Di whirled and faced the owner of the voice, a blond with long hair down to her tailbone, the face of an angel, and the body of every male fantasy in existence. She ignored Di entirely. Not surprising. Succubi literally didn't see the female of the human species—just like incubi didn't see the male—unless they had been deliberately targeted that way by their summoner. The two boys went slack-jawed and glaze-eyed, and their poor, worn-out little bodies were probably doing their damnedest to produce the appropriate salute.

It was fairly evident that Fay had left this "Janice" to cover her trail and maybe work some delaying tactics with the boys. She couldn't have expected Di to show up, or she wouldn't have left such a minor demon as a smoke screen.

The succubus slinked a little closer, and the boys licked their lips in an absurd echo of each other.

That might have worked if I hadn't shown up. Instead, this is going to work in my favor. I'll bet Deke still doesn't believe in the magic angle to all this, and I think even Alan still has a few doubts. Time to wake them up.

She gathered her power and blasted the shell of illusion surrounding the creature, revealing "Janice" for what she really was.

She was still a knockout—provided you didn't *mind* a lover with three-inch talons in place of fingernails, teeth like a shark, a long, pointed tail, and batlike wings that would have brushed the walls to either side of her if they hadn't been partly furled.

The boys' eyes bugged out, and Alan gripped Di's arm in a sudden spasm of unabashed fear. But before either one of them could do more than gasp, Di dropped *her* outermost shield. The one that hid the kind of power she controlled.

Now the succubus could see her, all right. *She* gasped, folded her wings protectively around her, and vanished in a cloud of what smelled suspiciously like Opium.

No brimstone for succubi, thank you. Lord. Little tarts always were show-offs. It's a damn good thing they're not as interested in combat as they are in sex. . . .

The boys were both standing stunned, their mouths hanging open, their faces dead white. Di could see identical thoughts running through their tiny little brains.

We screwed that?

She grabbed them both and hauled them around to face her.

"That *friend* of Fay's was a demon. Deke, dammit, I *told* you Fay was a—a witch of some kind! How the hell could you go and let her get her claws back into you like that?"

"Uh—" Deke couldn't look her in the eyes.

Alan just stared stupidly at her.

Di wanted to bash their heads together. "And where's *Fay*?"

Deke looked confused. "She just—left. I didn't ask her why. Then that blond came in—"

Di groaned. "Fay has been after Monica's hide ever since she came to Jenks, you idiots! And while you two were screwing your brains out—assuming you *have* any—Fay was probably kidnapping Monica! Now where the hell would she take her? The farm out near Catoosa?"

"But—" Alan began.

Deke was finally getting his act together.

"No, not there," he said, shaking his head. "That Sex Magick stuff—what you told Dad and me—the first time we—" He coughed. "—uh—"

"Spit it *out*, kid!" Di said impatiently.

"I thought she was just kind of kinky, like she just liked doing it outside. You kept asking me about cabins and things, and I guess I kind of forgot about this. She's got this place, this little place; it's a stable at the end of the runway where her dad used to keep horses. She never *lived* there or anything, and it's kind of run-down. I guess I must of figured it didn't count. We'd go there sometimes when we were in Tulsa and she couldn't—you know—wait—"

He gulped, and finished weakly, "She's kind of—enthusiastic. She used to say she liked the place 'cause she could scream all she wanted and nobody would ever hear her over the planes."

Shit, I'm a real idiot myself— Di thought in disgust. *She'd have to have an outside facility for some things, and any experienced sorceress would have a backup Power Point. She has to have figured out that we had her old place staked out when she tried to call her succubus. I would have checked my stronghold before I did a major spell, and I'll bet she did, too.*

Lord and Lady. I can't take the time to go pick up Larry and Mark. I'll have to use what I've got.

Two kids. Gods help me.

They were untrained, unknown quantities. Alan didn't even register much above normal. But they were all she had.

"Stand by for a shocker, kid," she muttered, pulling *all* the shields off Deke. " 'Cause I'm going to have to figure out what you're good for."

Deke had been surprised at what Di looked like before—when she was still wearing *her* outermost shield. Now he practically fainted. She didn't blame him; doing a quick scan on him, she'd already figured that he was just as Sensitive as his father ever was; he had some Wild Talent she couldn't figure yet—

And he was a living Power Point. He could quite easily shunt energy to, or drain it from, anything he chose—once he was trained. No wonder he'd survived Fay so long.

And no wonder Fay wanted her claws in him. At least a hint of that must have gotten through the shielding, and it must have driven her crazy, even if she couldn't identify it.

"Come on, you two," she ordered, shoving them in front of her and out the door. "Let's *move!*"

She briefed them on what they might expect when they got there, or tried to. It was a little difficult, since she didn't know what *she* was expecting. She could at least tell Deke what she expected *him* to do. He'd long since passed the stage of suspension of disbelief; he just hung onto the back of the seat and nodded at whatever she said.

She hoped she was getting through to them. She wasn't sure how clear she was being; it had been a long time since she'd had to brief mundanes under combat conditions. And it was a little difficult to talk and drive like a maniac at the same time.

Alan just looked at her forlornly. He wasn't *saying* anything, but she knew he was feeling utterly useless.

"Look," she said, trying to think of *anything* Alan could do. "In the glove compartment. Can you shoot?"

"I'm on the Jenks target team," he said, fumbling it open. "And I was with the Police Explor—Christ!"

"It isn't as big as it looks," she said acidly. "Shit, I can handle it." Alan removed the .45 revolver gingerly and stared at it. "If a little bitty broad like me can shoot it, so can you."

He just gulped and stared at her, and pulled the handful of speed-loaders out as well.

She didn't even have time to sigh with exasperation; at that point, Deke shouted *"There!"* and she slid a bootlegger turn into a half-hidden gravel drive on the side of the four-lane county road, a little turnoff that was buried in overgrown bushes.

They bounced through a series of washouts and over a one-lane bridge—

And suddenly the headlights spotlighted Fay, her blond hair and red silk harem pants and blouse unmistakable.

And beside her was Monica, held between two of Fay's little pets.

Di slammed the car into park and yelled *"Now!"* as she bailed out of the driver's side of the car, hitting the gravel and rolling into the weeds at the side of the road. Alan went out the other side, just as he'd been told. Deke stayed with the car—as *he'd* been told, since he didn't have any shields of his own anymore, he needed the ones on the car.

Come on *Deke, get your ass in gear!* Di could feel him fumbling around in the energy currents as she picked off Monica's left-side guard with a levin-bolt.

It shrieked and went up in a pillar of flame. She heard the gun go off as Alan shot at the right-side demon. The bullet wasn't more than a distraction, but between it and Di's actions, a distraction was all that was needed. Monica pulled free of the thing and came pelting back toward the car.

There was an inarticulate scream of rage from the sorceress.

And at that point, all hell—literally—broke loose.

Di didn't even have time to think much more than *Holy shit!* before she was running for her life, trying to put as much distance between herself and the kids as she could.

Fay was pulling power from sources even the most reckless of sorcerers would have left untapped—sources that bled into the protections around the One Below, sources that kept Tulsa's weather relatively stable, and sources that would leave her owing her soul a hundred times over to her allies. Levin-bolt after levin-bolt came winging at Di out of the darkness—and other things as well. Di was pretty certain they *weren't* illusions; illusions took a certain amount of mental control, and it was pretty obvious that Fay had lost any semblance of that. Di treated the things as though they were summonings instead of illusions, and they certainly went up with little screams of anguish when she hit them with her own levin-bolts.

She stumbled through the tangled brush and over tree roots, trying to keep her head down, trying to stay *alive*— Deke still hadn't figured out what he was supposed to do, and she wasn't sure he would in time to save her.

If she doesn't kill me, her allies are going to make chili out of her for what she owes them. They may do it anyway. But right now— She made a dive for the cover of some bushes as an ugly little thing with a long poisonous stinger made a dive for *her*. She managed to pick it off as it sheered away, but that gave away her hiding place, and a levin-bolt splashed off her shielding. —*right now I'm a bigger, shinier target than she is. Shit. I got the innocents out of the line of fire; very noble, but I'll bet that means that Guardian Magic isn't going to kick in.*

Wonderful. Just wonderful. Thanks a bunch, fellas.

A rumble of thunder overhead alerted her to yet another danger. Fay's uncontrolled magics were boiling up the atmosphere, and the granddaddy of all thunderstorms was building up at preternatural speed.

There was another storm brewing *beneath* the ground. The protections were thinning. The dreams of the One Below were taking on a disturbed quality.

Mark and Larry— She made a quick check; felt with relief that they were all right; still draining the site, like an attentive swimming-pool crew, oblivious to what was going on in Tulsa because of the shields around the place. *I have the power to take her down. But I haven't given her fair warning. And dammit, I can't do it while she's taking potshots at me!*

Within a few moments, the thunder and lightning were so continuous that the entire landscape was strobing around her, and she couldn't even hear the screeching of Fay's creatures.

The One Below was dreaming of storms, too.

She was right at the edge of the area covered by the headlights. *Not* a good place to be. She scrambled up out of her bushes, tried to backpedal, and tripped over something hidden in the darkness. Then a strange and stomach-lurching feeling distracted her for a moment, and, signaled by something deep inside her, she looked up.

Lightning played across the entire sky, illuminating the clouds whirling around a hole in the thunderheads.

A funnel-cloud.

And there was a definite stirring beneath the earth now; something beginning to wake and take an interest in the proceedings. The last of its dreams shredded away—

It wasn't pleased at having its dreams interrupted.

And was going to make every living thing within reach pay for being awakened.

Its reach was very long. . . .

Long enough to call down a hundred tornadoes on Tulsa, and send them ripping through every neighborhood in the city until there was enough peace for the One Below to drift back into dreams again.

Di spent a split second reckoning up the worth of her Oath, and her options.

I haven't got any. I'm going to have to bet it all.

And hope she hasn't learned the "reflect your enemy's power back at him" trick. Everything she's done so far is three hundred years old, and that trick dates from 1854. Please, oh gods—

Or there isn't going to be a Tulsa in the morning.

She made her "mirror"; grounded and centered herself, bracing it as well as she possibly could—

And dashed out into the cone of light from the headlights; then stood up in plain view, as if caught by surprise.

Di could feel the surge of triumph—and saw the blast of power coming straight at her.

The parabolic "mirror" held—and funneled the sorceress's power right back into her teeth.

Di's arcane "eyes" as well as her physical ones were blinded as a half-dozen lightning bolts lashed down, attracted by the pull of the power. Her "ears" were deafened by the scream of rage and pain, even as her physical ears were buffeted by thunder that literally pounded her to her knees.

And overhead, the storm died; while underfoot, the One Below growled in satisfaction and drifted back into sleep. . . .

After a while, sight came back, and hearing, and Di picked herself back up off the ground.

Oh, gods. Everything hurts. Absolutely everything. Maybe I'd have been better off if she'd fried me.

She staggered wearily back to her car; and as she came closer, she heard the sound of voices.

The boys.

Arguing.

Over just whose girl Monica was.

I can't believe this! she thought, gritting her teeth to keep from screaming. *Okay, granted Alan couldn't See anything but those two demons, and Deke probably couldn't See most of what was going on because he was trying to figure out what to do and had his eyes closed— but dammit, I'm out there getting my ass trashed, and—Lady of Light, if I had the strength, I'd strangle him!*

Monica could not believe what she was hearing.

I was kidnapped by a witch, she thought, stunned into silence. *I was going to be given to a couple of* demons. *I was nearly killed, we were* all *nearly killed. There was almost a tornado, we all saw it! And all they can think about is whose girl I am?*

The argument had started right after the huge bolt of lightning, when she'd cowered on the ground between them. That was when they both looked up, when *their* hands met, and each discovered a rival on the other side of her. It was probably all due to the fact that they were *all* an inch away from hysteria, but it was about to reach the point of blows, and suddenly she couldn't take it anymore.

"You—*assholes!*" she screamed shrilly, her voice cutting across both of theirs.

They stopped yelling, and stared at her.

"You can go fuck *yourselves!*" she screamed, shaking her clenched fists at both of them. "You're crazy, both of you! I'm going *home!*"

With that, she turned on her heel and flounced up the rutted road, with the lights of the car behind her, heading for the airport. If nothing else, she figured she could get a cab there, and her mother could pay for it when she got home.

They're crazy! They're both insane! If Fay ever shows up again, she can have both *of them!*

The light behind her grew brighter, and she heard the car engine right at her heels. She stumbled off the track into the grass, and the car pulled up beside her.

She peered suspiciously into the car, ready to tell the guys off, as the overhead flickered on. It was Diana; alone.

"I'm with you, kiddo," the witch said tiredly.

"God," Monica said, awed by the gray pallor of the woman's complexion, the sheer exhaustion that made her eyes look sunken clear into her head. "You look awful!"

"I feel awful," Diana replied. "Like death, only worse. How about a ride home?"

There were shouts behind them, as the boys suddenly realized that they were being left in the lurch. Monica looked back and could barely see them, stumbling along and waving frantically. "What about them?" she asked.

"Let 'em walk. It'll cool 'em down. By the time they get home, they'll be buddies again. They just needed something to take their nerves out on."

Monica managed a tremulous grin, then yanked the door open and jumped into the passenger's side. Diana Tregarde gunned the engine just as the two boys reached the side of the car, and pulled away, leaving them in darkness and a cloud of dust.

"Don't you think they could have done something instead of fight?" Monica asked plaintively.

"Yeah. Except that they're male. You know," Diana said as the boys' forlorn cries died behind them, "I'm twice your age, and I *still* don't understand men."

Dr. James Powell rubbed his hands together nervously. He hated to lose this patient—she'd meant a great deal in the way of a steady income to feed his coke habit—

Powell, that was one incentive you didn't need, he scolded himself. *You've been cold turkey for a month now. You can do just fine with the rest of your practice. And you got into this business to* cure *people, not make them dependent on you! Go back to being a doctor, not a goddamned drug addict!*

"You can let Mrs. Harper in now, Sherri," he told the secretary.

Rowena Harper moved gracefully through the door to his office and took the chair opposite his desk.

"Well, Mrs. Harper," he said quietly. "There's no doubt in anyone's mind. When you passed the certification board, it was only a matter of the paperwork. I want you to know that I was very happy to give you your release papers. And I'm happy to see you leaving us today."

"I never doubted it, Dr. Powell," she said, in a low, throaty voice. "I want *you* to know that I'll always be grateful to you for your help."

"I'm just sorry that it took such a shock—"

She bowed her head. "My poor daughter. What a horrible way to die. Lightning. Who would ever have thought something like *that* would happen to her? I still find it hard to believe she's gone. And yet—it's a paradox; if she hadn't had that terrible accident, might I not still be locked in my little world of delusions, insisting that I was her?"

"It's possible, I suppose," Powell said carefully. "I've learned never to discount anything when it comes to the mind."

She sighed, and twisted her hands in her lap. "I suppose it's just as well that I was so thoroughly drugged when it happened. You were able to break the news to me gently that way. Somehow I think that's why when you lightened the dosage, I was able to come back to my real self."

"That's entirely possible," Powell repeated. "Now, before you go—are you certain you'll be all right? All alone in that big house?"

"I won't be alone," Rowena said, still looking down at her hands. "Will I, Emily?"

Powell jumped; he hadn't noticed Rowena's sister Emily when she'd come in, nor that she had sat down on the couch behind Rowena. She was so quiet and subdued, she might well have been Rowena's shadow, or a piece of the furniture.

"No, Rowena," the woman said, in a soft, mouse-timid voice. "You will not be alone."

Rowena rose, and Powell realized that he could not delay the moment any longer. "All right," he said, rising to his own feet. "You take care of yourself. And stay in touch. You may need some help in adjusting. You might find yourself with too much time on your hands."

"I'm certain I'll be able to keep busy," Rowena replied, looking up at him. For a moment he thought he saw a hard, calculating look in her eyes. "I have a great deal of unfinished business to handle. A great deal," she repeated.

Then the look was gone, replaced by simple, warm gratitude.

It's the nerves, Powell figured, clenching his jaw. *Coke damages the nerves. I'm going to have to stop being so paranoid.*

He opened the door for her, and she and her sister slipped by him, both of them thanking him again, in sincere, effusive tones.

He watched her walk past his receptionist's desk and out into the hall. *God, she moves like that daughter of hers; at least she does now that she's sane again. Sometimes she even looks like her. Maybe that was the root of the delusion. There might be a paper in that. . . .*

Lord, she could be that sexy little thing all over again. Right down to the come-hither walk. . . .